PRAISE FOR Michael A. Stackpole's
ONCE A HERO

"Stackpole's rich world provides a brilliant tapestry across
which Neal and his fellows stride with all appropriate
pageantry, while the Reithrese are as nasty a set of villains
as ever complicated a fantasy plot."
—*Booklist*

"This sprawling medieval fantasy saga focuses on two people
separated in time but not in spirit. . . . Enjoyable."
—*Locus*

"I haven't believed elves this way since Tolkien!
The book is magic."
—Jacqueline Lichtenberg, *The Monthly Aspectarian*

"Magic, action, adventure, romance : . . This book has it all!"
—Jennifer Roberson

BOOKS BY MICHAEL A. STACKPOLE

MICHAEL A. STACKPOLE

EYES
OF
SILVER

BANTAM BOOKS

New York Toronto London Sydney Auckland

EYES OF SILVER

A Bantam Spectra Book / December 1998

SPECTRA and the portrayal of a boxed "s" are trademarks of Bantam Books,
a division of Bantam Doubleday Dell Publishing Group, Inc.

ISBN 0-553-56113-8

Published simultaneously in the United States and Canada

Bantam Books are published by Bantam Books, a division of Bantam
Doubleday Dell Publishing Group, Inc. Its trademark, consisting of the words
"Bantam Books" and the portrayal of a rooster, is Registered in U.S. Patent
and Trademark Office and in other countries. Marca Registrada. Bantam
Books, 1540 Broadway, New York, New York 10036.

PRINTED IN THE UNITED STATES OF AMERICA

OPM   10   9   8   7   6   5   4   3   2   1

ACKNOWLEDGMENTS

The author would like to thank Janna Silverstein and Anne Groell for convincing him to actually hammer this book into shape; and, as always, Liz Danforth for enduring the time I spend in the traces with projects like this.

In this book's writing the author found three books invaluable as resources:

The Great Game by Peter Hopkirk
What Jane Austen Ate and Charles Dickens Knew by Daniel Pool
The Fall of Napoleon by David Hamilton-Williams

Not only were they useful in research, but they were also fun to read.

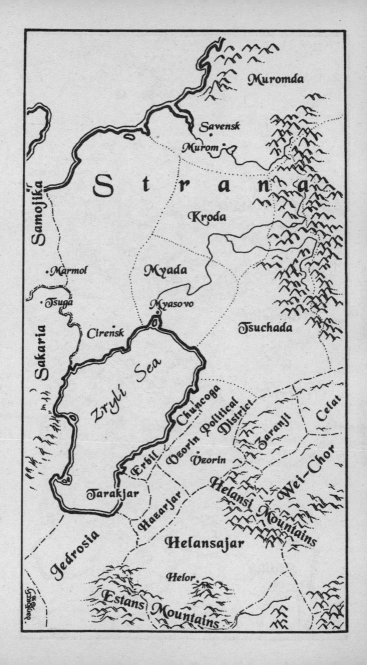

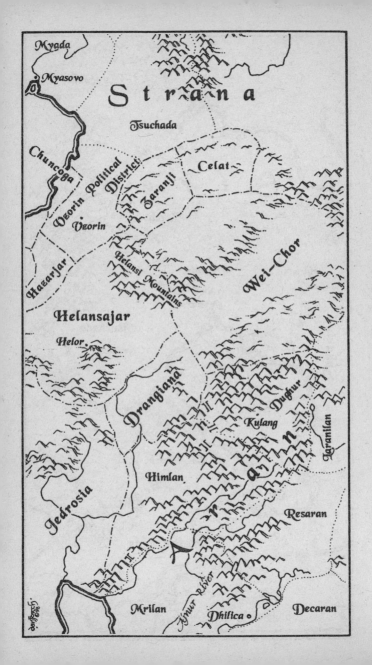

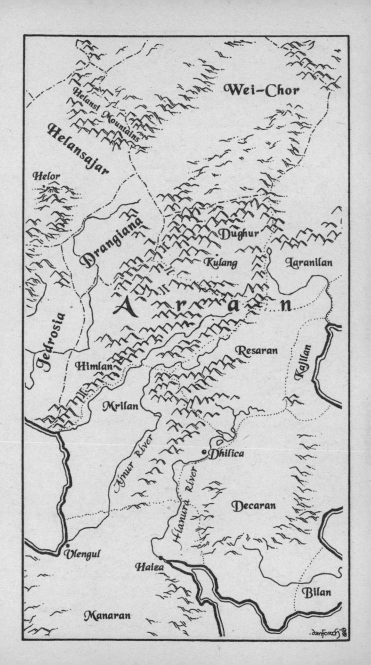

Prologue

Malachy Kidd rose silently from the alley's shadows, his left arm encircling the Lescari guardsman's throat. Malachy pulled back, less worried about stifling any outcry than having the man murmur a spell, and shoved his dagger into the man's arched back. The blade pierced the guardsman's ring mail smoothly, as if it were no more than flesh, then slid between ribs and found his heart.

The man stiffened, then slackened, but Malachy did not release his hold. He thrust up with the dagger again, deeper, then dragged the man further into the alley and gently laid him on his back. He reached down and shut the man's eyes, then crossed the man's hands over his heart.

Dropping to one knee beside him, Malachy covered the man's hands with his own left hand. "May God grant you eternal peace and forgiveness."

He felt a tingling in his right hand as the spell he'd earlier invoked on his dagger worked a pale blue bar of light from the crossguard down to the tip. The magick's main purpose was to keep the blade supernaturally sharp and enable it to puncture armor with little or no trouble. An ancillary part of the spell—*something one of the Augustinians doubtless thought elegant when he created the spell*—played the blue light over the blade, burning away the blood that coated it. The light vanished as a spark leaped from the blade's point, then Malachy slid the blade home in his boot sheath.

Malachy took quick stock of the man he'd killed. *Not really a man, more a boy.* The guard's youthful appearance didn't surprise him as much as he would have hoped, but he'd seen too many Lescari who had died in furtherance of the dreams of their Emperor Fernandi. The nondescript tabard the man wore suggested he was little more than a common conscript and Malachy was rather happy to see the crest of *Les Revisor Carmí* had not been sewn to the tabard's breast.

With prisoners this valuable, the Red Guards will be coming soon, which is why I had to act now. Malachy had begun the war

against Fernandi by spending two years in Lescar as a spy in service
to the King of Ilbeoria. The capture of Ilbeorian Prince Trevelien in
Lescar had prompted Malachy to rescue the Prince, blowing his
cover. The Ilbeorian King, pleased to have his son back, rewarded
Malachy by making him an envoy to the Tacier of Strana, Ilbeoria's
ally in the war against Lescar. Malachy had been attached as an advisor to the 137th Bear Hussars and had helped chase the Lescari
host in its retreat from Strana.

Vasily Arzlov, the Hussars' commander, and Grigory Khrolic,
the captain in charge of the battalion which Malachy observed, had
tolerated his advising—*or meddling*—well enough. Malachy had
prevented Khrolic's battalion from being trapped at Cirensk and
Marmol, which seemed to win Khrolic over. *Which is why he agreed
to send scouts out into the forest at my request, which resulted in
their capture.*

Malachy crept back to the mouth of the alley and crouched
there. The clothing he wore, save for the helmet and smooth battlemask, appeared in the dark to be little more than black linen, but the
magick he invoked on it gave it the tensile strength of steel without
the weight, deadened any sounds it might make, and sucked light in,
melding him with the shadows. The armor had been created in a
ritual at the Royal Military Seminary at Sandwycke and had served
him well in the few battles he'd seen in the last three years.

Tonight it will get sorely tested, I'm afraid. He'd asked Khrolic
to send a company out to the little town of Bauczeg to rescue the
captured scouts, but the captain had balked. He had said it didn't
matter that the two scouts who had returned had reported the town
was all but deserted; it was behind the Lescari lines and any assault
there might provoke a reaction that would upset Arzlov's battle plan
for the coming day. Malachy had then gone to Arzlov, but the
Stranan commander had dismissed him with a wave.

"Were you under my command, Kidd, I would order you to
no longer even think of a rescue attempt, but you are not mine
to command."

Malachy had taken that dismissal as a challenge, and chose to
read into it a certain sympathy for the captured scouts on Arzlov's
part. Malachy put together his own rescue kit and struck out through
the Gohazy Forest for Bauczeg. He left behind a note for Khrolic
telling him what he had done and how to deploy men to gather the
scouts back in.

Malachy looked at the moon's position in the sky. *Lieutenant
Smagolov should have delivered it to Khrolic two hours ago, so his
men should be in place. That means I better get to the rescue.*

What passed for a prison in the small town was the third floor of the government building at the square—the barred windows in the top floor being a clue Malachy would have been hard-pressed to miss. The simple way in seemed to be to go straight for the front door, but that would likely require a lot of killing on the way. Scaling the building itself would be tough, and while he had brought a coil of rope and looped it across his body, he didn't have a grappling hook to toss up to the roof.

I could always fly up there, but I'm not equipped with wings and that means the spell will weaken me rather seriously. He frowned for a moment, then a ghostly gray blur streaked across the square before him. It looked to be a wolf racing over the greensward and toward the alley to the left of the government building. *Saint Martin's Sign!*

Malachy immediately sprinted after the ethereal wolf, trusting in the omen. He and every other Martinist had heard countless stories of how a ghostly wolf had led lost travelers to safety, or searchers to a missing child. Even if half those tales were nothing more than fable, the core truth they surrounded meant Malachy did not fear detection despite so bold an approach. Saint Martin's Sign would never, he knew in his heart, lead him astray.

Ducking into the alley beside the Government House, Malachy smiled beneath his mask. Built into the side of the building was a staircase that wrapped around to the back and seemed to lead up to the roof. *Makes perfect sense—they don't want to be leading prisoners in through the Mayor's office while he's holding court.* He murmured a quick prayer of thanks to his patron saint, then mounted the steps and quickly reached the building's roof.

Malachy crossed to the iron-bound oak door capping a stairwell and tugged on the handle. *Locked, which is good for a jail.* He fished in a pouch on his swordbelt and pulled out a key. He slid it into the door's lock, then invoked a spell. He felt a trace of warmth where the key touched the bare flesh of his palm through a slit in his gauntlet, then he twisted the key and the lock clicked open.

He pulled the door open, then slowly descended the steep staircase to a short hallway that opened into a room fitted with numerous barred doors. In the center stood a long table with a number of chairs surrounding it, but only one was occupied. A heavyset guardsman, his doublechins resting on his chest, snored loudly enough to cover the sound of a cavalry charge. Off to the right lay a door similar to the one above and Malachy assumed it led to the stairs providing access to the rest of the building. Candles burning in wall-mounted lanterns provided a jaundiced light.

Malachy returned the key to his pouch and withdrew instead a slender braided leather thong. A strand of steel wire had been woven with it and Malachy looped the ends around his hands, leaving two feet of the cord between his thumbs. He crossed his wrists, making a loop of the cord, then slid forward silently.

He looped the garrote over the man's head, then tugged back hard, yanking his hands to each side as he did so. The snores dissolved into startled gurgles. The guard tried to get up, but Malachy crouched, pulling the man's neck down against the back of his chair, trapping him there. The guardsman's hands clawed at the cord as his face purpled. His legs kicked and the chair shifted, spilling him to the floor. He made one last attempt to get up, to twist around and get at his attacker, but with his eyes bulging and his tongue hanging out of his mouth, he collapsed.

Malachy hung on until he was certain the man was dead, then loosened the garrote. The dead man sighed the trapped air from his lungs, then lay there. The Ilbeorian coiled his garrote and returned it to his pouch, then crossed the dead man's hands over his heart and pulled out the key again.

He moved to the first cell and, using the skeleton-key spell, opened the door. Speaking in Stranan, he hissed a warning. "Carefully, my friends, come out. I've come to rescue you."

Two men, both with scruffy beards and tattered clothes, rubbed sleep from their eyes as they stumbled from the cell. Both had facial bruising and one had a crusted cut over his right eye, but did not look to be in very bad shape. One of them, Viktor, offered a semitoothed grin. "This is a miracle."

Malachy nodded. "It's a miracle only if we get you back to the Hussars. How many others are here?"

Viktor scratched his beard. "Two in the next cell, two more on the other side. We saw Dmitri and Zenon get captured, too, but they were badly wounded and taken elsewhere. I think the Lescari were going to have one of their witch doctors care for them."

Malachy nodded, easily reading the fear on Viktor's face. Fernandi had risen to power in Lescar as a result of a revolt that broke the power of the Eilyphianist Church and deposed the rightful King. Fernandi secularized the society and cleared the way for all manner of abominable magickal practices that the Church had suppressed. The Church taught that any magick that was not worked on objects, but on people themselves, was of the Devil. Fernandi decried that doctrine as superstition and, instead of making physicians use their magick on instruments and ingredients to fashion medicines, allowed the doctors to create spells that worked directly on their patients.

"Don't worry, Viktor. The taint from such practices only stains the souls of those who use the magick or consent to its use. Your friends will be fine." He moved to the next door and used the key to open it. "Take this rope and head to the stairs back there."

Viktor accepted the rope, then narrowed his eyes. "How is it that you, a Wolf-priest, know the magick of thieves?"

Malachy smiled and almost lifted his faceplate to let Viktor see his face. "When I was a spy in Lescar, this magick was useful to me. It saved Prince Trevelien much as it is saving you. Besides, wasn't Saint Yulia a thief before she became one of the Lord Shepherd's disciples?"

"A warrior and theologian?" The Stranan shook his head. "I would never have thought to find such a man here."

"Truth be told, Viktor, I only intended to be the sort of priest who would have his parish in a town like this." Malachy laughed as he went to the third cell and freed the last two scouts. He had known from very early on that he wanted to be a priest and the Church was happy to accept him. They tested him and discovered, to their delight and his surprise, that he was capable of wielding great magicks. As with all humans he had a magickal talent, but he'd not thought much of it. The Church, on the other hand, valued it greatly and offered him a choice of entering the Society of Saint Augustine or the Military Seminary at Sandwycke.

Neither choice had been exactly what he wanted. The Augustinians dealt with magick, creating and refining spells of all manners. They sought spells that would allow doctors to fashion cures for diseases and even developed the variety of combat magicks Malachy had mastered. While the idea of working with magick and creating spells did intrigue him, the Augustinians did not hold a strong enough attraction for him.

Malachy was Ilbeorian, which meant he had been raised within the Martinist Church. A sect of Eilyphianism, it had been introduced to Ilbeoria by a centurion of the old Scipian Empire nearly two millennia before. Saint Martin had seen a role for warriors in a Church that was, at its core, pacifistic. The Church had long embraced Eilyph as the Lord Shepherd and his believers as his flock, so Saint Martin saw warriors as the loyal wolves who helped the Lord Shepherd ward his people. Having been steeped in that tradition, and with the Church not offering him the chance of being a simple parish priest, Malachy chose Sandwycke. Once there, he mastered even the most powerful of battlemagicks with an ease that surprised his teachers and pleased his leaders.

Malachy helped the last man out of his cell. "To the roof with you all. Go. Take the stairs down, quietly." As they paraded out, Malachy dragged the dead guard into a cell, then locked all of the doors and headed up to the roof himself. There he locked the door to the roof, then joined the Stranan scouts in the alley below.

Crouching beside Viktor, he pointed toward the east. "You'll have to work your way around, but to the east is a ravine. Follow it until you reach a tall stone, go south until you find the stream and then take it back into camp. Captain Khrolic should have men out there waiting for you."

"You are not coming with us?"

Malachy shook his head. "Not immediately. Dmitri and Zenon are here somewhere and I should find them."

"We will help."

"No, just go. Let Khrolic know this area is still clear for tomorrow."

"It shall be as you ask, Wolf-priest. May God go with you, and His saints."

"Godspeed to you, as well." Malachy patted the man on the shoulder. "Go."

As the scouts left him, Malachy crossed his hands over his heart and bowed his head. "Ward them, oh Lord, and help me find their missing companions."

Looking up, he caught another flash of gray and saw the wolf loping toward a smaller building. Renewing the spells that strengthened his armor, Malachy slowly worked his way around to the northern section of the town square. He slipped into the alley beside the building the wolf had indicated, then caught a glimpse of the other two scouts through a narrow window. *Too small to go through. I should try the back.*

He turned toward the rear of the house, but someone standing in the alley unshuttered a lamp and shined light over him.

"Parada," the man commanded in Lescari. "Do not move. You cannot escape us."

In the backlight from the lantern Malachy could see just enough of the man's tabard to catch the Red Guard badge sewn onto it.

So they finally arrived after all. Looking back over his shoulder, Malachy saw two more men silhouetted by the alley mouth. "Three of you, to stop a Wolf-priest? Fernandi may believe that's possible, but you shouldn't."

The man with the lantern shrugged. "Resist us and the two Stranans here will be killed."

"Oh." Malachy let his head hang for a moment, then he slid his longsword from its scabbard with his left hand. He grasped the sword halfway down on the blade and proffered it in the direction of the man holding the lantern. "You know I cannot allow harm to come to them."

"A weakness of those who allow nonexistent gods to rule their lives." The man's ridicule was echoed by his companions at Malachy's back. "Reason will ever conquer superstition in this way."

"Oh, were I you, I would be thanking God for your good fortune." Malachy offered a hastily sketched salute to his captor. "Last I heard, your Emperor has a bounty of forty gold Suns on my head for my rescue of the Ilbeorian Prince."

It took the man with the lantern a second or two to realize what Malachy was telling him. About the time he puzzled it out and began to see himself accepting accolades from his Emperor for capturing such a hated enemy, Malachy eased his grip on the sword and allowed the hilt to slide back down toward his hand. He flipped it around, grasping the hilt firmly in his right hand, then lunged past the lantern and stuck the Lescari soldier in the throat.

The lantern crashed to the ground as the wounded man gurgled and clutched at his neck. Malachy spun, his sword's tip striking sparks from the alley wall and parried a lunge down, hard. Continuing the pivot on his left foot, he kicked out with his right, catching the Lescari warrior in the face. Bones crunched and the man sagged to the side.

The third Red Guard came at Malachy, his longsword held in cautious guard. The man mumbled something and his whole body began to glow a deep red, as if he were blushing from his boots to his helm. He lunged, coming in faster than humanly possible, slipping his blade past Malachy's guard.

The Lescari sword stabbed at Malachy's chest, but the armor he wore shifted and bunched. Part of it stiffened and deflected the blade, while more of it folded in on itself to pad the site of the attack. Malachy felt the blade hit hard and pain shot from a cracked rib to encircle his chest with lightning. The force of the strike drove him backward, where he caught his heels on the body of the throat-stuck man.

Malachy crashed to the ground on his back and no amount of armor shifting was sufficient to absorb the force of the fall. He lay there for a second as his assailant loomed up over him, an incarnadine nightmare. Malachy had known of the Red Guards' use of diabolical magick to speed themselves in battle, but never before had he engaged one thus enchanted. The Red Guard raised his sword in both hands, ready to plunge it down into Malachy's chest like a dagger.

Malachy locked eyes with his enemy, then, as the man thrust down, the Wolf-priest shifted his body to the right. The armor over his breast plated again, skipping the blade to the left. It passed between Malachy's chest and left arm, stabbing deep into the alleyway's packed earth.

The Ilbeorian whipped his sword around and down, catching the Red Guard in the flank. The Lescar's armor parted cleanly, as did the flesh beneath it. Blood gushed, glowing with little yellow tints, pouring out much faster than it should have from such a wound. The Lescari soldier grunted, then sank to his knees and fell to his side, only at the last relinquishing his grip on his sword.

Malachy rolled to his feet and watched his spells rid his blade and armor of the glowing blood. *Sped up the way he was, his body pumped his blood out far faster than it ever would have otherwise. With his magick he doomed himself twice: here and in the hereafter.*

The Wolf-priest could hear the call of voices, all speaking Lescari, ordering other Red Guards to converge on his position. He knew he had to flee, but he hesitated because he also knew it was his duty to free the other scouts. *Perhaps if I lead the Red Guards off in some chase, then I can return . . .* Hope sparked with that idea, but any plan to execute it died as a golden glow appeared in the center of the town square.

It immediately caught Malachy's attention for it looked as if the sun were dawning, right there, in front of the Government House. As the light grew in brilliance it eclipsed the Government House and Malachy found himself drawn toward it. He saw shapes in the light, but couldn't discern them clearly at first. He walked toward the alley mouth to get a better look.

The images slowly focused and gained in detail. A man appeared, naked except for a golden loincloth with long ends that hung down to his knees. His whole body had been formed of gold and decorated with silvery tiger stripes that ran over his limbs and torso. The metallic flesh was not lifeless armor, or the sort of reactive mail that Malachy wore—it seemed to be a metal veneer layered over taut muscles. The figure took a step toward him and Malachy saw muscles moving in the man's legs, arms, and stomach, all natural and very lifelike.

Malachy shifted his attention to the man's face, but now found it hidden by a cowl shaped from the skull of a bear. The rest of the bear's flesh hung down over the man's back, and the paws had been knotted at his throat to hold the cloak in place. Malachy felt certain the bearskin cloak had not been there when he first saw the man, but he couldn't remember it not being there, either. Studying the man's head and face again, Malachy suddenly realized that bronze ram's horns had curled up and out of the ursine skull.

What is this? The bear is Strana's national symbol and the horns are from Vandari armor. Is this an ally come to aid me?

A voice sounded in Malachy's head. *"Behold your enemy."*

"What?" Malachy staggered toward the dazzling figure. "Who are you? Who is my enemy?"

The figure never replied.

A glowing Red Guard slashed at Malachy's head from the right and the Wolf-priest never even got a chance to start a parry. The Lescari blade caught him in the face at the level of his eyes. Sparks exploded in his head and Malachy spun to the ground. The sparks faded into blackness, then another blow to his skull sank Malachy Kidd into oblivion.

BOOK I

THE
BOOK OF
THE WOLF

— 1 —

**Royal Military Seminary
Sandwycke, Bettenshire
Ilbeoria
15 Arcan 1687**

As he walked through the library, hugging a bound volume of maps to his chest, Robert Drury found the stares of the other students unsettling. He'd been much older than most when he entered Sandwycke— much bigger as well—and had even been a veteran of the Lescari War; so being stared at wasn't something he found uncommon. Those sorts of stares had died away over his four years at the seminary, so their renewal, especially in the library and at that moment, meant only one thing.

Robin sighed. *You must have really gone and done it this time, Uriah.* He frowned and that broke off a number of stares, save the positively icy glare from Brother Lucas. Robin offered him a weak smile, which prompted the old priest to shake his head and turn away.

Without knocking, Robin opened the door to the small study chamber he'd reserved. A long, lanky, loose-limbed youth with a shock of red hair sat sprawled between two chairs. He'd slumped down in one enough that his shoulder blades were pressed against the seat; the second chair served as a platform for his thighs. Uriah held two little painted blocks of wood, one in each hand, and rammed them together, vocalizing a sound that approximated the roar of a steam cannon firing a volley.

Robin's eyes narrowed. "Interesting exercise in tactical abstraction, Cadet Smith."

The wooden blocks flew as Uriah started, then grabbed for some portion of either chair to keep him from falling. He failed, tipping over the chair beneath his thighs and letting the other one skid noisily to the wall. The little blocks, painted to represent military units, danced around him as he crashed to the floor, then he looked up at Robin, anger gathering on his face.

"You scared me!"

"Uriah, you've been scaring me every single day we've been working on this project together." Robin set his book of maps down on the corner of the sand table in the center of the room. A boxy affair, it was open at the top and filled with sand that could be shaped into the terrain of any battlefield in the world. "I expected you to have our terrain ready."

Uriah climbed to his feet, then picked up the two wooden blocks. He set them with others on the edge of the sand table. "I couldn't do the terrain without those maps, could I?"

"You could have gotten started." Robin pointed to the troop designator blocks. "After all, you weren't busy painting up the troops the way I asked you to."

Uriah shrugged. "Why should I? Brother Lucas had them in his stores. He looked at me funny when he handed them over, but he always looks at me funny."

Robin shook his head. "You realize, of course, that Brother Lucas will give Captain Irons a list of the troops we requested, and that means he'll know we're doing a *hypothetical* for our Tactics seminar project."

"Does it matter? We're not doing a battle using his Cathedral Lancers, so he's bound to grade us down anyway."

Robin held up his hands. "Why don't you think about what you just said while you get the terrain ready?" He opened the book of maps and held it up for Uriah to study. "I want it exact."

"Okay." Uriah nodded, then waved the book away.

Robin raised an eyebrow. "Study it, Uriah. Apply yourself a bit. 'Exact' doesn't mean 'kind of close.' "

Uriah's green eyes narrowed. "I said, Cadet Drury, I have it. I have a facility for memorizing images, remember? That's one of the reasons I'm in your Advanced Tactics seminar even though this is only my third year here."

"Okay, do it." Robin closed the book. "Sooner rather than later."

Uriah pretended he'd not heard that last remark. Using a yard-long board, he smoothed the sand table's surface and leveled the sand over the table's six-foot length. Yawning, he swept a hank of red hair back from his eyes, then dug the board in at the far end of the table. Working the board forward and up, he heaped sand at the nearer end. Finally, with his hands, he built up a little mound to dominate the near end.

Brushing his hands one against the other to rid them of sand, he shrugged. "That's as close as I need for Jebel Quirana and its environs."

"I'm still waiting for exact, Uriah."

"And exact you'll get." The younger man then closed his eyes and placed his hands on two well-worn spots on the side of the table. He whispered a prayer to Saint Jerome, the patron saint of libraries and librarians, then gave one short, crisp nod.

The spell he invoked, though common and not very powerful, still caused a bluish incandescence to pour like mist from the nimbus surrounding his hands. It bled out to ring the table, then flowed foglike over the beige sand. As it sank in, the light shifted the sand, pulling some parts down and pushing others up. Where Uriah had left a rounded mound, Jebel Quirana appeared as a flat-topped mesa with its cliff sides etched in sharp relief. The fog even formed sand into the image of the city of Helor, though the mountain dwarfed it and the scale did not allow for much complexity aside from the shape of the walls.

Robin reopened the book and stared at the map he'd shown Uriah. Everything matched, from the broad valley that rose at the southeast end on up to where the cylindrical mountain stood with a city built at its base on the north side. The cartography was not particularly spectacular, but the contour lines gave a good idea of the slope of the land, and Uriah had matched things perfectly.

Robin closed the book and sighed. He knew the same spell Uriah had used, and was capable of wielding it with similar skill, but he would have had to section the table off and work on parts of it individually were he to get that sort of detail, studying the map all the while. *What he does without even breaking a sweat would take me nigh unto forever.*

"Great job, Uriah." Robin shook his head. "Given the nature of the battle we're simulating, the scale is too big to encompass the final stages of the battle—the siege of the city of Helor itself—but this will work perfectly for the preliminary stages."

"It's exact enough for you, then?"

"Definitely."

"I hope your city of Helor is up to your standards."

"*My* city of Helor? You're doing that map, too."

Uriah frowned. "Why am I doing all the work?"

"Ha!" Robin blinked his eyes and stared incredulously at Uriah. "This is the first work you've done on this project. If you actually worked hard on it we'd have been done a month ago."

"You're forgetting who translated all those Stranan unit histories for you."

"Uriah, your mother was Stranan; you learned the language while she dandled you on her knee. You translated those histories, but I was the guy who dug around and determined which histories you'd be working on, remember?"

The younger man nodded. "I remember."

"Good." Robin set the map book down again. "At least Irons won't be able to mark us off for the terrain in our presentation. I wish, though, you'd done as I asked and not let it slip that we were doing a hypothetical."

"I stand by my previous remark. We're not doing one of the Cathedral Lancer battles from the Lescari War, so Irons will hate what we're doing anyway. Why worry about it being a hypothetical?"

"Irons has a particular hatred of hypothetical battles, Uriah."

"You, doing something to provoke an instructor?" Uriah's green eyes filled with mischief. "I guess your working with me on this project has warped you."

"For someone who is so damned smart, you see a lot less than even Colonel Kidd." Robin rubbed his scarred hands over his face. "I'm not trying to provoke Irons, but I don't see any value in doing a project that hundreds of other cadets have done." *And if I had chosen such a project and picked you as my partner, you would have had absolutely zero work to do, which you would have gladly accepted.*

The younger man sighed heavily and began to pace the width of the small lantern-lit room. "Rob, you're a Firstie and you're a cadet company commander. You've got everything going for you. You'll be getting out of here come graduation a month hence. Now I've got one more year here—"

"If they don't bounce you out of here after this term."

Uriah's nose wrinkled with disgust as a hint of fear trickled into his voice. "And doing a hypothetical isn't going to improve my chances of staying, is it?"

Robin smiled, his dark eyes flashing. "Can't hurt them. At least with a hypothetical, Irons and the others will know we were using our brains."

Uriah sighed. "True. But I don't think it will make that much difference to him."

"I'm counting on the fact that you've actually applied yourself to stun him with surprise."

"I see you're working hard in your Witticism seminar, as well."

Uriah pointed toward the door and the library beyond. "There are plenty of battles we could have used for our project and shown Irons we were capable of thinking—and the chance for you to be graded down would have been much less. Many of the battles have been done before so we know where the holes in tactics and strategy are and we can plug them easily. All we have to do is pick one of these and you'll get the grade you need to get you on the *Saint Michael*."

"And you'll somehow convince yourself that warfare can be just as easy, just as simple, when you're commanding the *Saint Michael*."

"I don't think that's your problem, Robin."

"You're going into the same service I am, so it *is* my problem. And here, you're my partner, so it's even more of my problem." The older man folded his arms across his chest. "Sandwycke isn't going to send you away if I have anything to do with it. Your father wanted you here. You're in the accelerated group because your ability to wield magic is strong and because you're so smart. To lose you would be a blow to the service."

"Not as big a one as you might think. Besides, my father is dead and my brother has other uses for me."

"It doesn't matter that your brother is now the Duke of Carvenshire. The Church knows your value here. Your brother may want to marry you off to someone to seal an alliance, but his wishes amount to little when opposed by the Church."

"That's Tybalt, but you forget that my brother Graham is a priest and he has Cardinal Garrow's ear. If they start working together and if Tybalt stops the grant my father gave me to pay for my training . . ."

"If, if—you're worrying about hypotheticals." Robin shook his head. "Only a fool worries himself about hypotheticals."

Uriah exaggerated a laugh and pointed at the sand table. "Which brings us back to the wisdom of this one."

"This isn't a hypothetical, it's a reality that hasn't happened yet." Robin flipped his big book open and shifted through the yellowed pages.

"You really think this will happen, that Strana will attack Helor and try to dominate Helansajar?"

"Do you expect the sun to come up tomorrow?"

Uriah nodded. "Yes, and much too early for my tastes, too."

"I saw that coming. You'll need to apply yourself in your Witticism seminar next year, too." Robin leaned on the edges of the sand table. "Let's get the troops deployed. We've got to get this right, or Irons will have a field day with us."

Uriah's face brightened as he passed Robin the blue and gold blocks that represented the Stranan troops. "I could go back out and get the Cathedral Lancers troop chits and we could bring them into this battle. Irons never fails a project where his Lancers do well, no matter how weak the analysis."

Robin placed the units in the sand and began sorting them by type, then looked over at his partner. "Am I hearing you correctly, Uriah? Are *you*, of all people, suggesting we stroke Iron's ego for the sake of winning praise in a grades report? If you are, I'm going to ask for an Exorcist to speak with you."

That brought a smile to Uriah's face. "I suppose it does sound suspect. It's just that I know you need a good report to win the ethyrine command on the *Saint Michael*. Irons hates me, so you've got that going against you. In fact, I don't know why you picked me as your partner, anyway. I thought you were smarter than that."

"I am."

"But you did it anyway."

"You were perfect for interpreting any reports we had from Strana on their troops, and you did a great job at it." Robin picked up a Stranan unit that had been painted with a bronze base. "If you hadn't pointed out that the 137th Imperial Bear Hussars had a Vandari company attached to it, this project would have been doomed from the start."

"I would have reviewed the order of battle for you even if I'd not been your partner, Robin."

"I know, but I wanted you to share in this. We're doing a hypothetical, which means we have to think in unconventional ways." Robin gave Uriah a lopsided grin. "And you're about as unconventional as they come here."

Uriah nodded. "Insubordinate by any other name."

"That wasn't the last of my reasons." Robin started placing blocks on the miniature landscape. "What's the purpose of this whole exercise anyway?"

Uriah shifted his shoulders uneasily. "By studying what other commanders did and then trying new strategies, we can learn how to make the battle go better. We learn from their mistakes."

"Not only do you remember Iron's opening lecture, but you are close to having his voice down, too." Robin's expression sharpened. "What's the big mistake in that idea?"

"I don't think I see one."

"Open your eyes and take another look. Apply yourself, for once."

"I am. My eyes are open; they're just not silver. I'm still in the dark."

"Think of it this way, Uriah—why did we beat Fernandi at the end of the war?"

"The Warlord and his generals had learned how to counter Fernandi's tactics. They learned from the mistakes of the war's early commanders."

"You're getting there. And why did those early commanders get beaten?"

"Because they had never fought anyone using the tactics Fernandi did."

"Yet our commanders were Sandwycke graduates, and the Carinolians that Fernandi beat were schooled in the Vulcha tradition. Fernandi even beat the Tacier's best from the Savensk Academy, then burned the academy itself. They were the best military minds in the world, but Fernandi defeated them all. How did he do it?"

"Can't hazard a guess."

"Apathy I can handle, but don't play dumb. Think." Robin carefully placed the bronze-based block representing the Vandari company in the center of the Stranan line. "Give up?"

"Da."

Robin sighed. "As seminarians and students, when they had *their* Tactics seminars, all of them analyzed the *last* war. They perfected tactics for the last war. They were trained to fight the last war. And they would have won the last war, but Fernandi, he was fighting the *next* war. And our exercise here, this will be a battle of the next war."

"But this involves Stranan troops fighting against Helansajaran irregulars. You were the one who told me we've not had a survey of the area for thirty years, and Shukri Awan took Helor from the Khast family only a decade ago. There's not a book in this library that can tell us what his troops are like."

"True enough, but I have friends in Ludstone who tell me there are reports coming out of central Estanu. They contain only rumors about Helor at this point, but a lot of those rumors are stories about the city's conquest and the battling done in the area between the Khast faction and Awan's Helorian troops."

Uriah slowly shook his head. "Using substandard reports is not a way to win that berth on the *Saint Michael*, Rob."

"Despite not being military reports, this merchant stuff is not substandard. A cabin boy from the *Crow* now works for Grimshaw Mercantile. He's under the misguided impression I saved his life when we were fighting the *El Tauró*. He's been trying to pay me back for years and the information he's been giving me to do so is sketchy, but good enough for our purposes."

"You're putting a lot of faith in Irons allowing us leeway because this is a hypothetical."

"We're Wolf-priests, Uriah. Sharp swords, battlemagicks, and faith are about all we have to work with."

"You have a point, but I still have to wonder about your choice. Why this battle? We have no part of it—we can't even bluff about our hypothetical being a 'what-if' scenario pitting our troops against Lescari troops."

"I'd prefer to be doing the battle that liberates Helor from the Strananans, but—"

"But they haven't taken Helor." Uriah looked down at the handful of Helorian irregular designators lined up on the edge of the table. "The problem is that you can't be certain Strana will take Helor."

"They have to, Uriah—you should be able to see that better than almost anyone else. They have no choice. Helor is the key to all of Estanu and, one way or another, Strana has to take it."

Robin pointed toward the lowest end of the model and beyond it. "When Fernandi attacked Strana he overran the most progressive and advanced parts of the Tacier's Empire. He razed Myasovo and laid siege to Murom. Had Strana's ally, General Winter, not intervened when it did, or as strongly as it did, Fernandi would have brought Strana down. Not since the days of Keerana Dost has Strana been so close to falling."

"If Strana takes Helor, then they can bring pressure to bear on our holdings in Aran." Uriah shrugged. "They think their threat will cool our desire to expand the empire."

Now you're getting it, Uriah. Robin nodded. "But it's just as likely to trigger a war we'd both like to avoid."

"Maybe this isn't as hypothetical as I thought." Uriah smiled and slapped Robin on the shoulder. "You've thought your way through all the pitfalls."

"We can hope, but both know that when our plan gets studied with eyes of silver, gaping holes will appear as if by magick." Robin shivered involuntarily. "When Colonel Kidd gets a look at what we've done, he'll find the holes and exploit them terribly."

Uriah shook his head. "Don't worry; Viscount Warcross isn't part of the examination tribunal. Captain Irons has Knight-Commander Warren and . . ."

The older man arranged the Stranan steam-cannon batteries carefully near the gates of Helor. "I know the roster, but it doesn't matter who is *supposed* to be evaluating us. Malachy Kidd will be there. He always shows up for the Advanced Tactics seminar project evaluations. That's why no one ever re-creates the battle for Bauczeg, even as a hypothetical."

"Well, here's something that isn't hypothetical." Uriah pointed to the Stranan cavalry unit before Helor. "That's the 137th Imperial

Bear Hussars regiment. Pokovnik Grigory Khrolic commands it. Kidd knew him. Khrolic was commander of the battalion at Glogau when . . ." He hesitated and Robin saw goose bumps rise on Uriah's arms. "When the Lescari captured the Viscount. You should have picked another unit."

"I had no choice but to use it. The 137th Hussars have a company of Vandari attached to it and are stationed in the Vzorin Political District. When Strana goes in, the 137th Hussars will be the spearhead."

"I still wouldn't have used it."

"Because of Khrolic's popularity in Murom, and Duke Arzlov's infamy in Murom, it's one of the most documented and storied units in the Imperial Stranan Armed Forces. This hypothetical will be as accurate as we can make it."

"That's something, then." Uriah shivered. "I just don't like the idea of giving old Eyes of Silver more reason to go after us."

Robin pulled a sheet of notes from inside the cover of the atlas. "He doesn't need a reason to go after us—he just will. That's his nature."

"It might be his nature, but I don't like it. Don't you find it creepy, the way he wanders about? He's supposed to be blind, but there's no way I can tell he is . . ."

Robin's dark eyes hardened and Uriah fell silent. "Forget the stories you've heard about him and just remember what he is—someone who was broken by war. I saw a lot of people like that. Someone buys a commission in a regiment or on a ship and suddenly he's commanding troops in combat. War is *not* a place to learn your trade by making mistakes, especially when your mistakes get other men killed. Yes, Colonel Kidd ran into trouble in Glogau, but he spends his time here making certain we won't do the same. Better that than using your time here to make sure your own exploits live on gloriously in the minds of half-trained students."

Uriah nodded halfheartedly. "You refer to Captain Irons."

"Among others."

Uriah narrowed his eyes. "So, aside from giving Malachy Kidd something to concentrate on, do you have any more surprises?"

"If you'd been paying attention to what we've been doing, you'd know the answer to that one."

"Remember, I've seen the Stranan reports. You've not showed me the stuff you've gotten from Aran." Uriah dropped his voice to a whisper. "Anything really odd show up in those reports?"

Robin barely glanced up at Uriah and noted the faint blue tinge to his eyelids, bespeaking just a hint of Durranian blood in him through his mother. "You mean like rumors of the Dost's reincarnation?"

The younger man started, and that surprised Robin. "That would be a little bit of a surprise."

"It would, indeed." Robin folded his arms across his chest. "You think that the reincarnation of a conqueror who, eight centuries ago, emerged from Durrania and carved an empire that ran from the Arctic Ocean to the north, Aran to the south, from Tsaih in the east to Illyria and Glogau in the west, constitutes 'a little bit of a surprise'?"

"When you put it like that, ah, no." Uriah fidgeted a bit. "Still, it's commonly accepted in that area—and in some Stranan circles, too—that when he died he said he would return to rebuild his empire and protect his people. Stranan mothers have used his blood-thirsty image to frighten children into behaving for years, telling them that misbehaving children will be harvested when he comes back."

"Your mother among them?"

"Um, yes." The young man shifted his shoulders uncomfortably. "I know the Church says reincarnation can't happen, and I know it's just superstition, but . . ."

Robin smiled. "There are mothers all over the Urovian continent who are using the image of Fernandi to keep their children in line and behaving, and you have to know their Fernandi is scarier than the real one ever was."

"Good point."

"To your question, though, so far, yes, his return is completely hypothetical. There aren't even rumors of a pretender. Most soothsayers in Aran and Estanu, if the reports are correct, say the Dost has not yet been reborn."

Uriah started placing Helorian units on the sand table. "Just as well. If half the stories can be believed, the Dost has probably spent the last eight centuries in the grave mulling over the *next* war, just as we're doing. With all due respect for what you've got planned here, I think *his* hypotheticals would have a whole lot more reality in them than this one, and I don't think that's a reality anyone wants to see."

Robin nodded. "I think you're right there, so let's hope he forestalls his return until the battles *we've* waged are being studied in tactics seminars. Fighting Fernandi was bad enough. I've no desire to face the man who actually *did* conquer Strana."

— 2 —

> **Bir el Jamajim,**
> **Helansajar**
> **20 Arcan 1687**

In the high desert of Helansajar, water was life itself. The *Kitabna Ittikal*, the Holy Book of Ataraxianism, demanded of all civilized people the sharing of water with travelers. While many of the Helansajaran people would have proclaimed themselves to be worshipers of Atarax, and even offered prayers three times daily as prescribed in the *Kitabna Ittikal*, water was not always freely shared, and thus had the Well of Skulls earned its grim name.

In the stony bowl that surrounded the well and contained a sizable pool of water, bandits on horseback rode round and round the heavily laden camels and horses of the caravan, driving them to the water's edge. The bandits, all scruffy men wearing mismatched pieces of armor scavenged from dead enemies, waved curved shamshirs or nocked arrows to short, powerful horse-bows. With their bearded, dirt-stained faces contorted in fearsome grimaces, they screamed challenges and epithets at the tops of their lungs.

The caravan's dozen guards brandished their own blades, but the distance between the circle in which the horsemen rode and in which the guards stood was too far for them to counterattack. To make a run at the bandits was to maneuver away from the shelter of others too long. A lone man would be cut down easily, as a handful of bodies already attested. A couple of the caravan's horses had gone down, bristling with arrows, and a fat merchant in robes of blue and gold lay face-first in the dirt with a trio of arrows sticking up from his back.

A golden glow washed over one of the caravan guards, then he darted forward. He moved no more quickly than a normal man, so clearly his battlemagick didn't speed his reactions. As he closed with a bandit he leaped fearlessly up at the man in the saddle, slashing with his shamshir. The blade bit deep into the bandit's left flank, splitting armor and flesh.

The bandit's return stroke hit the guardsman in the left flank, as well. The curved blade sliced cleanly through the guard's leather armor, but slid across his golden flesh without doing any damage. The guardsman cried out triumphantly and grabbed a handful of bandit beard, then let gravity drag him and the bandit back to the earth. They landed in a heap and another swordstroke killed the bandit.

A second bandit, this one burning brightly red in the coming dusk, leaped from his saddle and engaged the guardsman. The bandit's sword slashed and cut almost faster than the eye could follow. It opened gaping rents in the guard's armor, shifting to the defensive only when the guard managed to aim a blow at the bandit. No blood flowed from within the guardsman's armor, but the ferocity of the bandit's attack drove him back, then the golden glow faded.

The bandit's next strike opened the defenseless guard from hip to hip and spun him to the ground.

Rafiq Khast had seen enough. The echoed thunder of the bandit horses' hoofbeats had covered the rumble of the Khast band's charge up and over the depression's southern berm. The thirty-man band had been directed to this spot and time by omens interpreted by Rafiq's uncle Qusay. Of the Khast warriors, only one in five had magickal talents that let them invoke battle spells; the rest relied on sharpened steel and the experience of living and fighting from the saddle for years.

Rafiq, with his black hair flowing from beneath his spike-topped helmet, raised his shamshir and drove his black horse at the red bandit. The bandit grinned and waved Rafiq on. Rafiq returned the smile, then invoked his own battlemagick, allowing an icy blue to spread from around his eyes to suffuse his flesh. The bandit's expression slackened, then he darted forward to strike at Rafiq.

It is a pity that your magick does not make you think more quickly, too. As the bandit charged at him, Rafiq leaned low to the right and slashed. The bandit flicked his own blade to the left to parry the incoming blow, clearly intent on continuing his rush forward to slash again at Rafiq's body. The two swords met with a ringing peal, then the bandit screamed as Rafiq's blow tore his shamshir from his grip. As the blade whirled through the air behind the bandit, Rafiq's cut crushed the man's helmet, spraying blood and brains over the ground.

To his left Rafiq saw his cousin Akhtar, Qusay's youngest son, split a bandit's shield with an overhand blow that took the man's arm off at the elbow. Others of his cousins skewered bandits on their spears or traded blows amid swordfights that drove horses and riders around in little circles. Some of the caravan guards charged out as well, while a small knot of bandits bolted for the other side of the well depression and rode off.

Rafiq slid from the saddle and stared down at one of the bandits who had been spilled from his mount by the band's charge. "You knew better than to be in this place, Feroze. It has been prophesied that you will die here."

The bandit leader rose to his feet and a red glow flowed over him. "You too are fated to die, Rafiq Khast."

"True, Feroze." Rafiq smoothed his luxurious black moustache with his left hand, then gestured casually at the rising moon to the east. "But I am fated to die beneath a full moon, which was ten days ago."

"The wounds I will deal you will allow you to linger until the next full moon." Feroze let a feral grin split his face. "I am the whirlwind."

"And I am the rock." Rafiq lowered himself into a fighting stance, his curved shamshir held easily in his right hand. The blade covered him from right hip to left shoulder and Feroze's stance aped his. Rafiq slowly extended his left hand and gently waved Feroze closer.

It is all a matter of timing. Feroze's battlemagick sped him up so he could strike more quickly and react faster than a man who had no battlemagicks. The whirlwind was a magick favored by Shukri Awan's courtiers because Awan had made good use of it in taking the city of Helor from Rafiq's father. *And yet none of them realize I have spent my life learning ways to liberate my family's birthright, which means I know how to deal with the whirlwind.*

Feroze darted toward Rafiq and the younger man gave ground quickly. Though Feroze used the same battlemagick as the man Rafiq had already slain, the older man didn't have the same speed. The magick could only optimize the man using it, and Feroze's age meant that while he was preternaturally quick, he wasn't so fast that Rafiq couldn't escape him.

Their blades clanged as Rafiq parried the cuts he could not leap away from. Feroze pressed him hard, chasing him back. Rafiq made a feint toward the pool, but the Helorian bandit cut him off. *He knows that if our fight moves into the water, his speed will be worthless and that with my heightened strength I will kill him easily.*

As he backed away from the bandit, Rafiq repeatedly tried to get to the water, or to lure Feroze into an area where enough sand had flowed into the depression to make footing treacherous. Again and again the bandit anticipated him, racing around to prevent him from setting a trap. Then Feroze would drive in, slashing back and forth, using his speed to slip under or over a parry. When Rafiq made to attack him, Feroze withdrew out of range, then danced back in with more cuts that split air and spilled no blood.

Feroze snarled at him. "You are not the rock, you are a coward. You do not fight; you run."

Rafiq stopped and lowered his guard. "I merely wanted the others to see your great speed, Feroze. Come now, do your worst."

The bandit sped forward, aiming a forehand slash at Rafiq's left flank. Rafiq made no effort to parry but instead dashed forward himself. Lifting his left arm, he took the blow on his ribs, but it did no serious damage. Feroze's speedy attack and Rafiq's move meant he'd slipped inside strike range, so the only thing that hit him was the swordsman's wrist.

Feroze's eyes grew wide as Rafiq clamped his left arm down on the bandit's swordarm. Rafiq brought his left hand under, up and around Feroze's elbow, locking the joint. Straightening his own arm, Rafiq brought Feroze up on his tiptoes, then pressed his shamshir to the man's throat.

"I am the rock, Feroze." He smiled coldly as Feroze's chest heaved with exertion. "I let you run around to tire yourself out. Warfare is not an old man's sport. Your master would do well to remember that. Your magick might make you fast, but your age makes you weak. Mine makes me strong, and my heart makes me stronger."

The red glow that surrounded Feroze drained away. "Will you kill me?"

"There is no need for that." Rafiq released him and let him stagger back a couple of steps. Feroze brandished his sword, then pure agony contorted his face. He dropped the blade and clawed with both hands at his chest. Feroze dropped to his knees, his eyes bulging. He screamed hoarsely and harshly, then slumped forward on his face.

Rafiq stared at the body for a moment, then turned to face the caravan's survivors. "As it is written: Atarax grants us our talents to be used in accord with his will. Misuse them and be denied Paradise forever. Feroze died of a weak and cruel heart."

Three gaudily dressed merchants stumbled forward and sank to their knees. They bowed deeply to him and came up with dust caking their foreheads and noses. "You are truly the instrument of God's Will."

"No." Rafiq gave them a warm smile. "I am the embodiment of Shukri Awan's worst nightmare. I am Rafiq Khast. Why is it that Shukri Awan sent Feroze and his men after you?" Rafiq pointed to some of the cargo bales on the camels. "You have just come from Helor. He should have robbed you blind there."

A slight breeze brought the scent of sand and blood to Rafiq as one of the merchants sat back on his heels. "My lord, we told Shukri Awan that we were bound for Kulang, to trade with the Ghur merchants."

Rafiq frowned. Toward the south and southeast the land began to rise. He could not see Helor itself from the well, but a gray smudge at the base of Jebel Quirana marked its position. To the east and west the land leveled out until it hit the foothills that marked the transition from lowlands to highlands and snowcapped mountains. They were known as the Helan and Estan mountains respectively and, along with the Jedrosian Plateau at the foot of the Estans, dominated the Helansajaran landscape. They defined the edges of the lowlands and made passage from Strana into the southern reaches of the Estanuan continent impossible except through Helansajar. The kingdom of the Ghurs lay far to the south, through the passes of the Himlan Mountains, and beyond it lay the warm, fertile land of Aran.

"It seems to me, my friends, that you are off course if you are bound for Kulang." He pointed past Jebel Quirana and smiled. "You have added several days' ride to your trip."

The merchant smiled, combing fingers through his black beard. "My lord, we lied about our destination to Shukri Awan because we are bound for Vzorin to trade for Stranan goods."

"I see. That makes much more sense."

Back north, too far away to be seen, lay Vzorin. The Vzorin Political District represented the Stranan Empire's southernmost penetration into the Estanuan continent. Rafiq had never been there, but his uncle Qusay had been enslaved there for a number of years as a young man. He told stories of wondrous things he'd seen; virtually all of it heretical to Ataraxianism, but fascinating nonetheless. Items of Stranan manufacture were often highly prized in the south, and opening trade with Vzorin would make the merchants very rich.

Rafiq's eyes narrowed. "You are clearly intrepid, daring to cross into Strana for the sake of gold. This is not the first time you have been there, is it?"

The merchant shook his head easily, but his two companions paled at the question. "There is a man in Vzorin, a merchant. His name is Valentin Svilik. He speaks our tongue and trades with us fairly. Were the Khasts yet lords in Helor, the trade would bring profit to all."

The blue flesh around Rafiq's eyes tightened. "Shukri Awan does not tolerate this trade?"

"His tariffs are enough to bankrupt us. You would be more reasonable."

"It is possible, but the Khasts no longer rule in Helor." Rafiq smiled. "We will again, however, when the Dost returns."

The merchants' faces brightened. "The Dost will return soon, we are certain of it. He must. It is time his empire is reestablished and his dominion over Estanu is made manifest." The eldest of the merchants nodded toward Rafiq. "You bear Durranian blood, so you will be elevated by his hand to the glory you deserve."

"So it has been told." Rafiq turned away from the merchants and looked at his band. He was blood kin to most of them and, like him, they too bore the marks of descent from the Durranian horde that had swept over the Estanuan continent centuries before. The blue tinge of the flesh around his eyes, and the sharpening of his ears, as well as his ability to wield stronger battlemagicks than most, were part of his heritage.

Strana too had once been under the Dost's dominion, and his uncle had told Rafiq that Stranan nobles resorted to cosmetics to heighten the Durranian coloring their diluted bloodlines had faded. Likewise their embracing of Eilyphianism showed their inferiority and a rejection of the heritage the Dost had given them. Even though he believed that fervently, Rafiq also knew the Stranans would be fierce foes if they ever chose to venture into Helansajar to wage war.

"Akhtar, we will stay here tonight. Send riders back for our spare horses and kits, then post guards in case the last of the bandits decide to return."

His cousin nodded, then turned and started giving orders.

Rafiq looked again at the merchants. "We will share this well with you this night if you do not mind. We will let fires burn here and Shukri Awan will think all your treasures will soon be his. When his bandits reach Helor tomorrow or the next day he will learn of his error and will be furious."

The eldest merchant nodded. "We shall bypass Helor on our return and go to Kulang. When we return, perhaps he will have forgotten about us."

"If he has not, if he does not grant you the hospitality demanded by the *Kitabna Ittikal*, the wrath of God will punish him." Rafiq smiled. "It is said of him that a falling star will mark his passing. It will be my pleasure to be the one to tickle that star from the sky."

— 3 —

Standing at attention at the front of the room, Uriah Smith resisted the temptation to lean forward on the sand table and send an earth-quake through the model of Helor. He thought he'd done a good job of re-creating the city—Robin had been impressed and gave him a smile—but clearly all his effort had been wasted. Tension rolled from the tribunal like an apocalyptic storm and sent lightninglike tendrils of dread through Uriah. *The most hypothetical thing about this project was our thinking it might be evaluated fairly.*

The three members of the tribunal sat there, each with his pate shaved as much as allowed by regulation and his remaining short hair lightened to gray or near white. Uriah had once marveled at how men trimmed their hair and colored it to lay claim to the wis-dom that normally came with age and natural hair loss; but in these men he saw it as a mockery of a very natural process. *Had these men truly been in a position to learn from their experiences, they'd bear scars that would show us how intelligent they were.*

Captain Irons, his red-faced outrage carrying color up onto his shaved pate, pinned their paper to the tribunal's table with a stiff fin-ger. Knight-Commanders Warren and Stubblefield kept their faces impassive, yet the number of place-markers sprouting from their copies of the report told Uriah they had a legion of points to attack in the plan. What made the whole thing worse was that the dressing-down had begun even before he and Robin had gotten very far in their verbal presentation of their project.

". . . Irresponsible, do you hear me?" Irons's angry words poured molten through clenched teeth. "This paper is indefensible and irresponsible. Fantasy has no part in the study of warfare. Yes, Drury, what is it?"

"Permission to speak, sir."

Surprised, Uriah looked over at Robin. *What are you doing, Rob?*

"Granted, Cadet Drury."

"Members of the tribunal, I convinced Cadet Smith to do this exercise. He noted that doing a hypothetical would be frowned upon." Rob's head bent slightly forward. "I should have heeded his insight in this matter."

"Cadet Smith should have heeded his own insight in this matter, Mr. Drury." Irons shot a hot glance at Uriah. "And I congratulate you in getting anything approaching cooperation or activity from Mr. Smith. The fact remains, however, that you deviated from the assignment both in choosing your subject *and* in second-guessing the intent behind the assignment of this planning exercise." Captain Irons's finger slammed again onto the report. "You cadets are given battle analyses so we can evaluate how you solve problems. That this battle *might* take place does not make it fact, and we have no basis upon which to evaluate your analysis. Moreover, this battle does not involve *our* troops. Are the two of you thinking of selling your services to Strana's Tacier or the Alanim of Helor?"

"After we convert the Alanim to Martinism, yes, sir," Uriah snapped in reply. "But maybe the Tacier would be a better choice, since after he takes Helor, Aran will be open to him . . ."

Irons's head came up and he spitted Uriah with a steel-gray gaze. "So you have a whole series of these hypotheticals planned, leading up to a Stranan assault on Aran, do you, Mr. Smith? Plenty more fantasy battles in mind, perhaps?"

"No, sir."

"Pity, Cadet Smith, because both you and Mr. Drury will want something to dream about while you repeat this course."

Robin glared at Uriah, then lifted his chin and spoke to Captain Irons. "In our analysis, sir, it seems likely Strana will have to take steps to secure its border with Helansajar because of the local political instability. Shukri Awan may control Helor, but he does not fully control the countryside of Helansajar. By taking Helor, Strana is pursuing a logical course toward stabilizing that region and opening new markets for their goods. By studying the tactics the Stranan forces would use in taking Helor, we can begin to look at how they might approach the conquest of Aran, which is likely the next target they will look at."

"Is that so, Mr. Drury?"

"Yes, sir. If you will look beyond the hypothetical nature of our report, I think you'll see that our reasoning is sound, as is our grasp of tactics."

"Oh, do you mean I might have overlooked something in your report?" Irons slowly sat back. The skepticism in his voice filled the large testing chamber. It brought hushed groans of sympathy from the rest of the cadets seated in the rows behind Uriah and Robin. Though Uriah didn't count many of the other students as friends, none of them wanted to see another cadet tongue-lashed this way. Most of them liked Rob—even found him something of a romantic figure since he had fought against Fernandi—and even admired him for daring to present a hypothetical. Still, the dangers of that sort of presentation were well-known, so none of the others would have thought the dressing-down unexpected or even undeserved.

"Mr. Smith, Mr. Drury, we have a problem here and it is very important you understand it." Irons opened his hands to take in the other tribunal members. "These exercises are graded based on a comparison with other analyses of the same battle and through the tribunal's knowledge of the troops, situation, and overall environment involved in the battle. When a battle involves the Cathedral Lancers, for example, I am able to bring considerable knowledge of that unit to bear in my evaluation. The same goes for my fellow judges here. A hypothetical that does not even include units with which we are familiar gives us no frame of reference within which to begin our evaluation process."

Uriah heard a sound from the back of the room, but didn't turn and see what caused it. He held Irons's gaze, knowing the man wanted him to turn away so he could blast him again. Captain Irons frowned heavily, then looked past him. The officer's open mouth closed, and his frown melted into a slightly more quizzical expression. He swallowed, and Uriah wondered if Irons's mind hadn't finally collapsed under the strain of his fury.

"I wonder," came a quiet voice from the back of the room, "if you are not underestimating your abilities, Captain Irons."

Irons began to shift uncomfortably in his chair. "I had not considered that possibility, my lord."

The soft voice grew louder, but only by dint of the speaker's approach to the front of the room. "You should give yourself that much credit, sir. You and the Knight-Commanders are known for being resourceful. While the bias against hypotheticals is well-known, I felt *this* work was inventive enough to warrant a closer look . . . to be studied in greater depth."

Slightly shorter than either Uriah or Robin, Malachy Kidd slipped between them. Uriah shivered involuntarily as Kidd's shoulder brushed against his and the man stopped inches away from bumping into the sand table. His white hair hung down to his shoulders yet, and unlike other men of his rank and position in society, the top of his head remained unshaven. Except for the length and color of his hair, Malachy Kidd might as well have been a cadet attending Sandwycke for instruction instead of an instructor dreaded by students and staff alike.

Captain Irons cleared his voice. "I think we would all agree, Viscount Warcross, that this project is imaginative, but you would also agree that imagination is seldom of benefit to a military commander."

"Undisciplined imagination, yes, Captain." Uriah heard something in Kidd's voice that gave it an edge, but one so delicate he could feel it slicing painlessly through Irons's ego. "I would agree undisciplined imagination is not good. This project, however, when read to me, did not appear to be lacking in discipline. If I might have your leave to ask a few questions of the cadets?"

"As you wish, Colonel Kidd."

Uriah smiled involuntarily and his tension began to evaporate. *Perhaps we have a chance at an intelligent assessment of our project, after all.* He glanced over at Rob and saw the larger man shift his shoulders uncomfortably. *Why be concerned over Kidd's evaluation? Irons has already told us we have failed, so how bad can this be?*

Kidd worked his way around the narrow edge of the table to position himself right behind Jebel Quirana. He pressed one hand to either side of the sand table, closed his eyes and frowned with concentration. Uriah saw the scar that ran from the corner of one eye to the other, and the bump it made over the spot where Lescari physickers had reconstructed Malachy's face with their diabolical magicks.

Malachy opened his eyes, light reflecting from the silver orbs sitting in his eye sockets. Because they were uniform in color and otherwise featureless, Uriah had no way of knowing if they moved the way real eyes did. They gleamed coldly and without compassion. Uriah suddenly understood Robin's concern. *This can be worse. He'll savage us worse than Irons ever could.* "My compliments on your model."

Uriah shrugged. "It was nothing."

Kidd canted his head, his white eyebrows arrowing together. "Cadet Smith?"

Because the eyes didn't move, Uriah couldn't tell if Kidd was looking at him or not, but he felt skewered by the man's argent stare. "Sir. Nothing. It was nothing, *sir.*"

"Good." The hint of a smile tugged at the corners of Kidd's

mouth, but the silver eyes remained mirthless. "Modesty becomes you."

Uriah shivered and looked down at the city nestled beneath Jebel Quirana, but he did not feel safe. Intellectually he knew Kidd could not see with those eyes. All the magick theory he had studied here at Sandwycke was clear on that one point without using Kidd and his eyes of silver as an example. While magicks could allow one the control of objects, it did not allow sensory reception through them. A burning poker might be thrust against his armor, yet the only heat Uriah would feel was that which bled through the armor. He would not feel the searing heat of fire against the armor, nor would he feel the sting of a sword cut or the prick of an arrow.

Even so, just because Kidd was blind, it did not mean he did not possess the ability to see things. *That was an aspect of the man I missed.* Uriah swallowed hard. *We fashioned this report to deal with someone of Captain Irons's intellect but, despite the warnings, we—I—didn't work hard enough to deal with Colonel Kidd, and Robin will be doomed because of it.* Uriah looked at his friend and slowly shook his head.

Kidd's voice came deceptively soft. "In your plan you allow for the destruction of roughly a third of Helor's troops in a defense of Bir el Jamajim, Bir el Bark, and Bir el Wuhush. These three wells are a considerable distance from Helor. Why did you think Shukri Awan would defend them?"

Robin answered. "Sir, we believed they would be defended to deny water to the Stranan troops. Water is of the utmost importance in the high desert there."

"Agreed, but does it not make more sense for Awan to let the Stranans take these wells and ship water forward to their besieging host—leaving these water caravans vulnerable to attack—than it does to try and hold them against overwhelming odds?"

Robin hesitated. "It does, sir, but Shukri Awan does not seem to have that strong a grasp of tactics."

Kidd raised an eyebrow. "Ah, so in this hypothetical you are hypothesizing that Shukri Awan cannot learn from mistakes he has made in the past? You suppose he is, in fact, stupid? Were this true, would you not have to hypothesize that such a stupid man would lose the throne to an imaginative member of the Khast family, in a reversal of what happened to put him on the throne?"

"Sir, it appears we may have artificially curtailed Helorian tactics based on the information we have at hand."

"Nice retreat, Mr. Drury, the kind that leaves bodies broken and bleeding over a battlefield." Kidd's head shifted a fraction of an inch toward Uriah. "Cadet Smith, you worked on the tactical situation here in Helor, correct?"

"Yes, sir."

"So, in giving the Helorians back their regiment of mounted irregulars, and having those irregulars operate behind Stranan lines, how would Pokovnik Grigory Khrolic change his tactics in assaulting the city?"

"I don't know that he would, sir." Uriah pointed to the blue and gold blocks of wood arrayed around the five walls of Helor. "The 137th Bear Hussars regiment incorporates an artillery company consisting of a dozen steam cannons. The walls of Helor are approximately thirty feet tall, yet only half that thick. They are built to defend against the primitive siege machinery that can be produced locally. The Stranan steam cannons, unlike preindustrial catapults and trebuchets, shoot projectiles on a flattened arc that makes precision targeting possible. Undermining and toppling the walls of Helor should not be difficult for the Hussars."

The flesh tightened around Kidd's eyes. "I commend you on your understanding of artillery theory, but there is a practical matter you may have overlooked in your answer. Why did Cadet Drury want Shukri Awan to deny the Stranan force access to the wells?"

"To deny them water, sir."

"And these steam cannons, what do they require?"

"Water, sir." Uriah began to sense a trap being formed, but he saw a chance to slip from it before it got him. "But the Stranans' cannons use steam-driven pistons to compress air and force it into the cannon's pressure chamber. The recovery and recycling of water vapor on these cannons is very efficient. In fact, the gunners will require more water after a day's combat than the cannons in each squad."

"I agree, Cadet." Kidd smiled easily. "I have . . . had experience amid the gunners of the Hussars regiment. Your analysis of their water usage is correct. You forget, however, that the Stranans use a single boiler to provide steam for each squad of three cannons. Destroy the boiler and the cannons are reduced to using a smaller boiler built into the gunne itself. While that boiler is likewise very efficient, it takes too much time to build up the pressure needed to destroy a wall."

"But the Helorians have no cannons with which to engage in counter battery barrages, so they cannot damage the boilers."

"No?"

The way Kidd asked the question screamed at Uriah that he

was wrong and that Kidd knew something he did not, but he continued to defend his position. "Sir, the Hussars will protect their cannons. No forces from the city can get at them."

Captain Irons sat forward. "We have Helorian troops operating in the Stranan rear, Cadet Smith."

Uriah frowned. "Sir, what troops?"

Irons's expression sharpened. "The remnants of the troops driven off from defending the wells."

Uriah frowned. *But I thought the colonel gave me those troops back to defend the city . . .* "Sir, that may be, sir, but they still will not have sufficiently strong equipment to destroy a boiler."

Irons frowned. "Surely you are aware, Cadet, that the Helansajarans have developed heavy crossbows sufficient for punching an iron quarrel through armor. That would be quite sufficient to put a hole through a boiler."

Before Uriah could curtly dismiss Irons's inquiry, Robin leaned forward. "Forgive me, Captain, but I was unaware the existence of such weapons has been confirmed. I understood their existence had been conjectured based on the occasional loss of Vandari armor when the Tacier has sent units into central Estanu. Our troops have encountered no such weapons when pressed by bandits from Drangiana or Helansajar."

"The reports you based your exercise on, Cadet Drury, have as much validity as the reports of these heavier weapons." Irons stared daggers at Robin. "If we wish to exclude conjecture from this discussion, you and your project are in serious peril."

"There is reality that deals with *your* fantasy, sir." Uriah started to point at the table, then brought his hands back to his sides. "Even if the larger boilers are destroyed, the cannons can be loaded with canisters of spike and grapeshot. The small boilers will produce insufficient pressure to bring the walls down, but the Stranans can use them to sweep the walls of defenders. That will leave the gates open to assault by more conventional siege machinery or the Vandari Rams. Stranan military doctrine, as reflected in the Lescari War, suggests that they may keep the cannons loaded with antipersonnel munitions specifically to keep your crossbow-carrying cavalry at bay."

He turned to face Kidd, sharpening the edge in his own voice. "And, Colonel Kidd, I hasten to point out that in our report we had His Imperial Majesty's airship *Zarnitsky* being used for resupply and refit missions. It has forty-eight steam cannons that could be used to shoot over the walls or to bring them down. And if the Helorians somehow destroyed its boilers, the ship could be loaded with rocks and then could fly up and drop them on the city—much in the same way the *El Malson* destroyed the bridge at Placé to keep the Cathedral Lancers from catching up with the fleeing Lescari Emperor."

In adding that last bit—which stung Captain Irons rather visibly—Uriah knew he had gone further than was wise. With that realization he also discovered he didn't care what Irons or Kidd could or would do to him. *Robin was right about our exercise. The wars in which we will fight will be in the future. Though we can learn from the past, if we learn nothing but the past, we will never be able to push beyond it.*

And, as the hypothetical and its defense pointed out, the distant future was far from certain—though the immediate future loomed before Uriah rather plainly. If the tribunal failed them in this exercise—and that result seemed rather obvious—Robin would lose his berth on the *Saint Michael. At least he will still be a soldier.* A failing grade for Uriah, along with the cancellation of his father's financial support, meant he would be sent away from Sandwycke and back to Carvenshire to become a pawn in his brother's schemes.

Better that, I suppose, than dying in some battle serving beneath some dull sot like Captain Irons.

Kidd's uplifted hand strangled Irons's muttered curses. "Yes, the *Zarnitsky* could intervene, but would that not put it at jeopardy? There are caverns in Jebel Quirana that could hide very large versions of these Helansajaran crossbows and they could shoot at the *Zarnitsky*."

Robin shook his head. "Jebel Quirana is the resting place of Keerana Dost. No one may enter its precincts except for the Dost reborn."

"Could not this Shukri Awan be the Dost's reincarnation?"

"Superstitious nonsense," grumbled Irons.

"Yes, Colonel Kidd, Shukri Awan *could* be the Dost reincarnated. However, the evidence we have rules against that possibility." Robin ticked two points off on his fingers. "First, reincarnation is a tenet of Ataraxianism. It is a false faith, so we know reincarnation does not happen."

Kidd arched an eyebrow over an argent eye. "Are you saying God could not cause a soul to be born anew?"

Robin hesitated, then glanced down. "I would not say it is impossible."

"Ah, so you would allow that God might do that, reincarnate someone, for his own purposes?"

Irons leaned forward. "If you will permit me, Colonel, your

question treads closely to the line of asking this cadet to espouse a heresy."

"I do not think it does, Captain." Kidd's abrupt reply drained color from Irons's face. "Is not the promised physical return of Eilyph in the end times a reincarnation of Him?"

"But He is God and God is Him."

"Then if we are reasonable men, we can agree that what God can and will do for His Son, He *could* do for another. For His own purposes, Captain." Kidd shifted his head to face Robin. "Forgive the frivolous digression, Cadet. You have another point?"

"I do, Colonel. Shukri Awan, *if* he could get soldiers positioned in Jebel Quirana's caves—there are tales told of demonic wards that bar passage—would have desecrated the mountain and that would cause the populace of Helor to revolt."

Kidd nodded. "Let us assume he can deal with that revolt . . ."

"Why?" Uriah curled his hands into fists and growled. "Why should we assume that? What evidence do you have, sir, that suggests Shukri Awan could deal with riots and unrest? Sir."

Captain Irons shot to his feet. "You are out of order, Cadet, and have entered new realms of insubordination."

"Did you ask *why*, Cadet?" Kidd's question came quietly in the wake of Irons's harsh rebuke.

"Yes, I asked why." Uriah let his anger with the way Kidd and Irons were shifting the circumstances of the report to suit their needs bleed fully into his voice. "Why do we assume Shukri Awan can handle a revolt? All of his troops are on the walls, getting raked by spike and grapeshot from the Stranan cannons on the plains in front of his city. All of the soldiers, that is, except the ones that you've got running willy-nilly behind the lines, shooting boilers. He'd have no one to support him. And his action of putting people in Jebel Quirana's caves would alienate the Imans. Without their support, and Atarax's implied favor, Shukri Awan would be killed by his own people and they would sue for peace with the Stranans."

Uriah felt his arms begin to shake, but fought to keep the quavering out of his voice. "The people of Helor know the Stranans are capable of atrocities, but that all they really want are outlets for their trade goods and a stable neighbor to the south. You can't sell stuff to dead people or enemies, and the Stranans know that. The Helorians would even agree to pay tribute to the Tacier because when the Dost returns—and you yourself said it's possible he *will* return—he'll take Strana and everything else and make Helor his capital again; probably with a Stranan satrap to rule over it anyway."

Uriah pointed at the sand table with a quivering finger. "*Our* hypothetical battle is based on the most solid information we can find. *Your* variations are pure speculation. You make Shukri Awan smart enough to have people operating in the Stranan rear, then you let him be stupid enough to desecrate Jebel Quirana. You can't have it both ways, Colonel. An enemy isn't going to be smart when you're smarter and dumber when you're dumb. We postulated actions based on the best information we could get. Things might not happen exactly as we put them in our report, but they will happen damned close."

"Cadet Smith, that will be enough!" Irons slammed a fist down on the desk. All three copies of the report hopped up in the air, then plopped down in echo of the blow. "Your conduct here is not befitting an educated man, much less a priest and a soldier. You are insubordinate, rude, and disrespectful. You will put yourself on report for your actions here and I will back Colonel Kidd when he asks for your dismissal from Sandwycke." Irons looked over at Kidd for confirmation of his words, but the silver-eyed man just stood there, slack-faced, shaking his head.

Irons frowned. "Sir, you will prefer charges to a court martial, yes?"

Kidd blinked, his head coming around quickly. "What? No."

Irons smiled. "Ah, you are right, sir, a court ecclesiastic would be better."

Uriah's guts turned to ice. Conviction by a court martial would get him dismissed from Sandwycke, but otherwise have little effect on his life. The positions his two elder brothers held within the Ilbeorian Church and political structure insulated him from the worst a court martial could deal out. A court ecclesiastic conviction could lead to wigging, prison, excommunication, torture, and/or exile, and his kin would be powerless to intervene. It would destroy his life utterly.

While he didn't think his life was all that great anyway, having it disposed of so thoroughly seemed like overkill. *That's what you get for antagonizing a Cathedral Lancer—they never use one sword cut where a half dozen will do.* Uriah molded his face into a defiant mask to hide the dread eating him up from inside.

"No, Captain Irons, I . . . will not do that, either." Kidd spoke haltingly, as if double- and triple-checking each word before using it. "I order you to prefer no charges. Cadet Smith did question me with enthusiasm, but he was not wrong to do so . . . He was right. I abused my position. I changed the conditions on which they based their project—ruthlessly so. Those conditions *are* the best available. Their report has to be evaluated on what it *is*, not by what you or I might have wanted it to be. Or thought it should have been."

Kidd rubbed at his eyes, then turned away from the table and began to walk out of the room. "No, he was right, quite right." Kidd's left hip bumped against the corner of the sand table, bringing Jebel Quirana down to obliterate Helor. "I was . . . wrong."

Uriah glanced at Robin and found him wearing the same slack-jawed expression as Colonel Kidd.

The blind man patted Uriah on the shoulder as he moved past. "Well done, Cadet Drury, Cadet Smith. Very good. Inventive. Good."

Uriah turned to watch Kidd drift from the examination room. With shoulders slumped and his steps tentative, he looked nothing like the fearsome creature who had haunted Sandwycke for more than a decade. *He looks so . . . beaten.*

" Eyes front, Mr. Smith."

Uriah turned back and came to attention. "Yes, sir."

Captain Irons's eyes blazed. "You may consider yourself lucky that Colonel Kidd is far more generous than I am. Your project will pass—just barely—and, Mr. Drury, you'll be gone from our midst. The *Saint Michael* will be welcome to you, though I fear for your troops. As for you, Cadet Smith, this is *not* over. Viscount Warcross may have barred me from bringing you up on charges for this incident, but there are other ways to send you away from here. Mark me, I know them all very well, and I shall enjoy employing as many as I need to send you from here as fast as possible."

— 4 —

┌─────────────────────────────────┐
│   **Marozac (The Tacier's Palace)** │
│   **Murom, Muromda**   │
│   **Strana**   │
│   **8 Census 1687**   │
└─────────────────────────────────┘

Stealing into the shadows behind her father's throne, Natalya Ohanscai watched his visitor, Duke Vasily Arzlov, carefully. The man's voice came in seductively deep and calm tones, as if he and the Tacier were discussing nothing more important than a game of chess, or the weather, or a fond reminiscence of some past adventure. Arzlov's stance and gestures betrayed no nervousness, nor any of the fatigue that should have resulted from his long trip to the capital.

Her father, the Tacier, listened to Arzlov quietly. On occasion he nodded his head or tugged at his long white beard to let the Duke know he was listening. Natalya recalled having been interrogated by her father many times before. *He sits almost motionless, but his amber eyes peer searchingly at you. They prompt full recall and full disclosure. Not many can deceive him, and many more believe they can than those who actually do.*

Natalya smiled at the man standing before her father. *You may be one of those who can fool my father, Duke Arzlov, but you do not fool me.*

Tall and elegant—especially in the Bear Hussars' uniform— Vasily Arzlov seemed to be quite at home in the Tacier's cavernous audience chamber. Natalya admitted to herself the young Duke did possess the dignity and bearing needed to avoid being dwarfed by the twelve carved pillars that upheld the vaulted ceiling. Each of the pillars had been carved in the likeness of one of Eilyph's disciples, including Nemyko the betrayer. It struck her as curious that Nemyko, complete with a hood hiding his face, was the pillar standing directly behind the Duke.

Part of Arzlov's dignity came from the uniform he wore. The navy blue jacket had two rows of gold buttons running from shoulder to waist, with gold piping linking them and fringed gold epaulets capping his shoulders. White riding breeches with a gold stripe down each side were tucked into tall brown boots at his knees. A gold gorget engraved with a bear's pawprint hung from a slender chain at his throat, declaring his allegiance to the Bear Hussars. The gold cord coiled on his sleeves made him a Naraschal of the Empire—a rank he had earned before being appointed the Duke of Vzorin.

Arzlov appeared almost completely comfortable in her father's presence. Respectful, but not overawed, he possessed a composure that inspired confidence in his ability to handle almost any problem he faced. *Were today ten years ago and did the Lescari host still threaten Strana, Arzlov would have been the only choice to act as Imperial Warlord.* Ten years previously he had been the man who defeated Fernandi, but the credit for the victory went to others, slighting Arzlov horribly. Because circumstances denied Arzlov his just reward—and because Vasily Arzlov was an ambitious man— Natalya felt certain he would only be truly comfortable when he sat in her father's throne and ruled the nation that had forgotten the debt it owed him.

"Rafiq Khast and his warriors provided this trade caravan an escort to the outskirts of the Vzorin Political District. The traders then came to Vzorin and met with Valentin Svilik, a trader who has done much to build ties with the people of Helansajar." The Duke smiled indulgently. "Svilik reported to me what had happened, and I immediately boarded the *Zarnitsky* and came here to give you the news of this caravan. We departed Vzorin eight days ago and arrived this morning."

"Thank you, Vasily, for bringing this matter to my attention. It would seem that, as your previous reports have indicated, Shukri Awan's hold on Helansajar is by no means secure. This problem vexes me, and should you as well, since the Vzorin Political District is where difficulties will likely spill over into our realm."

"I am quite aware of this, Highness, which is why I made this journey." Arzlov stroked his chin with a long-fingered hand. "There are numerous courses of action we could take to respond to this situation."

"And which would you, Duke Arzlov, suggest we follow? Is the uniform you wear a hint?" Natalya came forward from the shadows amid the rustle of her green gown's skirts. Her father smiled at her and Arzlov's blue eyes flashed with recognition. Though both of the men had known she was behind the throne, custom demanded they say nothing to her until she chose to leave her father's shadow. All of the Tacier's children—no matter which of his wives bore them— were considered insulated from the affairs of government and politics until and unless they chose to abandon the protection afforded them by the Tacier's shadow.

"Ah, Talya, you are most welcome here."

"*Spasib,* Father. It is good to see you again, Duke Arzlov."

"I undertook this journey with hopes of seeing you again, Tachotha Natalya. The mere sight of you brings me great joy. Grigory sends his most cordial greetings. I have been entrusted with a missive from him to you, which I shall be pleased to convey to you later. I look forward to having you visit us again in Vzorin."

"Thank you, my lord. I recall with much pleasure my journey to my realm." Her sea-green eyes flicked toward her father. "I believe, however, we were discussing your recommendation for action to my father."

Arzlov smiled, but that somehow failed to soften the crisp lines of the cosmetics with which he had painted his face. A light blue powder covered his face and a darker blue surrounded his eyes. Arzlov had then used scarlet to rim the blue around his eyes and to sharpen the line of his cheekbones. His makeup matched the enamel panels on his armor's battlemask. That particular red and blue pattern had been celebrated in Strana for Arzlov's contributions in the defeat of the Lescari Emperor.

"We have two distinct situations defined in this report, and should look at them separately. First is that of Shukri Awan. He rules Helor, and his possession of it means that by finding a way to work with him we will be able to strengthen our presence in that city and, therefore, the whole region. Since Helor is the key to Helansajar, we must take him into account in our planning. Second we have Rafiq Khast. He cannot take Helor from Shukri Awan, but he is free and powerful enough to range far north and attack Helorian forces without fear of retribution. He is favorably disposed toward us and has no love for Ilbeoria because they rejected his appeal for aid at the time Shukri Awan drove the Khasts out of Helor. Using his anger with Ilbeoria to turn him toward us would be wise."

"You say that, my lord, as if you think Ilbeoria is an enemy of my father's realm." Natalya watched him, seeing if he would take the bait she'd just laid out for him. "You do not think Ilbeoria is our enemy, do you?"

Arzlov's face darkened for a moment. "I serve your father, Tachotha, and in my capacity as Duke of Vzorin I must think about potential threats to my holding. Ilbeoria has the largest and strongest military presence in Estanu."

"But it is very far south, past the Himlans, in Aran."

"But it is capable of moving north."

"Talya, this is the not time to press this matter." Her father raised a hand. "Vasily's respect for Ilbeorian troops is well-known. We require from him now his opinion on recent events in Helansajar, not on affairs of state for the future."

"Yes, Father." Natalya bowed her head, but watched Arzlov to see if he would betray a smug satisfaction at her rebuke. What her father termed respect, she saw as rampant paranoia concerning Ilbeoria—and had seen it as such for years. She knew relations with the Wolf-King's realm were not what they had been at the height of the alliance opposing Fernandi, but neither were they in as dire shape as Arzlov had been rumored to think.

Paranoia and ambition can form the most lethal venom.

Leaving his legs slightly spread apart, the tall, slender man clasped his hands behind his back. "It is my opinion, Highness, that displaying our power to Shukri Awan or supporting Rafiq Khast would *appear* to require military operations in Helansajar. I am not convinced this would be our best course of action. The presence of a caravan coming to Strana, and Rafiq Khast's willingness to safeguard it, means we are not necessarily being seen as the conqueror lurking to the north and this is a change that is to our benefit."

The tacier nodded slowly. "You are saying that commerce may further this transformation and open Helor to us?"

"*Da*, Highness."

"This surprises us, Vasily."

"Forgive me, Highness."

The Tacier smiled. "You come here dressed as a Bear Hussar but you do not advocate military advances? We would have thought you would advise removing Shukri Awan and folding Helansajar into our Empire."

"Twelve years ago I would have wanted just that, but acquitting the responsibilities inherent in ruling the Vzorin Political District force me to think otherwise, Majesty." Arzlov opened his hands to the Tacier, then gently clasped them together again. "The Wolves in Ilbeoria would find much to be alarmed about if we were to send troops in any strength into Helansajar. On the other hand, complaints against our commerce from their merchants would hardly sound threatening to their warriors. The caravan that was attacked was not ours, so we do not even have the thin tissue of retribution to cloak any military operations. I believe, at this time, the best course is to approach trade with Helor *and* with Khast's faction. Whichever proves most loyal and strongest, this is the faction we support."

"Your plan has the added advantage of binding all peoples of Helansajar to us. Our borders will become safer." The Tacier nodded slowly. "Resistance to forays by the Ilbeorians will be stronger."

"Your thoughts are my thoughts, Majesty."

"Yes, good." The Tacier summoned a servant from the shadows of Saint Vohl's pillar. "We are aware you wish to return to Vzorin quickly, but we would have you dine with us this evening. It will give your Aeromancers time to recover from the journey here. Boris will conduct you to chambers set aside for your use. Rest now and he will come for you later."

"As always, it is my pleasure to enjoy your hospitality. I am in your debt."

"A debt you discharge when you house my Talya when she visits your realm."

"Again, my pleasure, Majesty, and one I anticipate repeating in future." Arzlov bowed and followed the barrel-chested servant from the room.

The Tacier waited until the echoes of their footsteps had died before he looked over at his daughter. "Your trust of Duke Arzlov is shallow, yes?"

"Yes, Father. I find him to be gracious and courteous, but this does not make him any less threatening to your throne."

"Daughter, you have told me before that he is a frustrated man, but we saw no frustration here when we cut him off from the easiest, speediest method of opening Helor."

"Which means, Father, he has already decided on new ways to open Helor." She shook her head. "There can be no doubt he is frustrated. There are nine provinces in the empire and each of the nine Naraschals who fought against Fernandi were made Tacarri of this province or that. Vasily Arzlov did more to drive Fernandi and his host from Strana than half of your Naraschals, yet he was appointed Duke of Vzorin Political District. To become a Tacarri he must do something which will make you raise Vzorin to provincial status. Opening Helor and Helansajar would do this, yes?"

"Da."

"Then there is nothing he will not do to accomplish that goal."

The Tacier smiled slowly and Natalya read amusement and mischief in his eyes. "Little Talya, what you tell me of Arzlov can also apply to your Grigory Khrolic, yet you trust him."

Natalya killed the instant denial on her tongue and thought for a moment. Grigory had been as ambitious as Arzlov when the time had come to fight against Fernandi. Though she had been only sixteen, she recalled very well the dashing cavalry officer's attempts to impress her. At the time there had been other distractions at court for her, so she had coldly rebuffed his advances.

After the war he had returned, changed and perhaps a bit chastened. He had come to see her, to tell her of those who had fallen in the fight against Fernandi. Natalya unconsciously wound a lock of black hair around her finger as she recalled Grigory's sorrow in speaking with her that day. The arrogant, proud officer had died in the war.

Gone was the façade, the bravado of a man who had not seen the cruelty of combat and the depravity of warriors caught in the throes of battle. In its place she discovered a maturity which, over the years, she had found very seductive. For three years the 137th Bear Hussars had been stationed in Murom and during that time she and Grigory had become lovers.

"Measure your words carefully, daughter. Whenever you coil your hair I know you are seeking to edit your thoughts before sharing them with me."

Natalya smiled and blushed, slipping her finger from the coil of midnight hair. "Grigory *was* ambitious, but war calmed him."

The mischief left the Tacier's eyes and voice. "Was it war that taught him restraint, or does he see you as his pathway to my throne?"

"No, Father, it is not that." Natalya recoiled, stung by her father's question. "I am the ninth child born to you, and the fourth Tachotha. Your preferences for the succession are well-known. My two eldest sisters are married to Tacarri and my brothers have strong backing among the Tacarri, so chances of my husband inheriting your throne are tiny. Grigory's ambitions, if he has any, are to serve you and Strana, even to the point of dying in your defense."

The Tacier held up his hands. "I accept your judgment in this matter, as do I accept it in the matter of Duke Arzlov. I think, in the month of Bell or Tempest, you will decide to visit Grigory Khrolic in Vzorin. You will enjoy this visit. You will stay for a month or two, then you will come home to tell me of all you have learned, yes?"

She felt her face flush at the idea of visiting Grigory in Vzorin. The last visit had been magical. While she knew another visit could never be the same as the first, she could hope it would be even better.

"I will do this for you, Father, but only because this is in our nation's best interest."

"And you will take no pleasure in this duty at all, Little Talya?"

"None, Father, unless, in the absence of alternatives, I must enjoy myself to keep my mission's true nature confidential."

— 5 —

> **Wolfsgate**
> **Ludstone, Midcastor**
> **Ilbeoria**
> **16 Census 1687**

Prince Trevelien genuflected at the foot of the gray carpet that led through the audience chamber to his father's throne. He came up slowly, even solemnly, as befitting his respect for the man in the throne, and the various offices embodied in him. *And,* the Prince told himself, *out of shame for having been so long absent.*

Despite having appeared before his father many times, the sight of Saint Martin's Throne still impressed him, even from the far end of the room. The saint's body formed the back of the massive stone chair, backing it just as the Martinist Church backed the government. Serene and strong, with his hands upheld in a welcoming gesture, the red-granite saint looked over the room as if all assembled were beloved members of his personal flock.

Two stone wolves, each rising to mid-thigh on Saint Martin, flanked the sides of the throne to form its arms. Carved from the same gray granite that had been used to build Wolfsgate itself, the wolves seemed to have grown up and out of the floor. When he was a child Trevelien used to think the wolves were really part of the castle—physical manifestations of the martial and spiritual nature of Wolfsgate and the man who ruled Ilbeoria from it.

A sheathed sword hung by a golden belt from the neck of one wolf, while the other had a golden shepherd's crook leaning against its outside shoulder. The sword and crook respectively represented King Ronan's political and spiritual leadership over the nation of Ilbeoria. Ronan ruled by the grace of God, blessed by Eilyph and warded by the Divine Wolf, his temporal earthly power being a reflection of God's favor for him, his line, and his nation. The sword and crook were brought to the throne when King Ronan officially held court, so in spite of the lack of courtiers, Trevelien knew his father had summoned him for state purposes, not some social courtesy.

This means he is ready to make official the matter we have corresponded on these past months. As he walked forward he recognized his older brother, Crown Prince Ainmire, and the Marquis of Marlborough, John Wellesley, standing in attendance on his father. He could understand Marlborough being present, since he advised the King on foreign affairs, but his sickly brother's presence surprised him. *'Twas not long ago that Ainmire was down with a bad case of black ague. He shouldn't be up this soon.*

"Good afternoon, Father." He took his father's outstretched left hand and kissed the wolf's-head ring. "Good to see you, brother, and you, Marquis Marlborough."

Sunlight streaming in through stained-glass windows splashed colorful spots on King Ronan's bald head. "How go your preparations for moving to Aran?"

Trevelien smiled slightly. "It is finally decided, then, that you will send me there?"

"It was decided, my son, before I wrote to ask you to accept this mission." Though the throne dwarfed his father, Trevelien heard power in the way his father kept his voice even and felt it in the way the King's restless eyes studied him. "You took convincing, and I had the time to convince you."

"Well, then, the preparations for the move are going as well as can be expected. Moving a household, even one as small as mine, is not easy." He glanced at his half-bald brother. "I think, Ainmire, you are fortunate to be staying here."

"Were my constitution as strong as yours, I would gladly go in your place." Ainmire coughed into his hand, then smiled. "I want you to know I am honored by your decision to allow your children to reside in my household while you are fulfilling your duties as Governor-general of Aran."

"How could I not trust Jeremy and Catherine to you? Not only are you heir to the throne of the Wolf-King, but you took very good care of them when . . ." A lump rose to his throat as he thought of his dead wife, Rochelle. "When I could not."

"They are good children. They love you and their mother, and they will miss you both." Ainmire nodded slowly at his younger sibling. "They will thrive here, and in a couple of years, we will come to visit you."

Trevelien clapped his brother on the shoulders but could not force words of thanks around the lump in his throat. Unlike his father and most other nobles at court, he had only taken a single wife. Rochelle Godeau had been a Lescari commoner he had met during his adventures in Lescar, as he sought to elude Fernandi's troops. Without her help he would have perished, but his sense of obligation to her formed but one strand in the cord that bound them together. They managed to escape Lescar, thwart Fernandi's assassins, and even win over King Ronan, despite the uproar over an Ilbeorian Prince marrying a commoner from an enemy nation.

When we were together there was no foe we could not defeat. They had produced two wonderful children and they had talked often of greeting the next century in one another's arms, with crowds of grandchildren surrounding them. At no time had Trevelien imagined life without her, nor could he imagine asking her to share him with another wife, despite the efforts of ambitious Ilbeorian lords with nubile daughters or spinster sisters.

Rochelle's death in the Red Pox epidemic of '85 had crushed him. *My world had ended, my future had died.* He had exiled himself to a dismal estate on a bleak Meridmarch headland where the howls of the wind mocked him and smothered his sobs. Ainmire had taken Jeremy and Catherine into his own household in Ludstone without complaint or being asked. He saw to their welfare for the two years that Trevelien's self-imposed exile lasted, creating a debt that Trevelien knew he could never repay.

Except, perhaps, through this mission to Aran.

Trevelien's profound grief had spawned an outpouring of compassion and also created a crisis for his father. Crown Prince Ainmire's poor health suggested to many that if he ever ascended the throne, his reign would be brief. While King Ronan remained quite robust despite having entered his sixth decade, everyone knew he would not live forever. Most people had assumed the crown would pass to Trevelien upon Ronan's death, but the Prince's emotional collapse had shaken their confidence in his ability to govern both the Church and the State. His being sent to Aran was a move calculated to show the clergy and nobility he was more than able to fulfill his duty to Ilbeoria when the time came.

Trevelien nodded his head. "I look forward to that visit, brother. I have no worries about my children."

"As well you should not." The Wolf-king smiled openly. "Jeremy and Catherine will be fine, Trevelien. No grandchildren of mine will be neglected. Besides, the climate of Aran would not be good for them. Leaving them behind is the right thing to do."

"I do not fear for them, sire, but for my heart in leaving them. It will take a month for letters to pass from them to me. They grow so quickly at this age. I will miss much in my five years in Aran."

"I understand, but this must be done." His father nodded solemnly. "It will pass quickly, and then you will be home again."

Trevelien lifted his head. "But I will not be able to calm their fears when they hear dire news from Aran. I would not have them be afraid for my safety."

"Nor would I." The King glanced at his advisor. "Marlborough has some new information that means your tenure there may not be as difficult as we first thought."

"Oh? Is that possible?" Trevelien arched an eyebrow at his father's aide. "With our merchants dominating trade on the Urovian continent, Strana has little outlet for its goods other than Estanu. Our merchants in Aran covet the same markets. The situation in Aran is just one big boiler with the pressure rising."

Marlborough smiled carefully. "Such speculation has been common ever since the Tacier posted Duke Vasily Arzlov to the Vzorin Political District. I too thought this a prelude to invasion, but Arzlov's lack of action is reflective of chaos in the Tacier's court. Whether it is fear over Arzlov becoming too powerful, or a desire by the Tacier to let his nation recover from Fernandi's predations, I don't know."

The Prince frowned. "Granted, being away from Ludstone and not following all the discussions in the Parliament, I may not be current in my thinking, but doesn't Viscount Hedgelee, Philbert Grim-

shaw, still lead a coalition of merchant-traders lobbying for a full invasion of central Estanu?"

Ainmire laughed. "I've heard him say, when deep in his cups,
we should just wade in and conquer Strana itself."

"Grimshaw is an idiot." Marlborough snorted as if he'd scented
something most foul. "Pity is that his brother is quite powerful in
Aran. He's one you will want to watch carefully, Prince Trevelien."

"Oh, that I intend." The Prince glanced at his father. "I gather
that, if not for men like him, I'd not be the new Governor-general of
Aran."

The diminutive King nodded once. "That is certainly part of it,
yes."

Marlborough interlaced his fingers. "It is my belief that your
appointment will send a signal to the Stranans that an invasion from
the north will be rebuffed and an invasion from the south fore-
stalled. Grimshaw and his people, on the other hand, will see your
presence as a possible prelude to war since your courageous exploits from the Lescari War are well-known. Everyone else will see
it as a test of your strength in the aftermath of Rochelle's death."

*And the romantic wags who write broadsheets will see the trip
to Aran as my chance to woo and win the hand of some Estanuan
Princess to mend my heart.*

Trevelien himself had no illusions about his assignment. He
stood in favor of preventing a war by letting the Stranans know Aran
would be defended, but he hardly saw his posting alone as sufficient
to get that message across, especially with Arzlov on the border. He
looked at Marlborough carefully.

"My lord Marquis, you can't imagine my presence will be
enough to frighten Duke Arzlov. I shall, therefore, assume your
opinion has more than wishful thinking behind it. What, then, have
your Stranan spies told you is the current thinking in Murom?"

Marlborough smiled with pure pleasure. "This report is com-
piled from a number of different sources, but most are Stranan, as
you suspected, my Prince. A caravan bound for Vzorin was attacked
by forces allied to Helor at a place known as the Well of Skulls.
Rafiq Khast's people drove the Helorians off, then escorted the caravan to the Vzorin Political District. A merchant there passed news of
the attack to Duke Arzlov and the Duke immediately flew to Murom
for an audience with the Tacier.

"Once in the capital, we believe Arzlov immediately asked for
permission to enter Helansajar to seek out and punish the Helorians.
The Tacier denied this request and, instead, suggested Arzlov actually send merchants in to open trade. Arzlov was not pleased, but the

Tacier asked, 'Why are you determined to take with blood what we can buy with gold?' The next day Arzlov retreated to Vzorin with his tail between his legs."

Trevelien frowned. "Vasily Arzlov *retreated*? He asked permission and then when he was denied he retreated?"

"That is what was reported to my people, Highness."

Is this possible, or have your spies been found out and fed this story to make us think there is no danger? The Prince caught himself. *With Arzlov there is always danger.* "The audience with the Tacier took place when?"

"On the eighth of this month."

"Nine days ago?" Trevelien's emerald eyes narrowed sharply. "That's barely enough time for that information to make it here, even by a Swift."

Marlborough smiled. "It arrived two hours ago on the *Elena*."

"Even so, my lord, you would agree that you have hardly had enough time to cross-check the story. For all we know Arzlov has already returned to Vzorin and launched an immediate attack on Helansajar."

The Ilbeorian spymaster shrugged. "For all we know the Dost has returned to the world and has already eaten Strana up."

Trevelien looked over at his father. "Does this report mean I will not be getting the regimental support we have been discussing?"

"It does appear, Trevelien, that Arzlov's teeth have been pulled."

The Prince tugged on a handful of the brown locks at the back of his head. "I know you do not want too many troops in Aran because you do not want the Tacier thinking we mean to attack Strana."

The King held his hand up. "The troop strength in Aran is adequate."

"But it is insufficient to repel a determined invasion from Strana."

"If we give the Tacier no reason to feel threatened by us, he will have no reason to attack us." King Ronan leaned forward, his hands caressing the wolf's-heads on the throne. "And if you do not have too many troops in Aran, the merchants can find no way to trick you into launching an attack that will bring Strana down on Aran."

Ainmire cleared his throat. "It is a circle, dear brother, in which troops engender a situation where more troops are needed. If escalation begins now, it will never end."

"I know that, Ainmire, but insufficient numbers of troops to defend Aran will make it a tempting target. If I have two regiments, I think that will be enough. The Danorian Pathfinders and the Wolf's-head Grimmands. They would be sufficient."

Marlborough shook his head. "Out of the question. If elite troops such as those were sent to Aran, the Tacier would allow Arzlov as much latitude as he wanted in central Estanu."

"What makes you think he hasn't already? What makes you think Arzlov is not already plotting something?" Trevelien held a hand up. "Let me amend that—we know he's plotting something; we just don't know what it is."

"Is he?" Marlborough crossed his arms over his chest. "Look at what he has been doing over the past ten years, Highness. Nothing. Absolutely nothing."

"It's not *nothing* I worry about." Trevelien waved that objection away. "I recall what he did when fighting against Fernandi. His tactical variations were brilliant. His battles were decisive and conclusive. Under his command the 137th Bear Hussars regiment hounded Fernandi from Murom to Ferrace. Yet the Naraschals got the rewards for Arzlov's effort. Either we have to consider the Tacier stupid for leaving such a dangerous man unrewarded, or the Tacier is planning to use Vasily's frustration to goad the man into taking Helansajar, adding a province to the empire and earning the rank of Tacarri that way."

"You have forgotten something, Highness." Marlborough smiled patronizingly at the younger man. "The Tacier does not trust Duke Arzlov. If he did, he never would have put Grigory Khrolic in command of the Hussars stationed in Vzorin."

"Even in Meridmarch I have heard this Khrolic-as-restraint idea advanced before, my lord, and I never subscribed to it." Trevelien shook his head.

Ainmire frowned. "I don't understand. Enlighten me."

Marlborough bowed his head graciously toward the Crown Prince. "After Fernandi was exiled, Arzlov was made Duke of the Vzorin Political District. This severed his ties with the 137th Bear Hussars because they stayed behind in Myasovo, rebuilding the city. That took them seven years, during which time Grigory Khrolic rose from a battalion commander to being Pokovnik of the whole regiment. After that they were stationed in Murom for three years. During that tour Khrolic became romantically linked to Tachotha Natalya, the Tacier's fourth daughter. The Marquis believes this makes Khrolic loyal to the throne, so the Hussars' new posting to Vzorin two years ago means that Arzlov has been restrained by the presence of his old aide Khrolic."

"Leaving him nothing to do but visit Murom and ask the Tacier for permission to attack Helor." Trevelien shook his head. "You can see, my brother, the wellspring of my concern."

"Gentlemen," intoned the King as he stood, "I believe this conversation is working its way well past usefulness."

"Forgive me, Father."

"And me as well, Highness."

Ronan nodded. "Trevelien, I cannot give you the regiments for which you have asked, but I will not have you unable to react if need be. The *Saint Michael* will take you to Dhilica, then will remain there. Prior to this we have left only corvettes on station in Aran. The *Saint Michael* has a hundred cannons, so it outclasses and outguns any other airship in the area. We will also place a full company of ethyrines aboard, so you will have some elite troops upon which you can call if things are difficult."

That is something. Trevelien bowed his head. "Thank you for your consideration, Father."

"I value your opinions very highly, Trevelien, and I trust you to the utmost. Your caution about Duke Arzlov is a good thing, one that will be remembered here at court. But something I want you to remember when you are in Aran: while Aran is not Ilbeoria, it is very much part of our empire."

Trevelien smiled. "I would have thought that obvious, Father."

"As would I, but reports from the current Governor-general worry me."

"How so?"

The King pointed to Ainmire. "Your brother discovered the kernel of it."

Trevelien nodded at Ainmire. "What is it?"

Ainmire shrugged modestly. "Anyone would have seen it. I had been in the archives studying dispatches from Brendanian Governors to the Crown just before the revolution a century ago. While some of the messages were quite alarmist in nature, other officials played down or censored all news about the anti-Crown feelings in the colonies. Those officials were the first to go over to the side of the colonials during the revolution."

Ainmire's smile began to grow and some color came back into his face as he warmed to his subject. "I happened to be with our father when dispatches from Baron Fiske came in from Aran. In reading them over I was struck by the similarity between the wording he used and that used by treasonous officials a century ago."

King Ronan leaned forward in his throne. "We have known for some time that certain of our subjects view Aran in the same way the colonists viewed all of north and south Brendania a century ago. They believe the distance from Ludstone means our laws do not apply and that their loyalty to their nation is optional. Brendania may have been lost to us, but Aran will not go the way of revolution. In Aran you will encounter people who are not awed by who you are and who, because of their own plans, may see you as a threat."

"But they do not think they could win a war against Ilbeoria, do they?" Trevelien frowned heavily. "Aran's economy is too closely tied to Ilbeoria to be able to survive independent of us."

"And we have taken steps to guarantee Aran's dependence does not go away."

"Hence the laws against the importation of steam engines, plans for steam engines, or the establishment of same in Aran." Ainmire shrugged his shoulders. "Because those are acts of treason, they are capital crimes, but some men will risk death for profit."

"So, Father, sending me to Aran is as much a message for those people as it is for the Stranans?"

"It is." The King nodded sympathetically. "It is not an easy task I am giving you."

"Were it easy"—Ainmire patted Trevelien on the shoulder—"he would have given it to me."

"Were it easy, neither one of us would be going, Ainmire." Trevelien laughed lightly. "Fear not, Father. Aran may not be Ilbeoria, but I *am* your son. Those who play because the wolf lairs far distant will find me much too close for their pleasure or comfort."

— 6 —

> **Royal Military Seminary**
> **Sandwycke, Bettenshire**
> **Ilbeoria**
> **17 Census 1687**

Malachy Kidd stood alone in his tower chamber, his left hand on his chin, his right hand cupping his left elbow. He held his head tilted forward, staring down at the chessboard. Part of him realized that orienting his head toward the board was ridiculous—he couldn't see the pieces. *Am I wishing I could, or do old habits just die hard?*

He allowed himself the hint of a smile. When his aide had communicated the move sent by his correspondent and had recorded the move on the game's log, Malachy had dismissed the young man and sent him on his way. Cadet Chauncy Malvern had, over the last year, been attentive to, if unimaginative in, pursuit of his duties, but as the date of his graduation drew closer, he had taken to nervously prattling on about all manner of nonsense. Malachy had often called him on it, dressing him down for being frivolous, but of late he had found it easier to be rid of him when his essential duties were finished.

While Malachy could not actually see the board, he was able to gently brush his hands over the pieces and rekindle his memory of their positions. The ability to visualize a chessboard and remember where all the pieces stood was not a skill he'd possessed before his blinding, but was one he'd developed while languishing in a Lescari prison until the end of the war. Through an elaborate tapping code he and other prisoners were able to communicate between cells with each other, and focusing on chess kept Malachy sane.

Or as close to it as I managed to remain. He turned away from the board, sidestepped a chair, and crossed to a sideboard. Reaching up, he took a crystal goblet from a shelf, then poured himself a glass of wine from a cut-glass decanter. The changing sound of the wine filling the glass told him when to stop pouring. In picking up the glass his thumb brushed over the Warcross crest that had been etched into the crystal.

He sipped the wine. Dry, with just a hint of sweetness to it. He knew it was a deep-ruby red from the Vurgunt district of Lescar. When living in Ferrace, acting as a spy, he had learned to like the vintage, and though he never authorized Chauncy or any of his other aides to buy it, the store of that vintage never seemed to run out. *Of course, with the war long over, importing the wine is easier, but still an effort for friends who wish to ease my pain.*

The Wolf-priest returned to the chair he had sidestepped before and sank into its leather-bound cushions. Holding the goblet before him in both hands he tried to imagine how the evening's fading light streaming through the western window would look. He knew that somewhere behind him the stem of the glass had fractured the light into a rainbow. He could also imagine a red-gold disk burning sharply, a pinpoint of light emerging from the wine's dark depths. The Warcross crest refracted the light differently, making the crest itself show up in chilly white relief.

It almost seemed to him, just for a heartbeat, that he actually could see the goblet, but he knew that was not possible, even with magick. Spells could affect objects and things without souls—at least that was accepted as truth within the Eilyphianist Church. Ataraxian magicks, and the secular abominations practiced in Lescar after Fernandi's anti-Church revolution worked differently, but were of the Devil. While Malachy prayed daily for a miracle that would return his vision to him, using a spell to accomplish that same end would cost him his immortal soul.

Vision in this life is not worth perdition in the next.

A strong, heavy hand knocked on his door and Malachy turned his face to the right in reaction to the sound. "Come, it's open."

The latch clicked and the door swung open on hinges that squeaked almost imperceptibly. The sound of the footsteps told him his visitor wore boots and time between footfalls told him that his visitor was tall. *And there is something familiar about that sound, a scraping . . .*

Malachy raised himself from his chair and bowed his head toward his visitor. "Highness, it is quite an honor."

The footsteps stopped abruptly. "Did you have word I was coming, or . . ." Prince Trevelien's voice trailed off to nothingness. "I shouldn't be surprised at anything you do, Malachy, but I am nonetheless."

"When you are tired the wound you took in the leg makes your left heel drag just a bit. I remember the sound from when you used to visit me." Malachy waved the Prince toward the other large leather chair in the center of the room. "You've traveled from Ludstone and quickly, hence your weariness. Sit down, please. Would you like wine?"

"You have that Vurgunt you liked so much?"

"One of the few pleasures of my life." Malachy returned to the sideboard and poured the Prince a glass. "I should thank you for it, I suppose, because either you're stocking my supply, or you know who is."

"It was a provision in the peace treaty—a tribute of sorts. Your wine comes from the budget made to provide for Fernandi in his exile."

Malachy smiled and followed the Prince's voice to his chair. He handed Trevelien his wine, then recovered his own glass and held it out for a toast. "To the wisdom of God and the faithfulness of his servants in fulfilling it."

The goblets rang clearly as they touched each other. Malachy sipped his wine, then returned to his chair and looked toward the Prince. "Acceptable?"

"Quite. I'd not mind more of this vintage at Ludstone."

"I shall have some sent up to you. I doubt I drink all I'm sent."

"I appreciate the gesture, but I'm not going to be there for long." A note of trepidation entered the Prince's voice. "It has been decided that I need to prove to our people that I am capable of ruling this nation and our empire if my brother cannot fulfill his duties. I'm being sent to Aran, to become the new Governor-general there."

"Aran?" Malachy sat back, his mind briefly flashing on the tactics exercise he'd critiqued a week and a half back. "You're being thrust into a very difficult position there."

"I am, and I know it." The squeak of leather and the shifting location of the Prince's voice told Malachy that Trevelien now sat forward, his hands on his elbows. *Probably staring into the depths of his wine.* "Fernandi's revolution overthrew the power of the Church in Lescar and helped undermine it here. In the colonies the effect has been heightened because of the example of the Brendanian revolt a century ago and the fact that our reliance on the colonies for raw materials and troops during the war meant that Ludstone turned a blind eye to excesses as long as we got what we needed. In the last decade there have been no strong Governor-generals in Aran and the Church has been more concerned with saving new souls than it is with reforming old ones."

Malachy nodded. "And you have the potential of the threat from Strana."

"Less so now than in the recent past." A hint of disbelief threaded through Trevelien's words. "News from Murom suggests that Duke Arzlov has agreed that military conquest of Helansajar and the city of Helor is not a good idea."

The Wolf-priest's goblet stopped short of his mouth. "Arzlov backed away from using his troops to carve out a new province for the Tacier? I find that hard to believe. He must have something else in mind."

"I agree, my friend, but that's a threat I can't deal with until it materializes." The Prince fell silent for a second. "What I wanted to ask you, the reason I came here, is that I want you to accompany me to Aran. I want you to advise me, help me with the situation there."

Malachy felt the tingle of flesh tightening on his arms and spine. "Me, in Aran? No, no; not possible."

"Why not?" Trevelien's voice grew stronger. "You'll be very important to me. With you I can discuss things and you'll point out the things I'm missing. I need your insight and help."

"I hear what you are saying, Highness, and I wish I could comply with your wishes." Malachy set his goblet on the arm of his chair, then leaned forward, aping the Prince's position. "The fact is, however, that you don't need me."

"I know what I need, Malachy."

"You said you needed my insight, so let me give it to you." He opened his hands. "I know what you've been through since Rochelle died. There are times you would think this place a society salon for the way gossip runs through it. I remember your wife well and I know her death was a stunning blow. Many said it had crushed you, completely, but I knew that wasn't true."

"Don't be so certain of your wisdom in that regard, my friend." The Prince fell silent for several seconds. "There's not a morning that I do not awaken wondering why she is not beside me. My father and others urge me to take another wife, or several, to help me over the hurt I feel; but I can't even think of doing that, even if wedding another would strengthen alliances. It seems too soon now, and likely will forever.

"I keep asking myself why God took her."

Malachy slowly shook his head. "But that's the wrong question to ask yourself. That's the question that keeps you in the dark and turned inside because you won't find an answer that will satisfy you."

"I don't understand."

"But you do, Highness. You graduated from Sandwycke; you have mastered the curriculum here. The reason your wife died is because she had played her part in God's plan. The grief you feel, that is part of God's plan, too. You focus on the pain and the hurt and think that a loving God would not do that to anyone, but the fact is that by feeling that pain you can understand the pain of others. For someone in your position that is vital, because you can soothe the pain of many people. The pain reminds you of your responsibility to the world and to God's plan."

"So God's plan for me is to go to Aran and govern?"

"So it would seem."

"Then what is God's plan for you that you cannot come with me?"

Malachy smiled and let his shoulders sag a bit. "I don't know. I thought I did until very recently. When I came back to Sandwycke— after you brought me back to Ilbeoria from that prison—I felt very much the way you did at the death of your wife."

The Wolf-priest raised a hand and traced a finger over the ridge of scar tissue on the bridge of his nose. "My Lescari captors used their magick to repair my face, but they couldn't save my eyes. I wondered why God would let me be touched and healed by the demonic, why he would steal my sight after giving me a vision I couldn't understand. Like you I withdrew into myself and wrapped myself in pity and anger. Then I realized, as I have told you, that I knew *why* what had happened to me had happened, but what I didn't know was what God had in mind for me.

"I spent the next decade here being nothing short of a vicious bastard in dealing with students and their military studies. I believed that by making them *think* I could prevent them from ending up like me. I thought *that* was what God wanted from me."

Trevelien's chair creaked as he sat straight. "And that wasn't the plan?"

"It doesn't seem so now, and never really was crystal clear." Kidd waved his left hand at the phalanx of shelves crammed with books lining the tower room's walls. "Many of these books concern military studies, but just as many are Augustinian writings about magick, its employment and theory. In looking back over my life, I wondered if my choosing to join the Martinist order was an error for which I was being punished. I considered asking to be transferred to the Augustinian enclave in Ludstone to pursue magickal researches—perhaps I could have even helped refine spells that would create the draughts that finally cured the Red Pox. I don't know. Still, even with that sort of incentive, leaving Sandwycke didn't seem to be part of the plan."

He traced a finger across his lower lip. "I still don't know what the plan is for me, but I think what I've been doing is not quite right. This is a realization, as I said, that I've come to recently, very recently."

"What happened?" A hint of the keen curiosity Malachy recalled in the Trevelien-of-old's voice returned. "Why are you questioning what you had previously accepted?"

"A week and a half ago two students offered a 'hypothetical' tactics exercise involving a Stranan siege of Helor. I tore into it rather brutally and one of the students took exception to my questions. He told me I was not being fair, that I was changing things as I went along and evaluating them not on what they had done, but on what I wished they had done. In all the time I'd been here no one else had ever done that, yet I'm certain every student who had me destroy a project felt exactly that way.

"I had, for the last decade, been shielded because of my blindness. Everyone here knew of how I lost my sight, what I had done in the war. Kindnesses like yours, seeing to it that I had the wine I liked—things like that were reminders for everyone that I was somehow special, and I took gross advantage of their pity for me. It was cruel and wrong."

"But those men whose projects you critiqued, they learned to be better and sharper. You did good things with them."

"A silver lining to a cloud, Highness, a cloud that was keeping me even more blind than I was before."

"Perhaps, then, Malachy, you are meant to come with me, to Aran. Perhaps that is what God wants you to see now."

Malachy sat back and sipped some of his wine. "What I see, my Prince, is this: as I was shielded by pity for my blindness, so you have been shielded by people's concern for your welfare. You've devoted yourself to your children, and that is a very laudable pursuit, but more is being demanded of you. You are a ruler, a civil authority; and you are a Cardinal Protector of the Church. Your duties there outweigh your responsibilities to even your own children, and now you are being placed in a position to acquit those duties. You're strong enough to do it alone."

"Am I?"

"I think there is no question of it. If there was, you'd not have come here to talk with me."

"What?"

Malachy smiled. "You, my friend, have just emerged from a long and terribly dark night. You're standing in a beautiful field at dawn and everything seems wonderful to you. And you, being the man you are, have looked back into that night and have seen me. You want me to come with you to Aran not because you think you need me, but because you think my traveling away from here will be good for me. You want for me the same dawn you now know, and I cannot thank you enough for that."

The Prince said nothing for a moment, then sighed. "I think I feel more like Saint Martin after his long, cold winter than a man who's been through a horrible night."

"An apt analogy, Highness. Your traveling to Aran will be akin to Saint Martin's going north through the Ferrines in the company of wolves to come to Ilbeoria, bringing with him his vision and wisdom." Malachy smiled broadly. "You'll not have beastly wolves with you, but plenty of your own soldiers to help you in your mission of protecting the Body of the Church. You will become the embodiment of the Martinist ideal: the faithful wolf helping the Lord Shepherd protect his flock."

"But I'll be dealing with pigs in sheep's clothing in that flock. Moneyed interests tend to be more concerned with consequences in this world than in the next."

"That is understandable, Highness, and your civil authority may be more suited to dealing with their excesses, but do give thought to their souls. Turn a man's heart and he will do more for you than is required by law."

"Your point is taken." The Prince sighed again. "Though I'm fairly certain some of the people I will be dealing with have no hearts."

Malachy leaned forward and reached out, patting the Prince on the knee. "It will be a grand adventure you're off on, Highness. I look forward to hearing from you about it. I was thinking, if you wish, we could even play a game of chess through correspondence . . ."

"You mean finish the one I abandoned after Rochelle . . ?"

"I was thinking to start a new one."

"That would be best. I couldn't continue . . . Rochelle, she took a keen interest in our game. She made me teach her how to play and we would discuss your moves and my—our—counters to them. She was good."

"A woman with a facility for chess is a blessing, Highness."

"She was that, and more." The Prince pumped a note of levity into his voice. "What I shall do when I reach Aran is to buy two matched chess sets and send one to you so we shall play on the same board with the same pieces."

"Thank you, Highness." Malachy stood and offered the Prince his hand. "Thank you for coming to save me from myself, but it looks as if circumstances have conspired for each of us to be saved at the same time."

"A good thing, indeed, Malachy." Trevelien enfolded his hand in a warm, strong grip. "I head back to Ludstone tonight, but I'll be back by the seventh of Bell with the *Saint Michael*. I'll expect you to join me for dinner on board the evening we arrive."

"And you're not going to kidnap me off to Aran, correct?"

The Prince laughed. "Not now that you've guessed my strategy, no. A tour, dinner, and perhaps I will avail myself of your thoughts about Aran and Strana and whole continent of Estanu."

"It will be an honor, Highness." Malachy nodded and waved his friend toward the door. "May the peace of God go with you, and the Divine Wolf keep your enemies at bay."

— 7 —

> **Royal Military Seminary**
> **Sandwycke, Bettenshire**
> **Ilbeoria**
> **18 Census 1697**

Uriah Smith raked an unruly hank of red hair back into place, then tugged on the hem of his gray uniform jacket. Even though regulations allowed him to wear the lighter cotton spring uniform, he stuck with the heavier woolen one because he felt the thicker material gave him more of a commanding presence. *It's not going to make much difference in a hearing before the Office of Faith and Discipline, but I'll take as much dignity as I can get before they destroy my life.*

He took a deep breath and tried to convince himself that nothing Irons had arranged could affect him, but the void that was sucking his guts into it told him that wasn't true. Ilbeorian society had him caught as firmly as a fly in a spider's web. Sandwycke had been his one bid to make a life independent of the wishes of his brothers and their mother, but now that fantasy was over.

His mouth tasted sour. *Please, God, at least don't let them wig me.*

Ilbeorians took baldness and hair turning white as signs of intelligence, experience, and wisdom. Young men who had risen in rank were allowed to shave their heads and lighten their hair as a reward for their service to the Church and State. Those who were disgraced or clearly stupid were wigged, and would be forced to wear a shaggy foolscap until they proved themselves remorseful or reformed. *If Captain Irons has been successful in his campaign to discredit me, I'll have locks down to the middle of my back for the rest of my life.*

The very thought of such a punishment tightened Uriah's hands into fists. His three years at Sandwycke had proved what his mother and father had always told him—he was very smart. He knew that was why his older half-brothers resented him and wanted to control his destiny. At Sandwycke his contempt for staid, slow-witted instructors and dense students had made him few friends. Only Robin, with his experience and age, had been able to tolerate Uriah.

At least, I think we are friends. The possibility that such was not the case surprised him and opened a doorway on the loneliness and isolation he'd felt all his life. The resentment of his father's first wife against his mother—a Stranan woman—had been transferred to him and kept him isolated from his own brothers. They had been much older than him anyway, so the distance was natural, and while Uriah accepted that as fact, he couldn't help but feel slighted by their remoteness.

As smart as he knew himself to be, he thought he should have been able to cultivate more friends. The problem was that, being as stubborn and headstrong as he was, he'd rejected everyone who didn't measure up to his standards. He realized, as he stood before the door, that he'd rejected all of them because he saw them as something less than himself. *If my brothers never accepted me, why would I accept anyone who was less than I am? If I had been smart enough to see that earlier, I might have avoided this whole situation. Perhaps I do deserve wigging.*

He sighed. *And when they wig me I should be made to powder it with charcoal on a daily basis.* For an irrational moment he wished he had dyed his red locks black before the trial, but he knew it was best not to antagonize the Inquisitor who had been given his case. *For once I don't need to look for trouble.*

He knocked once on the stout oaken door before him.

"The penitent may enter."

Uriah had to duck his head to get through the door, involuntarily bowing in the direction of the Inquisitor. He did not know or recognize the man in black, but judging by the size of his tonsure and the artificial-gray color of his hair, Uriah decided he was a Dean. That made him the rough equivalent in Church rank to Captain Irons. While someone from the Institutional side of the Church could not command someone in the Military branch, the Inquisitor would be able to rule in this venue and all parties would have to abide by his decision.

"Cadet Uriah Smith reporting as ordered, sir."

"Thank you, Mr. Smith. I am Dean Francis Webster of the Society of Saint Ignatius. I have completed my investigation of your situation." The Inquisitor looked to his right and then his left. "You already know Captain Irons and Colonel Kidd, do you not?"

"Yes, sir." Uriah read hatred on Irons's face, but Kidd's expression gave no clue as to what was going on behind those silver eyes.

Webster waved Uriah to a chair, then he seated himself behind a thick oaken desk. The only real illumination in the room came from two gas lamps flickering behind the Inquisitor. They were set between two arched windows through which the dawn's first light was beginning to pour.

The Inquisitor looked at his compatriots. "Let us begin. If you will join me in prayer."

Uriah bowed his head and clasped his hands together.

Webster crossed his hands over his heart. "Dear Heavenly Father, let Your wisdom be with us in the matter of this inquiry. Direct us toward the verdict You deem wise and just. Let the punishment fit the crime, tempered with Your mercy and in anticipation of Your forgiveness of the transgression. For this we pray."

"By Your will." Uriah looked up as his voice joined those of the other men in the room. *Please, God, let justice be done.*

"I have reviewed the charges made against you by Captain Irons. He has been rather forthright in advancing the case that you are disruptive and wholly lacking in military temperament. He has specifically cited numerous incidents of insubordination. He says you are a discipline problem, he suggests you are stupid and even advances the argument that you are physically unsuited to service."

What? Uriah couldn't help himself and blurted out a laugh. "Please, sir, if I might ask you, could you explain that last charge?"

The Inquisitor shook his head. "I could explain all of those charges, but I will not. It is not in the interest of those gathered here for me to do so. While I found the charges comprehensive, in investigating them I also found them largely without significance. For example, while my interview with Colonel Kidd did confirm what Captain Irons reported concerning your Tactics seminar project evaluation, Colonel Kidd did not seem to place the same weight on the incident as did Captain Irons. The same holds true for other incidents which were reported to me by Captain Irons."

Webster turned toward Irons. "In conducting my investigation I also learned of circumstances that could easily have explained and mitigated many of the incidents that were reported to me. Captain Irons, you neglected to mention that Mr. Smith's father had died in the middle of the month of Initibre, nearly five years to the day the cadet's mother was killed in a riding accident. Certainly you could see how this would not start the year off well for Cadet Smith. Even if you discounted the emotional impact of the death, the month he lost traveling to and from Carvenshire for the funeral could easily account for the aberrational dip in his evaluation reports."

Irons's head came up. "He wants to be a warrior; he'll have to deal with death."

"This is true, Captain Irons, but he is not a warrior yet. Were it not for something I uncovered in the course of my investigation, my time here would have been utterly wasted. Did not circumstances conspire against Mr. Smith, I would be recommending your commanding officer send you for a month's retreat to the Ignatian monastery at Beaconfield. You should look to your soul, Captain, because I do not think your relationship with God is all it should be. If it were, if you knew compassion, I would not be here."

Uriah kept a smile from his face. The Inquisitor's dressing-down of Irons threatened punishment barely on the benevolent side of wigging. The Ignatian order was famous for its physically demanding yet spiritually uplifting regimen. They stepped every cadet through a fortnight program prior to graduation that was supposed to be but a shadow of the ordeal one faced during a month-long disciplinary retreat. No one, save the Ignatians themselves, voluntarily undertook a course of their spiritual exercises, and being assigned a retreat was grounds for dismissal from some regiments.

Hiding his pleasure at seeing Irons pilloried was difficult, but he managed it largely because the Inquisitor turned back toward him and his gaze came hard and cold. Uriah began to feel very hot and nervous, sensing doom in the offing, but finding himself utterly unable to pinpoint where it was coming from. *If nothing Irons said made a difference to him, what can the problem be?*

Webster's expression eased momentarily. "I offer you my sympathy on the death of your father, Cadet Smith."

"Thank you for your concern, sir."

"You are welcome. You are an interesting young man, Mr. Smith. Save for Captain Irons and a few others, everyone I interviewed said you have the potential to be truly great, but that you never apply yourself fully to any task."

Uriah looked down at his hands. *Not the first time I've heard that.* "Yes, sir."

"Mark me, Uriah, this is not good. Were it not for your family's record of service to the Church and the King, I would doubt you were serious about your vocation. If you do not attend to this situation you could easily find yourself as spiritually troubled as Captain Irons, and I don't think you want that, do you?"

"No, sir." Uriah continued looking at his hands, not wanting to see the fire in the Inquisitor's eyes. Finally he glanced up timidly. "Do I take it from what you have said, I will be allowed to remain at Sandwycke?"

"Possible, yes. Unlikely, however." Webster shook his head. "In inquiring about you, I discovered that you were here under a grant from your father."

"Yes, sir, that is true." The Church offered each family with a member in service to the ecclesiastical branch a scholarship to Sandwycke for another child. His brother Graham's ordination meant Bartholomew's tuition for Sandwycke came out of Church funds. For Uriah a grant had to be arranged, and his father funded it.

But now my father is dead and so must be my grant. Tybalt must have canceled it. He has plans for me and for Carvenshire, but they do not appear to include my being a warrior.

"Duke Tybalt has petitioned to withdraw the grant and Cardinal Garrow intends to give him permission to do so."

Irons laughed aloud. "Yes! Without tuition, you must leave."

Uriah hammered a fist down onto his leg. In the split second it took to give Irons's scorn life, Uriah realized for the first time that he actually *wanted* to be at Sandwycke. It wasn't a question of staying to spite Irons—though that was nice, too—but of wanting to be there to prepare for the *next* war, so men like Irons wouldn't kill their own commands through stupidity.

I find something I want to do and it's taken away. Is this *justice?*

Webster nodded. "You are correct, Captain Irons. Without tuition Cadet Smith will be required to leave."

Uriah swallowed hard, then raised his chin, trying to force a lump from his throat. He leaned forward to get out of his chair, but Webster waved him back down.

"Going somewhere, Cadet?"

"Forgive me, sir, but I thought I could save us all time by . . ."— he glanced down—"leaving now and cleaning my room out."

"Are you that anxious to leave Sandwycke, Cadet Smith?"

Uriah shook his head. "No, but I have no money. I want to stay, but without tuition . . ."

"With faith, Mr. Smith, all things are possible."

"Begging your pardon, sir, but I thought God saved miracles for important things."

"Perhaps you are important to Him." The Inquisitor pressed his hands flat against the tabletop. "The grant your father gave you to attend Sandwycke is not the only grant available. As you know, cadets like Robert Drury are here on grants from factories where they or their parents work. Such grants usually come only after service has been performed for the factory, but these are not the only types of working grants we have."

Uriah's green eyes narrowed. "Sir, it is unlikely that my brother would allow me to work now to earn a grant, then return to Sandwycke at some later date."

"Yes, he said as much in correspondence I had with him. He did say, however, that if you could find a way to pay for your last year of schooling, he would allow you to stay." Webster's smile brightened. "As it turns out, there is a grant that has become available. The Earl of Meridmarch has a grant which is given for students who are worthy and willing to work at Sandwycke while continuing their schooling."

"Work here, sir?" Uriah frowned. *Sandwycke isn't in Meridmarch. Why does the Earl fund a grant for someone who works here?* "What is the job?"

"The job, Cadet Smith, is to care for the Earl's eldest brother."

"What?"

Malachy Kidd leaned forward. "You would serve as my aide."

Uriah's jaw dropped. "But you can't want that. I mean, after what I said to you . . . You couldn't want me to be your aide."

Kidd hesitated, then nodded slowly. "I requested it. My current aide will be graduating later this month."

Irons stood and stared harshly at Colonel Kidd. "Are you daft? Smith here is an insubordinate snake that's already bit you once. You should ask for some worthy student to be your aide, not this one!"

Webster looked up at Irons and forced the man back into his seat with a stern glare. "That's quite enough, Captain Irons. Are you going to persist in these outbursts, or will I be permitted to delay planning your retreat?"

Irons stiffened. "Forgive me, sir."

Webster's eyes sharpened. "Perhaps, Captain Irons, perhaps. You would do well to remember that Colonel Kidd is quite capable of making his own decisions."

Uriah looked at Kidd and was surprised at how fatigued the man appeared to be. "Sir, I appreciate your offer, but you can't want me. What I did to you at my evaluation was unforgivable."

"All is forgiven in the Lord Shepherd's eyes."

"Yes, sir, it is, sir, but . . ." *The blow that took his eyes must have scrambled his brains. He can't be aware of what he's doing.* Uriah shook his head. "There's no earthly reason why you should want me as your aide."

Kidd slowly raised his head, the appearance of weariness banished by the edge in his voice. "My reasons are immaterial to you, Cadet Smith. If you wish to remain here, you will accept the grant. If you do not, you will be required to leave Sandwycke. I did not think the man who opposed me so vociferously would be one to surrender the field to Captain Irons so easily."

Irons's face flushed purple. "I can't understand why you're doing this!"

"If I meant you to understand my reasoning, Captain Irons, I would spin for you some fable about the Cathedral Lancers and let you analyze it at your leisure." Kidd faced back toward Uriah. "Now, Mr. Smith, dare you accept this grant?"

The sharp tone of Kidd's question told Uriah that his service to the blind man would be nothing but hard work and pure hell. Whatever he imagined it to be, it would be different and annoying and far worse than anything Irons could ever serve up as punishment. The reasoning part of his mind begged Uriah to run as far and as fast as he could, but he hesitated. *I've never applied myself because I've never found a challenge suitable. Could Kidd be that challenge?*

He watched Kidd for a moment and then, with a nod, Uriah accepted the job.

"Mr. Smith?"

"Yes, Colonel, I nodded yes . . ." Uriah blushed. "I mean, sir, I accept the offer."

"Splendid." The Inquisitor clapped his hands. "I suggest we leave now and attend matins in the chapel. All of us should offer prayers of thanks for the resolution of this situation."

Irons stood with a snarl on his face. "I'm going to pray that God gives you back whatever brains you lost when your eyes were cut out, Colonel Kidd. I'll pray He reminds you of His true plan for warriors, and that He shows you your part in it."

"Then I shall be most obliged to you, Captain Irons."

"What?" The confusion in Irons's voice rode plainly on his face. "Why?"

Kidd's eyes waned into silver crescents. "Perhaps with both of us praying for the same thing, this time He will listen."

— 8 —

> **Royal Military Seminary**
> **Sandwycke, Bettenshire**
> **Ilbeoria**
> **19 Census 1687**

Standing on the edge of the Crucible of the Soul, Robin Drury felt the itchy weight of his thick woolen tunic and trousers. They dragged on him as if they were woven of lead. The fabric rasped against his flesh with each breath he took and each involuntary shiver. The new leather boots and leather gauntlets felt stiff, but his perspiration quickly worked at softening them. Where the collar on his tunic rose up to cover his throat it pressed uncomfortably against his Adam's apple. The woolen coif that covered his newly shorn pate and fell down over his shoulders left only his face bare.

He crossed his hands over his heart in prayer and lowered his head. The slender umbilicals that linked each garment to a different member of the Society of Saint Ignatius restricted that simple act ever so slightly, but not enough to shatter the contemplative mood in which Robin found himself. The past two weeks had been spent in the company of eleven Ignatians, praying, fasting, confessing, and thinking about himself and his calling to God's service.

He had done what they asked. He had answered their inquiries in accord with the formulae they presented him. He had attended Mass and taken the Sacraments. He had immersed himself in the mysteries of the religion that had claimed him since he was an infant, learning more about it in three weeks than he had in the previous thirty years.

Which brings me to this. Robin raised his head and stared out at the shimmering pool before him. Four of the Ignatians knelt at the corners of the pool, their heads bent in prayer. Sweat poured off them in waves, yet Robin knew it was not the heat that made them perspire so. Their prayers, woven into spells, were what made the pool molten, and their concentration on those spells made physical and spiritual demands upon them.

Robin bowed his head again, then spoke in a clear, resonant voice. "By my parents I was baptized with water. By giving me my vocation, God baptized me in His spirit. Eilyph too knew the baptisms of water and spirit. Upon His death, but before His return, He descended into Perdition and endured a baptism of fire. It burned from Him the sins He had accepted in our names, so that we could come to reside with Him in Heaven at the end of time. Through this baptism His body became as incorruptible as His soul. Here this crucible will burn from me my iniquities and cleanse me of my sins, so that I may ever serve to protect Him and His flocks, for ever and ever.

"By Your will."

The others echoed his last sentence, then continued in silent prayer. The Ignatians—aside from the four at the corners of the rectangular pool—held the slender woolen and leather umbilicals attached to his garments. Their prayers would imbue the clothes with protective and transmogrificating magicks which were crucial to preventing disaster during the Sacrament of Ordination Martial. The reddish light glowing from the pool transformed each of the Ignatians into some hellish parody of a priest, and the heat shimmer seemed unable to soften their images.

Robin stepped down to the first landing on the stairs. Molten metal lapped gently against the edge of the step, beckoning yet cautioning. Were he to falter, were his faith to wane, were he weak, he would be burned alive in seconds. Only by descending into and emerging from this hell on earth would he be able to lay claim to the power given one of God's chosen warriors.

Robin sank his right foot to the ankle in the liquid metal. "Soul of the Wolf, Sanctify me." His left foot descended to the same step.

He could feel the heat rising up through the soles of his boots, but it was distant and muted. The sensation was not at all the pleasant warmth of a fire on a cold winter's night. Robin found it harsh and almost cruel, like the scalding steam spraying about on the gun decks of an airship raked by enemy shot.

"Fangs of the Wolf, Strengthen me." He stepped forward, letting the liquid rise to mid-calf. The heat built, but did not sear his flesh. The first spark of panic in his soul was smothered by elation, but Robin prevented that emotion from becoming pride. *Careful, Robin. Here, now, the Seven Sins will truly be deadly.*

"Heart of the Wolf, Grant me courage. Cunning of the Wolf, Enlighten me." Two more steps sank him in up over his knees and the umbilicals fastened to his boots burned away. As the liquid pressed against the wool of his trousers the heat came through with more intensity. His scrotum tightened and his testicles retreated. For a heartbeat all manner of carnal reminiscences flashed through his mind, but he refused to surrender to lust.

"Passion of the Wolf, Fill me." Robin took the last two steps as one and the liquid metal lapped at his waist. The molten warmth engulfed his loins and pressed against him. He concentrated on the virtues of Temperance and Prudence to counter lust. As he did so his body relaxed and the umbilical on his trousers burst into flames.

"Oh Lord Shepherd, hear me; I am yours to ward Your flock." Moving forward, Robin felt the metal press against him, making his passage more difficult. The bottom of the pool sloped gently away from the stairs, sinking him deeper and deeper in the metal. The fluid swirled around him as he passed, tugging at his stomach and elbows.

"Suffer me not to be separated from Thee." The metal rose rib by rib to his nipples. It engulfed his bent arms from below the shoulder to wrist. The heat pressed in on him with greater weight than the metal, making each short breath painful. The smothering constriction of his chest made him wonder if he were strong enough to endure the Sacrament, but he pushed past that idea and continued forward.

"From the malignant enemy I will defend Thy lambs." Before him, floating inches below the surface of the molten sea, Robin saw a simple earthenware chalice. It appeared unremarkable, but in that Robin saw significance. *A cup very like this was used at Your last meal. With it You anointed Your followers. By drinking from it they shared Your salvation of humanity.*

Robin reached out for the chalice, plunging his hands into the burning metal to grasp the cup. The fluid steel coated his gauntlets, leaving only his head and shoulders untouched. Raising the cup, he bent his head forward then poured the flowing metal over his coif and shoulders. More umbilicals burned away.

The weight of the metal dragged at him as he once more moved forward. The steps leading up out of the pool lay right in front of him. The Ignatians, freed from their initial duty by the severing of the umbilicals, waited at the top of the steps to greet him. *Yet if I fail now, they will only be able to pray for the repose of my soul.*

One act separated him from brotherhood with them.

"In my hour of death call me; and bid me to come to Thee." Holding the chalice in both hands before him, Robin slowly began to kneel. Inch by blazing inch the metal rose past his shoulders and pressed against his throat. His body felt hot, too hot, as if only his sweat were what prevented him from bursting into flame. Down and down he sank, fighting the desire to flail his arms about to keep his face in the air.

Surrendering himself to the inevitable, he lowered his head to the surface and let the metal pull him down.

The sizzling agony he expected to feel as the metal burned its way through his flesh and into his skull did not come. He felt the metal press against his eyelids and seal off his nose and mouth, but it did not invade him. Its mass tightened the coif against his head, but the heat felt no more infernal on his bare flesh than it did through his clothes.

I am not found wanting! The thought came to him unbidden, chased by the panic of being found prideful. Though the Ignatians may never have detected it during their time with him, Robin knew, deep down, that he *did* harbor Pride in his soul. He was proud of having survived the war with Fernandi. He was even more proud of attending Sandwycke and graduating from the seminary. He even took pride in having stood up to men like Captain Irons. He had come to Sandwycke as his own man because that was the calling he had gotten from God and he had not changed despite the pressures put on him at the seminary.

He waited for immolation, but he did not burn. That fact brought with it great joy, but also a bit of sadness. *Were Uriah here, in my place, would You be so kind as to spare him?* In his friend Robin had seen great promise, but Uriah lacked something that would have kept him safe in the Crucible of the Soul. *Please, dear Eilyph, deal with Uriah in mercy and wisdom. He may be his own worst enemy, but he is not of the Enemy. Save him as You save us all.*

The cruel, harsh edge of the heat dissipated as the distance from it shrank. Even as the physical warmth moved into him to fill his spirit, Robin could not believe that here, deep in the place where sin was destroyed, God was not also destroying him. He was supposed to be contemplating his own sins, yet he had the temerity to acknowledge pride then dared to ask God for consideration for a friend. By what the Ignatians had told him he should have been melting like a votive candle tossed on a witchfire. They had been very diligent and descriptive in telling him what would happen if he were found wanting in faith, yet God had spared him.

During the spiritual exercises Robin had done what the Ignatians had asked of him, but he had continually had the feeling his prayers went to a God who was different than the one they espoused. Not different in that he worshiped Atarax or any of the myriad gods to be found in Aran, but different in that Robin's relationship with God had been forged in ways that the Ignatians would never understand.

Nor could they understand how that has shaped my vision of God.

The God Robin knew was more grim and yet more compassionate than the one the Ignatians worshiped. During the Lescari War Robin had seen the result of cruelties that no kind and loving God could allow to exist. No matter that those things were supposed to be of the Devil. If God were truly supreme, battlefield atheists used to say, He would destroy the Devil and all the afflictions of Perdition that He allowed to plague mankind.

Yet Robin had seen the reverse side of that coin as well. Stories of miracles heaped upon miracles could not be ignored. Why, when a steam cannon's boiler exploded, would none of the crew be scalded by steam or wounded by shrapnel? He had seen that happen himself on the *Crow*. Why did men report seeing angels standing above them, slaying enemy soldiers to buy comrades the time needed to take the wounded away? Why would downpours douse fires set by enemy arsonists or cause floods that washed away enemy supply trains?

God made man in His image, yet the images of man are vast and varied. Do You allow me my vision because it reflects an aspect of You?

No answer came to his question. He was not surprised by God's silence and took solace in the fact that he still lived.

Robin stood, raising his head above the metal, and finished the sacramental prayer. "With Thy saints I will praise Thee, for ever and ever. By your will."

Liquid metal poured off him as he mounted the steps of the pool. The physical heat drained away slowly, yet by the time he stepped from the pool, the steel cloth of his armor felt slightly chilled against his flesh. He handed one of the Ignatians the silvery cup he had borne out of the pool, noting that his family's crest now appeared in bold relief on one face. Reaching up, he grasped his helmet at the back of his head and beneath the edge of the faceplate, then lifted it up. With the coif melded to it, the helmet came away from his head easily.

Flipping the helmet around, he held it and started down at the distorted image reflected in the smooth faceplate's silvery surface. The mask had a gentle curve to it, peaking midway between his forehead and chin, just beyond the tip of his nose. Aside from the hollows and holes for his eyes, no features had been crafted into the mask. This surprised him because he had often seen other warriors whose masks resembled the face beneath or had taken on a wolfish cast. Legend had it that the mask's appearance reflected the aspect of the warrior that God found most pleasing.

Father Anselm smiled and rested his left hand on Robin's shoulder. "It denotes your implacability and refusal to surrender. This is a rare sign, God has much planned for you."

Robin looked over at the older man. "You have seen this before, a battlemask like this?"

"Yes, fifteen years ago, one that was almost identical to yours." The Ignatian smiled. "Another cadet stood here the same as you and pondered his fate as well."

"And God had much planned for him?" Robin arched an eyebrow. "Who was it? Perhaps I can learn something from his example."

"That would be a very good idea, indeed, Brother Drury." Anselm glanced down at his hands. "You see, four years after he stood where you stand, seeing what you see, Malachy Kidd lost his eyes. Learn from his example, but don't follow it, unless you want to be looking out through eyes of silver, too."

— 9 —

Vasily Arzlov drew a cup of steaming water from the samovar for his tea, then lowered the flame. Dropping a filled tea ball into the cup, he set it aside to steep. "Are you certain, Grigory, you will not join me?"

"No, thank you, my lord." Khrolic reached his arms out toward the center of the room, stretching.

Though Khrolic's blue tunic and black trousers were loose-fitting and free-flowing, Arzlov could not help but imagine the younger man was trying to emphasize his robust physique. Though only five years separated them in age, and both were of the same height, Arzlov did have to admit that his time as a political-district governor had trimmed from him the musculature of a warrior. He had maintained his leanness, but now lacked the hardness that Khrolic exhibited so effortlessly.

"I trust, from this languorous display, that civil order was not difficult to maintain in my absence?"

"It was simplicity itself. Rumors of what had befallen the caravan grew out of all proportion with reality, and resulted in citizens doing all they could to provide for the common defense of Vzorin in the face of instability and banditry in Helansajar." Khrolic glanced toward the glass double doors and balcony that overlooked over the sleepy district capital. "Every night was like this night, quiet and slightly fearful. Very conducive to order. I was out riding on patrol when you returned only because I did not wish my men to think I would willingly abandon them for luxuries you have here in your palace."

Arzlov smiled, more at the irony of Khrolic referring to his modest home as a palace than from any belief that Khrolic wouldn't have welcomed replacing him as the district's ruler. "This pleases me, Grigory. While your men suffer my wearing Hussar colors on my face, I would not want them angry enough with me to raise you into my place."

"They are your men, as well, Duke Arzlov, and would never act against you."

"But they follow your orders, Grigory." Arzlov swirled his darkening tea in the cup. "They might misinterpret those orders and I would be deposed."

"My orders are never ambiguous, my lord. I am your man." Khrolic sat back and rested his hands behind his blond head. "How was your visit to Murom?"

"It went much as I might have expected it would." The Duke took his tea and sat in a chair opposite Khrolic. The chair, with its boldly embroidered upholstery and spindly Lescari manufacture, had been looted from Fernandi's estate eleven years earlier. More ornate than the blocky furnishings surrounding it, the chair was still Arzlov's favorite despite the fact it was not wholly comfortable. "Tacier Yevgeny took the news about Helansajar calmly. Had I asked to send military force in, he would have denied my request. I told him I saw no real value in military action."

"You said what?" Khrolic sat forward, his hands clasped together in front of him, with his elbows resting on his knees. "Did I hear you correctly, my lord? You did not press for military intervention?"

"No, I did not." Arzlov removed the tea ball from his cup and set it on his saucer. "Did you think I would?"

Khrolic blinked his hazel eyes several times, then shook his head sharply, as if to clear it. "I am confused, my lord. Conquering Helor has been your intention for as long as you have been exiled to this hellhole. Shukri Awan has unwittingly given you the perfect excuse to ask for the troops necessary to take Helor."

"But I already have such troops." Arzlov sipped his tea and smiled at its woody bite. "I have you and your Hussars, your 3rd Sonasny Militiamen, and my two local regiments."

"*Da,* but you did not obtain the Tacier's permission to use them." Khrolic frowned gravely. "You let the perfect opportunity to move your plan forward evaporate."

To you it must seem so, Grigory, but your ambition is to better yourself by only one step. My ambition seeks for me greater heights. If you could plumb the depth of my plans, revealing what you know in Murom would accomplish all your goals, and it would get me a cold grave far to the east.

Arzlov set his cup of tea on a side table. "My friend, are we not of the same opinion concerning my posting to this place?"

"*Da.* His Majesty rewarded you with control of this district in hopes you would expand into Helansajar and take it to be part of the empire. All the Naraschals of his army know you deserved to have been made the Tacarri of a full province after the Lescari War. It was obvious what the Tacier wanted of you here."

"Correct. And if I had acted as he wished, what would have happened?"

Khrolic smiled. "You would have taken Helansajar in six months and would have pacified it in eighteen more. It would have been made a province and you would be a Tacarri."

"I would have been made a Tacarri when I was thirty-five years old. Most other Tacarri would have been twice my age." Arzlov opened his hands. "They are jealous. They are threatened. My throat is cut."

"But His Majesty would never condone that."

"No?"

"You think he would?"

"My friend Grigory, he would have little choice in the matter. Either assassins would explain afterward that I threatened the throne or, more likely, Ilbeoria would have seen me as threat to Aran. Killing me would kill the threat and, for all their pious mouthings of Eilyphianist Scripture, the Wolves are killers. I saw this, I knew what the Tacier wanted, so I waited. I thought, perhaps in vain, he would tire of this waiting before I would and give me other duties. He did not."

Getting to his feet, Arzlov paced the length of the small room. "Time was on my side. The old Naraschals grow older and lose their ability to present me with problems. I knew, to take Helor, I would need our very best troops, but I also knew His Majesty would never give me back my Hussars, especially not after you ascended into the Vandari and had one of ten companies of Vandari assigned to you. So, with you in Murom, I decided to send glowing reports about my native levies here. While they are good troops—this you know— they are not Stranan line troops."

"*Da,* but that is not the impression you gave in the reports you sent to court."

"I know." Arzlov smiled down at his subordinate. "My reports hinted that I might take troops mercenary to fight for Ilbeoria in Aran or, worse, hire out for use by Shukri Awan. Instantly I went from being a man who would conquer Helansajar to a man who might give Vzorin to the heirs of Keerana Dost."

Khrolic returned the smile. "His majesty reunites us by sending me here to be your watchdog. He has given you your troops. Why do you not use them?"

"All in good time, Grigory." The Duke returned to his chair and sipped more of the tea. It had begun to cool so he grasped the cup in both hands and wove the most basic of spells taught to Stranan soldiers with his magickal talent. The cup warmed immediately and a hint of steam drifted up from the aromatic tea. "In Murom I learned Ilbeoria is posting their Prince Trevelien to Aran as Governorgeneral. There was no news about troop deployments, but unless Ilbeoria moves several regiments with Prince Trevelien, we are not immediately endangered by this chain of events."

"Even if he brings troops, would he begin a campaign against us that would become mired in Aran's monsoons?"

"Probably not, but Trevelien is cunning, like the wolf he claims to be. Ilbeoria is the greatest threat to the Stranan Empire, and Trevelien's posting is a dagger pressed to our belly. This is a dire time for us, Grigory, because many nations covet what we have. They see in us today what Fernandi saw when he launched his invasion, and they will come after us. Not right now, perhaps, but they will come."

"You are not alone in your vision. Action is vital." Khrolic nervously tapped his index fingers together. "So, your plans for future are . . . ?"

"To proceed cautiously. I will continue trade overtures to both Shukri Awan and Rafiq Khast, as per the Tacier's suggestion. An unstable political situation is to our advantage. In return for profits we will be able to learn all manner of things about the defenses of Helor, and trade in arms and other goods can let us further destabilize Helansajar. This will be important."

"Agreed. What have you planned for my men and me?"

"Continue your patrols. We also need to send survey teams deep into Helansajar. Once we take Helor, I want to know the best ways into the country from the south."

Khrolic smiled. "Those would also be the best ways into the south from Helansajar."

"I suppose they would be, yes."

"Very good, my lord. After some sleep, I will begin to work up plans for a systematic survey of Helansajar to supplement the information we already have. Have I your permission to leave?"

Arzlov nodded. "Go, I can see you are exhausted from your patrol. I napped earlier, which is why I am still awake."

He kept his smile hidden until Khrolic closed the door behind him. *There are times, Grigory, when you can be insightful, but this only happens when you are not working so hard at being insightful.* Khrolic clearly thought the Duke's plan was to take Helansajar and immediately strike south into Drangiana and Aran. If he could conquer Aran, the question of elevation by the Tacier no longer mattered. Vasily Arzlov would be the ruler of central and south Estanu. He would have an empire that rivaled that of the Durranians and might easily be capable of conquering Strana itself.

Khrolic, in his burst of faulty insight, would not have seen how massive and difficult a process taking such an empire would be. Only Keerana Dost had been able to do such a thing and he had an advantage over his foes thanks to weaponry that was fabled for its potency. Khrolic, who had won a place among the Vandari, was in part heir to the Durranian warriors who swept across Tsaih, Estanu, and Strana. With his Vandari Ram company, numbering thirty suits of the terrifying Durranian armor, Khrolic could lay waste to all but the most powerful regiments in the world.

What Khrolic and so many others had forgotten was that the Vandari, all three hundred of them, were less than a third of the forces Keerana Dost had had at the spearhead of his hordes. The Durranians, with their sharpened features and bluish flesh, had been an alien and terrifying force boiling out of the mountain fastness of Durrania. They first swept into Tsaih and toppled the ruling dynasty inside a decade. Then they arrived in central Estanu where the Ataraxians proclaimed Keerana Dost an avatar of their god. This brought tribesmen flocking to his banner, swelling his armies to sizes so huge that their like had not been seen again until the Lescari War.

The Dost had conquered Strana, which, at the time, had really been nothing but a loose confederation of principalities linked by the hierarchy of the Orthodox Eilyphian Church. Keerana Dost killed the local ruling class and imposed his own order on Strana. He allowed virtuous and courageous people to rise within the society and this built a national identity for Strana that possessed a love/hate relationship with its Durranian overlords.

Then the Dost died. His empire was split between his three eldest sons and he was entombed, according to legend, in Jebel Quirana—along with the Ausdari armor belonging to the hundred warriors who had formed his bodyguard unit. The remaining nine hundred individuals in the special Durranian armor were split into three companies. The Vandari went to the son ruling in Murom. The Ostdari returned to Tsaih and the Kiidari remained in Helansajar, based in Helor.

All knowledge of the Ostdari were lost when the God-Princes of the Nine Cities revolted, overthrowing the Durranians. They somehow summoned the *Zihongde Fenluan*, the impenetrable wall of coruscating energy that marked the borders of Tsaih. For nearly eight centuries nothing had gone into Tsaih and only occasionally, during fearsome lightning storms that tore rents in the wall, did things escape.

The Kiidari were likewise lost as the Helansajaran Empire collapsed. This left only the Vandari. To earn one of the suits of armor, about which all manner of things were said, a warrior had to be capable of wielding powerful magicks. Arzlov had never been known for his magickal ability—the spell he had used to warm his tea was not his most powerful spell, but it was the one he found most consistently useful. He accepted that his magickal talent could be described as meager, but only if someone intended to flatter him.

Even taking the legends about the abilities of the Vandari armor with a large grain of salt—and acknowledging that they were still capable of incredible things—clearly the ability to make them work at their full capacity had atrophied over the years. Arzlov assumed that as armor passed from one old soldier to a younger one, the spells that powered the various abilities had been forgotten or incorrectly taught. Slowly, gradually, the armor became weaker as owners understood less and less about it.

Legends predicting the return of the Dost had caused Arzlov to think there might be a solution to the problem of the Vandari. The Dost's return and reconquest of Strana would only be possible if there was some way for the Dost's forces to again fully control their armor. Arzlov decided, therefore, that within Jebel Quirana's precincts he would find a hundred suits of Ausdari armor and the means for instructing people in their proper use.

With such a group of fully operational Durranian-type armor, re-creating the Dost's empire would be possible. The people of central Estanu held that the Dost would draw his armies from among them, through families that still had Durranian blood in them like the Khasts. What the Estanuans forgot was that the ruling class of Strana likewise had Durranian blood running in its veins. While each group saw the other as inferior, somehow Arzlov did not think magickal armor would care about their national allegiances.

And, for all he knew, *he* could in fact be the Dost reborn— some people had even whispered such heresy when he defeated Fernandi. Arzlov sincerely doubted he was the Dost reborn. This was less because he doubted reincarnation could happen than refusing to credit his military prowess to anything other than his own intelligence. *In some precincts, they would relish my adoption of Dost's mantle. I could not be more reviled than I already am, and proclaiming myself Keerana's heir would justify the harsh opinions held of me.*

While he did respect and even desire the power the Dost had known, Vasily had no desire to lay claim to the Dost's heritage as so many pretenders had done down through the centuries. As with most Stranan children, he had been weaned on stories of Durranian atrocities. Though he knew they paled in comparison with the excesses of the Lescari host, a trickle of fear still ran through him when he thought of the Dost's possible return.

More than just fear filled him, however, when the idea of the Dost's return came to mind. *He was the greatest military genius in history. Fernandi thought to usurp his title, but I ended those ambitions. How would I fare against Keerana Dost? Would he too covet Strana as do the Ilbeorians and Brendanians? I know I can keep them at bay, but would he be an enemy I could not defeat?*

He finished his tea and used its earthy flavor to return him from the realms of fantasy to the reality of his situation. Changing his status required the Ausdari. To get them he needed Jebel Quirana and the key to Jebel Quirana was the conquest of Helor. With the Hussars he could take Helor. With the Naraschals growing old at home, Strana would then be ripe for conquest. And after Strana, there would be no power in the world that could oppose him.

To gain full use of the Hussars, Arzlov needed to be certain Khrolic knew his future was brighter with him than with the Tacier and his daughter. He had not found the key he needed to lock up Khrolic's loyalty, but he knew it would come along. And soon, he hoped.

For though Vasily Arzlov could be a very patient man, he had already waited twelve years for his dreams to come true. Now the time for waiting was coming to an end, and he hungered for the time in which he would make things happen.

— 10 —

> **Wadi Hjara**
> **Helansajar**
> **20 Census 1687**

Rafiq Khast fought against the dreamsnare that had him caught tight. He knew, as did every blessed son who believed in Ataraxianism and worshiped Atarax in all the ways prescribed in the *Kitabna*

Ittikal, that the Most Holy Spider used dreams to read the true thoughts and fears of His people. In dreams He would grant the faithful tantalizing glimpses at the pattern He might weave for them in the future, or would reveal strands of His web that had been tangled unseen in their past.

Rafiq knew he had nothing to fear from examination. He was loyal to his God and to his heritage. Did he not thrice daily offer the prayer "There is no God but Atarax and the Universe is a web He has woven"? Even with the tragedies that had overtaken his family, he remained faithful. He knew that just as Atarax had been suppressed during the rule of the Jedrosians centuries ago, now was the time for the Khasts to be suppressed. Like his God, he planned a full and glorious return that would once again put his family on the throne in Helor.

The dream, though he struggled to escape it, swirled with promises of success in the quest to retake Helor. It showed him things, terrible things, all distorted and out of proportion. Huge dark forms swooped through the skies, releasing flights of silver angels. Massive metallic things—part man and more so insect or animal or machine—stalked across the open expanses of his homeland slaying all they encountered. From the north and south these titanic forces converged and promised death and destruction across the land.

Yet more dire, the tableau unfolded beneath the ivory disk of a full moon. *I am destined to die fighting beneath a full moon, so it has been prophesied since my birth. Is this dream to be a premonition of my death?*

A death omen being worked into his nightmare would have shattered the spirit of a weaker man, but Rafiq knew Atarax intended it as a test for him. As the metal monsters inched closer, growing higher than the *Jibal al-Estans*, and the black behemoths descended from the skies, he realized he was not meant to fight them. In his dream he stood alone, naked and unarmed, yet bathed in the shadows of a giant web.

There is a clue here for me. The web's shadow centered on his loins. Rafiq forced his mind past the initial reason he could think of for that symbolism, for this dream clearly had nothing to do with the sating of animal desires. *No, this dream speaks to my hopes for the future and for the Khast line. My loins represent my blood and bloodline.*

A second later the obvious logic of it all exploded in his brain. *My father, mad though he was, used to style himself as Helansajar's own Atarax. He sat in Helor, the center of the nation's web, confident he knew all that was happening around him. Then Shukri Awan came like a wasp and Helor's spider-king was driven from his home.*

Rafiq opened himself to the dream and realized everything around him was seen from the perspective of Helor. He was once again in the center of the web. Though formidable forces appeared ready to contest the ownership of the city with him, he was once again where his family should be.

Woven into the web's pattern he saw Voora Dost, the grandson of Keerana Dost. Voora had entrusted Helor to the Khasts when he took the Kiidari off to force Tsaih open and rescue his imperiled relatives. Rafiq had heard this tale from his father over and over again in fevered speech on cold winter nights, but until he saw it unfold in his dream, he had never fully believed it. *So Helor was ours by right, but we never occupied it until too late.*

For centuries the Khasts had been content to oversee their charge from the plains, never abandoning the nomadic lifestyle that had been the key to the Durranian success. Events changed during the time of Rafiq's great-grandfather, Tahir Khast. Strana had first looked covetously southward, so Tahir Khast took Helor and the Khasts ruled there for three generations to keep the Stranan bear at bay.

His father, Ghalib, had been the last Khast ruler of Helor. Ten years previously Shukri Awan, once his father's faithful lieutenant, had overthrown the rightful Alanim of Helor. Dark rumors of murder and blasphemy had begun to circulate about Awan, but when Rafiq had tried to warn his father, his words were given little weight. Ghalib had reminded Rafiq that Qusay Khast had predicted, at Awan's birth, that Shukri Awan would be father of the Dost reborn. "Such a person could never harbor treachery in his heart, Rafiq."

But Shukri Awan did rise up against the Khasts and drove them from Helor. They resumed their nomadic lifestyle, and other Helansajaran tribesmen had loosely allied themselves with the Khast band, but they never reached sufficient strength to oppose Shukri Awan directly. At best they managed to disrupt his plans—through acts such as thwarting Feroze and saving the caravan—but they posed no real threat to the ruler of Helor.

Rafiq's heart swelled with pride as he decided Atarax's message for him in this dream was a confirmation of the story his father had told him. The lingering bit of doubt about his father's tale drained from him as black blood suddenly began pouring from a slit in Rafiq's chest. He felt no pain, but the black flood gushing from his breastbone alarmed him. It became an ocean that swallowed the monsters and the flying things, then rose like a wave above him and crashed down on him, enveloping him in its sticky warmth.

Not really knowing which way was up, he struck for the surface and salvation. He succeeded by following the light of the full moon, making it save him at least once before it would kill him. He dragged in a lungful of cool air, then saw the black ocean had become a mountain lake. The water in it glowed blue and left his flesh with the same Durranian tint as the area around his eyes. He smiled at this, then followed the glowing ribbon of water with his eyes. It drained south then descended a precipice to flow out into the valley floor.

Suddenly he sat bolt upright. The cool mountain water that had been washing off him became the sweat soaking him and his bedding. He threw back his blankets and pulled on breeches. Tying sandals to his feet, he stalked from his tent and through the middle of the camp. The men tending the fire called out to him, but Rafiq ignored them.

At the far end of the camp he pulled aside the flap of his uncle's tent. He expected the man to be sleeping but instead found him already awake. Qusay Khast sat cross-legged on a carpet in the middle of his tent. He scooped up bits of bone and pieces of wood, shook them in his skeletal hands, then cast them down and laughed aloud.

"Uncle, what is it?" Rafiq squatted down and touched the man's emaciated shoulder. "What are you doing?"

Qusay laughed again, then turned to look at Rafiq. His leathery flesh bore the same bluish tint around the eyes as his nephew, and his left eye even matched Rafiq's hazel ones in color. His milky right eye peeked out from beneath a half-closed lid as Qusay gave his nephew a gap-toothed grin. That eye had been blind since birth and was said to let Qusay see things beyond the material plane, in the past and future.

"Watch, my nephew. The future is the past."

The man took up and cast down the bones and wood, letting them fall into an overlapping pile. He fingered pieces of it, casting some bits this way and that. The flickering flame of an oil lamp drew and repulsed shadows, as if they were strands of a black web being teased by the wind.

"I do not understand, Uncle."

Qusay turned at the waist and grabbed Rafiq's upper arms hard enough to hurt him. "It came to me as I slept. I saw before me an egg which I cracked open. In it was a strip of parchment on which was written, 'Thou art but an egg, and thou wouldst be the eagle. But thou canst the eagle be until thou art no longer the egg.' "

Rafiq recognized the quote from the *Kitabna Ittikal*. It came from the twenty-seventh chapter and in it the Prophet rebuked those who wished to embrace Ataraxianism without first absolving themselves of their sins and divesting themselves of the negative connections with their old life. "I still do not understand, Uncle."

"They have all been wrong, Rafiq, and this Scripture reveals that to me." Yet again he cast the bones and wood. Though they scattered in a different pattern—at least to Rafiq's eyes—his uncle stared at them as if no change had taken place at all. "The others have cast augury wands and never been answered. But this is because they were wrong."

"Wrong about what?" Rafiq rubbed his arms where the older man had grabbed him. "What have they gotten wrong?"

The older man laughed in low tones. "What is it we seek most of all, Rafiq?"

"Our reconquest of Helor."

"Why?"

Rafiq frowned. "Helor is the site to which the Dost will return and we are charged with maintaining it for him. In fact, my dream tonight indicates we will succeed."

If Qusay heard the latter part of his answer the old man gave no sign of attaching importance to it. "And for what do we wait?"

"This is the stuff taught to children, Uncle Qusay. Stop talking in riddles. Enough about eagles and eggs." He grabbed the old man and shook him. "What are you talking about?"

"The Dost, Rafiq, we await the Dost."

"Yes, yes, but the signs have not come to herald his birth."

Qusay freed his arms from Rafiq's grip with surprising ease. "When is the eagle born? When the egg is laid?"

"Yes." Rafiq thought for a second, then amended his answer. "No, when he hatches. Or both?"

"Becoming the Dost is a *journey*, not an event." Qusay fingered the bones on the carpet. "They have asked if the Dost has been born and have received no sign. I have asked if he who will *become* the Dost has been born, and I have a sign!"

Rafiq's jaw dropped open as he stared down at the augury wands. Magick, except for the obscene blasphemy practiced in the west, could only affect a person and bring him closer to the goals Atarax had woven into his future. Since the augury wands could only be manipulated by heretical magick—the sort none of them practiced—they fell from Qusay's hands as God intended and their rede was taken as true. Qusay was known for the accuracy of his foretellings—insightful interpretation of omens being the magickal talent Atarax had given him in exchange for stealing the sight from his eye.

"You say the man who will be the Dost has already been born?"

"Twenty years ago or so, here, in Helansajar." Qusay frowned. "He is in the mountains, to the west I think."

"To the west, in the *Jibal al-Estans*? On the edge of the Jedrosian Plateau?"

"This is what I read, yes, Rafiq." Qusay shook his head. "When I ask where, more specifically, all I am told is 'This is known.' What is it, Rafiq, you have gone pale?"

The younger man's mouth had gone dry and he began to shiver. "In my dream I found myself at the headwaters of the River of Stones. Here we camp on its dry banks but up on the plateau there is a lake. I was in the lake and my flesh was blue, as blue as if I were fully Durranian. What does this mean?"

Qusay gathered the augury wands in his hands and cast them down. Before they hit the carpet, they exploded into flames, momentarily blinding Rafiq. The bright afterimage on his eyes formed itself into the shape of a man and it colored him gold. The vision remained as long as it took for the blue smoke background to dissipate.

"Did you see, Uncle? The man? Was that the Dost?"

"I know not, Rafiq. When you saw your man, I saw the lake of your dreams." The old man pointed a quavering finger toward the west. "The destiny of the world awaits us to the west. We must go there immediately. The time for waiting is at an end."

— 11 —

> **Royal Military Seminary**
> **Sandwycke, Bettenshire**
> **Ilbeoria**
> **31 Census 1687**

Uriah Smith found himself a bit nervous as he reported to Malachy Kidd. With each step up the winding stairway in the tower, Uriah wondered if Viscount Warcross had decided to cancel the grant. He could think of a thousand reasons for Kidd's doing so, not the least of which was coming to his senses and seeing some wisdom in Irons's assessment of Uriah. *He can't think my service will be any easier on him than it will be on me.*

Reaching the iron-bound oak door at the tower's top, Uriah pounded on it heavily.

"Enter."

Uriah worked the latch and pushed the door open. The circular tower had been split into three rooms, and a short corridor led straight into the largest, which took up half the space. That room had been fitted with floor-to-ceiling shelves and cabinets of mahogany. Manuscripts, scrolls, and books filled the shelves with a haphazard tumble of volumes. Uriah would have guessed that while the number of books here came to a twentieth of the collection in the Seminary's library, there were volumes here that Brother Lucas would have coveted to the point of sin.

The room's other furnishings were equally elegant in terms of styling and richness of construction. The brown leather chairs and the one table had the spindly legs and gold-leaf tracery associated with Lescari manufacture, but these clearly predated the war. Some of it, he guessed, had been old when his father had been born and his father had lived a full threescore and seven years—in fact, Uriah had been born to his father's Stranan wife when the old man had long since passed the need for shaving his head.

"Cadet Smith reporting as requested in your note, sir."

Malachy Kidd oriented his head toward Uriah. "Thank you, Cadet." The white-haired man smiled. "In the future, you will not knock so loudly. I am *blind*, not deaf."

Uriah blushed. "Forgive me, sir, I didn't think."

"You thought, Cadet, but you did so incorrectly. You surmised that a deficit in one sense brought with it deficits in the others." Kidd's grim expression suggested the offense had been squirreled away for future use. "Sloppy thinking like that is what made Irons think you were stupid. Here you will learn to apply yourself and focus your mind correctly."

Silence hung in the air for a moment. Uriah shifted awkwardly from foot to foot, then clasped his hands behind his back. "You wanted to see me, sir?"

"Yes. I would have of you a favor."

A favor? "I'm your aide, sir. Order, and it shall be done."

Kidd smiled briefly, but Uriah felt no reason to take any joy in it. "Your term as my aide begins tomorrow, on the first day of Bell.

As this is the last day of Census I must settle my accounts for the month. Cadet Malvern is out preparing for his graduation a week hence, so he has neglected to come around and take care of this for me. I can and have forgiven him this lapse, given the circumstances."

The blind man pointed to the desk. "You will find an account book there on the desk—you'll need it when you return. From the drawer I want you to take a sheet of paper and write out a request for five gold Suns. Take it to Brother Idris in the Quartermaster's annex and he will give you the money. He will also give you a receipt for the money and a receipt for the money my brother has deposited with him for me. Bring them here, straightaway, make the ledger entries, then pay the money out to the appropriate people here at the academy and in Sandwycke."

"Draw a draft for five gold Suns, get the money from Brother Idris, come back here and do the accounts before paying the money out." Uriah crossed to the desk and turned up the flame on the oil lamp burning there. "I believe I understand, sir."

"And this will not be a problem for you?"

Uriah frowned. *Even my sloppy style of thinking can handle a task like this with ease.* "Should it be, sir?"

"Not at all, but that doesn't mean it won't, Mr. Smith. However, your school record suggested a facility for mathematics and geometry, which should handle it well." Kidd's expression wizened as he shifted from Ilbeorian to Stranan. "And it is said you have a facility for languages. Accounts shall be kept in Ilbeorian, yes?"

"*Da.*" The youth took paper from the drawer and inked a quill in the crystal and silver inkpot on the desk. "Brother Idris does not read Stranan?"

"*Nyet.*" Kidd laughed once, lightly. The lamp's yellow light burnished gold irises on Kidd's silver eyes. "You are different from Cadet Malvern."

"Is that good or bad?"

"What?"

Uriah sighed. "Is that good or bad, *sir?*"

"I suspect that is a question that will be answered in time. You've stopped writing. You have the draft written out?"

"Yes, sir." Uriah refrained from nodding, but rolled his eyes instead. "Shall I be off now, sir, or do you need something else done at the moment?"

"I have things under control, Cadet. You are dismissed."

"Yes, sir."

"Oh, Cadet Smith?"

"Yes, sir?"

Kidd pointed at the table. "Before you leave, lower the lamp's flame. No reason to waste the oil, is there?"

By the time he reached the Quartermaster's annex Uriah was fairly certain Kidd had known he had stopped writing because the quill was no longer scratching against the paper. *Not only is he not deaf, but he hears quite well, indeed.* How Kidd had known that he had not lowered the flame on the lamp still puzzled him. He didn't think the lamp had made a noise when he raised the flame, but he wasn't paying that much attention to it at the time.

Why do I have the feeling that I want to be as observant as possible in my new position? He smiled, realizing that Kidd would be far more of a challenge than anything he had faced before. Irons and others at Sandwycke had been as easy as his brothers to annoy and outthink. Until he met Kidd there had been no one—save his mother—who could anticipate or amaze him. Though he did not particularly care what others thought, or care about what drove them, people had been far too simple to read for him to find them interesting for very long.

Life in Carvenshire had not really been as bad as he had often allowed himself to think since his father had died. Yes, there had been much tension because Duke Leonard Smith had returned from his stint as ambassador to Strana with a pregnant Stranan wife. While Lady Alice chose to silently abide by the consequences of her decision not to accompany her husband to Murom, the Duke's three sons resented the woman who supplanted their mother and the child she delivered into their midst. When Uriah was growing up, his brothers had been merciless in picking on him, but he came to pity them and managed to avoid the worst of the things they tried to do to him.

His mother, Ludmila, had not provided him sanctuary. She let him endure the teasing, but then rewarded his bravery by sharing with him everything that was his Stranan heritage. He learned to speak, read, and write the language from her and delighted in reading the books her family would send to Carvenshire. While he acknowledged himself a Smith, he also took pride in his Stranan blood and took refuge in that part of himself when his brothers became unbearable.

In growing up, he also took joy in the exploits of Prince Trevelien. He saw the Prince's courage in taking a Lescari wife as the same as exhibited by his father in marrying a Stranan and his mother's in leaving her homeland to come to Ilbeoria. He took the

Prince as an example of true Ilbeorian nobility and clung to it when his brothers were exploring the depths of Ilbeorian barbarism in their conduct toward him.

The hollow ache started with his mother's death had almost swallowed him whole, but his father helped him deal with it and get past it. Princess Rochelle's death had also been a painful blow because it exposed his hero as human and vulnerable. That didn't lessen Trevelien in his eyes, but, as with many other Ilbeorians, left him frustrated because there was nothing he could do to help the Prince recover. Then his father's passing left Uriah utterly alone and without a purpose in life. If not for Robin's influence he would have been anchorless. *And probably cast out of Sandwycke months ago.*

He banished his maudlin thoughts as he entered the Quartermaster's office and smiled at the half-bald rotund man in the brown robe. "Greetings, Brother Idris. I have a draft here against Colonel Kidd's account."

The older man nodded abruptly and held his hand out for the document. "Word was that you would be the Colonel's new aide. Thought that started next month."

"Cadet Malvern has other things to do. I am helping out while he prepares for graduation."

Idris smiled slightly, but Uriah couldn't figure out what in his remarks would have prompted the change in his expression. *The lout probably has indigestion.*

He ignored Idris and went back to thinking about the lamp. *The flame gave off heat. Could he have felt that?* As he considered other solutions, Idris read the draft, stamped it front and back and shelved it, then counted out coins. Some he tucked in a little box on his desk, then he held the rest out to Uriah.

"Here is Kidd's money. I'll write out the receipts now."

The coins, gold and silver, clinked into Uriah's hands. *Wait, this isn't right.* The draft had been for five Suns, but to that Idris had added twenty silver Moons. That was two thirds of another Sun. *And then there were the coins he put in that box.*

Idris handed Uriah the receipts. "Here. See you next month."

Uriah looked at the strips of paper he had been handed. One was a receipt for five Suns and the other was a receipt saying the Earl of Meridmarch had sent sixty Suns for deposit in his brother's account. "There is a mistake here, I think?"

"Oh?"

"Yes, oh." Uriah tossed the silver Moons up and down in his right hand. "Twenty Moons' worth of mistake."

"That's your grant money."

"What?"

Idris smiled, but kept his voice low. "That's what Chauncy calls it. I guess it will be yours next month, since you're collecting for him now, what?"

"And the coins in the box?"

"You call the tune, the piper gets paid to play it."

Uriah's nostrils flared. "You're telling me, Brother Idris, that you help Chauncy Malvern embezzle a Sun a month? He gets eight Suns a year and you get four? Is that it?"

The older man hesitated, then sat up straight. Only the tremor running through his double chin betrayed his nervousness. "The bookkeeping is all in order."

"Certainly, because you probably short the accounts of what Earl Meridmarch sends by twelve Suns a year."

"What do you care, Cadet? You can't prove it." Idris laughed, but Uriah knew it was forced. "Your word against mine, with the books and Cadet Malvern speaking against you. Captain Irons would have you tried for an Honor violation and thrown out regardless of your grant."

"But you have given receipts to the Earl's couriers. They would prove you wrong."

"Oh, and you think the Earl will allow an audit of his finances to find twelve Suns a year? You know he's probably undertithing ten times twelve Suns per year. This is nothing. So are you."

"I can still expose you."

"Oh? Cadet Malvern may have come up with this scheme, but *I* like it. If you say anything I will say you proposed it to me. In a moment of weakness I agreed, then repented. Irons will have you." Idris's dark eyes sparked with anger. "Take what I give you and say nothing, or you will be ruined."

Muted by fury and shock, Uriah retreated from the office and stalked across campus. *How can they steal from a blind man?* That very idea outraged him, but he realized he was using his anger to shield himself from the real dilemma that faced him. *If I say anything, do anything, they will destroy me. I'll be wigged and imprisoned. And nothing will happen to them.*

But if I don't say anything . . . Uriah felt ice trickle through his guts. *My brothers used to joke I had Nemyko's red hair and green eyes, and now I'll monthly have the twenty pieces of silver for which he betrayed the Lord Shepherd to the Scipians. And I will get them for betraying my master as he did. If I say nothing I would deserve an Honor trial.*

Mounting the steps again to the tower chamber, he let the

debate rage in his head. He was tempted to throw the money away and run, but that would remove him from Sandwycke and Irons would hunt him down for being a thief. Saying nothing again and again presented itself as the easiest course—and certainly the most profitable—but Uriah rejected it. *If I do that, I'll be dancing to the tune Malvern is calling, and that won't work for me. I'm not going to become part of a crime because it would hurt me to expose it. Better to be innocent and falsely accused than guilty and overlooked.*

He knocked once on the door, then opened it and stalked into the library. "I have returned, sir."

"This I gathered."

Crossing to the table, Uriah let every Sun drop from his left hand to the tabletop. Each one rang with a deep, rich tone that was a credit to the skills and magick of the mintmaster that struck the coins. Then he let the twenty Moons cascade down through the fingers of his right hand. Their tones were not as deep, but the rustling sound of the pile building and collapsing was in its own way very pleasant.

Uriah waited for Kidd to comment, but the blind man said nothing.

"Don't you want to know why I have silver when you had me write out a draft for gold, sir?"

"Idris did not have a sufficient number of Suns?"

"Sloppy guess, sir." Uriah fished the gold coins out of the pile and again dropped them. "If you could hear the scratch of quill on paper, you can count these. There are five of them, as you requested. And twenty Moons."

"Idris made a mistake."

"A very big one, my lord." Uriah drew in a deep breath. "Cadet Malvern has been stealing thirty Moons a month from you. He gives ten to Idris to keep the deception a secret. Idris thought I had come on Malvern's behalf, so he gave me the money. He was quite brazen about it. He said that if I revealed the embezzlement scheme to you I would be ruined."

A grim smile came to Uriah's lips. He remembered very well the scourge of sarcasm Kidd had used to flay Irons. *Malvern will be wigged so badly he'll end up wearing a bearskin and Idris, well, his wife and family will soon find themselves among the beggars living in the shadow of Coldstone prison.* His smile grew as Kidd continued to ponder the problem he had been given. "What would you have me do, sir?"

The blind man sat very still for a moment, then nodded. "When you settle my accounts in Sandwycketown, distribute the Moons to the mendicants."

The young man's jaw dropped open. "My lord?"

"Yes, a Moon is a great deal when they are used to getting copper Stars, but possessing twenty Moons is a fell thing and I would be rid of them in a good way."

"But are you going to do nothing about Malvern and Idris?" Uriah ran his hand around through the pile of coins. "They have been stealing from you! You must do something."

"I have, Cadet Smith."

"I don't understand, sir. What have you done?"

"I've taken you on as my aide."

"That's not what I mean, sir." Uriah flicked a finger at the coins. "Something must be done about the thieves."

"I do not appreciate having my word questioned, Cadet Smith. I have said I have done something." Kidd's face darkened. "You are new, so I will explain myself, this once, then I want to hear nothing more about this, do you understand?"

"Yes, sir."

"Good. Idris came to me two years ago after the first incident. He confessed to me what he had done. The ten Moons he takes go anonymously into the poor box at Saint Nicholas's Orphanage down in town."

"You knew what would happen when I brought your draft to Idris?"

"I did."

Fury bubbled acid up through Uriah's throat. "So this was a test of my honesty?"

"It was a test of that and much more, Cadet Smith." Kidd slowly smiled. "I instructed Brother Idris on how he should deal with your possible reactions. He was not certain he could be convincing, but apparently he was."

"A test." Uriah shook his head. "I can't believe you trusted me so little."

"Would you have been inclined to trust someone with your record and attitude were you in my position?" Kidd shrugged. "Don't worry, you passed it."

"That means nothing." Uriah shook his head to clear it of confusion. "Would I have been discharged if I failed? No, obviously not. Malvern has not been discharged."

"He was quite cautious when he started stealing. He hid the money away after he got it." Kidd closed his eyes. "He became more brazen this year. He would have the silver clinking in his pocket when he came back from settling my accounts."

"And you did nothing?"

"It was not my place."

"He was stealing from *you*, sir. Who else would turn him in?"

Kidd's silver eyes opened again. "I had hoped he would confess voluntarily."

"But now you know he will not. You said yourself he had become more brazen. You have to turn him in."

"And if I do?"

"He will be punished."

"But will he repent?"

"He'll be sorry."

"Yes, but he will not *repent*. He will regret being caught, but never regret having stolen." Kidd opened his hands. "He will receive temporal punishment, but he will be damned eternally."

"That is his problem, sir."

"No, Cadet Smith. It is *my* problem and *your* problem." Viscount Warcross knitted his long fingers together. "Why were you willing to risk temporal punishment for a crime you did not commit?"

Because I'd sooner spit in Malvern's face than succumb to his coercion. But Uriah knew that answer wasn't what Kidd wanted to hear, so he never gave it voice. "I didn't want to be party to a crime, sir."

"But *why*?"

"It wouldn't be right." Uriah frowned. "It wouldn't *feel* right inside."

"Even if you knew you would not be caught?"

"It still wouldn't feel right, sir." *What is he looking for? Ah, yes.* "I'd not want to die with that sort of sin on my soul."

"Your tone is a bit more glib than it should be, Cadet Smith." Kidd nodded. "Your point is correct, however. A man's relationship with God is more important than any other possible thing he could face. If a person lives in the spirit of the Divine Wolf, in accord with the precepts laid down by Eilyph, he will know glory and salvation when he dies."

"But we all know that, sir. All our lives we have been told this lesson. Malvern knows it."

"But just as some people cannot grasp mathematics or language the way you do, so some people cannot understand the reality behind such theological concepts. To cleanse yourself of sin you must confess and truly desire redemption. Chauncy Malvern cannot understand this." Kidd frowned painfully. "If one does not understand mathematics, one can hire another to deal with accounts. But if one does not understand how to atone for sins and attain forgiveness, no other person can stand in their stead before God."

"But you can't let him get away with this." Uriah shook his head. "By making him face justice he will realize he was wrong."

"Punishing Malvern will drive him further from salvation." Kidd raised a hand. "It is my duty as a Wolf-priest to avoid doing that."

"Since when does your obligation to one man outweigh your obligation to the whole flock?" Uriah balled his fists in frustration. "This is not right! By letting Malvern go unpunished, you are loosing a thief into the midst of the flock."

"By showing him mercy in this world, I keep him close to earning mercy in the next." Kidd's head came up. "If he does not recognize and reconcile his transgressions, God will punish him and the punishment will fit the crime, all in accord with God's plan for Chauncy Malvern."

Uriah shook his head, not caring that Kidd could not see him. "I've never seen God's plans work so clearly."

"You're wrong, Cadet Smith, and will grow wiser with age. You'll gain in perspective so these things become more readily apparent. For now, trust me." Kidd clicked a fingernail against his right eye. "You would have to be even more blind than I to fail to see evidence of God's plans being made manifest in this world. You'll have to learn to open your eyes and see what he wants you to see, while you're still able."

—— 12 ——

> **137th Bear Hussar Headquarters**
> **Vzorin, Vzorin Political District**
> **Strana**
> **4 Bell 1687**

Looking out from the tower on top of his headquarters, Pokovnik Grigory Khrolic knew he was master of all he surveyed. With a smile on his face he included Pyimoc in this assessment. Though Duke Vasily Arzlov was a man full of cunning and intelligence, even he was one of Khrolic's charges. The men who guarded the Duke were Khrolic's men, so the Duke's life was his to preserve or destroy.

Because of you, Vasily Arzlov, I am trapped here. Vzorin's mud-brick buildings spread out around him in a haphazard sprawl. Most of the sand-brown buildings were square in shape, with flat roofs, and fire-blackened smoke holes and mud-daubed thatching. Despite the geometric regularity of the buildings themselves, differing dimensions and offset foundations made the city a labyrinth of narrow, overshadowed streets. People jammed new homes in wherever they could be made to fit, cutting off public access while creating a warren of interconnected buildings that might house three or four generations of a family in pitiable squalor.

Chickens and goats, dogs, pigs, and grubby little black-haired children ran, rooted, and played in open sewers. When the cold wind blew in from the north—not nearly enough during the summer for Khrolic's tastes—it carried away the stench of an unwashed human throng. The residents of the city were Stranans, but in name only. Racially and culturally they were part and parcel of Estanu.

Because of you, Vasily Arzlov, I will be leaving this place. Khrolic turned to look north toward the newest section of the city. Built in and around the area between the Hussars' home and Pyimoc, racial Stranans had created a real city. The streets, which had been paved with native stone, had sewer ditches dug along them and ran straight from the outskirts to where they collided with Old Town. Stranan architects had managed to teach local workers how to build proper structures. If one squinted enough—so the flat brown plains to the north could not be fully seen—it was possible to imagine being back in Myasovo or Savensk or even on the outskirts of Murom.

Grigory Khrolic very much wanted to be back in Murom. While many maintained that power centers other than Murom existed in the Stranan Empire, Grigory had noticed the strength with which they held that opinion was in direct proportion to their distance from Murom. No one—not even a Tacarri who was pleased with the power he wielded in his province—would refuse to abandon everything for a chance to return to Murom and seek his fortune at court.

Toying with the key that hung around his neck on a braided cord, Grigory began a slow descent down the narrow, circular steps. His footfalls rasped against the stone, the grit from dust storms helping grind it down. Native masons had been hired to build the tower, as well as to add to the Hussars' home, and the crudity of their craftsmanship provided the warrior with a nearly exact measure of his distance from Murom.

The reasons to return to Murom far exceeded his desire for power. Murom was the center of Stranan culture. Symphonies, operas, theatre dramas, and ballets were available for entertainment. Books that were the toast of Murom would arrive in Vzorin—if he were lucky—within a decade of their publication. The food and the accommodations in Murom were superior to anything else in the empire and perhaps in the world.

That certainly held true for the company.

He smiled as he thought of Natalya Ohanscai and fingered the gold *rubl* with her profile engraved on it in his pocket. He did truly love her—he knew that beyond question. He had wanted her since he first saw her, back when he first traveled to Murom as Vasily Arzlov's aide with the Hussars. He had been twenty-six years old and she a mere slip of a girl at fifteen. She ignored him at first, but he knew she was intrigued by him. He promised himself she would be his and launched himself on a campaign that would not bear fruit for eight more years.

At the base of the tower, Grigory emerged into his headquarters proper. The guardsmen standing at either side of the door snapped to attention, but Grigory ignored them. The posting of guards had more to do with a need to build a sense of duty among the Hussars than it did any fear of an attack. *Helansajar may be politically unstable, but the chances of an attack coming here in Vzorin are neglibible. An attack here would require a leader as audacious as I was in assuming I could win Natalya's heart.*

Another man might have been impatient, but Grigory had developed the ability to wait. Perhaps coming from a large family had aided in this. His great-grandparents, most of whom were still living when he was growing up, saw sixscore years. His parents preached "Haste makes waste" as if it were the Eleventh Commandment, and his family appeared to be long-lived enough to make proper planning a viable alternative to impulsive self-destruction.

Over and over again Grigory had seen people who appeared to be moving swiftly toward success and glory, yet, like shooting stars, they always flared out and fell as quickly as they had risen. The Ilbeorian, Malachy Kidd, had been one such individual. He had been brilliant—Grigory acknowledged his debt to the man for teaching him new tactics to employ with the Hussars—but because of Kidd's haste he did not see danger when it lurked nearby. His impatience had let Grigory destroy him, and in destroying him Grigory had learned yet another lesson.

No one is invincible.

That had been an important lesson for him to grasp as the Hussars had pursued the Lescari host back to their homeland. Grigory had learned to accept assignments but carry them out in a manner that saved him and his men undue casualties. Stranan doctrine always valued the weight of the army over the life of any one soldier, but Grigory modified that view substantially. While willing to shed his blood for Strana, he much preferred to shed the blood of the enemy for Strana.

His reluctance to pitch his men into the sausage grinder of war combined well with his ability to win battles through tactical advantages—inspiring his men to become personally loyal to him. As they moved into the ranks of other battalions his fame spread among the Hussars. By the end of the war he was the most popular officer in the regiment, so his appointment as Arzlov's successor came as no surprise—except to Arzlov.

Arzlov had offered Grigory a chance to accompany him to Vzorin, but Grigory agreed instead to be made Pokovnik of the Hussars. Vzorin was too far from Murom for him to pursue Natalya. More importantly, Arzlov's posting to Vzorin appeared as crippling to him as the loss of the Ilbeorian's eyes had been to Kidd. Grigory did not want to wither and die with Arzlov in Vzorin. His new posting took him to Myasovo, a city he knew well, and a city in dire need of his skills.

Walking down a corridor and then descending several broad steps, Grigory came to the arched doorway that led into the Vandari annex of the Hussar headquarters. Stranan laborers had been brought in to build the Vandari stable, and they worked from Grigory's own designs. Each suit of the armor had been given its own stall, as befit such fabled and valuable equipment. *No Estanuan mason could have produced work worthy to house them.*

For five years, using the engineering degree he had earned previously at Tacier's College in Myasovo, he had built a new Myasovo from the ashes left behind by Fernandi's forces. Once a quarter he took the three-day trip to Murom in an airship to report on his progress with the rebuilding. He also took time to socialize with the nobility, bringing them exotica that came through the port at Myasovo or up the Gold Route from Vzorin.

After two years his visits were greatly anticipated and parties were planned for the week he would spend in the capital. Though many wanted him to be their guest, he always accepted the offer from the Naraschal of the Vandari, Sergei Tsodov. Grigory's friendship flattered the military elder statesman and Tsodov made certain to parade Grigory around in the high social circuits of the inner court.

With the reconstruction of Myasovo all but finished, the only logical posting for the 137th Bear Hussars was Murom. Within a month of their arrival, on the Eve of Tenebre, the Hussars hosted a ball that was said to have been so impressive that, piqued at not having been invited, General Winter had stayed away from Murom for a whole month, until Mors.

Grigory's patience brought him more than just the posting to Murom and his chance to court Natalya. Positions within the Vandari had been hotly sought after and contested since the days of Keerana Dost. Vacancies within the three hundred were usually filled by the best graduates from the military academy at Savensk. Members of the Vandari always served with their company, not a separate command, and if they proved themselves good enough, they rose in rank within the Vandari.

Offering someone from outside the Savensk Cadre a chance to join the Vandari was all but unprecedented, but when a vacancy opened up in the Ram Guards, there was no question that Grigory Khrolic should be allowed to enter the contest to fill that slot. It also came as no surprise that he was able to best the other candidates in the majority of tests required. While he did concede a decade and a half to the others, those fifteen years had given him a wealth of experience that more than compensated for the superiority of their athleticism.

The only thing standing between him and joining the Vandari— the military elite of Strana, unequaled by troops elsewhere—was the initiation. Because the Vandari armor operated through magick, a warrior being given a suit of the armor had to be able to wield great amounts of magick. It was possible that in his first contact with the armor he would prove unable to coordinate all of the spells and handle all of the demands made on him by the armor.

If it went badly he would be driven insane.

If it went disastrously he would be consumed.

Grigory paused before the door to the stall housing his Ram, Twenty-seven. He brushed his fingers over the engraved nameplate set into the stone beside the door, feeling the letters of his name scrape past. Part of him still could not believe he had succeeded in joining the Vandari and touching the nameplate had become a ritual of his that brought back to him the reality of his success.

The twenty-nine other Rams had met with him in their headquarters an hour before midnight on the last day of the year. Initiation into the Vandari always occurred in the first hour of the month of Initibre. For 1682 the Rams had had only one replacement to make ready. If Grigory failed, Ram Twenty-seven would remain unoccupied until the next Initibre.

Grigory's left hand felt beneath his silk tunic for the bronze key that hung on a braided cotton cord around his neck. He pressed the piece of metal reassuringly against his breastbone. That key linked him to his Ram. It gave him entrance to it and control over it. It linked him with his success and symbolized the promise of a prosperous future.

It had not seemed so that first night. He had fasted for a week and attended Mass three times daily. He had had his confession heard before coming to the Ram headquarters, and kneeling on the cold stone floor, he wore nothing but a white cotton robe. Around him, wearing similar robes, the other Rams bore white candles and murmured prayers for his safety. A black velvet curtain hid the armor from his sight, but as he knelt there he could feel its presence.

The Rams' chaplain, a gray-beard Bishop, blessed him and then circled the curtained cylinder surrounding the Ram armor. Every two steps he flicked a censer at it, dribbling smoke over the curtain to frighten away any demons clinging to the hidden armor. Satisfied, the cleric said a prayer, then gave the key to Grigory. "God be with you, my son. If it is His will, your way will be without peril."

The irony of that statement had not struck Grigory until much later, for the same man, after hearing his confession, had suggested arranging a bequest for the Church if things did not go well. The chaplain had not put much faith in Grigory's worthiness to join the Vandari. *Or,* Grigory reflected, *he understood the true nature of the test I would face.*

As the Bishop stepped aside, the black velvet curtain surrounding Ram Twenty-seven parted. As if positioned to mirror him, the armor knelt on the floor. The candlelight glowed from the armor's bronze flesh and glinted from the sharp edges of the horns mounted on the head. The armor sat back on its haunches. Rounded thighs gave way to I-beam shins and elongated foot bones that ended in heavy cloven hooves. The arms likewise had rounded uppers that bled down past the elbow to mechanical I-beam forearms and cloven hooves. The barrel-chested body expanded up into massively powerful shoulders. The triangular head, which was featureless except for two glassed-over eyeholes, joined the shoulders without the benefit of a neck.

The machine—for that's what Grigory saw it as—had a majesty and power. Though it had been crafted by smiths eight centuries before in Durrania, it looked almost as if Strana's finest craftsmen—Vladimir Soloviev or Andrej Gorianov—had created it within the last decade. Ram Twenty-seven's history aside, only the fact that these two master craftsmen of jeweled miniatures had never worked on something this size precluded it from having been their invention.

And Ram Twenty-seven did have history. Just beneath its left breast Grigory saw a hole nearly twice the size of a gold *rubl*. Though no one told him what had happened, he had heard rumors, and during the Lescari War, he had seen the sort of damage the Vandari could sustain. Whether the armor was pierced by an iron bolt or crushed by a shot from a steam cannon, the results were the same. The body inside the armor would vanish—once joined to the armor the warrior would always be part of it—and the armor would remain damaged until it accepted a new master. Dragged back to Strana, it would wait for the start of the new year and the initiation of a new candidate.

Grigory Khrolic had stood and held the key before him as a priest might present the Eucharist to his congregation. He kept his voice even as he approached the armor. "I am Pokovnik Grigory Khrolic. I have been chosen through contest with others who would present themselves for your service. Together we will be more than we are apart."

When he got within six feet of the machine a number of things happened. With a metallic buzz-hiss, the triangular head rose up and revealed a hole easily twice the diameter of Grigory's neck. Below it the torso opened, splitting down a central seam that had not been visible before. Two doors pushed out toward him, then invitingly opened to either side. Aside from the little padded seat inside, and a cavity into which a leather-bound diary had been placed, the armor's interior appeared disappointingly spartan. Where the hole had appeared on the outside of the right-hand door, the interior had a thin film of metal already in place, as if the pilot's last act had been to place gold foil over the wound.

Grigory stepped up into Ram Twenty-seven. He placed his key in the little pocket sewn in over his heart on the robe, then turned and pressed his back against the cool metal of the armor. Reaching up, he inserted his arms through the shoulder-height holes and found his hands fitting snugly into leathery-feeling gloves. Easing himself down on the little seat, he placed his right and left legs through the holes into each of the armor's thighs.

Suddenly the head descended and the armor snapped shut, entombing him in black closeness. No light filtered in through the eyeholes. Heat immediately built inside the metal suit he wore. He fought the impulse to panic and, at first, he thought himself successful because his claustrophobic anxiety drained away. Then he realized his blindness and the fading of tactile stimulus meant something very, very odd was happening.

A blinding white light stabbed through his eyes—no matter that his eyelids were closed—and impaled his brain. A scream echoed in his ears. A deep, piercing pain carried straight through him, igniting fire in the left side of his chest with every breath. His hands tightened into fists and his teeth ground against the torment.

He fought against the agony, forcing himself to breathe. Choking back his own cries of pain, he started counting. *Breathe, one, two; exhale, three, four* . . . Filling his mind with numbers and logic, he shunted the discomfort aside. He could not, would not, let the armor kill him and take his dreams with it.

The situation began to change. The physical hurt began to diminish, but in its wake came something that frightened Grigory even more than the thought of dying itself. He started to shiver as cold nibbled at his hands and feet. It touched his knees where he had been kneeling, then the bare flesh of his face. He felt the tips of his ears and nose begin to burn with frostbite and fatigue pressed in on him heavily.

No! I will not be winterkill. Shaking off his lethargy, he started to pump his arms and legs. He invoked the ambulation spell he'd been taught as part of his initiation. *I must exert control or it will destroy me.*

The world swirled around him, disorienting him entirely. He felt himself falling. He reached out with his right hand to hold himself up and he felt the distant shock that stopped his fall. He saw sparks then brought his head up as the outside world swam into focus. The viewports provided him an abbreviated glimpse of his surroundings, but he saw enough to orient himself concerning up and down. Pulling his head and shoulders up, then pushing down with his right leg and extending his left arm, he managed to right himself.

He found himself breathing heavily with the effort. *It is as if I have wrestled this machine into submission.*

Muted applause built as he corrected his balance and then gingerly saluted his fellow Rams from within Twenty-seven. He could see the other Rams beaming proudly at his success, and some even looked amazed at his salute. Working hard, he managed to avoid having the right hoof dent the Ram's head or get caught up in the horn. Sitting the Ram back on its haunches, Grigory even allowed himself a smile despite his fatigue.

Standing there, he realized the sound of applause came to him as naturally as if he were not encased in tons of metal satyr. He assumed, somewhere, there was some sort of a funnel device carrying the sound to him. *The mechanical intricacies of this machine are incredible.*

Slowly he began to notice other things—magickal things—that surprised him about the armor as well. Black symbols on red tiles floated through his field of vision. If he tried to look at them, they eluded him, remaining at the edges of his visual field. He pondered them for a moment, but could not get a clear look at any one of them. Then he thought about the ambulation spell he had invoked and one of the tiles drifted down to where he could see it. Unlike the other tiles, this one had a red symbol on a black tile.

This means it is currently cast. Grigory began a mental inventory of the spells he knew and found each one was represented by a tile. During this process of taking stock, he discovered that simply by looking at the edge of a tile he could mentally command it to shift down into visual range. This brought to him two spells he had learned as a child and one last spell that he had not known he knew.

The symbol on the tile appeared to be an infant. Grigory smiled—he had been warned about that kind of symbol, for the tiles and their symbols tended to be individual to the pilots. *That tile will invoke the Initiation.* Being intelligent, and being still able to feel the pain of his initiation, he had no desire to invoke that spell and start the process over again.

Bringing the armor back to its kneeling position, he commanded it to release him. It did so, opening up as it had to accept him. Grigory freed his arms and legs, then half stumbled from the armor. He felt exhausted—so exhausted that he did not notice he was naked until he fell to the ground and felt the chilled stone against his flesh. Only later did he figure out that his garment had been woven into the braided cord from which his armor's key hung.

Grigory opened the door to his Ram's stall and smiled at the bronze monstrosity kneeling before him. Well polished, without a scratch on its flesh, Twenty-seven waited there, silent and grimly cold. Staring at it, Grigory could almost sense an intelligence there, but the viewports remained blank, and he killed an urge to enter the armor and parade around.

His success in joining the Vandari increased his fame a hundredfold. The Vandari companies normally operated independently, but in honor of his rank and position, Grigory was made the commander of the Ram company and it was attached to the 137th Bear

Hussars regiment. In 1685 the Rams moved south with the Hussars to Vzorin to aid Grigory in his mission of keeping an eye on Duke Arzlov and his actions on the empire's southern frontier.

Grigory stretched and then reached out to pat his armor on the broad thigh. He expected his exile to end soon. In ordering deep patrols of Helansajar, Arzlov had revealed more about his plans than he had intended. Grigory recalled that, at the peace conference that had ended the Lescari War, Arzlov and the Ilbeorians had not gotten along terribly well. Prince Trevelien had been part of the Ilbeorian delegation and Grigory knew Arzlov well enough to know the Prince had not been forgiven for whatever transgressions he might have committed. Bottled at the Ferrace conference, Arzlov's distrust of Ilbeoria had aged quite well and appeared to be nearing the time for decanting.

Trevelien's appointment as Governor-general of Aran made taking the Ilbeorian colony just that much more inviting for Arzlov. The political instability in Helansajar made taking Helor imperative, but having Trevelien in Aran would make it also a joy for the Duke. Grigory did not doubt the Duke could find a way to take the colony, though he did doubt the ability of the Hussars and the two native regiments in Vzorin to accomplish the job unaided. *Arzlov has a plan to deal with that, as well.*

For Grigory the only dilemma came from what he saw as an embarrassment of opportunities. If Arzlov's plan was viable, he would go along with it, adding to the empire and earning the Tacier's gratitude. If it was not viable, or things progressed with more difficulty than anticipated, Grigory would abort the campaign, consolidate whatever had been taken, and end the career of a reckless and ambitious noble before he could challenge the Tacier's rightful place at the center of the empire.

Smiling, Grigory stopped himself from trying to imagine how his plans might bear fruit. That sort of idle speculation prompted haste in others and Grigory did not want to fall into that trap. There was plenty of time for things to unfold. After all, only eight siblings stood between Natalya's husband and the throne.

He would live a *long* time. He could afford to wait. Not forever, but then it wouldn't be forever before Arzlov overstepped himself and the opportunity for Grigory to guarantee his future presented itself.

— 13 —

At the crest of the hill separating the seminary from the valley
where the airdocks lay, Uriah Smith stopped and gasped. Jaw agape,
he gently lowered the back end of the wheelbarrow. "May God have
mercy, it's beautiful, Rob."

"Enough to take your breath away." Smiling, Robin swept his
right hand toward the valley. "This is the *Saint Michael*, my new
home."

"It's big!"

"It is at that." Robin laughed. "A lot bigger than the *Crow* ever
was."

The airship *Saint Michael* ran 210 feet from bow to stern. Were
it not for the wings fore and aft, it might have been mistaken for the
capsized hull of a ship that had somehow been beached half a mile
inland—all without somehow being pounded into kindling by the
journey. The bow wing spread out in a gentle crescent from the prow
and thickened into the hull much as the head of a hammerhead shark
tapers back into its body. The aft wing, set above the open-air wing
deck, shared the same dimensions as the bow wing, measuring 150
feet from tip to tip. Above it the twin rudders added another 20 feet
to the ship's height and were mounted perpendicular to the plane of
the wings. The propellers were mounted at the aft as well, but remained idle with the ship in dock.

Uriah blinked. "It's really big."

Rob nodded. "One of the biggest airships in the world."

Uriah counted fifteen hatches on each of the three gunnery
decks and saw three more gun hatches on the starboard prow. He
knew the airship had four guns shooting aft, giving the ship a full
complement of one hundred steam cannons. That made the *Saint
Michael* one of the three biggest Airships of the Line in the Ilbeorian

fleet. Fully staffed, it would be home to over eight hundred airmen, including fifty-four Aeromancers whose magick would keep the ship aloft. In addition to the ship's crew, one hundred and fifty warriors shipped with the *Saint Michael*. Among them was a company of fifty ethyrines of which Brother Robert Drury was the new commander.

Uriah started pushing the wheelbarrow toward the squared-off aft end of the ship where twin smokestacks leaked black smoke above the twin props. He nodded toward the gangplank leading up to the wing deck. "Will you show me around after we stow your cloud chest?"

"We'll get a chance to look around *while* we're taking care of my chest." Robin pointed toward the belly of the ship and the trench dug beneath it. "Nice thing about flying is that the hull can be opened to give us direct access to the hold. No lowering supplies and having things break."

The younger man frowned. "But you're an officer. You'll be quartered in the wardroom and that's toward the aft. Hauling this chest down instead of up will be easier."

"I know, which is why we won't be doing it that way."

"Rob, I know you think I don't apply myself to jobs I'm supposed to be doing, but I *have* rolled your chest out here pretty far, haven't I?"

"True, but you offered to do that so you could see the ship." Rob pointed to the ship's belly. "We go in there."

"I don't understand why you don't want to board with the other officers, as is your due."

Robin waved Uriah after him. "You know I was on the *Crow* during the Lescari War."

"You were a gunner."

"And you said you didn't understand."

Uriah growled at the ethyrine. "Have you been tutored in harassment by Kidd?"

"No need, you just bring it out in me." Robin slapped him on the back. "When you've crewed a ship, there are things you remember about the experience. One of them is new-minted Sandies coming aboard thinking they're God's gift to the benighted folk lurking on the gunnery decks." Rob pointed to the triple row of hatch covers. "Save the officers sleeping in the cabins at the aft and a few others, all the crew sleeps in hammocks hung on those decks. They hang their beds in a space only fourteen inches wide. I spent five years sleeping there right above my cannon."

"So?"

"For someone so smart . . ." Robin rolled his eyes. "Uriah, I *know* the life of an airman isn't easy. I want the crew to know I know it."

"Oh." Uriah looked down at his hands. The space between the handles of the wheelbarrow was greater than what Rob described as available in which to hang a hammock. *Not much room on such a big ship, but there will be nearly a thousand people on board.* "You'll get more room than that in the wardroom, yes?"

"Prince Trevelien will get the Great Cabin, so the Captain will displace the First Lieutenant and so on. I imagine the wardroom will be crowded." Rob smiled wearily. "And it's right above the engine deck and our three engines. The noise and the stench will take getting used to."

"Three engines?"

"As you've said, Uriah, it's a *big* ship." Robin smiled broadly. "One for each propeller at the aft there and one to run the cannon-charging stations. I'll show you when we get inside."

"Good." Getting closer, Uriah looked at the flags flying from the trio of signal masts running along the air keel. "That looks like the Prince's flag. Is he aboard now?"

Robin shook his head. "It's possible."

"Do you think we'll meet him?"

"Probably not." The larger man smiled slyly. "He's likely at a reception for cadets who have sisters they want to get married off to him. I think Captain Irons was taking his daughter."

"No! The Prince will have enough trouble in Aran . . ." Uriah's eyes narrowed. "It's an honor-code violation if you lie like that."

Robin laughed aloud and thumbed the gold ring on his right hand. "I've graduated, so the board has no jurisdiction over me. Besides, do you think they'd believe *you*?"

"Only if Irons was accompanying his daughter to Aran." Uriah shrugged. "But it would be a thrill to see the Prince. Not meet him, you know, just see him."

The ethyrine stopped and rested his fists on his narrow hips. "Aside from recounting petty victories over instructors here, the only subject you've ever addressed with the least bit of enthusiasm was Prince Trevelien. He was a hero of yours, wasn't he?"

"Still is." Uriah let his gaze linger on the worn wood of Robin's cloud chest. "I used to thrill to stories of his adventures."

"As did all the rest of us. When his wife died . . ."

"Yeah, it hurt all of us." Uriah smiled a bit and looked up at the ethyrine. "Now he's heading to Aran where he'll show himself to be a hero again."

"He's not the only hero at Sandwycke, you know." Robin flicked a thumb at the distant seminary. "Colonel Kidd is a hero."

Uriah scoffed. "Sure, a hero. Do you know what he has had me doing? I've had to take down every book in his library, dust it, then he wants me to reorganize the library the way I think would be more efficient. I know this is another one of his tests, and that he'll tell me to put it all back the way it was originally, so I've fooled him and recorded the order of every volume just to be ready to put it all back."

Robin shook his head. "You know, you don't apply yourself to simple jobs, then you go overboard on other things. I think I'll be glad I'm in Aran when you finally graduate."

"Just for that I'll apply myself and request posting to Aran, then you'll be in trouble."

"I'll live in dread of that for a whole year, Uriah."

"I doubt that." Uriah smiled at his companion. "Hey, if the Prince *is* on board, going up to the wing deck and working our way down would be the most likely way of meeting him, wouldn't it?"

"Nice try, but we're not going that way."

Sighing in mock protest as they swung past three heavily laden oxcarts standing in the ship's shadow, Uriah followed Robin beneath the edge of the hull and entered the close tunnel below the ship. Two doors had been opened in the hull for loading. Sweating, bare-chested men worked at unloading a cart of wooden biscuit chests. They stacked them on a wooden pallet, then hoisted it up into the hold where more men unloaded it.

The loading master looked at Robin's cloud chest, then frowned. "Be a bit until I can get that aboard, sir. We want to clear these carts first."

"Don't worry, Mac. My load, my back."

The man squinted at Robin, then slowly smiled with a mouthful of crooked teeth. "Drury? Is that you?"

"Aye, Mac."

"I didn't recognize you with your head half shaved and out of your blues."

"It's been ten years, Mac." Robin turned toward Uriah. "Mac was on the *Crow*, too."

"Simon MacAllen, sir." The loading master extended a hand to Uriah. His grip was strong and his handshake as sincere as his smile. He let go of Uriah's hand, then embraced Robin. "Damn and all, I didn't know you were a Sandy."

"Factory life wasn't for me and the Lakeworth Carriage Works decided I wasn't for them."

"I knew you'd not take to that sort of work. I figured you for Coldstone."

Uriah blinked with surprise. "Robin in prison?"

MacAllen started to speak, but Rob silenced him with a glance. "Mac knew me in a time when I was a bit more boisterous, and thinking myself as smart as you think yourself. Mac, who's skippering this angel?"

"Prince Trevelien is on board, so there's only one man they'd put at the helm."

"Lonan Hassett?"

"Full Captain. I heard him read his orders at the change of command in Ludstone."

From the smiles on both men's faces, Uriah assumed they were pleased with the choice of captain. "Is Captain Hassett the one who stole the *Mockingbird* from the Lescari and got the Prince out of Lescar?"

"Aye, lad, he was the one." The glance Mac exchanged with Robin told Uriah there was more to the story, but neither man volunteered it.

"Tell me."

Robin smiled. "Uriah's compiling a biography of Prince Trevelien . . ."

"Oh, then we wouldn't want to tell him lies."

"Or rumors."

"So you're not going to tell me anything, are you?"

"Perhaps he's smarter than you think, Rob."

"One more year at Sandwycke will take care of that. Mac, we'll have more time to talk when we put sky below us." Rob grabbed the leather handle on the end of his cloud chest and hoisted the heavy box onto his back. "Good seeing you again."

"Wait for a moment, Rob, er, Brother Drury." Mac gestured impatiently at the men up in the ship's hold. "Get the pallet back down here, you larks. You have an officer here what needs to be aboard."

"The Sandy's got legs, hasn't he?" someone shouted from the dark depths of the hold.

"Aye, but it'll be the spring in your spine that welcomes him aboard. Before he was a Sandy he was a man, and the damned finest gunner the *Crow* ever had." The pallet descended rapidly and Mac waved them toward it. "Welcome aboard, sir. Glad to have you with us."

They mounted the pallet and it rose slowly into the ship's hull. From the outside the oaken airship had seemed huge, but inside

Uriah could see just how cramped it all was. The men working to unload things in the hold were all bent over. Boxes and casks were packed tightly together and wedged or roped into place so they would not shift as the ship flew.

The men hoisting them into the ship brought them all the way up through the hold's top hatch and onto the engine deck. Uriah stepped off the swaying pallet and almost knocked over a stack of crates containing live chickens. The birds squabbled at him and feathers flew into the air, but the pigs and four cows penned beyond them took no notice of the disturbance.

He was about to ask Rob why they had livestock on board, but he decided he didn't need to give him more ammunition for gibes about his intelligence. Thinking for a moment, he puzzled it out. All the foodstuffs being loaded into the hold below had been prepared by methods that would make them last. On the month-long journey to Aran, the *Saint Michael* might land only a handful of times on its journey to Aran—at coaling stations and on the island of St. Martin. Aside from that, the ship would have to be self-sufficient. Having a ready supply of milk, eggs, and fresh meat would be important.

Rob smiled as if he had read Uriah's mind. "Fresh, on an airship, usually denotes anything where there is more of the original food than there is of weevils or maggots."

Uriah smiled. "I knew there was a reason I wanted to be a foot soldier instead of an ethyrine. At least we get to forage."

"Yes, but we don't sleep in mud."

"Good point, that."

Rob nodded toward the aft of the ship. "The three engines are down there. The two that power the propellers are always kept fired in case moving quickly is necessary. The battleboiler is not—it consumes a lot of coal when in use—but pipes run from the smaller engines through the water tank in the battleboiler. They keep the battleboiler's water hot, so the engine can be fired and working in a relatively short time. It turns a shaft that uses belts, other shafts, and gears to drive the steam cannons' pistons in battle. If a prop engine fails, the battleboiler can be used to drive the propellers, but only slowly and only in emergencies."

Mounting the stairs in the center of the ship, Rob hauled his cloud chest up to the lowest gun deck. Thirty cannons, fifteen to a side, lined the deck. Cables and blocks were in position to pull the cannons forward so they could shoot out the hatches before them. Chains bound the cannon's truck to the hull to prevent the gunne from recoiling after a shot and careening around on the deck. Leather belts hung from a shaft running the length of the ship and fit into a geared assembly that would drive a cannon's piston when the gunner's mate engaged it.

"A good crew with a hot boiler can shoot twice in a minute. An eight-pound ball will travel six hundred yards, though at that range accuracy suffers." Rob patted one of the big guns. "The guns' boilers are kept cold just in case rough weather starts tipping things around. Having a fire started inside the ship is trouble."

"I can imagine." Uriah followed Rob up another flight of stairs to the middle gun deck and then toward the aft of the ship. He noticed what appeared to be a smallish enclosure near the center of the deck. What made it remarkable was that its walls had been plated with iron. "What's that?"

Robin glanced over, then nodded. "That's one of the Aeromancer stations. There are two more, one fore and one aft. Three Aeromancers occupy them for a six-hour shift and use their magick to keep the ship aloft. It only takes three Aeromancers, if they're good, and we have three stations in case they get hit in battle, so we won't go down."

Uriah winced. "It would make for a hard landing."

"And a lot of kindling."

Crew members made passage aft difficult because of the hammocks slung above the guns and the general bustle of sailors stowing gear they'd acquired while grounded. Uriah tried not to bump anyone, but that was impossible given the conditions. *Still, Rob is managing it.* "A bit crowded, eh?"

"It's because the folks not loading are here. Normally the watches have people elsewhere, attending to their duties. In dock the larks have got nothing to do." Rob hiked the chest up higher on his back. "In flight they earn their liberty."

At the aft end of the middle gun deck they came to the wardroom. The two ethyrines standing on either side of the hatchway snapped to attention when Rob approached them. He set his chest down and saluted them crisply, keeping his right hand with his palm hidden from them. They returned the salute, but refrained from smiling or otherwise lightening the serious expressions on their faces.

Uriah grabbed the back end of the chest and helped Rob carry it into the wardroom. He was immediately taken with the view. Windows made up the aft bulkhead, giving him a good look at the two huge propellers that drove the airship through the sky. "This is impressive."

"Imagine it when we're up so high that cattle look like fleas and clouds steal through our view like fog rolling in off the ocean."

"Wow." Uriah pressed his nose against one of the windows. "It's a bit hot in here, being up over the boilers. Why aren't the windows open?"

"They can't open." Rob slid his chest into an open spot beneath the padded bench that ran the length of the windows. "The propellers create enough suction that papers and charts would be whisked right out of the room. Conditions in here might seem nasty now, but I'll get used to it."

"Used to it? It's so hot."

Rob pointed toward the sky. "Not up there. When the air gets thin it gets cold. In wintertime it's no hardship to be a fireman aboard an airship. The smokestacks running up through the cabins back here provide heat. Of course, they can also be deadly if they get holed and fill the ship with smoke."

Uriah did an admiring turn in the cabin, then stiffened as he saw an officer wearing a bright red jacket with two gold slashes on the sleeves standing in the doorway. The Acolyte appeared to be as surprised as Uriah to find him there. The ship's officer moved quickly out of the way and drew himself up tight, then announced, "Captain in the wardroom."

Uriah and Robin both snapped to attention as Captain Lonan Hassett passed through the hatchway. Even if his jacket had not borne a gold star on each wrist, his tonsure would have marked him as a man worthy of respect. He moved with a humble economy of motion that would not have been unexpected of so slender and tall a man, but there appeared to be a bit of mischief in his step. It was reflected in his brown eyes and the hint of a smile on his face when he saw the two of them. He bowed his head to them, ignoring the fact that they had not saluted him, then turned to wave two more men into the cabin.

Uriah's mouth went dry as Prince Trevelien stepped into the wardroom. While he had entertained fantasies of meeting the Prince—who had not, after all?—such encounters had centered around his graduation from Sandwycke, or getting an award for his service to Ilbeoria. He had never anticipated such a casual meeting, so all of the brave things he had planned to say fled his mind instantly. *What do I do? What can I say? Do I bow or shake his hand? What if he doesn't offer? Or notice?*

Compounding Uriah's anxiety, Malachy Kidd stepped into the cabin behind the Prince. He carried a cane, though he held it more as if he were a gentleman out for a promenade than one who needed it to help him find his way.

"Good afternoon, gentlemen." Captain Hassett returned their salute. "Sorry to disturb you."

"Brother Robert Drury reporting for duty, sir."

"Ah, yes, the new ethyrine commander." The way the Captain looked at Robin gave Uriah the impression that he already knew a great deal about his new officer. "With rank, Brother Drury, you are allowed to come aboard on the wing deck."

"Yes, sir, I understand that, sir."

Uriah looked over at Robin. *He's nervous! Rob?*

"Old habits die hard, do they, Brother Drury?"

Robin's anxiety broke on the anvil of that lightly asked question. "Yes, sir, they do."

"Glad to have a Sandy on board who already knows his way around a ship." Hassett, clasping his arms behind his back, turned toward Uriah. "And who might you be?"

"I'm, sir, I mean, I am—"

Kidd stepped forward to Hassett's side. "I believe, Captain, this is Cadet Uriah Smith, my new aide. He and Brother Drury presented a most interesting case study of a Stranan assault on Helor this past semester."

"Ah, was that what Irons was on about?"

Uriah winced involuntarily.

Kidd nodded. "He did seem to find it quite memorable."

"Well, then, perhaps Mr. Drury will join His Highness and me for dinner one evening and he can tell us of this remarkable study." Hassett looked back at the Prince and was rewarded with a nod of assent. The Prince followed that with a step forward and Hassett smiled. "Highness, may I present Brother Robert Drury and Cadet Uriah Smith."

The Prince exchanged salutes with both men. "I look forward to hearing about your report, Brother Drury. And of you, Cadet Smith, I expect you to render as faithful service to Colonel Kidd as your father did mine. You may not realize it now, but you are enjoying a privilege that many would desire for themselves. You are in a position to study genius. Do not waste it."

"No, sir, Highness, I won't."

"Very well, then." Hassett turned and nodded to the Acolyte leading the tour of the ship. "We shall let you stow your gear, Mr. Drury. Please enjoy your time aboard the *Saint Michael*, Cadet Smith."

The two of them remained at attention until Hassett's party vacated the wardroom and the Acolyte pulled the hatch shut. Rob let out a big sigh. "Well, Uriah, you met the Prince."

"I know." Uriah frowned. " 'No, sir, Highness, I won't.' "

"You were eloquent, Uriah, but I don't think your remarks have quite the ring needed for immortality."

"I don't need to study genius to figure that out." The cadet dropped down onto the window seat. "I get a chance to meet Prince Trevelien, I can't even say my own name, and I mumble nonsense at him."

"At least you didn't make him angry."

"Yeah, no small miracle that, I suppose." Uriah clasped his hands at the back of his neck and looked up. "What was Colonel Kidd doing here? How does he know the Prince?"

Robin shook his head. "I don't know, but you're in the perfect position to find out. Ask him."

"And expect an honest answer? I don't think so." The younger man smiled slowly. "I tell you what, Rob, I'll nose about and see what I can learn about it, and you do the same. We can share notes and figure it out."

"Asking him would be easier and I've never known you to want to do a lot of work."

"Things are changing, Rob. I've already had a week's worth of studying genius and I know Kidd will make me pay dearly for the answers to any questions. If I can get them for myself, however, that will give me a leg up on him and I can use it to my advantage."

The ethyrine frowned. "Wasn't this how your difficulties with Captain Irons started out?"

"Yes, Rob, but this time it's different." Uriah Smith allowed himself a little laugh. "In Malachy Kidd I might just have found myself an opponent I'll have to work to beat."

— 14 —

> **Bahara al-Njûn**
> **Jibal al-Estans, Helansajar**
> **10 Bell 1687**

Rafiq Khast awoke abruptly and suddenly, as if in response to a scream or crack of thunder, yet he felt no fear. No sweat beaded up on his flesh. His heart did not beat fast. His hands did not tremble and his eyes did not burn with sleeplessness. He felt no desire to reach out in the darkness and grasp the hilt of his shamshir to reassure himself there was no danger.

He started to smile at himself and even laugh at waking up in the middle of the night, but then a word came to him, whispered on the night breeze.

"Rafiq."

His name, nothing more, came softly enough to have been a night murmur. Alone in his tent, camped with the rest of his band on the western shore of the Lake of Stars, he could have easily misheard. It could indeed have been a trick of the wind, or one of the guards calling out to him to report something odd. It could have been any of dozens of things, but Rafiq knew what he had heard.

"Rafiq."

The second time—Rafiq realized it must really have been the third, for the sound of his name had to have been what brought him to consciousness—the word came no more loudly or insistently than before. It sounded not as a question or command, but confirmation of what he had heard before. His name had been called and clearly the common courtesy of a response was expected.

He pulled on his breeches and tied sandals to his feet, then threw back the flap of his tent and emerged into the night's cool air. Around him he noticed his other men emerging from their tents. All of them looked about puzzled—all save his uncle Qusay. The bony old man had advanced to the lakeshore and squatted like a child at the edge. Water lapped at his toes and he pointed toward the center of the lake.

"A sign, Rafiq."

The lake itself hardly deserved the name and was considered special only because legend had it that the narrow body of water had no bottom. It was said that the stars mirrored in its dark surface at night were really showing through from the other side of the world. Rafiq had never believed that, but even he knew he could not dive deep enough to touch the bottom at the center of the lake. *What is said about the lake might not be wholly truthful, but it might not be entirely false, either.*

His first sight of the sign his uncle had pointed out sent a shiver through him. In the heart of the lake he saw a golden island. The disk had a diameter no smaller than the span of his arms, which meant it was worth an Alanim's ransom. Rafiq knew, since it was metal, it could not actually be floating on top of the water. At least he thought that was impossible, but the disk appeared to bob and undulate with the ripples raised by the wind on the water's surface. More disturbing came the realization that the flat surface of the island likewise rippled in a sluggish, imperfect imitation of the water.

Rafiq stepped closer toward the disk but before he could get his feet wet, the disk began to change. It flattened out, yet did not increase in size. Its resistance to the wind faded and thin edges flapped like silk flags flying from the walls of Helor. The gold rode the water like a reflection and appeared to become even more insubstantial, nearing transparency, before it became opaque again in spots.

Those spots turned into lumps. One rose above the two flanking it as a domed cylinder thrust up slowly through the golden sheet. Silver stripes began to bleed through as the rising thing began to slowly turn and twist the sheet around itself. Rafiq quickly recognized the lumps as a head and shoulders, then watched the gold film cover the rest of the rising body.

The body drifted up out of the water and hung in the air like a corpse shrouded in wet linen. The figure, clearly a man, began to breathe and the gold sheet tightened over the hollow of his mouth. Eyes flickered open and somehow looked out through the golden film, then the film flowed away from his upper body and limbs to finally resolve itself into a loincloth with tails that fell to knee-length.

Perfectly formed, the gold figure with silver tiger stripes etched into his flesh remained suspended a foot above the now placid lake.

Rafiq noticed the gold man's reflection in the surface of the water and this both pleased and frightened him. Had there been no reflection they would have been in the presence of an *ifrit* and would have been in jeopardy of losing their souls. The reflection proved this was no demon-spirit, but that left Rafiq to puzzle out what he truly was. That mystery gave Rafiq no comfort at all.

The gold man slowly opened his hands and splayed his fingers out. "Welcome, ten thousand times welcome."

Rafiq stiffened. The formula of his greeting was common enough, but the choice of words was significant. A *hundred* or a *thousand* welcomes would have been suitable for a reunion between long-lost friends, but *ten thousand* suggested a close relationship between families that had lasted for centuries.

It was also how the Dost was said to have greeted his most faithful retainers.

Qusay bowed until the lake's wavelets lapped at his forehead. "Our longing for your visit knows no end."

"It is the twin of my desire to return to you." The golden figure pointed casually to the ground. "Please be seated, my guests. I would offer you refreshment and hospitality but my time to play host is yet nigh." His legs melted together and flowed up toward his torso before re-forming themselves appropriately for a man sitting cross-legged amid peers.

Still stunned by the man's appearance, Rafiq sat abruptly in a spray of gravel and his men followed his example. He wanted to ask who the golden man was, but he feared the answer he might get.

The gold man looked directly at him. "You should not fear me or what I am. You have sought the Dost reborn and you have found him. When I was here before, I was known as Keerana, but now I am Nimchin. I have come again to fulfill promises made to your people, *my* people."

Akhtar, Qusay's youngest son, pointed at the metal man. "How is it that we know you are the Dost returned?"

"You know it by your fear and your hope." The figure leaned forward, resting one forearm across a knee, gesturing benignly toward Akhtar with the other. "You, Akhtar, know because you fear you are not worthy of your Khast birthright, for you are neither the wiseman your father is, nor the warrior your cousin Rafiq is. And you hope that I, in accord with the Dost's legendary wisdom, will have a place for you in the world I will shape anew. Is this not true?"

The defiance on the young man's face melted, then he nodded. "It is true."

"And I do have a place for you in the world I will rebuild. You voice the doubt they all share, for without it you would not be men. But my saying this has not reassured you."

Akhtar frowned. "The Dost has long been sought, and there have been pretenders to your title. How is it that you are different from them?"

The gold man opened his arms. "It is not obvious?"

Rafiq shook his head. "The display is impressive, but Stranans in their Vandari armor are likewise impressive."

"Yet they are not the Dost," he offered, completing Rafiq's thought. "Ahktar, when is it said I was to return?"

"In the most dire of times."

"Is this not the most dire of times?"

"When your Empire collapsed, generations ago, it slew thousands and scattered us." Wasim, one of the band's bolder warriors snarled angrily at the gold man. "*That* was the most dire of times."

"Is this true?"

Wasim nodded solemnly. "The glory of the Empire is but a memory to us. It is the fabric of dreams—night mirages that evaporate to leave one frustrated and bitter."

The gold man brought his head up. "Is it not written, 'Bitter dreams and a good life are preferred over the reverse'?"

"It is, but—"

"But you believe the Scripture is wrong on this point?" The

gold man's smooth face contracted, sharpening his eyes and brow with a click. "What is the greatest joy a man may know in his life?"

Qusay barked a short laugh. "A swift horse, a sharp sword, enemies to slay, women to warm his nights, and three prayers a day."

The gold man clapped his hands, sending a metallic peal ringing off the mountains. "When we took the empire, we knew that joy. Our sons and their sons forgot it and built themselves an empire of cities. Their lives were bitter and the dreams they were sent were of carefree days again roaming the world. They ignored the signs and were scattered."

Rafiq narrowed his eyes. "Then the Khasts were wrong in conquering Helor?"

"Do not think your forefathers fools for taking the city, Rafiq. They were correct in doing that. It was what was required for them to fulfill their duty." The hint of a smile twisted across gilded lips. "What you wish to know is why you lost the city."

Rafiq rocked back. *For the second time you have plucked my thoughts from my head. Do you know what I know?* "Why did the Khasts lose Helor?"

"So you could be here now. Had you never lost the city, you would not have seen all you have seen. You would not know what you know. You would not be the man you are—none of you would be the men I need."

The golden man slowly unfolded himself and stood, still four feet above the surface of the water. "It has been said I will return in the most dire of times, and so I have. When my empire collapsed it was not dire, it was a blessing. We, Estanuans of Durranian descent, were able to return to our way of life. We gained freedom unknown and unknowable to those who lock themselves in cities. They have softer lives. The line between life and death blurs for them. They fight to ease every pain, not taking joy in its conquest as we do. They push death away, making themselves thralls to it, winning extra years but years that are totally consumed in holding death at bay."

Nimchin—Rafiq suddenly found himself thinking of the gold man as the Dost—gestured with both hands at the water below him. A great wave rose up beneath him, but it did not splash back down. Instead the water sculpted itself into a relief map of all Estanu. Rafiq recognized it from the location of Jebel Quirana and saw that it spread far beyond the lands he and his forefathers had ever explored. To the south he saw the mountains of Drangiana and the nation of Aran. Above Helansajar, Strana lurked like a bandit waiting to strike an unwary traveler.

"This is our world, my brethren, and this is the most dire of times. Strana needs Helansajar. The foreign lords of Aran must deny Helansajar to them. Because of these conflicting needs, the life we know as the *best* life is threatened."

"Strana has wanted Helansajar before." Wasim raised a sheathed shamshir. "We have ever denied it to them."

"You did not listen, Wasim." Rafiq shook his head at the handsome warrior. "The Dost did not say *want*, he said *need*, and there is a vast difference between those two things."

"Want or need will not staunch their wounds."

"This is true, Wasim, but their *need* will open many more wounds than you know." Nimchin began to change as he spoke. His flesh grew harder and took on edges. "Barely a decade has passed since Urovia was locked in warfare the like of which has not been seen since my first lifetime. When Khasts were driven from Helor, how many warriors did Shukri Awan have with him?"

Wasim folded his arms across his chest. "Ten thousand?"

"Nearly a dozen years ago a Urovian tyrant lost ten times that number in his retreat from Strana. The next spring he returned to Strana with an army twice that size. And he was defeated." One of Nimchin's fingers elongated and stabbed down into the watery map at the place where the Stranans had their city of Vzorin. "The chieftan who led the Stranan army now resides here, barely a month's march from Helor."

Wasim sat back and seemed to shrink. Rafiq could feel his testicles withdrawing. *A hundred thousand men dead and he was able to raise an army twice that size over the winter? Even if all of Helansajar was united and all the tribes were one, our warriors would not number two hundred thousand.*

"This is why I have come." The transformation continued. Life drained from the gold man's body, leaving in its place hard-edged bars and plates and gears and other things Rafiq remembered seeing in rare Stranan goods displayed in Helor's bazaar. "Strana and the Wolf-Kings in Aran have great forges that create swords and armor in abundance. They possess huge ships that fly with fire in their bellies and a hundred mouths that spit out metal balls to crush and kill. Theirs is the power to raze cities and slay men in numbers that defy counting.

"They could destroy all we are, and will do so if we do not stop them."

"Can we stop them?"

Nimchin paused, letting his human form return, before he responded to Akhtar's question. "As great as is the Stranan need to destroy us, greater yet is our need to stop them."

Rafiq stood slowly. "To do this, all the tribes of Alansajar will need to be united. This you can do, but this is a task that will take time, and we do not have time, do we?"

"No, Rafiq Khast, we do not."

"With time being so important, why did you choose to appear to just us?"

The Dost's water map gently flowed back into the lake. "You are all Khasts or sworn to them. You have kept faith with the charges that were given to you by my descendants. You were destined to be first among those I called, and you are destined to be of the greatest use to me. In me and my service you will know the fulfillment of your desires."

The image of Shukri Awan lying in a pool of his own blood flashed through Rafiq's mind. *In service to the Dost, I will avenge my father and reclaim my family's honor.* The leader of the Khasts bowed his head. "I live to serve you, Nimchin Dost."

"Do not give yourself so freely." The golden man looked at Akhtar. "Have you been satisfied?"

The youth smiled. "I live to serve you, Nimchin Dost."

"Good." The Dost spread his golden arms out from his side. Linking his flank and the underside of his arms, a web of scintillating threads formed themselves into wings. Fingers grew out and long, like the fingers of a bat, and the filaments spread out to attach to them as well.

Beating his bejeweled wings once, the Dost flew higher into the sky. "Your first task for me is this. A month from now you will be at Vzorin. You will capture and bring to me a Stranan who speaks our tongue. How you do this is up to you. Bring your captive south. When it is time, I will come to you again and then the battle for our future will begin in earnest."

The Dost's ascent quickly took him up until he appeared to be nothing more than a star, then he shot across the sky, a golden streak dying amid the mountains to the south. Rafiq watched him go, a smile slowly spreading across his face. *You stain the sky in the same way as the star that will die to mark Shukri Awan's passing.* When he focused closer than the mountains that swallowed the Dost, he saw his men staring at him with excited fear and puzzlement on their faces.

"Blessed are we to whom the Dost has first appeared." He planted his fists on his hips. "Go, sharpen your swords and saddle your swiftest horses. In the Dost's service we have enemies to slay. There can be no better life."

— 15 —

Uriah Smith rubbed at his eyes in a vain effort to quench their burning. He didn't feel as physically exhausted as he had expected to, but he did feel mentally sluggish. Kidd demanded of him many things, and made his demands in a pattern that required all the mental agility Uriah could muster. It occurred to him that he might have underestimated Kidd when he told Robin he'd found a worthy opponent, but he couldn't allow himself to believe that he had.

From the very first Kidd challenged Uriah's conception of what his job would entail. Uriah had expected his job to concern doing a lot of busy work—serving food, cleaning up, and the like that sightlessness would make difficult—but Kidd had proved remarkably self-sufficient on those scores. There were no more blatant tests of his moral fiber, but Kidd found other ways to push him intellectually. Reshelving the books, which Uriah chose to do by first breaking them by category before alphabetizing them by author, had exhausted him and had forced him to make judgments about each book so he could do the task correctly.

And he didn't make me put them back the simple way Chauncy had shelved them. Kidd's question about Uriah's system did have him rethinking aspects of it, but he was pleased with how the library turned out. Even Kidd agreed that this organizational scheme was superior to the one employed by the seminary, where every book was shelved by author regardless of subject, ordered strictly by year of publication.

Making a last check of the tower suite before he headed off to bed, Uriah took a look around the tower's library and sighed. "I knew I'd be replacing his eyes, but I didn't think of what that meant."

His morning had been taken up with reading to Kidd from a

new theological text debating the nature of man and his position in relationship to God and the divine. The author, a Samojitan named Cort ip Harril, argued that a man's body was simply a vessel for his soul, and that the soul would live forever. Creating magicks that modified or affected a man's body would, in essence, defile that vessel and would lead to a corruption of the soul. Eilyph, on the contrary, was a divine spirit, a fragment of God Himself, made manifest in flesh. As God was incorruptible, so was Eilyph and his flesh, therefore the miracles he performed—though they mirrored proscribed magicks—were not evil. Because Eilyph had not passed on these magicks to his disciples, and instead only strengthened their abilities to use normal object-based magick, clearly his intent was for his followers to only use object-based magick.

Uriah found the reading fascinating, but tracking the actual course of the inquiry proved very confusing. Kidd often had Uriah pause in his reading of ip Harril's book to fetch another volume and read passages from it that clarified or obfuscated parts of the discussions. There were points where that subsequent source had led to another and so on. In no time he would find himself three or four books away from ip Harril's text, and miles away from points being examined.

He thought he would never learn how to remember where he was supposed to be, but Kidd never lost track of things, so he knew there had to be some method for retaining his place. Uriah finally hit upon the use of a series of numbered bookmarks to let him backtrack his trail. It was a minor victory, and earned only a nod from Kidd, but Uriah clung to it.

His study of the dualistic nature of mankind and the incorruptibility of Eilyph's soul continued until the post arrived. Uriah sorted through the letters, reading out the return addresses to Kidd. The blind man directed each letter to a different drawer in his desk save one. That letter had come from Ragusa and elicited a solemn nod from Kidd when Uriah informed him of its arrival.

"Before you open it, take the third drawer from the leftmost cabinet and bring it over to the desk."

This is new. Uriah crossed to where closed cabinet doors hid the lower half of a shelving unit. One of the doors banged slightly against the shelf next to it, prompting Kidd to hiss, "Be very careful, Cadet."

Uriah sneered silently, then added, "As you wish, sir."

The drawers were odd affairs in that none of them was more than three inches tall. Because of the handhold cutout on the front of the drawers Uriah thought of them as being much like serving trays.

As he pulled the specified drawer out he slipped his right hand into the dark recess and found a handhold opposite the front one, allowing him to easily pull the tray-drawer all the way out of the cabinet as instructed.

Once he had it out in the light he saw why Kidd had urged him to be cautious. A chessboard had been painted on the bottom of the drawer and chessmen were arrayed in the middle of a battle on it. Clumsy or hurried handling would have upset the pieces. Moving as carefully as a man carrying an overfilled bucket of milk, he conveyed the board to the desk.

"Remius is playing black. He will have sent a move in response to my last one. You will record his move on the log sheet, then you will move the appropriate piece to the proper square." Kidd's head came up. "You *do* play, of course?"

Uriah frowned. "My mother *was* Stranan. Of course I play. Sir."

"Good."

"No one in my family could beat me, sir."

"You mistake me, Cadet. I don't care about your level of play, I merely care that I do not have to instruct you in notation." The corners of his eyes sharpened. "You *do* know proper chess notation?"

"Would you like it in Stranan or Ilbeorian, sir?"

"Ilbeorian. The Stranan method is more economical, but less descriptive." Kidd steepled his fingers and pressed them against his chin. "What does Remius's message say?"

Uriah split the wax seal and unfolded the paper. "Emperor's rook to emperor's rank one." The youth furrowed his brows as he read the next line. "I don't understand this. He says, 'Ransom emperor's airship for warlord's champion and warlord's champion's pawn.' "

"You mean there is something about chess you do *not* know?"

"I do not mistake intelligence for education, Colonel. Even the most powerful steam engine is useless without coal."

"Ah, our first breakthrough." The blind man nodded, the muted light from the lamp on the desk flashing gold from his eyes. "Ragusa boasts a variant of chess that allows players to ransom back pieces taken by the other side. In this case he wants his emperor's airship, which will attack diagonally along the lines of white. For it he offers me a champion and a pawn. All of the pieces will return to their original starting squares if I accept the offer. While he concedes me an advantage on points, for an airship and a champion are considered to have similar value, he can employ the airship more quickly than I can my champion."

"So you will refuse."

"Perhaps." Kidd tapped at his teeth with a finger. "I will think upon it after we eat and after we read more."

"More theology, sir?"

"No, warfare, I think. You added the new Colistan volume to the collection, didn't you?"

Uriah groaned. That book weighed a ton and had been printed with very densely packed type. "Yes, sir, it's right over there."

"Good." Kidd gave him a cold stare. "Mind what you eat. You don't want to be sluggish when reading Colistan."

The rest of the afternoon and evening had consisted of reading, shelving books, unshelving books, and yet more reading. Colistan, in Uriah's opinion, had pointed toward the future of warfare pretty accurately. "His vision of warfare is correct, sir. In saying that armies of the future will have to be raised as cadres involved with the interests of the nation instead of localities, he's addressing the way the world is changing and incorporating that which works already."

"And that would be, Cadet?"

"The way *our* forces are organized. Sir."

Kidd's eyes narrowed. "You're saying you see a correspondence between Colistan's concept of a national army and the way Ilbeorian forces are arrayed?"

"I think it obvious, sir." Uriah slipped a bookmark into his place and closed the book. "You do not."

"Not at all, Cadet. Colistan argues that warfare is a logical outgrowth of a nation's foreign policy. His vision is of highly trained military units raised for the specific purpose of being an enforcement or harvesting arm of a government."

"Our troops are an embodiment of that concept, Colonel."

"No."

Kidd's flat denial surprised the cadet. Had he been speaking with Captain Irons, Uriah knew the denial would have been prompted by personality and not because of any reasonable exploration of the subject. "But Colonel, our troops are used all the time to promote Ilbeorian national self-interest. They were a century ago in trying to keep Brendania in the empire, thirty years ago in defeating the Ghurs in Aran, and a dozen years ago in fighting against Lescar. Our troops are employed in response to the dictates Colistan has outlined."

"You are in error, Cadet." Kidd's eyes flashed argent. "Our

troops are raised to fight as commanded by the dictates of God, to further His plans."

Uriah rocked back, the Colistan volume heavy across his thighs. "Sir, while that may be the moral basis for activity advanced by the King, Ludstone often dictates action that is later shored up with justification quoted from the Scriptures. After-the-fact justification does not sanctify actions taken for secular and political reasons."

"While what you say has validity, Cadet, especially outside Ilbeoria, God's dictates for *our* troops are clear and a foolish commander ignores them when he should not. During the Crusades against the Ataraxians, there were countless examples of times when local commanders went against orders from Ludstone, and we know the disasters that resulted."

"Yes, but that was before the invention of the steam engine made airship transit at all reliable. Airships that rely on the wind for propulsion are subject to the whims of weather. There was no way to predict when they would arrive, so orders would have no relevancy to the situation at hand. Orders issued from Ludstone are now done on the basis of good information, not bad information the way they were before. And the orders are timely, too."

"You consider month-old orders issued on the basis of two-month old information timely?" Kidd shook his head. "I doubt your friend Brother Drury will think the orders he gets in Aran to be timely."

"That could be, sir, but one has to ask if what he'll be doing in Aran is in God's interest or the interest of Ilbeoria and its economy?"

"If God is not pleased with what is happening in Aran, I am certain He will make His displeasure known."

Uriah raised an eyebrow. "Are you saying a just God would hurt warriors who are following orders from on high that displease God? Why would the local soldier be punished when he is doing what he was ordered to do? God must know the soldier assumes he's doing God's work."

"Interesting point, Cadet Smith. It ought to take us back to ip Harril tomorrow." Kid faced him. "Suffice it to say, if a warrior is true to his relationship with God, he will be given a sign concerning his orders."

"And if a warrior believes he's been given such a sign, but has not?"

Pain shot through Kidd's expression. "That too can be a disaster, Cadet." He rubbed his hands over his face, then stood. "I am fatigued. It is time I went to bed."

"What about your reply to Remius's move? If I prepare it now it can go out with the early morning post."

Kidd started to speak, then shook his head. "Perhaps, no, I think perhaps, no . . ." He frowned and turned toward the doorway of his bedchamber, then bumped his thigh against the corner of a table. "You may replace the board. I will sleep on my move."

"As you wish. Sir."

Kidd shuffled off to his bedchamber and closed the door, shutting Uriah out of the unlit room. The cadet waited to hear if Kidd would call out for any help and shelved books while he did so. When they were all properly returned to their places, he put the game drawer back into the cabinet.

Uriah took a step back and felt a sudden surge of anger course through him. Theology in the morning and warfare in the afternoon and evening, with the discussion circling around again to theology, made no sense to him. If the whole of the year he would spend with Kidd was going to be a repeat of that day, Uriah would be screamingly insane inside a month. *No wonder Malvern started stealing from him.*

Standing there in the midst of the books, Uriah felt as if everything were closing in on him. There were too many books and he knew he'd be expected to read from all of them and remember what he read, but to what purpose? All he wanted to do was to be a soldier and fight for King and country and, he allowed, the Martinist Church. Kidd was trying to prove his superiority by bludgeoning Uriah to death with more facts and philosophical viewpoints than anyone could possibly absorb.

He needed a way to strike back at Kidd and, as he looked at the cabinets with chess games shelved there, a plan slowly formed itself in his mind. *Just an outgrowth of what he's already had me do.* It occurred to him that Kidd had somehow memorized the exact locations of all the ongoing games in the room. Each cabinet held five drawers which meant Kidd was involved in thirty different games at the same time. Uriah had no doubt that Kidd carried in his mind the exact position of all the pieces and probably had thought several moves ahead on each game.

The battle between us is being fought on a battlefield of his *choosing.* As long as Malachy had more control over the local environment than Uriah did, the blind man would be able to maintain the upper hand. Any break in his control would be an advantage Uriah could use against him.

Smiling coldly, Uriah decided to alphabetize the games by the name of the opponent. *That way, when mail arrives, I will know where the drawer is and Kidd will not.*

To start, he slid all the boards from their cabinets and scattered them around the room. The boards all contained different types of chess sets. The main difference among them was the representation for the piece Urovians called the airship. Some, an antique set and two from Aran, used sailing ships, while others made that piece an assassin, a thief, or a concubine. One set had rather lewd figurines, but it came from Zante, so that was no surprise.

Rearranging the games proved no serious problem, though the list of opponents involved in correspondence chess with Kidd did have two surprises in it. The first came from a game twenty moves old in which Kidd was playing black against Prince Trevelien. The last move noted on the log had been Kidd's, and it had been sent on 14 Arcan 1685. That meant it probably arrived at Wolfsgate barely a week before Princess Rochelle died.

Uriah felt a chill run down his spine. His initial reaction to seeing Prince Trevelien listed as an opponent had been joy, because in this discovery he learned the Prince played chess *and* solved the mystery of how Kidd knew him. Yet that emotion seemed to mock the sadness that came with Princess Rochelle's death and denigrate the love her husband had felt for her.

In honor of her memory he shelved the game in the spot below Remius's game, using her name as its key.

The other surprise came on a board where no pieces had been moved at all. The maple and cedar set used all the common Ilbeorian forms for the pieces and was far more crudely carved than any of the other sets. The move log noted the game had begun on 12 Bell 1677, but Uriah attached no significance to that date—though he did recognize it as coming almost a year after the end of the Lescari War. He did not recognize the hand in which the play log had been written, but he assumed some other aide had started it. Kidd clearly had elected to play black and was waiting for his correspondent to send his first move.

What was most bizarre about it was that no opponent had been listed. *Had Kidd been waiting for someone to write him to start a new game, he would not have dated the move log, would he? Odd, but what isn't odd about Colonel Kidd?*

Uriah shrugged. "At least one person knew better than to get involved with old Eyes of Silver. Someday I'll be that smart." He shelved the game in the first position, for *anonymous* and closed the cabinets, eliminating all evidence of his perfidy. Taking a last look around, he nodded, then snuffed the desk lamp and retreated to his own little chamber.

Tired, he dropped onto his bed. He let images of wooden warriors battle through his mind, wandering fields overpainted with squares. He smiled at himself at first, feeling good about exerting his control in his new home, but that feeling quickly faded. Sleep would not come, and with each waking moment more shame began to creep into Uriah.

He shivered as if he had fallen asleep in a snowbank. *Regardless of how nasty a taskmaster Colonel Kidd is, he's still blind. But for the grace of God . . .* His stomach began to sour and bubble acid into his throat as he thought about having played so cruel a trick on a blind man. *The Prince said I was to study genius, and here I am being petty and stupid.*

He tossed back his covers and was about to slip out of bed, when a scream sent a jolt through him. The crashing and crackling sound of splintering wood that followed it made him vault out of bed. Wearing only underbreeches, he dashed out into the darkened room, then barked his shin on a table. Grabbing at it and cursing, he hopped forward.

"Who's there?"

An incoherent mumble mixed with a snarl made him look toward the cabinet that had previously contained Remius's game. He heard the clatter-click of pieces rolling around on a board, then felt chess pieces batter him like invisible hail in the darkness. Releasing his shin, he took one step in that direction, but his right foot came down hard on a pawn. As he hopped back in pain, a drawer hit him in the chest and toppled him over.

I need light! Staying down, he crawled in the direction of the desk. He heard chessmen clack off it as he drew himself up in a crouch behind it. Reaching into a drawer, he plucked out a match, then struck it and popped up to light the lamp. Turning the key to expose a lot of wick, he flooded the room with light.

His stomach folded in on itself as he whisked the lamp up and shielded it with his body. Looking like a fevered lunatic, Malachy Kidd tore the last drawer out of the cabinet, raked his fingers through the scattered pieces, then flung the whole thing carelessly aside. The drawer whirled through the air and would have exploded the lamp had Uriah not pulled it down to safety.

Kidd turned from that cabinet and darted across the room to the one containing the anonymous board. The blind man pulled it from the cabinet, then held it up triumphantly. "Yes!" He tossed it up in the air, then dropped cross-legged to the floor as if waiting for the pieces to shower over him. The board hit him on the shoulder and flipped off to his right, landing with a crisp clatter.

Uriah crossed to him and set the lamp on a table. "You're cut, sir, over the right eye." The cadet tore a strip from the Colonel's nightshirt and wadded it up against the wound. "What are you doing out here?"

Kidd looked up at him as if he could actually see through those eyes of silver. "I saw him."

"Saw who, sir?"

"The Dost. I saw him. I understand now." The man held his hands out in front of him as if he were cradling a baby in his arms. "He was so tiny, so vulnerable. And all of gold. Not a cherub or a work of art, but a machine. An infant machine. And He said, 'Behold your charge.'"

Tripping over that overturned chair and banging your head finished what the Lescari started in Glogau. Your brains are mush. "You heard an infant machine speak?"

"No, idiot, *God* spoke to me. I understand now." Kidd grabbed Uriah's wrists hard, making them hurt. "The pace of His revelation is speeding up."

"Sir, you've been hit in the head, *hard* in the head."

"I saw this before. The vision, it came to me as I slept."

"It was a bad dream, then, sir."

"No, not at all. It was a message from God. He has spoken."

Uriah twisted his wrists free from the man's hands, then forced Kidd to press the reddening bandage to his forehead. "Sir, you're hurt. You're needing to see a healer."

"*No!* I am fine. You yourself asked if God made His displeasure at human affairs known; well, He does. He did tonight. To me." Kidd grabbed his aide by his shoulders and a droplet of blood coursed down the right side of his face. "Look at the board. Look at it. Look at it!"

The insistence in the man's voice forced Uriah to look at the board. Uriah didn't even know if it had landed upright, but even if it had he knew what he'd see: a handful of pieces scattered and tumbled on a board. *Indulge him, then get help.*

Looking down, he started to tremble even before he fully comprehended what he saw. The drawer had indeed landed upright and every piece had landed on its base, on a square. Five pieces had been shifted from their starting positions. White's warlord had advanced one full rank beyond the pawn in front of it in what looked to Uriah as an illegal move. Black's warlord's champion had likewise jumped the pawn in front of it, but that piece was allowed to ignore pieces between it and its goal. In that position it protected black's king's pawn, which had moved forward two spaces. On the white side of the board, the king's champion had come out beside the warlord to menace black's pawn.

Uriah's mouth went dry. The chess set, when he had looked at it earlier, had been carved with Ilbeorian icons making up the pieces on both sides. Now White had bears for rooks instead of wolves. He knew it wasn't a matter of his having made a mistake earlier—none of the sets had pitted Ilbeoria against Strana, but this one did now. Making matters worse, the black king looked like Prince Trevelien, the king's champion looked like Robin, while the queen's champion had little eyes of silver.

And the advanced king's pawn appeared to be Uriah's twin.

More startling than even that was the presence of a thirty-third piece on a square attacked by white and protected by black. Carved from some gold-hued wood, it looked like an infant. It lay on its back in the center of the board. It appeared vulnerable, but the position of the black pieces meant taking it would cost white dearly.

"I don't understand, Colonel. A new piece, an illegal move. This is insane."

"Not insane, Uriah, not in the eyes of God." The blind man pointed unerringly at the tiny gold figure in the middle of the chessboard. "The warlord's opening-move jump is allowed in Helansajar. The Dost is there, between Strana and Aran. The message is clear."

"What's clear?"

"We're going to Aran." Kidd smiled up through a mask of blood. "The Dost is in danger and from Aran we will begin our quest to save him."

— 16 —

> **Airship *Saint Michael***
> **Off the coast of Ferrat**
> **12 Bell 1687**

The dying sun splashed pink and purple across the thin clouds as Robin Drury reported to the wing deck of the *Saint Michael*. He cleared his voice to preface announcing his presence. "Brother Drury reporting as ordered, sir."

Lonan Hassett, the only other person standing on the open-air deck on top of the *Saint Michael*, turned slowly and smiled. "Thank you for reporting so promptly, Mr. Drury. Please, be at ease. I wanted to commend you on your handling of the ethyrskiff."

Robin shrugged easily. "It was no problem, sir. I'm obliged to practice the spells I'll have to use if we're required to board another airship."

"But an ethyrskiff is a bit more difficult to manage than a pair of wings, and the currents down there off Ferrat's southern headland are rather tricky."

"Today must have been a calm day, sir."

Hassett slowly nodded. "Not many Sandies have your sense of modesty."

"Pride's one of the Seven Deadly Sins, sir."

"And not many of them have your skill with flight spells. You could have been an Aeromancer, but you chose not to be. Why not?"

Robin hesitated. His commanding officer had every right to ask any question he wanted of him, and Robin had a duty to answer. Privacy and secrets had no place in an organization where absolute trust had to be maintained between individuals. Still Robin would have preferred to let his actions speak for him instead of having his motives probed. *But if the Captain did not want the information, well, he'd not have been the kind of man entrusted with command of a dreadnought.*

"You'll have to remember, sir, that I served in the airfleet before I went to Sandwycke. I respect Aeromancers no end, but I recall doing my best to see to it that none of them were slain while we were fighting the Lescari. Myself, I'd rather be trying to kill enemy Aeromancers than to have the enemy trying to kill me."

"But it is those of us who are Aeromancers who move up to command airships like this." Hassett ran his hand over the oak rail forward of the deck. "You would be content commanding a contingent of ethyrines when you could be commanding their ship?"

Before answering, Robin looked out over the broad expanse of ship extending forward and up behind him. From the wing deck he could see all of the ship. Flags fluttered from the three slender signal masts extending up from the skywheel. The twin propellers at the back made a whirring throaty whoop as they spun and pushed the ship through the sky. The wind rushed past, chilling him slightly, and cloud threads swirled up and over the edges of the fore and aft wings.

It would be a grand thing to command this ship. "Permission to speak frankly, sir?"

Hassett, looking scarecrowlike as the wind plucked at his clothes and his brown hair, nodded. "Please."

"In the war I saw plenty of officers—Sandies and otherwise—who fell too much in love with the ships they commanded. Sure, lots of us come to think of ourselves as married to our ships, or that the ship is a mistress of some sort, being so demanding and all, but for these officers their ships were succubi. The officers would risk anything for the glory that would let them move up to a new and larger ship. They killed a lot of men in their quest for power."

Hassett's face became an impassive mask. "When the *Meridmarch* went down in Lescar, I lost a hundred airmen out of a crew of almost twice that number."

"I know, sir, but by bringing the *Meridmarch* in as you did, you stopped the *La Admiracio* from finishing the *Saint Brigit*. She got away, sir." Robin smiled carefully. "There wasn't a cloudbreather in the airfleet that didn't admire what you did. I know I'd want to make that same sort of decision, but I couldn't be certain that I could, so I'm best not in command of a ship."

"Again, Mr. Drury, you exhibit a modesty that becomes you." Hassett clasped his hands behind his back. "I should have expected this, given how you came aboard and all that Mr. MacAllen has said about you."

Robin sighed. "You shouldn't believe what Mr. MacAllen says about me, sir. He knew me a long time ago and thinks of me as the son he never had. As for how I came aboard, well, there are *fleet* officers and *crew* officers, and the pity is—saving yourself and a few other officers—rare is the man who is both. It might be nice to have friends at court when new assignments are being handed out, but in a fight it's the crew that will keep you alive or let you die. I'd rather be respected by the men under me than be the darling of someone over me when metal hail starts rattling through the clouds."

Robin smiled slightly. "I was hoping to make that very point to Cadet Smith. He's very smart, but he thinks that's enough to let him get by in life. If he actually applies himself, does some serious work and becomes a crew officer, he'll run one of the best ships in the airfleet."

"That will be something to see. I'm sure his time with Colonel Kidd will help in that regard." Lonan Hassett nodded solemnly. "I want *you* to know I very much appreciate having someone in my command who is willing to do more than his share, like taking a skiff down to our station on Ferrat or educate a headstrong cadet. Please let me know your thoughts and feelings about how we can make the *Saint Michael* a tighter ship than it already is. I am pleased with the crew, but in Aran things will be very different and I want things as much under control as possible."

"You'll forgive me, sir, for asking, but you seem to be expecting some sort of difficulty in Aran?"

Hassett pursed his lips for a moment before answering. "You were in the airfleet, Mr. Drury. You know a crew can become restive when far from home. Aran is an alien place. I understand it is hot and crowded, full of heathen temples, and has a caste system so rigid that the only way to pass from one level to the next higher is to die and be reborn."

"Descending is easier, sir?"

"As I understand it, yes. They have crimes for which we have no equivalent and their punishments are quite barbaric. They call for death by fire where we might only demand a flogging, and that's if your offense was against people, not the thousand and one gods they worship." Hassett shook his head. "Add to that confusing mix a resentment against us. We've been the power in Aran for thirty years, which means a whole generation has grown up in a homeland they no longer control. They chafe, with good reason, and that can be troublesome."

Robin nodded. "And then there are the Stranans."

"The Stranans," said a new voice, "are the least of our worries right now."

Robin turned and abruptly dropped to one knee. "Highness."

"Please, Mr. Drury, get up." Prince Trevelien's blue frock coat beat back and forth against his legs like waves against wharf pilings. "I have reviewed the paper you and young Smith presented at Sandwycke. I must commend you on your analysis—your premise is in line with my feelings about Stranan intentions concerning central Estanu. However, I found the idea of a Stranan conquest of Helor less disturbing than something else I found in your report."

"Yes, sir?"

"Your source for information about Helor."

"Skinny Hopper?" Robin caught himself. "I mean Simon Hopper? He is a clerk with Grimshaw Mercantile. He copied some things from reports they were coming from Aran for me. What got used was what Uriah and I distilled from rumors. Had anything been of military value, I'm certain it would have been turned over."

The Prince held a hand up. Though he stood inches shorter than either man, he had an air of peaceful confidence about him that made respecting him rather easy. "Viscount Hedgelee has been most cooperative in passing information on to the military, though his numbers—where we have our own for comparison—run to the high side of things. What disturbs me is that he seems to produce far more in the way of intelligence from central Estanu than we do. He clearly has agents in Drangiana and I expect him to have some in Helor by the end of the summer if he does not have them there already."

Robin frowned heavily. "I seem to remember, from a speech someone gave years ago at the factory where I was working, that our trade ran no further north than the Himlan Mountains. I was unaware the King had granted trading rights outside of Aran."

"He has not, but this has not stopped merchants from trying to extend their trade beyond the borders of Aran and into central Estanu. As you will recall, our Brendanian colonies revolted and won their independence a century ago." The Prince frowned heavily. "There are those among our people who believe history might be meant to repeat itself in Aran."

"But Highness, if they were to try to declare independence and actually win it from Ilbeoria, then there would be nothing to restrain the Stranans from falling upon them."

"Correct, Mr. Drury, unless one of two cases exists. The first is that their economic base is sufficient to allow them to buy and arm all the mercenaries they need to defend their holdings. Most of the trading companies already have their own militias, so steps have begun in this direction. If their economy was truly strong, they might even bribe Duke Arzlov to turn away from Aran and begin a civil war within Strana."

Robin shook his head. "Uriah did most of the reading about Arzlov since it was in Stranan, but I did not get the impression he could be bought."

"The most dangerous men do not have a price that can be reckoned in gold."

Hassett nodded at the Prince. "The second case involves creating a situation that would make it impossible for Strana or Ilbeoria to intervene against a rebellion."

The ethyrine swallowed hard. "The most obvious way to do that would be to spark a war in Urovia between Strana and Ilbeoria. A war would further cripple the Stranan economy and would occupy Ilbeorian forces closer to home than Aran. Even to think of such a thing is beastly."

The Prince looked disgusted. "Warriors dread war because they know its true cost is counted in bodies and blood. Merchants who might profit from trade in the war—or its aftermath—account for things differently."

Robin shivered. "Creating *that* situation would constitute an act of treason, would it not?"

"It would, indeed, Mr. Drury." The Prince nodded emphatically, his green eyes flashing. "Unfortunately we have no evidence of wrongdoing by anyone. That doesn't mean people are innocent, just careful. And we'll have to be that much more careful in counteracting their plans."

"It appears we're being thrust into the middle of a more difficult situation than I had imagined before." Robin shook his head. "Working out a hypothetical battle between Strana and Helor seemed strange enough. Pitting our troops against our citizens in Aran would have been even more odd and likely not to have earned me a berth here."

"Our intention, Mr. Drury, is to see to it that such a thing does not happen." The Prince smiled, but not nearly confidently enough to set Robin's mind at ease. "If we do things well in Aran, *all* fights there will remain hypotheticals."

"If you don't mind me asking, sir, what do you make of the chances of that coming true?"

"Good, I hope, Mr. Drury." The Prince's smile shrank to a grim line. "But make certain your ethyrines keep their blades sharp in case my estimate is grievously wrong."

— 17 —

Airship *Leshii*
Myada, nearing Myasovo
Strana
18 Bell 1687

Natalya swept wind-whipped black hair from her face as she stepped back into the Grand Cabin aboard the *Leshii*. Up on the brigantine's wing deck she had been able to see for miles and miles—and here, with windows on three sides of the huge cabin, the view seemed to go on forever. Fertile plains spread out in a verdant carpet below the airship. The Murom River had been a ribbon of silver cutting through the greensward and little villages had sprung up like mushrooms nestled in the lazy river's coils.

The transition from the hilly woodlands of Muromda province through Kroda to the green plains of Myada marked more than just a change in topology. The cold, forbidding formality of the Imperial capital melted here in the outer provinces. Naraschal Gennady

Cususov had taken Natalya's sister Marina for his primary wife and had been made Tacarri of Myada in reward for his efforts in the Lescari War. While fiercely loyal to the Tacier, Cususov did promote the maritime culture of Myada and the lazy, leisurely life enjoyed by the privileged.

Life in Myada and Myasovo came more easily and was less hurried than it was in the capital. Because of its being recently rebuilt, the city of Myasovo was very new and had all manner of conveniences. Not only were the new buildings equipped with gas-lights, but massive steam boilers in the basements were able to provide heat through cast-iron radiators throughout. While winter never was that cold in Myasovo, central heating seemed nothing short of a miracle, if her sister's missives could be believed. *And my magickal talent for kindling fires—valued in Murom in the dead of winter—is rendered useless by progress.*

Other advances, from the steel framing of buildings to the inclusion of lifts that moved people effortlessly from the ground to heights of seven or eight stories, made the city undeniably modern and confident of its shining place in the world. This positive view permeated the upper class and was reflected through nightly revels of the sort Murom only saw in the month of Festibre. The constant social swirl had overwhelmed Natalya when she last stopped in Myasovo—early in her previous visit to Vzorin—and she would have forgone stopping, but she missed Marina and very much wanted a chance to see her again.

Thinking about her sister, Natalya crossed to the window seat and dropped down on the plump cushions. Through the window, she saw the cruciform shape of the *Leshii's* ethyrskiff coming up from below and to the stern. Too small for a steam engine to drive propellers, it had a mast and a square-rigged sail that bulged with the wind. The little airboat gained on the larger ship quickly and disappeared from sight as it moved forward to enter the larger ship through the cargo hatches below.

Even if I had not wanted to see Marina, I would have stopped in Myasovo. Traveling straight to Vzorin would have seemed over-anxious and out of the ordinary. My father's mission precludes me from being so obvious. At least no one in Vzorin suspects anything unusual about my visit.

In their replies to her request for permission to visit, both Grigory and Duke Arzlov had been cordial and, in Grigory's case, anxious that she should make the trip as soon as was convenient for her. The sincerity of Arzlov's formal invitation made her wary and also prompted a smattering of guilt. She knew he was up to something, and she meant to prove it through her visit.

Part of her wondered if she were not jumping to conclusions. Though she considered caution concerning Duke Arzlov important, she realized her concern about him could be seen as almost as extreme as his paranoia concerning the Wolf-priests. In downplaying their threat because of her distrust of him, she knew she could be overlooking a legitimate threat to her father's realm. *In which case I should worry less about Arzlov, but that would mean his threat would be unmonitored.*

She shook her head, then lay down and stretched out on the window seat. "There will be plenty of time to chase those thoughts around in circles later." In the distance, from the wing deck, she had seen Myasovo. The Captain had told her they would reach the city in three hours, which would be just enough time to prepare for her reception.

Polina entered the cabin through the hatchway leading into the Grand Cabin's private galley. She bore a silver tray with two apples, some bread, and some cheese on it next to an empty crystal goblet. She set the tray down on the teak table in the center of the room, then took a glass bottle from beneath her arm and twisted the cork from it with a squeak. She poured a clear liquid into the glass, then rehomed the cork and put the bottle on the table.

"Captain Selov sends his apologies, Highness. In this area he trades with one particular family, but their patriarch died two days ago. His men arrived during the funeral. This is the best they had to offer you."

Sitting up, Natalya raised her right hand to her throat. "They were compensated, *da*?"

"They were honored to be serving you, Highness."

"That will not do. Draw my bath, then have Captain Selov send the skiff back to this family's home. Make to them gift of a bolt of that yellow cloth I was bringing for my sister. Marina will not miss one color from the rainbow, especially yellow. It makes her look fat. Be quick now."

"Yes, mistress."

The small woman opened the door to the bathing chamber and turned spigots. Steaming water shot from one faucet while colder water poured in from the other to fill a huge cast-iron and porcelain tub. Polina sprinkled some blue crystals into the water and the scent of roses rode the steam out into the main chamber.

As her maid departed again, Natalya began to disrobe. While

traveling on the airship she had chosen to wear clothes that closely resembled a man's riding costume, from boots and skintight breeches, to a white blouse and wool coat to ward off the cold of the clouds. She preferred skirts to breeches, but aboard an airship with its narrow passages and steep stairways they were impractical.

Of course, my arrival in Myasovo will require a gown of some sort. I'll have Polina choose it. Whichever of her gowns was chosen hardly mattered. Within an hour of her being conducted into her sister's company Natalya would be sewn into some new creation—cut in whatever fashion was this summer's rage in Myasovo—and whisked away to the evening's first party.

Leaving her clothes strewn behind her, Natalya made her way to the bathing chamber. She screwed the water spigots tight off and used a back brush to stir the water. She tested it with a toe, then turned the cold spigot full on for half a minute. Again she mixed and found the temperature a bit hot, but to her liking. Twisting her long hair into a black snake, she tied it up with a bathing band, then slipped into the fragrant, steaming bath.

Lying back, she smiled in recalling the best part of her previous visit to Myasovo. Everyone she met, it seemed, had known of her affection for Grigory Khrolic, and they all spoke highly of him. Myasovo, the city of his birth and where he had been educated, could not have been more proud of all he had done in rebuilding it. The people viewed him as the city's savior, for not only did he chase the Lescari horde away, but after the war he raised a new city from the ashes the Lescari had left behind.

To Natalya it seemed that she was held in higher regard because of Khrolic's love for her than because of who she was. That was a unique experience for her because she had become so used to being dealt with as the Tacier's daughter and expected the affection and homage people felt her due because of her blood. *With the people of Myasovo, things are quite different.*

Depending upon the approach of someone being introduced to her anywhere else in Strana, she could predict the course of their conversation. She found it easy to anticipate questions and deliver witty and charming answers to the most common of inquiries. She worked so her sincerity rivaled that of the greatest Stranan actresses and made her conversational partners think they had her captivated with their banter.

On her previous visit she found the people of Myasovo seemed more interested in Grigory than they were in her. She enjoyed sharing with them stories about him and getting the people's insight into Grigory based on what they told her about him. Their outright adoration of him helped expand her love for him and certainly broadened her understanding of him. Very quickly she learned Grigory Khrolic was very much a son of Myasovo, and that made him even more intriguing.

Myasovo did have one drawback for her. As she learned on her previous visit, Myasovo's citizens favored gambling games like backgammon and whist to her favorite, chess. Chess was thought to be too rigid and restrictive to be much fun. The wild abandon with which Myasovo's citizens wagered vast sums on almost anything surprised her, but she also found it charming. *And befitting a modern city where so much is new and delightful.*

Visiting his city before seeing Grigory again had opened her eyes to who he really was, and that openness, she was convinced, had been reflected in Grigory's reaction to her. While she dared not hope this visit would be as wonderful as the previous one, she wished to recapture some of the previous trip's magic. The informality and passion of the people outside the capital district might be alien to her, but like her sister, she could learn to adapt.

Yet I will not forget the primary purpose for my visit. Natalya nodded solemnly. *If threat to my father or nation exists, I will root it out and it will be threat no more.*

— 18 —

> **The Stoat**
> **In transit over Glogau**
> **18 Bell 1687**

"Ouch!" Uriah's head rebounded from its collision with the cabin's main beam. He scowled and sat down again on the wooden bench, almost upsetting the plate of food sitting there between him and Kidd.

The Stoat's grizzled old captain looked up and curled his lip into something somewhere between a grimace and a sneer. "Your nephew must like banging his head against the roof of my cabin, he does it so much." The rotund man laughed harshly, then carved another dark sliver from a piece of dried beef and tucked it into a bulging cheek. "Be careful, boy. Dash your brains out and we'll pitch you over the side."

Except that it would make you happy, I'd jump. Uriah rubbed at the rising bump on his head. "Dash enough of my brains out and I could join your crew."

Captain Ollis didn't like that at all. "Better men in that crew than you, boyo. At least they know which of their heads to think with. If you was as smart as the least of them you'd not have put the horns on the Right Reverend Cardinal Garrow, would ya? You were thinking with your little drossellstaff there, lad, and your sainted uncle saved you a lifetime of trouble by getting you on my *Stoat* here. Aran's likely the only place a lackwit like you can escape the Church. Still, and I say this for your own good, a fool like you will find trouble no matter where he goes."

Uriah let himself sag down in the shoulders, for he noted this sort of resignation usually brought a premature end to Ollis's lectures. As the man went on about someone he knew who had gone and done something stupid in Aran, Uriah picked up a biscuit and tapped it against the edge of the bench. The biscuit didn't shatter, but he felt the worms inside begin to move away from the point of impact. He hit it against the bench a couple more times, then snapped it in half and picked two black-headed white worms from the hard, dry bit of bread.

Nibbling at the edge of the stale biscuit, he nodded contritely. "Yes, sir, I'm a fool."

Ollis was not mollified in the least and continued telling his story of brainlessness and its dire consequences.

If your crew is so smart, why do you have so many stories of their stupidity to relate to me? At first, mindful of how important Robin thought it was to be on good terms with the crew, Uriah had pitched in and helped make the *Stoat* ready for the trip. He quickly mastered whatever tasks they gave him and even found ways to make some things go more easily. *Some of them did grumble when I pointed out how they could be more efficient, but they* did *end up doing things the way I suggested.*

While a bit crude and ignorant, the crew hadn't been that bad. On the first night out he'd even taken his meal with them, both to make friends and because Ollis made it apparent he didn't think Uriah deserved to be eating with "gentlemen." After dinner he joined a handful of them playing cards.

Lingering bad feelings from his earlier suggestions blossomed into full animosity as the game progressed. The airmen thought Uriah had never played cards before and he saw no reason to make them think otherwise. Being familiar with the games they chose, and being able to track cards and compute odds quickly, he had begun to win. He ended up ten Suns to the good, and a scruffy sailor named Philo mumbled something about cheating. Uriah immediately countered that a gentleman would never cheat and stalked off. His performance ostracized him from the rest of the crew. *Aside from being forced to spend time around Ollis, it's no great loss.*

As Ollis droned on, Uriah shot a hooded glance at Kidd. The Colonel sat there at the other end of the bench in silence, thoughtfully chewing on a piece of dried beef. The darkened glasses he wore hid his eyes and yet combined with his dark, somber clothing and brass-knobbed walking stick to make him appear to be nothing more than an old schoolmaster.

Sure, sit there as if nothing is wrong. Events had run out of control since Kidd had awakened with his vision. Uriah wanted to see Kidd as a broken-down, battle-weary dotard, but the strength of Kidd's belief in the vision scared him. Kidd had insisted on slipping away "like a thief in the night . . ." so no one would try to stop them. Uriah understood the wisdom of that precaution because the Eilyphianist Church had decided eight centuries ago that the Dost was the Devil incarnate. Uriah sincerely doubted the King and his Cardinals would be interested in supporting a mission to save the Dost.

Down in Sandwycketown they had purchased secular clothing and bought passage on a sea ship to Wroxter. While Wroxter was part of the Ilbeorian Empire, like Danoria and Klydlin it was peopled by folks who had once inhabited the whole Ilbeorian peninsula. Ages ago they had been chased into their respective corners of the country by Illyrian raiders who conquered Ilbeoria centuries before Saint Martin was born. Though the native folk tolerated political domination, they clung fiercely to their own culture and, some said, their own pagan religious practices. Their resentment against the Wolf-King and Ilbeoria made Wroxter a hotbed for smuggling and sedition.

It also made it a place where Kidd and Uriah were able to board a small airship bound for Aran. Kidd had explained to Captain Ollis in hushed tones how Uriah had bedded one of Cardinal Garrow's younger wives. The act of defiance against a Cardinal had won Ollis's admiration, though his cooperation in their escape had cost a dozen gold Suns each. It also cost Uriah an unending stream of homilies without which he would have endured the journey quite well.

Though he had thought the accommodations on the *Saint Michael* cramped and oppressive when he had toured it with Robin, they were palatial compared with those on the *Stoat*. The small ship had a modest engine, though Ollis relied entirely on wind to propel his ship. As a result the boiler went unlit and warm meals were a distant memory. The hold had been crammed full of all sorts of things—contraband, every bit of it, Uriah was certain—so the only place for Uriah, Kidd, and the twelve-man crew to sling their hammocks was over the cargo hatches.

The Captain did—albeit reluctantly in Uriah's case—honor his passengers by letting them take their meals with him in his cabin. He had avowed from the first that the crew's mess was no place for a gentleman like Kidd, but Uriah thought there were dogs that would have refused the Captain's hospitality. Salt-cured meat, worm-shot biscuits, and sour cider ale were faint inducements to join Ollis in his dim, crowded cabin, but Uriah knew their fare was better than what the crew ate, so he suffered through meals as best he could.

If Kidd saw the trip as difficult he gave no sign. His biscuits never seemed to have as many weevils as Uriah's did and Uriah hadn't seen him hit his head on beams and hatchways. His part in their little deception was even considered noble and seemed to have won the respect of the crew. They bowed and scraped when he was around, whereas they wouldn't so much as spit in Uriah's direction after the card game.

Kidd swallowed quietly as Ollis's story wound down. "I am certain, dear Captain, my nephew will be the better for the lesson of your story. I do not intend he should despoil any temples in Aran, nor bed any Ghur princesses, and I should think after this tale he would undertake to do neither."

"No, Uncle, never."

"See to it that you listen to your uncle, lad." Ollis bit into a biscuit then spat a worm toward the pissport in the corner. "He's a saint, lad, being blind and all but helping you."

"Yes, Sir."

Kidd reached out and patted Uriah's knee. "Captain Ollis, I gather by the roughness we encountered several hours back we are no longer over water?"

"That's right, Mr. Fletcher. We're in the skies over Glogau. I'd not planned going this far west, but we had the wind and there are saints over the ocean."

"Ah, yes, the *Saint Brigit* and *Saint Maurice* call Saint Martin their home port."

"Aye, and the *Saint Michael* put out from Sandwycke for Aran several days before we did. I was thinking to slip into the archangel's wake for the trip over Sakaria. Ethyrjacks have been skying out of Morea. I expect the *Saint Michael*'s Captain won't notice one more ship following like a duckling behind it—a fair flock of ships have been waiting for it at Saint Martin and in Scipia."

Uriah noticed some hesitation on Ollis's part in the last half of his statement. "I heard Lonan Hassett commanded the *Saint Michael*."

Ollis paled slightly, then shook his head. "My eldest, Thomas, just like me, he was crewed on the *Meridmarch*. Died when she went down. A Wolf-priest came to the house, talked to my wife, and read her a letter he said came from Hassett after he got away."

The man fell silent for a moment and the room seemed to get darker. Creaks and groans from the airship invaded the cabin like vengeful ghosts. Ollis took a deep draught of the cider in his tankard, then swiped at his bulbous nose with the sleeve of his tunic.

"I'd not give a cup of warm wormwood for most officers in the King's airfleet, but I would him. I never saw the letter, but my lady-wife said the priest read it pretty. Told how Tommy kept at his post, shooting and shooting at the *La Admiracio*. Hassett said my boy was a hero, that any who lived did so because of my Tommy. I don't know if that was the truth or just his conscience wanting to put us at ease. Said he remembers Tommy in Mass every year on the Ides of Tempest—Saint Swithin's Day it is and a holy day in Wroxtcr."

Kidd reached across the space between benches and rested a hand on the man's shoulder. "I am certain, Captain Ollis, that your boy knew the day on which he was fighting and Saint Swithin granted him the courage to stay at his post. I'll remember him in my prayers come that day."

Uriah kept his voice barely above a whisper. "Will we have reached Aran by then?"

Ollis wiped a tear from the corner of his eye, then nodded. "Make landfall there between the first and nones of Tempest, closer to the former than the latter. The *Saint Michael* is to be there on the first or so. We'll follow, but not that closely so we may get there later."

"I shouldn't think we want to be even that close to the *Saint Michael*."

"Here, lad, what do you mean by that?"

Kidd smiled reassuringly. "He means that your hold is stuffed full of things that smell wonderful and remind him of home. He coupled that with your willingness to smuggle a blind man and his fugitive nephew out of the country and figures you're carrying a great deal of cargo to Aran that might not have all the tax stamps in order on it."

Ollis gave Kidd a hard look. "You're blind, but you're not stupid. Could it be I'm smuggling *you* out of Ilbeoria and your nephew is just your traveling companion?"

"It would be easier to believe the Cardinal's wife found my nephew attractive than to think of her being interested in a blind man, would it not?" Kidd shrugged his shoulders, then tapped his nose. "This tells me you've a fair amount of Brendanian tobacco on board and sugar and coffee. Nothing to hurt a fellow."

"That's right, nothing to hurt a fellow." Ollis stood up and stuffed the last of his dried beef in his mouth. "Have to be making my rounds now."

"Don't let us stop you, Captain. You have done me a great favor, and I shall not forget it."

Ollis nodded, then stepped past Kidd and exited the cabin. He shut the hatch behind him, leaving the two of them alone.

Uriah bit a small piece of beef from the dried strip he had been given. "You actually could smell all those things in the hold? I only smelled coffee."

"It wasn't until I was stumbling about down there as we came across the coast that I discovered the other things. I decided it was best to let Ollis know we know he's smuggling without letting him know what he's really smuggling."

The younger man frowned. "What do you mean?"

"Describe the hold to me."

"Jammed full, except over the cargo hatch. Any rats on board would have to be hunchbacks."

"Quite colorful, Cadet, but hardly precise."

"Yes. Sir." Uriah stuck his tongue out at Kidd. "The hold is full, including around the boiler and steam engine. There's even coffee stored in the coal bin."

"Then even if the area around the boiler was cleared out . . ."

Uriah blinked. *Of course.* "It couldn't be used, sir."

Kidd nodded solemnly. "In fact, that steam engine has never been used. Remember, the key to the empire's economy is this: raw materials come into Ilbeoria, machine-factoried items go out to the colonies. Even though places like Aran are incapable of producing the quantity and quality of steel required to create a steam engine, transportation of even the plans for such things is considered high treason."

A cruel chuckle rolled from Uriah's throat. "Ollis is smuggling in a whole engine? And that bastard dares lecture *me* on stupidity?"

"I doubt he is the first to try, and he won't be the last." Kidd raised an eyebrow. "Smuggling, that is."

The younger man ignored the jibe. "But a new engine must have cost thousands of Suns. It's easily worth more than this flying dry-rot barrel. How could Ollis afford it?"

Kidd shook his head. "He couldn't, which means someone with a lot of money is paying him to get the engine into Aran. The opinion that Aran should go the way of Brendania is not unknown. The establishment of factories in Aran will bring it one step closer to independence."

Uriah scratched at his head. "First your God-touched vision and now this. Dealing with one problem was going to be tough enough, but now this makes two."

"Two? I don't think so." Kidd smiled enigmatically. "Anyone who wants a strong and independent Aran has no use for the Dost returning to Estanu to fold Aran into his renewed empire. Our being here to make this discovery is just one more sign from God that our mission cannot be allowed to fail."

— 19 —

> **Sorroc (The Tacarri's Palace)**
> **Myasovo, Myada**
> **Strana**
> **22 Bell 1687**

Natalya Ohanscai and her sister Marina looked over at Polina as the servant gave out with a little shriek. She jumped back from the newly opened packing case—just one of many strewn throughout the chamber.

Natalya frowned. "What is it, Polina? Is it a mouse?"

"No, mistress." The girl smiled sheepishly and pulled a dark wooden box from the piece of luggage. "This must have been in here since your last trip to Vzorin. We have not used this case since then."

Natalya thought the box looked familiar, but she couldn't identify it without a closer look. Marina darted over and plucked it from Polina's hand, then turned away to block Natalya's access to it. "Very nice workmanship on this box, Talya. The mother-of-pearl design worked into the lid, it has a bear seated upright, playing with an anchor line and cable. In Lescari, the words here, they say *El Os*. This means *Bear*, does it not?"

"Bear?" Natalya's right hand covered her mouth. *By the Saints, I had forgotten.*

Polina looked down. "I should have looked in packing cases when we noticed it missing, mistress. It is my fault it has been so long lost to you."

Marina's brown eyes widened. "This you got from your friend during the war."

The Tacier's daughter ignored her sister for a moment. "It is not your fault, Polina, and now it is found."

Natalya gave her sister a hard stare, which the older and slightly taller woman endured for a moment. "Please, Marina."

Marina's shoulders sagged slightly, then she held it out to Natalya. She took it from her sister and relished its weight. The box and its contents were precious—to her they were priceless. *Did I forget, or did I just want to forget?*

Marina looked at the servant. "You may leave us now, child. Fetch us some wine, perhaps some cheese. Not too much, for my sister already strains the seams of every gown I had made for her . . ."

Natalya heard her sister's remark but ignored it. Seating herself on the edge of a daybed covered with gowns in various hues, she opened the box and memories flooded back. *This I never could have forgotten.*

Natalya had grown up and become politically aware during the Lescari War. Fernandi's troops had completed their conquest of Samojita by her fifteenth birthday and with the spring they pressed on into Strana herself. By the middle of the summer they had sacked Myasovo and in only a month reached and occupied Murom. She and her family fled into the Transstranan Mountains and were saved, but the city was put to the torch and much of it was destroyed.

Miraculously, Marozac—the Tacier's fortress home—had not been burned and, even though Fernandi had stripped away much loot, his engineers had been unable to bring the building down. The Tacier and his family returned to Murom while Arzlov and the 137th Bear Hussars led the army in chasing the Lescari host from Strana. By the twentieth of Mors they succeeded in driving the remnants of that force from Strana and the Hussars were called to Murom to observe holiday celebrations.

As was fitting to reward the officers of the Hussars, they were invited to many of the celebrations conducted over Festibre. At these parties, dinners, and balls, Natalya had been introduced to Hussar heroes. Grigory Khrolic had been one of them, and a very dashing and handsome man at that.

Marina came to stand before her sister. "What are you remembering, little Talya? The first time you saw your lover?"

"Grigory was there, yes."

Marina laughed easily. "I do not refer to him, but to the man who gave you the box you hold in your hands. You saw him first, in Murom, when we returned from the mountains."

"Yes."

Though Grigory and all the Hussars officers had been impressive, with uniforms dripping with medals and faces painted up fiercely in Hussars colors, she had not found herself attracted to any of them. Drunk with victory and spirits, their gaiety seemed inappropriate for a city that had been laid to waste. She had withdrawn into herself, seeking some solitude, and found herself drawn to the quiet man the King of Ilbeoria had sent to her father's court.

She found herself entranced by Captain Malachy Kidd because he too seemed out of place in the celebration. While he did observe the Stranan custom of painting his face, he did so with subdued tones of red and blue, the Hussars colors. Unlike other Ilbeorians at court, he did not cut his hair short or shave his head and when asked why he did not follow the custom of his homeland she overheard him reply, "In Strana, the wise man cultivates hair as an ally against General Winter."

From other bits and pieces of gossip Natalya heard at the party she pieced together all the stories she'd heard of him while lurking in the shadow of her father's throne. Stories of Malachy Kidd had flooded through the Tacier's court when the man first arrived from Ludstone. He had lived in Lescar as a spy for two years, infiltrating *Les Revisor Carmi*—the Emperor's internal security apparatus. The Lescari never suspected him and were taken unawares when he helped commandeer the airship *El Os* at Clermon. He and his confederates—she had heard one was even Prince Trevelien—had eluded Lescari pursuit and escaped to Ilbeoria.

Her sister stroked Natalya's hair with a hand. "Oh, I remember your Wolf-priest well, sister. In light of his youth, the heroism of his actions, and the great honor of his being posted to Murom, I would have expected him to be an insufferable egotist. I never expected he would downplay his accomplishments as he did."

Natalya nodded unconsciously. "He was not like other of his countrymen at court, either. He worked hard to learn Stranan and happily ate and drank traditional Stranan foods. He fit in easily, making it simple to believe he had deceived Fernandi's people for so long. The way he often remained quiet and listened to others intently, this too was evidence of his patience, the patience that would have made him a good spy."

Marina picked up one of the gowns and draped it over her front. "I remember some of the Tacarri saying a man that quiet clearly

could not have done all the things attributed to him." She shrugged
and studied herself in a tall triptych of mirrors. "Men seldom have
learned the value of listening—and your Grigory is not among
them."

"Grigory listens."

"But not as well as your Wolf-priest." Marina frowned and cast
the gown aside. "Yellow makes me look fat."

An observation Malachy would have made, but never voiced.
That first night Natalya had seen in Malachy Kidd's behavior a reflection of herself and how she dealt with the social intricacies of
life at court. Natalya spent as much time as she could in her father's
shadow. There she learned far more about politics and the state of
the nation than any of her siblings. More importantly she came to
realize that by remaining quiet yet attentive, one could learn things
in addition to what others thought they were teaching. Just as she
found herself becoming a perfect little spy at court, so she recognized Malachy using those same skills to learn how to fit in within
Stranan society.

Natalya laughed lightly, earning a frown from Marina. "No,
sister, yellow does not make you look fat, for you are not fat at all."

Marina sniffed. "I am, but you are kind. I forgive you the
laugh."

"What I was laughing at was myself." Natalya gave her sister a
smile. "I remember that when I saw Malachy Kidd being quiet and
observant, I entertained the fantasy that Malachy had been sent to
spy on our father. I know now no spy would be inserted into Murom
as openly as Malachy had, but I was young then."

"Young, perhaps, but not foolish. I seem to recall you were
quite obsessed with him."

Natalya blushed. "I was *concerned*, not obsessed. I did make it
a point to learn about him."

"You stalked him like a hunter after a wolf." Marina smiled at
her own pun. "Very much like a hunter after a wolf."

"True, and I got him."

"He got you, I thought."

"Details. Try the red gown." Natalya set the box on the daybed
and handed the red gown to her sister, hoping to deflect her. "The
red will be perfect on you."

Her hunting of Malachy Kidd had required attending any number of celebrations in the capital—a pursuit that thrilled her siblings
but largely bored Natalya. Late in Festibre, Kidd caught her spying
on him at the same time she caught him indulging himself in what
was, unbeknownst to her, a passion of his. At a ball being given by

the Archduke Leonid Culechuc, she saw the Wolf-priest pause in front of a painting done a century earlier by the grande dame of Stranan arts, Irina Vorovsi. Titled *Men Playing Chess*, it depicted two older men huddled over a board that lay balanced between them on their knees. In the background children played soccer but one looked over his shoulder at the chess game.

Again and again through the evening Malachy stopped at the painting. He canted his head left and right, then would wander off again. Finally, after his fourth visit to the picture, Natalya stopped and attempted to discover what he found so fascinating about it. Try as she might, she only saw two men playing chess. While the artistry and technique made the picture one of Vorovsi's masterworks, Natalya had never found it to be *that* interesting.

"I believe, Tachotha Natalya, black is employing the Lescari defense."

Natalya nearly jumped out of her skin, but recovered herself quickly. "Then white will win because he is employing his pieces in accord with the Savensk opening."

Malachy moved from behind her into sight at her left hand. "Forgive me for startling you, Tachotha. It was not my intent to do so, but given your observation of me all evening, I thought certain you would know where I was."

She arched an eyebrow at him and flicked open a fan to half hide her face. "My dear Captain Kidd, you are mistaken if you believe I have been spying on you."

His blue eyes sparked impishly. "Forgive me. I lived by paranoia in Lescar and have not fully rid myself of it."

"Strana is not Lescar, Captain."

"Indeed not, Tachotha. There no one knows anything of chess." He frowned for a second. "Only Lescari intellectuals play chess, but in my time there I never met one."

Natalya smiled cautiously. "I cannot imagine going without playing at least once per week. To go without a game for two years would seem eternity itself."

"It is said Hell is a place where chess is not played."

"You have, of course, played since your arrival in Murom, yes?"

He gently shook his head. "Your father's Bear Hussars are fearsome warriors and they have fought valiantly to drive Lescari from Mother Strana. Time away from battle was time for sleep, not playing a game that mirrors battle."

"But does not chess teach strategy and tactics?"

Malachy smiled and pointed at the painting. "It does, but the

Lescari defense in the field is more spirited than in the game, and the Lescari emperor has more than eight pawns."

She lowered her fan to cover her bosom. "We will play, yes, you and I? Tomorrow, at Marozac?"

"I am honored by your invitation, Tachotha, but . . ." Malachy looked around the room.

"But?"

"Will this be acceptable?"

Natalya looked up and saw a number of people staring in their direction. Malachy's steel-gray uniform, with purple piping and stripes and gold buttons did stand in marked contrast to the white winter uniforms the Stranan officers wore. Her lavender gown complemented the purple of his trim, so they almost seemed to be a matched pair.

Puzzled by his concern, she frowned. "Why would this not be acceptable?"

He glanced down. "Our conversation seems to have attracted attention. You are a Tachotha and I am merely an Ilbeorian priest."

Natalya giggled lightly and fanned herself. "You have attracted attention here because of who and what you are, Captain Kidd. While I am a Tachotha, I have many brothers and sisters who will see the throne before I will. You are handsome, young, and gallant, which makes you very desirable among women at court. This means you also pose a threat to fat old balding Naraschals whose young wives have too much leisure time. And it is believed, as a Wolf-priest, you are celibate."

Malachy blinked. "I beg your pardon?"

"Your vow of celibacy is seen here as either pity or challenge."

"But I am not an Ignatian or a Donnist or a Neotian—I have no vow of celibacy."

"But you have avoided the snares and invitations by seductresses famed for their wiles and beauty."

A smile slowly spread across the priest's face. "Ah, I see. In seeking reasons for my refusals to be entertained—"

"Only a vow of celibacy could explain your resistance." She glanced around her with half-lidded eyes. "Now they wonder if one like me will be able to entice you to break your vow."

Malachy folded his arms and watched her for a moment. "How old are you?"

Natalya gracefully gathered her fan in gloved hands. "I will be sixteen in the spring." She tried to keep her voice even, but a bit of irritation with the question underscored her reply. "Many of the women at court have been married and have borne their first child by my age."

He shook his head. "I did not doubt you were nubile, and my own mother bore me just after her sixteenth birthday. I was marveling at how mature you are in thought and manner."

She smiled and chose not to hide it behind the fan. "Children at Marozac mature quickly or very slowly, and sometimes never at all." Natalya tapped him lightly on the shoulder with her fan. "So, will you be seduced from your vow by this Tachotha?"

Malachy laughed in sincere amusement. "Were I bound by vow to be celibate, I would be very tempted. And while I find the women here most beautiful and intriguing, I am here at behest of my King. This means I should not involve myself in intrigues, no matter how pleasurable or innocent. And, as I am a priest, I know grappling with and resisting temptation is good for my soul. Depriving myself and the ladies of Murom of mutual interaction brings all of us closer to eternal salvation."

"Without which you would find yourself in Hell," Natalya laughed, "where there is no chess."

"You know my mind, Tachotha Natalya."

"And I will know it even better after we play, Captain Kidd," I told him. Natalya sighed quietly and watched her sister preen before a looking glass.

Marina studied herself critically in the mirrors, then nodded. "Had I had this gown in Murom, I could have broken your Wolf-priest of his vow of celibacy. It will do quite nicely for this evening."

"It would have taken more than your gown, Marina."

"Yes, sister, me in it or me out of it." Marina laughed triumphantly, then gave her sister a quick kiss on the cheek. "I would have gone after him, but you were so taken with him. I thought it was wonderful how he indulged your taste for games."

Natalya narrowed her eyes. "You just didn't like the fact that he had no desire to indulge your taste for games."

"More true than you want to know, Natalya." Her older sister laid the red gown back on the daybed and picked up a sea-green one. "Here, this is for you. Hold it up; it matches your eyes. Stand there, very still, let me look at you. Think of something pleasant so you smile."

"Your wish is my command."

She tried to bring to mind bits of her last trip to Vzorin, but found her thoughts drifting back to her time in Murom with Malachy. The Wolf-priest had acquiesced to her invitation and over the next month and a half they played at least once a day. Natalya had found him a strong foe and an inventive player, though she regularly beat him. With him she could only count on the unexpected. By the end of their time together, Malachy had begun to force more and more draws and even stole a game from her on his last day in Murom.

Natalya smiled at her sister. "He was very strong and inventive, you know."

"In bed, that is a good thing."

Natalya blushed. "I meant as a chess player."

Her sister sighed. "Had I spent so much time with him, there would have been more between us than a wooden board."

"You mean *less*, don't you?"

Marina snarled and Natalya suppressed a laugh.

During her time together with Malachy, they became inseparable and insufferable. As the Tacier's daughter she could go anywhere Malachy could and was admitted to everything from military councils to troop exercises. When Malachy did not have work to do, they were playing chess or talking about life. At social functions the two of them often huddled together, sharing secret observations about people at court or going over the various strategies they had used in games played earlier in the day.

"That gown will be wonderful on you." Marina nodded slowly. "Truth be told, sister, I would have come after your Wolf-priest, but he was always so reserved and withdrawn."

"Like me?"

"In some ways, perhaps." Marina shrugged. "I prefer men with more fire."

"There was a reason you only saw him as stiff and formal. He was a long way from home, representing his King and country in a foreign land where he was learning the language, learning the customs. The discipline he imposed on himself was the discipline that made him a good chess player, allowed him to survive in Lescar, and made him a good soldier. In private he would open up more, speak of his dreams and desires."

"Desires that did not include you?"

Natalya frowned. "His desires were defined by his duty to the Ilbeorian Crown, but I knew what he had wanted back before he was sworn to his duty. He wanted a simple parish, a simple life. Where he was, what he was doing, what he had done had almost overwhelmed him."

Within two weeks of their meeting, she knew she was hopelessly in love with him. When she would take one of his pieces from the board, she would hold it out to him. She would wait until the fingertips of his cupped hand touched the underside of her wrist before she would drop the piece, and her fingers always brushed against the knuckles of his closed fist as she withdrew her hand. After the games she would insist on hearing what he had thought and planned while they played, and she held his hands so he could not get away until she had learned all she desired to know.

"Well, Natalya, it was obvious that he had overwhelmed you." Marina shook her head. "At balls and other parties, you would slip your arm through his, or lean against him when laughing at one of his jokes—you were quite shameless. When you whispered to each other you bent your heads forward, with your cheeks all but touching and your lips separated by only a few inches. And when you danced together, well, that actually was fascinating to watch. You moved as if of one mind and body, light and strong, graceful and swift, alone together within the crowd surrounding you. I so wished your Wolf-priest would teach my suitors how to do that."

"See what you get for being courted by men who do not play chess?"

"Yes, married."

Natalya winced as the remark stung her. She had known that Malachy loved her, too, from all the little signs he gave her. He thoughtfully preempted invitations to dance by ancient nobles and young officers he knew she detested. He learned to read her moods and deflect her away from dark reflections or towering rages with a joke or a quiet thought taken from Scripture. She saw his eyes eagerly flash when she entered a room and more than once caught a frown on his face when she danced with another or was late for one of their games.

Neither one of them spoke of their feelings for the other because of what Malachy had said at the Archduke's ball. With her he could be himself, and were they somehow exiled together to some uncharted paradise in the Cruciform Sea, they would have been free to espouse their feelings and become lovers. In Murom, with her being the Tacier's daughter and him being a representative of the Ilbeorian government, to openly admit what they both knew in their hearts would only lead to frustration and disappointment. Malachy was in her nation for his King, and he was there to help her people destroy the Lescari despot. His mission was important enough to supersede their happiness.

Natalya's voice softened to a whisper. "We both thought that when Fernandi was defeated—and our vision of the future allowed for no other alternative—things would be different between us. He would no longer have to represent his King and I might be married to him as a means to strengthen ties between our nations. Then, all too quickly, winter gave way to spring thaws. Rumors that Fernandi had raised a new army reached us. On their heels came reports that he was leading it east toward Strana, and the warriors left for the field."

On the night before the Hussars were to leave Murom, Malachy dined with her in her father's palace. At the close of the evening he took her hands in his and kissed both of them. "I'm leaving Murom a King's man, to watch the Hussars finish what we started last autumn. When that business is done, I will come back here for myself. And for you."

He handed her a wooden box with a mother-of-pearl bear on it. "I want you to have this to remember me. It came from the Lescari airship *El Os*. I found it in the Captain's cabin. He thought of himself as an intellectual."

Natalya let the green gown puddle on the floor and sat again on the daybed. She pulled the box into her lap and ran her hands over the wood. It felt as smooth as it had a dozen years before and its weight still impressed her. When she opened it she saw thirty-two figurines, half cast in silver, the other half in gold. Fernandi, his Marshals, and a host of his troopers made up the gold pieces. The Ilbeorians featured Saint Martin as the Warlord beside King Ronan, airships, armored priests, and wolves as the major pieces with plump and tonsured monks taking the place of the pawns.

"He gave this to me, for me to remember him by. He took it from the captured Lescari ship that brought Prince Trevelien to freedom. I refused to accept it. I knew how much it must have meant to him as a memento of the Lescari ship's capture. He insisted."

She lifted one of the silvery armored priests from its maroon velvet bed. *I told him then that I would care for the set for him and he promised to collect it from me after the war. And me with it.*

Her hand closed over the figure and she felt the coldness of the metal. Malachy had never come back for her. She had heard stories that he had died or had been captured, and she mourned for him. When Grigory Khrolic first came to Murom he had confessed to her that Captain Kidd's misfortune had been *his* fault. Had he found out about Malachy's secret mission and reacted sooner, Malachy never would have been maimed and captured.

Natalya felt her sister's hands resting on her shoulders. "I remember your tears when you heard of what happened to him."

"And I remember your kindness to me at that time."

Based on Grigory's report of all that had happened in Glogau, the Tacier signed a citation for conspicuous gallantry, making Malachy Kidd a Hero of the Stranan Empire. A request had been sent to Ilbeoria to allow Malachy to travel to Murom to receive this honor, but the Ilbeorian ambassador had said Malachy was "in retreat" and would be unable to attend any ceremonies. Repeated requests had always brought the same answer, so the requests stopped.

Natalya had not surrendered her hopes of seeing him again for years. She always waited for letters, and those diplomats being sent to Ludstone knew Tachotha Natalya would be happy to learn anything about Malachy Kidd. The story they brought back with disheartening regularity was that he had suffered horribly during his Lescari captivity. He was blind and broken. After being fitted with silver eyes, he had become something of a recluse, living at Sandwycke and occasionally leaving his tower to make life for students there a living hell.

Marina crouched and recovered the green gown from the floor. "It did surprise me, Talya, when you went from mourning your Wolf-priest to being courted by the man who accepted the blame for Kidd's maiming."

"That irony has not escaped me, either, Marina." Natalya shook her head. "There was something different about Grigory, after the war, after his time here. He had changed, and so had I."

When Grigory Khrolic returned to Murom with the 137th Bear Hussars, Natalya had been impressed by his maturity and how well he had organized his life. She saw she had been doing nothing but waiting for a half dozen years for Malachy Kidd to fulfill his promise to return. Though all the information she had about him indicated he would not be coming for her, in her heart she wanted to believe he would. In waiting for him she had done nothing with her life as a consequence, so she decided she would wait no longer.

Grigory sought her out, but his pursuit of her was not impassioned as it had been when he first came to Murom. While he did reveal his emotions to her when they danced together, or in private moments, the rest of the time he was a perfect gentleman. She realized, as she came to love him, that he had set out from the first to win her, and he had organized his campaign to do so as carefully as he had laid out the new Myasovo or planned action against the Lescari.

"Had he changed, Talya, or just devised a new plan to win your heart?"

"One required the other—a changed man executing an old plan or the same man executing a new plan. Either way, he was not the man I ignored in favor of Malachy Kidd. At least he wanted to be with me, and that was a big change from what I had known to that point."

She decided Grigory's efforts should be rewarded, so she gave herself over to him. She let her experiences with him replace memories of Malachy Kidd. She surprised herself in how easy a process this seemed to be and welcomed the relief of cutting her ties with the Wolf-priest.

"You are wrong, sister. The same man executing a new plan is not a changed man at all. There is much to Grigory Khrolic you do not see or do not allow yourself to see."

"Such as?"

"His ambition."

"His ambition is to serve the throne."

"His ambition to serve the throne could have been accomplished quite well without his winning a place in the Vandari." Marina's eyes tightened. "Grigory Khrolic wants to be more than just a military man. He has flaws, Talya, but you leave yourself blind to them."

"I've seen them. They do not matter." Natalya gave her sister a hard stare, but could not stop a shiver from running up her spine.

She had wanted her relationship with Grigory to completely supplant the memories of her time with Malachy, and this would have been accomplished but for one fault Grigory exhibited.

He and Natalya played chess only once, at her insistence. As a player Grigory was not terribly strong. She defeated him handily and looked up from the board expecting a smile and an offer of a re-match. She did get that, but only after a spark of outrage arced through Grigory's hazel eyes. In that instant she knew they would never play chess again and that a small part of Grigory would for-ever hate her for winning.

Prior to that game, Natalya had been determined to send Malachy's chess set back to him. After Grigory's reaction to his loss, she reconsidered. Her memories of chess would always keep Malachy alive in her mind and the momentary expression that had twisted Grigory's face was something she wanted to forget. It made her uncertain about him, just a bit, and she had brought Malachy's chess set with her on her visit to Vzorin the year before as if the pieces were a tiny army that could shield her from any unpleasantry.

Of this there was no need.

Her time in Vzorin had been one of true happiness. Grigory, having been separated from her for nearly a year, had been solici-tous in public, then ardently passionate in private. It seemed to her as if, away from the cold confines of Murom, Grigory had drawn energy from the desert and used it to fuel his love for her. *He was a man renewed, and a man from whom I needed no protection.*

It occurred to her, as she returned the silver priest to the box and closed the lid, that she had thought of neither that chess set nor chess itself since her journey to Vzorin. Grigory and their love for one another had taken over the portion of her life previously given to chess. She did not think about the game or care to play it, and she found herself more eager to complete her return trip to Vzorin than she ever had for any chess game she had ever played.

Marina snorted out a quick laugh, then shook her head. "Who is more blind, Natalya: your Wolf-priest who cannot see, or you who do not want to see?"

Natalya smiled at her sister and put the chess set down again. "Or the sister who insists on seeing shadows where there are none?"

"Believe that, if you wish."

"I shall, but no more about this now." Natalya fingered the fabric of the gowns. "We must dress for our party tonight, *da*? We can ignore the unimportant until after then."

"You know too well how to deflect me, Talya." Marina laughed again, then sharpened her expression. "What will you do with that chess set?"

Natalya raised her chin. "I will have my servant pack it away again. When I return from Vzorin I will be sending it back to its owner. I no longer have a need for it."

— **20** —

Vzorin **Vzorin Military District** **Strana** **27 Bell 1687**

Dressed in scruffy rags, with a soiled strip of gauze worn over his right eye, Rafiq Khast squatted in the dust of the street marking the border between old Vzorin and the newer sector of the city built by the Stranans. He rattled a chipped earthenware bowl at anyone passing by, flipping it with a flick of his wrist so the copper coins in it flew up into the air and clattered down again. Estanuan pedestrians gave him a wide berth and the Stranans ignored him completely.

Another time Rafiq would have been furious with his own people for shunning a beggar, because the *Kitabna Ittikal* admonished all believers in Ataraxianism to be generous with the poor. His anger would have come in part from a belief that a lack of sincerity in practicing their religion was why Atarax had not given his people back the Dost. Now, though, he knew the Dost had returned and he was engaged in a mission given to him by the savior of his people.

Akhtar, with the lower part of his right leg bound up behind his thigh, hobbled over and leaned against the wall beside Rafiq. Using both hands on his crude crutch, he lowered himself to the earth and winced as his weight settled on his leg. "There is something you will want to know, cousin."

"I am half blind, not deaf. Tell me."

The youth lowered his voice. "A number of Stranan servants have come to the bazaar on the behalf of their mistresses. They have asked Qusay to cast augury wands for them. He has and has learned much."

Rafiq smiled and bowed his head repeatedly as someone dropped a copper coin into his bowl. "God, in his wisdom, will smile upon you."

After the encounter with the Dost in the mountains, Rafiq and his band had pushed northward as swiftly as they could. Two days previously they had arrived on the outskirts of Yazdan—what they knew Vzorin to be prior to the Stranans moving in and establishing their new district. Infiltrating the city through the older, Estanuan half had been simple. The men divided up and, disguised as beggars, watched for someone who fit the Dost's needs. By asking around they learned of a merchant, Valentin Svilik, who had been aggressive in his dealings with Estanuans. He spoke the Estanuan tongue, understood customs, and had a keen eye for the sorts of trade goods favored in Helor and Strana. Once Rafiq had settled on Svilik as his target, they were rather quickly able to isolate the area where he lived and start studying him.

In many ways they were fortunate that Svilik was a merchant because he often moved through the older parts of the city searching out informants and contacts. The Khast faction quickly identified some of the people working with him. Rafiq had begun to plan on using one of Svilik's agents to betray him to them, though doing that seemed something less majestic than Rafiq wanted the first blow delivered in the name of the Dost to be.

Rafiq decided on the ride in that Qusay would be most valuable to their cause if he did divinations in the open in the bazaar. When the Khasts ruled in Helor, Qusay had kept three Stranan scholars as slaves, in turnabout for his own captivity in Vzorin. Qusay was fluent in their tongue and had taught Rafiq what little Stranan the younger man knew. In Vzorin, Estanuans purchased Qusay's services as entertainment, elaborating freely on whatever predictions Qusay made—and made yet more fun and cryptic by delivering them in deliberately broken Stranan.

"These women come and ask the same questions, all of them. They want to know if N'tala will like their dress or their home. She is important, this N'tala, and she is coming here." Akhtar held his hand up with all his fingers splayed out. "Five days. Perhaps *she* should be our target."

"No, cousin, because we do not know if she speaks our tongue, as the Dost demands of the one we bring him. We will, however, be able to make use of her, I am sure." Rafiq kept a smile from his face. *How you weave, Atarax, when you wish to reveal your power.* In three days warriors from some other Khast allies were to camp outside Vzorin. Rafiq had intended to have them harass trade, drawing the Hussars out of the city when he abducted Svilik. With this N'tala person coming into Vzorin the Hussars would not leave, but having them in place to defend someone was as good as having them away. They would not chase him to get Svilik back, if or when they noticed he was missing.

If he had his warriors threaten this N'tala, the Hussars would engage them in her defense. Rafiq knew his allies would be reluctant to face the Hussars in the city, but not if they knew the Dost required their services. He would send his most zealous men out to infect them with the fire the Dost had sparked in his heart and then the Stanuans would leap at the chance to do their part.

"Find out exactly when this N'tala is expected to arrive and how. Find out if there is to be a celebration." Rafiq fell silent as two Hussars strolled past. "Have Qusay tell them fortune will smile upon the person who first greets her when she arrives, or something like that."

Akhtar nodded and levered himself upright with his crutch. "It will be as you ask."

Five days. Rafiq knew he could make arrangements to have Svilik in that amount of time. Though the moon would be nearly full that night, he did not fear for himself or his effort. Though he did not know who N'tala was, he did know Atarax had deliberately woven her arrival into the tapestry of his life. *Through her arrival, we will realize the Dost's will.*

A cooper coin clinked into his bowl.

Rafiq looked up and smiled. "God is good, God is great, and blessed are those whose lives are woven with the weft of His will."

— 21 —

> **Dhilica**
> **Puresaran, Aran**
> **2 Tempest 1687**

The gray cravat snugged at Robin's throat like a strangling cord. Wearing his dress purple uniform jacket, with black boots, gray trousers, waistcoat, and white shirt, he felt more uncomfortable at the reception—where he was supposed to be enjoying himself— than he had on the entire, cramped journey from Ilbeoria. Given a choice, he would have been out leading a patrol through the Varatha Quarter of the city, no matter the risk, than to subject himself to having to dress up and be polite.

He smiled at himself, knowing that was not the core of his disenchantment. Even though he was a minor officer, his presence was expected at the party Prince Trevelien was hosting for the outgoing Governor-general, Baron Mortimer Fiske. It did not matter if the man deserved the honor or not; appearances had to be maintained, so the officers from the *Saint Michael* and its ethyrine contingent donned their uniforms and attended the party.

"Cheer up, Mr. Drury. No danger here tonight." A smiling ethyrine wearing a uniform almost identical to Robin's offered him a crystal cup of punch. "You'll be needing this soon enough. Drink up."

Robin sniffed at it suspiciously. "What is this, Brother Dennis?"

"They started with a negus, then added a lot of fruit juices. Less alcohol than the grog on your angel."

Robin sipped it. The drink was very sweet, which he expected from the negus, but adding the fruit had all but killed the sherry's taste. The drink had a tart afterbite which surprised him, and enough of a kick that he refrained from taking another hearty swallow. "Interesting. Thank you, sir."

"You'll learn to drink a lot here, Mr. Drury. We may be in the rainy season right now, but it gets deucedly hot in what ought to be a proper winter." The brown-haired ethyrine lowered his voice. "It's funny to see most of the high and mighty having servants spin bleached cotton into fluffy tangles to imitate snow for Eilyphmas come Festibre."

Robin nodded and sipped his drink again. Brother Dennis Chilton commanded the ethyrine company that served as Baron Fiske's Honor Guard. Despite being five years younger than Robin, Chilton was superior to him in rank. He'd graduated from Sandwycke a year after Robin had entered the school and had been posted to Aran immediately. He would return to Ilbeoria with Fiske, but during the transition he was doing all he could to acquaint Robin with the difficulties and pleasures of living in Dhilica.

"That will be a sight to see, lace snow. I imagine old habits are hard to break, sir."

"They are, indeed." Chilton ran a hand through his hair and patted it into place. "One thing you'll want to do, no matter how it seems wrong, is to get your boys some hats for the hot seasons here. They'll protest they're being wigged, but the sun gets very hot and we lose people to heatstroke even in winter and spring." He raised his cup and drained it.

Robin drank some more. "I'll have Sergeant Connor start scrounging hats after our patrol. Thank you, sir."

"Service here isn't that bad, Mr. Drury." Chilton looked out over the crowd. "Toughest thing is remembering that there are three standards for conduct here. The first is local custom, from which Ilbeorians and Urovians are immune. Local magistrates cannot enforce their laws and customs among us. For example, the cow is sacred to the Laamti, yet we are free to purchase, slaughter, and consume them. Generally we only do this with animals raised in herds started with imported stock, but not all of our citizens are concerned with what offense they might give the locals."

"But Urovians *are* subject to Ilbeorian law, yes?"

"That's the second standard. Our citizens are expected to act in accord with our law. Of course, there is leeway—assault is a crime, but assaulting a local servant is not the same as brawling with another Ilbeorian."

That wouldn't have been hard to guess. "And the third standard?"

Chilton nodded toward the swirl of people in the large ballroom. "You see before you the cream of Ilbeorian society in Aran. Many of these people are from noble families, albeit cadet branches. Many of them believe *our* laws are optional here and, God be merciful, Governor Fiske tended to side with them."

Robin frowned. "That might seem to be a dereliction of his duty."

"In Aran, it is said, we have the best government money can buy." Chilton looked across the room at where the rotund Fiske sat chatting with Prince Trevelien. "Baron Fiske will be buying his son a seat in the Lay Parliament and his brother is going to be made a parish Dean in Whartonfields."

"The way the colony is governed will all change now, I expect." Robin let himself smile slightly. "The Prince cannot be bought."

"I would love to see the change, but it will not come easy. They have people back home who have loud voices. But that notwithstanding, not all the folk here are bad. In fact, some are very special."

"I'm sure, Mr. Chilton." Robin looked out into the crowd, finding the mix fairly normal. In general Robin found that folks—save people who thought their blood blue somehow made them better than all the rest—were just folks. He started to turn back to Chilton to share with him that pearl of wisdom when a gap opened in the throng and a woman looked toward him.

The surprised smile of delight on her face sucked Robin's breath away. *I don't know her. Why is she looking at me that way? Why is she waving?*

Robin started to raise his hand to wave back, but the slap of Chilton's right hand on his back saved him from embarrassing himself. "Come with me, Mr. Drury. I have someone I want you to meet." Chilton laughed lightly. "She's one of the special people I mentioned."

Uriah Smith swore softly as he dug his hands through his leather satchel. Its contents had been thoroughly mixed up before his first search and this one, his third, guaranteed his clean clothes had been completely mingled with his dirty clothes. It also guaranteed that the leather purse with the ten gold Suns of his gambling winnings in it was missing.

Snarling, Uriah tossed the bag down and straightened up. His head hit a beam. "God's Blood!" He grabbed at the back of his head but felt nothing wet or sticky. Pain throbbed as a bump rose, but he realized frustration more than pain had prompted his profanity.

That thieving little monkey Philo took it, I know it! Uriah snarled and almost hit his head on the ceiling again. That money, which Kidd didn't know about, had been Uriah's ransom against misfortune. Uncertain of Kidd's sanity and the reaction of Church officials if they found out about their mission, Uriah knew he could survive with that money until he found a way to get back to Ilbeoria.

I saw that rat-faced excuse for a wigging skulking around near my berth down here. Since the card game he'd expected Philo to do something to get back at him and sneak-thievery seemed appropriate. "I should have kept the money with me."

Ducking his head, Uriah worked his way forward to where the crew was unloading the cargo through the open hatch. Uriah saw Philo down below and jumped down behind him. He grabbed the little man's shoulders, but Philo ducked and whirled out of his grasp.

"Do ye want trouble, boyo?" The snaggle-toothed man rubbed a hand across black stubble on his jaw. "Best get back up in the ship and get yer tings."

"I'm getting my things." Uriah pointed to the leather purse hanging from Philo's rope belt. "That money is mine. You stole it."

Philo smiled and looked at the pair of airmen to either side of him. "Could be, or could be I won it from ye like I told these men when I shared me good fortune with 'em." He spit in his hands, rubbed them together and made fists. "Calling me a thief means ye call 'em thieves, too."

Uriah curled his hands into fists. "You don't want the trouble I'll be for you."

The other four airmen spread out to surround him. "Talking a good fight, boyo, ain't the way ye wins fights." Philo advanced and the circle tightened. "Time ye learn Aran ain't home."

Robin deposited his glass on a side table, then followed in Chilton's wake. He smiled as the young woman leaned forward and kissed Chilton on the cheek. "Brother Dennis, I am so happy to see you. Since I had not heard from you, I assumed you would not be here. I did so want to have a chance to speak with you before you returned to Ilbeoria."

She looked up with surprise followed by a slight smile as her gaze met Robin's. Robin felt a jolt run through his insides. He smiled and knew, to be polite, he should look away from her, but he couldn't bring himself to do so. Her features had a strength to them without being sharp or without having surrendered a youthful softness. The strength, he decided, came from her straight nose and the animated fire in her hazel eyes. Her dark brown hair, which she wore up, accentuated the vitality and intelligence he sensed in her—and that, much more than her beauty or trim figure, attracted him to her.

She glanced down. "I beg your pardon, sir."

Robin shook his head. "No, I should beg your pardon, miss."

She paused, irritation and curiosity mixing in her eyes and the shape of her mouth. "Please, sir," she said, remaining proper by objecting to his speaking to her without a formal introduction.

Chilton laughed aloud. "Allow me to rescue you, Amanda, from this gross indignity. I should have thought he knew better, being just graduated from Sandwycke."

Robin's face reddened and he looked down. He hated the fact that he reacted that way, but he realized it was more in embarrassment of having caused her discomfort than over having made a fool of himself. At Sandwycke's gala balls he had observed all the social amenities, but only by default. When he attended the dances clerks had already decided who he would meet for what dance, then he was conducted to the woman, introduced to her, and would entertain her until they took him to his new partner.

Chilton let Robin's color get good and bright, then patted him on the back again. "Miss Amanda Grimshaw, it is my pleasure to introduce to you Brother Robert Drury, of the *Saint Michael*. He is a newly minted ethyrine from Sandwycke. Robin, this is Miss Amanda Grimshaw."

Robin took her proffered hand and kissed it. "Forgive my conduct earlier, please, miss."

"I must apologize to you, Brother Robert, for I spoke first. You merely replied to me, returning kindness for my breach of etiquette." Amanda smiled at Chilton. "Did you know Brother Dennis at Sandwycke?"

"No. He was far ahead of my class."

"But we are both ethyrines, which means we still have a bond. Rare are the men who choose to wear wings and fight." Chilton looked past Amanda and his expression sharpened. "Ah, Lisa Marsh is coming in this direction. I think I should speak with her. Excuse me."

Amanda raised her hand to her throat as she laughed lightly. "Of course, Brother Dennis. Luncheon tomorrow?"

"My pleasure."

Robin watched for a moment as Chilton intercepted a blonde woman with blue eyes who wore a ruffled yellow gown complete with a bustle. Amanda's gown, by contrast, was just as tight in the bodice, but had no bustle. Made of royal-blue satin and decorated with both white bows and pearls, it was cheery without being ostentatious or overpowering. "I assume Brother Dennis did us a favor?"

"You may correctly characterize it as such, though to him, I think, it is deliciously agonizing."

The ethyrine raised an eyebrow. "Are you free to explain what you mean?"

Amanda smiled up at him, then looked away. "I imagine you are quite clever enough to discern most of it. Miss Marsh's father is a rather successful import-export merchant here. The family has been here for over twenty years. Aside from the first five years of her life and four years spent back in Ilbeoria at school, Aran is all Lisa has known. She returned to Aran from school on the same airship that brought Brother Dennis here and they have been quite friendly since."

"I see." Robin noticed a subtle shift in her shoulders and a mischievous light flash in her eyes. "Or do I?"

"You see many things, I have no doubt, Brother Robert."

"Please, Miss Grimshaw, call me Robin."

"And you shall call me Amanda."

"Fair enough." Recalling bits and pieces of what he had done at Sandwycke's various celebrations, he offered her his right arm. "If you wish, we could repair to the dining room for refreshment, Miss Amanda."

"The story should last us that long, thank you." She slipped her left arm through his right and let him lead her out through the crowd. "A year ago a friend of mine from Saint Mary's Academy came out here to Aran for a visit. She is Jocasta Myles, the third daughter of the Earl of Norcliff. Do you know her?"

Robin aborted a curt laugh. "I am afraid, Miss Amanda, Earls' daughters and I do not travel in the same circles."

"But I had heard you served on the *Crow* before attending Sandwycke. Her oldest brother, Harry, was an Acolyte on the *Crow*."

"After I left the crew, I believe."

"Ah, I should have known. Harry is a frightful idiot, so I doubt you would have had much to do with him, would you, Brother Robin?"

Robin glanced down just as Amanda looked up with a smile on her face. He shook his head once. "You were speaking of his sister?"

"Ah, pretend you did not hear the question. That will work with me, but not some of the other ladies here in Dhilica. Be on your guard."

"I shall."

"As I said, Jocasta came for a visit and was very much taken with Brother Dennis. He was just as taken with her and dear Lisa had chosen this same time to evince an interest in a subaltern in the Mrilan Frontier Light Horse regiment. Her brave warrior went off and got himself killed in the Himlans and Lisa even felt obliged to wear mourning for a whole week during the hot season. By the time she was ready to take Brother Dennis back, Dennis and Jocasta were engaged to be married upon his return to Ilbeoria."

Her recounting of Chilton's labyrinthine personal affairs took them down the front stairs to the large banquet room beneath the reception hall. There huge tables had been erected and laid with all manner of foods. Robin saw a full squad of the ethyrines in Chilton's command had been dragooned into carving haunches of beef, huge hams, and six different varieties of large fowl. Aside from steaming platters of meat, all manner of fruits had been placed on tables separating the serving stations from one another. Bread and cheeses covered three other tables and the corners of the rooms held tables where one could get all manner of beverages.

Amanda smiled at him. "I do not feel terribly hungry, but some wine would be good."

Robin led Amanda over to a table where they each took a crystal goblet of a hearty red wine. Feeling subtle pressure on his arm, Robin allowed himself to be guided to a relatively open area midway between two wine tables, where they could stand and watch others feed without having their conversations overheard.

"Brother Robin, would you mind if I asked you some personal questions?"

"Not if you would answer me one first, Miss Amanda."

"Yes?"

Robin let the sly tone in her reply slide past. "Who is interested in the answers?"

"How do you mean that?"

The ethyrine sipped his wine. "You already know I served on the *Crow*. That means there is a brisk trade here in gossip. I want to know how far my answers will go."

She laid a hand on his arm and squeezed gently. "The answers are primarily to satisfy my curiosity about you."

"And secondarily?"

"You're right about the gossip." She laughed and the sound made Robin smile. "Your answers will serve as benchmarks for determining how much exaggeration our little community is given to here, but they'll go no further than that. You see, Brother Dennis and I are good friends. We have been socially acquainted since he arrived here, but we never courted. I think this made our friendship stronger. Dennis would not have introduced the two of us if he felt we could not be friends."

The way she said *friends* made Robin wonder which of the myriad definitions of the term she meant to invoke. "Brother Dennis has not known me for much over a day. He could have been wrong about me."

"In the three years Dennis has been here I have not known him to be wrong in his judgments of people."

"Ah, but if that were true he would not be above us speaking with Miss Marsh."

Amanda laughed again and Robin definitely liked the fullness and honesty of the sound. "Oh, he knew exactly what sort of a person she was when he met her. His problem was that, being young and far away from home, he did not realize she was not exactly what he wanted."

Robin thought that through, then nodded. "You have convinced me. Your questions?"

"Well, first the most important for most people here: how many wives do you have?"

"None."

"Widowed?"

"Never married."

"That is hard to believe."

"Been corresponding with my mother, have you?"

Amanda chuckled. "She doesn't believe it, either?"

"Not at all, but there are ample reasons I've never taken a wife. From the time I was twelve until I turned twenty, I served aboard the *Crow*. Because of fears about desertion, crew members were not allowed much liberty. While our efforts in helping drive the Lescari from Merida, Beregia, and Scipia did render some women grateful, finding war brides was much easier for the infantry than it was for men in the airfleet." Robin shrugged easily. "When I returned home I could only find work in a factory. Twelve hours there a day, plus helping my father on the farm, did not leave me much time for courting."

"But you are a resourceful man—Dennis tells me all ethyrines are. There must have been someone of whom you were fond."

He hesitated for a moment, then nodded. "There was. Her father owned the Lakeworth Carriage Works factory where I worked. I think she liked me because he did not."

"If that was her only reason, she was a fool."

"She did not have Brother Dennis to introduce us." Robin sipped his wine. "Her father paid for me to attend Sandwycke and she was married off to a local pig farmer—a gentleman, though."

"A gentleman, of course." Amanda nodded, then narrowed her eyes. "The awards on your uniform. What are they for?"

"The war."

She started to smile and he sensed an attempt at cajoling the answer from him. To forestall her attempt he frowned and her smile relaxed. "I cannot imagine, Brother Robin, it was a time filled with pleasant memories."

"Most bad, but some good. I still have friends today whom I knew on the *Crow*." Robin stared down into his glass and watched the wine drain away from the edges of the goblet. "Some people philosophize about war—Fernandi was a great one for his pronouncements—but they miss the core of it. War is where one man kills another because their conceptions of what is right and just do not agree. I'm not saying there are not times when there is no other choice, but some people spill blood too easily."

Amanda had narrowed her eyes as he spoke, then her smile became firm and she gave his arm a little squeeze with her left hand. "Dennis was not wrong about you at all."

The admiration in her voice left him speechless. He had said more about his feelings and had talked more about himself with her, a perfect stranger, than he had with anyone save Uriah since leaving the *Crow*. With Uriah he had been trying to show the boy that being smart and being wise were not always the same thing, especially at Sandwycke. Uriah generally missed the message, but glimmers of it came through—enough to encourage Robin to think there was hope for Uriah. As annoying as Uriah could often be, he wasn't one to betray confidences and Robin felt comfortable talking with him.

With Amanda he felt a similar comfort in sharing confidences, but he discovered a problem in speaking with her that he had not known with Uriah. He actually *cared* what she would think of him and his ideas. Her ready acceptance of his comment about war flattered him and he found himself feeling far younger and more foolish than he ever should have. That sensation, he decided, could be aptly described by her expression "deliciously agonizing."

Before he could remark on his discovery, a man shouted her name from halfway across the room. Robin instinctively took one step forward as an older man with matchstick-thin legs, a viciously hooked nose, and round little potbelly scuttled through the crowd toward her. Gentle pressure on Robin's arm let him know she did not see the man as a threat, but the way he waved his walking stick about to clear a path for himself made Robin doubt her judgment in the matter.

"There you are, Amanda. Come, we are leaving."

Robin looked down at her and raised an eyebrow.

Amanda smiled. "Father, where are your manners? This is Brother Robert Drury of the *Saint Michael*. Brother Robin, this is my father, Mr. Erwin Grimshaw."

"Pleased to make your acquaintance, Mr. Grimshaw."

"I'm certain you are, sir." Grimshaw looked at his daughter and then back up at Robin. "From the *Saint Michael*, are you?"

"Yes, sir."

"Well, sir, I have just met your Captain Hassett." Grimshaw swiped with a handkerchief at the spittle froth forming at the corners of his mouth. "I found him a thoroughly disagreeable man, thoroughly disagreeable. What, sir, have you to say to that?"

—— 22 ——

> **Vzorin**
> **Vzorin Political District**
> **Strana**
> **2 Tempest 1687**

Valentin Svilik scowled at the mirror. Forcing himself to relax, the strongly built man used a brush to deftly trace an exaggerated design around his eyes in a dark green. He carefully blended it into the lighter green on its interior, but tried not to let it blur into the light blue shades that colored the rest of his face. *Perfect, not that it matters.*

In the morning, which now seemed so long ago, he had anticipated a delightful evening escorting his mistress to the reception in honor of Tachotha Natalya's arrival. Antonia had agreed to attend with him even though her husband would be escorting his first wife to the reception. The man, a venerable but minor noble, had acquired his third wife for his prestige, and her family had surrendered her for the bride-price he paid them. It was not an unusual transaction and the man was remarkably sanguine about his newest wife having a lover.

His attitude about Valentin's liaison with his wife Antonia had improved measurably since Valentin's business had picked up with that first big caravan from Helor. The fact that Valentin had also been closeted with Duke Arzlov before the Duke went off on his trip to Murom also spoke well of him. That Valentin was held in such high regard meant some of that regard could reflect well on Antonia's husband. In fact, that regard and that notice had gotten Count Suiyev an invitation to the evening's reception and another to attend the actual landing of the *Leshii* at Pyimoc. Even Valentin had not been invited to the minor arrival ceremony, something for which he had been initially grateful.

But that had been when he counted on Antonia having some-thing of a brain in her head. Through his sources in the Estanuan community in Vzorin he had heard of a seer entertaining Stranan ladies and their maids with predictions of incredible good fortune befalling those who met the Tachotha first. He'd dismissed the seer's claims as nonsense—after sending one of his servants there to hear the seer's message firsthand—but Antonia had not. She convinced her husband to let her accompany him to the skydock at the Duke's palace.

This meant she would be with her husband throughout the eve-ning's festivities. She informed Valentin of her change in plans far too late for him to be able to escort anyone else. Aside from one or two dances with her, he would see a good deal less of Antonia than he had intended. It was one thing for the Count to have Valentin oc-cupying his wife's idle time and quite another to have the merchant taking Antonia from the Count's side.

Appearances must be maintained. Valentin finished off his so-cial painting, ran a hand back through a shock of black hair and smiled at the results. Because he was not a warrior, he was not ex-pected to wear the blue and red of the 137th Imperial Bear Hussars. Since the ballroom would be filled with Hussars, making himself noticeably different would be good. *It will make it easier for Anto-nia to see what she is missing.*

The door opened behind him and Valentin saw the reflection of his wizened valet enter the room. "Forgive me, sir, but an urchin from the street conveyed this to you." The man held out a folded packet of paper.

Valentin put his brush down, turned in his chair and took the message from the older man. He broke the wax seal and unfolded the paper. On it he saw drawn a crescent moon, a sword, a crossmark, and a small bird. He studied it for a second, then handed it back to Eduard. "Burn it. You will go to the Duke's palace and extend my re-grets for being late. I shall appear there as soon as I am able."

The old man nodded, then withdrew from the room.

Valentin stood and pulled on a cloak without donning a jacket, vest, or cravat. *Such finery would be lost on the crone Duah and make me look even more out of place in Old Town.*

Because the vast majority of his Estuan trading partners in Vzorin were illiterate, Valentin had created a simple set of images they could use to call for meetings. The crescent moon, for exam-ple, was a quarter full, indicating that Duah wanted a meeting al-most immediately that evening. Had the moon been half full the meeting would have come at midnight. The crossmark indicated a meeting, the location of which had been agreed upon by both of them the last time they met. In this case it would be at a small tea shop in Old Town. The sword indicated the meeting was urgent and the small bird was her signature. Had a skull or broken bone appeared in the message Valentin would have expected danger.

It does not pay to go anywhere here without anticipating danger. Valentin left his room and appropriated a sword cane with a heavy brass knob on it from an elephant's-foot stand beside the door. Grasping the wooden body of the cane, he twisted the knob and exposed several inches of the silvery triangular blade. He smiled and slid it home again.

"Forget pretty women, Valentin," he mumbled to himself, "duty calls and you must answer."

Natalya Ohanscai stood tall and serene on the *Leshii*'s wing deck as the ship slowly descended through the moonlit night. She wore a black cloak and dark veil to ward her and her gown from the caress of the sooty smoke drifting from the *Leshii*'s smokestack. Despite having her face covered, she could easily see the well-lit skydock to the east of Arzlov's castle.

For the briefest of moments Natalya felt sorry for the people gathered below where torchlight turned night into a jaundiced parody of noon. They all looked splendid in their finest clothes, yet had to be sweltering even in the early evening. She recognized uniforms from military units that spanned the breadth of the empire and marked a great deal of its history. The women wore spectacularly colored gowns of deep scarlet, verdant green, or dazzling blue along with jewelry to match. The gowns had tight bodices that emphasized ample bosoms, narrowed waists, then flowed out into full skirts draped over bell-shaped crinolines—from the air it looked as if from the waist down the women were satin-shrouded mushrooms.

Natalya slowly shook her head. *I should have anticipated this.* In Myasovo her sister Marina had indeed introduced her to the latest in fashions. Instead of the tight-bodiced gowns the women below her wore—or that she would have worn in Murom—the women of Myasovo had made a partial return to what Fernandi's Empresses had worn. The new fashion in Myasovo had been sleeveless gowns of gauzy material worn over silk chemises. A ribbon gathered the skirts loosely at the waist, riding low around the hipbones, then more substantial material flared out to the floor. The crinoline had been abandoned in favor of letting the silk skirts enfold the legs and outline them.

Were it not for the opacity of the jade chemise and skirts she wore beneath the nearly insubstantial white gauze gown, Natalya would have felt quite naked. Her sister and others of her circle had taken to wetting their chemises down so they would mold themselves to the bodies beneath—hastening an embarrassing consequence of a dozen turns on the dance floor. Natalya had refrained from letting her sister hydrate her gown in Myasovo and had no intention of even mentioning that idea in any discussions she had with others about the new fashion.

Seeing all of the women there and knowing they were gathered to meet her, Natalya was happy she had chosen to wear the cloak over her gown. The women would know, since the cloak did not bow out to conceal a crinoline, that she was not attired as they were, but she hoped they would put that down to her wearing something more practical on an airship. *Of course, this gown is practical only for seduction, but that is not such a bad thing since I know Grigory is down there, too.*

She felt only a slight bump as Captain Selov repeated the flawless landing the *Leshii* had performed at Myasovo. Airmen cleared the section of railing before her as, on the ground, men in Hussars uniforms lifted a gangplank and slowly extended it toward her. Two of the *Leshii*'s airmen knelt at her feet and reached out to guide it into place, then they secured it with lines and fastened the guidelines to the ship's rail.

Natalya barely noticed the activity around her. She lifted her veil and smiled. At the far end of the receiving platform she saw Duke Arzlov. Grigory Khrolic stood a rank behind him, tall and resplendent in his Hussars uniform. As if it were the bronze avatar of some demon-godling the locals worshiped, Grigory's Ram Twenty-seven knelt in back of its pilot. A length of red carpet passed between ranks of noble men and women to link her with Grigory. Two platoons of Hussars had been arrayed along the carpet to keep the people back at a respectful distance.

The two *Leshii* airmen descended the gangplank and tied the guidelines off at posts on the skydock. They snapped to attention, then one of them turned toward Duke Arzlov. "Permission to begin debarkation!"

Arzlov took one step forward and held his right hand out as if forty yards did not separate him from the airship. "Permission is most willingly granted. Tachotha Natalya, you are most welcome in Vzorin."

The *Leshii*'s fluid flight inspired both amazement and revulsion in Rafiq Khast. The wooden vessel hovered before the moon's ivory disk like a hawk riding desert updrafts. He found it beautiful and knew the man at the helm had to be very skilled indeed to bring so large a vessel down in the middle of a city.

Rafiq hoped his men would kill the pilot.

For his own good.

As beautiful as the flying ship was, it was a tool of evil. Magick was meant for men. Stories, wonderful, fantastic tales upon which Rafiq had grown up, told of enchanted carpets that flew and lamps that housed Djinn. They were always the creation of an evil sorcerer and even though a story's hero might use them for good, to defeat the sorcerer, those creations always perished with their evil master. Such things were an affront to Atarax and they had to be destroyed.

The Dost will lead us in the destruction of such abominations.

Akhtar came up onto the roof of the building where Rafiq stood. "The Stranan merchant is coming. He should be in the shop below in five minutes."

"Good." Rafiq bent down and lifted up a Stranan darklamp. "Do you remember the signal to begin the attack on the airship?"

Akhtar's face brightened. "Two long vertical lights, starting low and coming up. The verification is one to the side and then down."

"Excellent." He gave his cousin the darklamp. "Open the shutter, lift and close. You can do this, yes?"

"Yes, but should not the honor of signaling the attack be yours?"

"And I give the honor to you, Akhtar. The Dost needs men and to a trustworthy man goes this great responsibility." Rafiq pointed toward the northeast. "When Svilik gets here, let them begin the attack."

With Natalya yet a dozen feet from solid land, shrill war cries sliced through the polite applause at the airdock. Black arrows streaked in from the darkness. Cheers shrilled into screams as men and women fell wounded or dying. Out of the shadows men with curved swords and long spears forced their horses up the sides of the hillock and Hussars struggled to free themselves of the riotous crowd to oppose them.

One arrow hissed past Natalya's throat and stuck, quivering, in the airship's hull. Stunned, she stopped for a heartbeat. One of the *Leshii*'s airmen started back up the gangplank. "Get down,

Tachotha!" His mouth worked to shout more instructions, but blood poured forth instead of words. He toppled back against the rope railing, then pitched over to fall beneath the ship with an arrow in his back.

I am the target here. Gathering her skirts, Natalya ran as quickly as she could down the gangplank, then crouched in a puddle of black cloak. "Grigory! I am here!"

The terrified people scurrying around her turned away from the palace archway and ran past her and the ship. Natalya looked up and saw a swarthy man on a magnificent black stallion come up over the edge of the airdock. The Estanuan warrior shouted something when he saw her, reined his horse toward her, then he stabbed his steel-tipped lance at her.

The sharpened metal pierced her cloak and she cried out from surprise. The man clearly took her cry as one of pain, for he leaned toward her, thrusting the lance forward until it tore free on the other side. He hauled the lance back and up and Natalya came with it. The warrior's evident joy at his feat transformed itself into puzzlement when Natalya reached her feet and firmly held the wooden lance out at arm's length with her left hand.

Though others had always seen Natalya's magick as minor and suitable only for scullions and lamplighters, she had always seen it as hideously destructive. She invoked the spell that tapped her talent and fed the vehemence of her anger and fear into it.

Fire filled the lance's wooden shaft, exploding it like a lightning-struck tree. The blast stung her hand and knocked her down, but she refused to cry out. *I am a Tachotha, I cannot give voice to my pain.*

The warrior, having clutched the thicker butt end of the shaft tightly to his ribs, split the night with a mortal shriek. The fire ejected him from the saddle and burned his right arm off at the shoulder. The blackened limb dropped smoking to the airdock's stone surface beside Natalya. The man's terrified stallion bolted past too quickly for her to get to it and escape on it. The warrior's body fell within the crowd and vanished from her sight.

Natalya whipped her smoldering cloak off and cast it over the crisped arm.

Another Estanuan horseman spotted her and began to cut his way through the crowd to get at her. His shamshir slashed left and right, scattering gaily dressed people. Women in crinolines jostled and toppled one another. A woman in scarlet went down, in an instant going from beautiful to being an inelegant flash of white underskirts and legs flailing in terror. People tripped over her, then clawed yet other people down in their insane attempt to rise to their feet again.

The horseman slowed as the crowd parted around Natalya. He grinned, blood running in a little rivulet from his sword's curved blade. For a moment she read lust in his eyes, then disgust swallowed it. Glaring at her cruelly, he raised his sword to kill her.

Though he had regularly traveled through the older sections of Vzorin, and often enough at night, never before had Valentin Svilik been able to determine what made it seem so *foreign*. He smiled at himself for having that thought. He knew he was the interloper in a city that had been old before the state of Strana had come into existence. *Here,* I *am foreign.*

Yazdan's antiquity provided some of the things that made the city feel alien to him. Modern conveniences, like gaslighting for the night, were unknown in Old Town. Layers of dust seemed to cover everything with a perpetual twilight that was only exacerbated by nightfall. Shadows here seemed thicker and more sinister. The buildings had not aged at all well and open sewers occasionally flooded the streets when the body of a dog or man diverted their flow.

Making all of this worse was Svilik's realization that the seemingly haphazard array of narrow streets and alleys was not the result of random building spurts over the centuries. He knew enough of the Estanuan culture and Ataraxian philosophies that governed the people's lives to know they did little by chance. Imans were regularly consulted on the layout of streets, the locations of buildings, and even the placement of doors and windows. All was to be done in accord with the *Kitabna Ittikal.*

The result of such consultations meant Old Town Vzorin resembled a web formed of streets and alleys. In reality it was a maze that hid far too many things for Svilik to feel secure, even living in the Stranan quarter of the city. Rumors abounded of underground temple complexes dedicated to Atarax, of places where devout young men learned to be assassins and of pleasure palaces where Stranan women were enslaved to sate the desires of wealthy Estanuans.

Svilik had built up his network of informants in an effort to pierce the veil of secrecy that shrouded Old Town, so he could know the people, determine their needs, and be able to fulfill their desires. The District Governor before Arzlov had angered the local population by demolishing a huge swath of buildings to construct Pyimoc, the airdock, and what had become the Hussars' headquarters. Whether the man had been subtly poisoned or just died of a heart attack no one knew for certain, but Arzlov assumed the worst and took steps to calm the people of Vzorin. Aside from consulting Imans over details of Pyimoc's completion, he cracked down immediately on two bandit gangs that terrorized Old Town.

This action on the behalf of the people of Old Town had made Svilik's efforts to recruit agents easier, but saying that was to suggest lighting one small fire in Initibre could somehow bring an end to winter. Appeals to greed brought Valentin most of the information he gathered, though bribing local officials to free individuals who had been imprisoned for minor offenses also worked. Thieves were considered thieves throughout the city, and if an Estanuan man caught stealing in the Stranan section of town were turned over to the Imans for punishment, he'd lose a hand. Dismissal of charges against him, with a promise of secrecy about the offense, earned gratitude that was repaid in information.

Duah had been different. An older woman, she came to Valentin because her pubescent daughter, Thurayya, had been kidnapped by a Stranan nobleman's son. The young man had been exiled from Murom by his family and Svilik learned he had been sent away for "abominations." Without writ or warrant, for Valentin knew no one could obtain neither to deal with the matter, Svilik burst into the man's home and threatened to kill him for having taken the girl, whom Valentin represented as his own mistress. The noble apologized and released the girl unharmed—babbling something about the moon not having yet reached the proper phase for his work anyway.

Svilik sent the girl back to her mother, then befriended the noble. And on a night when there was no moon, which was suitable for the work Valentin had planned, he led the noble into Old Town. Valentin even paid the local constabulary to write a report that concluded, "While it is true that the fatal wounds bore superficial resemblance to knife cuts and stabs, eyewitnesses verified that a pack of wild dogs killed the Count. The dogs were subsequently slain."

Duah had then become one of Svilik's most important and valuable sources. Her information was always good and always aimed at making a profitable deal for Valentin and various traders. Because he had recovered her daughter and because she knew who had led the Stranan noble to his death, Valentin trusted her.

He ducked his head as he entered the small tea shop Duah maintained as an adjunct to her family's home. A number of men sat at tables near the doors leading back to the street, but Valentin did not find that at all out of the ordinary. Duah appeared through the doorway leading into the kitchen and pointed him to a table. He nodded and seated himself, expecting her to join him.

He looked up and blinked with surprise when a hazel-eyed Estanuan with dark hair and a neat moustache sat down across from him. "What is this?" he asked in Estanuan.

"Do not be alarmed, my friend Valentin. I am Rafiq Khast. I am here to offer you the greatest opportunity of your life." Khast smiled carefully. "I have wonderful news for you. The Dost has returned."

"I see no profit in this news for me."

"But you will, my friend." Rafiq's hand closed over Valentin's right wrist. "He has sent me to fetch you to him, and by doing his will, we shall all prosper."

A huge bronze hoof backhanded the Estanuan warrior threatening Natalya from his saddle. The warrior flew past Natalya and slammed hard into the *Leshii*'s hull. The whole left side of his body had been crushed, with jagged bits of bone showing through gaping rents in his mail. The man's horse scrambled away from the corpse and the creature that created it, leaving Natalya alone, as if in a small protective bubble, with a bronze killing machine.

The Vandari Ram towering protectively over Natalya made her feel like a child trapped in a nightmare. The Ram's right forehoof gathered her in as the creature sank to its haunches. She wanted to flee after the horse as the Ram pulled her toward it, and would have bolted, but the metal creature had an astonishingly gentle touch.

The Ram flicked its left forehoof down. Natalya found the movement reminiscent of a woman angrily snapping open a fan. She marveled as layer after layer of the hoof splayed out in a semicircle that shielded her completely from a hail of black arrows that arced in at her. Clinking loudly, most of the Estanuan arrows hit the hoof-shield and bounced away to clatter on the ground. One actually punched through between two of the wedge-shaped hoof segments, but they closed again on the shaft, trapping it.

Natalya clung to the cold, lifeless metal of the Ram's right thigh. The right arm swept out and battered another Estanuan rider from the saddle. Natalya only saw the blow in isolated little flashes of light and shadow, but the imprint of a huge hoof in the man's crushed chest would stay with her forever.

The high-pitched Estanuan war cries shifted in tone and the Ram lifted its head above her. "Do not be alarmed, dearest Natalya. They are breaking and running."

"Grigory, it *is* you!"

"Your servant, Tachotha."

Natalya shivered. She had known the Ram *had* to contain Grigory. She had seen the suit and had even seen it on parade, but neither of those situations were what the Vandari armor had been created for. It was an implement of war. She had always known its potential—or had imagined its potential—but never as anything this violent and forbidding.

In spite of the metallic ringing accompanying it, Grigory's voice had been recognizable. The little grates in the neck from which it seemed to come did rob his voice of the emotion she had expected to hear when he spoke to her. At least, she assumed his words would have emotional content—fear, love, anxiety, concern, remorse—but in the sound she heard none of that. It was as if the armor kept his humanity to itself.

Or as if in the armor Grigory was less the human he was when free of it.

In the same way she had known the armor was a weapon of war, she had known Grigory was a man of war. Until now, she had never seen him at his trade, making use of the skills he had honed in years of training. When he spoke to her of war it was always as it had been when he had returned from the Lescari conflict. He had always spoken of his feelings about the men he had lost and the men who had been killed under his command. He never seemed at ease with the nature of his vocation.

But here, moving swift and certain through the milling throng to reach her and protect her, he had been very much himself. Had the Aralans not broken off their attack, she had no doubt Grigory the Ram would have laid waste to them. They would have been curs worrying a mighty bear. He would have destroyed them.

Because it was his duty.

And to keep her safe.

Natalya heard a hiss and a click above and behind her. She moved out from beneath the armor's shadow and smiled as Grigory stepped from the Armor's interior. Instead of the red and blue uniform he had worn on the airdock he was clad in a sweat-soaked single-piece garment made of blue flannel. It covered him from above the knees to his shoulders and fastened up the front with white buttons. A key hung around his neck on a braided cord and was visible because the garment's top two buttons were unfastened.

Natalya reached out for him and stroked his cheek, smearing a bit of the blue color around his eyes. He smiled and she hugged him to herself as tightly as she could. "I will ever feel safe in your arms, Grigory."

"You shall fear nothing while I am alive, Tachotha Natalya." He kissed her once, quickly, on the mouth, then loosened his hold on her. "The Duke comes this way."

Natalya reluctantly released him, but remained beneath his left arm. She kept her left hand pressed against his stomach, ignoring the way the wet flannel felt in favor of feeling him breathe. She took strength from just being near him and smiled when a bead of sweat fell from his nose and anointed her forehead.

Vasily Arzlov strode purposefully around the wounded as he crossed the airdock to where they stood. Despite bearing a bloodied saber in his right hand and having a ragged slash in the cloth over his right thigh, he managed to appear elegant and very much in command. Injured people on the ground drew strength from him and ceased their whimpering as he walked past them.

He bowed respectfully to Natalya. "You are unhurt, yes, Tachotha?"

"Yes, Duke Vasily."

"Then my prayers are answered, due in no short part to Pokovnik Khrolic's gallantry. You are unhurt, Grigory?"

"Just tired, my lord." Grigory looked back at the armor. "My Ram took more from me than my uniform. I am not complaining about such sacrifice, but tailors and sleep will be required to put things right again."

Arzlov smiled. "You worry about sleep, Grigory. I will gladly have my tailors fill wardrobes full of uniforms for what you did this evening. Had you not been here, the slaughter would have been epic. Go, and take Tachotha Natalya with you. I have your men rounding up surviving attackers for treatment. Our guests will be dealt with first, of course."

"Of course, sir."

"Tachotha Natalya, I will have the men unload your luggage. Your maid is still aboard the *Leshii* and can inventory your baggage? Good. I would like then to use the *Leshii* to track these bandits as they run from our city. We will find them and they will pay for what they have done here."

The grim threat in Arzlov's words did not surprise Natalya and did not repulse her. "Captain Selov and the *Leshii* are at your disposal, Duke Vasily. I wish you luck in your hunting."

"Thank you, Tachotha." Arzlov bowed his head to her. "Those who are enemies of Strana cannot be allowed to go unpunished."

On this we agree, Duke Arzlov. Natalya shivered as the man mounted the gangplank and marched up to the *Leshii*'s wing deck.

Grigory hugged her closely to himself. "There is no need to shiver, my Talya. I will protect you."

It did not surprise Rafiq to see the Stranan look over at the old woman whose note had summoned him. "Why, Duah? Why the betrayal?"

Rafiq tightened his grip on the man's wrist. "You saved her daughter and destroyed the man who would have despoiled her. This was good, but Thurayya was seen here as soiled. I will take her with us and offer her to the Dost as a wife. If he will not have her, then I will give her to my cousin, for he is of an age to have a wife. She will marry into the Khast family, Valentin, and her honor will be returned to her."

The Stranan opened his mouth as if to protest, then closed it and shook his head. "I gave the girl her life, and you give her life with honor. I understand."

Rafiq smiled. "I have promised Duah that we will not harm you if you do not resist."

"The men behind me are yours?"

"Four of my best, as are the four waiting outside." Rafiq's grin broadened. "And there is me."

Svilik nodded. Rafiq could almost hear the thoughts galloping through the man's mind. He knew, were he in Valentin's position, he would be calculating odds, then weighing them against the value of the news about the Dost's return. "The Dost sent you for me?"

"He asked for someone like you, yes."

"How did he know there was someone like me here in Vzorin?"

"He is the Dost. He knew."

Svilik laid his cane on the table with his left hand, then crossed his left wrist over his right. "You will want to bind my hands."

"And you will want to share bread and water with me before we depart."

Svilik looked surprised at that offer. "I know enough of Ataraxianism to know this means you will not slay me. I will trust you and go with you."

"As the Dost knew you would." Rafiq smiled and motioned for Duah to bring food. "The journey we begin tonight will be one that shapes the future of your nation and mine. How auspicious it is to begin it in trust."

— 23 —

Five of them, Uriah noted, *but none look as tough as my brothers.*
Despite the impossibility of his situation, Uriah did not consider
running an option. Chances were, if he ran, they would catch him
and beat him bloody. He'd learned early on that fighting was better
than running.

Against such odds he wanted to do the most damage possible
to his enemy. During his three years at Sandwycke he had been
schooled in all manner of very powerful and devastating battlemagicks, but without a weapon to bring to hand, they were useless.
Like everyone else, he'd heard stories of warriors improvising and
modifying spells to make shoe-lacings into enchanted whips or tav-
ern tankards into maces, but all he had to work with were his fists.

Luckily, not *all* the training at Sandwycke involved magick.

Darting forward at Philo, Uriah feinted with a right hand at the
man's midsection. Philo dropped both of his hands to cover his
belly, leaving his head open. Uriah's roundhouse left arced in and
clouted Philo's right ear with the force of a sledgehammer. The
scruffy thief's knees wobbled in and out, then the man collapsed
into a gibbering heap.

Leaving his right foot planted, Uriah pivoted back to the left
and drove his left elbow into an airman's gut. That man jackknifed
forward, holding his stomach. Uriah brought his fist up and mashed
the man's lips into a leaking red pulp. That man reeled away, leaving
Uriah with his back to a crate and three stout airmen ready to fight.

Here's where it could get nasty. He set himself, hoping they
would come in individually, but they were not entirely stupid. Their
scarred faces and torn ears proclaimed them survivors of many
dockside brawls. They came in as one. Uriah hammered two punches
into the face of the centermost man, but it didn't matter. The sheer
weight of the trio's bodies jammed Uriah back into the crate.

Uriah heard things snap and wondered for a second if the sound came from his ribs or the crate's rough wood. That line of inquiry became academic as one man's knee found Uriah's groin. Pain exploded up into his gut, paralyzing his lungs and washing away all rational thought. The airman brought his knee up again, compounding the damage and effectively taking the fight out of Uriah while not taking him out of the fight.

Breathless agony robbed Uriah of any conscious thought. Fire burned in his lungs and he wanted to breathe, but it seemed to him as if he'd forgotten how to do so. Kicks and punches caught him in the ribs, compounded the pain in his chest. Other blows exploded stars before his eyes. Warm sticky blood from a scalp cut poured over his face, half blinding him, then a particularly savage kick to his stomach pitched him forward. He caught himself on his hands, leaving his ribs open for attack again, then vomited the remains of his supper all over the airdock.

Uriah collapsed, tasting both blood and vomit. Hard kicks continued for a few seconds more, then they slackened in ferocity. Rising laughter, bold boasts, and verbal insults started in as the sailors congratulated themselves on their victory. Uriah barely noticed their comments as even the loudest couldn't fully penetrate the ringing in his ears. Blood bubbled up when he exhaled through his nose, and the aching in his ribs made every breath shallow and difficult.

Fingers tangled in his hair and picked his head up. Philo's face swam in and out of focus. It looked lopsided, but Uriah couldn't tell if that was because of swelling from his punch or his own inability to see clearly.

"Oh, boyo, ye done it now." Philo reached around to the small of his back and drew a knife from the sheath there. Highlights glinted from the blade's edges. "Fighting's made me blade-thirsty and yer blood's what will slake it."

Robin stiffened in response to the question. "You are referring to Captain Lonan Hassett, sir?"

"I am, sir." The little man shook himself angrily. "He is a very annoying man."

Amanda rested her right hand on her father's shoulder, interposing her presence between them, yet linking the two men at the same time. "You did not enjoy your time at the whist table, did you, Father?"

"The man won a month of Suns from me." Grimshaw glowered over at Robin. "And then he had the unmitigated gall to demand a promissory note from me right then and there. He was assured, by all and sundry, that when I said I would have the money sent round with a servant in the morning that it would be there. He said—"

" 'I won it from you, sir, and I will have it from you, sir.' " Robin smiled as he completed the quote. "You *have* met Captain Hassett."

"As I have said, sir." Erwin's expression sharpened. "So you have lost at whist to this man, as well?"

"I have played whist with him, sir." Robin looked at Amanda. "There is little free time on an airship, but at Saint Martin we had a day of liberty."

Erwin stepped in closer. "And Hassett always demanded money from your hand when you lost?"

"You mistake me, sir. I said I played with him, I did not say I lost to him." Robin lifted his head slightly. "However, those who lost to him were admonished to pay quickly and personally. It is a habit from the Lescari War—widows seldom acknowledge gambling debts."

"Those same debts are probably seldom paid to widows."

Robin nodded at Amanda. "Word in the fleet in those days was that dead men shared in Hassett's prizes, and gambling debts were worked out during the division."

Amanda's father stroked his chin and nodded slowly. "A man of principle."

"A man who is true to the vows he took in entering the officer corps."

"Very good, Brother Robert, was it? Very good."

Robin looked at Amanda, a bit surprised that she did not correct her father into using the more intimate version of his name. He would have not liked it, of course, but he expected Amanda's apparent affection for her father to prompt her to share it with him. When she did not, Robin smiled at her. *You are as shrewd a judge of people as is Brother Dennis.*

When he looked back at Erwin Grimshaw he saw the man had undergone a transformation almost as startling as that of a frog turning into a prince when kissed by a princess. He had straightened up and his flushed face had returned to a more normal shade of pink. His glance did not dart about furtively, though Robin still thought him calculating.

"It would seem, Brother Robert, that my demand on my daughter's time will steal her away from you. This separation would seem to be a burden upon both of you, and this I regret." The older man smiled carefully, almost in a friendly manner. "However, tomorrow is to be an early day for me, so we must depart now."

Robin nodded, then took Amanda's right hand and kissed it again. "It has been a pleasure meeting you, Miss Grimshaw."

"The pleasure was all mine, Brother Robert." Though she used the formal version of his name, the slight squeeze of her fingers let him know she had not forgotten what she should be calling him.

Robin offered his hand to her father. "It was likewise a pleasure meeting you, sir."

"And you, sir." The warrior found Erwin's grip surprisingly strong and dry, though his hand did feel a bit chilled. "Perhaps, Brother Robert, you would consent to dine with us at Gauntlan Manor? I believe my daughter would enjoy renewing your acquaintance. Shall we make it a week from this evening?"

"Please do come."

"As much as it would please me, I will have to refuse." Robin frowned, honestly wishing he would be able to accept the invitation. "Before Governor Fiske leaves Aran, Captain Hassett wishes to have Brother Dennis Chilton guide us on a patrol of the Himlan border and Mrilan. We will be gone for the better part of a week, then after that I will have to settle my people."

"Two weeks or three, then. I shall send an invitation around to you." Grimshaw reached into his waistcoat pocket and withdrew a calling card with his name upon it. "While you are settling in here, please avail yourself of any assistance my people may be to you. Grimshaw Mercantile and Transportation, Limited, has many resources here. We very much value the sacrifice you and your men are making to be here on our behalf."

Robin accepted the card and tucked it away in his waistcoat. "Thank you, Mr. Grimshaw. And if there is anything I can do for you or your daughter, do not hesitate to send for me."

"I can think of nothing right now, Brother Robert," the old man said, "but by the time you come to Gauntlan Manor, perhaps that will have changed."

Uriah got his hands beneath himself and tried to pull away from Philo, but his strength failed him. Philo ruthlessly dragged him up into a kneeling position, then forced his head back to expose the full length of his throat. "Me knife will drink deep."

Before the man could slash his throat open, Uriah saw a bright flash up in the ship's dark hold. Kidd leaped down to the airdock, his eyes blazing incandescently behind his dark glasses. He landed nimbly, then lashed out with his walking stick. The wooden stick took on an eerie blue glow a second before it caught Philo in the side of his face. Uriah heard a sharp crack and saw one of Philo's eyes pop from the socket before he was swept from Uriah's sight. The wretched little man crumpled as if he'd been hit with an iron pole.

Uriah forced himself up, trying to regain his feet. He knew Kidd could not possibly fight the other airmen. He was blind. One lucky blow did not a fight win. *Without my help they will swarm over Kidd and kill him.* Heaving himself up, Uriah stood for a second or two, wavered, then sat down hard on Philo's chest.

Kidd fought like a man possessed. He slapped one man across the chest with his cane, knocking the burly man flying as if he were nothing more than empty clothes. A quick spin slammed the stick's silver cap into another airman's stomach, folding him in half. As that man sagged down, Kidd ducked beneath a flailed fist from another sailor. Already on one knee, Kidd shifted the stick up and around, slashing the tip into his third assailant's groin. As that man sank to his knees, Kidd snapped the stick's cap off the man's forehead, dumping him on his back.

The last man started to flee. Without turning toward him, Kidd whipped the stick back and threw it. Whirling through the air, it tangled in the running man's feet, tripping him up. The man landed face first on the deck, bounced once then crashed heavily into a crate. The man rebounded from it and rolled onto his back, with the shoulder that hit the crate looking very much misshapen.

"Uriah, where are you?"

"Here." He shook his head gently but the twin images of Kidd refused to flow together. His white-haired mentor crawled forward, hesitantly. "I'm here, sir."

Clearly orienting on the sound, Kidd worked his way toward him and followed Philo's legs up to where Uriah sat. "Are you all right? No, stupid question. How badly hurt are you?"

"Cuts, bruises. I can't see straight." Uriah kept his left hand pressed against the tear in his scalp at his hairline. With his right hand he reached down and took Philo's purse. It felt heavy enough for ten Suns, so he tucked it in his jacket's pocket. "I'm not going to be in very good shape for riding into Helansajar."

"But you've recovered enough to steal from a dead man." The disapproval in Kidd's voice stung.

Uriah winced. "He stole the money from me. I won it playing cards."

"I didn't know."

"I hid the money from you because I thought you would not have approved."

"You're right, I wouldn't have."

"Nothing wrong with gambling, is there?"

Kidd shook his head. "You have better ways to spend your time. Perhaps you'll learn from this, Cadet. Your ill-gotten gains brought you to this. And you doubted temporal punishment for crimes."

"Please, sir, I *hurt* too much for this now." He groaned to emphasize the point. "But I can still thank you for saving my life."

That appeared to surprise Kidd. The dark expression on his face lightened appreciably. "You're here because of me. You are my responsibility."

"I'll try to remember I'm here to help you, not the reverse, sir." Uriah tried to inject levity into his voice. "And I'll thank you to teach me the spell you used to fight those men."

Kidd's face closed down again. "The spell?"

Uriah felt his stomach begin to tighten as Kidd turned away from him. He had seen Kidd tear through the airmen with the ease of a giant wrestling with toddlers, yet he no longer possessed the confidence and fury that had defeated his enemies. *He's confused and . . . frightened?*

"Yes, sir, the spell. I saw your eyes glowing. Could you see the airmen?"

"See them? No, that's impossible." Kidd's brows piled up on each other in a frown. "I—I just knew where they were. Probably their breathing and footfalls—I used Philo's voice to identify his location, and yours to find you just now. When you've been blind as long as I have, you learn to sense things or memorize their locations."

Memorize a place you've never been? You were helpless when I rearranged your chess games. What is happening? "Yes, sir, that must have been it."

"Yes, sound and memory." The expression on Kidd's face told Uriah the Wolf-priest knew that answer made no sense. "Do you need medical attention?"

"I'll need some stitches in my scalp, and even if you *are* sensing things, I'll not want you to be sewing me up."

"No, I agree—though I favor cautery." Kidd smiled briefly, but his expression slackened as he stood. "Did you say my eyes were glowing?"

"Yes, sir." Uriah let Kidd help him to his feet. "What does that mean?"

"I don't know." Kidd shrugged. "But given that it accompanied my miraculous victory in the first brawl I've fought during the last twelve years, I shall assume it means we're on the right track and God wants nothing to gainsay us from saving the Dost."

— 24 —

Office of the Governor-general
Government House
Dhilica
Puresaran, Aran
3 Tempest 1687

Prince Trevelien clasped his hands together as he looked around at the colonial Ministers gathered at the conference table. He smiled cordially, but let an edge enter his voice. "Let us pray."

A number of heads came up and stared at him. That a number of the men appeared unprepared for his first words did not surprise the Prince. To open the reception the previous night, Baron Fiske had offered a cursory benediction—one that did not task his intellect to compose and did not challenge the audience with a message. *That oversight I will rectify this morning.*

"Dear Heavenly Father, though we find ourselves in a rich and delightful land, full of natural beauty and a wealth of opportunities, do not let us forget from whence we come and that Your judgment will be upon us when we die. Let us not be distracted by temporal pleasures from our duty to You, oh Lord. Let us not be tempted away from our responsibilities for the members of our flock—responsibilities that exceed those we have to ourselves. In Your Holy Name it has been said that to lay one's life down for another is the greatest love a man can show for his fellow man. Let us not forget that *all* of our actions should reflect our love for our fellow man. You are a wise, loving, and forgiving God, and we will emulate You to the best of our ability. Grant us the patience to do so and the wisdom to mete out justice where it is demanded.

"I ask this in the Name of the Father, His Son, and the spirit of the Divine Wolf.

"By Your will."

As his head came up, Trevelien was pleased to note perspiration had begun to appear on some of the shiny pates in the room. "Good morning, my lords and gentlemen." He nodded his way through returned greetings, then cut them off by slapping his left hand on the long mahogany table. "You will be seated, *now*, and I will make a statement. After that you will report to me on your activities and you will answer all questions I put to you in detail that will satisfy me."

The Ministers, all wearing frock coats, waistcoats, and cravats in somber colors, took their seats like a company of frightened schoolboys. Some tried to appear nonchalant. Others let narrowed eyes imply anger to mask their fear, but Trevelien knew the prayer and the abrupt slap had them wondering if he were insane or angry or God's vengeance incarnate.

Better they think the latter.

The Prince stripped off his own coat and hung it on the back of the chair at the end of the table. "My father admonished me that Aran was not Ilbeoria. Last evening, when Ilbeorian citizens here in Aran gave me glowing reports of Baron Fiske's administration, they made this more apparent than my father ever could have, and I set great store by my father's ability to be convincing. I saw, I heard, last night, that Aran is not Ilbeoria, and I find the fault for that perception—at least in the area of government—lies with you."

Trevelien unknotted his cravat and used it to mop sweat from his own forehead as he paced around the table. "At this moment some of you are thinking what others will think when you tell them of this meeting. This is: we have powerful friends back home. The Prince can be recalled.

"Perhaps you are correct, but you should take everything into consideration when it comes to my recall. It will take a month for you to ask your friends to recall me, and a month for that recall to come back here. Then it will take another good month for my appeal of that order to reach Ludstone and then another month for my father or my brother to come and physically remove me from office. Four months before you are rid of me, gentlemen, Tempest, Majest, Autumbre, and Tenebre.

"In four months I can break and beggar all of you."

He stopped abruptly and pointed at a scarecrow man who had grinned at his last remark. "So, you think you have amassed too much in bribes for me to make you a pauper, Lord Farnham?"

The man's grin turned to a horrible grimace. "No, Highness, I was thinking of the reaction of others to your actions. Their arrogance melting to the heat of your resolve."

"Ah, of this I am certain." Unbuttoning the cuffs of his white linen shirt, he rolled his sleeves up to his elbows. "I know that under Baron Fiske, and under the Governor-generals before him, favors have been returned for favors. I know many of you have profited from various enterprises that go against the interest of Ilbeoria and the Martinist Church. That will stop now."

His circuit having once again brought him to the head of the table, the Prince opened his hands. "Let your people know I am quite serious about arresting corruption in Aran. If a colonial officer, administrator, or clerk takes a bribe and circumvents regulations, he is committing treason. If someone offers him a bribe to overlook violations, that too is an act of treason. Any offer of a bribe to permit, condone, approve, or conceal an unlawful act is treason and shall be dealt with accordingly. Am I understood?"

The dozen Ministers gathered around the table nodded solemnly. Smiling, Prince Trevelien pulled his chair out and seated himself. "Very good. You should also understand that I intend to hold everyone in this government responsible for actions taken before I assumed this office. At the same time, I will prepare for each of you a full and complete pardon. It will be given to you contingent upon two things: your continuation at your post and a full, accurate report on the covert and overt ways this Crown Colony functions. I realize you might be very reluctant to implicate individuals in crimes. I would point out to you that Ilbeorian law allows for some or all of a traitor's property to be rewarded to the patriot who brought the treason to the attention of authorities."

Trevelien let them sit in silence for a minute, considering what he had said. The lot of them were thieves, but they were thieves who happened to know the identities and methods of operation of all the other thieves in Aran. Promising them pardons in return for their cooperation did seem like a subversion of justice, but Trevelien had no doubt God would exact a greater punishment from them than *he* could ever threaten.

Some of them, he knew, would accept his offer and then try to profit in spite of it. Others, he hoped, would become his men body and soul. The conflict between those two groups and the thieves outside government would make his reign difficult, but the job was never meant to be an easy one. By daring to challenge those who saw themselves as the real power in Aran, he had a chance at making the changes that would keep Aran in the empire.

"Well, if no one feels an urge to resign and return to Ilbeoria, we may proceed." The Prince smiled, then sat back in his chair. "You have a month to prepare your reports or your resignations. Today, just tell me the most pressing and important things I need to know to govern here."

— 25 —

Breathing in through the myrrh-scented handkerchief blocked much of the odor of sizzling human flesh, but Vasily Arzlov had taken no precautions to mute the Estanuan's screams; though he had long since stopped being bothered by them. As in the interrogations of the other captured warriors, vocal chords ceased producing the most penetrating tones after the first hour of screaming.

The torturer returned the iron to the fire, the flesh on it flaring up for a moment, then looked up at the officer serving as interpreter. The interpreter, in turn, looked toward the Duke. "I believe, my lord, we will learn nothing more from this man."

Arzlov nodded, then waved the victim and the torturer away with his white handkerchief. "Very well. Kill him and dispose of him with others."

The torturer nodded and bent to the task of throttling the Estanuan while Arzlov slowly rose from his chair. The long hours spent in the close chamber had allowed his muscles to stiffen. The wound on his thigh pulsed with pain, but Arzlov had chosen to ignore it. The Estanuan sword had only cut skin, not muscle, so he decided the pain was out of proportion with the damage done. After having it washed and sewn shut, he had put the wound out of his mind.

Lieutenant Vorobiga opened the chamber's door and stood by in case the Duke had difficulty negotiating his way up the stairs. Arzlov appreciated that much insight in a junior officer and liked the fact that Vorobiga knew enough to wait to be asked to render aid. *This means you are thinker, Anatoly, and I have uses for thinkers.* "Walk with me, Lieutenant. You will remember things I may not."

"At your service, my lord."

Arzlov nodded, then began the arduous journey up the steps to

ground level in his castle. The weight of the information produced
from the Estanuans who had survived the attack burdened him more
than his wounded leg, but deep down inside he knew he would overcome both things. *My leg sooner than what I heard, no doubt.*

The survivors had been surprisingly forthcoming about the
raid. Some of them had almost gloated about it. That annoyed Arzlov because that meant they truly believed what they were telling
him. Their arrogance continued even under torture, confirming their
belief that the Dost had returned to Alansajar.

The Dost's return was something every Stranan had been
taught to fear as he grew up. Evil children were told they would be
harvested at night to feed the Dost's appetite for human flesh. Jebel
Quirana supposedly hid a doorway to Hell—every child believed
that as fervently as he believed Eilyph would someday appear in
Murom to herald the end of the world. Even Fernandi's threat to the
nation of Strana had not been seen to be as dire as that of the Dost
because the Dost had *succeeded* in conquering Strana already.
The Stranans opposing the Lescari host had taken fierce pride in the
fact that *only* Keerana Dost had conquered their nation and they
fought as hard to preserve his legend and his blood-descendants'
right to rule Strana as they did to save their homeland.

And the Dost clearly had helped defeat the Lescari host. The
Vandari, all three hundred of them, had been effective in occupying
Fernandi. While the Vandari nipped at his northern flank, Arzlov
and the 137th Imperial Bear Hussars had been able to repeatedly
penetrate the Lescari line and force a retreat. In pitched battles the
introduction of a single Vandari company had been enough to get
the Lescaris to retire from the field.

The Dost's return would be a disaster, both for Strana and
Vasily Arzlov. *Why now?* His plans had been going very well. He
knew he could count on Khrolic to lead the Hussars in the conquest
of Helor. Arzlov had no doubt Grigory believed he would turn south
and go after Aran next, but what Khrolic believed had absolutely
nothing to do with what Arzlov would do once Helor was his.

The presence of the Dost, whether he was truly the Dost or one
of myriad pretenders who had arisen over the years in central Estanu, would make things far more difficult. The most successful pretender, Arzlov remembered, had started in Drangiana four hundred
years earlier. Pandit Dost had turned south and had conquered most
of Aran. He established the Varatha Empire, remnants of which still
existed in Ilbeorian vassal states like Mrilan and Manaran.

The Dost could unite the tribes of central Estanu and organize
stiff resistance to the Hussars. If the Dost managed to do just that,

Arzlov's plans would collapse. His success demanded a swift and efficient campaign to take Helor. From there he would return to Strana and ride a groundswell of pride in his accomplishment into the Tacier's throne. That there would be opposition he did not doubt, but he knew he could neutralize any military forces arrayed against him through mutiny, bribery, or force of arms.

The Duke turned to look back at the subaltern following him. "All prisoners claimed to be Khasts or allied with Rafiq Khast, *da?*"

"*Da*, my lord. They took pride in it."

"*Spasib.*" During the interrogations, Arzlov had thought it odd that the prisoners traced their connection to the Dost through the Khast family. Those who were members of the family had told a fanciful tale of a man made of gold speaking to them in the mountains while all the allies told distorted versions of the same story. He had noted that those who claimed to have seen the Dost themselves had greater resistance to the pain inflicted on them, again verifying the depth of their belief in the story they told.

Identification of the Khast family both gratified and worried Arzlov. The Tacier knew the Khasts would be capable of raising a pretender to the Dost's throne, and a pretender would be quite a threat to Strana. Khast involvement meant the situation in Helansajar was deteriorating, but Arzlov was there to keep things under control. Requests for additional troops might even be granted because of this new information.

The fact that Rafiq was not operating in the logical manner he had been lead to believe was characteristic of the man did disturb Arzlov. The Duke would have seen Rafiq's choosing to proclaim *himself* the Dost as a brilliant political move. The fact that Rafiq subordinated himself to the Dost lent credence to the claim that the Dost had returned. Unless Rafiq planned to use a false Dost to inflame people, then have the Dost proclaim Rafiq his agent in Alansajar, Arzlov saw no way for Rafiq to benefit from the Dost's appearance.

Perhaps Rafiq himself has been deceived into believing this Dost is genuine. A couple of the victims had said their attack was meant to occupy the Hussars while Rafiq and others kidnapped the merchant Valentin Svilik on the Dost's orders. Svilik's home had been searched and his servant had been questioned, but neither action resulted in any clues about Svilik's location. Svilik had gone missing before, but not without someone knowing where he was headed or whom he was seeing. The prisoners had said the Dost had asked for a Stranan who spoke Estanuan, but Arzlov didn't see a merchant as exactly the sort of information source he would want when planning a military campaign.

Perhaps the Dost's time in the grave has weakened his mind.

The effect of reports about the raid and rumored return of the Dost would be explosive in Murom. If an expedition were organized to find and kill the Dost, Arzlov knew he would not be at its head. The Tacier would undoubtedly consult the Wolf-King about destroying the threat to their mutual holdings in Estanu. Prince Trevelien's presence in Aran provided a logical choice for an expedition leader. *Put Wolves in Helansajar and they will never leave.*

Regardless of the threat posed by the Dost—and Arzlov refused to believe he *had* returned—allowing the news of the raid and the threat to Tachotha Natalya to reach Murom would be suicidal. Arzlov's enemies would use the attack to show he could not be trusted with a backwater command. He would be said to be a shadow of the man who had driven Fernandi from Strana and the Tacier would take the threat to his daughter as a personal insult. Arzlov would be removed from Vzorin, stripped of power and rank, then stationed in Murumyskda. His final days would be spent staring across the Boreal Straits at the frozen tip of North Brendania.

Arzlov limped from the dungeon stairs into a marble foyer with a vaulted ceiling and one each of four columns in the corners. He turned and smiled at Vorobiga. "Lieutenant, I want you to take a squad of your men and seal off the airdock north of Vzorin. All flight from Vzorin is suspended until we can determine that the attack last night was not part of a plot to kill Tachotha Natalya and overthrow her father."

The man frowned for a moment and glanced back toward the dungeon, then nodded. "It shall be as you ordered, sir."

"Also, you will tell no one what you heard down there. This Estanuan fantasy will probably be coursing through the rumorstream in Old Town soon enough, but I believe the story is merely an attempt by Helansajaran elements to prompt a popular revolt here. We shall give it no currency."

"Yes, my lord."

"Good. Before you go to the airdock, find Pokovnik Khrolic for me." Arzlov smiled grandly. "Ask him to see me once Tachotha Natalya no longer requires his presence. There is a minor matter upon which I would like his opinion."

— 26 —

Clad in a gray cotton tunic, liturgical-purple pants, and black boots, Robin Drury joined Captain Hassett and Brother Dennis Chilton on the *Saint Michael*'s wing deck. At the forward railing Acolyte Foster stood beside the helmsman—a strapping fellow named Sorrell—and kept an eye on the compass as the ship slowly rose away from Dhilica. Deep in the bowels of the ship the steam engines thundered and the twin propellers dissipated the boiler's black smoke.

"Coming about to 315 degrees, sir."

"Very good, Mr. Foster. Steady as she goes." Hassett clasped his hands behind his back, hiding the gold stars on the cuffs of his cardinal jacket. "I believe the advantage height offers us will enhance your geography lesson, Mr. Chilton."

"Yes, sir. As I was pointing out on the map below, Dhilica is located in the heart of the northern part of Aran. It is the capital of the state of Puresaran and through the ages has been the seat of many dynasties and kingdoms." Chilton pointed down at the brown snake of a river undulating through the Dhil Valley. "The Hianura River carries silt down from the Himlans to the north and from the Decaran Plateau to the south. It floods every winter, laying down a new layer of fresh earth. This is why the Dhil Valley is probably the most fertile valley in the world."

Robin looked up from the river north to the snowcapped peaks of the Himlan Mountains. The chain ran in a jagged line from the southern border of Tsaih far to the east all the way to the Jedrosian border in the west. In his travels Robin had seen all manner of mountains, from the Ferrines between Ilbeoria and Merida, to the mountainous spine of Jedrosia. Magnificent though those mountains might have been, compared to the Himlans, all other mountains were hillocks with pretensions. The Himlans' sharp faces and the way huge sheets of snow clung to the peaks made them forbidding and yet majestic at the same time.

Chilton continued his explanation. "The Himlans have watered the valley and have kept it safe from invaders. Further west, near the headwaters of the Ajmur, there is a pass leading north and another even further east that allows Jedrosian renegades to raid in Mrilan from time to time. That pass is called the Khac Pass, from the Jedrosian word for *dust*. The northern pass is the Varatha Pass."

"Named after the empire?"

"Yes, Captain. The empire is also the source of the name for the more dangerous section of Dhilica itself." Chilton nodded to the port side of the airship. "The Varathans largely inhabit Mrilan now, though a solid population of them lives in Dhilica. They are mostly Ataraxians, but there is an undercurrent of Laamti in their version of the religion. The Mrilani Princes have been very friendly to us and Frontier Guard units drawn from Mrilan are the most effective troops we have here."

Robin absorbed that with a nod. "What sort of trouble can we expect on our patrol?"

Chilton shrugged his shoulders. "Not much, really. The countryside is rugged and the people are relatively poor, so they have nothing to steal. This does not prevent bandit bands from forming and raiding, but that usually happens in the fall or spring after the harvest or after calving time. Most often the bandits prey on trade routes, but the Frontier troops are good at hunting those raiders down and killing them.

"The most consistent threat to Ilbeorians and Urovians here comes from Ghur nationalists and religious extremists. The Ghurs have chafed under our rule and their new ruler, Prince Agra-sho, is using anti-Ilbeorian sentiment to keep his people from deposing him. Fortunately for us he only holds sway in the Himlans and doesn't have that much influence in most of Aran.

"Closer to home things can be a bit more explosive. About a year ago in Dhilica an intoxicated Ilbeorian bludgeoned a flatulent cow to death and that almost sparked a riot. Some Eilyphian missions in outlying areas have been harassed, but nothing dire. I think the fanatics are waiting for the fabled return of the Dost before they try to murder us all."

Hassett frowned. "I was under the impression the Dost had never included Aran in his empire. Why would Aranans be looking forward to his return?"

"Keerana Dost's troops did raid down here, and local kings swore fealty to him, but he did not hold power here as he did in

Strana, Estanu, and Tsaih, so your point is well taken, Captain. It's really the Varathans who want his return. They formed their empire under the leadership of someone who claimed to be the Dost, so they have that history. And they are mostly believers in Ataraxianism. The Dost was seen as an avatar of Atarax when he was here the first time. It all gets tied up together, but I do not think the threat posed is very serious. While the Varathans do hold themselves as different from the majority of Aranans, they would not want to anger Ilbeoria by staging an open revolt."

"Why not, Mr. Chilton?" Robin looked out at either side of the ship. "It's a beautiful country, well worth fighting for."

Chilton nodded in agreement. "There are two reasons why a revolt is unlikely. During the days of the Varathan Empire, each official, noble, and warrior drew his yearly income based on the productivity of a land grant. Half the money raised for the produce would be sent to the Varathan Emperor and half would go to the officeholder who collected it. In order to prohibit any officeholder from garnering too much power, his salary would come from an area well away from where he served the empire, and land grants were redistributed every four years on the basis of merit.

"When we arrived, we changed the system so each official drew his income from the area in which he served. This tied him to the land, and since we allowed his holding to be passed on to his children, guarantees of his family's prosperity were contingent upon the loyalty of the family to Ilbeorian authorities. This landed class of people owe their prosperity to us and they are not wont to forget it."

"That's one reason, Mr. Chilton, and a good one. What is the other?"

"Two years ago some Ghur bandits were marauding in eastern Mrilan. They used an old, abandoned Laamti monastery as a stronghold. Baron Fiske sent the *Kestrel* up from Dhilica to deal with them. We flew up and did four ovals, two north of it and two south. We hit it with all our midguns and put sixty shots into it. Reduced the monastery to rubble. That was a lesson many Aranan nobles took to heart."

Hassett nodded appreciatively. "I can understand how they might have indeed done that."

Chilton smiled. "Yes, sir. The display would have been even more impressive with the *Saint Michael*."

"With luck, we will not need to use such a display, Mr. Chilton." Hassett looked off to the east. "As I understand it this northern patrol takes us south of Dughur, along the Himlans to the

Bay of Vlengul, then down and around past Dhilica to patrol the
northeast reaches of the Dhil Valley."

"It has every time I've been on it, sir."

Robin caught resignation in Chilton's voice and saw Hassett
raise an eyebrow. "I don't know about you, sir, but I would certainly
like more of an explanation of that reply."

Hassett smiled. "You may speak freely, Mr. Chilton. You sound
disappointed about the course of the patrol."

Chilton drew in a deep breath, then frowned. "It is no secret,
sir, that there is a fair amount of smuggling that goes on here in
Aran. The patrol route dips south and returns through the middle of
the country because Baron Fiske ordered it to be that way. Our pass
from east to west is enough to scare off bandits, and in our wake, a
lot of little ethyrskiffs head out to trade. Until now, with the supreme
authority in the country being a man who very much wanted to
curry favor with wealthy merchants, there was nothing I could do to
enforce the laws of Ilbeoria. Perhaps, Captain, to get your Aeromancers accustomed to the winds around the Himlans, you would
want to turn at the bay and come back along this route."

"I shall take that under advisement, Mr. Chilton, thank you."
Hassett patted the rail of the ship. "We'll reach the bay in three days
at this rate. If these merchants make decisions with the same skill
they use at whist, a return trip by the mountains might well be a
profitable gamble."

— 27 —

Varatha Quarter,
Dhilica
Puresaran, Aran
5 Tempest 1687

Uriah awoke with a start as two squabbling monkeys dashed past
his shuttered window then thundered over the roof. It took him several seconds to collect himself enough to remember where he was,
what he was doing there, and why he hurt so much. Rolling over
onto his side, he slowly levered himself into a sitting position.
Fighting dizziness, he turned the wick up on the night-table lamp
with his left hand.

As yellow light flooded the room he saw Kidd sitting across from him in a broken-armed chair. The accommodations at the Wilton Hotel lacked youth and structural integrity, but Captain Ollis had assured them the owner was discreet when he wasn't drunk, and couldn't remember anything when he wasn't sober. He got them a room there and told them to remain in it until he got back to Dhilica.

Uriah glanced at the window and saw reddish light bleeding in from the west. "Getting to be evening, is it, sir?"

Kidd nodded. "How do you feel?"

"Fine."

"I can't believe that, Cadet. You took a severe beating."

Uriah winced. *It hurts too much to try to keep up any pretense.* "I don't feel as bad as I . . . look, I imagine. Ribs are still tender and my nose is sore. I'm one big bruise." Uriah hesitated for a second, then leaned forward with his elbows on his knees. "Do you think it is wise for us to be waiting here on Captain Ollis?"

"He'll come back, Mr. Smith. He may be a Wroxterman, but he'll be as good as his word this time."

If his crew hasn't killed him by now. Ollis had followed Kidd from his cabin and had seen the blind Wolf-priest dispatch five of the crew. Ollis realized he could be in serious trouble for his crew having assaulted a Wolf-priest and his first temptation had been to run. Unfortunately for him most of the rest of his crew—six Aeromancers, a navigator, and a helmsman—were exhausted. In trying to convince them to try to get the *Stoat* up and flying again, he'd learned that the men Kidd had laid out had been bullying the rest of the crew. Led by Philo, the four cargomen were planning to kill Ollis and take his ship for their own.

Realizing that Kidd had saved his life, Ollis found them the room at the Wilton and arranged with an Aranan family to bring them food. He disposed of Philo's body, dismissed Philo's companions, and hired new cargomen in some of the dockside taverns in the Varatha Quarter. Ollis said he was bound to deliver his cargo "up north," but he promised to return and help them do whatever work it was they were doing in Aran.

"I'm not inclined to trust him." Uriah started to stretch, but the pain in his shoulders and ribs made him abandon that plan. "He has to have guessed you're a Wolf-priest and he knows we know he's a smuggler. Disposing of us as he did Philo's body would save him a lot of trouble."

"Captain Ollis is not willing to accept the consequences of murder."

"But smuggling a steam engine out of Ilbeoria is already a capital crime. You can only hang a man once."

"I referred to the *eternal* consequences, Cadet." Kidd slowly exhaled. "He knows he can escape the hangman in this world, but eluding God is impossible. Ollis may not respect Ilbeorian law, but he holds God's laws a bit more dear."

"You're right. I remember about his son and Saint Swithin's Day." Uriah scratched at the crusted scab on his scalp. "I'm sorry for delaying our departure."

"You were savagely beaten. You're young, you'll heal quickly, but you need rest." The blind man hesitated, then sat forward. "Regardless, I had not planned much beyond getting here to Aran. I had intended for us to purchase horses and provisions, but Captain Ollis pointed out difficulties with riding from here to Helor."

"It would take us two months to make the trip on horseback, with the mountains to cross, and about six days for the *Saint Michael* at full speed."

Kidd raised an eyebrow. "I was not aware you were awake during my discussion with him."

Uriah shook his head, then stopped as the room began to wobble. "I figured it out as part of the tactics project. I assumed Irons would assume I didn't know that stuff."

"And you were set to ambush him?"

"I was planning to exceed his expectations of me."

"Interesting euphemism for *ambush*, Cadet." Kidd grinned in appreciation and Uriah would have smiled if it hadn't hurt to do so. "Captain Ollis indicated there are bandits who operate throughout that area and he says even attempting the trip to Helansajar without guides would be impossible."

"What is the plan now?"

"Captain Ollis trades regularly with a village a good way up into the Varatha Pass. He believes we can get a good head start from there and he's willing to take us with him when he makes his next run. He can even get us local guides. A week or less traveling north from there would put us in Drangiana, with another two to Helor."

The bed creaked as Uriah shifted his weight in a vain attempt to get comfortable. "Have you told Ollis you have come to save the Dost?"

"He is not my Confessor." Kidd's eyes narrowed. "I have led him to believe we are on a mission to convert the Alanim of Helor."

"But Martinist Warrior-priests don't do missionary work and only have limited authorization to perform the Sacraments. We can only baptize and give last rites." Uriah snorted. "On our mission at least one of those should be useful."

"Keep your comments away from blasphemy, if you don't mind, Mr. Smith." Kidd shrugged. "Captain Ollis's knowledge of the intricacies of the Church is weak and might have contributed to a misunderstanding of our mission. Still, he does know even a lay member of the Church may perform a baptism in times of need, so he is not inclined to question what I have said."

"Well, then, blessed is he who furthers the Lord's work."

"You should not mock him or God, Mr. Smith." Kidd's face became a mask of resolve. "Captain Ollis, engaging in illegal commerce against Church and State, needs all the blessing he can get. His ignorance will save his soul. That it will also save the Dost is not a matter for his concern."

— 28 —

Pyimoc
Vzorin, Vzorin Military District
Strana
5 Tempest 1687

So lost in thought was Natalya Ohanscai that she did not realize she was not alone until she turned from the window and discovered a man standing just inside the doorway. It took her a couple more seconds to register his presence and even longer to realize who he was.

A ringlet of hair trailing from her index finger, Natalya covered her surprise with a smile. "Grigory, it is you."

"Yes, darling." He looked back at the door. "I knocked and called to you, but I heard no reply. I would not have intruded, but after what happened when you arrived . . . I did not want to chance another Helansajaran attack."

"Do not apologize for your concern about me. It makes me happy and drives fear away." She began coiling dark hair around her finger again. "Come, sit, I have something to discuss with you."

Natalya had been given a right-angle suite of rooms on one of the fortress's third-floor corners. Grigory had entered into the sitting room and, at her invitation, moved toward the couch in front of the fireplace on the suite's interior wall. That hearth opened on the other side to provide heat to the master bedroom. A small room for Polina sat opposite the bedroom's expansive closet and dressing area, sandwiched between the sitting room and the master bedroom.

The Tachotha sat opposite him on the couch, turning to press her back against the scrolled arm. Grigory leaned forward as if to sit closer, then stopped as if he sensed the seriousness of whatever she was going to say. "Grigory, I have been told, albeit politely and properly, that the *Leshii* is now under Duke Arzlov's command and that I am not allowed to report to my father about what has happened here. This has me very worried."

"Talya, you should not worry. Duke Arzlov, he has reasons for what he has done—"

She held a hand up to prevent Grigory from continuing. "Please, Grigory, I know you do not mean to patronize me, but you are preparing to tell me that Duke Arzlov's reasoning makes sense from a military viewpoint. I will not accept that. I am trying to think of his reasons, to puzzle out his mind in this, and I cannot. This is why I am worried."

Grigory's denial of her first sentence died. His mouth closed and he glanced down at the couch. *I've hurt him.* Natalya wanted to reach out to him, to let him know that she was not angry with him, but his closeness would distract her from the concerns she felt compelled to share with him.

"Grigory, Helansajarans organized an attack here, in Vzorin, on Pyimoc. Even had I not been here, this would be serious. With Duke Arzlov preventing reports from going back to Murom, I am given to wonder if other attacks like this have gone unreported."

The blond Hussars officer shook his head. "I give you my word, Natalya, as an officer in the Imperial Armed Forces and as a man who loves you, that there have been no other attacks like this."

"Of which you are aware."

Grigory frowned for a second, then nodded. "Of which I am aware. But I would stake my reputation on being aware of any and all attacks against our forces since I have been here. This was unprecedented."

She sighed. "If no other attacks like this have taken place, why will Duke Arzlov not send a report back to my father? Is he hiding something?"

"Natalya, I know you are not stupid. I also know you do not trust Duke Arzlov." Grigory's broad shoulders sagged slightly. "Please do not let your lack of trust of him blind you to his intelligence and his true love for Strana."

Her denial of his words died in a frustrated nod. "You are correct, Grigory, my love."

"Duke Arzlov has his reasons, Natalya. First and foremost among them is his inability to learn who was behind this attempted assassination of you."

She frowned. "I thought you knew. Helansajarans attacked. You have prisoners, they can be questioned."

"They *have* been questioned. They acknowledged being led by a Helansajaran chieftain, but none of them knew who might have been behind him."

"Ask them again; they may have remembered something else."

Grigory shook his head. "It is too late for that."

"They have been murdered?"

"Please, Natalya, do not jump to conclusions." Grigory breathed in slowly, flaring his nostrils, then gave her a level, hazel-eyed stare. "Helansajarans—actually *all* Estanuans—are a primitive people. They worship a foul, dark god. They understand life and death, but none of the gradations in between them. These prisoners were questioned then slain and their bodies were left in Old Town. With them we sent a loud message to Rafiq Khast and his allies. They will know better than to attack us again."

"But they were slain without benefit of trial."

"Natalya, dearest, think what you are saying. They tried to *murder* you. Hundreds of our best citizens and bravest soldiers saw them. Of their guilt there was no doubt. A trial means that in one week or two we would have found them guilty and had them executed. If convicted of trying to kill a child of the Tacier they would have been beheaded and then burned. By returning them to Old Town we warned others against making the same mistake. *Swift* justice is understood by the Estanuan mind; formalities of a trial are little more than a game for them. This was a better way to deal with the problem."

Natalya frowned heavily. "I cannot believe anyone would have motive to assassinate me."

"Perhaps not, Natalya, but would someone have motive to have you assassinated here, in Vzorin?"

"What are you saying?"

Grigory smiled. "Natalya, you are beloved by your father and at court. Were you to die here, in an attack that took place at Duke Arzlov's castle, his reputation would be destroyed—and that is the best that could come of it. If your father did not order him executed for incompetence, he would strip him of his rank and exile him to Murumyskda to guard rotting fishheads. Arzlov's accomplishments against Fernandi would be forgotten. This man who has very much to offer our nation would be disgraced and discarded. He is too valuable to let that happen."

He glanced back at the door, then scooted forward on the couch and lowered his voice. "I have spoken with Arzlov. He believes it is possible that this attack on you was engineered by Ilbeoria. The Wolf-priests have no love for Duke Arzlov and only his presence here prevents them from driving north through the Himlans to attack us. If he is discredited—and many men at court in Murom would love to have that happen—he will be removed from Vzorin. Anyone replacing him would be less competent than he. Prince Trevelien is now Governor-general in Aran and he brought with him the warship *Saint Mikhail*."

"But this is impossible." Grigory's low, conspiratorial whispers tickled remembrances of Marina's warnings about him. *Could Grigory be plotting himself? No, not possible.* "How could the Wolf-priests have known of my arrival?"

Grigory shrugged as if the question had no merit. "It is enough they knew of your trip here last year and had news you were planning another. As you saw by the number of people waiting to welcome you, your arrival was not a well-kept secret. All the Wolf-priests had to do was set a bounty on your head and the Helansajarans would track your progress themselves and kill you."

Natalya raked both hands through her hair. The scenario Grigory presented had a logic that was seductive. It was plausible, but created such a large conspiracy that she could not believe it was true. Prince Trevelien's placement in Aran could have been accomplished for any of a host of reasons, yet in this plan it was to press for the conquest of Strana from the south.

She realized many of her countrymen feared such a thing, but she thought it very unlikely. She didn't think it was any remnant of her feelings for Malachy that made her reject the idea of an Ilbeorian plot. Ilbeoria, with its superior industrial base, would force Strana into concessions eventually, so such an overt act made no sense. *Then again, perhaps because it makes no sense, it has merit since it would be unexpected.*

It seemed obvious to her that Grigory believed this scenario largely because he had heard it from Duke Arzlov. She had no doubt that Grigory held Arzlov in high esteem, but she also knew that Grigory knew better than to accept everything Arzlov said without question.

"Grigory, I think your concern for me has blinded you to a very basic flaw with this scenario. Recall Saint Kristov's Axiom: apples on the ground likely grew in the branches of the tree beneath which they lie."

"What do you mean, Natalya?"

"Simple explanations are best, Grigory. Duke Arzlov is correct— news of an attack would be devastating to his position at court, but this is true regardless of that attack being part of a plot or just a random attack against a target with assumed value. Since we need not presume a conspiracy for this to embarrass Duke Arzlov, it is best to discount the presence of a conspiracy. These actions Duke Arzlov has taken are to protect his own reputation and to presume otherwise is to blind ourselves to reasons why he wishes to maintain his reputation."

"He does not want to lose his post here."

"Yes, Grigory, but why? We all know he is wasting away here. Everyone expects him to do something that will enhance his position. If this attack embarrasses him before he has put his plans into effect, he is doomed."

Grigory's face slackened for a moment, then his eyes narrowed. His voice became a whisper. "If you are correct, what do you think he will do?"

Natalya lowered her voice to match his. "I believe he will use your Hussars to strike at Helor. Moving now, he would be able to take it before Ilbeoria could push troops up from Aran to oppose him. Since winter will leave Strana before it will leave the Himlans, we will be able to reinforce Helor in spring before the Ilbeorians can move."

She did not add that she felt Arzlov would use the acclaim from his victory and any reinforcements put under his command to try to force her father from his throne. *Grigory might believe Arzlov wants glory, but then desiring to be Tacier is something Grigory could never understand.*

The Hussars' commander nodded slowly. "Then if he asks me about invading Helansajar, we shall know his game."

"And you will report it to me, so I may report it to my father."

"Of course, my love. That goes without saying."

"Good, Grigory, very good." Natalya leaned forward and kissed him on the cheek. *And something else that goes without saying is this: as much as I love you, Grigory, I love Strana more. Fail me, fail your nation and support Arzlov, and I shall be forced to see to your destruction.*

29

Though the Khast camp had settled into its nighttime routine, Rafiq Khast felt the evening was somehow different. Tension filled the air and Rafiq was able to attribute some of it to their captive. Valentine Svilik had seen an airship silhouetted against the waning full moon and assumed his countrymen were out looking for him. Though the airship did represent a flying abomination to him, Rafiq did not fear it. Eventually it would return to Vzorin for more supplies and even well before then he expected his band to have eluded it.

The group's calm confidence in the Dost and his ability to deal with any possible problem seemed to both amuse and frighten Svilik. His amusement came from what he'd described to Rafiq as Helansajaran innocence—especially in light of their complete belief in the Dost. "Even you, Rafiq, as shrewd and far-thinking a man as there is in Helansajar today, has surrendered your future to the Dost. You have been as wily a foe as Shukri Awan could have, but now your faith in the Dost has made you a mindless tool."

Rafiq easily understood how his unquestioned devotion to the Dost scared Valentin. The Stranan did not know who or what this Dost was supposed to be—and no Stranan could allow himself to believe the Dost had actually returned. For Svilik, the fact that the Khasts believed so fervently meant that an attack from central Estanu against Strana was close to becoming reality. *Were I threatened with my homeland being conquered by warriors who are led by the Dost, I, too, would know fear.*

At the moment, though, Rafiq felt he had very little cause for fear. Reports from backriders indicated they had not been pursued from Vzorin. There was rejoicing in this, and mourning for those of their number who had died at the airdock, but little reaction beyond that. The company had remained alert while they were still in the Vzorin Military District, but once they were back on their home soil, the Helansajarans relaxed as if they were a continent away from Strana and immune to attack. *Things are going well, in full accord with the Dost's plan.*

Seated in front of a small tent, Svilik raised his bound hands and accepted a bowl of tea from Rafiq Khast. "Thank you," he said in Estanuan.

"You are welcome, Valentin." Rafiq squatted on his haunches next to the Stranan. "You have been quiet. Are you angry your people have not come for you yet?"

"No, I have been trying to puzzle out how a man like you can have been deceived into believing the Dost has returned. How you can have so much faith in him."

Rafiq raised an eyebrow, then slowly smoothed his moustache with his right hand. "I have been waiting for this to happen all my life, Valentin. The faith I show in him is fully his due."

"I am trained to observe, Rafiq." Svilik nodded toward the men sitting at the fire in the middle of the ravine where they camped. "Your men show no discipline. You have not posted pickets. You light fires though you know the *Leshii* is up there, watching. You are not acting as I would expect you would."

The Helansajaran smiled slowly. "Ah, I understand your dismay. There is a reason for this, but one you would not believe because you are an infidel."

Svilik sipped his tea, then frowned, "Do not insult me, my friend. Yes, I am an Eilyphianist, but am I not also knowledgeable about the *Kitabna Ittikal*?"

"Knowledge is not belief."

"Lack of belief is not ignorance."

"This is true, Valentin." Rafiq looked up and pointed in a lazy circle around the campsite. "Do you see anything special about this place?"

"It is suitable for çamping, less so for defending, but acceptable."

"I have seen this place before, Valentin."

"As I would expect of one who makes his home in Helansajar."

Rafiq shook his head. "No, I have seen it, as it is now, before this night. I have seen it like this every night we have been riding from Vzorin. We are meant to be here this night."

Svilik again drank from the cup of bitter tea and frowned with concentration. "I know that you believe Atarax speaks to you through your dreams. The story of how the Dost appeared to you strikes me as very dreamlike in its aspects."

"You think we all shared this dream, imagined all this?"

Valentin nodded. "I must consider that as an answer."

"Because, if the incident is true, the Dost is clearly invested with incredible power. You cannot allow yourself to think that."

"No, I cannot." The Stranan looked at Rafiq. "Why are we meant to be here this night?"

The Helansajaran pointed up into the night sky. "Behold."

Svilik looked up. At first, his face registered nothing. The stars twinkled in the blackness, but then a golden speck streaked through the sky. Even Rafiq first thought it was a shooting star, then it approached the *Leshii*'s dark form and spiraled around it before swooping down toward the campsite. As it did so, Svilik's mouth gaped open.

A golden harpylike creature with the head and body of a man but bat wings in place of arms descended through the sky to their little valley. As it came close, Svilik's hair streamed back as the air displaced by the flapping of its wings buffeted him. He blinked in clear astonishment as the figure stopped moving through the air and just stood there, six feet above the campfire, as if the air had become solid beneath his feet. Silver highlights flashed from the tiger-striping on its torso and limbs, then the wings withdrew as the fingers shrank and a normal man replaced the monstrosity that had been there seconds before.

The tea bowl fell from Svilik's hands. "He is made of metal!"

Rafiq stood and shrugged. "He is the Dost."

The gold man started toward Svilik, stepping down as if on an invisible stairway. He reached the ground a man-length away, but his footfalls made no sound. He looked down at Svilik and, even though the Dost had no eyes per se, the Stranan reacted to the gilded stare as if he'd had someone reach into his chest and grab his heart.

A shiver shook the Stranan. "Who are you?"

The gold man's head came up. *"Minya zavoot Nimchin. Ya Dost."*

Svilik's face fell as the Dost answered him in Stranan. "Have you truly returned?"

"Da, Valentin Svilik." The Dost nodded slowly and reached his left hand out. He touched Svilik on the crown of his head. Rafiq thought the gesture gentle, almost paternal, and it won a smile from the captive. Then the man's face slackened, and his eyes closed peacefully.

Rafiq Khast stepped back for a moment as the Dost's flesh flowed like water over the huddled Stranan. For several seconds he could see Valentin's outline, then the gold liquid appeared to become more solid. The form of a seated man disappeared as the gold flesh hardened into the shape of an egg.

The Dost kept his hand pressed to the top of it. "You have done well to bring Valentin Svilik to me, Rafiq Khast."

"We ask only to serve, my lord." Rafiq nodded toward the egg. "Had we known what you desired, we would have only brought his head. How had he offended you?"

The Dost shook his head slowly. "He gave me no offense. He is not dead. He will be of use to me, as you are, but not of as great use."

The gold man gestured at the ground as if using his open right hand to smash a stinging scorpion against the earth. The ground trembled as if a great weight had been slammed into it, and a little dust cloud rose out of the dry gravel between Rafiq and the Dost. As it settled back down, Rafiq saw the gravel and sand had been pressed into a three-dimensional map of central Arala.

A brilliant ruby the size of Rafiq's thumb stuck out of the ground from their approximate location. The Dost gestured. The ruby toppled over and inched along through the central Helansajaran valley, past Helor and Jebel Quirana, to a point in the Drangianan highlands, the northern foothills of the Himlans. "Do you know where this is?"

Rafiq shook his head. "I have never traveled that far south, my lord. In that area a Ghur bandit, Haytham Kasi, and his people range far and wide. He styles himself the lord of the Varatha Pass and collects to him warriors who pick over villages and caravans like jackals. We do not fear him, but only a fool goads a rabid dog without reason."

"I require you go to this place."

"Then this is reason enough." Rafiq nodded solemnly. "We shall do this gladly, Nimchin Dost. Shall we go alone, or may we share the glory of destroying Haytham Kasi with other Helansajaran brethren?"

"My purposes would be better served if only your band goes, but I will not send you out to be slaughtered. It will take you how long to reach this place?"

"Three weeks, perhaps less."

"Good. Within that time Haytham Kasi will be dead."

Rafiq frowned. "If you would not have us destroy him, what will you require of us in his land?"

"You will go to this place. There you will meet two men, foreigners. They will not be easy to mistake because one of them is young and the other has eyes of silver." The Dost gestured and the map flattened itself. Rising up through the cloud, the ruby hung suspended in the air. "When you find them, hold this ruby pressed against your heart. Think of me and I shall come."

"What if they run from us?"

"They will not run, Rafiq." The Dost lifted the egg with Svilik in it and placed it on his back. His flesh melded with the shell of the egg to hold it in place. He reached his arms out and this time they formed themselves into the wings of a gigantic bird. With one powerful downstroke the Dost launched himself into the air. "Worthy of fear you Khasts are, but these men are warriors of the Wolf."

"Wolf-priests have run before, my lord," the Helansajaran shouted after the Dost.

"They will not run, Rafiq, because they have come far seeking me." As the Dost rose higher into the sky, Rafiq heard light almost melodic laughter. "They seek me for their own reasons, but what they desire of me and what I need of them are, tragically, not the same thing at all."

— **30** —

Saint Michael
On Patrol
Mendhakgaon, Mrilan
Aran
10 Tempest 1687

Letting his wings hang by their harness strap from one shoulder, Robin Dury descended from the armory to the *Saint Michael*'s engine deck. He could feel his heart pounding away in his chest in time with the thunder coming from the battleboiler's engine. "Archangel Platoon, form up forward of the bay, Dominion Platoon aft of it. Partner up and gird your wings. Unfurl them only after you have dropped from the ship."

He heaved his own compact wings up over his head, then slipped his arms through both shoulder straps and let the rectangular package drop into place. He buckled the straps in an X pattern across his chest, then attached the leg straps and waist belt. Pulling his elbows back, he was able to seat his hands on the unfurling handles with ease.

"Brother Robin, check my wings, please."

Robin turned and smiled at Dennis Chilton. "Gladly, if you will do the same for me." He tugged on the straps and tightened one, then nodded. "You're fledged."

Robin's wings felt heavy as Dennis tugged on them. The rectangular package felt awkward in contrast to the lightness of Robin's steelsilk armor, but he knew he would not even notice them once he left the *Saint Michael*. Once he was out and had his wings unfurled, the Aeromancer magick he would use would allow him to float, climb, or dive and land softly enough to avoid hurting himself. Once down he would drop his wings and fight on foot, though if required he could always redon them and fly out of the immediate area.

The problem with sustained flight was that the magick that made flight possible also drained the person using it. An ethyrine who saw himself as some sort of human warhawk would end up exhausting himself before he ever entered battle. Using as little magick as possible to get to a battlefield worked the best, which meant the wings and the magick made the drop from an airship little more than a barely controlled fall.

Chilton smiled. "You're fledged, Mr. Drury."

"Thanks." Robin nodded. "God be with you."

"And with you."

Robin turned toward his platoon and saw most of them had already donned their helmets. Half of the faceplates looked like the men wearing them, the other half had animal aspects—the majority were lupine, but a number of raptor faces were represented as well. *This will be our first time in battle together, so our crossbows better shoot straight and our swords cut cleanly. I pray it goes well for us.*

"Hear me. The situation below is this: a Donnist mission and the village of Mendhakgaon appear to be under attack. The village is burning and the mission is under assault. The attackers appear to number between fifty and a hundred; they have horses, swords, spears, and bows. Archangel Platoon is to ground at the southern end of the village and move north toward the mission. Dominion will ground to the west of the mission and move toward it. Our goal is to relieve the mission and drive the attackers northeast toward the Varatha Pass. We do not pursue once the mission is secure."

A throaty steam whistle sounded shrilly from above, cutting off the sound of the cannons above them being run out their gunnery ports. Down below the clanking ring of a chain falling slack and a flood of light marked the cargo hatch being opened. Robin reached over and pulled the bar up from the rail around the hole in the engine deck.

"Archangel goes on two whistles, Dominion on three. Remember, jump, count three, then go to wing. The mission is on the north side of the village." Robin took his helmet from a peg on one of the ship's beams. "Let us pray. Dear God, Your blood was shed by hatred and Your wounds were healed by love. Know we act now in love for You, protecting those You have claimed to Yourself, and casting into the pit Thine enemies. We ask this in Your name. By Your will."

Robin pulled on his helmet and felt it mold tight to his head. He wanted to smile, but the fear bubbling around in his guts stopped him. It was the same fear he'd known as a gunner on the *Crow*, but more concentrated because he was alone, not a member of a team loading the cannon, charging it, aiming it, and shooting it. This time the fear was more personal and that much more consuming because of it.

He felt a hand on his shoulder. He turned and saw the wolf-face of Chilton's armor. "Baptism of steel, Mr. Drury. Don't worry about yourself; just remember the people we are here to save."

"Thanks." Robin hefted his crossbow. "Archangels, get ready."

Two short bursts from the ship's steam whistle echoed through the engine deck. Robin stepped to the space in the railing, hooked his thumbs through the unfurling handles, and leaped into the hole in the *Saint Michael*'s hull.

The scream of air rushing past his helmet blasted into his ears. For a half second he forgot who he was and what he was supposed to be doing, then he focused on the whitewashed building in the distance and the burning village between him and it. Grasping the unfurling handles firmly, Robin invoked the wing spell. A blue glow spread out from his hands and down the handles.

Behind him the magick went to work. The wings had been folded in on themselves a half dozen times. As the first three-foot length snapped out parallel to Robin's shoulders, a small support rod telescoped out and locked the first pivot joint in place. Again and again the joints clicked open. With the last one, the layered and folded metal feathers fanned out. Suddenly Robin's fall slowed and he bounced up a bit higher.

The prevailing wind in the valley blew southwest to northeast, which is why the two platoons were landing on the clear edges of Mendhakgaon. Fire had engulfed the scattered collection of wooden houses built on terraces carved from the mountainside. The smoke shrouded much of the area around the mission and, if their luck held, would hide the ethyrines' arrival. If they remained unnoticed until they had grounded and advanced to attack the raiders from behind, Robin doubted there would be much of a battle after all.

Through the smoke he thought he caught a glimpse of a banner and a dozen or so men riding south. *They'll reach our grounding zone before we have a chance to molt. If we have to fight with wings on . . .*

Without a second thought, Robin let his crossbow dangle from the lanyard on its stock, drew his sword, and tipped his wings toward the ground. As he started into a steep dive, he grasped the sword with both hands around the hilt. The pommel pressed against his navel and the tip angled out and down toward a point a good yard in front of his toes. Twisting his hands around so his palms faced up toward his head, he tightened his elbows in against his belly. Breathing a prayer to Saint Jude of Lost Hopes, he cast the spells that made his armor work and enhanced the nature of his sword, then leveled his glide out and swooped low into the smoke.

He saw nothing but black and gray and feared he might have gone too low. The whistling of wind past his helmet deafened to any sound from the ground, then the smoke curtain parted. A silhouette loomed in the smoke before him, then resolved itself into a swarthy bandit. Robin brought his head up, arching his back and gaining a foot of height. The plume on the lead rider's helmet slapped down across Robin's faceplate, then the shock of his sword slicing through the man's torso threatened to tear the blade from his grip.

He hung on tightly, and half a dozen feet past the dying man, he boosted the spell on his wings. He started to pull back up into the sky and thought he'd make it, but his left wing hit something. The stout rattan pole upholding the standard he'd seen from above splintered with the impact. The heavy, red and black woolen pennant came away and wrapped itself flapping around his broken wing tip.

The wing's shoulder straps dug into him and, suddenly, Robin found himself rotating to the left. His right wing pointed into his glidepath and began to angle down as he tried to get his left wing up. In response, the right wing dipped even more, then caught something on the ground. The wing bowed and twisted, the metal spars forming its leading edge screaming in protest. Finally, with a thundercrack, the spars snapped halfway along the wing's length, but by then Robin was tumbling through the air, out of control.

The ethyrine smashed into the ground hard, hitting square on his back. He bounced and continued to roll along the dirt roadway, tucking his arms and legs in as best he could. The left wing curved under him for a moment or two, as if it could vault him back into the sky, then it ripped itself apart. Metal feathers sprayed out in his wake, interspersed with dirt clods gouged out of the ground by his disintegrating wings. As he came up and over, the stub of his right wing jammed into the ground, then snapped off at the shoulder. It sent a jolt through him, spinning him laterally through the air, but nearly killing the tumble's momentum. With sword and crossbow flying off into the gray smoke, Robin somersaulted on through a muddy puddle, then rolled to a sodden stop in the middle of the road.

His armor had helped dissipate some of the force of the impact, but the crash landing still left him shaken and battered. His ears rang and he tasted blood in his mouth. His back hurt, but he could move his arms and legs, so he didn't think he'd broken his spine. His limbs all seemed in perfect working order. Somewhere, he realized as his head cleared, he'd lost his weapons and recovering them was vital.

Out of the smoke a riderless horse dashed past him, running from the south to the north.

He clawed at the release buckle on his chest and got the shoulder straps loose. Drawing the knife sheathed in the top of his right boot, he cut himself free of the waist and thigh straps and rolled away from the wings. He looked around for his sword and didn't immediately see it. *It can't have gone far, unless it flew into one of these buildings.*

A curtain of smoke flowed along the dirt street. In its wake, Robin saw his sword leaning up against the stone foundation of a smoldering building. He ran over to it and grabbed it, then slid his dagger away in its boot sheath again. *Next step, work my way back to my people.*

Ducking into an alleyway to get himself oriented, Robin found himself face-to-face with a frightened little brown-skinned boy. Tears had eroded twin tracks through the soot on the child's face. He wore two rags, one wrapped round his loins and the other around his head. Shivering with terror, the child squatted in the shadows and clutched to his chest a foot-long figurine made of gold.

Had it not been for the eight arms on the figure, and the fact that she wore no clothes, Robin might have thought it a statuette of a saint. *Laamtist idol, I would guess, some local pagan thing.* Robin looked at the boy and smiled, but only realized his mask did not ape his face when he saw no easing of the child's frightened expression.

"You're safe now, son." Robin winked at him. *Saint Martin, if you want to give me a sign here, I could use the help.*

The pounding of hooves drew Robin's attention away from the boy. He invoked the spells on his armor and sword again. A lightning-bright spark worked up the soiled sword from its hilt to the tip and leaped off into the smoke, leaving the blade shiny and bloodless in its wake. Robin heard the boy gasp, then guttural curses and the crisp slap of leather on horse flesh filled the roadway.

Not quite the sign I had in mind.

Four of the five riders seemed surprised to find Robin crouched in an alley. The fifth saw the child and pointed wildly at him. The lead rider shouted orders and they all spurred their horses forward.

Robin darted into the street, keeping to the right. This placed him between them and the child and forced the riders to reach across their own bodies to attack him with their swords. Yet despite that disadvantage, they came for him, swords held high, shields positioned to protect them.

Robin's blade took a large chunk out of the round shield the lead rider bore, trimming a crescent off the top. His blade continued on its arc, taking an even larger chunk out of the lead rider. That man screamed and slumped from the saddle, bloody froth rising from his chest wound and his shield arm hitting the ground before he did.

The riders reined up short, eyes wide at their comrade's fate. Another cloud of smoke billowed down into the street, cutting them off from Robin, but before it closed, he did see a red glow rise from the flesh of one man. Though Robin could see nothing, he drove straight at them, remaining low, angling toward the last man in their line. As a breeze thinned the smoke, Robin found himself right where he wanted to be, beside the last rider. Coming up, he drove his sword through the man's spine, then levered him off the horse.

Gathering the reins in his left hand, he hauled himself up into the saddle. He slid his toes into the stirrups, then slapped his sword across the rump of another horse that the dissipating smoke revealed ahead of him. It leaped forward, crashing into the two horses in front of it and they lurched forward as well.

Digging his heels into his horse's belly, he urged the black beast forward, splitting the knot of riders. Ignoring the man on his left, he slashed at the two riders on his right. He caught the glowing man on the left shoulder and watched blood spurt high into the air. Another cut missed the second man, but both of them turned and headed north at a gallop. Having been attacked from the air, then watching a lone warrior slaughter their friends, was more than they had a stomach for.

Reining his horse around, Robin saw the last man leap from his saddle and pounce on the child. The man grabbed the statue and tugged at it, but the boy would not let it loose. With his teeth flashing white in a dirty brown face, the boy bit at the man's hands. The bandit drew a curved dagger from the sash at his waist with his right hand and raised it, ready to strike.

A quick slash with Robin's sword took the man's hand off at the wrist. The bandit clutched at his bleeding stump and turned, pain and fury all over his face. He started to say something, but an overhand blow from Robin's sword crashed down on the man's bronze helmet. It split the metal and crushed the bone, spilling the man to the ground.

Robin leaned down from the saddle. "Come boy, I'll get you to safety."

The boy turned away from him, shielding the idol with his body from Robin's gaze.

"Not *it*, you!" Robin pointed to himself, then the child, and patted the horse behind himself. "Come, up here."

Half cringing, the boy held one hand out to Robin. The warrior took it and hauled the boy up over the dead man and settled him on the horse, back behind the saddle. He hooked the child's free hand through his belt in the back. "Hold on."

Robin started the horse trotting back toward the south and thirty yards on met with the rest of Archangel Platoon. The men on point raised their crossbows toward the sky and shook their heads while the men behind them just stared. Robin couldn't read their masks, but the way they brandished their weapons he knew they had not believed he had survived his stoop into the smoke and were happy to see him alive.

"Come on, we have a mission to rescue." Robin lifted the boy down to Sergeant Connor, then pointed toward an overturned wagon. "Wait there."

He couldn't tell if the child understood him, but the boy obediently ran to the designated hiding place. He still clutched the golden idol to his chest, but Robin ignored that fact. *Heathen he might be, but right now he needs defending as much as any Cardinal.* Touching his heels to the horse's ribs, he urged it forward, but kept pace with his men as they worked their way uphill.

In less than a minute they reached the northern edge of the town. The smoke cleared around the mission, revealing Dominion Platoon in position to the west. The bandits gathered around the mission appeared to be in some disarray, centered on a vocal argument near the middle of their line. As the smoke dissipated, one of the men in the argument screamed and the knot of men around him parted to look back at Robin and the Archangels.

Robin raised his sword, then pointed in the bandits' direction. "Archangels advance. Be prepared to flatten if they charge." Giving the horse some heel, the Wolf-priest let it prance forward of his line.

One of the bandits, a big bald man with a hooked nose and luxurious moustache, leaped into the saddle of a horse and drew his shamshir. He banged his sword against the iron boss of his shield and screamed out a challenge. Holding his curved sword high and back for a big slash as he passed by, the bandit trotted his horse forward. He rode directly toward the Wolf-priest and it seemed to Robin that the bandits and ethyrines were waiting to see if he would accept the challenge.

Robin twirled his sword once, then brought it up in a guard that mirrored that of the bandit. An ethyrine offered Robin a shield from a fallen bandit, but Robin shook his head. *If I actually need a shield, I'm in serious trouble.* He nodded toward his foe, then started his horse into a gallop. As the horse picked up speed, he brought his arm forward and held his sword straight out, as if it were a spear or lance. He made his horse drive straight in at his opponent.

The bandit, realizing the thrust would take him before he ever got a chance to cut Robin from the saddle, brought his shield up a bit. The iron-edged disk covered most of his chest. His blade came forward to shorten his stroke, clearly intent on getting in a quick strike as they rode past each other.

When only ten feet separated them, Robin brought the tip of his blade up to aim at the man's eyes. The circular shield rose to block him, temporarily blinding the bandit. The Wolf-priest rolled his wrist and cocked it, pulling the tip of his blade back toward his right shoulder. As the two men passed, Robin cut his sword down and around, beneath the shield's trailing edge.

The ethyrine's blade passed cleanly through the bandit's studded leather jerkin. Robin felt a tug as his sword caught for a moment on a rib, but he pulled it free as he ducked away from the bandit's return slash. The shamshir whistled past his ear, narrowly missing his head.

Robin reined his horse around, trapping himself between cheers from the ethyrines and the wail from the bandits' line. The bandit he had cut wavered in the saddle like a drunken man, then tipped to the left. He hit the ground all boneless, his sword and shield bouncing up into the air. His horse galloped off all wall-eyed, trying desperately to outrun the broken thing that had fallen from its back.

Before Robin's blade could finish cleaning itself, the ethyrines charged the bandits from the west and south. Glittering blades held aloft, steelsilk armor encasing them, wearing helmets with fierce visages, they looked like an army of metal men rushing forward. Robin fought to keep his horse under control as the ethyrines reached him and swept past.

Some of the bandits countercharged on foot, but the majority broke when the first crossbow volley scythed through them. Those who didn't go down, and didn't start to flee, came rushing forward all ragged and dirty. Their curved blades skittered off the ethyrine armor, their shields splintered catching ethyrine cuts. One ethyrine sword sliced through a neck, spinning the head through the air so the turban it wore unwound itself. Another bandit reeled away from a fight, his sword arm gone from elbow down and his life pulsing from it. The bandits screamed defiantly at first, then in pain, and then stopped screaming at all.

The rest of the bandits took to their horses and galloped off toward the northeast. The ethyrines' lead elements cut some of the fleeing bandits, but couldn't hold a line against a cavalry charge—even one as desperate and ragged as the bandits' attack. More than one ethyrine was bounced off the shoulder of a wild-eyed horse as the bandits made their break for freedom.

The bandits' route out of the village took them thundering along a dirt track that cut up and around on the mountainside opposite Mendhakgaon. More properly thought of as a cattle trail than a road, the brown path cut across green pastures and eventually continued northeast and out toward the Varatha Pass. The horsemen strung themselves out along it, with riderless horses, reins flying, ranging above and below the bandits' retreat.

The ethyrines captured what horses they could and half a dozen of them rode toward Robin, eager to pursue. Robin shook his head. "We have driven them away from the mission. To go after them would be foolish and suicidal."

Comforted by the lack of pursuit, the fleeing bandits screamed threats and challenges. Robin could not tell what they were saying because he did not speak their language, but the tone made the intent of their words very clear. They brandished swords and slowed their horses to a walk. Some even argued with others about running, and pointed their blades back toward the village.

Sergeant Connor, sitting astride a gray mare, shook his head. "They'll be coming back for us, sir."

"They may think so, Sergeant," Robin said, sheathing his sword, "but they are wrong."

A cacophonous throbbing built in the valley, echoing from stone canyon walls and the burning town's buildings. The sound pulsed loudly, its rhythm akin to a heartbeat, but more steady and even more insistent. It didn't speed up with passion as it neared the battlefield, but kept on relentlessly even and strong.

Robin turned in the saddle and looked up, his face blossoming into a hidden smile. "They are very wrong."

The *Saint Michael*'s bow broke through the smoke hanging over the village and surged forward. Smoke curled down around the tips of the wings like snow clouds blown from the heights of the Himlans. The thrumming of the engines sent a vibration through Robin's chest as the whole of the ship slipped into the clear air. Sooty vapor billowing out of the twin exhaust stacks trailed tendrils in the ship's wake, linking it with the destruction of Mendhakgaon.

Cruising along a hundred yards above the valley floor, the air-ship turned until its stern came about, pushing the *Saint Michael* on a course running parallel with the bandits' line of retreat. Some bravely brandished their swords at it, but others spurred their horses forward, cutting high and low around their fellows. Those who understood what they were seeing cried out in terror, while the ignorant laughed and watched.

The *Saint Michael* loosed its thunder, drowning out the bandits' voices. One second Robin could see the bandits, then in the next huge white clouds of gun mist hid them. The dreadnaught's starboard cannons went off as one, sending out a huge shock wave that reverberated through the valley. The gargantuan wooden warbird heeled over to port then began to climb up and out of the valley, pulling much of the mist in its wake.

The evaporating white clouds revealed a torn landscape, with what had been green pastures now blasted into a brown sea of mud. The cattle track no longer existed and weathered stones that had dotted the hillside had been sprayed into gray stains over the earth. Fluids glittered dark against the earth, and some scattered bits of color dotted the ground; but aside from that and a lone lathered horse galloping fast and furiously up the mountain, Robin could see nothing of the bandits.

From the way the ship had reacted in flight, Robin knew Hassett had given the bandits a triple-deck broadside. Forty-five canisters of grapeshot, each containing dozens of lead balls no bigger in diameter than a hen's egg, had ripped the bandit force to pieces, churning the earth into a ruin. Looking more closely, Robin saw a little movement on the hillside, but it came spasmodically, arhythmically, and slackened quickly to nothing.

As the sound of the *Saint Michael*'s engines drained from the valley, human and equine cries of pain from half-buried and broken creatures rolled down from the hillside. Robin knew something should be done to help the wounded and dying, but healing them to hang them made no sense. The haunted expressions worn by the bandits' surviving victims atop the mission's wall further prevented him from taking action. *These people look as if they have seen Hell, and those men soon will. May their pain make them penitent.*

Having long since removed his helmet and faceplate, Robin frowned at Sergeant Connor. "You seem to have a few more knives there than you did when you came down, Mr. Connor. There are regulations against looting."

"Begging your pardon, sir, it's not loot." The beefy veteran rested his hands on the hilt of one of the knives thrust into his belt. "I thought it would be good to have some for training the men, sir, since they're likely to run into them here."

"Good thought." Robin saw Connor's concerned expression ease. "Turn them over to our Quartermaster when you get back."

"Yes, sir."

"Except for the one or two examples you'll want to keep with your collection, in case we need one quickly."

"Yes, sir." Connor's face brightened. "And I'll see to it there's no looting, sir."

"And take care of that little boy."

"I've already seen to it, sir."

"Carry on, Mr. Connor." Robin turned and walked over to where the first ethyrskiff from the *Saint Michael* was landing. "The village is secure, sir."

Captain Hassett came over the side while the ethyrskiff was still a yard off the ground and landed squarely on his feet. "Very good, Mr. Drury. How are the people from the mission?"

"They survived, but they're still pretty nervous. If you'll follow me, sir, you can see for yourself." Robin led him over to the shadow of the mission where the village's survivors had gathered. "Captain Hassett, this is Father Loughlin Ryan, Society of Saint Donnan. Father Ryan, this is Captain Lonan Hassett of the *Saint Michael*."

Hassett extended his hand to the diminutive priest. "Pleased to meet you."

"And I you, Captain, and would have even under other circumstances." Though the redheaded man barely topped five feet and was scarecrow-gaunt, he had a strong grip and a defiant spark in his green eyes. "I'd be lying if I said I thought I'd be alive right now."

Hassett looked out at the small group of people who had

followed Ryan from the mission building. "Are these the only survivors?"

"They are." Ryan pointed at the two white women to one side of the group. "Sister Mary Denise and Sister Elizabeth Catherine are Sisters of Compassion. The rest are converts."

Robin directed Hassett's attention back toward the burned-out village. "The bandits sent an advance party and demanded tribute. During the negotiations to determine what would be paid, the bandits scouted the town and decided they could conquer it. Father Ryan felt suspicious and invited the people to take refuge in the mission, but the majority refused."

"Can't blame them, Captain. They thought the presence of Eilyphianists would enrage Kasi and make him specifically go after our mission. I think a lot of them would have been happy to see us driven off. The Ghur bandits forced everyone into the headman's home, that big building in the center of things, then set the city alight." Ryan nodded in the direction of the boy Robin had saved. "Little Nataraj appears to be the only survivor outside the mission. He ignored their order to stay in the house and stole back a gold statuette of a Laamti goddess the bandits had looted from the local temple."

Hassett smiled. "Brave act for so young a boy."

"The image was of Devinataki—a minor goddess of the dance. His namesake is linked to her in Laamti tales." Ryan shrugged. "We've plenty of children who would act to prevent the desecration of a church. Such strength of faith makes me hopeful when we are able to convert them."

The *Saint Michael*'s Captain nodded. "Since there are so few of you here, I am uneasy about your safety."

"We'll be fine. You've killed the bandits."

"And in doing so, we may well have made your mission here a symbol others will feel compelled to destroy." Hassett frowned heavily. "You are rather far away from help."

Ryan folded his arms. "If you think I'm afraid to be out here—"

Robin shook his head. "The Captain's not saying that, Father. He hopes you realized that just because Saint Donnan was martyred when his church and converts were burned down by pagans in Culordain, tempting the same fate for yourself is not a good idea. Martyring will make you a saint certainly, but there are other ways to be canonized."

"What I *am* asking, Father Ryan, is for you and your survivors to come back to Dhilica with us." Hassett rested his right hand on the priest's shoulder. "You have knowledge of this country that I need, and I believe the Governor-general would likewise appreciate your perspective on things."

"Fiske? The only thing he wants to know is how to turn one coin into two, with no sweating on his part."

"No, I don't suppose you have heard up here. Prince Trevelien is now the Governor-general. I can guarantee he'd like to hear what you have to say about Baron Fiske."

Ryan smiled slowly. "And I'd be very much liking to tell the Prince what I think of Baron Fiske. It was because of Fiske that I left the Donnist mission in Dhilica and came up here. It's difficult to convince folks to convert and agree to act properly when some of our most prosperous citizens carry on like frenzied heathens."

The little priest nodded. "Well, Captain Hassett, if you'll get us to Dhilica, I'll have us put up at our mission there, then I'll be at your disposal."

"It would be my pleasure to have you aboard the *Saint Michael*."

"And my pleasure to be letting the Prince know all about Aran." Then the priest's eyes narrowed and Robin felt a chill tickle his spine. "Although there are some things he may wish he didn't know, and others he'll wish he could just make go away."

— 31 —

Pyimoc
Vzorin, Vzorin Military District
Strana
12 Tempest 1687

Grigory Khrolic felt a jolt of surprise when he saw the condition of Duke Arzlov's desk. Neat orderliness had given way to a confused jumble of charts, rolled maps, books, and loose sheets of paper covered with writing and diagrams. Even during the Lescari campaign things had never gotten so chaotic. *Nor had Arzlov ever looked this fatigued.*

"My report is brief, sir."

Arzlov looked up and appeared to take a second or two to recognize Grigory. Fatigue had darkened the flesh around his eyes, taking it from cerulean to near black. Yet despite his lack of rest, Arzlov's bright eyes quickly sharpened and showed the same fire

Grigory had been used to seeing a dozen years earlier. "Signals from the *Leshii*?"

"*Da.*"

Arzlov laid his goose-quill pen down and sat back stiffly. "Please tell me what was said."

"The *Leshii* is forty miles south and returning here for recoaling. The last sighting of Khast's group puts them west of Helor and heading south. The *Leshii* broke off to return two days ago, but was able to use her mirrors to signal scouts we have there. Our scouts will track Khast and leave indicators. The *Leshii* should be here in four hours and could be ready to go back out by tomorrow morning."

The Duke shook his head. "*Nyet.* When the pursuit resumes we will use the *Zarnitsky*. It has enough guns to deal with gathered tribes or anything else that might be encountered in Helansajar. It would look, from their path, that they mean to reach the Varatha Pass and sell Svilik to Ilbeoria in return for support opposing Shukri Awan."

"This is possible, sir."

Arzlov frowned. "You disagree?"

"It is my feeling that drawing any conclusion based on what evidence we have is premature." Khrolic shrugged. "Soliciting Ilbeorian support is sensible for Khast, but is it sensible for the Dost reborn? Why would he see *us*, heirs to fully one third of his old empire, to be a threat for which intervention by foreigners is sought?"

"If this Dost even exists."

"You make an excellent point, sir. His return has not been substantiated except by the hallucinations of dying men. Hardly reliable."

"Your news of Khast's location makes me wonder if the tale about the Dost's return is not some sort of fiction created by the Wolf-priests to distract us from what is truly happening here."

Were your paranoia a prancing horse, you would have ridden it to death by now. Grigory shook his head. "Possible, my lord, but unlikely."

"You are probably correct, Grigory, but Wolf-priests would like us to be looking away from them and Aran." Arzlov nodded and closed his eyes for a second. Had he not steepled his fingers, Grigory would have thought the man finally succumbed to sleep. "You would agree these events—whatever they are—demand action?"

I have heard this sort of question from him before. It is invitation to danger, and, possibly, great reward. "I think that conclusion is inescapable, my lord."

"You would not also agree that we are at crossroads in history, Grigory?"

The younger man shifted his hands around behind himself as he evaluated the question. *The question suggests others might disagree, even to the detriment of Strana. Will my answer make him see me as willing to conspire with him to act in his favor?* He formulated an answer that would not trip the snare being laid for him. "Your interpretation seems valid, sir."

Arzlov smiled slowly. "You are wise, Grigory, for these times demand caution." His arctic eyes snapped open. "They also demand vision. Sit. Let me explain to you what all of this is. At the end I will ask you to make a decision—a decision that will determine my future, your future, and the future of your nation and probably that of the whole world."

Grigory dragged a chair over—another from the estate of the Lescari Emperor—and lowered himself into it. The last time he had heard Arzlov speak in such serious and grave tones was when they faced the final battle with Fernandi in Jajce. *Then he noted destiny would be decided by us. His vision then was accurate, but is it that way now?*

The Duke smoothed his brown hair down with both of his hands, then quickly studied the items on his desk. He nodded once, then glanced up at Grigory. "It may puzzle you to hear this, but the presence of the Dost is immaterial to what we must consider. His presence, if it is him or just another pretender or even nothing more than a rumor, acts only as a catalyst. His actions will hasten our actions or hasten the demise of Strana.

"You are intelligent, Grigory. You know many things. You know, having rebuilt Myasovo, how primitive Vzorin here is in comparison to your creation."

Grigory smiled in spite of himself. Myasovo had risen from the ruins of an old, decrepit city to become a monument to the advancement of mankind's knowledge. Sewers had been dug to carry away waste. Streets were wide and straight, facilitating and encouraging commerce. Gas lighting, trash haulage, a professional police force, and water pipes to individual buildings had been put in place. Modern methods had been used in constructing those buildings and the streets had all been paved. He had worked a miracle and he knew it. Sinful though it might have been, he took pride in what he had done.

"You also know, Grigory, that Murom and the rest of Strana is primitive compared to Myasovo. And yet, as wonderful as your Myasovo is, you know there are cities in Ilbeoria and even Lescar which incorporate even newer conveniences. You know of the new, very powerful steam engines and railroads in Ilbeoria. You know of how their factories and mills function at higher levels of efficiency and productivity than ours could ever possibly manage. You know that for every day we do not move forward, we fall back two. You know the gap between Ilbeoria and Strana widens and soon it will be insurmountable."

Grigory nodded slowly. "This is true."

Arzlov stood slowly, more consumed by thought, it seemed, than fatigue. "You are from Myasovo. I understand there the fisher-folk have a saying: a fish rots first in the head."

The younger man's flesh went cold. *You dance on the border of treason, Vasily.*

"You need say nothing, Grigory. This is dangerous ground. I shall blaze a trail and you may decide to follow me or betray me. All I ask first is that you listen to me."

"I will, sir."

"Thank you." Arzlov unrolled a map of Estanu and pinned it to his desk at the corners with books. "When we fought Fernandi, we fought with men and steel. Ilbeoria did their share of that, but they also fought with gold. They put up a blockade, both on the ocean and in the air, that isolated Lescar from its Brendanian colonies. Lescar fell as much because we killed their troops as it did from Il-beoria gutting Lescar's economy.

"Now Ilbeoria has that same blade pressed to *our* belly, and we must act or we shall surely die. Our leadership is made up of old men who revel in the glory we won them when fighting Fernandi, and their goal is to rebuild Strana the way it was. They do not re-spect your vision, Grigory, and seek to re-create the past when we are facing a future that will consume us. Their inactivity gives the Wolves great opportunity to gobble us up."

"I agree with you, my lord." Grigory leaned forward in his chair. "This is why I have been surprised that you have not used the Hussars against Helor before this. We can take that city and with it secure the area and open new markets in central Estanu. From there, Aran can be ours."

Arzlov began chuckling and Grigory wondered if exhaustion had unhinged the man. Grigory frowned heavily. "Did I say some-thing to amuse you, my lord?"

The Duke calmed himself, then gave Grigory the full force of his stare. "Do you think I believe you so naïve as to suppose you see conquest of Aran as the solution to the problem I advance? You? You, he-who-created-Myasovo? Conquering Aran would be equiva-lent for us to pouring a gallon of vodka into a pint flask. Strana cannot possibly benefit from expansion into Aran except to deprive Il-beoria of its colony."

"Exactly, my lord. Our presence in Estanu could threaten the Wolf-King, making him grant us trading concessions."

"Let us follow this line of thought, then." Arzlov tapped the map with a long finger. "Let us say that tomorrow I direct you to take Helor. Your Hussars will arrive there in the middle of Majest and will have secured Helor in another two weeks. You could take Drangiana in Autumbre, but by the first of Tenebre snows would fly, making any trek through or over the Himlans impossible. Agreed?"

"Agreed."

"Good. With such conquests to your credit—"

"In your name, my lord."

"*Da,* in my name, Vzorin will be elevated to the status of a province and I will be made Tacarri. Perhaps."

Grigory's head came up. "There is a question of this?"

"You have been in Murom. You understand politics." Arzlov balled his fists. "The same Naraschals who deprived me of my just rewards after Fernandi's defeat will point out, in justice, that *you* conquered Helansajar and Drangiana. They will point out that in ten years here I did nothing. Vzorin will become a province with me as its Tacarri. Helansajar and Drangiana will be made into a province of central Estanu and you will be its Tacarri. You will marry Tachotha Natalya and will eclipse me."

Grigory, secretly pleased with the Duke's assessment, shook his head defiantly. "I would never stand for such a betrayal of you, my lord."

Arzlov chuckled again, but without the lunatic undercurrent. "You would protest this injustice to the Tacier. He would tell you that I had surrendered my chance to you. You would then press to have him let me lead the expedition to take Aran in spring. He would say that such action is not warranted. He would tell you that when you sit in his place, you would see what you do not now see. You would be hobbled."

The younger man frowned. The scenario Arzlov presented to him rang absolutely and completely true. General Winter, which had always helped defend Strana, would arrive early in the Himlans, preventing Grigory from using the momentum created in the conquests of Helansajar and Drangiana to gain even a foothold in Aran. The winter would allow the Ilbeorians to reinforce Aran, making its conquest impossible. It would also give the Tacier and all the other Taccarri time to plan a way to neutralize him as a threat to their power.

An uncharacteristic frustration ripped through Grigory. Though he had known that he would betray Arzlov to further his own career, now he was being shown how he would be betrayed in turn. The Tacarri and Tacier would do to him what they had so effectively done to Duke Arzlov. Worse yet, in doing that, they would doom Strana. They were a stop block in the path of progress, not realizing that Ilbeoria was a threat that had to be dealt with lest Strana be bought up by Ilbeorian merchants.

Grigory's hazel eyes narrowed. "Have you a solution to this situation?"

Arzlov hesitated, looking down, then nodded slowly. "I will share it with you, Grigory, because I realize you have an opportunity to place yourself where I cannot. What I will say to you amounts to high treason. If you do not think my logic holds, you can topple me by telling Natalya what I have said and sending her home. You will replace me and can work your magic on Vzorin as you did on Myasovo."

Grigory shivered as Arzlov unrolled another map. This one, slightly smaller in scale, showed all of Estanu and Urovia in detail. "We have agreed, Grigory, that modernization is what we require and modernization is a laborious process. We have three methods for modernizing: inventing technology, trading for technology, and stealing technology. Invention is slow and can only build on what one already possesses. We will forever be reinventing that which Ilbeoria has invented. Trade requires us to have something someone else wants. Ilbeoria wants little of what we have, and not enough of it to get them to trade us their technology. Theft means we must occupy some place with technology greater than our own—Ludstone, for example—and this means a conflict our Tacier will not condone or permit."

Grigory nodded. "Your assessment is sound."

"I have worked on it for years. I had thought I would act myself on this information, when circumstances became dire enough. The current crisis did not come to boil as quickly as I had anticipated, which means you will benefit from what I have planned."

Arzlov brushed his hand lovingly across the map. "As before, you will take Helansajar and Drangiana this year. After things are secure, we bring the Hussars and your Vandari company by air to Murom to accept our nation's thanks for what you have done. All the Tacarri will be there to praise you. You will be elevated to Tacarri, but with your troops there, you will stage a mutiny, kill those Tacarri who will not support you, and will topple Tacier Yevgeny from his throne."

"But—"

Arzlov held a hand up to forestall the protest. "Tacier Yevgeny must be put aside. He is sixty-five years old. He was married before the steam engine was invented. He has a nostalgia for the old ways that will forever bind us to those old ways. We need your vision to be able to move into the future."

Grigory nodded. "If this were to come to pass, what would we do then?"

"You immediately send a message to the Wolf-King in Ilbeoria telling him you have no desire for aggression in Aran. You tell him you consider Drangiana and Helansajar to be buffer states, under your rule, but open for trade."

"But that will give Ilbeoria more markets, which is not what we want to do."

The Duke smiled. "Deadly daggers are often concealed in pretty sheaths."

"I do not understand."

"You shall." Arzlov tapped Lescar on his map. "Ilbeoria cut Lescar off from its colonies. Lescar had a very small market for its goods. Come spring, we will do the equivalent to Ilbeoria. You will permit me—for this is what *I* want from you, Grigory—to lead our armies in the conquest of Urovia. We, you and I, swept over Urovia a decade ago. We know no one and nothing can stand before us. We take Urovia, depriving Ilbeoria of substantial markets and, at the same time, opening these markets to our traders. In Lescar, which Ilbeoria has been helping to build up, we may steal technology. In return for opening those markets back up to Ilbeoria we can trade with the Wolves for technology."

"But if we take Urovia, Ilbeoria will have to oppose us there."

"Yes, Grigory, but it is as with the chess move: we have them in champion's fork. They fight in Urovia, we threaten Aran." Arzlov smiled like a fox. "Strana has ever had one resource that dwarfs that of any other nation: people. We have enough troops to defend our entire empire. Ilbeoria does not."

"What if Ilbeoria refuses to trade technology to us?"

"Their government might, but their merchants will not. Ilbeorian merchants in Aran are greedy. If offered sufficient gold, they will sell the hangman all the rope he will need to hang them. We offer them money, trading opportunities, and perhaps support if they decide to revolt as Ilbeoria's Brendanian colonies did. We play them against Ludstone and we win."

Grigory frowned slightly. Not only did he find the logic of Arzlov's plan unassailable, he found the thinking behind it frighteningly brilliant. Even though Grigory had ambitions himself, he had been content to wait. He saw this was his weakness because there came times, as now, when taking action was the only way to prevent a greater disaster.

Vasily Arzlov had waited and circumstances had been arranged to freeze him out of power. *If I wait, will forces come to view me with suspicion and block my path to power?* More important than that was the very real risk of having his *best* opportunity slip away.

That very idea started writhing through Grigory's guts as if it were a snake with razor scales. He had felt that same sensation once before and knew it came from a conflict between what he knew to be a prudent path and what his heart knew was the *right* path. That other time he had followed his heart and the decision had proved to be correct. *There are times when swift, decisive action is not impulsive but necessary.*

Still, the plan Arzlov had presented had one flaw from Grigory's point of view. "There is no reason, my lord, why I must be Tacier to make this plan work. You could be Tacier."

Arzlov shook his head solemnly. "I am ambitious, Grigory, but I am also a patriot. When I was sent here to Vzorin, I could have revolted. You and others would have followed me. I could have deposed Tacier Yevgeny and reigned in his place. I did not do so because that would have hurt Strana, and that I will not do.

"You, Grigory, are Strana's future. You will live long, you will have great influence. You have vision and the will to change Strana. And you have a talent for it. I only have a talent for war. As your Warlord, I will bring you Urovia. I will enter our history as the greatest Stranan warrior ever. And while I live, anyone who wishes to depose you will either enlist me—and I will turn him over to you—or oppose me. Opposition I will crush. I am a warbow and you are an arrow. I will live on in fame in the nation you create."

The Duke shrugged, then looked up from his map. "But this is only if you are willing to take the steps necessary to put this plan into operation."

Grigory nodded. "I am."

Arzlov raised a hand. "There is one last detail to which you will have to agree."

"This is?"

"Tachotha Natalya."

Grigory's breath caught in his throat. *I should have seen this before.* He knew she would oppose Arzlov's plan, *if she knew of it.* That meant she could not know of it. Packing her off to Murom would have been the logical thing to do, but the attempt on her life meant she could not be sent to the capital. If she was, Arzlov would be called to account for his lack of action in preventing the attack. That would kill the plan.

The young officer sat back. "We can never deceive her about our plans. She will have to trade her freedom for Strana's future."

The Duke nodded. "This was my assessment, though I felt she might refuse to marry you later because of taking this action."

Grigory shrugged. "Was this not always possible? Marriage to her would legitimize my claim to the Tacier's throne, but I am permitted many wives and she has many sisters. You will expect me to take wives from the Urovian nations you conquer. Natalya *could* be first among them, but if she refuses me, she can be replaced."

His own bloodlessness surprised him. He loved her, but the preservation of that love was not as important to him as his dreams, especially with the path to achieve them that had been opened in this conversation with Arzlov. Winning Natalya had been a goal for itself *and* as the furtherance of his dream. While he wished her to accompany him and be part of his future, if she were to become an impediment, she would have to be set aside.

A quizzical expression passed over Arzlov's face. "I had forgotten you could be so pragmatic."

"Yes?" the younger man asked, enjoying the anticipation of Arzlov pointing out one of Grigory's greatest personal victories.

"You sacrificed a company of scouts in Glogau just to rid yourself of the Wolf-priest who had excited Tachotha Natalya's passions."

"Yes, I did." Grigory smiled slyly. "Then I began my campaign to win her by telling her of my sorrow at her loss. It was an opportunity I would have been stupid to fail to recognize and negligent to fail to use. Just like this."

The Hussar stood. "When do you anticipate initiating the campaign, my lord?"

"Once we have a report back from our scouts or the *Zarnitsky* about Khast and his band we will know how to take his forces into account. By the end of the month, easily." Arzlov smiled. "Seven or eight days from now you should start exercises that take the Hussars to the border with Helansajar. Send them out, and when the *Zarnitsky* comes back, you may fly to your command. In a month or so you will own Helor and it will be the first jewel in your crown as Tacier."

— 32 —

It occurred to Uriah Smith, as he clung to his saddle on the back of a stout mountain pony, that he was a good two thousand miles from Carvenshire as the crow flies, and had traveled even further than that to get where he was. *In one journey I have traveled further distant than my father did when going to the Tacier's court.* He shook his head as he realized most Ilbeorians couldn't even conceive of traveling so far, much less surviving the trip.

All around him the Himlans rose up as if jagged pieces of granite pottery shoved up through a crust of earth and snow. Though the season was still summer, in the high passes the cold winds howled down from the mountaintops. Swift-moving clouds swooped low at times, hiding the peaks. Whenever the clouds withdrew, Uriah found himself looking up, half convinced the mountains had grown even taller while concealed.

In front and behind of them rode two Himlan villagers whom Captain Ollis had convinced to guide them into Drangiana. Ollis had told them that getting guides would be difficult, but the people of Thandragaon were more than happy to guide the Wolf-priests. Ollis had looked surprised at first, then smiled and told them what the people were saying.

" 'Pears your *Saint Michael* wiped out a Ghur bandit company that had ranged down the pass from Drangiana. Report of the cannons echoed through the mountains and some herders found the bodies. Couple of survivors told a powerful tale. A single Wolf-priest on horseback killed the leader then scattered the bandits. The *Saint Michael* came in and used its cannon on the retreating force. Since there are two of you the people figure you'll be cleaning up whatever is left in Drangiana."

The cost of the guides' services was fixed at two pounds of

sugar and some pots and pans of Ilbeorian manufacture. The rest of
the cargo Ollis had with him—cargo that had been loaded in
Dhilica—was traded for blankets, carpets, embroidery, and some
very fine pieces of jewelry. Uriah, when he helped unload the *Stoat*,
noticed the steam engine had been removed from the ship. He also
saw that the crates containing the Ilbeorian products used for barter
had the Grimshaw Mercantile & Transportation, Limited, logos almost completely burned from them. None of the crates had tax
stamps and he sincerely doubted the items from Thandragaon
would pass through customs on their way out of Aran.

The openness with which Ollis conducted his business surprised Uriah. Ollis had complained about the *Saint Michael* being
off course when it destroyed the bandits, but he said the *Stoat* had already been returning to Dhilica before he saw the warship bringing
survivors back to the city. Aside from that mild irritation, Ollis had
not appeared concerned about official scrutiny of his actions. He
had hidden nothing from Uriah and, not caring for more lectures,
Uriah refrained from asking a lot of questions.

Of course, being a Wroxterman, Ollis saw smuggling as a national imperative, not a crime. Because Uriah and Kidd had traveled
surreptitiously from Ilbeoria, Ollis counted on them being less than
legitimate. Then, when Kidd saved his life, Ollis saw them as close
and dear friends. He had helped them and trusted them not to betray him.

*Ollis is an idiot. He has no reason to expect we would not be-
tray him. He smuggled a steam engine out of Ilbeoria, and he knows
we know he did that. Turning him in would grant us all sorts of rewards and favors. He never should have come back for us. He
should have sailed back to Ilbeoria and prayed we died in Dhilica
or on the road to Helor. Or he should have had someone kill us.*

Uriah looked to his right where Kidd sat tied to his saddle.
"Colonel, can I ask your opinion on something?"

Kidd appeared not to hear at first, then nodded. "You can. And
may."

The younger man ignored the grammar reminder. "Why did
Captain Ollis come back for us?"

"He is a man of his word. Abandoning us would have been beneath a man of his honor."

"Ollis, a man of *honor*?" Uriah laughed aloud and heard deri-
sion echo back from the Himlans. "He could spend the rest of his
life in a confessional and never come close to being shriven."

"Ah, so a man who is a sinner cannot have honor in your view of the world? Interesting." Kidd turned his head toward Uriah and the sun glanced dazzlingly from his eyes. "What makes you think Ollis has any sins to confess?"

"Well, sir, he is smuggling. He is stealing from the government. His crimes devolve from envy and greed." Uriah sniffed to emphasize a shrug for the blind man. "Clearly he must be sinning."

"You're being an untidy thinker. Your reasoning is actually far from clear." Disappointment washed over Kidd's face. "Apply the analytical skills you showed in your project to this problem. What are the conditions under which a sin can occur?"

Uriah's nostrils flared. *Ask for an opinion, get a debate.* "The sinner must know the action is against the law, and he must fully consent to committing the act with full knowledge of its unlawfulness."

Kidd nodded. "It is the law of Himlan that cows are sacred and cannot be eaten. You know this. Would you be sinning to eat beef here?"

"No."

"But it is against the law of this place to eat beef. You know this, therefore you have consented to committing an unlawful act. Is not that *your* definition of sin?"

"Yes, but the law does not apply to me."

"So, you're above the law now? Why doesn't it apply to you?"

Uriah frowned. "Because that is a law for the people of Aran. To them it is wrong, but not for me."

Kidd's expression sharpened. "So sin is situational? There is no absolute judgment of what is sinful and what is not?"

"Evil is sinful. Performing evil acts is sinful."

"Ah, then what is evil?"

"Isn't this getting a bit far afield from my original question?"

"You mounted the charge, now deal with the pikes, Cadet."

An image of a pike and Kidd's head mounted on it flashed through Uriah's mind. "Evil is the opposite of love."

"Then what is love?"

Uriah snarled silently. "The greatest love one man can show for another is to lay down his life for that person."

"Nice recitation of Eilyph's admonishment to his disciples, but you could do better." Kidd sighed and shook his head. "It will do for the moment, however. You would say, then, that love is a sharing of self, a selflessness that is freely given?"

Uriah nodded. "Yes."

"Good. What is the opposite of that? What is at the core of the Seven Deadly Sins?"

The younger man scratched at his head. "Sloth, gluttony,

avarice, greed, lust, envy, and pride. They're all centered around self."

"So then it would seem that evil is the ultimate expression of selfishness and self-absorption."

"I guess so."

"You aren't sure?"

"Well . . ."

"Why is selfishness evil?"

"It's obvious."

"If it were obvious, Cadet, you would give me a complete answer. It might require you to be a bit more generous with your mental capacity, more loving and less selfish with it, if you will."

"Philosophers and theologians have wrestled with this problem, surely it is beyond so poorly schooled a cadet as me." Uriah glared at the man, angry at being read so easily. "Please, sir, enlighten me."

"I doubt even *I* can do *that*, but I will explain evil to you." Kidd closed his eyes. "Self-absorption sets man apart from God. It seeks to make man the center of life, supplanting God, working into the clutches of the Devil himself. It is cause for concern because a man who keeps himself separated from God will never know eternal life and instead will endure eternal damnation."

Kidd's calm delivery surprised Uriah. Cold tickled the base of his spine. Uriah shivered. "Thank you, sir."

"You could have gotten there, Cadet Smith, easily and without overmuch effort, had you applied yourself. You are intelligent, but you look to your own comforts first, and to making the world come up to your own standards. Doing so is fraught with danger and pain."

"Speaking from experience, Colonel?"

Kidd stiffened and Uriah knew he'd driven a spike deep into Kidd's soul. The Colonel's voice came slowly in reply, and deeper. "I have never pretended to be without fault, Cadet. I too fall prey to the sin of pride—I allow myself to believe I can help others, but this does not always turn out to be true. What sets us apart is that I have looked into my own soul and identified my weaknesses, you have not. If this self-examination comes to you before too late, you will be capable of great things. If not, I think you will find yourself very much like Captain Irons, older and bitter, which would be a waste."

Kidd raised a hand to forestall any comment from Uriah. "This, however, is a point that we could belabor right now and get nowhere; and it's quite off the point of your original inquiry. So, tell me, is Ollis a sinner or not?"

Uriah struggled to swallow his anger. *The gall of the man to speak to me so!* Even though anger shook him, Uriah did feel a trickle of fear playing as a countercurrent to it and found the truth in Kidd's words to be at the source of that fear. He acknowledged that because, growing up, he had fought so hard to establish his own identity—one that gave him value without linking him to the brothers he loathed—being judgmental was part and parcel of who he was. In asking the question that had started the whole debate he was attempting to assign Ollis a rank beneath him, one worthy of contempt, but it dawned on him that there was no purpose to that exercise. *Regardless of who and what he is, Ollis did us a favor or two, and the Eilyphianist thing to do would be to thank him and think well of him for it.*

The suggestion that he would end up like Captain Irons stung, yet Uriah knew that was the best of what he might become if he didn't begin to amend his ways. *Kidd's purpose in life is to seek and fulfill God's plan for him. My purpose, to this point, is to prove how good I am, how much better I am than others. I serve no one but myself, which means I am wallowing in evil.*

Without admitting the possibility that he was afraid of what he'd discovered about himself, Uriah took the way out the Wolf-priest had offered him. "Ollis knows smuggling is against the law, and he consciously does it, and he does it for personal profit—clearly selfish—so I'd have to say yes, Captain Ollis is a sinner."

"But he is a Wroxterman who lost his son on an Ilbeorian warship. Does he have a valid position if he argues that what he is doing is in protest of an illegal and oppressive government that rules his nation?"

"He could say that, sir, but that wouldn't make it true, would it? Wroxter is part of Ilbeoria. The avenues to make changes in the government are as open to him as they are to anyone else."

"Suppose the Wolf-King decreed that on every Churchday we were to punch every old woman we saw. Would you do it?"

"No, because that law is clearly wrong."

"Even if the King says God told him it was necessary."

"God would not do that."

"Perhaps, then, Wroxtermen see the Customs Acts as nonbinding upon them, the same as you obviated the Laamti prohibition against eating beef."

"So he is *not* a sinner?"

Kidd smiled slowly. "You were correct the first time; Captain Ollis *is* a sinner."

"Then why argue around in circles?"

"Argument is of the mind, Cadet, but it's the heart that knows evil." Kidd tapped his own chest. "Sin resides in the heart and you have to judge men by the content of their heart, not their minds. The mind can agree that the ends justify the means, but the heart never can."

Uriah pondered that for a moment, then nodded. "So Ollis and Fernandi are brothers under the skin."

"Hardly. Ollis is a man like all the rest of us. His sins, because he is convinced in his mind and a bit of his heart that his crimes are not serious, are venial. He will not be damned for all time if he dies unshriven, as Fernandi will be. And that is the key that too many people forget: sins, all sins, can be forgiven if forgiveness is sought in earnest, with an open and loving heart. Sin is a fault within us, an imperfection, that keeps us apart from God."

"Are you saying Fernandi can never be forgiven, Colonel?"

"Fernandi, Cadet Smith, will never *ask* to be forgiven."

"But if someone did ask, he would be forgiven?"

Kidd nodded. "Any man, any sin."

Uriah looked away to the highest mountain peak. "You once told me that God sometimes punishes people while still on this earth. He might visit upon him an affliction as punishment for that sin. How is it that Fernandi escaped such divine retribution, when his sins were so great, and yet other suffer for more minor transgressions?"

Kidd shrugged and fatigue washed over his face. "I have no answer for you, Cadet. My . . . affliction—"

"No, sir, I didn't mean to suggest—"

"My affliction is a reminder from God, a goad to action. The last thing I saw before my eyes were taken was a vision the meaning of which it took years for me to begin to understand. You were there when God reminded me of it and you saw what I saw with the chess set. It is what led us on this journey."

"So if you succeed in saving the Dost, God will give you back your eyes?"

"I don't know. I don't know if I am worthy of seeing again because of the sins my pride in having that vision and my dedication to puzzling it out has caused me to commit."

"What sins are you talking about?"

"Cadet, inspiring fear in every student who presented an Advanced Tactics project is but one example. When I lost my sight I abandoned friends, I did other things that were selfish, all because I was in pain and angry and clinging to this vision as if it were my only salvation. It has taken me a long time to see how wrong I was, and when I reached that point, God again granted me a piece of a vision that told me I was again on the right path." Kidd pounded a fist against his breastbone. "In my heart I know this is right, but I also know there are sins for which I must atone. If God, in His wisdom, grants me absolution and, by some miracle, restores my sight, I will be very happy. If not, I will strive to grow closer to God so that in the next world I will enjoy all I have missed here."

Uriah shook his head. "I think I would be more angry at God than you are."

"I tried that for a while, and discovered the only thing worse than being blind was being blind and stupid." Kidd gave Uriah a half-smile. "Hating someone who will forgive you any transgression seemed the height of stupidity to me."

"That's something that never occurred to me."

"It's a lesson many fail to learn, Cadet." Kidd nodded thoughtfully. "Fernandi once told me that if he allowed himself to believe in God, he would do so only so he could hate Him. I told Fernandi that if he was wrong, if there was a God, he'd burn in Hell. Fernandi countered that if I were right, at least we'd be warm and have an eternity to laugh over how wrong we'd been. I'm here to make sure that prediction does not come true because, truth be told, I've never been that cold, and conversing with Fernandi for eternity would indeed be Hell itself."

— 33 —

> **Gauntlan Manor, Dhilica**
> **Puresaran, Aran**
> **20 Tempest 1687**

As he lighted from the carriage in front of the sprawling Grimshaw home, Robin Drury realized he wished he were again dropping into a pitched battle from the *Saint Michael*. He did not feel comfortable all dressed up in proper evening wear—one of the last things of which Dennis Chilton had convinced him was that for a dinner at the Grimshaw mansion he needed a good suit of clothes. Robin would have preferred to be wearing his dress uniform, but the tailor Chilton had recommended had told him such things were not done by *gentlemen*.

I should have told him I am not a gentleman. Robin forced a smile on his face as he proceeded up the white crushed-stone walkway to the front door. *If I were a gentleman I would not feel so uncomfortable. I am a Wolf-priest. I was chosen for a higher purpose.*

Robin allowed himself a bit of a smile. *I don't think being ill at ease among the rich is that much of a bad thing for me.* His brush with the aristocracy and how they dealt with those they saw as their inferiors during his days at the Lakeworth Carriage Works factory had left a sour taste in his mouth. While there were individuals like Dennis Chilton and Amanda Grimshaw who clearly were able to escape their upbringings, Robin found most aristocrats to be hopelessly prideful and out of touch with the realities of the world. *They view others the way a chess player views his pieces and that level of detachment is hideous.*

Even at twilight, with the surrounding palm trees and shrubs beginning to engulf the house in darkness, Gauntlan Manor was a sight to behold. At the center the structure rose to three tall stories with a steeply pitched roof of red ceramic tiles capping it. All around this central tower the ground floor spread out to fill a square of sufficient size that were the tower to fall in any direction, it would only land within the confines of the manor. A red-tile roof covered a verandah that surrounded the building.

The factory I worked in back in Ilbeoria was smaller than this house. Robin mounted the steps and crossed to the door. The big brass door knocker shined without tarnish despite the humidity. Robin raised the weight and let it crash down against the plate beneath the ornate wolf's-head.

He noticed that if he lifted the weight all the way up, he could have rapped it against the wolf's skull and he thought he spied wear there that suggested others might have done just that before. Flipping a knocker like that was a sign of contempt for the Church that he recalled doing when he was but a boy. He suspected those who had done it here were filled with less boyish mischief than true contempt for the King and his long reach into their affairs here in Aran.

He stepped back to look at the house again as he waited. *Come to think of it, the village I lived in was smaller than this house.*

An Aranan dressed in Urovian attire—save for the white turban wound round his head—opened the door. "Good evening, sir."

"Brother Robert Drury."

"You are expected, sir." The Aranan managed his Ilbeorian in clipped crisp syllables that lacked the singsong undercurrent of the pidgin language used by most Aranans. "Please follow Pradeep."

Robin entered the foyer and followed another Aranan down a

central corridor which ran the length of the house. Pradeep said nothing, but then from his limited experience with footmen Robin knew it was not the servant's place to speak to a guest save in an emergency or under great duress. Not that the man needed to say anything—his size alone impressed Robin. Even discounting the inches added by the turban, the servant exceeded Robin in both physical height and the width of his shoulders. Robin had seldom found himself smaller than anyone and he secretly wondered if Grimshaw had hired such a large footman to make Robin uncomfortable.

Or did he hire such a large man because it gave him pleasure to be commanding someone who could break him in half like kindling?

Pradeep opened the door to the drawing room and ushered Robin in. The Wolf-priest immediately found himself the center of attention and started to feel he had been ambushed. Chilton's instructions about such dinner engagements had included an admonishment to be fifteen minutes late. Robin knew Chilton would not have misled him, which meant, in turn, that the other guests had been urged to arrive before half past seven.

Robin's unease began to wane as Amanda Grimshaw turned and smiled at him. Excusing herself from a conversation with two older women, she strode boldly over to where he stood before the doors. The rustle of her gold satin gown filled the awkward silence created by his arrival. "I am happy to see you again, Brother Robert."

Robin bowed his head to her, then took her hand and kissed it. "The pleasure, truly, is mine."

"I have heard you had a most extraordinary adventure in Mendhakgaon."

"How did you hear about that?"

"I have my sources."

Erwin Grimshaw cut between two men whose girth strained the seams of their waistcoats. "Excellent, you have arrived. Pradeep, tell Lutley we are all here." Focusing on Robin, the host smiled. "News of your exploits traveled swiftly through our community. When I had said we would invite you to be our guest, I did not realize we would be having such a hero with us."

"I am no hero."

"False modesty will not survive here, sir. You are among friends who understand."

Understand what? There was something in Grimshaw's oily tone that sent a shiver down Robin's spine.

The doors to the drawing room opened and an Ilbeorian of moderate build and a full head of flowing white hair announced, "Dinner is served."

The people in the room quickly moved to join their dinner partners. Amanda slipped her left arm through Robin's right and guided him into position behind her father and a woman she said was her aunt.

"Is your father widowed?" he whispered as they moved into the hall and turned left.

"No, my mother is still in Ilbeoria." Amanda's smile hardened around her eyes. "She is not of a temperament to deal with Aran. Aunt Philomena is here to see to the proper running of our household."

"I see," Robin murmured politely. He had the impression that while Amanda had not lied to him, she had not shared with him the whole truth about her mother. The way she reached over with her right hand to hold his arm suggested to him that she had not wanted to mislead him purposely, and further that she was ashamed of herself and her act. That did not surprise him—women of her breeding were not given to lying easily and especially not to members of the clergy.

He glanced back over his shoulder at the other guests. Most of the men looked to be anywhere from five to thirty years older than he was, with all of them in the various growing stages of corpulence associated with prosperity. He had a military man's disdain for such an obvious lack of physical conditioning and it was exacerbated by the liquor blush on their faces and the extreme degree to which all of them had shaved their heads. While the military had definite regulations about how much tonsure was allowed with each rank, laity had no such hard-and-fast rules. *Most of the men look as if the cut of a razor exceeds their wisdom by miles.*

The women all looked older than their male counterparts. Most of them dripped jewelry and had swathed their full figures in thick layers of silk. Several wore long fingernails that were only suited to a life of personal idleness. The remaining women were slender to the point of being skeletal. While nothing in their color suggested they were ill, their smiles appeared to have been chiseled into their faces beneath their hollow, dead eyes.

Robin smiled down to Amanda. "It would seem Aran treats blessed few Ilbeorian women well."

"I shall take that as a compliment, Brother Robin."

"As it was intended. You have obviously flourished here."

Lutley led the way into a room on the right side of the corridor. Erwin Grimshaw took his place at the head of the table and put Philomena at his right hand. Robin stood next to her and Amanda next to him. The other six couples distributed themselves around the table, leaving Michael Crowe at the far end and Anthony Ekins, publisher of the *Dhilica Monitor*, across from Robin.

Erwin Grimshaw open his arms. "Welcome, my friends. Please enjoy the hospitality of Gauntlan Manor." He pulled his chair out and moved to seat himself, but stopped when his daughter coughed lightly. "Yes, Amanda?"

"Perhaps, Father, Brother Robert would like to say grace?"

Irritation darkened Grimshaw's face for a second, but a smile chased it away. "If you would be so kind, Brother Robert."

Robin bent his head. "Dear Father, we offer thanks for this meal and this company. By Your will we enjoy this bounty, fruits of men's labor, but gifts from Thee regardless. By Your will."

The men held the chairs for their partners, with Grimshaw being the exception. Lutley seated Philomena then directed Pradeep and another footman—similarly attired from turban to buckle shoes and identically sized—in presenting the guests with their soup. Service proceeded in what Chilton had termed "Stranan style." A footman appeared at Robin's left elbow holding a steaming tureen of beef consommé from which Robin ladled out enough to fill his bowl halfway.

He returned the ladle to the tureen carefully so as not to splash the man with hot soup. It struck Robin that the man, while wanting to avoid being scalded, might well have been more concerned about the source of the broth instead of its temperature. Across the table he noticed Diana Ekins, one of the scarecrow women, all but toss the ladle back into the tureen, heedless of the Laamtist footman's discomfort.

Chilton's instructions had been comprehensive when dealing with dinner and the first rule was one with which Robin had no difficulty complying. "Brother Dennis tells me that it is my duty to engage you in conversation, Miss Grimshaw, if you would not find the idea of same oppressive."

"I should enjoy speaking with you very much, Brother Robin." She smiled invitingly. "As Brother Dennis told you, such conversation should be of little consequence, but that is a convention I would flaunt. I am compelled by curiosity to ask you what you thought of Mrilan and the Himlans."

"Aran, as a whole, is very beautiful country. There are pristine places that look much as I imagine the Grove of Urjard must have been before the Fall of Man." Robin, prompted by other questions from Amanda, supplied a travelogue throughout the soup and two fish courses. She countered with a description of a trip she had taken a year before to Vlengul and that saw them through oysters, lamb cutlets, and Aranan antelope steaks. Erwin Grimshaw demanded a recounting of the battle of Mendhakgaon, which Robin truncated and sanitized for the sake of the ladies present. That story occupied the duration of the roasted game hen course, bringing them to the final entrèe, roast tenderloin of beef.

Dennis had told Robin that he was not expected to eat everything he was served. He had to keep reminding himself of that because the food was wonderful. Even though he had been in Dhilica since the twelfth of the month and no longer forced to endure shipfare, airfleet rations were neither as good nor as plentiful as even the wastage at the Grimshaw table. Even having eaten sparingly, by the time Pradeep offered him slices of tenderloin, Robin almost felt too stuffed to take more food.

To be polite he took one filet, but his hesitation had been noticed. Others at the table seemed to collectively let their breath out when he placed the meat on his plate. Robin couldn't figure out why his action would have been of concern to them, but then he noticed how everyone else took very generous portions of beef.

Are these people that *vulgar?* The only reason Robin could see for such gluttonous behavior was that the servants could not eat beef. Forcing them to serve it and watch the guests eat it, then to clear the plates, meant the gulf between Ilbeorian and Aranan was emphasized in precise and even insulting terms. Robin, having been a common laborer in Ilbeoria, had no doubt the servants knew very well the size of the social chasm between themselves and the guests. He wondered why the guests felt it necessary to stress the differences so bluntly.

Robin put his knife and fork down without eating any of the tenderloin. He noticed Amanda did the same and shared with him a brief smile. The rest of the assembly did not notice what they had done. They devoured their meat quickly, eating as if they had consumed nothing for days previous. Enough of them left one or more filets behind on their plates that Robin felt certain they believed he and Amanda had eaten their fill.

Mangoes and cheese arrived as the final dish, but Robin had lost all appetite. The other diners finished their desert in short order, then Philomena set her linen napkin down and rose from her place. "Ladies, shall we repair to the drawing room for coffee?"

The other women murmured farewells to their dinner companions and followed Philomena from the room. Amanda's good-bye had been delivered with a neutral tone, but the way she let her right hand trail across his shoulders gave Robin the impression she did not want to be going. He smiled at her, knowing he would see her again when, after port and cigars, the men returned to the drawing room for coffee themselves. Given that her father was so keen on whist, and the party had sixteen people, Robin even anticipated cards might end the evening.

After Amanda left the room, Lutley closed the doors near the head of the table, then walked to the far end of the room. Robin didn't watch him or what he did, but when the Wolf-priest heard a panel sliding away into the wall he looked up. Erwin stood and pointed toward the hidden doorway and the stairs visible beyond it. "Gentlemen, if you will join me in the tower, we may see to our pleasure."

Chilton's instructions had not addressed this sort of thing specifically, though it had included a general rule that the host's invitations should be accepted graciously. The other guests were up and out of their chairs even before Grimshaw finished his invitation to relocate, so Robin stood and moved off with them.

Because of the size of the men preceding him up the stairs, Robin was on the landing to the first floor before he got a look at their destination. The room into which they walked occupied the center of the tower and had narrow, arching windows in the north and south walls. In the place of windows to the east or west Robin saw doorways that led into small, dark rooms. Another stairway, located at the opposite corner of the room, led up to the tower's top floor.

The room had been decorated opulently and in sharp contrast to the lower level of the house. Down below the furnishings had been typically Ilbeorian—heavy and strong, built with right angles from dark wood. While some locally woven carpets had provided splashes of color, the somber brown and deep mahogany dominated Guantlan Manor's living area. Save for the humidity and the race of the footmen, on the ground floor Robin could easily have imagined himself back in Ilbeoria.

But here, gaudy silk sheets of the sheerest nature hung from the ceiling. They appeared to have been woven from a rainbow of vapors and helped make the large space intimate and even dreamlike. Huge cushions lay scattered about, piled one upon another atop thick, lush carpeting. The only chairs Robin saw in the room were ornate and styled after Lescari Imperial designs which had become equated with decadence in the minds of most Ilbeorians.

The two footmen closed the doors then moved to a sideboard where they picked up trays laden with half-filled brandy snifters and a box of cigars. They circulated through the company, their faces impassive, but their movements slightly wooden. Once everyone had been served—Robin accepted brandy but refused a cigar—the footmen retreated back to the doors. One of the men—Harald Sinclair, an engineer—displayed his magickal talent by lighting the cigars with a touch.

A cloud of white smoke drifting from his mouth, Anthony Ekins leaned forward conspiratorially. "So, your telling of the battle of Mendhakgaon differs from what I've heard really happened. You don't have to soften it for us now that the ladies are gone. What really happened?"

Robin shrugged uneasily as Ekins's question focused everyone's attention on him. "It was much as I described it at dinner. The village had burned and the bandits were laying siege to the mission. We fought them, killed a few, and the rest ran off."

Ekins brought his cigar swooping down with smoke trailing behind it. "Then the *Saint Mike* came in and gave those thieving wogs what for."

Grimshaw snorted smoke like a dragon. "Good sign for the heathen to see. Smart of you to bring the survivors back to Dhilica so they could spread the news. Took the *Kestrel* to settle things a year ago, now the *Saint Mike* has reinforced the message. Still, son, your part hasn't gone unnoticed. Story goes that you cut the leader in half and that put the fear of God into the ragwigs. Takes a brave and wise man to know how to break the enemy. We have need of such men out here."

"I believe, sir, you are presuming too much based on rumor."

Grimshaw blew his objection away with another gust of smoke. "I think not, sir. I have made inquiries about you, sir, since we met and I have been favorably impressed with what I have learned. I am confident Aran is better for having you here than not."

Robin knew Grimshaw had something on his mind and wished the man would come to his point directly. He also knew he would not because Grimshaw was cautious. "I hardly think, sir, I can be of enough influence that a nation would notice me or my contributions to its history."

Ekins gestured toward Robin with his snifter, spilling a dollop of the amber liquid. "You are wrong, sir. You have already killed a bandit raiding into Aran from across the border in Drangiana. You and your ethyrines showed yourselves to be competent and fearless, and that counts for a great deal here in Aran. While all of us, for our various enterprises, have our own little militias, you command the most potent fighting force on this subcontinent."

"We're less than a hundred men."

"But Aran is a place where one man, in the right place, at the right time, can divert the course of history into a channel he wants." Grimshaw's gray eyes became slits. "You know, of course, that the

Beregians first reached Aran three hundred years ago. Julio De Souza went to the Hranje of Vlengul and said he was an envoy from the King of Beregia. He talked the Hranje into writing up an agreement for exclusive trading rights to Vlengul with Beregia, then returned to his home country and talked King Gervasio into ratifying the agreement."

"I know that history, sir, and it is entertaining, but the fact is that those times have passed." Robin coughed lightly into his hand. "Aran is a big place. I am here to serve our nation as best as I am able. Nothing less."

"But perhaps something more?"

The Wolf-priest eyed Grimshaw carefully. "Excuse me, sir?"

"Your service here can benefit you, as well. This dinner, for example, is held in your honor. These men, my friends, will extend other invitations to you—though none of them have a daughter as lovely as mine is." Grimshaw smiled easily through the smoke. "We are a small community here, Brother Robert, and we acknowledge the debts we owe one another. We repay favors in kind."

"But my service requires no repayment."

"But our gratitude requires us to thank you very directly. In fact, toward that end, you shall go first."

"First, sir?"

Ekins smiled at him. "After this honor, you'll slay whole companies of wogs."

Grimshaw drained his brandy, then took Robin's partially filled snifter from him. "If you please, stand over by that red pillow."

Dread stiffened Robin's legs as he paced over to the point in the middle of the room. He heard someone—Grimshaw probably—clap twice. A draft blew into the room from the far corner where the stairs were. The wind billowed the silken cloths up, parting them, then letting them undulate back together.

Women followed in the wake of the breeze and Robin's mouth gaped in surprise. Ten of them came down the stairs and filed through the doorway. They varied in height and shape, yet were all unfailingly beautiful. They wore embroidered silk vests that were cut so high that he could see the softly rounded underedge of their breasts. Their skirts, which had been gathered around their slender waists by belts made of linked gold Suns, had been cut from the same sheer cloth as was draped throughout the room. They wore silk in enough layers that he had to imagine what he could not actually see, but their attire was a tonic to his imagination and sent it off in all manner of directions.

Robin looked at the women each in turn. Some were dark-

skinned and full-lipped, with long black hair typical of the people
from the deserts of Decaran. Others had complexions barely darker
than his own, with features more closely approximating those common in Urovia. He assumed they were half-castes. Still others,
slightly taller with a golden hue to their skin, had sharpened ears
and a bluish tint around their eyes. He marked them as Alansajarans
of Durranian descent. The two of them were a long way from home
and, as with anything that was imported, Robin knew they had to be
expensive.

The women smiled at him with their mouths, and he felt the
stirrings of lust in his loins. They were undeniably attractive and,
from the sensuous ways they shifted their hips or the subtle and self-
conscious hand motions they made, Robin knew they would be very
good at what they did. He'd seen that look before, felt the caresses
their smiles promised, in Urovian harbor towns during the war.
Memories of his adventures bubbled back up into his mind as another breeze ruffled skirts and brought to him their perfume.

Lust. To Robin it was the most obvious, basic, and insidious of
the Deadly Sins. When the Durranian woman on the end ran the
glistening tip of her tongue over her lips, his body wanted to respond to her. The way her hands slowly brushed down her flat stomach, then out to rest on her hipbones, started his heart racing. Her
hands came forward, palms turning outward, as she stretched casually. That motion deepened the hollow between her breasts, something she clearly knew would quicken Robin's breathing.

His physical, animal nature urged him to select her. At his core
he wanted to steal away with her, carry her to one of the little pillow-
laden rooms. He wanted to tear her clothes off and ravish her. He
wanted to lick the sweat of their exertions from her body, then have
her again and again. His body wanted him to lose himself in the he-
donistic carnality of the moment, to stop thinking and just to act.

*And once upon a time, I would have stopped thinking and just
acted.*

"This is how you mean to thank me?" Robin turned slowly to
see seven men leering expectantly at him. "With a concubine?"

Grimshaw nodded. "Take two if you like; there are enough for
all of us."

Robin regarded his host carefully, uncertain if he'd really heard
what Grimshaw had said. "Two, sir?"

Ekins laughed. "He's a young buck of a man, fresh from war.
He might want *all* of them."

The Wolf-priest's face closed down. *I don't believe this is happening. These men are mad.* "This is wrong."

Grimshaw looked surprised. "The law of the land allows men of sufficient means to keep concubines."

"It's not the law of the land I'm worried about." Robin folded his arms, his eyes narrowing. "You can't do this. It's *wrong*."

Ekins laughed. "Come now, you're a healthy man. You have appetites. Have you never indulged—"

Robin cut him off. "What *I* have or have not done is not an issue here, sir."

"We're sinning, yes?" Peter Marsh yawned. "You want to tell us we're imperiling our souls."

Ekins waved his cigar through the air. "Do not worry yourself, Brother Robert. Message received. Tomorrow or the next day I'll nip on down to a church, confess my sins to one of your brethren, and I will be right again with God."

"You *are* imperiling your souls and mocking God by thinking you'll be forgiven when you have no remorse. Even so, that's not my major concern here." Robin pointed back toward the doorway. "Your wives and daughters are down there. They must know what you are doing up here. What you do here hurts them; it must."

"Not likely." One of the men pointed to a panel of wooden scrollwork set in the west wall. "My lady wife likes to watch."

"I suppose I should not be surprised at that, but I am." Robin shook his head. "But even if your wives sanction your activities, they're still wrong. Think of what you're doing to these women."

Grimshaw shrugged. "We're asking them to practice skills they have perfected, skills for which they were purchased. We are most appreciative and we help them fulfill their purpose on this earth."

"I doubt very much, sir, if what *they* wanted out of life is what they have *now*."

"Do you, Brother Robert?" Grimshaw's face hardened. "These women, were they not here, would be in a brothel in the Varatha Quarter, bedding with cockroaches, eating garbage, and rutting with all manner of unwashed, lice-ridden scum. Most of them would already be dead and all would be diseased, with their teeth rotted out, their hair oily and matted, their full breasts flat dugs flopping against bony chests.

"Their life here is one without want."

"Except Mr. Grimshaw, they go without *freedom*." Robin looked at the women, then back at the men lusting after them. "A well-groomed mare in a clean stable may have a better life than a plow horse tilling a field, but it is no less property. I'm certain, Mr. Grimshaw, that you and your friends believe you're doing these women a grand favor by saving them from the life they would have known, but you're not saving them for *their* sakes, you're saving them for your sake. That's wrong, and I'll take no part in it."

Robin marched forward and split the line of men. He headed straight for the door, but the two footmen stepped into his path. Robin stopped.

"Tell them to let me pass, Mr. Grimshaw, or I will hurt them. Badly."

"You rebuke us for lust, yet you pride yourself on thinking you could best them."

Robin turned back and stared down at Grimshaw. "You apparently believe you are not done with me, but I *am* done with you."

"You're correct, sir, for once." Grimshaw glanced at his other guests. "These men and I represent the true power here in Aran. I want you to know this so you will understand why your life becomes miserable here. You have insulted us and clearly have shown you deserve no consideration from us. Therefore you will be crushed beneath our heels. It is the way life works here in Aran— you are with us or against us. We offered you a chance. You shall have no other."

When Grimshaw finished speaking, Robin took white gloves from his internal jacket pocket, drew them on and nodded curtly. "Understand this, Mr. Grimshaw, gentlemen, I am not someone you own, nor am I someone you will *ever* own. And *if* you were as powerful as you believe you are, you'd have no need to enslave people to enjoy your company."

"We don't keep these women because we *have* to, we keep them because we are *able* to." Grimshaw let a little laugh rattle from his throat. "Power is nothing if it is not used."

"Power unused is still power. Power misused is *nothing*." Robin turned on his heel and faced the doors again. Breathing a prayer to Saint Martin, he raised his hands and balled his fists. The magick invoked by the prayer made his white gloves glow a bluish-purple. "Tell them to step aside."

"Pradeep, Harinder, let him pass, then pour us more brandy."

The twin Aranan giants opened the doors for Robin, then closed them after he stepped through. He stood on the landing for a moment, alone in the dark except for the glow of his gloves.

Echoes of derisive laughter seeped through the doors and washed over him.

They laugh because they believe they have humiliated me and expelled me from the ranks of the wisest men in Aran. Robin unknotted his fists and looked at his glowing gloves. He began to smile and, taking the steps two at a time, even started laughing. *And I laugh because the wisest men in Aran believe gloves that do nothing more than glow are a sign of power. They might not be stupid, but they don't know as much as they think they do, and that may well prove to be Aran's salvation.*

— 34 —

Matrah Ghul
Drangiana
24 Tempest 1687

Am I even supposed to be here? Uriah asked himself yet one more time since he and Kidd had left the Himlans. Trekking through the mountains had been difficult—physically and mentally. Not sharing a language with the guides, he could only communicate with them in a very rudimentary fashion. *I know little and clearly am not the aide Kidd needs in this quest. Robin should be here, or someone else.*

At the border of Drangiana the guides turned around and headed back home. Uriah was sorry to see them go because they had been the ones who picked their campsites, fetched water, collected firewood, saw to the horses, and prepared meals. He had learned a little about surviving in the area from them, and when they abandoned the trek, the meals and choice of campsites suffered to the point of making the journey on the *Stoat* seem like luxury itself.

Uriah fed more wood into the fire he'd kindled to keep the twilight's chill at bay. While the trail heading north toward Helansajar had descended quite a bit from the heights of the Himlans and Varatha Pass, the Drangianan highlands still had thin air and cold nights. More annoying than the cold, though, was Uriah's discovery that in thin air he had no stamina. He had to do the work of two men, but he only had the strength of half a man with which to do it.

His inability to keep up with physical tasks had burrowed down into his brain and started eating away at who he was. He realized that even *he* couldn't live up to his own previously high standards, that he was being pushed to his limits and beyond. Before he had never been driven to the point where he might fail at something, and doubting himself was a new and terrifying experience. *I've clung forever to the* me *I built myself into, and now that's crumbling. What will I have left if it goes?*

He glanced back at where Kidd sat with his back against a big rock and the heels of his boots hooked over the edge of a crack in the rock on which he sat. Shrouded in a black wool blanket, the older man stared silently into the distance. The evening's rising breeze tugged at his white hair, but Kidd gave no sign of noticing it. Unmoving and bleached of color by the onset of twilight, he exhibited as much life as a stone.

Kidd doesn't even seem to notice how hard things are. He has his goal and that's what sustains him. The youth shivered, more from fear than cold, and started to rummage around in the saddlebags for food. Kidd had done no complaining about their pace after the Himlanan guides headed back, but Uriah knew he wanted to be pushing on faster. *We've come all this way and yet he keeps his impatience bottled up!*

"Colonel, do you want your beef dry, or should I boil it up?"

"I'm not really that hungry."

"Sir, you need to eat something. You're all in, you just don't see it." Uriah clapped a hand over his mouth. "I'm sorry, sir, I didn't mean it the way—"

"Don't worry yourself, Cadet, I understand." Kidd shook his head. "Take care of yourself, Uriah, I'm fine."

"I don't mind boiling yours up same as mine." Uriah smiled. "A little broth will do us both well, and the boiled meat will be easier to chew."

"It would be at that, Uriah." Kidd shuddered and clutched the blanket more tightly around himself. "Still, your effort will be wasted. Neither one of us will eat tonight."

Uriah's stomach growled in protest. "What do you mean?"

The older man blinked his silver eyes. "Tonight it is over. Tonight the Dost comes."

"What?" Uriah stood and looked around. "I don't see anything, don't hear anything. How do you know?"

"I know."

Uriah heard some sadness in Kidd's voice. "Are you thinking about what will happen now, if you're wrong or you're right?" The young man tossed a large chunk of wood into the fire and watched sparks swirl up into the sky. "I don't know how you can be so calm."

"I'm not really calm, Uriah, more contemplative. I was allowing myself to imagine how my life might have been different had I made other choices." Kidd shook his head. "It's an idler's game and I really shouldn't indulge myself."

"No harm in that is there, sir? If you'd not made the choice you did to take me on as your aide I expect my brother would have me betrothed to someone right now." Uriah sighed and refastened the straps on the food satchel. "Don't know if I'd like that or not. I'd be warmer, probably, and better fed."

Kidd smiled. "And would find a fiancée more interesting than me, I suspect."

"It's possible, but she'd have been my brother's choice, not mine. I think the woman I'd like would be one who would want to be here."

"Someone worthy of your high standards, Uriah?"

"Yes, sir." Uriah allowed himself a little laugh. "If things had been different for you, Colonel, would you be married now?"

"Being a Wolf-priest doesn't preclude my marrying, you know that." Kidd drew his knees up to his chest and held himself tightly. "I would have thought I'd be married by this time but, then, my eyes . . ."

A wistfulness had entered Kidd's voice and prompted Uriah to glance down at the rock. "What was she like, sir?"

"You're assuming there was someone, Cadet." The older man glanced over, his eyes pale orbs in the starlight. "And, in this case, your assumption was correct."

"Was she someone you met in Lescar, sir, like Prince Trevelien's Rochelle?"

"No, I met her later, but she was very much like Rochelle in some ways. Intelligent and willing to accept responsibility for all manner of things. She had a curiosity that was tempered with common sense. Her laugh could shatter the most dour of moods—though I never felt dour in her company. I actually had every intention of making her my wife after the war, but . . ." Kidd closed his eyes.

"She sounds as if she was wonderful, sir." Uriah shrugged. "Still and all, having her man be blinded, well, that would be a burden. You can't really fault her for not wanting to shoulder that much responsibility, at least not when the shock of it was still on her."

"Don't do her a disservice, Uriah. She was not so shallow." Flickering tongues of firelight danced golden reflections onto Kidd's unseeing eyes. "I decided I'd not burden her with my care, and not because I thought she couldn't or wouldn't handle it. I just didn't want to see myself as being a burden. It—"

"It robbed you of being who you thought you were, and you had to hold to that, thinking you could get back there, to keep you going."

Kidd blinked his eyes. "Very good, Mr. Smith. You deduce in a heartbeat what it took me years to learn."

"Truth be told, sir, I've been working that same way for my entire twenty-three years and have only just come to see it myself." Uriah tossed the food satchel aside and scrubbed his hands over his face. "For the longest time I wanted to be my own person, distinct from my brothers. I didn't really want to go to Sandwycke because my brother Bartholomew had already gone, but the other choices were worse. The fact that I can wield some powerful battlemagicks—at least I have the potential to, once I finish my training—that was something to be proud of. Still, my brother's having been there before me and all—"

"Made you uneasy and even resentful. That's why you would excel when you could, but only in places where he had not?"

"I guess, sir, yes, that's it." Uriah snorted. "Seems so shallow now."

"Selfish, even?"

"Yes."

Kidd laughed aloud. "Congratulations, Uriah Smith, you've reached a point in your life few people ever do, and one that even fewer use as a stepping-off point for the rest of their lives. You've seen that who you want to be and who you think you are may not be sufficient. There is more out there, God's plan is out there. I've accepted it and now I'm here. If you accept it as well you will move on to far greater things than you could ever have imagined."

"Yes, sir. I'll work on accepting what He has in store for me."

Kidd nodded solemnly. "Your only regret will come if you retreat from this point."

The scrape of metal on a rock brought Uriah's head up before he could frame a reply. It took his eyes a second or two to adjust to the darkness outside the campfire's circle of light, then he saw the shadowy forms of half a dozen men weaving their way through the rocks at the south end of the hollow. Turning slowly, he looked past Kidd and saw yet more men entering the hollow. "I don't like the looks of this."

Kidd threw off his blanket and stood. As he peered into the darkness, the men at the hollow's north end gasped audibly. "How many, Uriah?"

"The place is alive with them, sir. They're cautious, but they're carrying more knives than I've seen at Sandwycke's mess hall." Uriah looked around again. "Twenty, maybe more."

All of them were swarthy and dirty, though Uriah thought he probably looked none too savory himself. Most of them stayed at the edges of the firelight. A tall, clean-limbed man with dark hair and a full moustache stepped forward, then crouched down. He fished in a pouch on his belt for something, then pulled out what looked to Uriah to be a ruby. He pressed it to his heart and closed his eyes. His men likewise crouched, and Uriah grew more anxious as they watched their leader and waited.

A humming started low then built in intensity, but Uriah couldn't place its point of origin. He saw a number of the intruders look skyward and he followed their gazes up to study the white splash of stars streaking the night's black void. He saw something gold flash through the sky, then spiral down toward them. At the same time the sound grew louder and Uriah began to shiver.

"Something odd, Colonel."

"What?"

"I don't know. It isn't natural." What Uriah saw was so incredible that he really had no way to even begin to describe it. It started out looking like a huge dragonfly with a golden body, with flesh so polished that it caught and reflected the firelight back. The wings, which looked to be silver and crystal, moved so fast they blurred. Beyond its size and being made of metal, the thing wore the wrong head. "It has a man's head. It's all metal and big and has a man's head, sir."

Uriah focused on that fact then realized the humming had died and, while he'd been looking at the head, the body had changed. The bulbous insect body had narrowed in some places and broadened in others, with multiple limbs and wings combining to form arms and legs. Yet even without wings and sound it managed to hover in the air, a good yard above the rock. Silver tiger stripes streaked the golden statue's body. Just at the moment Uriah had accepted that somehow the statue was going to hang frozen in the air, the limbs became fluid, then the creature slowly stepped down to the floor of the hollow as if descending invisible steps. *"Dobry vyehchyir."*

Kidd raised an eyebrow. "He speaks Stranan. Is he in Vandari armor?"

"Too small, too strange." Uriah looked over at the Colonel. "He's made of gold, sir. The humming . . . he was a dragonfly. Now he's a man of gold with silver tiger stripes."

"Gold with silver stripes?" Kidd shivered. "Does he look like a bear?"

"No, sir. I said a *man*."

The man of gold spoke to the intruders in a tongue Uriah could not identify and they drew their curved swords with the unmistakable rasp of steel on scabbard.

"*Nyet, nyet.*" Kidd tapped his own chest. "*Minya zavoot Malachy Kidd. Drauka.*" Kidd's identifying himself in Stranan and claiming to be a friend did nothing to stop the circling men.

The gold man pressed his hand to his own chest and the fingers seemed to merge with it as if his flesh was liquid. "*Minya zavoot Nimchin. Ya Dost.*"

Uriah's jaw shot open. "The Dost?"

"Yes."

"So it *does* end tonight."

The Dost spoke again to the men accompanying him. They swarmed forward and grabbed the two Ilbeorians.

Kidd shouted in Stranan, but Uriah saw words weren't going to do any good. The younger man jammed his elbow into the stomach of the man on his left, then brought his left fist around and tried to punch the man on his right. That man brought his own head forward and smashed it into Uriah's face. Pain exploded from the bridge of Uriah's nose to the back of his skull, then rebounded toward his face again. A foot clipped his heels together, knocking him off his feet, and he sat down hard.

The man he'd elbowed cuffed him, then sat on his legs, but Uriah barley noticed that. Across the fire from him three men had wrestled Kidd to the ground near his rock. With one on his legs and one each holding his arms out to his sides, Kidd could do nothing to resist them. He struggled for a second, then laid his head down and stared unseeing at the sky.

"Leave him alone, he's blind."

The Dost stopped in mid-stride and looked back at Uriah. The firelight slithered over his musculature, making the Dost appear to be an idealized human. The Dost spoke and the men restraining him tightened their hold on his limbs.

The Dost lowered himself to one knee at Kidd's side. He reached out with his right hand and brushed it over Kidd's face, as if gently closing a dead man's eyes. Uriah saw Kidd's body convulse violently enough to pitch off the man holding his legs, then the Wolf-priest lay very still.

Uriah tried to pull himself free, but could not. "What are you doing to him? If you killed him, you'll pay."

The Dost looked back at Uriah. "He . . . not be . . . die."

The shock of hearing Ilbeorian from the Dost slackened Uriah's resistance for a moment. "What did you do to him?"

The Dost again touched Kidd's forehead, but the body did not react at all. The man of gold looked at the other two Helansajarans restraining Kidd and spoke to them. They released the unconscious man's wrists, then the Dost took Kidd's right wrist in his left hand. He tugged the Colonel's body a foot to the left and laid the wrist across a dark crack in the bedrock.

"Leave him alone!" Uriah tried to pull his arms free, but he couldn't. "For God's sake . . . Leave him alone!"

The Dost's body shimmered for a second, then his left hand became fluid and poured down into the crack. Where the Dost's hand had encircled Kidd's wrist, a gold manacle bound Kidd to a post sunk into the crack in the rock. As the Dost pulled the stump of his arm back, another hand grew in at the end.

The Dost stood. "It be . . . is time to depart." He said something in Aralan and Uriah found himself jerked roughly to his feet.

"Wait, you can't leave him there." Uriah tried to pull his captors toward Kidd's body. "He's blind. You can't leave him there. He'll die."

The gold man looked from Uriah to Kidd and back again. "I am the Dost. I do what must be done."

"You can't leave him."

"It is not for you to be concerned."

"He's my responsibility, dammit!"

"And poorly you have acquitted your responsibility, then." The Dost shrugged. "No matter. It is time for him to be responsible for himself."

"Don't leave him. Don't." Uriah snarled at the men holding him. "He came here, all the way from Ilbeoria. He came here just to save *you*, save *your* life."

"It matters not that Malachy Kidd came looking for me." The Dost shook his head. "His fate does not concern me."

"How can you say that?"

"It is simple." The Dost shrugged his shoulders and huge angel's wings sprouted from his back. "I did not come here to end his quest, but to further mine. I came here looking for *you*, Uriah Smith, and now that I have you, I am one more step closer to reestablishing my dominion in this world."

Thus ends the Book of the Wolf.

BOOK II

THE
BOOK OF
THE BEAR

— 35 —

Malachy Kidd opened his eyes and discovered he was still blind. That fact surprised him. And his surprise further surprised him. *I have been blind for a dozen years, why should I expect things to be different now?* Still, something nagged at the back of his mind to tell him that he should have expected things to be different . . .

He started to sit up, but pressure and pain at his right wrist stopped him. He tried to pull his arm free but only a grinding pop in his shoulder rewarded his effort. He started to panic, then fought it and imposed some order on his thoughts. As he did so, images and impressions seeped into his brain and slowly resolved themselves in startling detail.

The inclusion of visual elements with his impressions of the previous evening startled Malachy, since that sort of thing had not happened in over a decade. His memories of the discussion he and Uriah had had remained black, but with the entrance of the intruders and especially the humming that ended it, he saw a bit of a golden spark. It grew brighter, a simple spot in the void that was his life, as the hum died and a voice started speaking in Stranan.

I tried to tell him we were friends. Malachy's flesh puckered with goose bumps. *He said he was Nimchin, the Dost.*

With a shiver he pushed himself past the possible significance of that bit of information. He remembered being wrestled to the ground and held there, then he had felt a cold hand on his forehead, brushing down over his eyes. For a fleeting, incomplete moment he had a vision of a golden man standing over him. Through the metal fingers he could see a redheaded Ilbeorian being restrained by Helansajarans, then a lightning jolt ran through his body. Then nothing.

No, not nothing. Kidd felt his mouth go dry as another image resolved itself in the darkness of his brain. Carved in gold from

black shadows, he saw a wolf's-head. Though he had nothing with
which to compare it, he knew it was huge. Featureless silver eyes
stared down at him, yet in them he saw a reflection of himself.

The words *Behold yourself* echoed through his mind.

Another shiver shook him. He linked that vision with the ones
he had seen in Glogau and at Sandwycke. "A bear, a babe, and a
wolf. All were metal and all had a role: enemy, charge, and me. I
thought there was a logic at work here, identifying my enemy and
the person I was to save, but I thought *my* role was clearly implied in
saving the babe from the enemy. The third vision seems redundant."

Why would God employ a miracle for no apparent reason?

Malachy laughed at himself. "The reason is just not apparent to
you, Malachy Kidd. You're still blind to the whole of his plan. It
would seem that *if* you are to save the Dost, it is not here and not
now. Perhaps the Dost is not ready to be saved or perhaps I am not
ready to save him."

He tugged at the restraint binding him to the rock. *Especially
not in this condition.*

Lying on his right side, he probed all around the shackle and
stuck the fingers of his left hand as deep as they would go into the
crack in the rock. He felt the cool metal as far down as his fingers
could get and assumed the slender post ran yet deeper.

Curling up into an awkward sitting position, Malachy used his
left hand and left leg to try to move the post. Nothing happened. He
tried to wiggle it back and forth but made no progress. He pressed
down on it, hoping to drive it further into the rock, but again his efforts were frustrated.

He felt around the shackle again and could find no seam or
hinge or clasp. He knew—absent great and powerful magick—it
was impossible for a manacle to be formed that way. The manacle's
smooth surface reminded him of his armor's featureless battlemask.
*Powerful magicks created that mask. Escaping this manacle must
be a test of my skills—if I succeed then my mission continues.*

For half a second Malachy thought it somewhat unfair for him
to be given such a challenge in light of what he'd already endured to
get where he was. He dismissed that thought immediately, letting it
be crushed beneath his belief that God would only demand of him
that which would make him better able to play his part in God's
plan. *The fact is that I've not used powerful magicks for years. I've
let my talent lie fallow and now I'll need it to free myself.*

Intellectually Malachy knew there was a way to escape from
the manacle. Anything that had been created through magick could
be broken by it. For every spell there was a counterspell, or another

spell that would warp what had been created. Had he been an Ignatian he would have known the spells necessary to soften the metal, since Ignatians learned them to help cadets form their steelsilk armor and battlemasks. He didn't know those spells, but knowing they existed meant he had a place to start. His reading of Augustinian texts further provided him with some background information that made it possible for him to improvise something.

A bit more analysis of the situation focused on a problem with the manacle binding him. The Dost, if in fact his captor had been the Dost, would have been raised in the Ataraxian tradition and would have used their magicks. *Could he have made my flesh flow around and into the manacle's opening using Ataraxian magick? And how was it that I actually felt I saw him and Uriah and the men with them? Was that Ataraxian magick, too, or something else? Does the Dost use some sort of other magick—Durranian magick—that combines aspects of Urovian and Estanuan magick?*

Malachy laughed aloud and shook his head. *Stick to the primary problem; you are not in your study sending an aide scurrying through books. Think later, act now. Regardless of what tradition the Dost is using, the nature of what he has done with the magick makes him a very powerful sorcerer. A good thing to remember, and something that means I'll have to push myself to get out of it.*

Ultimately it didn't matter if the metal had been made to flow around his hand or his flesh had been made to flow into it. The fact was that the manacle was metal and it was that metal he had to deal with. *Stay focused on the problem and you can solve it.*

Every graduate of Sandwycke learned how to modify and improvise spells. The spell Malachy had used on his walking stick to defeat the *Stoat*'s airmen had been a war-enchantment normally cast on maces and flails. Almost without thinking he had altered it, stepping down its power, since the walking stick could not have contained it and his opponents had worn no armor. Yet even in its reduced state it had crushed Philo's skull.

After devoting a bit more brainsweat to his predicament, Malachy realized what he needed to do first was to free the post from the rock. Once he had his freedom, he could work on getting his wrist free of the manacle itself. To do that he wanted to employ spells that would soften the metal enough for him to twist it free of the crack. While he knew no smithing magick, he did know simple spells to infuse heat into things—a spell found useful on cold nights in the field when a fire is not a good idea. *It's as good a place as any to start.*

Malachy brought his hands together in prayer. While modifying or invoking spells did not always require prayer, saints had been known to insulate the foolish from the consequences of their actions. Given that improvising spells and increasing their power levels could be dangerous, Malachy decided to offer a prayer to Saint Dunstan, the patron of metalworkers. Malachy called to mind a stained-glass portrait of Saint Dunstan from St. Vohl's Cathedral in Ludstone and firmly fixed that image in his mind.

With the image of a muscular Dunstan hammering on a pair of gold bracers he had presented to King Edgar in 825 foremost in his mind, Malachy bent his head in prayer and invoked his spell. "Saint Dunstan, please intercede on my behalf with the Almighty and Ever Living God. Tell Him that His imperfect servant Malachy Kidd seeks to do His will, as best he is able, and needs to affect this metal to do so."

The Wolf-priest felt heat building in the metal encircling his wrist. He tried to move the post, but it still would not budge, so he pushed more of his personal energy into the spell. The warmth continued to increase, chasing the last of the night's chill from the metal. *Progress, good.*

Malachy tried to move the post again and thought he felt it shift. He fed more energy into it, repeating his prayer to Saint Dunstan, then the heat started to rise quickly. The Wolf-priest felt his skin become uncomfortably hot, then he caught the acrid scent of singed hair.

Too much, too fast. Either Saint Dunstan is giving me a big boost, or there is something very strange about this metal. He tugged at the post and felt it shift—the strength panic was lending his muscles making that possible—but pain shot up his right arm. *If I don't do something to control this magick, I'll burn my hand off!*

He pushed himself past his panic and concentrated on the image of Saint Dunstan in spite of the pain. He focused on the saint's bulging muscles and the bracers, seeking the painless strength of the stained-glass limbs. Malachy offered another hurried prayer. "Saint Dunstan, your aid is near freeing me, but I have not your skill for dealing with what I face here. Please, I beseech thee, direct me such that my work will please the Lord Shepherd as your work on the bracers did."

The pain reduced the last part of the prayer to hisses and yelps. Malachy felt the pain peaking and a suffocating sensation closing over him. He began to feel faint and knew that to lose control would doom him. He'd pass out, the spell would drain him of life, and he'd become an incinerated corpse in the middle of nowhere. Screaming at the top of his lungs, he grabbed the post firmly in his left hand, hooked his heels into the crack and, pushing off with them, heaved back on the post.

It slid from the ground immediately, offering only a fraction of the resistance it had before. Malachy fell back and bounced off a stone, then rolled onto his right side. He held his hands out in front of him and felt the heat continue to grow. Coming up on his knees, he held the post out as if it were a snake and tried to shuck it from his wrist, but the metal would not come off.

To his horror, Malachy felt the searing heat of molten metal coil up around to trap his left wrist as well.

The heat did not increase at all, but neither did it abate. Instead it spread out, working its way up both arms from wrist to elbow. The stinking of yet more melting hair combined with the scorched scent of his shirt as the sleeves began to burn. From wrists to elbows his arms felt as if they had become torches. He imagined his flesh blistering up and bursting, his forearms becoming shriveled, blackened twigs that would shatter against the rock into countless slivers of charcoal.

Keeping his arms flung open wide, Malachy screamed so sound could override his pain. When his throat had become raw and felt as if a fire had been kindled in it, too, he coughed and fell silent. He leaned back, exhausted, letting the weight of his outflung arms pull his shoulders toward the ground.

The heat and pain had vanished, but he feared that just meant his arms had been burned clean off and frayed nerves were gathering strength to begin a new assault on him. *If I do not think about my arms, they will not hurt.* He tried mightily to think of anything but his arms, which doomed his effort and left him waiting for the next wave of agony.

Which was when his right forearm hit a rock.

It clinked.

Clink? Malachy frowned. *Burned arms shouldn't clink.*

Still leaning back, and aware of the growing discomfort in his thighs, Malachy wiggled the fingers on his right hand.

They worked.

He wished he could have seen them work. He snapped his fingers.

They snapped. He felt it. He heard it.

Slowly coming upright, he snapped the fingers of his left hand.

He got sound and feeling in that hand, too.

Extending only his index fingers, he brought both hands together in front of him.

The fingers touched each other tip to tip.

Okay, I have forearms and hands, but the clinking?

He let his hands slide past each other and on up until they encountered cool metal on his forearms. Running from wrist to elbow, a metal cylinder circled each forearm three quarters of the way around. On the right cylinder Malachy felt the raised image of a sword and on the left a shepherd's staff. *The Sword and the Crook.* Above each of them he also felt a wolf's-head.

These are just like the golden bracers Saint Dunstan made for King Edgar. How did that happen? He thought for a moment and then nodded. *My second appeal asked for skill to be granted to me, so my work could please God as Saint Dunstan's had. I guess my prayer was taken a bit more literally than I'd intended, but the result seems to work.*

Malachy felt around the open edges of the bracers and tried to slide a thumbnail beneath them. He couldn't. As nearly as he could tell with his fingers, the metal and his flesh had been fused together seamlessly. Still, when he tapped on the bracers, he could feel the vibration coming through, but had no direct sensory input through the bracers. *They're a lot like my armor in that respect. This fusion is odd, but there's bound to be some sort of an explanation for it.*

Right now, all that matters is that I'm free.

Malachy nodded and leaned back, raising his face toward Heaven. "Dear God, I thank You for lending me the skill needed to free myself. Thank you, Saint Dunstan, for your timely intercession and inspired intervention on my behalf. These bracers will serve to remind me of your devotion to God, which I will do my best to emulate. By Your will."

Exhausted by the spellcasting and decidedly thirsty, Malachy climbed unsteadily and leaned heavily on the rock to his left. Uriah had told him a small stream ran to the south and, assuming it was still morning, he knew he could determine which way was east by turning in a circle and determining when the sun felt warmest on his face.

Uriah. I had forgotten about him. "Uriah, where are you?"

He heard a sound to his left and turned toward it, then heard something else behind him. Before he could spin toward it, a sudden sharp blow to the back of his neck stunned him and dropped him to the ground. *What?* He tried to get his hands beneath him and get back up, but a booted foot ground its heel against his spine. "Uriah?"

He got no response to his question, though the man standing above him did speak. "*Da,* Dmitri, it is an Ilbeorian."

"Why would the Khasts take most of the Wolf-priest's things and leave him here with gold bracers and silver eyes?"

"I do not know. This is why I am a scout and here, not a noble and in Vzorin. The *Zarnitsky* is due to head back to Vzorin for recoaling tomorrow. Let us signal it to take us and this man with it. Your question deserves an answer and Duke Arzlov will find a way to get it from this one."

— 36 —

Pyimoc
Vzorin, Vzorin Military District
Strana
27 Tempest 1687

"Thank God you came, Grigory." Natalya launched herself into his arms and clung to him. "Duke Arzlov's guards have kept me here in my suite for the past four days. They say their orders come from you, but I know this is not true . . ."

She felt his arms move from enfolding her to her shoulders. She reluctantly allowed him to slip from her embrace. Praying she would see a smile, she looked up into his face.

What she saw chilled her. "What is it, Grigory?"

The blond warrior's expression stopped short of being stern and formal, but only just barely. "Please, Tachotha Natalya, may we sit down?"

Natalya nodded and took his left hand in hers as they walked over to the couch. She gathered one leg beneath her as she sat down. "Grigory, you need not be so distant."

The Hussar sat on the edge of the seat with his right hand massaging his forehead. "I do not mean to be distant, Natalya. I know I have not spent much time with you in the last fortnight—"

"We have been together four days, Grigory, and fewer nights than that."

"Yes, yes, I know." He swallowed hard and gathered his hands in his lap. "I have been mistaken, wishing to shield you. I see this now. It was unfair, but I did it out of my love for you. You must believe that."

Natalya frowned in confusion. "Shield me? From what must you shield me?"

Grigory sighed heavily and ran his fingers back through his long blond hair. "We have uncovered a plot concerning you. There is to be another kidnap attempt on you. What was believed to be an attempted assassination was meant to be a kidnapping. Shukri Awan, ruler of Helansajar, wanted you taken. Unbeknownst to him, his agent was really in the employ of Rafiq Khast. Khast made the kidnapping into an assassination to cause Awan great trouble."

Her jaw dropped open. "That makes no sense whatsoever, Grigory. Kidnapping me would invite Stranan wrath to fall upon Helansajar. Shukri Awan is not suicidal."

"Oh, beloved, he would not be killing himself." Grigory's hands curled into fists. "We have learned that Shukri Awan has been negotiating for a full year with one of the Stranan Tacarri. This is the reason why you were to be kidnapped. This Tacarri wishes to use Shukri Awan to disgrace Duke Arzlov and have him removed from Vzorin. The Tacarri will step in to negotiate your return, winning great national favor. This favor he will translate into a revolution that will topple your father from his throne."

Natalya shook her head, trying to deny the wave of numbness sweeping over her. In its wake she felt angry that someone would use her so cruelly in a plot such as that. No one could believe one of the Tacarri would stoop so low. It was true that some Tacarri in the past had become Tacier, but they were always drawn from cadet branches of the current dynasty. Because of the Lescari War and the rewards the Tacier gave all his Naraschals, none of the current Tacarri were from the Ohanscai family, though several had married daughters of the Tacier, officially entering them in the line of succession for the throne.

Who would do this? Marina? None of the Tacarri she could think of would back such a plan. Most of them were insufficiently political to have imagined all the ins and outs of such a plot. *Could one of my sisters be doing this to promote her husband?* It was possible, she allowed, but unlikely. Natalya knew she, being the Tacier's ninth child and unwed, occupied a truly small place at court and in the minds of her countrymen. While her father might reward whoever rescued her, the act of rescuing her would hardly provide the momentum needed to depose her father.

Her green eyes sparked angrily. "Who is it, Grigory. Tell me."

"I cannot. We do not know yet."

"No, with a plot this complex, learning the identity of the leader would be difficult." Natalya slowly curled hair around her finger. "You have ordered me confined here so the kidnappers cannot get to me?"

"Yes, Tachotha."

"And since you do not know the identity of the treasonous Tacarri, for me to return to Murom would put me at risk?"

Grigory nodded sadly and sagged a bit forward, as if he were being bent over a chopping block by an executioner. "I feel . . . impotent . . . at not being able to solve this mystery and protect you." His head came up. "I love you very much, Natalya, and I would never cause you pain, but your confinement here is for your own good. You must understand this."

Natalya forced herself to relax. She leaned forward and caressed Grigory's cheek. "I do understand, Grigory, and I will comply with your wishes. In return, you must keep me informed. I want to know everything. I know you have the *Leshii* patrolling. The *Zarnitsky* is doing the same, *da?*"

Khrolic managed a bit of a smile. "The *Zarnitsky* is returning. It should be here by midday tomorrow. It will help us learn more."

"Good." Natalya looked down and bit her lower lip. "Grigory, I need your strength. I want you with me tonight. I will show you that you are far from impotent. I will show you how much I love you and remind you why you wish to keep me safe."

The Hussar nodded solemnly. "I wish to be no other place than with you, Natalya. You are all my heart desires."

Natalya let ringlets of raven hair slide from her index finger. "And you supply me with my reasons to live." *Which now have become two: learning how Arzlov forced you to lie to me and learning how to thwart his plans.*

— 37 —

> **Dayi Marayir**
> **Helansajar**
> **28 Tempest 1687**

In the four days of travel since Uriah had left Malachy shackled to the earth, the youth went from shock and outrage to a simmering anger. Few of the Khast band spoke Stranan so the language gap between him and his captors meant that his early outbursts concerning

Kidd were rewarded with cuffs, kicks, and punches. Uriah kept all signs of pain hidden from the Helansajarans so they could get no satisfaction from abusing him.

The bruises and the residual ache in his nose from the struggle that first night reminded him of the fight from which Kidd had rescued him. *And then he stayed with me in that hotel, taking care of me when I was supposed to be caring for him. I repaid him by letting them abandon him in the middle of nowhere.*

For as long as he figured Kidd could survive, Uriah resolved to escape the Estanuans and go back to rescue him. As he tried to plan an escape, it occurred to him that an education he had thought comprehensive really was nowhere near what he needed it to be. He'd been schooled in how to handle weapons and some battlemagicks of a defensive nature in his first three years at Sandwycke. He'd had strategy and tactics added to things, as well as some magickal theory, but none of that was applicable to his current situation. Where the Sandwycke training failed him in particular was in the area of escape and evasion techniques.

In his darkest moments he did not think that at all strange: Martinists who didn't escape, like Malachy, would be martyrs and thereby become saints. While the theft of the *Mockingbird* from Lescar was hailed as a great victory by Ilboeria, it was seen as such primarily because it embarrassed Fernandi so badly. Since all the civilized nations ransomed and exchanged prisoners—and the size of the ransom demanded could be seen as indicative of status— escaping was seen as a low-class exercise in poor sportsmanship.

The central problem Uriah faced when considering escape lay in the fact that the Helansajarans grossly outnumbered him. He could wield some fairly powerful magick, but all of it required items upon which the spells could be focused. By happenstance or design, the clothes he wore, the ropes that bound him, and the saddle upon which he sat were the most dangerous items to which he had access.

How can a wolf be expected to ward his flock when he can't escape the snares and traps others set for him? Stupid strictures and ideas of honor—the sort of thing that kept the starch in Captain Irons—meant Uriah was without the tools he needed. *In the wild a trapped wolf would chew its own leg off to be free, yet we allow ourselves to be hobbled. That is insane.*

After three days Uriah conceded defeat. Even if he escaped, he could never get back to Kidd before the Colonel died of exposure or thirst or by a wild animal attack. *Even if I could find him, it would be too late.* He found it ironic and unfair that Kidd should have come all the way to Drangiana just to die so unceremoniously. *He deserved a better death than that.*

A day after Uriah had given up hope for Kidd, the mounted company, with Uriah riding in the middle, entered a narrow canyon. Tall redstone walls rose up to confine the sky to a thick blue channel. From the twists and turns it took, Uriah assumed the canyon had been carved out of the stone by eons of wear from a river. What water had roughed out generally, harsh winds had finished, further torturing interesting forms from the rocks. The Ilbeorian youth saw a number of manlike shapes that could have been taken for miraculous manifestations of this saint or that, and that thought brought him around again to memories of Kidd.

Now another martyr for the Church. Saint Malachy.

Before his anger could flare again, the canyon's sides squeezed together above them and tightened down into a tunnel. As it curved back and forth, worming its way beneath the eastern edge of the Jedrosian Plateau, it descended slightly and the air grew warmer. Uriah sniffed expectantly and was rewarded with the heavy scent of sulfur in the dry, dusty air. *Perhaps I'll be seeing you sooner than I expected, Colonel.*

Around a turn the tunnel began to brighten with a lurid red glow produced by a licking wall of flame. As they drew closer to the end of the tunnel and the bright circle where it terminated, he heard a whistle. The red light faded a bit. Passing into the cavern at the tunnel's end, Uriah saw large flaming metal-lattice barriers drawn to either side of the opening and he smiled.

It seemed obvious to him that when the barriers—which could be stuffed full of wood, oily cloth, and sulfurous coal—were lit afire and set before the opening, they provided a suitably hellish impression for anyone who came upon them accidentally. Scant few people, Eilyphian or Ataraxian, would venture close to what so obviously had to be a passage to Hell. Imagery aside, the heat put out by the barriers was enough to prevent even the most determined explorer from trying to get past them.

The cavern into which they rode impressed Uriah for a host of reasons. It was larger than St. Vohl's Cathedral in Ludstone—though not quite as deep, it was taller and wider by far. Three sides of the cavern had been worked by artisans who smoothed the walls then raised pillars and tiger symbology out of the rock. Though the big cats had been rendered in a style that made them more sinuous than Ilbeorian heraldic tigers, the power and majesty in the carvings impressed Uriah. The artisan's love and respect for his subject came out in the work.

A dais had been raised at the front of the cavern. In the center of it sat a throne which almost seemed to Uriah to be a parody of the Wolf-King's throne at Ludstone. Instead of wolves forming the arms, crouching tigers flanked the stone chair. A huge rearing bear made up the back of the throne and a reclining wolf formed a footrest. Uriah did not like the implications of that symbolism, but the wolf looked neither abused nor dead.

The Dost sat in the throne unmoving. Though silver and gold striping alternated over his body as it had when Uriah saw him before, the Dost's form had changed. He had taken on hard edges and bits of gearing could be seen in his elbows and knees. He seemed to Uriah to have been re-created by a blacksmith with a basic knowledge of anatomy.

At his feet knelt a man clearly of Urovian ancestry. As far away as he was, Uriah couldn't get a good enough look at the man to place him as being from one nation or another, though his beard and their current proximity to Strana helped him to form his first guess.

Behind that man stood a tall figure clad in red with black tiger stripes worked through her clothing, from the hood and veil to jacket, blouse, and long skirt. Uriah hadn't settled on the figure's gender as female because of the veil and skirt, though that had certainly pointed him in that direction. She, and the four other similarly attired figures who joined the Dost on the dais, possessed a fluid grace that he didn't expect of men. He found them very catlike and confident.

Leaning forward in his throne, the Dost gestured in the direction of the barriers. They slid closed again and Uriah's mouth went dry. Urovian magick allowed for the manipulation of items, but one had to be in physical contact with those items. The diabolical magick practiced by the Estanuans worked on people, enhancing them and their abilities. Neither school of magick allowed for the manipulation of items over a distance. Uriah looked back to see if he had somehow missed people or a mechanical device bringing the braziers back into place, but he saw neither and fear started gnawing at his insides.

The riders dismounted and two of the tiger-women came down to lead their horses away through an opening into a side cavern. Still bound with his hands behind his back, Uriah needed help getting down and an overbalanced Qusay nearly toppled over beneath his weight. Just as the men seemed ready to go down, Uriah felt pressure against his face and chest that stopped his fall and allowed Qusay to get a better grip on him.

Looking up, Uriah saw the Dost nod and lower his hand. The Ilbeorian shook his head. *That is impossible. Magick like that cannot exist.*

The Dost stood and his body flowed from the mechanically emaciated form to the more human shape Uriah had seen before. He spoke to the Helansajarans in their own tongue. Uriah had learned a few words during his travels, but understood nothing the Dost said. It came to him as a mild surprise when the company turned and headed off in the wake of their horses.

Uriah turned to follow them, but Rafiq grabbed his arm and kept him in the larger room. The man the Dost had spoken with was taken off by the woman who had stood behind him and guided deeper into the cavern complex through an opening hidden in the shadow of a pillar. Another of the women on the dais stepped forward and took Rafiq away, leaving Uriah alone with the Dost and the last of the tiger-women.

"You have fared well on your journey here?"

The muscles of Uriah's jaw twitched. "You left a man bound to a rock. He's dead now."

The Dost frowned. "Is he? You know this?"

"It's obvious, isn't it?" Uriah struggled against his ropes but could not free his hands. "Do you think he could have survived all this time the way you left him?"

"No, but then I did not expect him to remain the way I left him."

"What?"

"Your Malachy Kidd was capable of freeing himself. Whether he did or not is not your concern. Discussing him is not why you were brought to this place." The Dost looked at the woman on his left. "This is my sister Turikana. She will see to your needs while you stay with us."

Uriah scowled at her. "All I need is my freedom."

The gold man frowned for a second, then stared hard at Uriah. The Ilbeorian's head suddenly seemed crowded. He felt a tingle course up and down his spine, as if someone were walking on his grave. That sensation passed up through his neck and into his head, sifting his memories as if a child's hand were letting sand dribble away through its fingers.

Uriah covered his face with his hands and the presence in his mind fled. "What were you doing to me?"

The Dost ignored the question. "Freedom has to be earned, and you do not yet have the knowledge you need to let you earn your freedom. She will be responsible for you until that time, and you will be responsible to her."

"I will?"

"Defiance I expect, but you are not foolish. You will find her quite able to deal with you."

Uriah looked at her again. Though not as tall as he was, nor as heavy, she was not a petite woman who could be physically over-whelmed. Still, he thought he could deal with her until he met her steady gaze. Her green-gold eyes burned with an intense, almost feral light. He felt a jolt run through him and bleed off a bit of his self-confidence.

The Dost smiled. "You will learn from her our tongue and she will learn Ilbeorian from you. She is fluent in Stranan, so you may use that as an intermediary language. When you are not teaching her, you and I will speak from time to time about your home, your life, and your philosophies. The other man you saw here before is a Stranan and I have learned much from him about how the world has changed since I was last here. I expect further enlightenment from you."

"I'm not going to tell you things that you can use to conquer my country."

"This should not be a concern of yours, Uriah Smith."

"You already said you were going to reestablish your empire."

"And I will do just that." The golden man shrugged casually. "I am the Dost. My empire has been neglected. What I learn from you will neither hasten nor prevent the conquest of Ilbeoria. It will merely determine how I choose to deal with your people once they realize the true import of the Dost's return to the world."

— 38 —

Government House
Dhilica
Puresaran, Aran
29 Tempest 1687

Prince Trevelien refrained from offering his hand to Erwin Grim-shaw as the little man entered the Prince's office. Were it not for the recent riots and the disruption of the government's ability to func-tion, he'd not have been meeting with the man at all. *He arranged for all this so I would be required to seek his counsel.*

"Mr. Grimshaw, I have often heard your name mentioned in discussions with my Ministers."

The wizened man smiled as if not offended by the Prince's refusal to shake his hand. "I hope all that is said is good, Highness."

"It is certainly remarkable."

"Ah, that is something, but not always the same as *good*."

"Those who said you were perceptive have not lied, Mr. Grimshaw." The Prince pointed the merchant to a straight-backed chair, then walked around his own desk and sat down. "Since you requested this meeting, I suppose it is up to me to ask what I can do for you."

Grimshaw seated himself on the edge of the chair. "Perhaps, Highness, you should ask what *I* can do for *you*."

What you can do for me is to stop tampering with my government. After he demanded loyalty and full disclosure from his colonial Ministers, his government slowly ground to a halt. The Ministries did what they were supposed to do, but they did it slowly. They did everything they could to hinder the Prince's ability to rule the colony. Matters that should have been routine and handled at the most basic levels were referred to him for his approval. The avalanche of paper that tactic created had buried his office.

After he reined in his fury at the bureaucratic assault, Trevelien had to admit the Earls of Commerce in Aran were not the utter simpletons he had at first believed. Just because their operations did not appear to be very sophisticated did not mean the men who were behind them were incapable of being very tricky. They had made no attempt to hide their business before because no one was watching over them before.

The gauntlet had been thrown down with his explosive first meeting with his Ministers. Grimshaw and the others had taken it up enthusiastically. Their counterassault had exploited the inherent weakness of the colonial government. Whereas before the level of work had been light because so many regulations were being ignored, the workload created by full compliance with the laws brought the colonial administration down faster than an airship that had lost its last Aeromancer. With the government constipated by a glut of papers being filed, the Earls were left as free to act as before.

And this time they saved money on bribes. The Prince let his anger go and snorted a quick laugh. "Very well, what is it that *you* can do for *me*?"

"First I will thank you for your indulgence." Grimshaw smiled weakly, as if in pain but manfully bearing up. "I believe, Highness, that this first month in Aran has not been all it should have been for you. Initial misunderstandings have created some acrimony and I am of a mind that such divisiveness is not productive."

"I will agree with that. Now what have I misunderstood about the Ilbeorian Crown Colony of Aran?"

"Highness, Aran is not a place like Ilbeoria at all. It is a land of opportunity that demands husbanding and guidance if it is to reach its full potential."

Trevelien nodded. "This is what has brought me here, Mr. Grimshaw."

"Is it, Highness?"

Trevelien did not like the oily tone in Grimshaw's voice. "Why did you assume I had come here?"

"Many people come to Aran to forget unhappiness . . ."

The image of his dead wife, her silken hair, her deep blue eyes, flashed through the Prince's mind. *Rochelle . . .* The Prince sharpened his stare and focused it on Grimshaw. "I am here for the welfare of Aran, nothing else."

"Of course, Highness, as you say, for Aran's welfare. Unfortunately you have arrived and tried to govern with an Urovian viewpoint. The perspective shifts when one is in Dhilica, as I believe you have discovered." Grimshaw gestured toward the bank of windows behind the Prince. "Here, in Dhilica, you can experience in full the problems and promise of Aran that, I believe, have only ever reached Ilbeoria in muted abstracts and incomplete reports.

"It is this belief on my part which has caused you some discomfort. When your Ministers came to me with the allegations of wrongdoing you had laid against them and, by implication, myself, I fear I overreacted. I told all of my peers that we would have to do things in the Ilbeorian manner. This, I gather, has overloaded the government."

The Prince nodded. "Our resources have been somewhat strained." He kept his voice even despite his disbelief at what he was hearing. *Who does this man think he is? How can he come here and tell me he is responsible for shutting my government down? Rochelle, you would laugh so at his antics.* "In time we will adapt."

"Agreed, my Prince, but civil unrest seems to be keeping a swift schedule. As you know a number of us have brought our factory militias into Dhilica to help keep the peace."

The government's paralysis had led to citizen frustration with the bureaucracy. Native workers who could not get travel permits were barred from going off to work or from returning home, which resulted in angry mobs protesting at the Labor Ministry. The territorial police had been fairly brutal in breaking up the crowds, forestalling riots but producing a growing level of anxiety throughout Dhilica. Vandalism and physical assaults against Ilbeorians had begun to rise and the population's reaction to those incidents fed back into the overall fear and dissatisfaction with the new administration.

"Someone less understanding than I, Mr. Grimshaw, might think you have brought your house troops to Dhilica as a prelude to some sort of revolution."

Grimshaw adamantly shook his head. "No such thing is intended, Highness. We have wives, children, and loved ones here in Dhilica. We merely wish to see to their safety, sir. We mean no challenge to your power. In fact, we have high hopes for your future in Aran, provided our initial difficulties can be straightened out."

"Does this mean you will advise the Ministers to speed things up?"

"I believe they could be so advised, if things come to an agreeable conclusion." Grimshaw smiled again, this time showing some teeth. "You are a reasonable man. We should be able to reach an understanding."

Trevelien nodded warily. "Used that way, those words usually suggest that I, being reasonable, will come over to your point of view."

"Then please forgive that implication." Grimshaw's gray eyes narrowed. "I truly do believe you are a reasonable and reasoning man. If I did not think so, Highness, things would be progressing differently right now. In fact, I have the utmost respect for you and sincerely wish you were in line to rule from the Throne of Saint Martin before your brother Ainmire."

The Prince allowed himself a smile. "Certainly, then I would be in Ludstone and Ainmire would be here."

"That is not what I meant, sir."

"Perhaps not, but having my brother in my place would not pain you overmuch."

Grimshaw slid back in his chair. "No, no, it would not."

"That, sir, is the first truthful thing I think you have said so far."

The little man let the barbed remark pass as if he had not heard it. "I would prefer to see you on the Throne of Saint Martin because I believe you are a man of vision. You came here to Aran and you saw that what was happening here was unacceptable. You decided to make the changes that would make Aran acceptable to you. I would argue that your only error in doing that came from viewing Aran and its problems from an Ilbeorian perspective, not an Aranan one.

"Highness, Aran's area is four times as large as Ilbeoria and includes a dozen smaller nations, each with its own heritage and history. Two major world religions dominate the area, with Eilyphi-anism and Martinism spreading quickly. There are two growing seasons and the Dhil Valley is so fertile it supports a population twice that of Ilbeoria. The climate is generally agreeable, the mineral wealth is great but underexploited, and the pool of inexpensive labor knows no end."

Grimshaw's eyes sparkled as he spoke about Aran. "People back in Ilbeoria cannot understand the problems and potential of this place. Aran has known empires that rivaled those of Scipia and Fernandi and they survived far longer than even the Dost's Estanuan Empire. Had Ilbeoria been born here, were Dhilica now Ludstone, Ilbeoria would be the greatest nation on the planet."

Trevelien frowned. "The Ilbeorian Empire *is* the greatest nation on this planet."

"It is now, yes, but for how long will that continue to be? The North Brendanian Combine is blessed with the same riches as Aran. You will see in it what Ilbeoria could have been and in it you will see the rise of the rival that will break Ilbeoria's supremacy in the world. With its natural resources, the Combine will be able to deal with future challenges more swiftly than Ilbeoria."

"But Mr. Grimshaw, Ilbeoria has Aran's resources."

Grimshaw's nostrils flared slightly. "Highness, you know that might not always be true."

"What are you suggesting?"

"I suggest nothing, Highness. I presume that an intelligent man like you knows there is a time when a child will outstrip the parent. The Brendanian colonies were able to revolt and win independence from Ilbeoria because of their distance from their mother country and because forward-looking people decided they could not reach their full potential living in the shadow of Ilbeoria.

"Brendania is not the only place where people look to the future. In Aran, for example, the Laamtists believe in reincarnation—a chance to repeat life until perfection is achieved. They see life as a big wheel. Perhaps their view is not so wrong."

Trevelien leaned forward over his desk, supporting himself on his elbows. "Prince Lorcan had several Grimmand regiments in Brendania before he began his revolt. There are no such troops to support such action here in Aran."

"There are various house troop companies here in Aran, as well as Mrilani warriors who are not averse to fighting for money. Jedrosian and Ghur mercenaries and even some of the Drangianan tribes could be purchased."

"But surely Ilbeoria or Strana would react in the case of this revolt."

Grimshaw smiled like a fox, with enough spittle gathering at the corners of his mouth to hint at a rabid froth. "Not if Emperor Fernandi were surreptitiously returned from exile to Lescar. His arrival in Ferrace and the resulting upheaval would preoccupy both nations."

Free Fernandi? Why not rip open the gates of Hell and bring forth demonic legions to lay waste to the world?

Trevelien forced himself to sit back in his chair because what he really wanted to do was lean forward and snap Grimshaw's neck. He knew he could not afford to indulge that bloodred whim, but such rational thought in no way dulled his desire. What Grimshaw had suggested was the moral equivalent of giving a knife to a homicidal lunatic and turning him loose in a house full of children. That Grimshaw could imagine such a thing, and suggest it as part of a plan to sever Aran from the empire and make Trevelien Aran's ruler meant two very dire things.

The first was that Grimshaw thought Aran could function as a fully independent nation in a modern, industrialized world. Part of the reason Brendania had succeeded in declaring and maintaining its independence was because patented inventions had been stolen from Ilbeoria and duplicated in the colonies. Finished goods that could previously only have been made in Ilbeoria were being made in Brendania. The revolt taught Ilbeoria a bitter lesson which was the reason the export of steam-engine parts and design had been made a capital crime.

It was true that the Lescari had stolen that technology and Fernandi used it to build his war machine. Ilbeoria had given the secrets of steam to Strana so they could oppose Fernandi. The Lescari had traded the information and a huge tract of land to the Combine in return for raw materials during the wars, though Brendania maintained an official neutrality. But even Fernandi, desperate as he was near the end, did not export steam technology to his colonies.

Grimshaw's belief that Aran could survive meant he knew of working steam industry in Aran.

Trevelien acknowledged that efforts to stop the spread of new inventions would always be doomed to failure. Once an advancement had been made, there was no turning back, but unwise use of that advancement could cause more trouble than it prevented. Ilbeoria's economy depended on the factory jobs that would move to the colonies if factories were allowed to spring up. Markets would collapse, unemployment would rise, and anarchy would reign in the wake of that sort of disaster. *This cannot be allowed to happen.*

The second and more disturbing thing about Grimshaw's suggestion was that it revealed how close to revolt Grimshaw and his fellows truly felt they were. Modern industry was the key—one steam-driven factory could make for them the parts to produce other steam engines and other factories. They had troops and money. The only thing they needed was a leader, and Grimshaw had offered the job to him.

Trevelien knew the offer to rule in Dhilica was not genuine. Men who held the leadership in Ludstone in such contempt clearly would have no use for him. Grimshaw's brother had been one of the lords who had most loudly protested the Prince's wedding to Rochelle, so he had a serious indication of how little the Grimshaws thought of him. Since his posting to Aran was a test to see if he could truly rule, people like Grimshaw would assume he could not. Their offer to him was simply an expedient added on to a plan that had already been put together in order to buy them some time to finalize their true plans.

Trevelien had not been fooled. Fernandi could just as easily come to Aran as he could return to Lescar. Word that their Emperor had escaped exile and had established himself at the head of Ilbeoria's largest colony would be enough to spark an uprising in Lescar. If Fernandi renewed relations with the Brendanian Combine's ruling triumvirate, the former colonies might unite in a war to conquer Ilbeoria and possibly all of Urovia.

Father, you had no idea how bad things have become.

The Prince brought his hands together. "You are correct, Mr. Grimshaw. The view from Dhilica is decidedly different than the one from Ludstone. I will need time to consider what all this portends."

"Of course, Highness. I think it should be a month before any notice of recall arrives from Ludstone. Things will keep until then."

"I believe they will, Mr. Grimshaw. Good day." Trevelien watched through slitted eyes as the man walked from his office. *I have one month to determine exactly who is in this conspiracy with Grimshaw, to find their factory, and decide if there is any way to forestall their revolt. And if I can't—I must, I absolutely must. If I do not, the world will again be at war and the blood of millions will flow.*

— 39 —

Robin Drury frowned as he looked down at the grubby child tugging at the hem of his service jacket. "Yes?"

"Fathasay gokwic." The boy pointed off through the gathering twilight toward the Varatha Quarter of the city. "Gokwic, gokwic, go-go."

Ignoring the stares and laughs of the other ethyrines in front of the barracks, Robin dropped to his haunches and rested his hands on the boy's shoulders. "What are you saying? Catch your breath. Again."

The boy got louder and just a bit slower. "Fatha say go kwic. Go mission, go-go."

"It's a trick, Brother Robin. Ragwig alley bashers will get you."

"Thank you, Mr. MacBride, for that opinion." Robin looked at the boy and suddenly realized why the boy looked naggingly familiar. "You're Nataraj. Father Ryan sent you?"

"Hanji, hanji." Nataraj took a step back and pulled on Robin's right hand. "Go mission, go-go."

"Mind your rings, sir, the little wogs are quick."

Robin took Nataraj's hand in his, then stood and turned back toward the ethyrine who had spoken. "Mr. MacBride, did I invite you to address me?"

"No, sir."

"And were you taught to slouch when addressing a superior officer?"

MacBride straightened up and snapped to attention. "No, sir, Brother Drury, sir."

"Good. I think you should report to your cell and spend the next four hours contemplating the virtue of Charity. There are Ignatian

exercises available to help you focus if you cannot manage it yourself, do you understand me?"

"Yes, sir."

Robin shifted his gaze to the heavyset older man standing beside MacBride. "Connor, get your platoon, save Mr. MacBride here,
ready to move. I don't know what trouble there is down at the Donnist mission, but I want you ready to respond. If I'm not back here
inside an hour, notify Captain Hassett I'm missing and bring
Archangel in to take care of the situation. Understand?"

"Yes, sir."

Robin looked down at the boy. "Let's go."

"Brother Drury."

Robin turned. "Yes?"

Connor tossed him a *katar*, one of the punch-daggers native to
Aran that Mrilani warriors favored. "Take this now. If there's trouble, I'll bring your sword."

Robin snatched the scabbarded knife out of the air. "Thanks."

By the time the ethyrine turned around again, the little Himlan boy had already crossed the square in front of the barracks
and headed off down Suhana Road. Shoving the *katar*'s leather-
wrapped wood scabbard through his belt at the small of his back,
Robin ran after the boy. He knew he would never catch Nataraj, but
he really didn't need to. He knew where the mission was located and
had created a plan of action for evacuating it in case religious intol-
erance made it the focal point of the growing civil unrest.

Even with religious hatred being the key problem in Mendhakgaon, he hadn't considered trouble all that likely in Dhilica. The
recent labor problems *had* suggested to him that resentful Aranans
might decide to burn the mission down, but most of their anger had
been directed at the Labor Ministry. The local constabulary had
taken care of those problems, albeit without any lessening of overall
tension. If there *was* trouble at the mission Robin could see Father
Ryan sending for him instead of the Territorial Police—even if it
was just to have him on hand to try to control the Territorial Police.

Barely able to keep Nataraj in sight, Robin did avail himself of
some of the shortcuts the boy used. The alleyways were a bit
crowded and a dog tied beside a door snapped at him, but otherwise
the journey proved uneventful. The shortcuts brought him out on
Murgi Street. Heading east along it, he came to the square just north
of the mission.

The situation did not look good. A group of a hundred or more
Aranans filled the square but remained a good ten yards from the
front door of the mission. Father Ryan, dressed in a black cassock

with a green chasuble draped over it, stood between the crowd and the mission. Whatever he was saying to them appeared to be holding them back. Nataraj remained behind Ryan, but stole the occasional glance at the mission.

Robin ran up to the priest. "I came as quickly as I could."

"Saints be praised."

"What's the matter?"

The small priest wiped the sweat from his forehead. "I was saying Mass when a man entered the mission and demanded that I hear his confession. I told him he would have to wait—he was drunk, I could see that. I told him to go outside and wait. He left the mission, then came back about a minute later. He was hysterical. He had a knife and took one of my volunteers hostage. He said the mob wanted to kill him."

Robin looked at the crowd in the square. "They chased him back here?"

"Only ten or so of them. The crowd has grown."

"Why were they after him?"

"It's not clear. The couple in the front of the crowd there are the Chands. They say this man took their son away to work at a job far away. They offered Sohal good money—the boy was supposed to be very smart and good with his hands. He went away a week ago and the family was informed yesterday that he had been killed. They were paid for his death, but no one will tell them what happened to him.

"I tried to convince Venner to tell them what happened. He won't, he's afraid they'll kill him. I did get him to let everyone go save his hostage, but I'm not going to be able to get him out of there. He wants to have his confession heard before he goes anywhere. He feels very guilty—what he knows must be horrible. I told him I couldn't hear his confession if he had a weapon in hand. I suggested you could, being a Wolf-priest and all."

The ethyrine frowned. "You know the martial branch of the Martinist clergy can only administer two Sacraments: baptism and extreme unction."

"Aye, I know that, but Venner doesn't."

Robin pulled the *katar* from his belt and handed it to Nataraj. "Hang on to this like you did the statue of Devinataki."

"*Hanji,* go kwic."

Robin tousled the boy's dark hair. "Pray for me, Father."

"Go with God, Brother Robin."

The ethyrine walked slowly and easily toward the tall, arched doorway in the mission's front wall. One of the two doors was closed, the other stood open a couple of feet. The thick stained-glass windows on either side of the door provided Robin the barest of warped and colored views of what was going on inside before he poked his head through the doorway.

Robin offered a prayer and invoked the same magick on his jacket that made his armor work—some protection being better than none. *Saint Martin, be with me.* Taking a deep breath, Robin slipped through the open doorway and into the mission's interior.

The mission was really rather plain. It consisted of a huge room in the middle of which wooden benches had been arranged to form a small chapellike setting. Low cots, tables, and chairs took up the space in either wing. A wooden altar had been built against the back wall and a small tabernacle of gold sat in the center of it.

Most impressive of the decorations was the wooden statue of Eilyph hanging above the altar. Carved of native woods, it showed a man with a serene expression of love on his face. His chest and out-stretched hands bore the stigmata from when his false disciple Nemicus the Betrayer had thrust a sword through Eilyph's crossed hands and into his heart.

Eilyph's chiseled serenity contrasted sharply with the sweaty panic on the face of the man crouched in the altar's shadow. Venner had a stubble on his narrow face that matched that on his pate, and a haunted look to his deep-set brown eyes. While of average height, Venner had a whipcord slenderness that belied the strength with which he held his hostage. The flush that alcohol had brought to his cheeks provided the only real color in what would have otherwise been gray flesh.

He had his left arm around the waist of a young woman who wore a dress with a volunteer's white apron over it. Her black hair and a shadow hid her face, but Robin would have been surprised if it were anything but a mask of terror. *At least she's not whimpering, which is good. There's some steel in her.*

Venner raised the knife he held in his right hand so Robin could see it, then brought it back down to press against the woman's pale throat. "Stay away."

Robin opened his hands. "Peace be with you, my son. Father Ryan sent for me. I came to hear your confession."

The man licked his thick lips. "My confession, yes."

The ethyrine smiled and walked forward. "You might wish to speak more softly, my son. God will hear you. We need not excite those outside."

"Right, those outside."

"Perhaps you want to sit down on this bench here." Robin

pointed to the first bench in the row nearest the man. "You and your friend will be more comfortable."

Venner shifted his left hand down and caught hold of the volunteer's apron tie. "Go, miss, to the bench like the good priest says." The knife didn't move from her throat as Venner got to his feet and pulled her up with him.

When the woman stood up, her hair fell away from her face. Though she had paled and her hazel eyes were wide with fear, Robin Drury had no difficulty recognizing her.

What is Amanda Grimshaw doing here? Robin kept himself from reaching out to her. "Do as he asks, miss, and nothing will go wrong."

"Y-yes, s-sir."

Watching Venner and Amanda move together toward the bench, Robin's mind shifted and he began a tactical evaluation of the situation. The knife the man held at Amanda's throat was a singled-edged, cant-bladed knife. If the spine were held parallel to the floor, the front two thirds of the blade would be seen to broaden out and slope sharply downward. The inner razored edge had a nice elbow angle that Venner used to trap Amanda's throat. Had it not been for the protection provided by the frayed collar on her dress, she'd have already been bleeding from several small cuts.

Venner himself did not appear to be as drunk as Father Ryan had suggested. He moved a bit sluggishly, but he looked alert and he wasn't slurring his words. Robin suspected that fear of the mob had contributed to what Father Ryan had seen as the man being out of control. Clearly the time spent nestled against the altar, thinking about the likely fate awaiting him, had somewhat sobered Venner.

Robin came around the end of the bench as the two of them were seated. "You really ought to put the knife down. Confession should be heard absent the tools of violence."

"Consider this battlefield conditions. You make exceptions there, yes?"

"We do, indeed." Robin lowered is head. "Let us pray. In the name of the Father and of the Son and of the Divine Wolf . . ." As he intoned the words, he first turned his right hand palm out, then his left and completed the ritual by bringing both palms up to cover his heart. He hoped Venner might ape his movements, removing the knife from Amanda's throat for a second.

A second in which he could act.

Venner twisted the blade so its spine tapped Amanda gently on her chin. "You'll have to make the signs for me, miss."

Amanda complied, but her hands trembled.

"Please say this with me. Dear God, I am a sinner. Born with the stain of the sin that entered the world in Urjard, I can only gain forgiveness from You through the intercession of Your priests. I hereby confess my sins, renounce my wrongdoings, and pledge myself to live in the manner Your Son, our Lord Eilyph, has laid down. Grant me strength. By Your will."

Both Venner and Amanda repeated the prayer, though she closed her eyes through most of it.

Robin looked at the end of the bench. "May I sit down?"

Venner frowned, then nodded.

Robin sat down facing the altar, then turned toward his left to face them. In doing so he cut the man-length separating him from Amanda in half. If they reached out to each other their hands would touch, but Venner's knife guaranteed that would not happen.

The Wolf-priest smiled slowly. "Please, my son, unburden your soul. What happened to make those people so angry?"

Venner glanced at the doorway. "I was having a pint down here with some of my mates when one of the wogs saw me and started in on me about a man who died at a job I'd given him. He was making out like it was my fault, but it wasn't."

"Calm yourself." Robin glanced down for a second, carefully measuring the distance between himself and the knife. He would have had an even chance at getting it had Venner let Amanda sit straight up, but her captor didn't. He'd pulled her back against himself so Robin's lunge would have to take the ethyrine up and over the length of Amanda's body before he could get at the knife. "Do you know how the man died?"

"I was there, wasn't I?"

"And having been there you feel some vestiges of guilt, deserved or not. You brought him to where he died, but it is not as if you pushed him. You would have saved him if you could have, yes?"

"Of course. I was on the other side, using the levers to move it over when he got crushed."

Robin raised an eyebrow. "What crushed him?"

"It was . . ." The man faltered. "It was heavy, Father. God knows what it was, doesn't He?"

"Of course, my son." Leaning forward, Robin kept his voice soft. "I am ready to absolve you of your sins, but you must let the woman go first. You're causing her pain and we can't have that."

"All right."

Venner began to pull the knife away from Amanda's throat when the mission's door flew open. Two men wearing the black shirts, khaki jodhpurs, and black boots of Grimshaw's Mercantile Militia burst into the room. They both held crossbows at the ready. Venner stood up abruptly and pressed the knife to Amanda's stomach. "Get away."

"Miss Grimshaw!" cried one of the two militiamen.

Venner looked at Amanda. "You're a Grimshaw?"

She nodded.

Venner looked at Robin and the priest saw all hope go out of the man's eyes. "Grimshaw's come for me. I'm all done in, ain't I?"

"Step away from her, Cobb Venner, or we'll be forced to shoot."

"Pray for me, Father, I'm Hell-bound now."

Breathing a prayer under his breath, Robin dove from the bench at Venner and Amanda. He hit her at the knees with his shoulder and gathered in a handful of her skirts. As they went down Venner swiped at Amanda's belly with his knife. When they hit the ground, Venner released Amanda and rolled away to Robin's left.

Robin slid Amanda back behind himself, then went for Venner. The man slashed at Robin twice with his knife. Robin ducked beneath the first cut, then parried the second one with his left forearm. He felt the sting of the blade as it sliced through his jacket and into his flesh, but he brought his right fist around anyway and doubled Venner over with a blow to the midsection.

Clutching his stomach, Venner reeled backward and dropped the knife. Robin scooped the blade up with his left hand, then held his right hand out. "It's over, Venner. No one else needs to die."

The purple-faced man straightened up, struggling to draw in a deep breath. He began to nod, then two crossbow quarrels slammed into his body. One punched through Venner's right hand, nailing it to his abdomen. The other drilled its way through his neck, spraying blood over the man's shoulders and up the wall behind him. Without even a gurgle, Venner pitched over backward and writhed briefly before a final convulsion left him lying very still.

The two militiamen reloaded their crossbows before approaching the body. Robin turned away from them and knelt beside Amanda. "Are you hurt, Miss Grimshaw?"

She had her hands pressed to her stomach. "He tried to kill me."

"He was not a well man, Amanda."

She shuddered. "No, he tried to kill me and you couldn't stop him. But his knife didn't cut me. How can that be? Was it a miracle?"

Robin winced as he pressed his right hand against the cut in his left forearm. "Not quite a miracle. I couldn't get the knife, so I grabbed your skirts and magicked your dress into makeshift armor.

As you can see from my arm, if he really tries to cut hard it doesn't do much good, but his heart wasn't in slitting you open. I think hurting you was more a blow at your father than any act of malice against you."

One of the two militiamen came over and grabbed Robin by the shoulder, then tried to haul him to his feet. "What did he say to you?"

Robin remained on his knees. "Anything he said is confidential because it was said during the Sacrament of confession." He glanced at Amanda. "Even Miss Grimshaw must remain silent about what she heard or face excommunication."

The militiaman frowned. "Come tell that to Mr. Grimshaw." He gestured at Robin with his crossbow, then jerked his head toward the door.

Amanda sat up and untied her apron. "He's going nowhere, Mr. . . . What is your name?"

The militiaman took a half-step back. "Elgar, miss."

"Robin is going nowhere, Mr. Elgar, until I get him to a doctor to get his arm stitched shut." She wrapped her apron around Robin's arm and used the lacings to tie it tight. "You go report to my father what you've done. If *he* decides he needs to speak with me, my father knows where I live. And given my impression of your needless murder of Mr. Venner there, I would think the last thing you want me discussing with my father is what went on here."

Robin slowly stood. "Since you did not know Miss Grimshaw was here when you arrived, perhaps her presence need not be mentioned at all."

Elgar thought for a second, then nodded. "She'd not be able to tell him anything anyway."

"Correct." Robin looked toward the doorway. "You have your troops out there keeping the crowd back?"

"Yes, sir."

"Then why don't you take Venner's body out there and let everyone know this is over? We will leave through the rectory and no one need ever know Miss Grimshaw was here."

Elgar nodded. Robin led Amanda past the altar and through a doorway into a small room that functioned as the sacristy. The door on the other side of it led into the rectory. "We'll be safe in here until everyone leaves."

Amanda frowned angrily. "I am sincerely tempted to tell my father about what happened here. That man did not have to die."

"I wouldn't, if I were you."

"Why not?"

"Your father and I had words in the tower."

"The tower." Amanda glanced down. "My father was furious with you. I wanted to tell you I was proud, but he forbade me from seeing you or writing to you."

"So you volunteered here, at the mission, in hopes I would come by?"

"I did hope you would come by." She smiled and stroked his cheek with her left hand. "But I have worked here as a volunteer for a long time. Over a year, in fact. Ever since I learned what happens in the tower."

"If you tell your father what transpired today, he will forbid you from returning here." Robin frowned. "And I have to say I think those men had no choice but to kill Venner."

"Why?"

"He was holding *you* as his hostage. You were in jeopardy and had I not been here, you would have died. If they had let him live, your father would have learned how close their arrival came to killing you. Your father makes terrifying threats, and his men probably believe all of them."

"They murdered a man out of fear of my father?"

"They probably thought they were still protecting you. Venner was dangerous, and I've ample evidence of that soaking my sleeve and your apron."

Amanda glanced back in the direction of the church. "I've never seen a man die before."

"It's never pleasant."

"I should hope not." Amanda shivered, then looked up at him. "I shall pray for Venner later, I think, but now we must go get your arm looked after."

"Please, let's get away from here." Robin tucked the bloody knife through his belt at the small of his back and followed Amanda from the rectory. *The longer we stay, the greater grows my suspicion that Elgar and his friend meant for Venner to die all along. They asked me what he'd told me, which means Venner knew something Grimshaw wants kept hidden. Whatever that secret is, at least two men have died because of it, and I fear they are but the first of far too many more.*

— 40 —

Vasily Arzlov shook his head, well aware that such a gesture was wasted on his prisoner. Though it had been a dozen years since Vasily had seen him, there was no mistaking Malachy Kidd. Despite the scar linking both eyes, the Ilbeorian Wolf-priest still possessed the handsome nobility that had made Vasily certain that Khrolic would never win Tachotha Natalya's heart unless he found a way to eliminate Kidd as competition.

"Captain . . . no, you are a Pokovnik, *da?* You call the rank Colonel, as I recall. Do you see irony in our meeting again, after all these years, here in Vzorin?"

Kidd rattled the chains binding his hands behind his back. "I would have thought, Duke Arzlov, that you would not feel the need to bind a blind man."

"I have too much respect for your abilities, Colonel."

"I am no threat to you." Kidd's white hair spread over his bare shoulders as he shook his head. "As last I recall we may not have been friends, but we were certainly not enemies."

"I had that impression, as well, but tensions between our governments put me in an odd situation. You present me a problem. I know you to be a very able strategist. I know being robbed of your sight did not atrophy those skills." Vasily paced in the small cell, letting the crisp crack of his footfalls fill it. "My men, tracking Helansajarans who raided Vzorin, found you, alone, with no equipment, wearing a pair of bracers that no one, including you, can remove from your arms. Last I knew you were at Sandwycke. We found you in Drangiana. Can you explain this?"

"You would not believe my explanation."

"Malachy, how can you say this? Wolf-priests are known for their honesty. Please, how did you come to be in Drangiana?"

"I had a vision that required me to travel."

"And you were borne to Estanu by litters of angels?"

"I flew, though there were no angels in that crew."

"Malachy, you disappoint me. More importantly you are disappointing Sebsai here." Vasily looked at the torturer and the man pumped the bellows on his coal fire. "Though he is a local, not racially Stranan, he is truly skilled in eliciting truth. He has chosen to work with hot irons this evening because I want information from you, and I want it quickly. He is actually capable of being gentle, but not if you will not cooperate."

Kidd's face turned toward the brazier where irons were beginning to glow a dull orange. "You're going to burn me?"

"Tearing out fingernails and teeth do work, but most subjects shy from the sight of hot metal. Being blind, you will be spared that. You will hear a sizzle and smell your flesh roasting. This makes it most effective." Arzlov nibbled at a corner of a fingernail. "Why were you in Drangiana?"

"You don't have to do this, Duke Arzlov."

"Give me a choice, Malachy. Why did you leave Sandwycke?"

"I had a vision of the Dost. I was sent to save him."

"The Dost is a myth."

"If he is, then I'm not really here, but back in Sandwycke, sleeping through a long nightmare."

Arzlov laughed. "Perhaps I was wrong, my friend Malachy. I had thought you still a military man, not some priest out to redeem a demon that has taken fleshly form. Saving the Dost's soul will not neutralize him. You Ilbeorians are fools. I will have to see just how foolish. But I cannot know that until I know what you know." Vasily nodded at Sebsai, prompting the torturer to draw a red-hot iron from the brazier. "This will hurt more than anything you have ever known, Malachy, but do not worry, there is a way to end your torture. As it is said in Scripture, 'The truth will set you free.'"

"I'll remember that."

"Yes, you will, and much, much more before your time here is done."

— 41 —

The small cave room in which Uriah found himself housed made for very close quarters. The entire area given to him was the size of a blanket folded in half. It had been laid out beside the room's entrance, over an uneven and lumpy section of the floor. On a little shelf above it Uriah was allowed to keep his pillow, an earthenware bowl, and a small pitcher.

The rest of the room was not that much more sumptuously appointed. A carpet and pile of pillows in the far corner showed where Turikana slept. Twin curved shamshirs were crossed on the wall beside her sleeping area. On a low table next to the sleeping area, located almost directly across from the door, an oil lamp's flickering flame sent black smoke up where it drifted out through a crack in the rock above. A closed chest sat beside the table and Uriah assumed it contained Turikana's clothes.

Entering the room, she smiled down at him. "Your place, good?" Her Ilbeorian came haltingly and accented with a mixture of Stranan and Aralan pronunciations. "Good, yes?"

Uriah nodded and scooted around to a more comfortable place to sit. "It is good," he said slowly.

"It is good." Facing away from him, Turikana removed her hood and veil, then shook her head so her dark brown hair spread out and down over her shoulders. She turned back toward him slowly, her dark eyebrows drawn together in thought. Bluish flesh surrounded her eyes and spread across her cheekbones, enhancing the exotic nature of her green-gold eyes. Though slightly larger than some might think attractive, her straight nose added character to a face otherwise unmarred by age or experience. Full lips marked a mouth that was neither peevishly small nor overwide. She had a strong chin and a solid jawline without either seeming mannish.

Her smile grew a bit as she regarded him, then broadened fully as she looked up toward the doorway.

The Dost nodded to her, then looked down at Uriah. "I beg your forgiveness for your accommodations. We have little space and even less in the way of things. We are nomads and must always be prepared to move."

Uriah shrugged. "My berth on the *Stoat* was smaller."

The Dost's face went blank for a moment. "You came here on a weasel?"

Uriah laughed aloud. "No, no, the *Stoat* was an airship. It brought me to Dhilica and then to Thandragaon."

"How long did that journey take?"

"About a month."

The Dost nodded slowly. "Valentin tells me the Stranans also possess airships. Whose are more powerful?"

The Ilbeorian smiled proudly. "Ilbeoria has the largest airships in the world, but our enemies say they just make for bigger targets. The North Brendanian Combine uses Stalkers—airships that ride very close to the ground. All of their cannons are set to shoot up through the hold of an airship. With them, and a moderate number of other airships, Brendanians were able to fight off Ilbeoria and gain independence. Strana has a lot of ships, most of them in the middle range, same with most other nations. Our airfleet knows no equal."

"Do you realize that to a devout Ataraxian, your airships are huge, floating castles of evil?"

"Because of their view of our magick?"

"Precisely so."

Uriah shrugged. "What Ataraxians think about western magick doesn't matter because their magick sells their souls to the Devil."

The Dost smiled. "How curious that each side accuses the other of exactly the same thing."

"But only one of us can be right."

"Is that true?"

For a half-second Uriah thought he heard Kidd's voice coming from the Dost. "Atarax is a false god. He is only one of the demons ruled over by Shaitan. He was chased from Heaven for his rebellion against God. The fact that Ataraxian magick works on people proves it is evil."

"But did not Eilyph heal through magick?"

"He was the Son of God. He was God Himself."

"So it is permissible for Him to do things that are evil when done by others."

The Dost's lips may be moving, but Kidd's words are coming through. "Yes, because Eilyph harbored no evil in his heart. His acts were selfless. Ataraxian magick is evil in part because it mocks the miracles of Eilyph and seeks to mislead people into abandoning the True God. Besides, many of Eilyph's miracles used items to effect them. During His last meal with His disciples, He showed them spells to work on bread and wine to create powerful items through which His love for all could be made manifest."

The Dost's metal features flowed into a smile. "You quote dogma quite well, Uriah. Perhaps, as we speak further about Martinist theology, you will tell me what *you* think, not what others want you to think. Now I have other things to which I must attend. I will leave you with this." He held his right hand out with the palm down and from it grew a gold globe about the size of a small apple. It detached itself from his hand and fell.

Uriah caught it and was surprised by how light it appeared to be, despite being formed from gold. More important than that, the force of the drop gushed a bit of it out through his fingers. The tendrils of gold hung down from between his fingers like wax dripped down the side of a candle, then it retracted and the slightly flattened globe made itself into a perfect sphere.

Puzzled, the Ilbeorian looked up at the Dost. "What is this?"

The Dost shook his head. "There is no word in your language for it. I could comment on its nature, but I would prefer to have you manipulate and study it for a while, then report back to me what you think it is. Play with it. Apply yourself and learn its secrets."

Uriah bounced the fluid metal from one hand to another. "What if I break it?"

"You cannot do that." The Dost shook his head and turned to walk away, then stopped. "Rather, if you *can* break it, you will be the most dangerous man alive."

— 42 —

Government House
Dhilica
Puresaran, Aran
30 Tempest 1687

Robin Drury entered Prince Trevelien's office and saluted both the Prince and Captain Hassett. "Reporting as requested, Highness."

Trevelien returned the salute then pointed Robin toward an empty chair beside a small round table. "Please, Brother Robin, be seated. Would you care for some tea?"

"No, thank you, sir." Robin moved to the chair indicated, but waited for the Prince and Captain Hassett to be seated before he lowered himself into the chair. Though neither of the other two men were dressed in anything more formal than everyday uniforms like the one Robin wore, Robin felt underdressed. To accommodate the bandage on his left arm, he'd rolled his sleeve up to his elbow. While a practical thing to do, it seemed to him to be somehow disrespectful.

The Prince glanced at Captain Hassett. "Lonan and I were discussing a matter of importance and your name came up in connection with it. He told me you have had some dealings with Erwin Grimshaw."

"I have, Highness."

"Please, tell me what you think of the man."

Robin frowned. "I met his daughter, Amanda, at the reception after you took over for Baron Fiske. Brother Dennis Chilton introduced us. I subsequently met her father and was invited to their home for dinner."

Trevelien watched him intently as he spoke. "Did you accept the invitation?"

"Yes, sir. I went to dinner there on the twentieth of this month. I was one of sixteen guests at the house. If the service and fare was any indication, Mr. Grimshaw has done very well here."

The Prince lifted a teacup and saucer and held it in his left hand. "You seem reluctant to give me an opinion about the man, Brother Robin. You may be frank here."

"Yes, sir, I understand that." Robin looked down at his hands. "It is just that, Highness, I have found his daughter to be an intelligent and thoughtful person and I am afraid that anything I might say about her father would reflect badly on her. I know she knows of some of the things he has done, and she has taken steps to redress the resultant ills, but I don't think she knows the totality of what her father does."

"Your caution is well taken, Brother Robin, and I shall bear it in mind." Again the Prince looked at Captain Hassett. "Lonan has only given me the impression that your dinner at Gauntlan Manor ended disagreeably. What happened?"

"Two things, Highness. After dinner all of the men retired to the tower and were offered brandy and cigars. There the guests all spoke about the future of Aran. It was noted that I commanded the most formidable fighting force in all of Aran. They said they wished to thank me for my service in Mendhakgaon, but I had the impression that they were hinting at rewards in the future if I were to become their man. No offers were tendered, but it seemed obvious that my acting in their interest would earn me more rewards."

"Such as?"

Robin shook his head. "That was the second thing, Highness. In that tower Grimshaw keeps a number of concubines. They appear to be drawn from throughout Aran and even up into Helansajar. To reward me for Mendhakgaon they offered me first choice among them—and said I could choose more than one—for an evening's entertainment."

"They offered you the services of concubines?" Trevelien looked very surprised and set his tea back on the table. "Has Grimshaw no shame?"

"It's power, Highness. He keeps them because he *can* keep them."

Hassett shook his head. "It would appear the rot runs deep at Gauntlan Manor."

Robin frowned. "Not Amanda, sir. When she learned what her father did in the tower, she began volunteering her time at the Donnist mission in the Varatha Quarter." He held his arm up. "She was taken hostage by a man who worked for her father. I tried to talk him into surrendering to the authorities, but got cut for my trouble. Two of Grimshaw's Militia shot him dead."

Trevelien rose from his chair and walked over to his desk. He opened a drawer, drew a small box from it, and came back to the table. He set the walnut box on the table, then opened it. From the red velvet interior he drew a gold ring set with a large ruby. He slid it onto the ring finger of his right hand, then held it out for Robin's inspection. "Do you know what this is?"

The ethyrine nodded slowly. "It's a Cardinal's ring."

"Correct. Do you know why I have it?"

Robin thought for a moment. "If I recall something Cadet Smith once told me, part of your duties within the Church is to serve as the Cardinal Protector of the Empire."

"Right again. When I wear this ring I add to my civil powers as Governor-general the privileges and responsibilities of the Church. While I trust both of you implicitly, I will have you swear before God on this ring that you will reveal nothing I am about to tell you to anyone save my father or his successor, and that only upon or because of my death."

Robin blinked as the Prince laid his hand flat on the table. He could not imagine what could be so delicate and dangerous that such an oath would be required, and this frightened him. Still, he did not hesitate to lay his hand over the Prince's. "Before God I swear on the Cardinal's ring I will reveal none of what I am about to hear except to the King or his successor, and that only upon or because of the death of Prince Trevelien of Ilbeoria."

Hassett also took that oath. "What has happened, Highness?"

Trevelien leaned back in his chair and suddenly looked very tired. "Yesterday Mr. Grimshaw came to me and offered to make Aran into a kingdom where I would rule. He said that the country would be capable of competing with Brendania and suggested the possibility of returning Fernandi from exile on Zlora Isle to Lescar as a way to keep Ilbeoria and Strana occupied while Aran revolted and the situation stabilized."

Robin stared at the Prince. "Fernandi?"

"Yes, the Lescari Emperor." Trevelien opened his hands. "I know the offer was not serious and I suspect the true plan is to install Fernandi here in my place. Personally I believe that Grimshaw is mistaken in thinking he could control Fernandi, but I also believe Fernandi would promise Grimshaw anything to win his way out of exile."

The ethyrine nodded slowly. "There was a rumor that ran through Sandwycke a year ago saying Fernandi had offered his daughter Lisette in matrimony to you, Highness, to win his freedom."

The Prince sighed. "There is some truth to that, but my brother was the target of her affections and the offer was rejected. With that avenue of escape closed, it appears Fernandi began to look at alternative ways of gaining his freedom."

Trevelien leaned forward in his chair. "Having Fernandi here in Dhilica would not make the country viable, and this is the core of our problem. For an independent Aran to be able to make its way in the world, it will need modern industry. While this nation has enough waterways to make waterwheel factories possible, true factories with steam engines will be needed to turn out steel and all the other necessities of a modern nation. For Grimshaw to suggest Aran can be self-sufficient, I must assume there is already one or more steam engines in Aran. They may even have a working factory or two."

Captain Hassett frowned. "So, we need to locate those factories and destroy them. It will only be a temporary solution to the situation—having gotten one engine in, they can get more, but it will be very expensive for them. Without those engines and factories, there's no way Aran can become independent."

The Prince nodded. "I was half hoping, Mr. Drury, you might be able to renew acquaintance with Mr. Grimshaw and regain his confidence. It would take time, but we need to know— Why are you laughing?"

"Forgive me, Highness, I apologize." Robin held his hands up. "I don't think Grimshaw will ever trust me—"

"Damn!"

"—but finding the factories you mention might not be as difficult as you imagine."

"What?"

The ethyrine glanced at Captain Hassett. "Do you recall Sergeant Connor from my platoon?"

"Older man, rather big?"

"Yes, sir. Connor is very much a student of the enemy—he studies whoever he sees as an enemy at the time. He learns about them and their weapons. In the short time we've been here he has amassed a collection of weapons that is nothing short of remarkable and rather comprehensive."

Hassett smiled. "I seem to remember most of that collection coming from Mendhakgaon."

"It did, sir, and a good thing, too." Robin held his left arm up again. "Yesterday a Grimshaw employee, Cobb Venner, cut me with a strange-looking knife. I showed the knife to Connor and he said it was a Ghur *kukri*. He showed me a number of them he picked up on our expedition against that Ghur bandit band and he told me about them. It turns out the Ghurs lavish a lot of care on their knives, working sigils corresponding to the date and location of birth into them. Just as all the villages in Culordain use a different knitting pattern on the sweaters their fishermen wear—so the bodies of drowned men can be returned to the right village for burial—similarly the designs on a *kukri* allow it to be returned to the place of manufacture so it can be melted down and made into another knife when the owner dies. The Ghurs are supposed to be the fiercest fighters in Estanu—they were the last to be conquered by the Dost and the first to win independence—so their knives are highly prized."

The Prince nodded. "They gave us a lot of trouble before we defeated and disarmed them. Melting their knives down did seem to kill their spirit."

"Yes, sir. Connor says the *kukris* from Mendhakgaon looked just like the one that had cut me. More importantly, the steel was good, very good—better than the steel generally used here in Aran." Robin smiled. "Since the Ghurs are known for their metalwork, I didn't attach any significance to the quality of the steel, but this talk of factories dovetails with something else.

"This Venner hired Aranans to work outside Dhilica on a project both he and Grimshaw's Mercantile wanted to keep very secret. I'm wondering if he got the knife on a visit to one of the factories." Robin cradled his arm to his chest. "Prince Agra-sho has his palace in Kulang. It's common knowledge the man is itching to return the Ghurs to their warrior ways. Grimshaw is buying their cooperation with weapons manufactured there, I would bet. With the Ghurs as an army to enforce Grimshaw's will, even Fernandi might have to think twice before betraying Grimshaw."

"Grimshaw did mention Ghur mercenaries to me, but I missed the significance of that slip, too." Trevelien frowned with concentration. "Knowing the factories exist and are producing weapons is a bit more vexing than fearing they exist. Finding them in Dughur is not going to be easy."

"It will not be that difficult either, sir. As I said, the Ghurs inscribe dates of creation and location sigils on the knives they make." Robin smiled. "All we have to do is find someone to read the knife that cut me, then the *Saint Michael* can guarantee *that* factory joins Venner in the grave."

— 43 —

Vasily Arzlov furrowed his brows. "Grigory, I refused your request to add my two Vzorin Uhlans regiments and the Vzorin Dragoons to your force for good reason. I have legitimate concerns about Vzorin's security. If Khast was willing to attack when your Hussars were here, Vzorin will be that much more vulnerable without you."

Grigory's hazel eyes remained hard. "Without them, I may not be able to take Helor quickly enough. Speed is critical."

"Agreed, but so is the integrity of Vzorin. What will it matter if you take Helor when Khast raids Strana and leaves Vzorin in ashes? Your attack would not be the gallant contest needed to raise you to the status of an Imperial hero. You would be a laughingstock and we both would spend the rest of our time frozen in Murumyskda."

The Hussar officer took a deep breath and nodded reluctantly. "The *Zarnitsky* brought no word of the Khast band when it returned?"

"No. We do not know where they are."

"Last report said they were in Drangiana. They cannot threaten Vzorin from there." Khrolic frowned heavily. "I expected more co-operation from you in this, Vasily."

The Duke hid his anger at being addressed with such familiarity. *Before now I would not have guessed at this side of Grigory Khrolic.* Arzlov had always seen Khrolic as a talented and methodical, if plodding, officer. He was not the sort of individual to act in haste, yet now, after he had made his decision to abandon his normal caution, he was set to race on forward as fast as possible.

"Grigory, the Uhlans and Dragoons must remain here to protect Tachotha Natalya. You cannot take her with you, and she cannot be sent back to Murom. This is the best way."

"Perhaps."

Perhaps you will only serve as the battering ram that opens

Helor. Arzlov smiled, pleased that he had decided to refrain from revealing to Khrolic the identity of the man the *Zarnitsky* had brought back from Drangiana. He had only told Khrolic the man was an Ilbeorian agent and left the impression he was a half-caste scout making a preliminary survey of Drangiana. Grigory had dismissed the Duke's lie as unimportant and having no bearing on his campaign to take Helor.

Arzlov did not feel Ilbeoria was an immediate threat, but Kidd's presence bothered him. Despite Sebsai's inducements to speak, the Duke knew that Kidd had been holding something back during his interrogation. It appeared to have something to do with the traveling companions who had scattered when the Khasts raided the Wolf-priest's camp. The scouts said he had called out for someone—the name they repeated was "Yuria," which the Duke took to be some Himlan woman who served as Kidd's trail-wife.

At worst it means the Wolf-priests might know the Dost is rumored to be in Estanu, though Kidd was convincing when he said no one knew of his vision. The Ilbeorians can do nothing now, but that will not be the same in the future. I must guard against disaster, and this means Grigory Khrolic's usefulness to me is in decline. Were he not my hedge against the expedition's failure, I would destroy him now.

Arzlov had thought he could use Khrolic repeatedly to push his plan, then betray him and assume the throne himself. He had wanted Khrolic out in front, making himself a target within the circles of power that surrounded the throne, but Khrolic's inability to balance caution with ambition made him too unreliable for plans to continue without modification. *Adapting my plans will not be too difficult, however. I will play to his strengths, and those of the other pawns available to me.*

"Believe me, Grigory, for I have your best interests at heart. I am a bow launching you into the future. The Hussars, the Third Sonasny Militia, and your Vandari Rams will be more than enough to handle Helor."

"But if it takes too long to take Helor, I will not be able to take Drangiana."

"No matter. Drangiana may fall to a feint, but it would have been just gilding on the jewel that is Helor." Vasily looked down at the map on his desk. "Helor is the key to your future. Make your farewells, then take the *Zarnitsky* to your troops, Pokovnik. Your destiny awaits you in Helansajar."

———

Deep in the bowels of Pyimoc, Malachy Kidd lay shivering in a pile of moldy straw. Sebsai had succeeded in keeping him in agony without allowing him to slip into unconsciousness. Whenever Malachy felt he was going to faint, the hot iron would be withdrawn and angry nerves would begin to calm themselves. Then more questions would bring more answers and they would bring more pain.

The blind man smiled ever so slightly. The pain from the hot irons had been extreme, but Arzlov had been wrong. *I had felt pain like that, and pain beyond that, when I freed myself from the Dost's trap.* The worst of the pangs had stabbed right through him, but they never hit the point where they became unbearable. Malachy knew he was feeling pain that should have driven him out of his mind, but a soothing sensation pulsed out from the bracers and allowed him to retain some control.

During torture, Malachy made conscious decisions about what he could reveal and what he had to hide. He told Arzlov everything he knew about troop strengths and placements in Aran. Malachy knew nothing of a confidential nature about those troops, and anything he told the Duke could be confirmed by Stranan spies in Aran. Though he feigned reluctance in divulging the information, that bit of his interrogation would be useless to the Stranans.

He also allowed himself to hide behind Arzlov's assumption about his vision of the Dost. It surprised the priest that Arzlov treated the vision as nothing more than a misguided delusion. For Arzlov the world was men and machines and motives, conquest and defeat. Searching out an enemy to convert him from one religion to another was stupid. Doubting the Dost's existence was, Malachy thought, even more stupid—and really wasn't the sort of mistake he would have thought Vasily Arzlov would have allowed himself to make.

Believing my mission to save the Dost proves me insane is another mistake he's made. What Arzlov thought of him, or believed about the Dost, was really immaterial to Malachy. *My mission is paramount and my captivity here is just another test. I must escape, so I shall.*

Gingerly shifting himself around to sit with his back against the rough stone wall, Malachy cataloged the problems he would have to overcome to escape. He did not know exactly where he was, or how many guards were stationed between him and the outside. He had no weapons and his only clothing consisted of ragged trousers and some badly worn boots and the bracers. He had no money, was easily recognizable, did not speak Estanuan, and had no easy route to a safe haven.

And he was blind.

I'm sure everyone, including Duke Arzlov and even Captain Irons, would see this little exercise as the most ridiculous of hypotheticals. Wolf-priests are not thieves to be schooled in the ways of escape, but most Wolf-priests are not members of Les Revisor Carmi de Fernandi. Malachy allowed himself a little bit of a smile. *Using the skills I learned to get Prince Trevelien away from Fernandi to free myself from Arzlov just has a delicious irony all its own.*

Malachy Kidd pushed himself to his feet and began pacing off his cell. *Information is where I start, and freedom is where I will end.*

Grigory could not determine if Natalya were hiding anything from him or not. "Were there any other way, dearest, I would not leave you here. You know that. Had I a choice, I would not go from your side, but my Hussars are out on exercise and I must go to make certain they do nothing to jeopardize Strana."

Her eyes rimmed in red, Natalya looked up from her end of the couch. "You should recall them, Grigory."

"I cannot." He felt a thrill from her crying about his departure, but her weakness repulsed him. *She is crying like a child denied a toy or a treat.* "My love, Duke Arzlov has correctly deduced that only through a slow advance on Helor will we provide the renegade Tacarri with the impetus to ask your father to *recall* my Hussars. Once we know who has made such a request, we know who the traitor is. At that time we will be able to move against him. I agree that having the Hussars outside Vzorin makes it a tempting target, but the Vzorin Uhlans and Dragoons will keep the city safe. I do not fear Rafiq Khast staging another attack while we are away. We know where he is and it is too far from here for him to menace Vzorin."

"Is this what you learned from the prisoner brought back on the *Zarnitsky*?"

Grigory felt an icy viper coil in his stomach. *Does she know more than I suspected, or is she bluffing?* "The *Zarnitsky* brought no prisoner to Vzorin, only scouts."

Natalya looked toward the window overlooking the airdock. "But I thought I saw guards conduct someone from the *Zarnitsky* after it landed."

"When was this?"

"At night, late at night."

Grigory shook his head. "You were dreaming, Tachotha. I have myself talked with all who traveled on the *Zarnitsky*. Our scouts followed Khast far south, into Drangiana. He has no support, no army. He is not a threat."

"I was awake. I know what I saw. Guards brought a hooded, cloaked man from the *Zarnitsky* into Pyimoc." She frowned. "I was not dreaming."

"No, you may not have been." Grigory watched her breathe in and out for a second. Memories of time spent wrapped in one another's arms flooded through him, but did not supplant his devotion to his goal of becoming the Vandari Tacier.

That devotion made his lie come easily. "Because the Estanuans view our magick as diabolical, our Aeromancers have been threatened. What you saw was one of them being escorted from the airship. Duke Arzlov has been keeping them on board in case another attack demands getting the *Zarnitsky* aloft quickly."

Natalya looked down. "You are correct. I have been foolish."

"No, Natalya, you are looking for a means of making sense from all that has happened. You are trapped like a pawn on a chessboard." He leaned forward and kissed her gently on the forehead. "You need not fear, my love, for I will protect you."

"I know this, Grigory, I do."

Confident and smiling, Grigory stroked the back of her hand. "I should ask of you a favor."

Natalya's eyes narrowed ever so slightly. "Favor?"

"This lock of hair, one you have wound round your finger." Grigory plucked at it playfully. "I should ask for it as a token, since it is your favorite, one I can keep with me always."

Reaching down, Natalya slid a dagger from the sheath in Grigory's left boot. "It is yours, Grigory." She sliced the curl free and let it uncoil into the palm of his hand. "With it goes all significance it holds for me. Take it as a sign of my true feelings for you."

— 44 —

Dayi Marayir
Helansajar
31 Tempest 1687

Uriah Smith trailed a step behind the Dost as the man of gold strode down the rank of men forming Khast's band. Uriah would have felt like a general reviewing troops, but the Helansajarans were a fairly ragtag band of men. Instead of maintaining proper military decorum, they smiled, spoke to one another, and watched the Dost with absolute devotion in their eyes.

Each of the Helansajarans opened the neck of his tunic and bared the flesh at the base of his throat. The Dost reached up and touched his index finger to the hollow between their collarbones. The fluid gold that made him up pooled around the tip of his finger as if it were sealing wax and filled that small space. When he withdrew his hand, the gold resolved itself into a small medallion that had fused with their flesh, featuring a spider's web that had trapped five stars.

Uriah assumed the image had its roots in Ataraxianism, but he could not puzzle out its meaning. He looked over at the Stranan keeping pace with him and raised an eyebrow. Svilik shook his head. *Either he does not know, or he wishes to conceal his knowledge from me.* Though the Stranan had been nothing but cordial to him, Uriah sensed resentment from Svilik that made him reluctant to trust the Stranan fully.

The Dost came to the end of the line and touched Rafiq Khast. The leader of the Helansajarans smiled broadly. Uriah found himself smiling in sympathy with him because the look on Rafiq's face mixed respect with his adoration for the Dost. Whereas the other Helansajarans seemed to mindlessly venerate the Dost for who he was, Rafiq consciously held him in high regard.

The Dost began speaking to the Helansajarans and Svilik translated his speech into Stranan for Uriah. "The Dost is explaining that they are now to be his *b'idsayih*."

"That is . . . ?"

Svilik listened for a moment or two more with puzzlement on his face, then he nodded. "Do you know what *sabbakrasulin* are? In Strana we have called them *besbegoon*. That is *demon-runner* in Ilbeorian."

"I am able, friend Valentin, to translate Stranan into Ilbeorian myself." Uriah smiled tightly and recalled a legend he read of while researching his Tactics project. "Their magickal talent is for running supernaturally fast. I thought they were mythical."

"They are rare enough to be mythical, but they are highly valued in Estanu. Chieftains use them to relay information. They have their own brotherhood and are known to be incorruptible. No one knows their true speed. I doubt they are substantially faster than a running man, but their spells allow them to keep running for hours on end. That ability, and their use of mirrors to flash simple messages from one watchpost to another, means they relay information very quickly throughout Helansajar and Estanu."

The Stranan nodded toward the Dost. "He says the talisman he has made part of them will identify them as his spokesmen. It will also allow each far-traveler—that is a direct translation of *b'idsayih*—to move faster than any *sabbakrasulin*. He says that merely by looking at one point on the landscape, then invoking the talisman by saying *'issa hunak,'* his *b'idsayih* will be delivered to that point."

Uriah frowned, believing Svilik mistaken. If he were correct, the Stranan would be describing a situation where magick, focused through a device, had a material and substantive effect on an individual. Uriah knew this was impossible because magick could affect items, not people—excepting the demonic magick the Estanuans practiced.

The second Uriah made that judgment about the impossibility of what he was hearing described, he second-guessed himself. *A magicked sword will slice through flesh. That's magick having a material effect on an individual.* He scratched at his forehead. *No, that's what swords do; the magick just helps it slice through armor and things it could not normally penetrate.*

But the amulets are part of them, blended with their flesh, so are they objects, or part of them, or something else entirely? Uriah drew the ball of golden metal the Dost had given him from his belt pouch and rolled it between the palms of his hand. *This material seems almost to have a magick all its own. Does it defy all known traditions or define yet another?*

Rafiq stepped away from his fellows and peered off toward the entrance to the large audience cavern. He drew in a deep breath, stared off into the darkness, then said, *"Issa hunak."*

In an eyeblink he vanished. Uriah stared at where he had been standing, then started looking all over for him. He did not see him, but the sound of laughter came through a narrow gap of blackness from the other side of the flame wall. Then, a second later, Rafiq reappeared in front of the Dost and continued his laughter.

Uriah grabbed Svilik's arm. "Did you see?"

"Da."

"What does it mean, *issa hunak?*"

Svilik thought for a moment. "It means *now there*. It's a tortured formation of the phrase, unlikely to be uttered accidentally. The Dost is cautioning them to be careful. Traveling in this manner can take them as far as they can see and will do so in a heartbeat, but their bodies will react as if they have walked all that distance. Rafiq agrees. The Dost says any *b'idsayih* could kill himself if he tries to go too far."

The Stranan fell silent and his face hardened as the Dost spoke to each of Khast's men individually. "This is not good."

"What?"

"The Dost is telling each of these men which tribe in Helansajar he is to visit. Leaders of these tribes are to be told of the Dost's return. They are to be asked to come here to meet Nimchin Dost and then to help him retake Helor."

The young Ilbeorian heard the dread in Svilik's voice, but didn't feel it echoed in his own heart, despite acknowledging himself half-Stranan. Svilik clearly thought the conquest of Helor would be the first step toward the inevitable re-creation of the Durranian Empire. The Dost had said nothing to suggest that was not his intention, but Uriah didn't take that as given for two reasons.

First and foremost, the Tactics seminar project showed that Helor could fall to an attack by Stranan forces. Even if the Dost were able to bring the equivalent of Stranan Vandari armor into a battle, that alone did not constitute an unbeatable defense for the city. The Dost's presence in Helansajar would cause difficulties for the Stranans, to be certain, but having the Tacier focused on dealing with the Dost meant the nation's vast industrial resources would be brought to bear on eliminating the Dost.

What worked against Fernandi would probably suffice to destroy the Dost.

His second reason for not despairing along with Svilik is that Uriah had a hard time reconciling the gore-filled tales of the Dost his mother had told him with the reality of Nimchin. Nimchin Dost had been cordial and solicitous of him and his well-being—so much so that it was almost possible to forget he'd left Malachy Kidd to die in Drangiana. And even that charge against him wore thin because the Dost just didn't seem like the sort of person who would have engineered a cold-blooded murder. Uriah knew that general impression counted for nothing in the long run, but it still made it difficult to imagine Nimchin Dost at the head of a host sweeping across Strana.

The Dost came to Rafiq Khast to give him the final assignment. Svilik remained locked in thought so did not translate. Khast's eyes grew wide as the Dost spoke to him, then he bowed solemnly and kissed the Dost's hand. Rafiq turned away and focused on the doorway, then was gone.

Uriah smiled as the Dost walked toward him. "You made Rafiq happy."

"I entrusted him with the most urgent of the embassies. If we are to be as strong as we were before, we need to be reconciled with

old enemies and free of attack by new enemies. Rafiq's mission will
guarantee both things."

"Quite an order for one man."

"He is the leader of the Khasts. He will succeed." The Dost
nodded slowly. "All that is required is that he convince Prince Agra-
sho that his Ghurs need not be worried about me and instead should
look to reasserting their power in Aran."

— 45 —

> **Pyimoc**
> **Vzorin, Vzorin Military District**
> **Strana**
> **31 Tempest 1687**

The rhythmic tapping sound brought Malachy out of his sleep with
a start. For several seconds he could not remember where he was.
The sour scent of rotting straw almost convinced him that eleven
years had spun away while he slept, depositing him back in the
Lescari prison camp at Mont-de-Veri. *No, no, not even the Devil
could be that cruel.*

As he came awake and his mind cleared, the tapping began to
resolve itself into a coherent pattern within which he could discern
repetitions. One set of taps, no more than six, would be followed by
a brief pause, then a second set of no more than six taps. The pause
after the two sets of rapping sounds would be longer than the one
between them, then a new set would begin.

Malachy pressed his hand against the wall and could feel the
microtremors coming through. More than the sound, the tactile sensation brought parts of his experience at Mont-de-Veri back to him.
The Lescari had used an old Donnist monastery as a prison, holding
their captives in solitary confinement. The prisoners, defying their
captors, communicated via a simple system of tap codes. Ilbeorian
had twenty-six separate letters in it, but one of them, *c,* could be replaced by either a *k* or an *s,* reducing the number of letters to twenty-
five. The prisoners placed the Ilbeorian alphabet on an imaginary
five-by-five grid, beginning with *a* and ending with *z.* They then
transmitted words to another prisoner letter by letter by tapping out
the correct two-number code for each letter. Malachy smiled, recall-

ing one prisoner insisting on reordering the grid so the most commonly used letters required fewer taps, speeding up transmission, but the basic grid served everyone else quite adequately.

Spelling out each word—regardless of grid used—made transmission of information slow, so the prisoners developed slang abbreviations for words. The term *cavalry*, for example, underwent two reductions. First it became *kvlry* then *kv*. That sped up communication and would cause difficulty for non-Ilbeorian literates trying to determine what they were saying to each other. Long pauses marked the end of sentences and the repetition of the verb at the end of a sentence was used to signify a question, so punctuation marks were superfluous. Grammar suffered horribly as well, but at least the prisoners were able to communicate with each other and that gave them hope for the future.

By shifting to an eight-by-eight code he and others were even able to play chess. Malachy thought that forcing his mind to remember where pieces were on an imaginary board was what kept him sane in captivity. *Better fighting new and imaginary battles than listening to others endlessly repeat tales of their exploits in the field against Fernandi. Enduring that would have driven me entirely insane.*

He listened for a moment, then nodded to himself. *The Stranan alphabet has thirty-three letters.* He quickly calculated what their code had to be like and mentally ordered a Stranan grid. *A, b, v, g, d* . . . The alphabet required a six-by-six grid that had three empty places at the end which he chose to ignore until he ran into someone using them.

Malachy dug around in the straw and found a small fragment of stone. He tapped it against the wall several times in quick succession to get the other prisoner's attention. Silence followed in the wake of his rapping. Malachy tapped out the Stranan word for *yes, da,* then hit the stone once against the stone. He paused for a second then tapped out the code for the four-letter Stranan word for *one.*

Things remained quiet, then the person on the other side started tapping back. Malachy counted the little sounds. *One, five; one, three; one, one.* He smiled as he translated the numbers into Stranan letters, then translated that word back into Ilbeorian. Two. *He got it.* The transmittal of the simple one-two sequence meant they had ordered their grids in the same way and were using the same values for the appropriate letters.

The Wolf-priest laughed as he arbitrarily assigned a gender to the person on the other side of the wall. It was possible it could be a woman, though Kidd doubted that to be the case. He supposed he made the other prisoner male based on his experience in the Lescari War. The handful of women prisoners were housed in a camp other than Mont-de-Veri. After a moment's more reflection he realized the decision went deeper than that. There was something about how the vibrations coming through the wall felt to him that marked his communicant as being male.

That's a conclusion I can verify as we go along here. Malachy nodded as rapping started from the other side of the wall. Though confined by the cell, communication with another prisoner gained Malachy a fragment of freedom. *Ignorance is impotence. Learning what this man knows will bring me closer to escape, and closer to renewing my crusade to save the Dost.*

— 46 —

> **Dayi Marayir**
> **Helansajar**
> **1 Majest 1687**

Uriah watched with open admiration as Turikana sparred with her brother. Clad in black boots, red pants and blouse and with a black cloth belt around her waist, Turikana seemed constantly in motion. Her sword appeared to be a shamshir of sorts, but the hilt had been elongated and curved to make the whole weapon look like a stretched-out S. The balance point appeared to be right at the circular hilt guard and Turikana kept the blade spinning around that point as she moved in, slid to either side, or backed away from one of the Dost's attacks.

The Dost bore no weapon and wore no clothes. Where his sister struck at him, his fluid flesh hardened into plates of armor. It appeared to Uriah that this armor rose like the scales of a snake from the depth of his limbs and torso, then sank away again when the threat had been defeated.

When the Dost chose to go on the offensive, his hands would flatten and grow into silver blades equal in length to her shamshir. Sometimes the blades were held in conventional guard positions. At other times the Dost became scythe-handed or his fingers splayed out into a tridentine form. The blades appeared to be razor sharp, but they never cut when they reached Turikana's body.

Turikana came in low at her brother, her blade spinning in a narrow cone above her right shoulder. She extended her left leg toward him, then withdrew it as he made a stab at it with his left hand. Bending her right leg, she brought the sword down as if intending to sweep it through the Dost's left knee. As the joint armored itself, she shifted the blade's angle of attack and came up through the Dost's left armpit.

Gold splashed in the air as the sword cut through what should have been the Dost's chest muscle. Uriah heard him yelp in pain, then felt a quiver run through the golden globule he held in his hands. A second later Uriah felt a stinging pain in his own chest, right where the blade had cut the Dost.

Uriah dropped the gold, took a step back, and clutched at his own chest. "What was that?"

The Dost, whose flesh had repaired itself, held his hands out to his sister. "Stop." He bowed to her and she returned the gesture of respect, then retreated from the cavern's grand chamber toward the small one she shared with Uriah.

The Ilbeorian felt a warmth seeping into his left armpit. He probed it with his right hand and it came away bloody. "What?" Uriah pulled off his tunic and saw a thin red line scoring his flesh. "I'm cut where you were cut."

The Dost approached, his gold lips pursed. "So it seems. I had not anticipated this."

"Had not anticipated what?"

The Dost looked down at the gold globe between them. "I gave you a piece of this shell I wear. It is rather resilient and, when damaged, repairs itself by drawing energy from the person wearing it. At least I *thought* it was the person wearing it and invoking the magick to make it work. It appears that anyone in contact with it can be affected by it. You were in close proximity to me. Were you further away I doubt any of the physical damage would have transferred to you. Fascinating."

Uriah eyed the Dost with open suspicion. "You wear something that eats your soul?"

"I said *energy*, not soul, just as your Urovian magick requires you to put some of your own vitality into spells. I feel a slight chill, which means the armor has drawn heat from my body to use to repair itself." The Dost raised a gilded eyebrow. "Are your hands perchance cold?"

Uriah pressed the backs of his hands against his face. "Slightly."

"Very interesting. I never encountered that before."

Uriah frowned. "But if you are the Dost and you created this shell, how is it that you do not know all about the armor?" The Ilbeorian held his hands up to forestall an answer. "That question sounds as if I accept your claim to be reincarnated, which I do not. It is not possible."

"Isn't it?" The Dost flowed down into a sitting position with his legs crossed. "Please join me. I would discuss this point, in context of your beliefs, which I very much want to understand."

Uriah sat warily. "I'm not a theologian."

"No, but you have been a Martinist all your life, have you not? You entered a Martinist seminary. You must have some understanding of the doctrines of your faith."

"Of course." Uriah raised his head. "Even so, there are intricacies."

"I understand. We will speak generally. Why is reincarnation impossible, from the Martinist view?"

Uriah took a moment to organize his thoughts, though nagging memories of Kidd's comments about reincarnation began to undermine his confidence. "The reason reincarnation is not possible is that each individual is a unique creation of God, endowed with free will and given a lifetime to choose good or evil, God or the Devil as his master. God so loved Mankind that he sent Eilyph, his only begotten Son, to show us the way to eternal salvation. God is merciful, but so is He just. At the end of our lives we await the Judgment Day, when our souls will be found pleasing to God and gathered unto Heaven, or found wanting and cast into the flaming pit of Perdition."

The Dost's hand merged with his chin as he supported his head.

"Your Eilyph, when he was given to you, was he a man first, and then made a god, or was he a god masquerading as a man?"

Uriah shifted his shoulders uneasily. "The theologians say He grew into His knowledge of His divinity because it was God's intention to have Him gain a true understanding of the travails of humanity. After His death, His soul experienced what all human souls experience, then He returned to His body to show us that through Him there is life after death. As His soul was able to live after the death of His body, so our souls can live on after our deaths, if, on Judgment Day, we are accepted into Heaven."

"So you Eilyphianists accept that man is both body and soul."

"Yes, but only the soul lives on after death—save for that of Eilyph and Lilith, His mother. They have ascended bodily into Heaven."

The Dost narrowed his metal eyes and for a moment Uriah had the uncomfortable feeling Kidd was staring at him. "You have related all this as a child might. How much of it do you believe?"

Uriah's quick response died unspoken. "I am not a theologian. Nor are the people in the martial branch of the Church overly schooled in dogma and doctrine. I can only tell you what I have been told."

"That is not what I asked."

The Ilbeorian looked down at his hands. "I don't know how to answer you."

"Try truthfully. Faith unexamined is worthless."

Uriah shifted uncomfortably. "I believe Eilyph was born, lived, died, and rose again. The Scriptures are full of parables and allusions. I can't say I believe one passage and not another. I don't know. I have grown up accepting all of it as true, but I have questions, the same as anyone might."

The Dost's expression eased. "That is a fair answer." He freed his hand from his chin. "Let me ask you about this: you said each person was a unique creation of God. If this is true, would you say the soul and the body are created at the same time, or, given a soul's eternal nature, could a soul be prepared before the body is ready?"

"It doesn't matter, since each soul is suited to only one body."

"Good point. Let me ask you this: do you more closely resemble your mother or father?"

Uriah shook his head and tried to figure out where the Dost was heading with the radical change of subject. "My father. He had red hair and green eyes, too."

"Good." The Dost held his hands up and his thumbs became sharpened spikes. He stabbed one into the palm of the opposite hand and vice versa. Turning his hands with the palm down, he let liquid metal flow out like blood. It hung in the air, but the droplets did not merge. Instead they stayed distinct. The fluid from his right hand assumed a cubical shape while the liquid from his left hand became round.

"Let us assume that you are a mixture of your parents, yes?"

"Yes."

"Good." The Dost brought his hands together. As he did so the piles of spheres and cubes mixed together without losing their individual shapes. "We shall assume that your siblings are likewise a mix, but not the same one. Now if you have children, they would be half of you and half of your wife, yes?"

"Yes."

With a gesture the shapes split themselves into ten randomly determined piles. "I give you ten children, which are half you and half their mothers, which means they are a quarter of your parents each, yes?"

Uriah nodded. "Yes."

"Generation after generation, you become more dilute, but you still exist in your children and grandchildren and so on." The golden piles split and split again until a cloud of tiny golden objects slowly spun around the Dost. "Some of your lines will die out, but what has been lost could be found in the children of your brothers and sisters. You, and your parents through you, still exist, you see?"

"I believe so."

"You have seen among the Khasts, some Stranans, and even in Turikana the coloring and sharpened ears that mark us as being of Durranian descent. Because Durranian traits and blood are valued here and in Strana, efforts have been made to preserve these traits. Matches are made between people who exhibit them—not entirely unlike breeding done by horse traders." The Dost laughed lightly.

Uriah joined him and poked at one of the floating cubes. "My mother was Stranan, so perhaps even I have a fraction of your blood inside me."

"Indeed, I should think so." The Dost's voice remained even. "A bit, in any event."

"I've probably tainted it forever, too, judging by that reaction." Uriah sighed. "Please continue."

"It is possible, then, that all of these scattered traits have slowly been gathered back together, yes? In me, these traits combined and were reborn." The Dost opened his arms, then brought his hands together. All the floating bits of gold returned to the cradle formed by his palms, then were absorbed back into his flesh. "When my soul, *my* eternal soul which was created for *my* body, found in my physical makeup a body it recognized, it returned to my body and I was born again."

The logic of the Dost's explanation hammered Uriah. *If it is as he suggests, then reincarnation is not only possible but cannot be considered sinful, can it?* "But God only gives each person one life."

"But who is to define what constitutes that life? You said God gives us one life in which to choose good or evil. He has given us an objective, much as a commander might give you a military objective to be attained. If we look at each individual attempt you make toward that objective, we might say you had multiple chances. If we step back and judge your success based on other parameters, such as the amount of time you were given, then the number of individual attempts has no bearing on your success because you took your objective within the allotted time. With this perspective, what we consider *lives* are merely fragments of what God might consider a *life*."

"But if you are correct, if what you are saying happened has indeed happened, then . . ." Uriah felt his stomach knot up. The Dost's rebirth cast serious doubt on the nature of certain fundamental truths upon which Eilyphianism was based. Over the centuries theologians had worked out solutions to all of these problems. Heresies had been suppressed and lives lost fighting for or against some variation in philosophy. The whole basis for civilization was in question.

The Ilbeorian's mouth slowly hung open. "This makes everything a sham, a fraud."

The Dost shook his head. "No, Uriah, not a fraud. What we have discussed here does not invalidate your faith or any other. Eilyphianism may just represent one path, one very direct, difficult path, to attaining eternal life. It may represent the *only* path, in fact, and reincarnation is merely your God's merciful way of letting those who cannot choose between good and evil try until they do make their choice."

That could also be true. Uriah frowned. "There's no way of knowing, is there?"

The Dost shook his head. "Now *I* do not know how to answer *you*. You now confront what I must face. You find conflict with centuries of thoughts and rules created by men to justify their beliefs. Likewise I must battle all the expectations foisted upon me between incarnations. The two of us, we must remember that at the center of all the artifice and presumption there are truths that need no justification. We must examine these truths and challenge ourselves to further the goals they represent."

— 47 —

Pyimoc
Vzorin, Vzorin Military District
Strana
1 Majest 1687

Malachy sat quietly, listening to the echoes of a cell door being slammed shut and guards walking away from it. The noise had not originated close enough to have been the door to the cell next to his, the one housing his communicant. The guards had dragged the

Hussar out hours ago and had not returned with him yet. Had a sharp pain in Malachy's left armpit not awakened him, the Wolf-priest would not have been clearheaded enough to make the judgment about the sound. By the time he recalled what had awakened him, the pain had subsided.

Anxiety about his friend's fate would not go away.

His communicant had been reluctant to let Malachy know why he was in Pyimoc's dungeon, but slowly the story had come out. The man was a soldier, one of the 137th Imperial Bear Hussars. He had deserted when Grigory Khrolic had held a briefing in which he told his troops that they were going to march to Helor and lay siege to the city. Duke Arzlov only wanted the Hussars to go to Helor, show the flag, and come back as a warning to Ilbeoria to stop any thoughts of expansion into Helansajar or central Estanu.

Spies in Helor had reported a large Ilbeorian warship arriving at Helor. It had left a company of ethyrines behind as a courtesy guard for Shukri Awan. The presence of Ilbeorian troops had prompted Arzlov to send the Hussars out, but Khrolic wanted to use the opportunity to further his own career.

The Hussar had chosen not to go because he found the assignment dishonorable. Khrolic had denounced him as an agent of Arzlov's enemies in Murom, which was what had caused him to be placed in the dungeon and subjected to tortures to learn what he knew. Since he knew nothing and could say nothing, the tortures would continue until he was dead. Since Khrolic had convinced the Duke that the Hussar was in service to his enemies, the Duke would never believe the truth.

The Hussar had also said Khrolic boasted of wanting to capture the ethyrines and put their eyes out as he had arranged to have done to another Wolf-priest during the Lescari War.

Malachy shivered again as he recalled piecing together that information tap by tap. *Khrolic had never acted on the message I'd left him, so he never rescued the scouts and made no attempt to get me back.* He had never before suspected Khrolic of having been involved with the disaster in Glogau, but it made perfect sense. Khrolic had learned a great deal from Malachy but never seemed to like it. And, Malachy admitted to himself, he'd whisked Natalya away from Khrolic at various parties in Murom. He and she had laughed about Khrolic's frustration and made a game of inciting it, but he'd thought it was a good-natured bit of mischief.

Grigory clearly did not. I created an enemy and never saw the danger. It would have been child's play for Khrolic to get information to the Lescari lines that warned of the scouting mission and the attempted rescue. In retrospect, the late arrival of *Les Revisor Carmi* and the segregation of the wounded scouts made perfect sense. *It was one big trap and I wandered blindly into it.*

Malachy laughed hollowly at his own choice of words.

So, now I know who the bear with ram's horns was. He was my enemy at the time of my blinding and he is still my enemy. He must also be the threat to the Dost against which I must act.

Malachy shivered in his straw. The ethyrines, probably fewer than fifty total, had a better chance of standing against the Hussars than Malachy did of convincing his jailers to let him borrow an ethyrskiff for taking a tour of the city—but not that much better. Without warning or a chance to prepare Helor for a siege, neither the ethyrines nor the citizens of the city would be able to resist the Stranans for very long. Even *with* warning the chance of defeating the Stranans would be minimal.

The Wolf-priest shook his head. *In Glogau, Grigory Khrolic knew my plan and used it to slaughter the men I was out to rescue. Here, I know his plan, and may be able to use it to prevent the slaughter of a whole city. It does not make escape any easier, just more imperative. What happened in Glogau will not happen again.*

Vasily Arzlov bowed after entering the Tachotha's suite of rooms. "Forgive my intrusion, Tachotha. I do not mean to presume, but with Pokovnik Khrolic gone, I thought you might have questions or worries I could address. I know you are chafing beneath your confinement here, but it is for the best, I assure you."

Natalya glared at him darkly. "I appreciate your concern, Duke Arzlov. I shall report it to my father when next I am in Murom. When would you suppose that to be?"

"Please, Tachotha, as much as you do not trust me, I am not your enemy here. Grigory has pointed out, and I agree, that you are very much in danger. His punitive bombardment of Helor will warn Shukri Awan away from ever attacking Strana again. What is wrong, Tachotha?"

"The Hussars are going to *attack* Helor?"

Arzlov nodded. "Grigory thought a simple bombardment would be best. He expects Shukri Awan to offer reparations and peace. He must have told you that. He told me you agreed with his thinking."

Natalya's eyes narrowed. "He said what?"

"He told me you said his thinking was sound and that you encouraged him in this effort against Shukri Awan. Did you not?"

Vasily scowled at the carpet. "I thought your feelings natural, given how close you came to death, so I did not question them."

She looked up at Vasily. "What about the renegade Tacarri and the plot against my life?"

"I beg your pardon, Tacotha?" Arzlov blinked at her. "What has any Tacarri to do with Shukri Awan's attempt on your life?"

"Grigory told me first that you said Ilbeoria was behind the attempt on my life, then the story changed so that a renegade Tacarri was working with Shukri Awan to kidnap or kill me." Natalya pressed her fists to her temples. "It makes no sense when I try to explain it. Did it ever make sense?"

"Tachotha Natalya, are you telling me that you did *not* approve of Grigory's plan?"

"Nyet!"

"What could his game be?"

"If *he* were to do what everyone expected you to do—take Helor—he might be elevated in your place to rank of Tacarri."

"Yes, but why press the attack now? It is late enough in summer that reinforcing Helor will be difficult. A spring campaign would have been better."

"Unless he thinks to forestall another campaign next spring." Natalya's green eyes flashed dangerously. "Did the *Zarnitsky* bring an Ilbeorian here to Vzorin?"

Vasily rubbed his hands together in a nervous fashion. "Did Grigory tell you this?"

"No, he denied it."

The Duke let relief briefly wash over his face. "No, it did not."

"But I saw—"

"What you saw was a member of the Khast band we brought here for interrogation. No connection to Ilbeoria at all."

"I see."

I am certain you do, Tachotha Natalya. "When questioned, the prisoner told us nothing."

"Pity. You disposed of him?"

"Yes, yes, he is gone." Arzlov exhaled loudly. "He did not like being a prisoner."

"I can sympathize with him."

Vasily worked a pained expression onto his face. "No, Tachotha, I would not have you feeling this way. Grigory had you imprisoned here, not I. If you will give me your solemn word that you will not go to Murom or communicate with anyone in Murom before the Helorian matter is settled, you are free to roam where you will in Vzorin."

"My father *should* know of what is happening."

"Yes, but later. I owe it to Grigory to do what I can to stop him. If he is not stopped, his career will be over and a good officer will be destroyed."

"Yes, of course." Natalya's concern for Khrolic deadened her face. "I give you my word I will not return to Murom, Duke Arzlov, nor will I send messages there. Grigory must be stopped, and I urge you to do all you can to prevent disaster."

"Your wish is my command, Tachotha Natalya." Arzlov bowed. "If you will permit me, I will review the plans Grigory discussed with me and try to see if there are flaws we can exploit to stop him."

"Do not let me detain you, Duke Arzlov." Natalya smiled graciously at him. "Please do keep me informed."

"Thank you, Highness, I shall do so." Vasily retreated to the door. "If I may be of further service to you, please do not hesitate to call upon me."

"Thank you, Duke Arzlov. I believe I will be able to handle myself without burdening you."

Vasily smiled as he closed the door behind himself. "This I do believe, Tachotha Natalya. Do what you think you must. Your help will be most appreciated."

— 48 —

Kulang Valley, Dughur
Aran
1 Majest 1687

The ethyrskiff dropped silently from the belly of the *Saint Michael*. Robin helped the two airmen in the crew cast the lines off the flat-bottomed boat, then took up his position in the bow. Behind him the airmen raised the short mast and pegged it upright. Beyond them the skiff's Aeromancer sat in the pilot's chair, using his magick to keep the boat flying. The rigging lines went past the Aeromancer to the navigator, who sat in the stern and guided the boat along its course.

The airmen got the sail unfurled and the midnight breeze filled it. The wind came from the southwest, which was perfect for them because they wanted to scout out the upper reaches of the Kulang

Valley. Below and ten miles to their stern, the city of Kulang had been built on the shores of Lake Namardgi. In coming up from Dhilica the *Saint Michael* had traveled east into Dughur and had skirted the city. Though their charts were the best available, the last survey of Dughur had taken place thirty years earlier. The map did not show a village with the name engraved on the *kukri* Robin had taken from Venner, but it did have a couple that were close. All of them were located in the upper Kulang Valley, so that's where they began their search.

The *Saint Michael*, all but invisible above them, changed its heading and flew off to the east. It would come around and wait for them at the north end of the valley. While Hassett did not think the Ghurs would be expecting any action against their factory, he did not want the thrumming of the steam engines to give away the airship's presence. The ethyrskiff, moving silently on the wind, could scout out the valley and locate the factory.

Robin had volunteered for the scouting run. Having had experience working near a steel mill in Ilbeoria, he knew what to look for. *And what to smell for.* Robin felt certain that any sort of steel mill would be kept working around the clock. That meant it would need a lot of fuel and would be belching out smoke even in the dead of night. Since the steel appeared to be turned over to individual smiths to make weapons, he also assumed there would be numerous outbuildings surrounding the factory, as well as warehouses in which to store the weapons that had been made.

The night breeze carried them along at four knots per hour. In the six hours before dawn they would be able to traverse the section of the valley that lay a comfortable day's ride from Kulang. He'd settled on that arbitrary measurement because it would make it convenient for Prince Agra-sho to visit the facility. Likewise any airships putting in to Kulang for trade would be able to swing up and deliver workers or take away goods without adding suspiciously to their itineraries.

In the first two hours they saw nothing of note. The thin sliver of waning moon shed very little light on the ground. It illuminated the snowy peaks above the floating boat, but gave definition to little else. Then, as the skiff came about on a northerly heading, they came into a part of the valley that ran north for a couple of miles before turning back to the northeast.

Down below Robin made out the silhouettes of buildings with firelight pouring out their doors and windows. The largest one had twin smokestacks that looked like volcanoes as they spit sparks in the night. Surrounding the factory like disciples seated at Eilyph's feet, a dozen smaller buildings rang with the sound of hammer on anvil and glowed red from forge fires. Beyond them Robin saw buildings that were not characteristic of Dughur or Aran, but that he recognized as Ilbeorean-style factory longhouses meant for worker lodging.

Robin worked his way back to the navigator. "Make as fast as we can for the *Saint Michael*. We've found what we were looking for. The sooner we get back, the sooner we can finalize plans for our salute to the industriousness of Erwin Grimshaw."

Rafiq Khast learned one important fact about being a *b'idsayih* as he came through the Himlans and it saved him a lot of time in making the trip. He started by moving point to point conservatively, largely to learn how quickly he would tire traveling magickally. He did notice fatigue and a chill, but moving south a mile or two at a time did not seem to tax his strength overmuch. He discovered that if he ran a bit after a "jump" and began to feel hot, the next jump would cool him down and tire him even less.

Even with the running, the longer leaps did wear him out more quickly than the short ones, but still did not exhaust him as quickly as actually walking that same distance might have. Forty miles between points might involve walking over sixty miles of terrain, yet the *b'idsayih* amulet only made him feel as if he had walked the shorter of the two distances. He proved this to be true when he started to move from hilltop to hilltop and into the Himlans, managing to effortlessly pass from one peak to another without suffering from hiking the terrain between them.

The sensation of jumping from point to point was not something Rafiq found wholly pleasant. His body seemed to stretch out to the point at which gauze would have seemed a steel wall by comparison. He seemed to become fluid and drain back into his body at the new location. He suffered a second or two of disorientation on arrival, but that seemed to pass into an unbelievably clear state of mind.

He took refuge with some shepherds that first night in the Himlans after it became too dark for him to see very far. The last thing he wanted to do was try to move to the crest of a silhouette mountain, only to find himself actually looking at a star well beyond it. The shepherds were quiet men who shared their food gladly with Rafiq. He told them nothing of his mission, but gave them a gold coin from Helor when he left at dawn.

The journey to Nagmandir—Prince Agra-sho's palace—

should have been exhausting, but Rafiq was too excited to feel tired
when he reached his goal. He spotted the huge white edifice the moment he stepped through Kulang's eastern gate, then in an instant he
was beside the central courtyard's fountain. His sudden appearance
surprised the guards at the palace doors, but they were cautious in
their approach to him.

After a brief debate, one of them came walking over to where
Rafiq stood. "May the joy of warm nights be with you always."

"May you have more wives than problems." Rafiq bowed to the
soldier. "I am Rafiq Khast of Helansajar. I am come to speak with
Prince Agra-sho on behalf of the Dost."

That declaration etched astonishment on the soldier's face.
"I—I will return." He spun on his heel and continued past his fellow
guards on into the palace.

Rafiq almost followed him in, then decided against it. Looking
out from Nagmandir's courtyard he saw the eastern half of Kulang
and found it an interesting city. Most of the buildings had been
painted the color of snow, though around the doors and over the lin-
tels brightly colored lines served as decoration. Rooftops of thatch
or pottery tile seemed evenly matched in distribution throughout
the city. Out on the lake, which was by far the largest body of water
Rafiq had ever seen in his entire life, ships with sails of red and blue
raced through the waves.

As a b'idsayih *I am like those ships. No matter the lay of the
land beneath the water, I pass over it all.* For one irrational moment
he thought about traveling out to the deck of one of the ships, but
feared somehow ending up in the middle of the lake itself. *The nomadic life may be the best life, but moving through deserts does not
a good swimmer make.*

Still the ships and the way they glided over the water reminded
him of the airship he had seen coming in to land at Vzorin. While he
knew it to be demonic and sinful, he could appreciate the ease with
which such a craft was able to travel from place to place without
worrying about terrain.

It occurred to him that the amulet the Dost had fused to his
flesh could be seen as a diabolical focus for magickal energies and
thereby something a devout Ataraxian should refuse to use. He dismissed that idea instantly because the Dost had given the talisman
to him. Since Keerana Dost had been worshiped as an avatar of
Atarax, and Nimchin Dost was him come again, clearly there could
be nothing evil about the amulet. Items into which magick was woven were evil because the men using the magick did not know the
proper way spells were to be employed. Clearly Nimchin Dost *did*,

and had made it a part of Rafiq's very being, hence the amulet Rafiq used was not evil.

At the sound of footsteps Rafiq turned around and saw the soldier to whom he had spoken leading a bald man in an orange robe out to him. Rafiq bowed. The soldier and the other man returned the bow. "I am Rafiq Khast. I am come as an envoy to Prince Agra-sho from Nimchin Dost."

"So I have been told." The bald man sighed. "The Prince is away from Nagmandir at this time. I do not know when we will expect him to return."

"But you do know where he is at present?"

The bald man straightened up. "Of course."

"Please point me in the direction he has gone and tell me how I may find him."

"I cannot."

"I come from the Dost."

"So you say."

"And you doubt?"

The bald man watched Rafiq through half-lidded eyes. "There have been many Dosts and many more who have pretended to be from these Dosts. The Ghurs have never been fooled or defeated by *pretenders*."

Rafiq reached out and grabbed the shoulder of the bald man's robe. Glancing back over his shoulder at the tower in the northwest corner of Nagmandir, Rafiq breathed *"Issa hunak."* In an eyeblink they both appeared on the tower, with the bald man screaming hysterically and Rafiq on his knees with his hands clutched to his stomach.

Crushing weariness dampened the fire in his stomach and limbs. The nerves in his body could not muster the energy to complain. He felt *cold*, far colder than he ever had before. He recalled feeling stretched, as before, but then the other man's being became entangled in his own. As they both materialized on the top of the tower, their essences were ripped apart and the segregation had been brutal.

I hope none of my fellows are so rash as to have tried this.

The other man dropped to the tower's top beside Rafiq. "Please, sir, do not do that to me again. I don't doubt, I don't . . ."

Rafiq swallowed hard and slowly forced himself up to dwarf the cringing bald man. "The Dost would not be pleased that such a display was necessary. Where is Prince Agra-sho?"

The bald man got to his hands and knees, then crawled to the edge of the tower. "He's there." He pointed off to the northeast.

"Follow the valley until you get to the village of the smiths. Where the valley goes north, he is there. You'll find him there."

Standing beside Captain Hassett on the wing deck, Robin Drury caught his first glimpse of the factory complex in daylight. The smokestacks still shot sparks into the air, but he could barely see them even against the thick rope of black smoke pouring into the sky. To the north of the factory lay a huge pile of coal that had been invisible in the night. A line of men with wheelbarrows moved from the factory to it and back.

Hassett looked over at Robin. "Are your men prepared to descend?"

Robin nodded. "Archangel and Dominion platoons are ready to go."

"Good. I intend to shoot one light-pressure charge volley of grape against the factory roof with our forward cannons. That should bring everyone out and away from the factory. Two broadsides will level the factory itself, then the forges, then the housing and warehouses."

"Yes, sir, then we go in and determine how complete the damage is."

"Correct." Hassett slapped Robin on the shoulder. "Good luck."

"And you, sir."

Hassett nodded, then yelled down to his helmsman. "Mr. Foster, bring us down below the level of those smokestacks, but keep us back so they won't hit us when they go down. Make the heading four points off the starboard bow. Signal the gunners to be ready for my order to shoot. The buildings won't be moving, so every shot better count."

The hour he had spent in Prince Agra-sho's company had Rafiq Khast thinking seriously about staring at the steel mill's molten heart and uttering the words *issa hunak*. Agra-sho's squeaky voice seemed appropriate for someone with so scraggly a beard and such a youthful face, but it grated on Rafiq mightily. So did Agra-sho's massive girth, which the Prince seemed intent on using to pin Rafiq against things hot or uncomfortable or both.

The Helansajaran realized his presence and mention of the Dost scared the Prince, but it need not have. "Please, Prince Agra-sho, the Dost is not attempting to press a claim on Dughur. He hopes

Dughur and his realm can be allies. He wishes to work with you to your mutual benefit."

"I have powerful protectors, Rafiq Khast." The Prince opened his arms and waved his pudgy hands at the factory surrounding him. "This mill took two years to build, but it was well worth the expense. It produces as much steel in a day as most smiths could create in a lifetime. I have hundreds of smiths working on knives and swords. I don't need the Dost. In fact, your master should *tremble* at the mere mention of the name Agra-sho."

As the Prince accented the word *tremble* his body shook, sending ripples up and down through layers of fat and flesh. Rafiq refrained from laughing and instead nodded solemnly. "Is this the message you wish me to bring back to the Dost?"

"You have seen my factory, Rafiq. You know of my power. You may tell him what you wish." The Prince frowned, his lowered brows all but eclipsing his piggish eyes. "Unless you think he would not like that."

Before Rafiq could answer he heard a sound like thunder echo through the valley. Immediately thereafter a series of sharp cracks sounded from the roof above as if a steel monsoon had suddenly blown in. Rafiq looked at the windows and doorway to the east and saw shards of red tile cascading down like an avalanche.

"Issa hunak."

In an instant Rafiq stood just outside the factory's open doorway. A huge black shadow slid across the ground from the north end of the valley heading south. Rafiq wanted to run and wanted to jump away, but he found himself unable to think about anything but being devoured by that shadow. As it swept over him he felt the chill left by his jump deepening, then he looked up and his jaw dropped open.

A massive airship passed slowly overhead. It flew low enough that looking up into its belly he could see silver men, and could pick out individual planks that had gone into its construction. At its aft he saw two spinning blades, twin smokestacks, and above them, two rudders mounted atop the vast expanse of the aft wing.

The airship began a lazy turn toward the east. As it did so it slid out from beneath the sun, leaving Rafiq blinded by the noonday brilliance. Rafiq went to his knees and pressed his hands to his eyes. *If I cannot see, I cannot jump. Atarax, do not allow the Dost's servant to be caught in a web woven to ensnare others.* He opened his eyes and saw angry round red afterimages, but they quickly faded.

Another angry round image replaced them in his sight as Agra-sho fought his way through the crowd of fleeing Ghurs. "What has happened here, Rafiq? You are really a spy for them! You are an

Ilbeorian spy!" Agra-sho plucked a dagger from his belt and held it aloft. "The Ghurs will never be dominated again!"

Snarling, Rafiq hit Agra-sho hard in his ample belly. The Prince squawked hoarsely, then toppled back on his expansive buttocks. The blue silk pants he wore split on all their seams while the gold silk tunic popped open from waist to armpit on each flank. Rising from his knees, Rafiq kicked the *kukri* from Agra-sho's right hand, then grabbed a handful of the man's black hair and rolled him into an upright position.

"However much you fear the Ilbeorians, Agra-sho, you should fear the Dost that much more."

The throbbing rumble of the airship's engines filled the valley as it flew back north. Forty-five cylinders poked from the port side of the ship, then vomited steam and iron. Whole sections of the factory's roof and upper walls evaporated when the volley hit. Shots from the cannons sliced through the smokestacks like scythes through wheat stalks. The brick cylinders slowly tottered and fell, shattering when they battered down the factory's eastern wall.

Above them the airship heeled a bit to starboard, but leveled out quickly. Another volley ripped through the smoke and dust cloud rising from the factory shell. Flames shot up into the sky as cannon shots damaged the smelting crucible. The huge vessel pivoted forward all at once, cascading a wave of molten steel across the factory's floor. In its wake the metal tide left burning islands and sprayed steel rain over the ground when the wave hit the edge of the factory's foundation.

The bravado Rafiq had mustered to frighten Agra-sho fled along with his courage. Releasing his grip on Agra-sho's greasy hair, the Helansajaran stared at the roof of the longhouse beyond the smithies and *jumped* there. He landed, shivering, then immediately fell to his knees as tiles shifted and slid away beneath his feet. Pain shot up through his knees, but he lunged for the roof's crestline and caught hold of it. Breath hissed in between his teeth as he pulled himself up and stared back toward the factory.

From that vantage point he watched as two barrages from the airship blew the forges to smithereens. Tiny buildings exploded, and finished weapons whirled through the air like debris caught in a windstorm. Then the airship turned back toward the south and blasted the factory's warehouses into twisted and broken debris.

With the airship coming around and heading toward the longhouses, Rafiq realized the Ilbeorians were nothing if not thorough. He *jumped* to the top of the coal pile and then further up the valley. Behind him the thunder of forty-five cannons marked the reduction of the longhouses to flinders. Huge timbers, splintered at the ends, danced across the landscape, while other scraps bounced free of the dust cloud or burned.

Rafiq watched as the airship lowered ropes, then men of silver slid down them and started searching the ruins. He wasn't certain what they thought they would find, but far be it from him to criticize warriors exercising their right of plunder. *If they have left anything complete enough to plunder.*

As he watched them he compared his first vision of the valley with what he saw after the attack. Destruction of the factory and surroundings had been utter and complete. With a thousand men he could not have so totally destroyed a village, even if given a whole day. The Ilbeorians, in less than half an hour, had pulverized what it had taken men two years to build.

Rafiq smiled as he saw the Ilbeorian soldiers herding a far little form toward a cage being lowered from the ship's hold.

"Perhaps the Ilbeorians will *tremble* at the mention of your name, Agra-sho. Not me. Not the Dost."

Rafiq's mirth died quickly as he took a last look at the smoking ruins. *It is good that you have returned now, my Dost.* Rafiq looked further north and prepared himself for the trip home to report what he had seen. *Dire times are upon us and only you can keep us safe.*

— 49 —

> **Pyimoc**
> **Vzorin, Vzorin Military District**
> **Strana**
> **2 Majest 1687**

Excepting the distant tolling out of the hour and the rustling of rats in the cell, silence reigned in the bowels of Pyimoc. Malachy's communicant had never returned to his cell and the resulting sense of abandonment hit the Wolf-priest hard. Sitting wedged into the far corner of his cell, he felt as if he were the only man alive in the world.

Intellectually Malachy knew he was not alone. The intense loneliness and urgency of doing something twisting him up inside were all aided and abetted by hunger, the aching burns, fatigue, and frustration. He had responsibilities to the ethyrines in Helor and to the Dost, but he just felt too weak and drained to act.

Through prayer and meditation he realized his sense of impotence was baseless. He had originally been chosen for Sandwycke because he was able to handle many very powerful spells. He was qualified as an Aeromancer and could have been an ethyrine, but had chosen to accept his first assignment in Lescar so he could spy for Ilbeoria. His training for that role taught him spells he could use in conjunction with the proper equipment to get him out of his dungeon. *No other Wolf-priest has the training needed to complete this mission, which is why God placed me here. It's time to be more concerned over His designs than my own wretched position.*

Yet even in trying to motivate himself, he could not get away from the fact that escape was difficult. From the sounds the guards made on their rounds he knew the direction he would have to travel to get out, had a fair idea of the number of guards and doors he would face, and even knew which of his captors liked to nap on the job—significantly delaying their rounds in the wee hours of the day.

Had he a single key to operate as a blank for his skeleton-key spell, he could have been up and out to ground level in Vzorin inside ten minutes. However, he didn't have such a key, nor even a pilfered fork or spoon. The guards, who amused themselves by watching him eat, felt utensils were optional for a blind man, and their laughter as he drank down gruel made the fluid food even less palatable than it was.

And he had no desire to know what the crunchy bits he ingested really were.

His hands contorted into fists and he used his anger to shatter his apathy. *No sense in concentrating on what I do not have. I need to use whatever I do have to get out of here.*

Calming himself, he opened his hands and held them out in the air with fingers splayed out. He slowed his breathing and concentrated on listening. He tried to draw in every sensory impression he could, from the moist, cloying odor of the mildew on the walls and the cool draft coming under the door, to the noise made by rats and the position he occupied in relationship to all these other things.

He knew the framework into which he placed all these impressions came from his quick memorization of the room and its dimensions. Two paces deep and three wide, it had two steps that led up to the door in the middle of a wide wall. The door, which was made of wood bound by rusty metal, had a two-inch clearance at the floor and hung funny so the upper corner squeaked against the jamb when it was opened or closed. Guards often had to kick the door to open it, the sound of which combined with the noise of the key in the lock to alert him to their arrival.

The floor beneath the musty straw was made of mortared stone, the same as the walls and ceiling. The floor sloped down to the exterior corner opposite where he sat. The rats largely congregated there and Malachy suspected there was an open drain in the corner. The squealing rats had never let him get close enough to it to be certain, but the territory they defended was too small for an opening through which he could escape.

As he sat there absorbing and cataloging all the sensations in his cell, he began to understand something he had ignored before. He had assumed, since he had been diligent in memorizing as much of Sandwycke as possible, that his ability to navigate had depended solely on his mental map and a few subtle clues like noises or scents. Alone in the cell he realized the subtle clues were far more informative than he had previously imagined. When being tortured he could pinpoint the location of a hot poker based on where its warmth seemed concentrated well before the Duke's torturer ever applied it to his flesh. *But I can feel the warmth of sunshine on my flesh, so this is not that remarkable, is it?*

More importantly, though, he realized he could almost *feel* the rats milling about in the corner of his cell. He knew, under normal circumstances, that was impossible. Magick, of course, could hardly be considered normal and with his training it was possible for him to modify and develop spells. Even so, he had never undertaken any effort to create a spell that would give him the impressions he was getting.

Is it possible that out of need I subconsciously created and now employ magick to compensate for my sightlessness? He almost rejected that idea out of hand, but then he remembered his fight with the airmen from the *Stoat*. He had known where to strike, yet in the chaos of the fight all the subtle clues would have been lost.

The evaluation of Uriah's semester project also came back to him. He had been fine and had navigated well until Uriah's pointed criticism had undercut Malachy's concentration. *After that I stumbled into things, bumped things. And the night of my vision, I had lost my ability to navigate in my own home.*

The fact that armor and weapon spells functioned without further conscious attention once they had been cast supported the idea that magick could work without conscious control. *That still is a long way from suggesting a spell could be created without the caster knowing what he was doing. Then again, that is exactly what the* first *magicker must have done. And teachers always caution against improvising spells without proper forethought, suggesting an ill conceived spell could be triggered by careless or inattentive individuals.*

The Wolf-priest rubbed a hand over his stubbly jaw. *This sensory spell seems to exist and work. What it probably does is employ the air as a medium for it, reflecting back to me air currents and other disturbances. If the fight at the* Stoat *was any indication, it functions well in combat situations, which means I'm not nearly as helpless as I or, more importantly, my captors, are likely to think I am.*

The possibilities opened by this discovery buoyed Malachy's spirits. It made jumping a guard a viable strategy for obtaining the items he would need to escape. *Now I just have to get one close enough to handle, but that won't be hard.*

Malachy had chosen to sit in the back corner of the room because guards, when making their rounds, could see him there from the little window in his cell door. The one time he had fallen asleep in a corner that put him out of sight, the guard entered his cell and kicked him awake. *I have the bait to get him in, but I need a weapon of some sort to deal with him.*

At least I have some armor. He clacked the edges of his gold bracers together. *These are fine for protecting me, but they are of no use offensively. Perhaps a garrote made from braided strips of my pants leg . . . That takes the first one. His keys and truncheon should get me the rest of the way out.*

He brought his hands together at the cuff of his pants, but before he could start to tear the cloth, the bracers began to heat up. He felt the warmth on his face and burned areas of his bare chest, but not where the bracers actually touched his arms. That flesh actually felt *cold*, as if all the warmth had been leeched out of it.

As if the bracers had become living creatures, they writhed and shrank. Undulating sluglike along their edges, the bracers crawled down his forearms to his wrists, then they flowed out over his hands. He held his hands out away from his body and felt the gold coat them like a second skin. Then a tendril of metal stretched itself from the palm of his right hand to link it with his left palm. Pulling his hands further apart stretched the tendril. He met resistance when the wire garrote reached the optimal length of two feet.

How is this possible? More unconscious magick, or something else?

The sound of footsteps in the corridor outside his cell distracted him from any analysis of the bracers' transformation. Malachy stood quickly and crossed the cell. Standing with his back against the wall near the door, he held his hands up. *Wait until he steps down, loop the wire over his neck and haul back hard. Done, and I'll be on my way out.*

A key scraped in the lock. Malachy smiled and readied himself to strike.

Dressed in black and wearing her long black hair done up tight against her skull, Natalya Ohanscai sneaked from her suite in the dead of the night. She did not trust Duke Arzlov and she found herself doubting Grigory even more than she did Arzlov. She hated thinking Grigory had lied to her on his own, but Arzlov's surprise and his reports of words Grigory had put in her mouth seemed to indicate Grigory was no longer worthy of her trust.

Because she already knew Arzlov to be a skillful enough deceiver to fool her father, she did not feel comfortable accepting evidence of Grigory's treachery based on the Duke's word alone. Grigory's insistence that she remain in her suite and refrain from sending messages to Murom had started the erosion of her trust in him, but before she allowed the process to be complete, she needed to determine how truthful Duke Arzlov was being with her.

Arzlov had tried to hide from her the fact that there *had* been an Ilbeorian prisoner on the *Zarnitsky*. He had seemed to be quite relieved when she feigned acceptance of his story about the prisoner having been eliminated. Grigory's denial of the prisoner's existence still bothered her, but she found it easier to believe that Arzlov had fooled Grigory and was manipulating him than to accept Grigory lying to her to advance some plan of his own.

Since neither one of them wanted to admit to the existence of an Ilbeorian prisoner, Natalya realized that prisoner had to be of some importance. Interviewing the prisoner could provide her with whatever information both men had tried to hide from her. *And with that I can decide what I must do to protect Strana.*

The Tachotha made her way silently through the halls of Arzlov's fortress. The building had the massiveness of traditional Stranan architecture, but the use of sand-colored local stones made the building seem less daunting. Oil lamps hung from the ceiling at the intersection of corridors and along staircases. Their guttering light sent shivers through shadows and had Natalya constantly looking around for guards.

She had planned to convince the guards in the dungeon to let her see the prisoner on the strength of her identity, and then swear them to secrecy, but when she reached the first watchpost she discovered this was not necessary. Only one guard sat at this station and his snores were loud enough to cover the approach of galloping cavalry. A big ring of keys hung on a peg in the wall above the gray-haired man. Natalya grabbed it without waking the guard, then started fitting keys into the first iron-barred door's lock.

The fourth key in the dozen worked. She opened the door as narrowly as possible and slipped through to a small landing above a steep staircase. After closing the door behind her and locking it, she descended stealthily. The oil lamps down in the dungeon were spaced more distantly, but they offered sufficient illumination for her to proceed easily.

The staircase had another iron-barred door at the bottom of it. Natalya fumbled with the keys a bit, but managed to locate the right one quickly enough and opened the door. She shut it again after she passed through and locked it, then moved into a narrow corridor with only one oil lamp burning along its length. Fortunately for Natalya, the lamp hung across the corridor from the only closed door. The other three doors stood open and the interiors looked to be what she would have expected in a dungeon cell.

She peered in through the closed door's little barred window, but saw nothing. Undaunted by appearances, she inserted a key in the lock and it worked. *That was lucky.* She pushed the door open, then had to push harder when it stuck up near the top. Putting her shoulder into it, she shoved and the door swung open. Her momentum carried her forward and she stumbled down a step or two.

Natalya heard movement behind her, then felt something press against her throat. The pressure tightened, then with a metallic *ping*, it stopped as the garrote parted in the middle. Without thinking, she drove her left elbow backward and hit something solid. She heard a loud *ooofff*, then she pivoted on her left foot and brought her right knee up, catching the doubled-over prisoner in his chin.

The man flew backward and hit hard on the room's stone steps. He lay there, stunned, his arms and legs spread out wide. Natalya stepped forward, lifting her right leg in preparation to stamp down on his groin, but he looked up at her, pain and surprise mixed on his face, and she stopped. She knew that she should press her advantage, cripple him and escape, but she stopped and slowly lowered her foot.

It took her a second to realize why she had stopped. When she did her right hand covered her mouth while her left arm lay pressed against her stomach. *His eyes, they are silver.* She sank slowly to her knees. "Tell me your name."

The man's artificial eyes widened, then he winced and laid his head back on the stone. He mumbled something in Ilbeorian, but too low for her to understand, then shook his head. "You are Tachotha Natalya Ohanscai, *da?*"

"I know that. Who are you?" She asked the question again, but seeing the outline of his face in the lamplight, she no longer needed an answer.

"Are you hurt?" The man shivered, then held his gold hands out, palm up. "I thought I hurt you."

"Not as badly as I hurt you." Natalya rubbed at her throat. "Your garrote broke."

The man struggled up into a sitting position. "Yes. I caught the scent of your hair and, well, it broke before I could hurt you."

"You knew it was me?"

"I knew you weren't one of my captors." He smiled slightly. "They don't bathe, for which I am now thankful. I'm glad I didn't hurt you. I would never hurt you."

"But you did, Malachy Kidd." She reared back and stood. "You broke your promise to me."

"Broken promise by a broken man, Natalya. You knew me . . . before. What happened to me . . . I am not the same person who danced with you in Murom."

"I see that. Eyes of silver; hands of gold." She folded her arms across her chest. "You could *not* come to Murom, but you *do* find your way to Vzorin. More duty for your King?"

"Duty to my God, Natalya. He demanded it." Kidd sat up and hugged his hands around his knees. "I would have been going to Murom for *me*, for a man I no longer was, to make a claim on you I did not feel I could press."

His words sank deep into her heart. Echoing his promise, his tone said that what he wanted had become impossible for him to deliver. "Malachy, I wanted you to return to Murom for *us*. Whatever happened to you did not matter—*you* mattered."

"*Da,* Natalya, I understand how you felt then, and I can never make up to you the pain I caused you. In Glogau, things changed for me. Not just my eyes." Kidd raked white hair out of his face. "God gave me a vision before he took my eyes. I have spent my life since then trying to do what I think He wants of me."

She tapped a foot impatiently, crunching straw beneath it. "And I could not have helped you with this work?"

"I did not think so, Natalya, but your being here, now, and having opened this cell suggests to me that God certainly had different things planned." The Wolf-priest reached back and steadied himself against the wall, then stood slowly. "This assumes, of course, you are willing to help me in my work."

"What does your divine vision demand of you?"

"Keerana Dost has been reincarnated in Arala." Malachy reached out and rested his hands on her shoulders. "I was sent by God to keep him safe."

"You cannot." Natalya pulled away from him. "The reborn Dost will destroy Strana."

"*Nyet.* God would not bring me here to be Nemyko the Hooded One for your nation. He may work in mysterious ways, but treachery is not one of them. I do not know how the Dost will be important to the future of Strana, I just know he is." Malachy stared at her as if he could really see with his metal eyes. "I need you to trust me, Natalya."

"How can I trust someone who says he is here to aid a demon who covets my nation?"

Malachy smiled and on his face she saw echoes of the times they had shared. "I could have lied to you about my mission, Natalya, but I didn't. I would not have lies divide us."

"Have you forgotten the division your failed promise has caused after being so shortly reminded of it?"

Malachy grinned in a manner she found easily recognizable. "I said I would return to Strana, Natalya. Here I am, as promised."

"You said you would return to *Murom*, Malachy."

"I'm blind. How am I going to read a map properly?"

Despite her not wanting to, Natalya laughed at his remark. "The wonder is that you are here at all, then?"

"My appearance did seem to surprise Duke Arzlov, *da.*"

The calm confidence in Malachy's voice and the warmth of his smile dented her anger and fear. *He is correct. He has returned, which means he is more truthful than Duke Arzlov and Grigory.* She hesitated for a moment, seeking out any other obstacles to her trusting him, and found none. The memories she did have of him, the ones Grigory had not supplanted, came from their time spent playing chess together. Nothing in those memories caused her to doubt him, his word, or his intelligence.

"I have decided to trust you, Malachy Kidd, at least for the moment. Your mission threatens my nation, but it is minor compared to the other threats to it right now."

Kidd nodded. "The attack on Helor."

"How do you know of that? Was that part of your vision?"

"No. I will explain later. Right now we need to escape." Kidd mounted the steps to the doorway. "We have to get an ethyrskiff. If you will navigate, I will fly."

She shook her head. "Duke Arzlov has grounded all ethyrcraft."

"Then we will have to improvise. We need a craft and a sail. We'll think of something once we're away from here."

"Agreed." Natalya took his left hand and tucked it into the crook of her right elbow. "Before you were injured, when I thought of our futures, I never considered becoming a fugitive in my own nation with you."

"Nor did I. Having surreptitiously left my nation, though, and having slipped through Aran illegally, I can tell you it will be an adventure." Malachy coughed lightly, then followed her from the cell. "You've probably already guessed, of course, we'll be going to Helor. We will become *international* fugitives."

"Of course, Pokovnik Kidd, I should have known." Natalya smiled and hugged Malachy's hand against her ribs. *I am off to an enemy nation to stop my lover from conquering it so a blind Wolf-priest can save the life of an individual who may destroy my nation.* She laughed momentarily. *I doubt this is what my father expected when he suggested this trip to Vzorin.*

Kidd gave her arm a squeeze. "What do you find funny?"

"Well, Malachy Kidd, after our adventure, your next trip to see me may require your going to Murom after all." She smiled broadly and led him down the dungeon corridor. "If we succeed in doing what we must, I suspect my father will never let me out of his sight again."

— 50 —

Government House
Dhilica
Puresaran,
Aran
4 Majest 1687

Robin Drury saluted smartly and stared straight ahead at Prince Trevelien. "Brother Robert Drury reporting as ordered, Highness."

Trevelien returned the salute crisply. "Please, Brother Robert, be at ease. I believe you recognize His Highness, Prince Agra-sho of Dughur."

Robin clasped his hands behind his back and widened his stance. "Yes, Highness, we had the pleasure of the Prince's company on the return trip from the Kulang Valley." The ethyrine glanced down at the rotund potentate. Agra-sho had been given new clothes, though he strained their seams and likewise stressed the joints in the chair from which he all but overflowed. "Good to see you again, Highness."

Agra-sho waved his right hand at Robin as if dismissing him, never looking up from the bunch of grapes perched on his chest.

Prince Trevelien sat at his desk and picked up a sheaf of papers. "Mr. Drury, I have read your report on the raid in the Kulang Valley. Your chronicle of destruction was very complete. You report the remains of two or three steam engines in a steel mill. Were you certain of what you saw?"

"Yes, Highness."

Trevelien smiled slightly. "Prince Agra-sho has suggested you have no idea what you were looking at."

"Begging the Prince's pardon, Highness, but I worked at the Lakeworth Carriage factory as a spring smith for a total of four years. I've seen the inside of a number of steel mills. Even with the damage done by the *Saint Michael* there is no mistaking what I saw. That was a steel mill on a par with any in Ilbeoria ten years ago. And it had steam engines."

Agra-sho noisily chewed a grape, but it seemed to Robin that some of the color had begun to leave his face.

"In your report you also note the presence of weapons in a warehouse at the site."

"Yes, Highness. I saw mail, helmets, *kukris,* a variety of *tulwars*, spearpoints, and armor for horses. We brought back several crates of the stuff. All high-quality weapons made from steel that a modern mill would produce."

"And you plucked Prince Agra-sho right out of the middle of all this?"

Robin nodded. "We did, Highness."

Trevelien sat back in his chair. "Would it surprise you, Brother Robert, to learn that the Prince here says he knew nothing about the factory's existence until that very morning, when he came up from Kulang to discover it quite by chance?"

"It is true, you know, it is." Agra-sho waggled a finger at Trevelien and back at Robin. "You should believe me about this."

"The Prince's statement aside, sir, when we found him he was weeping about how all his hard work had been destroyed."

Agra-sho cast the grape skeleton down with all the force he

could muster and it could sustain. "I must protest! You would take the word of this common soldier over *my* word? *I* am Agra-sho, Ruler of all Dughur. I do not lie."

No, you probably just have servants do it for you. Robin frowned at the plump man. After he had finished groveling and begging for his life—which had not been in jeopardy—Agra-sho had wept about the loss of the factory. Then he wept about the condition of his clothes and asked to be allowed to retrieve new clothes from his cottage. Then he wept about the fact that the *Saint Michael* had reduced his cottage to kindling.

Trevelien rubbed a hand over the shaved portion of his pate. "Prince Agra-sho, I believe Brother Robert Drury. I believe him because what he tells me coincides with every other report I have had concerning your factory. Those reports all add up to your willing cooperation in the smuggling of forbidden technology from Ilbeoria, the establishment of forbidden industry in Aran, *and* the militarization of Dughur. All three of these things are capital crimes in Ilbeoria *and* in the Constitution of Dughur."

"You would not execute me! I am *Agra-sho*."

"*That,* sir, I will use as your epitaph." Trevelien came up out of his chair and leaned over his desk toward Agra-sho. "You are not a stupid man, though you are given to acting like one. You gambled and you lost. Executing you for these crimes would be problematical, but not insurmountably so. Luckily for you, I believe Brother Robert *could* be mistaken. So too could be Captain Hassett and every other crew member of the *Saint Michael*. It could just be that the factory was placed in the Kulang Valley without your knowledge or authority. It could be that you heard rumors and chose to investigate."

Agra-sho blinked his way through confusion. "It could be?"

"Certainly. I think, in your position, I would have dismissed these reports as fatuous until . . ."

"Yes, fatuous, until . . . ?"

"Until I heard a *name*. I think if I had a name of a man, an Ilbeorian, who was making all the arrangements, then I would be curious. I would go from Kulang up the valley and find this factory. I would be ordering it shut down when the *Saint Michael* came up and flattened it." Trevelien looked up at Robin. "Could *that* be consistent with what you saw and heard, Brother Robert?"

Robin nodded. "Yes, sir, I suppose it could, Highness."

"I thought so, Brother Robert." The Ilbeorian Prince looked at his Ghur counterpart. "Were I in your position, I should think I would make that name available to the Governor-general of Aran, so the criminals could be dealt with appropriately. Otherwise misunderstandings could sour relations between Dughur and the Governorgeneral."

Agra-sho made an effort to lean forward, which meant chins pulled up against his chest for a second before he sat back again. "This is exactly what I have been trying to tell you, Prince Trevelien. This is how it happened exactly."

"The name, Highness."

"He was a representative of Grimshaw Mercantile and Transport." Agra-sho's voice sank into a conspiratorial whisper. "His name is Cobb Venner."

— 51 —

| Dayi Marayir |
| Alansajar |
| 4 Majest 1687 |

Rafiq Khast tried to still the fatigue tremors, never allowing himself to think they might have had their beginnings in the fear knotting his stomach. "I must report failure to you, Nimchin Dost."

Silver highlights flashing from his stripes, the man of gold sat forward in the tiger throne. "Prince Agra-sho has rejected our pledge of neutrality?"

"It is worse than that." Rafiq glared at the Ilbeorian standing at the Dost's right hand. "The Dughur Prince was a fool, but his fear of your power would have made him our ally. He had a giant . . ." Rafiq sought the right word, but could not find one in the Estanu vocabulary. "Giant place that created steel. He had dozens and dozens of smiths fashioning weapons and armor."

The Stranan, standing to the Dost's left, looked over at Uriah. *"Zavot."*

Uriah's surprise showed immediately on his face. He said something in Ilbeorian, but out of it Rafiq only recognized the word Agra-sho had used. "Yes, fahktori. This is what Agra-sho said it was. It had taken two years to create and had parts brought all the way from the land of the Wolves."

The Dost held a hand up to silence his two foreign guests.

"Will Agra-sho be using these arms and armor to oppose us? I am unclear on this."

"No, my lord, he will not." Rafiq took in a deep breath. "While I was there in the fahktori a huge airship came into the valley. A man could ride for a day on a fast horse and never have escaped its shadow. It produced clouds amid thunder and they rained metal down on the fahktori. This storm crushed it, but they used a second cloudburst to further the work of the first. Then they destroyed the smaller forges and everything else in the valley. Then men made of silver slid down ropes and captured Agra-sho."

The Dost sat back slowly. "Could it be as he says?" the Dost asked in Stranan. "Could an airship from Ilbeoria lay waste to a valley settlement so easily?"

Uriah nodded. "The airship *Saint Mikhail* is on station in Aran. It is the most powerful airship in the world. If Ghurs were arming themselves and if their factory used steam engines brought from Ilbeoria, I would expect such swift and harsh tactics being used."

"How does one defeat such a powerful weapon?"

Svilik shrugged. "Steam cannons on the ground, Stalkers or other airships and even ethyrskiffs that become fireships. Airships are not invulnerable and are often limited in range based on coaling stations and amount of supplies they can carry."

"Strana has such ships?"

"Nothing as big as the *Saint Mikhail*, but we have some. The largest one in Vzorin, the *Zarnitsky*, is half the *Saint Mikhail*'s size."

The Dost fell silent. Though he stared at Rafiq, the Helansajaran had the feeling the Dost did not know he was there. The Dost's silence frightened Rafiq because it meant the Dost could be surprised. While Nimchin Dost had acted with prescience before, now something he had not anticipated gave him pause.

The Dost closed his eyes, then opened them and smiled weakly at Rafiq. "This is distressing news and gives me much to think on. We will have a week before chieftains I have asked to be assembled will arrive at the meeting point. All four of us will have to use that time to plan out a strategy that defeats the *Zarnitsky*."

Valentin Svilik shook his head. "I am a prisoner, but I am not a traitor to my nation."

"No, Valentin, you are not, nor would I ask you to be." The Dost's eyes glinted brightly. "Understand me: if we cannot take Helor and maintain it against a Stranan threat, this world will enter a period of warfare for which the Lescari War was but an inferior prelude. Neither your nation, nor mine, nor even yours, Uriah, will survive."

Standing on the balcony outside his office, Vasily Arzlov stuck his right index finger into his mouth, then raised it into the breeze. It felt chilled on its left side and this made him smile. *East wind blows gently, two or three miles per hour. Even in their makeshift ethyr-skiff they will progress easily toward Helor.* A quick and conservative calculation put Natalya and Malachy in Helor by the ninth of Majest, a week and half before the Hussars would arrive.

He allowed himself a chuckle, for his plan was unfolding as expected. Grigory Khrolic's unpredictability meant he had to be eliminated. The Hussars and Sonasny Militia could defeat the Vzorin troops Arzlov commanded, but only if they were at full strength. By letting Khrolic batter his troops against Helor, they would be weakened and the Vzorin units could defeat them.

Of course, Vasily did not anticipate having to fight them. Khrolic would take Helor and Arzlov's troops would be welcomed as reinforcements. Vasily would then place Khrolic under arrest, charge him with treason, and have him executed. And Tachotha Natalya would agree Khrolic had acted on his own. Helor would still be conquered and Vzorin would become a province, with Vasily as its Tacarri.

Natalya's decision to go to Helor was obvious because there she would be able to try to stop Grigory. With the ten days of advance warning provided to Shukri Awan by Kidd and Natalya, the Helansajarans would be able to prepare a defense that would weaken the Hussars. Even if Shukri Awan were as superstitious and idiotic an individual as rumors made him out to be, Kidd was no fool. Even a blind man could arrange a defense that would bleed the Hussars before they took the city.

Vasily wondered what Kidd's reaction would be when he

learned there were no ethyrines in Helor. Arzlov had enjoyed playing the deserter on the other side of the wall from Kidd. The Ilbeorian had been very skillful in ferreting out the story behind the desertion. But what Arzlov found most telling was the silence that followed the admission about Khrolic having previously arranged an ambush for an Ilbeorian. That must have been quite a shock, though the Wolf-priest recovered quickly enough to continue the interrogation.

What Kidd thought really did not matter in the long run—his acting with and for the Helansajarans would be sufficient for Vasily's purposes. While Natalya would defend Malachy and his actions, Arzlov knew he could convince her father that she had allowed her emotions to cloud her thinking. A Wolf-priest's presence in Helor was damning in and of itself. That Natalya and Kidd would both tell of a Hussar deserter who told them about ethyrines being present in Helor—a story even the Ilbeorians would deny—would serve as proof that Kidd, who once had been a spy, had been in Helor for nefarious purposes and was reduced to spinning such a weak tale to cover himself.

Vasily knew his plan was not as neat and trim as he might have liked, but it did not matter. What would matter would be results, and taking possession of Helor would be an impressive result. Uncovering signs of Ilbeorian adventurism in central Arala would make the Tacier see that Ilbeoria was a true threat to the Stranan Empire. From his position in the Tacarri Council, Vasily would be able to use his influence to direct the Tacier against his real enemy in the world: the Wolf-King. He would ask of the Tacier what he had told Khrolic he wanted when the younger man ascended to the throne. What Fernandi had failed to do, Vasily Arzlov would accomplish and then *his* name would live forever in the annals of history.

I leave Vzorin as a mere Duke. Within a month I will be a Tacarri, and within a year I will be the conqueror of all Urovia.

Thus ends the Book of the Bear.

BOOK III

THE
BOOK OF
THE TIGER

— 53 —

The sweet scent of an orange filled Malachy's nostrils as he dug into the rind. The gold flesh on his hands hardened at the point of his thumbs and extended into a shallow blade designed perfectly to separate rind from fruit. He peeled the orange easily, tossing fragments of the skin off to his left, well away from Natalya and their makeshift ethyrskiff. Though he could not see either of them, he did feel aware of their positions and did his best to miss them.

He shook his head. "Good thinking on your part, Natalya. You secured us transport *and* food at same time."

Her voice carried an amused lilt to it. "Again, I tell you this is more your doing than mine. You asked for a wooden box to which we could afix a sail. The first thing I saw that early in the morning in the streets of Vzorin was a fruit vendor's wagon, complete with a canvas canopy. I offered him Stranan gold for it and he accepted my offer."

Malachy popped a section of orange into his mouth and chewed. It struck him there had been some pretty hard bargaining going on before the exchange, but Natalya passed it off as if it were nothing. He had known from before that she had a strong will, but he had only known her as a young woman. In the dozen years since he had been with her, she had grown to fulfill the promise of her youth.

Their flight from Vzorin had not been easy. The canvas awning had made for a passable sail, but the wind did not always come from a useful direction. When it did not, the only way they could travel would be for Malachy to lift their skiff into the air, then put it into a gentle fall. The wagon possessed the gliding prowess of a millstone, but through subtle manipulations of the aeromagick and by having Natalya shift the sail around to direct them, Malachy was able to make progress.

The process of flight followed by a controlled fall was very exhausting and would have been impossible to continue had they been without food. Having a fruit wagon for their skiff worked to their advantage, and the more they ate the lighter the load became. Neither one of them mentioned the fact that when the load was the lightest Malachy would not have enough strength to lift it, but by then they hoped to be in Helor.

They flew most of the first day, and toward dusk Natalya reported being able to see a mountain in the distance that had to be Jebel Quirana. Nearer their position she also saw the Hussars' camp. To avoid them Malachy flew southeast toward the Helansi Mountains. They also decided to stay hidden during the day and only fly at night. Aside from hiding them and saving exertion until the heat of the day had passed, they got an added boost from the cooler air filtering onto the Helansajaran plains from the mountains. The prevailing night breeze ran south, moving them closer to their objective.

The open camaraderie created by the surprise of their meeting had dulled a bit because of apprehension after they left Vzorin. While they had once been friends, they had changed enough in the last dozen years that they didn't really know one another anymore. Their trip became measured in a procession of disjointed conversations. Assumptions each had made about the other proved to be false, and that led to some disappointment and just a hint of betrayal.

It is ridiculous to believe we would not have changed, but we somehow expected the other would not have after all these years. Some of the resulting surprises are good, but many are jarring.

Malachy also sensed her disappointment and hurt from his failure to come for her surfacing from time to time. He very much wanted to heal that wound he'd dealt her, but the pain she harbored kept him back. Her emotional wariness did not surprise him, and he realized it was probably a good thing that it held them apart. *I have been so long alone, I do not know how to handle the sort of strong feelings we once had for each other.*

He hoped, at the very least, they could return to some neutral state where their friendship could blossom again.

Malachy drew his knees up to his chest, then bit the end off an orange segment. "I am very sorry, Tachotha Natalya, for any pain I caused you. What I did was unforgivable, really."

"Malachy, I understand." A slight hitch in her voice betrayed the true feelings her words hid. "You were blinded."

"Blinded, yes, to many things, but I never should have allowed myself to be blind to who my true friends were. My feelings for you

led me to think of my staying away as somehow protecting you."
Malachy frowned, hoping his argent stare would not frighten her.
"Twelve years ago I committed an evil act—I let my belief in God's
mission for me turn me away from you and others. I arrogantly assumed that if I had His work at the center of my life, I would need no
one else. That wasn't true, of course, but I refused to let myself believe it. I also refused to let myself realize that by cutting myself off
from friends I was hurting them as much as I was hurting myself."

Her voice came from a point closer than it had moments before. "You do not owe me an explanation."

"But I do, Tachotha Natalya, because, in my selfishness, I was
cruel to you. In Ilbeoria I spent my time at Sandwycke, studying and
learning all I could about military affairs and magickal theories. I
would evaluate projects by students and I would tear them apart.
They feared me so much they would curse my eyes of silver and I
took pride in this. I belittled all the best students we had in Ilbeoria,
just to convince myself that I was the only logical choice for God to
use in His plan."

He popped the rest of the orange segment into his mouth. "I
knew I was being cruel but I justified my behavior because I believed it made the students better soldiers. This may or may not be
true, but even if it is, it does not justify what I did."

"You were doing what you thought best."

"Yes, but I should have demanded better of myself." Malachy
smiled slightly. "I was proud about being better than so many
others—even being blind. Deep down I knew they did not fight back
because they pitied me, and I took full advantage of this situation.
After a while, when they did not fight back, I began to believe they
did not because they *could* not. But that changed this spring."

"What happened?"

"I evaluated a project that postulated a Stranan assault on
Helor."

"Fortuitous, *da?*"

"*Da,* but such coincidence is not what made the difference. I
was twisting project parameters and changing things on the student
presenters, altering circumstances they had presented then pointing
out why their analysis failed. One of the students challenged me. He
told me I was wrong to be doing what I had done. He told me their
project was the best job possible, with information they had, and I
knew he was correct. I realized that I was failing students and myself and God. I made that student my aide."

He shook his head. "Together we came to Estanu, following
my mission to save the Dost."

"He was not in the Vzorin dungeon."

"No. In Drangiana he was taken by the Dost. I do not know where Uriah is or even if he lives."

"If he was tough enough to make it to Estanu, then do you think he could be dead now?"

"Probably not—he *was* half Stranan."

"Good; this bodes well for me in our present situation." Despite the levity Natalya injected into her voice, Malachy could still hear her nervousness in the background.

"Without a doubt. Since we will be together, I want you to know that I was incredibly foolish not to go to you in Murom, even blinded." He sighed. "I owed you more than that, and I hope we can still be friends."

"Malachy, the feelings I had for you then were very strong, and when they died, the hurt was terrible." She sighed heavily. "I am older now, wiser, I hope, and capable of understanding, in part, why you did what you did. And I, too, would like for us to be friends. This trek will be impossible if we are not."

"I know you've changed, Natalya. I appreciate the person you have become."

"One thing, Malachy, that you must understand." Her voice shrank a bit. "I am in love with Grigory Khrolic and he loves me."

"Ah, I see." Malachy sucked on an orange segment, then chewed it up and spat the seeds out. The irony of her declaring her love for the man who blinded him sent a shiver through Malachy. For a heartbeat he wanted to reveal Khrolic's perfidy to her, but he stopped. *To what end would I do that? I hurt her in the past by abandoning her, and now I would try to blame that abandonment on the man she loves? Perhaps her love for him changed him, redeemed him. To say anything would be cruel, and I've hurt her enough for one lifetime.*

Still, something in the emotional undercurrent in her words cast doubt upon the statement's meaning. It seemed to him that, in part, she meant her words to hurt Malachy, and they did, but they also covered a hurt of her own.

Natalya clearly has loved Khrolic, but she is no longer certain that he returns her affection. The fact that we're bound for Helor to stop Khrolic's Hussars from attacking the city confirms her doubts about Khrolic's feelings and intentions. He shook his head and fought a desire to walk to her and gather her into a hug. *Nothing for me to do but pray that her strength will see her through the trials that lie ahead of her.*

"I remember Grigory Khrolic very well. He is a most fortunate

man to have won your love. I wish for you all possible happiness."
He forced a smile to his face. "I ask of you one indulgence."

"Yes?"

"It is this: if I act in a familiar manner which causes you discomfort, please ask me to refrain." He hung his head. "I don't want
to hurt you any more than I have in the past."

"Granted, provided you return an indulgence."

"Name it."

He heard mischief enter her voice. "After you left Murom, I
had tutors teach me Ilbeorian so I could speak with you in your own
tongue." She switched to Ilbeorian. "The lessons cost a small fortune, which the Tacier paid, and I would now like to get full use of
them."

"You are an amazing woman, Natalya."

"So says the blind Wolf-priest in the desert." Natalya laughed
aloud. "Perhaps, then, there is a grain of truth in it."

— 54 —

Lord Norcliff Gardens
Dhilica
Puresaran, Aran
5 Majest 1687

Robin Drury smiled. He saw Amanda Grimshaw standing in front
of Lord Norcliff's statue as, earlier that morning, Father Ryan had
suggested she would be. Her high-waisted canary gown had been
tied with a bow at her back. Her yellow gloves and parasol matched
the color of the dress perfectly, though neither had the embroidery
or lace trim that decorated the gown. Amanda's hair had been gathered up at the back of her head, exposing the nape of her neck, and
the yellow bonnet she wore hung at mid-back on long straps.

"Forgive me for intruding on your thoughts, Miss Grimshaw,
but I must say I am happy to see you."

Amanda smiled up at him. "Why, Brother Robin, how did you
ever come to be here at this time?" Before he could answer she
added, "Father Ryan swore he would not act as a go-between."

"I do not think he meant to be, either." Robin offered her his
left arm and she took it. "Nataraj has taken to spending his time

around the ethyrine barracks and my men are beginning to treat him like a mascot. He's supplementing the Ilbeorian you teach him at the mission with some of the more colorful vocabulary ethyrines tend to use, and Father Ryan is not pleased."

Amanda feigned shock. "I cannot imagine what would be the matter with the way ethyrines speak."

"Father Ryan came over to get Nataraj and drag him back to the mission. He happened to mention you would be here this afternoon. He told me he didn't want to be a go-between, but said he had passed this one message on so you'd stop urging Nataraj to visit our barracks."

She smiled slyly. "I offered to fetch the boy back myself."

"Did you?" Robin smiled back at her. "I'll have to encourage Nataraj to visit more often."

Amanda laughed, then turned to face him and walked backward for a few steps. "I trust you will not think me too forward in, in essence, asking you to meet me here. My father has forbidden me any contact with you, but I cannot abide by his judgment in this matter. He does not know you saved my life."

"I doubt that would change his mind about me."

"And even if you had not saved me from Venner, I would disobey my father." She stopped walking, eliminating the physical distance between them, and surreptitiously brought his left hand up to her lips. "I find you quite a remarkable man."

Robin felt the urge to gather her into his arms and kiss her. He could see in her eyes that she would permit him that degree of familiarity, but he held back. What they both desired had to remain hidden in public. His reputation mattered little to him—though the idea of casting aspersions on Captain Hassett because of his conduct did cause Robin concern. More importantly, though, the innocence of a walk in a garden could become a scandal that would dishonor Amanda, and he would not be a party to such a thing.

"And you, Amanda, are a jewel of incredible warmth and brilliance." He looked about, then back down at her. "We should continue walking lest tongues begin to wag."

She hesitated for a moment and kissed his hand again, as if to flout convention, then spun back to his side. "You are right, of course."

"No one regrets it more than me."

Amanda chuckled deep in her throat. "Are you ever exhausted by the difficulty of living for appearance's sake?"

"I'm not certain I follow you exactly."

Amanda's parasol described a circle that took in the entire gardens. "Look at this place, Robin. The shrubbery, the topiary, the flowers, they're all from Ilbeoria. All the people here are from Ilbeoria and are dressed as if they were in Ilbeoria. If God scooped this garden up and carried it to Ludstone, no one here would notice a difference."

"Except in the heat."

"Yes." She nodded emphatically. "Beyond the boundaries of this garden, the natives of Aran wear clothing appropriate for the weather. Wouldn't you be more comfortable in short pants, sandals, and a light shirt, or no shirt at all?" She plucked at her gown. "I have three layers of material on here, each one as thick as the gauzy dress worn by Aranan women at this time of year."

Robin scratched at his tonsure. "It is amusing that we mark a bare skull as a sign of intelligence, and walk about here without hats, risking sunfaints."

"Another example." Amanda frowned. "It goes beyond clothing, of course. While I should like to kiss you and be kissed by you, custom frowns on such conduct in public, and you and I would never be allowed to be alone in private. Those who would castigate us for a public display of affection are wives of men who join my father in his tower escapades. A blind eye is turned to those debaucheries because, after all, the women in the tower are not Ilbeorian."

"It makes them sound as if they are animals."

"Oh, certainly, but we know this is a fraud. If my father had a flock of *sheep* in that tower those women would not be so tolerant, nor would society be so forgiving. There is something morally repulsive in a society where the welfare of animals is viewed with more concern than the abuse of other human beings."

Robin let that thought roll around in his brain for a moment, then he nodded. "Saint Martin's message for all of us is that we must act to protect those who cannot protect themselves, and we must act to prevent others from exploiting the vulnerable."

"For once, Robin, just once I would like everyone living behind a mask of civility to look in some Mirror of Truth to see what he really is in the reflection."

"It will happen, Amanda, when they die and are judged."

She sighed. "I know, and patience is a virtue, but I would like people to work toward making the world more like Paradise. If Heaven is going to be more fantastic and magnificent than we can imagine, then let us imagine and create all we can here and Heaven will be that much more rewarding."

The ethyrine nodded in agreement. She spoke of personal sacrifice as being needed to make the world better. Too many people thought of sacrifice in terms of proxies—money or goods in exchange for time and concern. While that form of charity was better than nothing at all, using it as a screen behind which all manner of antisocial activities could be shielded was abhorrent. Whatever good was done by the charitable gift became negated by the evil perpetrated by the benefactor.

Robin patted her right hand. "By teaching at the mission, you are doing a great deal to change the world."

"But I could do more." Amanda shook her head. "Working around my father is . . . complicated."

Her voice layered meaning into the word *complicated*. Aside from making her father angry, she risked ruining her life by defying him. If Erwin Grimshaw were to disown his daughter, she would have nothing. If she possessed any personal wealth at all, which was unlikely, chances were excellent it would have been tied up through trust agreements, with her father as trustee. All of the various techniques for denying wealth to a woman had been carefully explained to Robin by Lord Lakeworth at the time he offered Robin the scholarship to Sandwycke.

Robin recalled the session with Prince Trevelien and Prince Agra-sho the previous day. If Agra-sho's identification of Cobb Venner gave Trevelien any leverage against Erwin Grimshaw, Amanda's father would have more to worry about than her activities. "Life itself is complicated, Amanda and, perhaps, as things change, your concerns will be simplified."

She looked up at him as they rounded a corner on the garden walkway. "That's the first time I've heard you talk in vagaries, Robin."

"Forgive me, but I am not at liberty to reveal to you everything I know—not now, perhaps never. I would never let anything hurt you, if I could prevent it." He sighed heavily. "I hope you can find it in your heart to trust me."

"You are a charming man of strong moral fiber and good character who saved my life." She stopped, stood on tiptoes and kissed him on the cheek. "There is scant room in my heart for anything else *but* trust in you, Robin."

— 55 —

Rafiq Khast could barely believe his ears. Wearing the Dost's red and black colors, he stood at the right hand of the Tiger Throne. Before him, arrayed in a semicircle, were the chieftains and warlords of the seventeen most powerful tribes in all of Helansajar. The Dost had spoken to them and solicited their support.

To a man they denied it.

Rafiq could no longer contain himself. "Have you not heard what he has said? Do you not know who he is? Have you not seen, by his nature and the amulets that allowed his couriers to reach you, that he is a man of great power? Are you all fools?"

Ismat, chieftain of the Shalandut, stroked his long white beard. "It would seem to me, Rafiq Khast, that the fool is the one who believes what his peers hold to be false."

"And I, Ismat, would say that is the mark of a visionary. You have seen but a fraction of what I have seen, yet I knew from the first who this was."

Another chieftain, this man midway between Rafiq and Ismat in age, narrowed dark eyes. "But you yourself know the claim to being the Dost has lost its value over the centuries. Your great-grandfather was proclaimed to be the Dost reborn when he took Helor."

"Yes, Faraj-al-Faruhk, what you say is true. Recall, however, that he never claimed that title for himself."

"Ah, then you believe all those who claim the title for themselves *are* the Dost?"

"Enjoy your semantic games, you will need them to prove you were right when it is shown how wrong you really are." Rafiq caught his breath to launch into a further rebuke of the chieftains, but he felt the heavy warmth of the Dost's hand on his arm. "Forgive me, my lord, for speaking thusly."

The Dost flowed into a standing position, emphasizing his power and abilities. "No pardon is needed, Rafiq Khast. Your family has always been the most loyal and least blind." He looked out toward the gathered chieftains. "And these men are not wholly blind, but have their vision hampered by concern for their people. If they were to support me their tribes could be devastated. They would be willing, but only if it could be shown that such support would not be a disaster."

The Dost opened his arms. "What would you have from me as a sign?"

The chieftains and their warlords turned to each other, speaking and gesticulating rapidly. They reminded Rafiq of hens squabbling over feed. He turned to the Dost. "Dawn has broken the night, yet they would ask of the sun a sign that it is truly risen."

"You stand on higher ground, closer to the horizon than they do, Rafiq. They see a lightening of the sky, not dawn yet." The Dost rested a hand on the Helansajaran's shoulder. "When they have this sign, they will flock to my banner."

"They should flock now."

"But they cannot. Your loyalty blesses you and the Khasts. All others must be secondary to you."

The discussion among the visiting chieftains ended and Faraj-al-Faruhk stepped forward to offer their verdict. "We will believe you are the Dost if, in twenty days, beneath the full moon, you possess Helor."

An unsettling chill ran down Rafiq's spine. Faraj-al-Faruhk and the others all knew Rafiq was fated to die beneath a full moon. They chose that date specifically to further isolate the Dost. They didn't think Rafiq's support of the Dost would extend so far as to put himself in jeopardy.

Rafiq forced himself to laugh, and it banished most of the chill. "You are named 'the Judge' in our tongue, Faraj, but you have judged me falsely. In my life I have seen three hundred full moons, and I have survived each of them. I may be fated to die beneath *a* full moon, but it does not mean *this* full moon. The Khast warriors will be there with the Dost, to win Helor for him."

The Dost nodded to the men before him. "I accept your challenge. I will possess Helor by the night of the full moon, but I do not accept this challenge without demanding something from you. Because I know who I am, I cannot allow you to deprive your people of accepting me. The Khasts are valiant, but number fewer than one hundred warriors. What I demand of you is to tell your warriors about my return and let those who wish to join Rafiq Khast in the taking of Helor to come forward. From you, in accordance with what is written, I will draw the warriors to form my host."

Ismat of the Shalandut nodded. "This is acceptable."

"Then have your warriors assemble here within two weeks. Go now, with the peace of the Dost on your souls."

Rafiq waited for the chieftains to withdraw before he turned and spoke to the man of gold. "I will be beside you, full moon or no."

"Of this I have no fear, Rafiq." The Dost seated himself in his throne. "But I do have two duties I will ask of you."

"Your wish is a sacred duty to me."

"You will assemble your people here and accept the warriors who come without rancor. You will find this place well laden with food and weapons. You will eventually have seventeen companies of fifty warriors each. You will bring them to the plains north of Helor by dawn of the day of the full moon. You will attack when you receive a signal—a signal you will feel through the amulet I gave you."

Rafiq touched the gold amulet with his right hand. "I understand."

"Good. I will be going from this place in six days, taking with me all of my sisters save one. She will remain with you here." The Dost smiled. "You remember Thurayya?"

"The girl I brought from Vzorin when I brought Valentin Svilik to you?"

"The same."

"Will you take her to be your wife?"

"No."

"Then I will arrange for her to marry my cousin Akhtar."

"No." The Dost shook his head. "I have adopted Thurayya into my family. She is now one of my sisters. While your cousin is a good man, Thurayya is not meant for him. I would have you take her to be your wife."

"My wife?"

The Dost smiled. "When Keerana Dost came out of Durrania, his brother Vertil was his greatest general. I would have a brother with me when I take Helor, and, for Thurayya, I would have a noble husband who will get bold sons upon her."

"You have honored me, my lord."

"Your courage honors you. This marriage is done, by my order." The Dost stood and clapped Rafiq on both shoulders. "Your wife awaits you in your chamber, my brother."

"Thank you, my brother."

"One more thing, Rafiq."

"Yes."

"It was said of the Dost's brother that he would die at a time of his own choosing." The Dost smiled broadly. "Vertil died with his great-grandchildren surrounding him. I know you will choose just as wisely as he did."

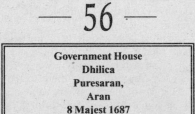

— 56 —

> **Government House**
> **Dhilica**
> **Puresaran,**
> **Aran**
> **8 Majest 1687**

Prince Trevelien ignored the glare of pure malevolence focused upon him by Erwin Grimshaw. "I'm not sorry in the least my summons prevented you from leaving for your month's holiday in Vlengul. You have some serious questions to answer, Mr. Grimshaw, and I had best like your answers."

Clad all in khaki, from his riding boots and jodhpurs up to his shirt and pith helmet, Grimshaw looked uncomfortable without the armor of more formal attire. "I am certain, Highness, any questions *you* have for me could have waited my return."

"I think not, Mr. Grimshaw, and since I am the Governor-general of Aran, *my* thoughts are the ones that matter, not yours. Be seated."

Grimshaw clasped his riding crop in both hands at the small of his back. "I do not believe I will be here long enough that standing will be uncomfortable."

"Your choice." Trevelien seated himself at his desk and shuffled some papers. When he saw the tip of the crop vibrating with Grimshaw's poorly concealed rage, he looked up. "Do you understand the penalties for treason, Mr. Grimshaw?"

"I hardly think, Highness, that any of the remarks I have made to you could be considered treasonous."

"Your opinion is noted, but that is not what I asked." The Prince narrowed his green eyes purposefully, and let the tones of anger slip into his voice. "Do you know the penalties for treason?"

"They vary from wigging to death."

Trevelien selected Captain Hassett's report about the factory raid and moved it to the top of the papers before him. "Less than a week ago the *Saint Michael* discovered and destroyed a steel mill in Dughur. Evidence was found of multiple steam engines on the premises. The mill was making steel that Ghur smiths were fashioning into weapons—beginning an armament of the Ghur that has been prohibited for the past twenty years."

"That is shocking, Highness."

"I thought so, Mr. Grimshaw. In an interview with Prince Agra-sho I was told one of your people, Cobb Venner, arranged for the construction of the factory and the importation of the engines."

Grimshaw nodded. "I know."

"You dare admit your involvement with this factory?" Trevelien shot to his feet. "You are far more arrogant than I ever would have imagined, Mr. Grimshaw."

"And you, Highness, must think me as stupid as you think me arrogant." The riding crop lashed down with a snap against Grimshaw's riding boot. "At dinner last evening I was informed of your interview with Prince Agra-sho, by the Prince himself. I immediately returned to my office and started an audit of accounts with which Mr. Venner had workings. I noticed, in a preliminary look at his accounts, a higher-than-normal shrinkage rate on shipments to Dughur. Mr. Venner had noted that *gifts* were required to conduct business in Dughur."

Trevelien snarled at Grimshaw. "You expect me to believe that Mr. Venner had hatched this scheme by himself, without your complicity?"

Grimshaw's head came up and his chin thrust forward defiantly. "You are welcome to conduct your own audit, Highness."

After you have destroyed records? "Since Venner is dead, there is little hope anyone would be able to contradict or correct any errors in such an audit."

"This is true, Highness." Grimshaw actually managed to get a pained look on his face. "And I cannot be one hundred percent certain that members of the auditing staff were not working in concert with Venner, so they may cover up or destroy evidence. While I find this crime as monstrous as you do, and the thought of corruption in my firm absolutely abhorrent, I am not certain I can assure you that all of the guilty individuals will be caught.

"Of course"—Grimshaw shrugged—"we have begun procedures to revoke the pension being paid to Venner's family back in Ilbeoria."

"No doubt." Trevelien fought to keep his frustration from his face. Having been schooled as a warrior, he had maintained an unhealthy contempt of the merchant class. Granted most of his dealing with it had come while merchants and more common folk had sought to curry favor with him. He found their efforts transparent and, therefore, ineffective. This led him to think of them as inferior strategists. While that judgment might well have held for most of the group, Erwin Grimshaw clearly was not representative of the majority.

I should have known he would have covered himself. Rochelle used to say I believed too much in the strength of justice to realize the depths and labyrinthine precautions inspired by evil. The Prince wanted to hammer a fist on his desk. *Instead of breaking Grimshaw as I wished to do, I have shown him that he has successfully anticipated and defeated me. Instead of fear, I get contempt—but that can be used too if it makes him underestimate me.*

Grimshaw licked his lips with the tip of his little pink tongue. "I believe this has cleared up our difficulties, for now. May I take my leave?"

Trevelien affected an air of petty resentment. "You may go, but not to Vlengul."

"What?"

"You yourself said your auditing staff could not be wholly trusted." Trevelien gave Grimshaw a smile that fell halfway between triumphantly broad and firmly cruel. "You will remain in Dhilica until this audit is done and I have reviewed it to my satisfaction. *Then* you will be allowed to leave."

The color in Grimshaw's gray flesh slowly rose. "If I were you, Highness, I should not want me nearby. I think time spent in Vlengul should let me forget just how angry I am with you."

"That well could be, sir, but I care not for myself, only *your* discomfort." Trevelien folded his arms. "You would like to be in Vlengul and *I* would like a means to prove you guilty of treason."

"I suspect then, Highness, we shall both be disappointed."

"And I suspect, Mr. Grimshaw, we have actually found a point upon which we both agree." Trevelien pointed toward the door. "I'd wish you a good day, but you'd doubt my sincerity."

Grimshaw spun on his heel and stalked from the office. Trevelien winced at the door slammed behind the man, then he smiled. "Rochelle, this is one you would have found a very evil man," the Prince whispered to himself. "And you would have been my strength in fighting him. The depths of his evil are unplumbed and the labyrinths are uncharted. I'll just have to hope that in his anger with me he'll lose his way, then I can give him all the justice he deserves."

— 57 —

> **Alanim's Palace**
> **Helor, Helansajar**
> **9 Majest 1687**

The diplomatic skills Natalya had absorbed in her father's court had her thinking that flying a fruit cart into Helor in the middle of the night might not be the proper way to enter the city. As Malachy brought the cart down into the palace's ivory inner courtyard, she knew they were dropping too fast and tried to correct him. Pain and exhaustion contorting his face, Malachy managed to slow them at the last second, but still the cart hit hard.

The rear wheels hit first, shattering spokes and warping iron wheel rims with a scream of metal. The front wheels hit next and ripped away from the axle. As they skidded and wobbled deeper into the courtyard, the wagon bounced once, then split in the middle and slewed around in two pieces. Oranges, lemons, and limes rolled and hopped out of the wagon, spraying out over the courtyard's marble surface. The wagon's front end caught on something and tipped over, throwing Natalya clear and onto a bed of citrus fruit.

Natalya rolled as she hit the ground and spent the energy of her flight without injury. Regaining her feet, she ran to where Malachy sat slumped in the aft portion of the wagon. For half a second she thought the landing might have killed him, but then she saw his chest rise and fall in the courtyard's yellow torchlight.

He's alive! She smiled, then shook her head. Malachy might actually be living, but he did not look that far from death's door. Exhaustion had sunk his eyes into gray hollows, and the grime from their flight etched the outlines of his bones against his jaundiced flesh. His hair had matted and clumped, and the weight he had lost on the journey added a sharp gauntness to his cheekbones, jaw, and limbs. The various sores and wounds from his torture added to his overall appearance to make him look more like Death personified than any human being.

She knew she did not look much better and that impression was made very apparent by the astonished and horrified expressions worn by the guards who ringed the broken cart. Some had drawn their shamshirs, but most just gaped slack-jawed at her. She broadened her smile and stood slowly. "Do any of you speak Stranan?"

The guards jabbered among themselves, then one of them ran off. Natalya kept her smile in place, then tried using simple sign language to communicate with the Helorians. She pointed to Malachy and then herself, tapped her right eye and spoke the name Alanim Shukri Awan. The message she wanted them to get was that she and Malachy had come to see Shukri Awan.

The net effect of her message was to get the guards to back further away from her. This apparent failure displeased her in part, but was not completely without merit. At their new respectful distance the chance of their being able to attack without warning was reduced. Content with that, she sat down and took Malachy's right hand in her own.

The gold coating his hands felt less like metal than actual flesh. She could not see lines or pores in it, but she felt a slight indentation at the cuticles. Malachy had never offered to explain what the metal was or how he had gotten these golden replacements for his hands. She had not pressed him about his eyes or hands, though there had been times when curiosity had almost gotten the better of her and prompted questions.

Two soldiers arrived escorting a tall, slender man in very fine robes. The tall man bowed to Natalya and began speaking in Ilbeorian. "I am Suhayl ibn-Hakim, advisor to the Alanim. Who are you and what is your business here in Helor?"

Hearing the irritation and hostility in the man's voice, Natalya hesitated a second before answering him. "I am Talia Konev and this is Martin Childs, a merchant from Ilbeoria. We were prisoners in Vzorin. We came here to warn you and your Ilbeorian troops of an invasion force coming from Strana. You must take us to see the Alanim immediately."

Suhayl snapped orders at two guards and they immediately ran off into the palace. In Stranan he said to her, "I shall speak your native tongue for your convenience. You shall see the Alanim, but only after you have been made more presentable. I will speak with Alanim Awan and convey to him your reason for visiting. If you will follow these guards, they will conduct you to your chamber. Others will follow with a litter to bear your companion away."

Natalya did not want to leave Malachy behind, but Suhayl's firm tone gave her no choice. As Tachotha she could have defied him, both by rank and by spirit, but revealing her true identity to him would be dangerous. With a Stranan army on the way, she would be a valuable hostage in Shukri Awan's hands. While holding her captive might seem like a good way to turn the Hussars back, she knew it would provide Grigory with enough justification to attack and take Helor with her father's blessings.

And take it he would. With that realization she saw how much her thoughts about and feelings for Grigory Khrolic had shifted in just two weeks. At *that* time she had believed Grigory to be deceived by Vasily Arzlov. Her duty to her lover had been to protect him and to try to point out to him that Arzlov was using him. She had found him singularly difficult to convince about this point and had wondered at how he could not see what was very apparent to her.

He did not see it because he did not want to see it. Natalya did not doubt Arzlov had his own plots in place, but clearly Grigory did, as well. She had kept herself focused so completely on watching Arzlov and assuming the worst about him, that Grigory's plotting had gone all but unnoticed. In thinking about Grigory and how easily he had fooled her, she wondered how far back his deceptions went.

Her face burned with embarrassment. *Too far, much too far. He must have seen me as his route to power, but then Helor presented itself and I was set aside.* She swallowed against the sour taste in her mouth. *I should have known I was incidental to him when he reacted so badly to losing at chess. He wishes to be subordinate to no one.*

The guards guided a silent Natalya into a long wing of the palace that had cool marble floors and tiled walls. The corridor rose high enough above them that the ceiling remained hidden in the shadows cast by the guards' lanterns. Unlike her father's castle, this place had no statues or murals on the walls, just various weblike designs on the blue and white wall tiles.

The lead guard knocked gently on a door and Natalya thought she heard a number of girlish giggles from the other side. Having prepared herself to see a woman open the door, the appearance of a tall, heavyset bald man surprised her greatly.

Her unkempt appearance seemed to surprise him as much as he had surprised her. A guard said something to him in Helansajaran, then the eunuch shooed the man away with a chubby hand. Moving out of her way, the man invited her into the room and then closed the door quickly behind her.

They've put me in a seraglio! Natalya folded her arms. *"Nyet, nyet!"* The eunuch looked deeper into the darkened room. "Dobrila!"

Natalya heard a rustling of fabric as a petite woman with dark brown hair rose from a bed of pillows and pulled on a sheer skirt of silk. The woman wore slippers and gold glinted from a fine chain around her right ankle, but she was otherwise naked. The woman's small breasts and overall physique made her appear almost boyish, but the breadth of her hips and the way she stalked forward banished that thought immediately.

The eunuch spoke to Dobrila and she, in turn, addressed Natalya in halting Stranan. "This is Jabr. He keeps the Alanim's mistresses."

"I am *not* here for the Alanim's pleasure."

The Stranan woman spoke to the eunuch, then nodded at his reply. "Jabr says the guards said Suhayl wants you cleaned and made presentable." She wrinkled her nose. "You stink of rotten fruit and look as if you have not bathed in months."

Natalya started to snap a rebuke at the woman, then stopped and laughed lightly. *I would have rebuked her, and for what? Telling the truth?*

"Please, then, you will show me where to bathe?" Natalya smiled politely at Dobrila and the Stranan woman nodded.

While following Dobrila around the perimeter of the room, Natalya was able to count a dozen sleeping women. She was certain that the gauzy veils hanging down from the ceiling and the shadows deeper in the room hid dozens more woman. *How many of them have been taken from my nation and reduced to this state?*

Dobrila led Natalya into a tiled room with two pools of water. The larger of the two steamed while the other did not. "Use small pool for bathing. I will find you clothes and perhaps food, *da?*"

"*Da.*" Natalya smiled gratefully. "Bread, please. No fruit." The Tachotha rested her hands on her stomach. "No fruit."

The Stranan slave took a cake of soap and a brush from a small hollow on the tiled wall and handed them to Natalya. "You should be diligent. Shukri Awan may call for you at any moment. I shall return with food."

Natalya stripped off her clothes and tossed them into a stinking mass against the wall. She tested the water with her toe and found it lukewarm. She sank herself in it, letting the water close over her head. Coming back up, she raked her fingers through her hair and was horrified to discover how matted and tangled it had become.

Not wanting to let the water calm enough so she could see her reflection, she applied brush and soap to her skin with a zeal that reminded her of the scrubbings her nurses had subjected her to as a child. What she had hated then she could appreciate now. She shivered when she looked down and saw how filthy the water had already become. She washed her hair, rinsed it, and washed it again.

Once it was clear of soap she seated herself at the edge of the small pool, spun on her backside, and slid into the hotter pool. By contrast the water seemed scalding. The sunburned patches of flesh at her throat and on the backs of her hands hurt because of the heat. Working her way around the edge of the pool, she found a shallow area and lay back, letting the warm water lap over her belly like waves flowing across a flood plain. Resting her head on the edge of the pool, she tried to relax.

Almost immediately she wondered what sort of care Malachy was receiving. She pictured him in a similar position elsewhere in the Alanim's palace but found her mental image of him came complete with his worn boots and threadbare black pants. This struck her as odd. She tried to imagine him naked and found she could not, which struck her as yet more odd.

When she had first known him, back before he lost his eyes, he had often been the object of her fantasies. Whether held privately or shared amid giggles with her sisters, she'd never had a problem visualizing him unclothed. Since she had never actually seen him naked, her fantasies varied in anatomical particulars, but her mind had never before denied her such detail.

Natalya frowned. She and Malachy had been in closer contact over the past week and a half than ever before. Together they had huddled beneath their wagon to escape the sun. They had fallen asleep in one another's arms and awakened there, as well. The circle of his arms, even offered innocently, seemed to banish the worries and furies that would have otherwise kept her awake.

Malachy had been timid and tender in his solicitousness of her and her needs. He had always been on guard against intruding on her thoughts or against placing his hand inappropriately on her. She often woke to find herself on her side, nestled with her back against his belly. In that position Grigory would have had his arm draped across her stomach or a hand gently cupping a breast, but Malachy did not. His free hand always capped her shoulder like an epaulet, keeping her secure but not presuming intimacy where none existed.

Natalya marveled at his consideration and his control. The hesitation in his voice when a conversation began to veer toward emotional subjects had caught her off guard at certain points. In the dark, while their skiff flew through the night, she had found it easy to imagine herself a dozen years younger. She found herself speaking to Malachy with an openness and ease that she had not known since the days of the Lescari War. There were times it seemed as if the intervening years had been a long dream, then Malachy would abruptly shift the subject and she would be reminded that they both had changed.

Malachy's self-discipline had been admirable—frustratingly so. She admitted that to herself without hesitation, but a bit of surprise. Before they had flown the last leg to Helor she had tried to convince Malachy to wait an extra day, to rest. She did think that a good thing, but she had also wanted more time with him, alone. When he refused, reminding her that time was critical if lives were to be saved, she was glad he could not see the pouty expression that swept her face.

He had spent their time together being careful not to deal with her as if the feelings they had once shared still lived.

She had spent their time together slowly letting those same feelings be reborn. They didn't flood back all at once, but seeped up slowly. Bit by bit the memories returned and when Malachy's behavior had been compared to Grigory's, the Hussar had been found wanting.

Just as Grigory had not been able to supplant Natalya's memories of playing chess with Malachy, she had no memories of the Ilbeorian to replace intimate remembrances of Grigory. There had been times when she lay awake, pressed against Malachy, hoping and wishing he would let his hand slip from her shoulder and stroke her stomach. She wanted him to act on the emotions she was coming to feel for him, but he had not.

Natalya knew pure exhaustion had to be at least partially responsible for his lack of ardor, but other things played a part, as well. Malachy had always been possessed of a keen sense of responsibility. Just as he was rushing to protect other Ilbeorians from the advancing Stranan force, so too did he protect her from himself.

Even though she did not want that protection.

She tried to identify the catalyzing element that had turned her from being angry and hurt—as she had been years ago—to falling in love with him again. Part of it was the emotional distance he placed between them. It showed respect for her and that he was willing to place her well-being above his own feelings. *He was willing to subordinate his feelings to mine, something Grigory would never do.*

She also realized that the Malachy Kidd she had been angry with had been a monster she conjured up from her imagination. The man with whom she traveled had not been a thoughtless beast, but just a man who apologized to her and admitted his failing. She had managed to vilify him, then refused to accept in her heart that her characterization of him could have been wrong. *At least, I did not accept it all at once. But, gradually, on the journey, my heart learned what my mind knew.* She smiled with that thought.

Dobrila's return brought Natalya back to the real world. "We must hurry. Alanim Awan wishes to see you quickly." The slave dried Natalya's hair with a towel and combed it out. The eunuch entered the chamber bearing a green robe which Natalya cinched around her waist with a black sash. Dobrila pulled on a cloak of dark blue velvet, then led Natalya back through the harem and out into the hallway.

"Follow me."

They proceeded on through darkened corridors, working their way deeper into the palace. Natalya knew they would have to stop at some point and move to one of the wings because the palace itself butted up against Jebel Quirana. One could only go so far south before running out of building.

At just that point Dobrila opened a door and started down a wide winding staircase. On three landings they were admitted through locked doors by pairs of guards. Finally, at a depth of what Natalya estimated to be fifty feet, they entered a large chamber with an arched roof that crested half the distance back to the surface. Oil lamps burned everywhere, but smoke drained out through a latticework hole in the center of the roof.

The chamber itself was at once striking and chaotic. Across the room from them, twenty yards away, a stone throne stood in an archway that, had it not been walled off in brilliant cerulean tile, would have led into Jebel Quirana. Up on the surface—visible from a long distance to fliers—a similarly colored, titanic archway backed the palace, likewise blocking the entrance to Jebel Quirana.

The throne had two tigers as arms and a stone slab with a gold web worked into it as a back. The style of carving looked archaic and the presence of the animals surprised Natalya. Ataraxian tenets prohibited the production of idols and that generally meant believers only used geometric or botanical patterns in their decorations. *Could the throne be from before the time when Ataraxianism came to Estanu?*

Between the doorway and the throne, every manner of treasure Natalya could think of seemed to be gathered in piles and stacks and rows. The collection of things had been organized to the degree that it was sorted like with like, but beyond that she could detect no order to it at all. Coins lay piled nearest the throne and handwoven carpets had been stacked beside the doorway, while everything else lay around and between.

Shukri Awan looked up from the pile of gold coins and smiled. "Thank you, Dobrila, you have done well. You may leave."

Dobrila bowed and retreated to the stairs. Natalya did not try to hide her surprise. "You speak Stranan?"

The bald man stroked his black beard and nodded. "I have Stranan slaves, as you have seen, who serve me as I once served in Vzorin. I learned some of your language there, but have kept current. I believe it is important for a leader to know the tongue of his subjects, *da?*"

"I did not know Helor has a large Stranan population."

"Please don't be so coy, Tachotha Natalya."

Natalya smiled to cover her surprise. "You have me mistaken for someone else, Alanim."

Awan flipped the coin in his hand. "Please do not insult my intelligence. As you can see, I collect things, and one of them is coins. My formal collection is up above, and I will gladly show it to you later. Suffice it to say, I have countless coins with your profile stamped on them—they might be seven years old, but as I saw during your bath, you have not aged at all badly."

Natalya's face burned. "You watched me while I bathed?"

His blue eyes glittered with amusement. "Calm yourself, Tachotha." He touched the blue coloration around his own eyes, then flicked a finger against the slightly sharpened tips of his ears. "While you carry enough Durranian blood for me to consider you breeding stock, I do not lust for you. Even the least of the women in my seraglio know more about carnal pleasure than any ten women of Strana. *Those* needs I satisfy there.

"Your presence presents me another need, however, part of which was satisfied by seeing who you really were. The engravers of this coin were spectacular. Are they still alive? I will have them do my coin." Awan turned and pointed toward the throne. "I think I will have that throne pictured on the reverse, while I am on the obverse. I know a profile is customary on a coin, but I wonder which side I should choose. Right or left? Which do you think?"

As Awan turned his face right and then left, Natalya considered his question for a moment. Immediately something in her brain told her the matter was utterly ridiculous and not worthy of thought, especially now. "Where is my companion?"

Awan looked at her as if seeing her again for the first time, then smiled. "Your Wolf-priest?"

"How . . . ?"

"Did I mention I collect medallions, as well? His profile is not as exact on the medal you gave to the *ravadcheka* that fought with him in Glogau as yours is on your coin, but then currency demands accuracy, don't you think? If people can look at a coin and see a confident, strong leader, they will support him, *da?*"

"Where is he?"

"Suhayl will bring him when he is ready." Awan flipped the coin back over his shoulder and it clinked into the pile. "I am so happy to have you here. You are my first true visitor—well, visitor of rank. Are you here as an ambassador?"

Natalya shook her head. "No, we came to warn you and the Il-beorians here about a Stranan force that is coming this way."

"Yes, yes, a delightful fantasy to distract my guards." The man smiled as if they were close friends. "I have sent a company of my cavalry out to destroy this host of yours, just so others will think I take this subterfuge seriously. Now, no, it could not be."

"What could not be?"

Awan covered his mouth with a hand. "Your father didn't think that sending you to me would prevent me from conquering Strana, did he? You were not sent as a *bribe*, were you?"

"No, of course not!" None of Awan's chatter made any sense to Natalya and her fatigue eroded her self-control. "What makes you think you can conquer Strana?"

Awan's laughter filled the chamber with echoes of insane mirth. "Oh, it is true, they never see what should be obvious. Forgive me, Tachotha Natalya. Permit me proper introduction, one in context." Shukri Awan stepped up on the dais. "Stand before me and know true fear, daughter of Strana. I, Shukri Awan, am the Dost re-born. Before this year is out I will again be master of all Estanu."

Malachy awoke with a start when a hand pressed roughly against his chest. "Who is it?"

"A friend. There is little time." The whisper came in heavily accented Ilbeorian, but Malachy understood it. "You are a Wolf-priest."

"Yes, just like the others here."

"There are no others here."

"What?" Malachy reached out and grabbed a handful of tunic from right below where the man's voice came from. "The airship, the *Saint Michael*, left troops here."

"Wah, your eyes." The man grabbed Malachy's left wrist with both hands but could not break his grip. "You are mistaken. There are no troops here."

Then what I heard in the cell was a lie. Why? Malachy let his grip slacken as everything dropped into place. *I was tricked. Arzlov deceived me and deceived Natalya. She freed me and I took her to Helor, to save my people. He tells her father that I kidnapped her and the Tacier will authorize anything Arzlov wants to get her back. I wanted to prevent a war and I've gone and started it.*

"You said you were a friend. What does that mean?"

"It is possible to get a message to Aran."

"How?"

"Signals, mirrors, *sabbakrasulin*."

Malachy grimaced. *Sabbakrasulin* were Ataraxian demon-runners—men who enslaved themselves to the devil to run fast. *If I use them I encourage their damnation. But if I do not, a greater disaster looms.* "What do you want?"

"Wolf-priests are rich."

"I guarantee you as much gold as you can carry."

"I am but a weak man."

"Bring friends."

"I have five very strong friends."

"Only five?"

"They will bring their wives. They have many wives."

"Yes, make it a family affair, good." Malachy levered himself up on his elbows. "Get word to Prince Trevelien. A Stranan Hussars regiment is on its way to lay siege to Helor. Tell him to send help immediately—whatever he can manage as fast as possible. If he doesn't act with all due dispatch, come next summer Vasily Arzlov will be sitting in Government House in Dhilica, grinding the spine of our economy to dust beneath his heel."

— 58 —

> **Gauntlan Manor**
> **Dhilica, Puresaran**
> **Aran**
> **15 Majest 1687**

Fear tore through Amanda Grimshaw as she paused in the doorway to her father's study. Her father capered around in a tight little circle at the center of the room, arms flapping up and down in time with the midnight chiming of the clock on the mantel. With his head thrown back and a rhythmic wheezing issuing whisper quiet from his mouth, he looked as if he were dying or possibly—impossibly— laughing. Tears rolled down the old man's cheeks, making Amanda think he might indeed be laughing, and that scared her even more than his death.

My father only laughs at someone else's misfortune. "Father, what is the matter? Who was your visitor?"

The old man spun around a couple more times, then stopped abruptly, frozen in place like an animal preparing to spring away from a predator. Erwin's gray eyes brimmed with tears, but were not ringed with the red of weeping. "Matter? Absolutely nothing, my dear. Edwards brought me this from the office and now everything is perfect."

He held up a paper, then pulled it back in front of his face. His eyes tracked over the words written there, then he laughed again. "This is better than perfect."

Amanda pressed her left hand against her throat. "What is it, Father?"

Erwin gave her a sidelong glance over a hunched shoulder and his lip almost curled up in a snarl, as if he were a cur protecting a morsel of food. Then his shoulder dropped and he smiled. "This, Amanda, is the solution to all of our problems. We have been proved right about everything we've been saying. Those fools back in Il-beoria made a fatal mistake in not listening to us." His face darkened. "The debacle in Dughur will complicate things slightly, but I think we can handle the situation for the time being."

"You're scaring me, Father."

Erwin's face softened. "No, no, I would never do that." He glanced at the message again, conquered his broad grin and waved her to a chair. "Let me explain this to you, Amanda. This message is from Helor. I had made arrangements with certain groups of people to send me information. I have been able to use it to maximize our profits. Usually this information is just commercial rumors—good harvest, bad floods, and so on. Sometimes, though, it is more of a critical nature. Like this."

Amanda leaned forward, but her father spun away and began to pace before she could read the crabbed writing on the page. She knew the news must be utterly devastating to someone her father hated. She hoped it did not involve Robin, but since he was so closely tied with Prince Trevelien, she could not help but think anything making her father happy would make Robin miserable.

"I think you do not trust me, Father."

Erwin hesitated for a moment before turning back to face her. "Not trust you?"

Amanda gave him a big smile. "I was teasing you, Father, just as you have been teasing me with the news in your message." She leaned forward, resting elbows on her knees, and peered up at him. "It must be very exciting."

"The most exciting, my dear." Erwin held the paper aloft as if written on it were a message from God Himself. "The message was sent by a Martinist priest named Fiddauyun. It asks the Prince to send help because an Imperial Stranan Hussars regiment is marching on Helor. The message started out about four to five days ago. What kind of name is Fiddauyun? Danorian? Culordainian?"

"I don't know, Father." Amanda glanced down at her hands and forced herself to still their trembling. "Will you tell the Prince what the message says? You've long predicted this would happen. Now you can be proved right."

"Amanda, dearest, I am already proved right. I had the vision and I have taken precautions. Since the Stranans won't be able to ship supplies through the Himlan passes, we have until spring to prepare for their assault. We will be ready, with Grimshaw's Militia spearheading the defense of Aran."

"But Father, if you told the Prince now he might be able to help Helor. It might forestall the war."

Grimshaw frowned slightly. "To what end, daughter?"

"It would save lives, Father."

"It might save Ataraxians, but their salvation is not my concern and their deaths would be on the souls of those Stranans who killed them." Erwin shook his head resolutely. "If I give this information to the Prince . . . well, I won't, I just won't. It's on his head. If I had been in Vlengul as I wanted to be—as his pettiness and peevishness prevented me from being—my deputies would have given this message to him. He had his chance, but he failed."

Erwin stared hard at his daughter. "If I were to give this to the Prince, he would take the *Saint Michael* north and might be able to do something. Then he would be the savior of Aran. His power would increase, his rule would become more harsh. Giving the Prince this information would destroy me and Grimshaw's Mercantile, and everything we have worked for in Aran. I won't have that. Prince Trevelien is the greatest enemy Aran has, and withholding this information from him guarantees he will be recalled to Ludstone."

Her father began laughing again. "Yes, I will have my brother Philbert propose for me to be the new Governor-general. After we drive the Stranans back into their own country, I will be the logical choice. Yes, that will be perfect."

Erwin held the message out and touched it to the flame of the oil lamp on his desk. The paper caught quickly, blackened and curled. After all the writing had been consumed, he dropped the burning paper to the floor and crushed the flames with his foot. "This is a wonderful day."

Amanda forced a smile to her face. "It is, Father."

"It is the end of one era and the beginning of a new one that demands courage and attention to duty."

Can you read my mind, Father? "Yes, sir. I understand that."

"I know you do." Erwin patted himself on the stomach. "I think celebration is in order. You and your aunt should have a glass of port. I think that is appropriate."

"Will you join us?"

"I will be in the tower; you go ahead without me."

"Yes, Father." Amanda stood and kissed her father on the forehead. "I love you."

Erwin Grimshaw took a step back, his surprised expression melting into joy. "I am blessed to have a daughter such as you, Amanda. Good night."

"Yes, Father, good night." Amanda hugged her arms around herself as her father walked away. *Courage and duty, Father, your words. The era that ends tonight is the era of my being your daughter. I now begin life as a citizen of Ilbeoria. God grant me the courage to accept and accomplish my duty to my nation.*

— 59 —

Bir el Jamajim,
Helansajar
15 Majest 1687

Grigory Khrolic would not have thought it possible for Vandari armor to move through the desert of the Helansajaran lowlands unnoticed, but the silhouetted Helorian guards marching around the perimeter of the enemy camp sounded no alarm. Only thirty yards separated the elite Vandari Rams from the Helorian cavalry company camping around the well at Bir el Jamajim, yet the stealth of the Rams' approach meant the men they would kill remained unaware of their impending attack.

Most would die in their sleep.

Three tiles with red on black imagery hovered at the top of

Grigory's vision. The first, displaying a cloven hoofprint, marked the magick that allowed the armor to move and function. A second showed a silhouette of the Ram armor. It represented a spell that cloaked the armor in shadow and made it blend in with the night. The last one, a human ear that had been torn in half, dampened the sound of the armor's movement. Employing those spells, which were draining but not overwhelmingly so, the Vandari had moved beyond the main body of the Stranan troops to attack the cavalry spotted by the *Zarnitsky* earlier in the day.

Conventional Stranan doctrine would have had Grigory bring the *Zarnitsky* down to pour a couple of broadsides into the Helorian camp. Grigory had rejected that idea because the sound of the airship's engines would be enough to waken the Helorian riders. Once awakened the riders could scatter, rendering a broadside less than effective in getting them all. The purpose of attacking the Helorian riders was to delay discovery of their force until the last minute, and having survivors fleeing to the city would not do.

More importantly, the Ram Vandari needed to draw first blood in this campaign. They had served well in the Lescari War, but their duty since then had been relatively soft. One of the Vandari had become so complacent he had been killed attempting to track down bandits—thereby making Ram Twenty-seven available to Grigory. While he had used his armor to repulse the Helansajaran attack against Natalya, the other Rams had not seen real combat in years.

They must remember what it is to be in a crucible of war. Grigory made Ram Twenty-seven stand tall, no longer in the half-crouch of the advance. He raised his forelegs, pointed forward, then waved his men on with him. Pumping his legs to propel the armor into a sprinter's gait, he galloped the armor forward. Sparks shot up where metal hoof met half-buried stone, but even that much light failed to alert the pickets around the Well of Skulls.

When a guard did turn—Grigory guessed the vibrations of Vandari hooffalls caught his attention—his face registered surprised terror. A hoof flicked out and the man flew, his chest crushed flat. Before he hit the ground, the thirty Vandari Rams had boiled up over the crest of the depression and poured down into it. A metal stampede, they blew through the middle of the camp to the southern end of the depression, then worked back north again to kill the stragglers.

Tents hooked on horns snapped like pennoncels as the Vandari pursued and smashed their quarry. Grigory would have thought it obvious that swords could not prevail against the might of the war engines, but this did not stop the Helorians from drawing their shamshirs and attacking the Rams. Blades snapped on forelegs raised to parry, then swordsmen died as glancing Vandari blows shattered limbs and ruptured organs.

The shrieks of dying men and the ringing clang of metal filled the firelit bowl. The shadowed shapes of giant Rams twisted through a complex dance of destruction. Vandari Rams soared as they leaped over compatriots to pounce on fleeing Helorians. Circles of gore marked where men had been flattened beneath metal hooves. Where men ran, Vandari followed; where men slowed, Vandari did not. A quick twist to the right and an impaled Helorian would writhe on a horn, then be spun off to die in the darkness.

Up on the edge of the depression, Grigory watched delightedly as his company annihilated the Helorians. The cavalrymen scurried about like rats, seeking escape where there was none. Defiant, cowering, agile, no matter their behavior, the Helansajarans were crushed out of existence by the Stranan Vandari. In less than five minutes, aside from the horses that had brought the Helorians to the well, the only signs of life came from prowling metal beasts.

Grigory felt no remorse for the dead Helorians. They had been foolish enough to place themselves in opposition to him. He knew it was not a conscious choice on their part, but they blindly followed a master who should have known better than to fight against his superiors. In the struggle between Stranan and Aralan, the superior people would always win. It did not matter that both of them claimed their nobility based on their share of Durranian blood—what made the difference was the stock into which the Durranian lords of old had bred.

Grigory looked down on the Vandari assembled in the depression. "You have done well. Extinguish their fires so the *Zarnitsky* will know we are finished here. They will go ahead and attack Helor with barrages at dawn and dusk, to let them know fear before we arrive. When we do, they will see us. Our fearsome aspects will spark dread in their hearts. Six days from now they will open the gates of Helor to us. If they do not"—Ram Twenty-seven opened its arms wide—"I can see you will not shrink from what must be done."

Prince Trevelien leaned forward on his desk, forcing calm onto his face for Amanda Grimshaw's sake. Sitting across from him, with Robert Drury resting his hands on her shoulders, she trembled violently enough to be in the throes of a malarial seizure. "And you are certain this message arrived for your father from Helor?"

"Highness, forgive me, but I could not look at it. I only know what he told me."

"Yes, of course, Miss Grimshaw." The Prince smiled reassuringly at her. "I know it took a great deal of courage for you to come here this morning. I think your action may save the life of the Ilbeorian who sent the message. You are a brave woman."

"What will you do, sir?" Amanda dabbed at red-rimmed eyes with a handkerchief. "To my father?"

The Prince sat back and scratched his shaved head. "Your father is a minor concern at the moment. I will think of something, but I suspect all that will happen will be his recall to Ilbeoria. At best he has been willfully negligent and I doubt I could get a court here or in Ludstone to convict him. Exile is the most I can do." He frowned. "And it is what I will do."

Relief washed over Amanda's face, then horror followed it. She reached a hand up to her shoulder and laid it on Robin's hand. The ethyrine's face betrayed no emotions, but his hands gave her shoulders a gentle squeeze. Both of them clearly knew that her father's return to Ilbeoria would mean her departure from Aran. Echoes of the grief he had felt at his wife's death ran through Trevelien as he remembered comforting his daughter in the same way that Robin comforted Amanda.

Love for another and duty to country all too seldom run on parallel roads. Trevelien closed his eyes for a second and cleared his mind. The problem he had to deal with was Helor and Strana's assault on it. Running at flank speed, with no head winds or storms to slow it down, the *Saint Michael* could reach Helor inside a week. The problem with that was that the airship would be at the extreme edge of its recoverable range. If it *did* make it to Helor, the coal it would have on board would be enough to get it back to Dhilica. Without secure supply stations between Dhilica and Helor, the *Saint Michael* would have to come all the way back to the capital to refuel.

Trevelien looked up at Robin. "On the trip out here I read a report you prepared about a siege of Helor, correct?"

"Yes, sir."

"Can the city hold out for long?"

Robin shook his head. "My partner and I worked from the Stranan point of view, using sketchy information. In our analysis the city would fall quickly, but in the testing Colonel Kidd pointed out a number of things we had not taken fully into account. Given the storms that will be rolling into the Himlans soon, I doubt we can deliver enough troops to lift the siege before next spring."

"Could it hold out that long?"

"The Stranans probably have a company of Vandari."

"Could a company of ethyrines oppose them?"

"We'd give them a lot to think about, Highness." Robin nodded confidently. "We're offensive troops, though, sir—our tricks will slow them down but I don't think we can keep them out. Defeating a siege will require different tricks than the ones I know. Someone else would be good for coordinating the defense. God willing, that person is already in place."

"Indeed, Brother Robert, God willing, the Alanim will listen to him, too." The Prince and Robin shared a resolute nod. Before coming to report to him, Robin and Amanda had inquired of Father Ryan what the name Fiddauyun meant. The priest had told them it was Estanuan for *silver eyes*. Both Robin and the Prince took that phrasing to mean only one thing, yet neither of them could imagine how it was possible. *God is willing, I guess.*

The Prince pressed his hands together. "Miss Grimshaw, this news you bring me requires me to take action. I will speak with your father. Quite frankly, I will lie to him and tell him that I learned of the news through a spy I have in his company. Though I do not know your father well, I think that information will occupy his mind enough to preclude him from noticing your absence from his household. I would have you stay as a guest in my home for the duration of this crisis."

"Highness, I don't know what to . . ." Amanda looked up and back at Robin and the ethyrine nodded at her. "I would be honored."

"Good. I will see to it that you have everything you desire." He looked up at Robin. "Get your people together. There is a Ghur uprising with which we need to deal. I'll be going along as an observer. Make certain your men attend Mass. We'll leave this evening."

Again Amanda's hands sought Robin's. "So quickly?" She looked at the Prince imploringly. "Of course you must go; I'm sorry."

Trevelien stood and came around to the front of his desk.

"Don't worry, Miss Grimshaw. Brother Robert will join you and Captain Hassett for dinner with me before we leave. It will be dire business ahead and dinner with you will be the pleasant memory to sustain us through it."

— 61 —

> **Dayi Marayir**
> **Helansajar**
> **15 Majest 1687**

Until the party had been assembled, Uriah had not realized how many "sisters" the Dost had claimed. Aside from Thurayya—who was staying behind with Rafiq, Svilik, and a host of servants—he counted fifteen women in the red and black tiger livery. Turikana led a squad of eight, saw to their pack animals, and reported to the Dost that all was ready for their journey.

As he swung up into the saddle of the horse he had been given, Uriah frowned. "Turikana, why are we traveling out now? We should wait and go with Rafiq's force."

She shrugged and spurred her horse out of the cavern. "It is the will of the Dost."

Uriah smiled. "Your Ilbeorian is getting very good, but that answer does not explain the wisdom of leaving before the army is ready to travel."

The Dost floated toward him as if sliding on a frozen stream. "There are things that must be done before I enter Helor."

"Things?" Uriah urged his horse forward and the Dost kept pace with him. "You usually strive for precision in your speech. *Things* is a rather ambiguous term."

"Agreed, but the application is appropriate in this case." They moved through the cavern, past the fires, and into the long tunnel leading out. "When I was laid to rest we knew I would return. We also assumed, my brother and I, that many would try to lay claim to my mantle. We decided it would have been irresponsible if precautions against pretenders were not taken. We must work through these precautions before I can assume my full power."

Uriah looked down at the gap between the Dost's feet and the ground over which he floated. "You seem quite powerful now."

"True. By the standards here I am."

"Here? In Ilbeoria or Strana you'd seem just as powerful."

The Dost's metal mask smiled. "That is what I meant by using the word *here*."

"As if there is somewhere else to be." Uriah caught himself. "Aside from Heaven, Purgatory, Hell, and Limbo, that is."

"And if I tell you there are dozens and dozens of other places to be?"

Uriah felt gooseflesh rising on his arms. "The discussion about reincarnation prevents me from saying the existence of other places is impossible. And, I admit, at times when I have felt the whole world was against me I have wished there were other places to be." The Ilbeorian shrugged. "So, tell me, are there other places?"

The Dost nodded solemnly. "There are many other places in Creation, each one different, like facets in a gem. All part of the same rock, but each is unique. They are similar in nature, but different in society and culture. The boundaries that separate these places from one another are not easily permeable, but travel between them is possible. It is from another place that I and my people, those you think of as Durranian, came to this world."

"How?" Uriah knew he should consider the whole idea insane, but the concept of other places and travel between them felt right to him. "Why?"

"The answers to your questions are bound up in each other. Where I came from was a land of great power. The magicks that the greatest of your kind can wield would be child's play to us. I came from a family of nobles who were known for the power of our magicks. My father accused my brother and I of plotting against him. He had been unable to accept that *our* generation, not his, was the subject of a prophecy. He took us prisoner and exiled us to this world. Through his magick he tore a hole through the dimensions and left us and our followers here, on a magick-poor world, in a desolate mountain valley."

"Durrania."

"Yes." Golden sunlight glinted off the Dost as they rode into the open and began their meandering trek northward. "We raided out from there, feeling weak and vulnerable in our armor, then discovered two things: as weak as we were, we were more powerful than anyone here. More importantly, we found that the product of our interbreeding with native men and women were fertile. This meant that whatever *we* could take, our heirs could hold."

"You intended to create an empire as a base from which you could go back home, right?"

The Dost shook his head. "We knew we could not. This world is too poor in the magickal energy required to return us to our home. We had hoped—in vain, we knew—that some place, some point, might be a focus for magick here. It might have enough power to send us home to Valascy, but no such place exists.

"We created our empire because we had the power to do so and nothing else to do with that power."

"You had power with no direction. That is a fell thing." Uriah sat up tall in his saddle. "If the stories told in Strana are true, the uses to which you put your power were horrible."

"The stories told are doubtless exaggerations but not by much. We allowed our frustration at being trapped to dictate how we treated the people we found here." The day's dying sun flashed off the Dost's forehead. "Exerting control over such emotions is not easy."

"But it is necessary." Uriah frowned. "It is this need for restraint that sustains the Church."

The Dost considered this for a moment, and then a moment longer. As he thought his progress slowed. Uriah reined back to keep pace with the man of gold. "Restraint—perhaps this is the lesson I need to learn in this lifetime."

"It is one that eludes many men."

"Save you, perhaps?"

Uriah blinked. "What do you mean?"

The Dost's metal eyes shrank. "You have restrained your curiosity from allowing you to figure out the secret of the metal ball I gave you. I had thought it would intrigue you."

"It did." Uriah glanced down at his horse's head, feeling the weight of the golden ball in the pouch on his belt. "Something about it feels familiar, but it is also elusive. I cannot quite grasp all it is."

"Apply yourself and you will." The Dost nodded solemnly. "As I shall apply myself to learning restraint and the proper use of the power I wield. It is very important I do so.

"Eight centuries ago, by carving out an empire, I assumed responsibility for millions of people. Before this month is over, I will

own up to it or, as many of your Martinist martyrs have done, I will
die in the attempt."

— 62 —

> **Government House**
> **Dhilica, Puresaran**
> **Aran**
> **15 Majest 1687**

Prince Trevelien took great joy in the way Erwin Grimshaw's jaw
worked up and down at the base of the man's purple face. Rage stole
Grimshaw's sanity, but fear stole his breath. The Prince could easily
imagine the abuse the man wished to heap upon him, but the word-
less wheeze issuing from his mouth seemed far more eloquent than
any string of words.

"Yes, Mr. Grimshaw, I did take a page from your book. As your
clerks learned to bribe *my* officials, so I too learned to bribe *your* officials. I believe I had a translation of the message from Helor before you did. I have spent a day considering my reaction to it. I am
now prepared to share it with you."

The man standing across from him closed his mouth, but pure
venom shot through his gray stare.

"You, Erwin Grimshaw, are undesirable. I *know* you were arming the Ghurs to create a private army, loyal to you, that would win
Aran independence from Ilbeoria. I am aware of attempts to solicit
support from myself and men in my service. You have been careful
and no evidence of these attempts exist, beyond personal recollections, which you can deny. Even so, you and I know this is all true.
You and I also know that the only civil penalty I can visit upon you is
exile."

"Your decree will not keep me out of Aran for long."

"No, I suspect it will not." The Prince opened a box on top of
his desk and slipped a ring onto his finger. Bloody fire shot through
the ruby. "I am not without other resources. As the Cardinal Protector of the Ilbeorian Church, I fear I am compelled to have you
excommunicated."

"The Church has no jurisdiction in this matter."

"No?" The Prince let the hint of a smile onto his face. *You have no idea what a gross blunder you have made, do you?* "The message you refused to pass on to me was from a priest. You interfered with the transfer of a message from a priest in my diocese to me. You have tried to disrupt the conduct of Church business and have endangered a priest in the process."

"This charge will not stand. I thought the message a fraud."

"That was not a decision for you to make. Perhaps if I place you in custody of the Society of Saint Ignatius and they begin to work with you, then you will see the error of your ways. They will subject you to spiritual evaluation and, even if my order of excommunication is overturned in Ilbeoria, you will remain in their care until they are certain you are strong in your faith. That could take you months or *years*."

The color drained from Grimshaw's face, but his expression remained defiant. "I would convince them to release me."

"I doubt it. You are a notorious fornicator and adulterer, as well as a whoremonger and slavemaster. You appear to have a weakness for carnal sins, but the Ignatians know how to cure that." The Prince opened his hands. "It might take you the rest of your life, but you will not die in a state of sin."

Grimshaw's shoulders sagged. "If you remove that ring, my only penalty is exile?"

Trevelien nodded. "But I am not convinced I should remove the ring."

"Name your price."

"Bribery? I knew that was your stock-in-trade."

"Do not insult me, Highness. I will not contest exile and will never return here, this I promise." Grimshaw's eyes narrowed. "What must I do to avoid Church involvement in this?"

Prince Trevelien tugged at his ring. "One simple thing. If you do not do it . . ."

The small man nodded with resignation. "The ring returns to your finger."

"And you'll know Hell on earth before you get a chance to experience the real thing." Trevelien saw Grimshaw nod once more. "Good, we have an agreement. Now, let me fill you in on the details."

— 63 —

The sharp crack of shattering rock brought Natalya awake immediately. Any thoughts about thunder died as she looked toward the window and saw a clear pink dawn sky to the east. *Not a cloud in sight.* Then a thunderlike thud sounded a second before more rock exploded noisily.

Sweeping her black hair from her face with her right hand, she got out of bed and stumbled barefoot to the window. A cool breeze puckered her flesh and reminded her of her nakedness. She glanced back at the bed and thought about returning for a sheet to wrap around herself, then she saw the airship hanging in the sky.

The *Zarnitsky* flew to the north of Helor and let go with a third salvo. A vapor cloud condensed around the side of the airship when the cannons shot. Iron cannonballs arced down through the air, but they landed in a portion of the city shielded from her view by the curved wall of her tower chamber.

Natalya ran across her room, her long hair flying behind her. Through the western window she saw the buildings crushed and collapsed by the barrage. Smoke rose from the ruins. People scurried about with buckets of water while others—shaken and dirty and bleeding—sat wailing in the narrow streets.

The door to her room burst open. Natalya turned, covering herself with her hands. "Who dares?"

A disheveled Malachy Kidd stood framed in the doorway. "Are you unhurt?"

She sighed and lowered her hands. "Yes, I am fine. Please close the door."

Malachy complied with her request, then bowed his head. "Forgive me for intruding like this. I . . ." He raked his fingers back through his thick white hair. "I was not sleeping well and the shots woke me. I pulled on pants and came running because I feared . . ."

"I am not hurt."

"Thank God."

"I would thank Him for weather that grounded the *Zarnitsky*." Natalya sighed heavily. "I counted three salvos."

Malachy folded his arms across his chest. "Dawn and dusk, with one salvo added each day. The *Zarnitsky* chases Shukri Awan into a hole at night and back out again at dawn. If this sort of barrage keeps up, resistance to any Stranan assault will be minimal. No one is safe, no one can strike back. The fear is palpable and growing."

"Grigory was always cautious." Natalya felt a bit of a chill and decided to wrap herself in a sheet. "He will win with terror what it would otherwise cost him blood to take."

As she moved back toward her bed, Natalya noticed how Malachy's head moved to follow her. When Grigory had seen her naked, he had always watched her with sidelong glances. Evidence that he found her stimulating became painfully obvious, yet his reluctance to look directly at her was something she had thought of as a cute idiosyncrasy—boyish modesty and embarrassment.

She knew contrasting Malachy's openness with Grigory's secretiveness was ridiculous. Malachy was blind, so he could not be responding to the same stimuli that had aroused Grigory. Despite that impossibility, she suddenly wanted to know how he would respond to her nakedness. She *wanted* him to respond to her nakedness.

"If you would, Malachy, hand me the robe on the peg at the back of the door. It is too cool at dawn to be unclothed."

Malachy turned away at the start of her request, but his golden right hand froze after clutching the robe. He turned back toward her, the robe hanging down from his hand. His cheeks colored. "You have my apologies for violating your privacy this way. This is, however, one of the few times I've found being blind actually useful."

"You think I have become ugly in the last twelve years?"

"That is not what I said, nor what I meant. I have clearly embarrassed you, however."

"I am not embarrassed. Did not God create the first man and woman naked? Why would this embarrass me?"

The blush on Malachy's cheeks deepened. "Tachotha Natalya, I have acted improperly in bursting in here. I must leave. Please forgive me."

"No, wait." The uneasiness in his voice surprised her. "You do not need forgiveness, Malachy Kidd." Natalya felt her own face flush with color. "I do."

"You? Why? I'm the one who has caused you discomfort."

She shook her head, not for him to see or hear, but to rebuke herself. "I asked for my robe to see how you would react. I was . . . I was trying to trick you into my bed."

"Why, Natalya?"

"Of you I have many good memories, Malachy, and more from our time here together. I choose to think on them and cherish them and want more of them. I wanted to use *new* memories to banish memories of intimacies I shared with Grigory Khrolic." She turned away from him and felt tears filling her eyes. "I wanted to use you to replace him in my mind, much as he replaced you. I feel alone and afraid. Grigory figures in recollections of times when I felt neither, and I did not want that."

She did not hear his footfalls as he crossed the room, but she felt his presence and warmth as he settled the robe over her shoulders. "Do not berate yourself, Natalya." The light touch of his hands tickled her neck as he brushed the hair back away from the right side of her face. "This is a dangerous place and these are dangerous times. This barrage, it just adds pressure. We are isolated and threatened. We would have to be as mad as our host not to feel the need for reassurance and friendship."

"You, Malachy Kidd, are lonely and fearful?"

"I was the one who could not sleep, as you might recall. Loneliness and fear tend to make my sleep fitful, at best." His hands settled on her shoulders reassuringly. "We are friends and really are alone here together, since we have little in common with the Helorians. It is only sane for us to cling to each other to keep away terror and despair."

Natalya turned to face him and pressed her body against his. Her arms circled his chest, her hands slid over taut muscle while his arms slowly enfolded her. She kissed his chin. "It is wrong to seek sanctuary in each other?"

"If fear and despair are all that are bringing us together, yes, it is a bit of a selfish act, and that's never right. We would be taking for ourselves from the other person." Malachy kissed her forehead. "It wouldn't be terribly wrong, not mortally wrong, but wrong."

She kissed his throat. "And if we come together out of love for each other?"

The Wolf-priest shook his head. "If we love each other, then there is nothing wrong with it."

Natalya leaned heavily against him and tried to urge him to walk backward. "Then you would join me in my bed?"

"I would like that very much, yes, Natalya." The Wolf-priest gently tightened his embrace but did not move with her toward the bed. "I would love to, but I cannot."

She looked up at him. "And you did not tell me of your vow of celibacy before now because . . . ?"

Malachy laughed aloud and kissed her forehead again. "I have no such vow, and would repudiate it now if I had taken one. No, the reason I can't be with you has something to do with this place. Something about Helor distracts me constantly. It lurks there, in the back of my mind. I feel as if I'm being watched, or as if I'm supposed to see something, but it hovers out of sight, just barely out of sight. I do not know what it is and I do not know how to stop it from intruding."

He leaned his head forward and kissed her on the lips. "When I come to be with you, Natalya, I want no distractions."

Physical frustration prompted a groan from Natalya, but she hugged Malachy more tightly for fear he would try to pull away in response. "I will allow no distractions when we are together." She laughed and laid her head on his shoulder.

She realized she felt closer to Malachy than any man in her life she had ever known, including Grigory. A kiss, a hug, a smile, all of these things could be counterfeited and she had allowed her physical intimacy with Grigory to blind her to the small bits of himself that he hid away from her. *I took his physical ardor as a sign of his feelings for me, and I was deceived.*

Never again.

Natalya looked up into Malachy's argent eyes. "I will tolerate no distraction because I want to be the sole focus for the man I love."

Malachy stroked her cheek with a golden hand. "I promise you that, Natalya, forever more."

"Good." She kissed his neck lightly. "Now, let us determine how we fulfill your mission here so we can begin to have the rest of our lives to spend together."

The rising thrum of the *Zarnitsky*'s engines brought Natalya out of a restless slumber. The sound sent vibrations through her as the airship dropped steadily toward the city. Each day the volleys had increased in number by one—*this morning it will be six*. Dressing quickly and pulling a cloak on over her shoulders, she rushed from her chamber and down the stairs. Taking a corridor that led across the length of the main palace building, she reached another set of stairs and went up to the flat roof.

She found Malachy already there. Silhouetted against the blue tile archway built into the mountain behind him, he appeared a statue carved of ivory and onyx. She could read fatigue in the dark circles beneath his eyes. His face turned toward her as she stepped out onto the wooden viewing deck. "You should not be here, my love."

Natalya shook her head, then smiled. "The *Zarnitsky* will not shoot us. Grigory will want the palace intact so he may ensconce himself on Helor's throne."

"His desires will not stop the gunners from aiming poorly—no offense intended to the Tacier's Airfleet." Malachy slipped his left arm from beneath his black woolen cloak and pointed toward the sky. "The attack run begins now."

Flying slowly west to east, the *Zarnitsky* swooped low. The first volley wreathed the ship in shot-mist. Below, twenty cannonballs blasted into the city's poor quarter. Daub-and-wattle buildings crumbled beneath the assault. Their collapse raised a huge cloud of dust and smoke, cutting off any chance for Natalya to detail the damage done, though piercing screams told her more than she wanted to know.

From the city a cloud of arrows and rocks rose up toward the airship, but none of them reached their mark. Defenders on the walls and on other rooftops shouted at the ship and cursed it, but the airship lumbered along seemingly heedless of their words and impotent attempts at retaliation.

That illusion vanished with the *Zarnitsky*'s second volley. It proved the city's attempts at defense had not gone unnoticed. Twenty cannons vomited grapeshot, spraying the rooftops and walls with deadly metal hail. Natalya saw some people just disappear in red explosions while others fell, writhing and screaming. Yet more numerous were the bodies of people killed instantly, lying twisted and broken and often in pieces. The morning's first cold light brightened the blood running from walls and trickling through gutters, but failed to add warmth to the corpses in the streets.

The *Zarnitsky* started a turn toward the north so it could bring the guns on the port side of the ship to bear on the city. "The *Zarnitsky*'s Captain wishes to have all his gunners practice, it seems."

Malachy nodded slowly, then cocked his head. "Wait, something is odd here."

Natalya bent her head forward, trying to hear what Malachy had heard, but she found nothing out of the ordinary. With the airship turning its bow north, the sound of the engines grew and echoed loudly back from Jebel Quirana. It had been that way every morning. *But this morning . . . What is that? Another noise? Another engine?*

Craning her neck, she saw the largest airship she had ever seen cruising past the top of Jebel Quirana and gliding forward like an eagle riding the wind. It seemed endless—she kept waiting for the ship's stern to appear, but by the time she saw enough of the ship to match the *Zarnitsky*'s size, only an open cargo hatchway had appeared. Despite its size, the airship came on swiftly, clearing the top of the mountain before the *Zarnitsky* could finish its maneuver.

With a belch of black smoke, the *Zarnitsky* aborted its turn and went to full speed in an attempt to elude the larger ship. The *Saint Michael*—Natalya read the gold letters on its stern—shifted its course slightly, bearing north by northeast, positioning itself to cut across the *Zarnitsky*'s stern at a ninety-degree angle. When the Ilbeorian ship had the *Zarnitsky* halfway between its own bow and stern, the *Saint Michael* loosed a broadside.

Gun-mist clouded the *Saint Michael*, but nothing hid the damage done to the *Zarnitsky*. The Stranan airship's stern crumpled inward as if it were a flimsy toy crushed in a child's grasp. The starboard aft wing tore away above the wing deck and slowly spun toward the ground. Pieces of shattered propellers whirled off into the air, followed by tumbling sections of the smokestacks. Trailing black smoke, the ship began to list badly to port and slowly drift toward the ground.

Then the boilers blew.

A gout of steam jetted from the *Zarnitsky*'s stern, boosting the ship forward and up at the bow. A secondary explosion spit out flaming debris. Smashed timbers and crippled bodies arced out onto the plain in front of the city. The ship shuddered with another explosion, spilling more men and equipment out. As the smoke cleared, Natalya could see that everything at the stern, from the keel up to the wing deck, had been reduced to jagged planking and burning wreckage.

The airship's stern swung down and smashed into the ground. The *Zarnitsky* snapped in half amidships, suddenly bristling along the break with splintered boards. The bow wing gained altitude for a second, as if trying to escape destruction, then it began to dip, too. The aft half of the ship rolled along the ground then tore itself apart, flinging wood and metal and men out along a hideous path gouged in the earth. In its wake the port bow wing caught on the ground, accelerating the rest of the ship's descent. The rest of the bow came around in an arc and plowed into the ground, disappearing in a cloud of dust that transformed itself into a pile of burning wood in a matter of seconds.

Joy and sadness warred in Natalya's head, driving her to her knees. As happy as she was that the barrages would end, every airman on the *Zarnitsky* had believed he was on a mission to punish Shukri Awan for his attempt on her life. "All of those men, they were loyal Stranans. They were here because of me. Three hundred, four hundred, their deaths are on my soul."

Malachy stood over her. "Their deaths are not your responsibility. Those men carried out orders that were clearly immoral in nature. They shot at innocents. They, and the man who gave the orders, are responsible for their deaths."

She looked up at him. "But they have left widows and orphans behind."

"And they made widows and orphans here." Malachy closed his eyes. "I am not without compassion, Natalya, but the choice to make war or refrain from making war is one that carries with it great responsibility. Those men did not die because of you. They died because of choices they made—they sowed the wind and reaped the whirlwind. All we can do now is to care for the people, both here and in Strana, who have been hurt by their action. And do what we can to prevent more deaths."

Natalya heard a thump followed by metallic clicks on the roof behind them. She turned and saw a tall man dressed all in silver. He unfastened the last restraining straps and a boxy metal apparatus with attached wings dropped from his back to the decking. He reached up to the corners of the jaw on his plain facemask and pried his helmet loose. He immediately snapped to attention.

"Colonel Kidd, Brother Robert Drury reporting."

Natalya saw Malachy turn slowly, surprise on his face and hesitation in his manner. "Brother Robert Drury—Robin—you are a long way from home."

Robin smiled. "Yes, sir. The same could be said of you, sir."

Malachy nodded. "Yes. How is it you happen to be here, Brother Robin?"

The ethyrine's dark eyes became narrow crescents. "Your message to Prince Trevelien got through. We came as quickly as we could, and burned a lot of coal in the process. We were lucky the *Zarnitsky* went down so easily because we only had one more volley."

Malachy grew distant and thoughtful. "Does the *Saint Michael* have enough coal to make it back to Dhilica?"

"Barely. Captain Hassett dropped his ethyrine company and two ethyrskiffs of supplies to lighten the load. It is heading back now."

Natalya looked up and could no longer see the Ilbeorian ship. "He is right, Malachy, the *Saint Michael* is gone."

She expected, by reminding Malachy she was present, to get an introduction, but Malachy seemed lost in thought. The distraction he had mentioned previously had increased with the time spent in Helor, eroding his ability to sleep or concentrate. *This place takes a toll on him that is terrible.*

Malachy frowned heavily. "How long was your trip up here?"

"Five and a half days at flank speed."

"Eleven days before they can return, then they will only have one shot."

"I believe so, sir."

Natalya reached out and touched Malachy's right shoulder. He twitched, then she felt the tension running through him. "Your allies are here, Malachy. The *Zarnitsky* is no more. Perhaps Grigory was on it, supervising the barrage."

"No, not possible. He's out there, with his Vandari."

Robin nodded. "We were able to see fires of a camp about two days' ride out."

"At Bir el Wuhush."

"Yes, sir, fifty miles or so north."

"Two days." Malachy shook his head, then another jolt ran through him and he sighed heavily. "Forgive me, I'm not thinking. Brother Robert, let me present Her Imperial Highness Tachotha Natalya Ohanscai. Tachotha Natalya, this is Brother Robert Drury, Ethyrine commander for the *Saint Michael*."

Natalya extended her hand to Robin and he kissed it most respectfully. "You are most welcome here, Brother Robert."

"The honor is mine." Straightening up, the tall man shook his head. "I would ask how you both came to be here, but from what Prince Trevelien has said, Colonel Kidd's participation would make even the most impossible explanation the truth."

Malachy took Natalya's hand in his own. "The Prince is fond of hyperbole."

Robin laughed. "He said you'd say that. He said I should tell you that he's also fond of not having died in Lescar. He's confident that with you in charge of the defense of Helor, the city will be able to hold out until the *Saint Michael* returns."

Natalya became aware of Malachy's drift back into thought when his grip on her hand slackened. "Eleven days. The city should be able to survive that long."

Malachy frowned again. "With fifty ethyrines and the supplies they brought? It will be very difficult, very costly."

The ethyrine looked surprised. "You have Helor's troops."

"Lost some already in a defense of Bir el Jamajim."

"Shukri Awan defended the well?"

"And lost his people, just as you and Uriah predicted."

"And as you rated us poorly for suggesting." Robin shook his head. "But now we'll have the siege. Surely Shukri Awan will be reasonable in defending his city?"

"You've yet to meet him, Brother Robin."

A loud voice rolled over the roof from the doorway leading below. Natalya turned and saw Shukri Awan stride through the doorway. He had two shamshirs bared and a look of ecstatic joy on his face. His robe matched the blue of the tiles in Jebel Quirana's archway. "This is a day ordained by the one true God to proclaim his favor toward me," he bellowed in Stranan.

Still speaking loudly, he turned his back to Natalya and pointed both curved swords out toward the burning pieces of airship. "Yes, it was wonderful. From this clear sky Atarax sent webs of lightning to bring our tormentor to disaster! And now He gives us silver angels with which to oppose our enemies. Need there be more proof that we are the Dost?"

"What is he saying?"

Malachy looked at Robin with a slack expression on his face. "He says, in essence, that he's as mad as a hatter and will be of no help at all in defending his realm from conquest."

— 65 —

> **North Helorian Plain**
> **Helansajar**
> **24 Majest 1687**

Charred wood crackled beneath the soles of his boots as Grigory Khrolic crouched amid the wreckage of the *Zarnitsky*. He'd not seen the ship go down, but the smoke from its wreckage had stained the sky and had been visible from Bir el Wuhush. His forward scouts had mirrored back a message laying blame for the airship's destruction on an Ilbeorian airship. From the description he knew it was one of the Ilbeorian dreadnoughts, which meant it had to be the *Saint Mikhail*.

The Ilbeorian intervention in the Helor affair proved Duke Arzlov's paranoia had not been as extreme as Grigory had once thought. *He was a visionary when fighting Fernandi and again when he decided to support my ascendancy. The Tacier proved himself foolish by making Vasily waste himself in Vzorin. For a dozen years we could have been doing what we will next year—sup in Ludstone amid the ruins of Wolfsgate.*

Grigory's scouts had reported new construction on the walls of Helor over the past three days. He had come forward himself to see what the Helorians were doing and decided these new constructions were further evidence of Ilbeorian interference. Steel armor plating fronted three sides of the hexagons built atop the walls. The central plate had a cross cut in it and, though dusk made for tricky shadows, when an internal armor plate rose up, Grigory thought he saw a barbed head on a shaft resting on a ballista assembly.

Vandari harpoons. He realized that any weapon created to be able to shoot through Vandari armor would also be able to pierce the mobile boilers that drove the pistons of the Hussars' mobile steam cannons. Without the cannons, breaching the walls would prove difficult. While the Vandari could easily top the walls, the harpoons could cost him men in such a direct assault.

He had anticipated a siege that had consisted of rolling his cannons up and shooting at the gates until they collapsed—nothing more. The harpoon stations gave him other targets and made him realize more caution had to be used in getting close to the walls. All it would cost him was time and, if his estimates of the *Saint Mikhail*'s resupply times were correct, he had more than a week before the ship arrived again.

Even its reappearance did not daunt him. Properly dispersed— as his men would have to be to cut off access to Helor—the Hussars would not be good targets for antipersonnel barrages from the Ilbeorian ship. Dug in, as he now realized they would need to be, the earth itself would protect them from Ilbeoria's wrath. They would wait the ship out and then renew their siege when it withdrew again.

Entrenchment was the key. As soon as possible he would bring his sappers up and get them digging trenches parallel to the walls. Once he had his cannons in position to cover any advancement, the sappers would dig in on a diagonal to a point twenty or thirty yards forward. There they would begin another parallel trench and the cannons would move forward. At longer ranges they would be able to shoot grape and spike with enough force to keep defenders down. In closer their cannonballs could bring the city's walls down.

Bringing the Vandari up to aid in the digging would permit things to progress swiftly enough to complete the job before the Ilbeorian ship could return.

His cavalry companies would patrol the perimeter, preventing anyone from slipping out of the city. He could not afford having Helorian irregulars operating in his rear area. The Hussars' cavalry were more than a match for anything they would meet on the plains, so he had no doubt as to their success. The trick with them was to vary their patrols so no one could count on where they would be at any one time, day or night.

Grigory Khrolic looked at the city at the base of Jebel Quirana and knew his plans would bring success. "Our dance may be longer than I desire, but you will be mine, soon enough."

**Gate of Princes
Helor, Helansajar
24 Majest 1687**

Robin smiled with pride as the workers settled the oversized crossbow on the carriage built at the center of the second harpoon platform. As they pounded home the wooden dowels that kept it in place on the platform pivot, Robin placed the drawing hooks on the woven metal bow wire and used the lever and pulleys to draw it back. The ropes tied to the hooks groaned and the wood creaked, but the steel bow bent without protest. Back at full draw, Robin settled the trigger lever in place and flipped the draw hooks off the bow wire.

He looked over at Natalya. "You can tell his nibs that this one is ready, too. If his smiths keep working, we can have two more of these up here tomorrow."

The Stranan princess translated his words and Shukri Awan nodded. "He is happy. He says this will be the Dost's harpoon station. He will defend the city from here."

"I hope he aims at what's out there and actually shoots, instead of waiting for divine intervention to kill Vandari." Robin bowed to Shukri Awan as the city's leader clanged his twin swords against each other. The ethyrine stared after him as the man began a quick march with his bodyguards back to his palace. "Long locks and dark, that one."

Natalya frowned. "I am not certain I know that expression."

"Sorry, I forget your training in Ilbeorian is formal." Robin grabbed a tuft of his own short hair. "In Ilbeoria, the less hair you have and the lighter the color, the wiser we suppose you to be. That being the case, the Alanim's probably got yards and yards of hair tucked up in that turban of his."

"I see your joke." Natalya's face darkened. "Malachy wears his hair long. Is he taken for a fool in Ilbeoria?"

"Colonel Kidd?" Robin shook his head. "His rank entitles him to shave most of his head, if he wishes. He doesn't for his own reasons. But even if his hair weren't white, there'd be no mistaking his intelligence. Someday, if I live that long, I might be halfway as smart as he is."

"But you are not a stupid man. You created these giant crossbows with these steel springs. This is not something a lackwit could do."

Robin patted the leaf spring that made up the bow. "No intelligence here. After the war I worked in a carriage factory. Leaf springs make the ride good. Back at Sandwycke, because of a comment made by someone arguing with Colonel Kidd, I started thinking about how one could make a crossbow that could hole your Vandari armor. This is it."

"You are too modest."

"Humility is a virtue." Even as he said that, he knew he was painfully close to the sin of pride. The pivot girdle on which the crossbow rested had been built so the aim point could be raised, lowered, or traversed. Likewise, with the help of a rope-and-pulley system, the whole platform could be moved to the right or left by a crew of men below the parapet walk. A foot lever raised the armor plate that closed the shooting cross and protected them from counter battery shots by Stranan cannons.

While he would have preferred a bank of steam cannons to repulse the Stranans, the gunner in him was proud of the lethal potential of his crossbows. "I think these will serve us well. With some spells to augment their performance, we'll have a few surprises for your Colonel Khrolic."

"Do you think we will be able to defeat the Hussars?"

"I don't know, Highness." Robin looked back toward the Alanim's palace. "Shukri Awan does, and that might count for something."

Natalya shrugged. "Since he was young he was told he is destined for greatness. It is said a falling star will mark his passing. Defeating Strana here will be part of his legend."

"It makes some sense, I suppose, if you believe in those sorts of omens." Robin depressed the foot lever, raising the armor plate, and looked out through the cross in the front of the platform. He saw campfires off in the distance. "And why is it he thinks he's the Dost reborn?"

"At the time of his birth it was foretold that he would be father to the Dost—or so Shukri Awan says." The Stranan Princess wore a disgusted expression. "He says he puzzled over that and, having gotten no sons on anyone, he decided a quote from the *Kitabna Ittikal* held the key to the prophecy. It says, roughly, 'The child is father to the man.' "

Robin whistled. "So he decided then that he was his own father?"

"*Da.* He then took Helor from the Khasts because they were holding it for the Dost against his return."

"And I have the feeling that he firmly believes webs of lightning brought the *Zarnitsky* down, not the *Saint Michael.*"

"He considers that a fact more solid than Jebel Quirana itself."

Robin felt a cold shiver run down his spine. The Helorian troops he had seen appeared to be ready to fight to defend their city, but they took a lot of their courage and determination from Shukri Awan. Demented though he might be, he had a charisma that Robin knew had to be enhanced by being able to hear his pronouncements in Estanuan, not translation. Shukri Awan's inherent unreliability bothered Robin because of its effects on the Helorian troops. If the Stranans decided to attack at dawn or dusk or some other time at variance with Awan's whims about fighting, the ethyrines might be the only people in place to defend the city, and that meant it would fall.

As if she read his mind, Natalya hugged her arms around herself. "Malachy thinks Grigory will attack at this time of day, at dusk."

"When the Alanim has decided to hide himself away from falling stars?" Robin thought for a moment, then nodded. "Colonel Kidd is probably right. Nothing we can do about that, though."

She smiled ruefully. "But Malachy keeps working at it."

"He has been a regular hermit." Robin glanced at the palace tower where Malachy worked. "His ideas about stockpiling sand to put out fires and organizing watches are good. Every day we get before the final assault is another day he can make this city more ready to resist."

"And is another day he goes without sleeping or eating."

Robin heard the concern in her voice and knew exactly what she meant. Kidd had not been eating very much or getting much rest as he studied and measured and planned based on the information he could glean from a sand table representation of the city. Oddly enough, when Robin had visited him, Kidd's most useful ideas had seemed to be afterthoughts or solutions offered as a spur-of-the-moment response to a question.

"I think, Highness, we should go to Colonel Kidd and convince him to eat and rest. He has to know he'll be no good to us if he can't think."

"I agree, Brother Robin."

"Good. I need to check one more thing, and then we can be off." Robin took one of the four-foot-long tapered iron quarrels and fitted it into the crossbow. "Connor, traverse this platform to due west."

"Aye, sir."

Robin steadied Natalya as the platform jerked and rotated to the right. "That's good." He raised the armor and sighted down the shaft at the first platform on the western side of the city gate.

"What are you doing?"

Robin smiled at her. "The Alanim says he'll be on *this* platform defending his city, yes?"

"Yes."

"Well, I'll be on *that* platform doing the same thing. These armor plates are strong, but I want to be certain they're strong *enough*." Robin pressed down on the trigger lever and with a bass vibrato the crossbow launched its shaft at the other platform forty feet away. With a resounding clang, the iron bolt dented the armor plate, then bounced away to clatter on the street below.

Natalya looked at him. "Satisfied?"

"Yes, but not enough to be stupid. I'll put stop blocks in so we can't aim at each other."

"But what if Vandari reach the other platform?"

Robin shook his head. "If that happens, there won't be enough time for me to regret my error, and Shukri Awan will be the least of my worries."

— 67 —

Alanim's Palace
Helor, Helansajar
24 Majest 1687

Malachy Kidd felt the wooden edges of the sand table dig into the palms of his hands through the thin gold tissue covering them, but he forced himself to ignore the pain. If he released his grip on the table, he would fall down. He wasn't certain he would be able to get back up if that happened, and though he felt an intense need for food and sleep, he couldn't let go.

If I let go, I lose contact with the table. He knew, from the moment he touched the sides of the table, that it was special. Never before had he touched a sand table that was contained within the confines of the space represented *on* the table. In theory the sand table's Helor contained the room he was in with its own sand table, and *that* sand-table-Helor had a room and so on. The sequence would carry on infinitely, just like the image trapped between two facing mirrors.

That recursion gave the sand table power and trapped within it part of the essence of the city itself. Malachy knew inanimate objects did not have souls in the spiritual sense, but no one doubted the connection between images and their reality. This was why so many Eilyphianists wore medallions representing saints or Eilyph himself. It seemed to Malachy, were he a sufficiently powerful magician, he could make a change in the face of the sand table and it would be reflected in the city.

Exhausted as he was, he knew that was a fantasy that would have to be explored by theoretical magicians back in Ludstone or elsewhere in the world. The possibility that he could do something like that was not what kept him hovering at the sand table's side. The recursion effect amplified the distraction he felt. When he touched the sand table, when he concentrated, he felt something. It was there, some clue or sign that would prove the solution to their problem, but it only flirted coyly with him. He could feel it, yet focus his thoughts as he might, he could not locate it.

This sensation both angered and frightened him. Its elusiveness had him on the brink of insanity. It lurked out there, like a half-forgotten word or an insect buzzing about just out of sight. In so dire a situation to have the solution elude him so steadily angered him.

The existence of the sensation was what had him scared. There were times when he thought he felt footfalls in the tiny corridors and streets of the model Helor. He knew that could not be true because it meant he was getting sensory information communicated through magick. For a priest like him this was impossible to do—unless one had succumbed to temptation and had demons supplying that sort of information. Yet he had not called upon demons—at least not consciously—and he *had* regained his sight when in proximity to the Dost.

Reconciling what he had been taught about magick with the experiences he had known while pursuing a mission for God was not easy. The simple answer to it all would be that God had not given him a mission—his visions had been inspired by demons and God had taken his eyes so he would see no more visions. The problem with that was that demons were supposed to tempt men away from the path of God and Malachy had not strayed. He still held to his beliefs.

Of course, all that has come up to this point could be luring me into a sense of security that sets me up for a grand fall. The conflict of dogma with the action demanded by any given situation was a harbinger of danger. If he dared second-guess teachings that had been handed down for centuries, claiming he had a direct route to God's Wisdom, he would be condemned as a heretic. *Many are the men and women who have fallen prey to such misconceptions.*

Just to be on the safe side of things he knew he should release his grip on the table and try to let all traces of sensations vanish from his memory. Since what he was feeling was something he couldn't account for within what he had been taught, rejecting it as demonic was easy. *Walk away now and you won't risk your soul, Malachy.*

At the same time as that course of action suggested itself another argument arose to keep him there. *God's Wisdom is said to be made apparent through a series of Revelations. What if this sensory ability is meant to reveal a new gift from God?* In rejecting it Malachy would be turning his back on something meant to enhance his ability to combat evil in the world. The reactionary response would be evil in and of itself. If he gave in and did not face the challenge of determining what was going on, he could easily be shrinking from the mission God had entrusted to him.

When the sensory information came to him, it did not feel wrong. Peculiar, yes, but it seemed he had been getting that same sort of information unconsciously since after he lost his eyes. Why was it benign when coming through the air to him, yet malignant when he used a sand table to discover it? There was no space to draw the line there, either both were evil or both were good. Assuming God had sent him on the mission—a mission he accepted well *after* developing the sensory magick to replace his eyes—the sensory magick had to be good.

But if the magick was evil, then the second vision could have been from Shaitan to lead me astray. The Devil could easily appropriate the imagery God used at Glogau to twist Malachy into acting for him. *But if the Devil is doing that, why has the mission become one of saving lives instead of triggering a war?*

Frustration made him snarl, but he transformed it into a laugh. "Dear God, You did not make things easy on Your Son, but He was

God-made-man. I'm nowhere near that level, so this is difficult. I will do what You ask of me, but more direction would be helpful. *Very* helpful."

He didn't hear the door behind him open. He *felt* the click of the latch through the table. That brought a smile to his face, but his inability to follow that sensation broke his joy. "Who is it?"

"Malachy, we have come to take you to food and rest."

"I appreciate it, really, but I can't leave now, Natalya." He nodded at the sand table. "I am very close to understanding—"

"You're very close to falling down, Colonel." Malachy felt a strong hand on his upper arm and it surprised him that Robin had gotten that close without his awareness. "I might be insubordinate, but I'll carry you if need be."

"Robin, I can't leave. I'm close, very close."

"Colonel, you're *too* close. A watched pot never boils. You need food and rest."

Is this my help, God?

Malachy nodded, knowing both of them were correct. He tightened his grip one last time and got enough of a flicker to know his solution was out there, then he let the table go. "You win."

Robin laughed gently. "We will win, provided you're sharp enough to direct us."

"Don't put all your hopes in me, Robin."

"He will not, Malachy." The Wolf-priest felt Natalya slip beneath his right arm to help hold him up. "He has Vandari-killing crossbows at the gate and his ethyrines are training others to fight. We have the tools, we just need an artisan to use them."

"I will do my best." Malachy's hands slipped from the table and he sagged between his friends. "God willing, I will do my best."

— 68 —

Dost's Camp
Southeast of Helor
Helansajar
27 Majest 1687

Uriah had a bad feeling as he threw open the flap of the tent he shared with Turikana and found her running a whetstone over the curved edge of her shamshir. Her sharpening the sword did not surprise him—she did that with the same unconscious ease his mother had exhibited when knitting. "What are you doing here? You always take the first watch."

Turikana shrugged uncomfortably. "It is the will of the Dost."

"Why is it that every question I ask you gets the same answer?"

She started to use her standard reply, then stopped. "There are many things which only his will can explain. This is one of them."

Uriah fished the gold globe from the pouch on his belt. "And this is another. I have played with it and studied it. I can manipulate it a bit, but I still don't understand it. What am I supposed to do with it?"

Turikana held her sword aloft and watched the golden glow from the oil lamps slide along the razored edge. "I do not know, Uriah. My brother cloaks himself in mystery because it is deemed necessary. Things are unfolding according to a plan set down in the *Kitabna Ittikal*. I believe he knows or fears certain events, but does not offer warnings in an effort to let things unfold naturally."

Her comment reminded Uriah of various conversations with the Dost. "Your brother *is* something of a fatalist."

"I think he believes he is practical."

Uriah caught an undercurrent of disbelief in her words. Rubbing his hands together, he rolled the globe into a short cylinder, then concentrated to make it retain its shape. "The Dost must have been very different as a child."

She shook her head. "I do not know. I met him ten years ago. I was lost in a *samun*. I had drunk alcohol and wandered away from the caravan with which I was traveling. The wind came up. Sand and rocks flew within it and would have killed me except for Nimchin Dost. His shape grew into that of a huge turtle and covered me. He adopted me as a sister and I have been trained with the others since that time."

"I've seen you use a sword. You are very good."

"I worked very hard to be good." She pointed to the gold baton in his hands. "Had I your mental quickness, or if you had my stubbornness, both of us could be great."

Uriah shrugged and let the baton melt back into a globe. "Manipulating metal—one more useless skill."

"Not useless in and of itself, but unrealized by you." Turikana shook her head. "We will all need to be skilled. The Storm Blows from the North."

"What does that mean?" The Ilbeorian knew she had not chosen those words by chance. "Strana is invading Helansajar?"

"Now, later, it does not matter." She laid her sword down on the pillows beside her and pulled her knees to her chest with her arms. "In your Scriptures you have a description of the end of the world, yes?"

"Revelations." Uriah tried to fashion the globe into a set of scales, but gave up when the chains proved difficult. "Eilyph returns and the good are separated from the evil in a huge war."

"For us the world ends in a Storm that Blows from the North. This storm does not have the intelligence of your Eilyph. It chooses the strong and slays the weak."

"An invasion from Strana would do that." Uriah heard thunder rumbling in the distance. It sounded from the north and that raised the hair on the back of his neck. "The Dost sees this storm as another sign pointing to his return?"

"Yes. And perhaps he does see it as a Stranan invasion." Her hand fell to the hilt of her sword. "That is why he told me not to set out pickets."

"No sentries?" Uriah's blood ran cold as the thunder sounded louder. "Saints help us, that's not *thunder*, those are horses! Riders! We're under attack."

Turikana sprang to her feet and brandished her sword. "Get to the Dost, now. Help him."

Uriah almost denied her request, but something in the lifelessness of the gold ball in his hands pulsed urgency through him. He followed her out of the tent just as the lead rider of the Stranan cavalry squad entered the valley at the far end. While Turikana shouted orders to her sisters, Uriah sprinted to the Dost's tent and burst in.

"Stranan cavalry!"

His jaw dropped open as he saw the Dost struggling with the blanket that had been laid over him. Above and behind Nimchin the golden armor he wore stood stiff and lifeless, its chest a dark hollow, its face gone. At its feet, nestled in the pillows like an infant, lay Nimchin Dost. The blue most Durranians had around their eyes spread across his cheeks and up over his forehead. The sharp points of his ears rose almost to the crown of his head. While slightly alien, his strong features made him a most handsome man. The piercing nature of his coppery eyes heightened his majesty.

His body mocked his power. He had no arms or legs to speak of, just hands and feet connected at his shoulders and hips respectively. Lying there, naked and helpless, fighting off the last of sleep, the Dost clearly could do nothing to save himself. The Storm that Blows from the North had come and would carry him away as easily as a *samun* would drive before it grains of sand.

No! Uriah snatched the Dost up and ran from the tent. At the north end of the valley Turikana had raised a defense, but horsemen poured around her tiny knot of defenders and rode on. Their sabers slashed guy lines, withering tents and trapping people within them. Two riders spotted Uriah and the Dost and spurred their horses deeper into the camp.

"Run, Uriah." The Dost's voice, freed of the metallic tones that had filled it before, carried fatigue with it. "Leave me to my fate. Run. Save yourself."

"No!" Shifting the Dost around to his left arm, Uriah brought his right arm back. "We have to do something to save the others."

Whipping his arm forward, he threw the gold globe. It appeared to be on target to hit the rider on the right, but it veered sharply at the last. As it did so the sphere flattened out and stretched until its profile became a thin gold line. He saw the horses gallop on through it even though it should have smacked them sharply on the snout. They passed beyond the point where it hung in the air, drawing closer, their swords aimed for sweeping cuts.

Uriah knew he and the Dost were dead.

Then the horses and riders began to fall apart. Where the line had passed through them they went to pieces. Blood spurted from the horses' severed necks. The beasts stumbled forward, but the lower half of their riders stayed firmly in the saddle. Their torsos fell backward until they hit the horses' rumps, then were catapulted through the air to land with wet thumps behind Uriah.

Uriah dashed to the left to stay clear of the tumbling, thrashing bodies. "I did that?"

"*We* did that." The Dost clutched at Uriah's shoulder with his right hand. "Hold me up. Up above your head. You are right. We have to save them."

The Ilbeorian lifted Nimchin up above his own head. He grasped the man's feet and thrust him as high up in the air as he could. Though lacking arms and legs, the Dost weighed enough for Uriah's arms to immediately begin to protest. Uriah locked his elbows in response and snarled defiantly at the pain.

Above him the Dost began chanting in a tongue Uriah had never heard before. The words hissed in serpentine tones and cracked like thunder, at once melodious and yet hard-edged. Something about it sounded deliciously familiar. Even from the first syllable Uriah realized this was a language meant to harness and shape power.

And power it did command. Uriah felt himself rooted to the earth, linking it and the Dost. Energy surged up through him. The hair on his head stood out and resisted the teasing buffets of the rising wind. Above them, illuminated by the light of the nearly full moon, dark clouds began to gather with unnatural speed. Rocks and swords in the valley began to glow with a purple light.

Off in the distance, high in the mountains, lightning flashed. Beneath the clouds Uriah saw dark sheets of rain falling. With each passing heartbeat lightning struck again and again, getting closer and closer to where they stood. The storms ate up miles in seconds, and the full fury of the storm broke over the Dost's camp before any of the combatants had any chance of taking cover.

Hail the size of eyeballs battered Uriah like grapeshot. Horses reared up, riders spilled from saddles as lightning seared the air and the stink of ozone filled the valley. Then the rain came in waves. The first icy curtain drenched Uriah thoroughly and a second sank cold bone deep into him. Lightning marched down the valley toward him and the Dost, prickling his flesh and half blinding him.

Uriah could see little in the midst of the deluge. He heard screams and the occasional skirl of steel on steel, but he could not tell who lived and who died. Argent flares silhouetted combatants, but rain-soaked figures seen only as shadows gave him no clue to their identities. He hoped Turikana yet stood unharmed.

Fear for the Dost's kin spread the storm's chill to his soul.

Onward the lightning came. It blasted past the battle, igniting tents and bursting rocks. *It's coming too close!* Uriah realized it would sweep over them and tried to run. His feet refused to move. His arms would not unlock. He looked up and saw the Dost raise his hands toward the heavens.

Then the bolt hit. Pain turned Uriah inside out. He felt on fire, but it was a *cold* fire that consumed him. The lightning seemed to split and split into more and more forks, dividing and dividing until every square inch of his body was pierced by its own individual needle. Brilliant light filled his eyes, then shadow rushed in to blind him.

Uriah felt himself falling but never felt himself hit the ground.

— 69 —

Robin Drury surrendered his position at the sand table to Malachy Kidd. "As you can see, Colonel, the Stranans are starting on their third trench. They have rigged up mantlets with wood salvaged from the *Zarnitsky*'s wreckage. That's let them bring their Vandari even closer to help with the digging."

Kidd planted his golden hands on the two darkened spots on either side of the table's corner. He closed his eyes, then nodded. "Yes." The word hissed from his mouth, half confirmation and half sigh. "By tomorrow afternoon they should be ready to proceed."

"You still assume a twilight attack?" Robin moved around to the other side of the table. "You expect Khrolic to ask his troops to operate in darkness?"

Kidd's eyes opened and locked on him. "You do not?"

"You know Khrolic better than I do." Robin shrugged, feeling uneasy beneath Kidd's silver stare. "I would not think him that shrewd. Asking men to fight at night is not easy."

"Neither is defending in the dark." Kidd nodded and leaned in over the table. "Grigory will use anything he can to make things go better for his troops. Lower light will hamper your ballistae more than it will his Vandari. Also the Helansajarans tend to be uneasy about fighting at night. If Shukri Awan retires for the night, we are in trouble. The troops here are stalwart, but if their leader runs, they may not be inclined to remain in the battle."

The ethyrine nodded as thunder rumbled distantly. He glanced at the window. "That's odd. I would have thought it was going to be clear tonight."

The blind man looked out beyond the tiny simulacrum of the city. "It comes from the north?"

Robin glanced out the window again. "Yes, sir. And it's moving rapidly, too. *Very* rapidly."

"The Storm that Blows from the North."

"What?"

"Ataraxians believe the world will end in a storm that blows from the north. It's similar to our apocalypse, but more elemental and less benign." Kidd's body twitched involuntarily. "This is not a good omen."

"The local troops will be spooked." Thunder exploded out on the plains and lightning illuminated the Stranan trenches. Robin turned to comment about how lucky it was for the Stranans to have to endure the storm, but before he could he distinctly heard the thunder echo from the sand table. The whole expanse of it glowed green and the corrupt color bled up to cover Kidd.

Lightning struck outside again and again. On the sand table little puffs of smoke rose from invisible strikes, leaving blackened droplets of molten glass behind. "Colonel, what's happening?"

"He's close, it's all close."

"What's close?"

Ribbons of smoke curled up in front of Kidd. "The Dost, the end of everything, it's close." Kidd mumbled on, Ilbeorian words getting mixed with other sounds Robin could not place. "The end is here!"

"Get away from the table." Buildings in the model Helor exploded as invisible lightning hit them. The flashes from outside became brighter and the thunder deafening. "Let the table go."

"No!" Green light suffused Malachy's silver eyes. "I'm close to finding the key. It's here, now, I know it!"

"Get away!"

"No!"

Feeling the hair rise on the back of his neck, Robin grabbed the edge of the table and vaulted over it. He caught Kidd in the chest with both feet, then released his grip and tumbled over Kidd's falling body. Robin let his momentum carry him as deep into the room as he could get, scattering chairs and overturning tables. He stopped when he slammed his back into the room's south wall, then he looked up.

A dazzling lightning rope curled in through the open window and struck the tower's twin on the sand table. The wooden box exploded, spraying flaming splinters throughout the room. The sand itself followed, smothering most of the fire. Beneath where the lightning had hit a blackened globule of glass bubbled and smoked.

His ears ringing fiercely, Robin scrambled across the floor to where Kidd lay on his face. The ethyrine rolled him over and beat out the smoldering patches on the Colonel's clothes. Other than a trickle of blood from his nose, Kidd seemed unhurt. He was breathing without difficulty, but remained unconscious. Robin felt the back of the man's head to see if he had hit it when he fell, but he found no lumps.

Robin laid him down again and snuffed the one bit of burning debris that remained. He rubbed a hand over the back of his neck. "Lightning ravaging Helor like that is a bad omen, indeed. The locals will assume nature is Strana's ally. Helor's troops will be nervous and the best strategist in this hemisphere is unconscious.

"Might as well follow his lead and get some sleep." Bending down, he hefted Malachy over his shoulder and straightened up again. "If the Stranans do come tomorrow, absent a miracle, the next sleep I get will be death and that prospect pleases me not at all."

— 70 —

**Within Jebel Quirana
Helansajar
27 Majest 1687**

It occurred to Uriah, as he awoke in dry darkness, that he finally knew what it felt like to be straw on the threshing-room floor. Every fiber of his being hurt worse than it had after his beating in Dhilica. Not ache, not sting, *hurt*. It was as if every bone in his body had been pounded into little bits and they all grated on each other when he even thought about moving.

"The pain will pass, Uriah."

It took him a moment to recognize the Dost's voice. The chamber in which Uriah lay gave the Dost back a hint of the echo, but without the metallic ringing his voice did not sound quite right. Uriah tried to roll up on an elbow, but agony defeated that attempt rather quickly. He sighed. "I wish I was dead."

"I have been, my friend; you would not like it."

"How can you make jokes after that?"

The Dost laughed lightly. "You have more body to hurt, my friend."

Uriah summoned all his strength and shifted his position about an inch to face the sound of the Dost's voice. "Why didn't the lightning kill us?"

"We were creating the storm through a Durranian spell. The lightning, when it hit us, would have killed us, but I was able to shunt it into another magickal process. I brought us here, inside Jebel Quirana."

"Where?"

"We are in a chamber deep in the mountain, almost all the way to Helor. I did not plan to get here this way, but the opportunity presented itself."

Uriah winced and slowly turned onto his side. "Your armor was left behind."

"It will find us."

"How?"

"I don't really know how. I just know it will."

"I don't understand."

"What? About the armor or about me?"

Uriah blushed. "Both. You."

Silence pressed down in the darkness until the Dost's soft voice began to rise. "I was born this way—no arms, no legs. I know when I was first here, so very long ago, I was not this way—I was like you, able-bodied. This time, though, something went wrong. My mother may have drunk *gulholla* when she carried me, or sinned somehow or suffered in some other way. My father, because he believed he was destined to be father to the Dost, had secreted my mother away, here, in Jebel Quirana."

"But that is taboo."

"And that is perhaps the sin for which I have paid with my arms and legs. I do not know." The Dost's voice fell silent for a moment. "I was born in Jebel Quirana. My father served as midwife and saw I was a monster. He rode off into the night with me and left me out in the desert to die. He knew no imperfect creature could possibly be the Dost—the *Kitabna Ittikal* confirms this. He meant for me to perish alone and abandoned me before he returned to Helor."

"You have said you are the Dost, but if you are imperfect, how can that be?"

"How can I know what God has planned for me? Do you know God's plan for you?"

"No." Uriah forced himself into a sitting position and accepted the pain as punishment for his stupidity. "How did you survive?"

"The armor found me. Just as my soul had a link with my body, so too was my armor of old bound to me. It sensed my presence and my need. It cut a portion of itself out and came to me. It found me in the desert and took me into itself. It sustained me and fed me memories of who I had been. Keerana Dost's memories instructed me in survival and magick. I became my own father and learned what it was to be the Dost."

"Your sisters . . ."

"Not blood, adopted. Like me they are all desert-kill saved from death. There were times when I just cleared my mind and *sought*. The armor brought them to me and I took them to Dayi Marayir to train. They are to inhabit Ausdari armor and help us defend the city against the Strananss."

"But we left them behind."

"They will find us."

"Are you sure?"

"Those who were meant to survive the storm will be here."

Uriah shook his head. "I wish I could be as certain of things as you are."

"I am certain of nothing, Uriah."

"You know exactly how things will happen."

"I do not . . ." The Dost's voice trailed off for a moment. "Tonight, lying there in my tent, I was ready to die. I am imperfect. I doubted my identity as the Dost and I waited for a sign to show me I was meant to inherit the title I claimed. You were my sign."

"How could you doubt? You are so powerful. You brought up the storm."

"With your help."

"I did nothing."

"Except save me." The Dost fell silent for a moment, then sighed. "When I was here as Keerana, I was much like you. I was stubborn and brash. Things came to me easily so I did not see the efforts others had to put into things. I found it easy to destroy because I did not understand what it was to build."

Uriah felt a cold chill course down his spine. *Does that describe me?*

"I think, perhaps, your God or Atarax or blind fate trapped me in this body so I would understand the difficulties and trials others faced. It provides me another sign of the direction into which I must channel the gifts I have been given and the power I will assume."

"That is a good thing." *And a lesson I should learn.* "So what is our next step?"

"We rest now. Earlier, before I abandoned my armor, I was able to determine that Rafiq and his people are in position. There are fewer than a thousand of them, but they will suffice. When my sisters arrive, we will push on deeper into Jebel Quirana. At the end of our journey our true ordeal will begin."

"What happens then?"

"I do not know for certain, but I can tell you this: life as we know it will never again be the same."

— 71 —

Helor, Helansajar
28 Majest 1687

Standing in Ram Twenty-seven's shadow, Grigory Khrolic returned Lieutenant Vorobiga's salute. "You have a report for me, Anatoly?"

"*Da.* The encampment our cavalry patrol hit was completely destroyed. They went back after the lightning storm and found nothing but the dead. It was of no consequence."

"But stopping refugees from fleeing Helor is good, Lieutenant. It establishes some order for our regime." Grigory nodded solemnly. "Our cannons are ready for the next phase of the operation?"

"*Da.* Our cannons are in place to begin working on the walls and gate. We have brought the battleboilers up to drive them and have shielded them with mantlets. They've begun to fire them. They should be ready soon. The gunners tell me they could probably destroy the crossbow batteries on the wall if you wish for them to try."

"*Nyet.* The mantlets seem proof against their bolts. Keep six cannon using grapeshot and spike shot to keep the defenders behind their armor. Have the rest concentrate on the gates."

"Yes, sir." The junior officer nodded. "When shall we begin?"

Grigory looked down at his Ram's shadow. "Patience, Anatoly." Stepping beyond the shadow, Grigory scratched a line in the dirt with his heel. "When this shadow gets here, it will be soon enough. Shukri Awan will fight for an hour or two, then his city will be ours."

"Princess, I do not want to argue with you. You cannot be here." Robin Drury shook his head adamantly. "Their battleboilers are smoking real good. We have a couple of hours of daylight left. The attack is coming now."

Natalya's nostrils flared. "You would allow Malachy to be here?"

"Yes, but—"

"But he is blind." She grabbed one of the iron quarrels from the rack on the interior of the battery's armored facing. "I am not. I can help."

"It's not the same thing."

"Brother Robin, if you would take his help, then I am here to help in his stead."

Robin frowned. "He's still sleeping?"

Natalya nodded. "I tried to rouse him but I cannot."

"He must have caught more of that lightning than I thought." Robin ran a hand down over his face. "If you load for me, you have to get clear when I tell you to. If you don't, you could lose a hand."

"I understand."

"You realize you are shooting at your own people."

Natalya raised her head and her eyes burned brightly. "The *Zarnitsky* killed people in this city. The Hussars and Vandari will kill more of them. I came here with Malachy to forestall the attack, but that was not possible. Now I must help defend against it."

The steel in her voice made Robin glad she was fighting with him and not against him. He looked over at another ethyrine crouched in the battery's shadow. "Nugent, boiler reports."

"One and four are still being coaled up. Two and three are having belts run out to the cannons."

"Good." Robin looked down below at where Connor and four other ethyrines stood next to a Helorian and an ancient trebuchet. "Ready for ranging shot."

"Aye, sir."

Robin looked at Natalya. "Load."

"Da."

"Clear."

She raised both her hands. *"Da."*

"Shield up."

Nugent hit the pedal. "Clear."

Robin sighted down the quarrel at the mantlets covering one of the boilers. He hit the trigger lever with the heel of his hand. With a deep *thwang* the ballista shot the iron shaft. The bolt traveled on a straight course, but fell short by a third again the distance it traveled.

Robin turned and crouched down on the edge of the platform. "Range it at four hundred yards."

Connor translated the request for the Helorian and the man looked at the arm of the trebuchet. The man raised his hand, then started moving it downward, all the while yelling *"Wati, wati, wati!"* The ethyrines hauled on a windlass, cranking the arm of the trebuchet lower and lower. When it came close to touching the ground, the Helorian clapped his hands.

Connor fitted a trigger hook through the leash on the end of the trebuchet's arm. His men laid out the sling, then rolled a three-hundred-pound rock into it. The sling closed over the top and fastened to the trebuchet's arm. The ethyrines stood back away from the rock and shouted, "Clear."

Connor grabbed the trigger hook's lanyard and gave it a yank.

The trebuchet consisted of a six-ton counterbalance on the shorter end of the arm, and a framework to uphold the bar on which the arm pivoted. The three-hundred-pound stone—which had been pried from the foundation of a ruined building—accelerated as the counterweight plunged earthward and the long half of the arm whipped up toward the sky. Just past the apex, one end of the sling slipped free of its hook and the stone began a long, ungainly flight through the air.

Simple mechanical siege machines were not known for their accuracy for a number of reasons. Primary among them was the fact that the projectiles, which varied in size, shape, and weight, flew in a high, arching trajectory toward their target. This gave the missile a lot of chances to miss its target, long or short, so hitting the same spot twice was not easy to do.

Unfortunately for the Hussars their advancement had elicited only weak shots from the ballistae mounted on the walls. Thinking themselves outside the effective range of the crossbows, they made no attempt to protect their battleboilers beyond assembling and positioning mantlets. In digging their trenches, they created very basic and easily recognizable boiler and cannon emplacements, giving the ethyrines all the time in the world to spot and aim for them.

The rock landed short of its target by twenty feet, but this proved particularly lucky for the Ilbeorians. The rock landed smack on top of the center cannon in the formation around battleboiler three. It smashed the cannon flat to the ground, crushing the carriage and spinning the freed wheels off across the plain. Then, because the bulk of the gun prevented the rock from plowing into the ground, the stone bounced farther out and went into a tumbling roll, scattering mantlets like playing cards and slamming into the front of battleboiler three.

The purpose of a boiler was to create pressure which then could be transferred by pistons and belts to the cannons to charge them up. When the rock hit the boiler, it decreased the volume of the boiler itself, immediately raising the pressure inside the boiler to well above the tolerances intended by the engineers who created it.

Rivets holding steel plates in place sprayed outward, killing half the boiler crew instantly.

Without rivets to hold it together, the boiler exploded. Metal plates sliced through the air—and the men—as a steamy mushroom cloud rose into the sky. The expanding gas cast the remaining mantlets about, shattering them and sowing them all around the Stranan position. Boiling water gushed out, flooding the gunnery emplacement and sending screaming men running.

Before Robin or the ethyrines could even begin to cheer their success, the other three cannon batteries started shooting. Grapeshot rattled off the battery's plating and ricocheted from the wall's merlons. The Gate of Princes creaked and groaned under the impact of a half dozen cannonballs, but it held.

Nugent glanced up over the edge of the wall, then ducked back down. "One of the Rams is coming up, zero degrees."

Robin hooked the retractors on the bow wire and cranked it back into place. He set the trigger lever. "Load."

"Da."

Robin flicked the hooks free. "Clear."

"Da."

"Shield up."

Nugent again stomped on the pedal to raise the shield. "Clear."

"Now we show them a trick." Robin invoked a spell. A bluish glow suffused the ballista. He followed the movement of the Vandari armor, tracking left to right. As the Ram began to slow, Robin hit the trigger lever.

This iron bolt shot out decidedly faster than the first one. The trajectory remained flat. The bolt looked like a black dot to Robin, a black dot centered on the Ram's flank. At the last second the man inside the Ram appeared to have seen something out of the corner of his eye because the Ram turned away, but that only made the target bigger, not smaller.

The bolt hit the Ram low in the back and a bit right of center. The giant armored figure convulsed, then its limbs froze in place. It pitched forward on its face, but remained up slightly at the right side, where the protruding head of the bolt held it off the ground.

More grapeshot clattered against the battery's armor. On the other side of the gate Shukri Awan arced a long shot out at the Stranan lines, but it failed to hit or damage anything.

Robin dropped to his knees as the world swam around him. *That took more out of me than I expected, or is it that I'm just more tired than I should be?*

Natalya squatted next to him. "Are you well?"

"I will be. That spell increased the power of the bow, giving it greater range. It was originally designed for use by ethyrines using normal crossbows. Applying it on a larger bow shooting a heavier projectile really drained me." *One more shot like that and I'm through.*

Natalya rested her hands on his shoulders. "You will recover?"

"I have to. It's a tough spell to use." He smiled. "Colonel Kidd could probably manage it a half dozen times, if he could see."

"Shall I get him?"

Robin shook his head. "Not going to matter. Khrolic has to know he has to come now. We've showed him he's more vulnerable than he thought he was. We killed one of his boilers and cannons and we killed one of his Vandari. Attrition will favor us. We'll kill half a dozen Vandari before they make the walls, then they're into the city. They won't have their cannons then, and fighting in a city will be tough. It would be nice to have the Colonel here, but a blind man isn't going to be able to help us now. He did his bit in the planning."

"But he didn't think it was enough."

"We better hope he was wrong."

The distant sound of an explosion brought Malachy Kidd to full consciousness. Throwing back the blanket, he swung his bare feet out of bed. Wearing only a cotton nightshirt, he stood and stumbled toward the window in the northern wall of his tower room. Off balance, he fell heavily against the palace's stone wall and caught himself on his hands.

The moment his hands touched the stone he felt the same sensation he'd had in touching the sand table, only stronger. *The solution is here, I can feel it.*

He heard a noise behind him and turned toward it. In the blackness he caught a fleeting glimpse of a golden wolf with silver eyes darting out where the door to his room should have been. The vision reminded him of the image of the wolf that had led him against the Lescari *Revisor Carmí* in Glogau.

Saint Martin's Sign!

Without thinking, without doubting, he pushed off the wall and ran across the floor to the doorway. He slammed hard into the closed door, and rebounded from it, landing on his backside on the floor. He shook his head, then laughed, stood and jerked the door open. *A miracle may show me where I need to be, but it's not going to get me there. That's my job.* Still chuckling, with his left hand held before

him and his right hand trailing along the wall, Malachy ran through
the palace and leaped down whole flights of stairs from one landing
to the next.

He felt strange and more alive than he could remember feeling
before. Through his fingertips he pulled in information about his
surroundings. In jumping from one point to another he knew he was
employing Aeromancer magick, but was doing it with precision he
had never known before. Landing, he would crouch and touch his
hands to the stone, then leap again and begin running down new
corridors. As he did so the sense that he was closing in on his target grew.

He reached ground level and found yet another passage taking
him down further beneath the level of the city. At the far edge of one
landing he bumped up against an iron-bar door. He pressed his hand
against the lock and the gold metal coating his palm flowed into it,
then the lock fell to the skeleton-key spell he had learned for his
mission in Lescar. Two more times he had to open similar doors on
landings, and he found he didn't even have to wait for the gold to enter the lock, the spell just opened them with a touch.

Finally he found himself on the threshold of a large room.

Malachy knew it was large because he could sense his goal being close but not too close. He started walking forward and could
feel obstructions in his path. He picked his way through a rat's warren of things. With every twist and every turn he knew he was getting closer and closer until his hands itched beneath their gold flesh.

So distracting was the sensation in his hands, he nearly tripped
going up the steps at the room's far end. Reaching out with his
hands, he touched tile and could feel its chill against his fingertips. *I
can also feel its color. It's blue.* As he shifted his hands around, feeling the edges of the archway that contained the tile, the temperature
rose beneath his hands. He noticed the heat became almost painful
at the edges of the arch, but shifted to cool and soothing toward the
middle. His hands felt best in the center when thumbs and fore-
fingers were pressed together to form a triangle.

Malachy pushed and nothing happened. He knew his goal, the
solution to saving Helor, lay on the other side of the wall, but he
could not get through. *If this were a door, not a wall . . .* He let his
head slump forward and bump against the tile. "I can't feel any
weight of the building above on this tiled wall, so it's supporting
nothing. It is meant to move."

He invoked his skeleton-key spell and heard a click. He
pushed—pushed hard—and the door disguised as a section of wall
slid back about two feet. Malachy heard another click and the wall

held in place. Shuffling to his right, he squeezed through the opening and found himself in what felt like a narrow corridor.

He started off along it and felt a plate in the floor shift slightly. Behind him the door crashed heavily shut. Concern that he might be trapped forever beneath the city of Helor flashed through him for a second, then vanished. He moved on deeper, his feet moving of their own accord. Though he walked through a level corridor and entered a chamber with a level floor, it felt to him as if he were walking downhill and he had to restrain himself from breaking into a run.

Off in the distance he saw—actually *saw*—a golden speck. His heart began to pound. As he got closer, it grew and took the shape of Saint Martin's Sign, the golden wolf he had seen in his chamber above. Yet again it increased in size until it became a giant gold Wolf with silver eyes in which he saw his own reflection.

Malachy stopped three feet from the apparition's thrusting muzzle. As he did so, the gold flesh on his hands peeled off and fell to the floor. He could not see the twin gold spheres, but through his feet he could feel them rolling off further into the cavern. He reached a bare hand out and touched the Wolf's nose.

With a hiss the head rose up and exposed the interior of the metal creature.

Malachy jumped back and sucked on his fingers. When he touched it the Wolf felt as cold as a corpse, yet he could not say it was dead. Nor was it alive. He had sensed something there, a *presence*, for which neither he nor his theology could account. He would have called it a ghost, but he thought of them as negative creatures, but this wasn't negative.

It is almost as if what I felt was this thing's potential.

"That is exactly what you detected, Wolf-priest," a voice echoed through the cavern. "Now it is up to you to decide if this potential is to be for good or evil."

— 72 —

Helor, Helansajar
28 Majest 1687

As the dying day slowly bled scarlet into the sky, Rafiq Khast led his riders up to the plains to the west of Helor. Cresting a rise, he was surprised to see the Stranan lines so close. With an upraised hand he signaled a halt.

Below him the Strananas had arrayed themselves in a semicircle around Helor approximately two thousand yards away. Thin smoke rose from the ashes that marked what had been mantlets. In the center of their line cavalry companies formed up behind two dozen or more giant metal Rams. Rafiq had never seen their like before, but he had heard enough stories to easily identify them as Vandari.

Amjad Nasra, a Warlord from the Tomri tribe, rode up beside Rafiq. "Wahhh! We cannot fight metal demons. To fight them is suicide."

"We will fight them and their allies. And we shall win." Rafiq shook his head.

"You are more confident than I would be in your place, with the moon about to rise."

Rafiq turned and looked at Amjad. "You do not understand, do you? We are fighting for the Dost. He has given me a wife. He has told me I will have sons to carry on my line. I am his brother and I shall not fail him."

"All that will not save you from death."

"Death does not matter now that the Dost has returned." Rafiq reined his horse around and signaled his men to form up in companies of one hundred. He placed the Khast company in the center, with the other six split evenly to make up the two wings of his formation. He drew his shamshir and the Helansajarans did likewise.

Bringing his horse back around to face the battlefield, he smiled at Amjad. "The Dost says I will die when I choose. I do not choose to die today."

"You are blessed, Rafiq." Amjad allowed himself a nervous laugh. "When do we attack?"

Rafiq fingered the amulet at the base of his throat. "Soon, I think. We will get the signal soon."

Including the Dost and himself, Uriah saw that only thirteen of the people who had traveled from Dayi Marayir had survived the assault and storm to find their way to the heart of the mountain. He did not include the gold armor in that tally because the moment it arrived it engulfed the Dost. Turikana had made it and Uriah greeted her with a hug.

The Dost took the assembled party deeper into Jebel Quirana. They marched on in silence, following in the light of the golden aura that glowed around the Dost. Though the mountain was supposed to house the Dost's tomb, and the others seemed to be silent out of reverence for that fact, Uriah did not find the place frightening. Though he did not know what he would face within Jebel Quirana, he had a sense he could overcome any challenge that came his way.

It also struck him as odd that the Dost and his party had the same number as Eilyph and his company of followers. *I wonder if one of us is a traitor, like Nemicus.*

The Dost looked back at him. "My Nemicus is ahead of me, not behind me. He tried to kill me once, he will try again."

"You know my thoughts?"

"If they concern me."

The Dost faced forward again and brought them into a square chamber. Opposite the doorway Uriah saw a steel panel set flush in the opposite wall. Rivets ran around the perimeter, suggesting to Uriah that the panel was more than a single sheet of steel and that it hid some sort of mechanism inside. What surprised him was that the panel clearly had been worked by skilled artisans, yet no one in Estanu possessed such metalworking ability.

"This is of Durranian manufacture?"

"My brother created the door and he was quite good." The Dost smiled slowly. "Into the floor of this chamber he put a pressure plate that closed the door when it was stepped upon. When my armor came out in search of me, it sealed the room beyond."

"Interesting." Uriah folded his arms. "So open it."

"I cannot."

"What?"

"Vertil made this door. It contains a locking mechanism." The Dost shrugged. "It requires magick to open it, but I do not possess a suitable spell."

"Then how are we going to get in there?"

"Do you not believe your God moves in mysterious ways?"

Uriah nodded. "Would you have me pray for intercession?" *At least that would explain why I am here.*

"While effective, I think that would be premature." The Dost closed his eyes and a soft click sounded from the panel. The door retracted into the stone cavity above. In the doorway lay two golden gloves that melted and rolled together into a ball, then sprang up into the air and splashed into the Dost's chest.

Uriah looked at him. "Was that my globe?"

"No, your globe was reabsorbed when the armor sought me out after the storm."

"And only Rafiq still has an amulet." Uriah's mouth dropped

open as the Dost swept past him into the cavernous chamber. "That means . . ."

The Dost nodded and turned to face to his right. "That's exactly what you detected, Wolf-priest. Now it is up to you to decide if this potential is to be for good or evil."

Grigory Khrolic looked down at the man on horseback in front of him. "Yes, Lieutenant, I saw the horsemen on our flank. They are nomads, bandits, watching us. If I thought they were of consequence, I would have done something about them. *They* do not matter."

Another volley of cannon shots hammered Helor's weakening gate. Already the rampart above it had fallen apart. The gates themselves were cracked and splintered. Cannonballs had bent and torn metal fixtures. One door hung by only a single hinge as other shots had gouged the rest of its support from the western wall. One more volley, perhaps two, and they would topple. Then the Vandari could rush in and the cavalry come behind them.

A sense of dread oozed up through Khrolic's dreams of glory. "Anatoly, what banner are the horsemen flying?"

"They have seven companies. Each company's standard is different, with a gold pennant flying above and a traditional flag below. Some of them are Khasts, the rest are various tribes."

Perhaps Rafiq Khast has decided he is Dost after all and has convinced others of this. "This changes things. Take your battalion and position yourself to defend against them. Second battalion will follow us in as planned."

Vorobiga saluted. "Yes, Pokovnik."

As the junior officer rode away, Grigory glanced to the west and saw the sun's disk touch the horizon. Back to the east a full moon had begun to rise. He smiled. "It is fitting that sun and moon watch us this day. Never before has there been such an important battle. Never again will they see such a battle bring mortal man glory equal to their own."

— 73 —

Malachy Kidd spun on his heel at the sound of the voice. Walking toward him, isolated in a field of black, he saw the Dost's golden form. "I can see you."

"I suspect you can." The Dost raised a hand to his face. "I too see through metal eyes. You have invented your own spell for enhancing your senses, but you lack vision. Your spell is melding with the one I use and you gain sight through it. This is very good."

Trailing behind the Dost, as if ghostly portraits drawn with gold chalk on black stone, other people entered the cavern. Malachy recognized one of them from the brief glimpse he'd had at the time he had been taken. "Uriah?"

The phantom dashed forward, past the Dost, and filled Malachy's sight. "Colonel Kidd, you're alive!" Uriah opened his arms as if about to hug Malachy, then blushed, snapped to attention, and saluted smartly. "Good to see you again, sir."

Malachy returned the salute, then hugged the youth. "I'm glad to see you have survived, as well." He looked over Uriah's shoulder toward the Dost. "I am not certain how long survival will be for any of us. The Stranans are attacking Helor."

"This is what we have come to stop." The Dost spread his arms out and the eleven other people with him moved into the shadows. They vanished from Malachy's sight for a moment, then metallic statues lit up around the room. Ten Tigers the size of the Wolf before which he stood ringed the Dost and the two Wolf-priests. "With your help, in the Wolf, we should be able to prevail."

Malachy released Uriah. "This is Vandari armor?"

"No. This armor was originally part of the Ausdari company."

"But it functions in the same way the Vandari armor does?"

The Dost slowly shook his head. "It will work in the way the Vandari armor *could* work. Their armor is crippled because they deny themselves its full power."

Malachy frowned. "I've never known a Stranan to do anything by halves."

"No? Their use of the Vandari employs a fraction of its power. The Stranans use it only as armor and it can be much more." The Dost shrugged. "They suffer from self-imposed limitations, much as you do."

"What do you mean?"

"You are seeing with eyes of silver, yet your Church teaches this is impossible, does it not?"

The Wolf-priest caught himself before he answered by reflex. The Dost was right, he was seeing through silver eyes. Moreover he had already determined that he had long been able to sense things through magick, though this was not a conscious process. *What I can do unconsciously, I can do purposely by invoking a spell.* The fact that scholars of magick had never done this before, and had subsequently declared it impossible, did not mean it truly was impossible.

"It does, and the Stranans are Eilyphianists." Malachy frowned. "You suggest they could have their Vandari operating at full strength, but they do not."

"They have the key, but they do not use it because, long ago, they found another way to make the Vandari work. They think they are powerful, but they are men trapped in toys, as you will see."

The Dost pointed toward the Wolf. "Only the most elite from my company ever occupied the Dari. Your being here, your mastery over the bit of armor I left you, means I am honored to accept you into their number. This Wolf was destined to be yours eight centuries ago. It has waited faithfully all this time. Make it whole."

His stomach roiling as if vipers nested in it, Malachy climbed into the hollow in the Dari's chest. Inside the armor he found his sight had returned enough that he could make out a host of details and colors that he had not seen in over a decade. He pushed his feet down into the holes at the top of the thighs. His hands and arms fit snugly into black tunnels beyond the shoulder holes. Pressing his back against the Wolf's metal flesh, Malachy nodded and the armor sealed itself.

An explosive brilliance pressed against his eyes with physical force. He felt as if it had burned through his head, but he found it did not hurt him. The light—whatever it was—probed his mind and sifted through memories, but lingered over few of them. It withdrew quickly and seemed to have taken part of him with it, yet Malachy did not feel anything missing. *What has been taken has just been borrowed.*

His vision went from black to gray. He saw triangular black tiles with red symbols on them hovering at the edges of his sight. By concentrating he appeared to be able to force one toward the center of his vision and he identified each as corresponding to a spell he had been taught. An exquisite rendering of an airship covered his Aeromancer magick. A host of sword tiles represented the various spells he knew for dueling and a simple key marked his lock-picking magick.

The only tile he could not identify was one depicting an infant. Malachy summoned it to the middle of his visual field. *If the other tiles are magick I know, this must be magick I do not. It is part of the Wolf and, I would guess, is part of becoming acquainted with the Wolf.* Closing his eyes, but still seeing the tile, Malachy invoked it.

A convulsion shook him and he immediately broke out in a cold sweat. The brilliant light slammed into his mind again with the force of a wave crashing into a breakwater. Images of tile after tile poured into his head. Each hexagonal tile fitted together in a perfect honeycomb pattern, but Malachy could not recognize the symbols on them. *They appear to be pictograms, like the script used in ancient Tsaih.*

The light flickered, then surged into him again. One by one, the hexagons flattened and sharpened into triangles. As they underwent this transformation the symbols on them changed to become something he could recognize intuitively. Seven tiles—one for each of the senses—lined themselves up to his right and went from black on red to the reverse. As they did so, Malachy became able to see and hear and smell and feel through and with his Wolf.

A tile depicting a running wolf shifted color and Malachy found himself able to control the armor's movements. He invoked a claw tile and the Wolf's right paw produced claws the length of broadswords. Choosing one of the tiles he had contributed originally, Malachy started a blue glow on the claws, magickally enhancing their abilities.

The Wolf-priest at once marveled at what the armor could do, yet trembled with the implications of what it meant. In the Urovian tradition, magick could only affect objects. In the Estanuan tradition it could only affect people—and practitioners of the other art were seen as possessed by evil. Durranian magick appeared to be a synthesis of both schools, which could make it acceptable in both, or reviled by both. In his heart Malachy knew it was not evil, but he also suspected his superiors would not look upon it with joy.

Anyone who seeks to limit or claims exclusivity in interpreting

God's actions is a fool. If God has created this magick and makes it available, it must be something we need. A new trail is being blazed for His purpose. Perhaps this *is the true reason behind everything I have endured.*

Malachy brought the Wolf up to its full height in a bipedal stance, then looked down at Uriah. "I can see you, truly see you. Red hair, green eyes, and all. This is incredible. So many capabilities."

"Many of which you will not have the time to learn right now." The Dost stepped back away from Uriah, then raised his hands toward the heavens. He floated up, four feet above the floor, then brought his hands down to his side. From a crevasse hidden above by stalactites, a river of gold poured down over the Dost. Malachy expected it to splash all over the room and run out in a great puddle, but it did not. Instead it filled an invisible mold in the rough shape of a man that stood as tall as Malachy's Wolf.

The body's shape slowly sharpened and attained the definition of the Wolf and the eleven Tigers surrounding it. The Dost's armor became a larger analog of the form he had worn before, with powerful thews and crisp, noble features. It had the pointed ears of a Durranian and pressed a hand to its own chest with a gentle, imperial grace.

The Dost's armor smiled and Malachy's Wolf opened its jaw in lupine imitation. "Enemies have come to the Dost's city, to enslave the Dost's people. You are but a dozen, yet possess the courage of a dozen dozens. Come with me and they shall not prevail."

Robin caught Natalya around the waist and hauled her back into the battery as the final cannon barrage brought the gates down. "They're coming now, Princess. You better go."

She snarled at him, defiant fire burning in her eyes. "You shoot, I load."

Robin nodded. "Clear."

"Da."

"Shield up."

Nugent hit the pedal. "Clear."

The Wolf-priest squinted down the shaft as the shielding came up. He swung the ballista to the left. "I have one sighted." He invoked a spell, the bow glowed blue, then he depressed the trigger lever.

The Ram he had aimed at cut slightly to the right. The bolt hit the Vandari in its left hip, puncturing it and shooting all the way ate1

through. The golden Ram stumbled and went down to its knees, but it did not freeze the way the other one had. After a moment's hesitation, it got back up and kept coming despite a pronounced limp.

"We have time for three shots." Robin set the retracting hooks and cranked the bow into a cocked position. "Load."

"*Da.*"

"Clear."

"*Da.*"

"Shield up."

Nugent stamped down the pedal with his right foot. "Clear."

Robin shot again, this time without invoking the magick. The Rams had picked up speed as they stampeded forward. They closed quickly into lethal range for unaided shots. Because of their assault the cannons did not shoot again for fear of hitting their comrades, giving Robin time to aim. He really didn't need it, as quickly as they came. With each step they loomed larger and easier to hit. He shot into the bobbing mass of golden giants and prayed for the best.

One of the Rams stumbled and went down, but the dust cloud raised by his comrades hid him. The other batteries also sent bolts into the crowd, but one of them ricocheted up into the air without killing a target. Robin couldn't see if any more Rams fell.

If I hadn't put the stop block in I could have shot into the city. Damn. Cocking the ballista, Robin felt sweat from his brow sting his eyes. "Load. And once you've done that, Tachotha, start praying."

Uriah looked from the Wolf to the Dost and back again. "Where is my Dari?"

The Dost shook his titanic head. "You have no armor."

The youth's stomach folded in on itself. "But how can I fight if I have no armor?"

"This fight is not for you, Uriah." The Dost squatted down and reached out as if to pat the Ilbeorian on the shoulder, but held back. "Had you mastered the globe, then you could have used the armor."

"You should have told me."

"I told you that learning all you could about it was important." The Dost's disappointment echoed through the cavern. "You should have applied yourself to the task of learning about it. Colonel Kidd and I could only bring you so far. It was up to you to complete your journey."

Uriah thumped himself on the chest. "Wait, I have combat training. And you know things come easily to me. I could do it."

"Even your Sandwycke training is not enough. And that you are intelligent and learn easily does not help." The Dost pointed off to a large archway with a stone wall sealing it off. "What we will do out there should not come easy to anyone."

"I don't understand."

The Dost nodded. "You should. Do you recall the suggestion that I had been trapped in my true body to teach me what it is like to be normal?"

Uriah nodded.

"This was correct. You were separated from your family and teachers in hopes you would learn those same lessons."

Uriah looked down and felt a shiver run through his body. *Like the armor, I have so many capabilities, but I limit myself by not going full out. I'm selfish that way. It is my sin.* "Nimchin, I understand the wisdom of what you are saying. Please, now, let me join you."

The Dost's Dari shook its head. "It is not enough to understand it in your head, you must know it in your heart."

As Colonel Kidd had said, you have to know your heart, and I am wanting. A lump rose in Uriah's throat as he realized uncounted leagues separated him from the selflessness that motivated the Dost to protect his people from the Stranans. *I have always wanted to be great and I squandered my chance before I even realized I had it.*

As Uriah let all of this run through his mind, two of the Tigers stalked over to the stone slab blocking the giant archway. Hooking gold claws beneath the stone, they heaved upward. The rock ground in the sockets on either side of the arch, but the stone curtain rose slowly. Lifting it above their heads, the Tigers braced it, then let others hold it aloft as they slipped into the dark corridor beyond it.

The youth looked up at the Dost. "What am I to do?"

The Dost's armor shook its head. "I do not know. I only know what I must do."

"Is there no way I can help you?"

The Dost's right hand traced a fingernail across his left breast. The scraping that gathered beneath the fingernail formed itself into the golden globe Uriah had so often handled before. It dripped down into Uriah's outstretched hands.

"If you *can* help, you will have to find out how yourself." The Dost looked to the corridor leading out. "This way will be blocked to you."

"I am to wait here?"

"If that is what you believe you must do, yes."

"Is this it, then? Is *this* the reason I came all this way?"

"Not the reason, my friend, but the result."

Uriah looked over at the Wolf. "Colonel?"

The Wolf shook its head. "I don't even understand *my* role in all this."

The Dost smiled. "You're to begin your healing. When you lost your eyes, you allowed another to steal your vision. It is time to claim what is yours again." The gold colossus froze for a moment, then joined the Wolf in upholding the stone curtain. "The signal has been sent to our allies. It is time for us to go. Farewell, Uriah."

Uriah's legs folded beneath him and he sat down hard. The stone curtain crashed down behind the Ausdari armor, the echoes of its closing filling the chamber. Then the sound died, leaving the Ilbeorian alone in utter darkness and complete silence to roll the gold ball between his hands.

Rafiq Khast felt a trickle of urgency through the medallion fused with his flesh. He smiled and drew his sword. "The Dost beckons us forward! Onward, my brothers! Today we please God and make history that shall be sung of forever."

— 74 —

Helor, Helansajar
28 Majest 1687

Robin triggered his last ballista shot at point-blank range. The iron bolt deflected off the upraised hoof of one Ram, then caught another in the forehead, between horns and eyes. The Vandari staggered, but remained mobile though it presented a ridiculous image as it continued forward with a bolt sticking out of its head.

The Rams boiled in through the gap where the gate had once been. Metal hooves further ground the doors into a crackling mass of splinters. Two overturned the trebuchet, then another smashed it with hooves. Wood cracked apart and ropes snapped, sending pieces of logs bouncing and tumbling further into the city's narrow streets.

Robin jammed his helmet on and pulled his faceplate into place. Uttering a prayer to Saint Michael, he invoked the magick of his armor. He drew his sword, said another prayer, and it glowed with a coruscating red light.

"Robin, no, you can't fight them."

The Wolf-priest looked over at Natalya. "Have I any choice?"

Down below the Vandari had slowed. Their initial charge took them into the small courtyard just beyond the gate, but the narrow tangle of debris-strewn streets impeded progress from that point forward. Defenders on the roofs of the buildings surrounding the courtyard heaved rocks and building stones down on the Stranans. Though their efforts seemed to do little actual damage, the ferocity of their resistance surprised and stopped the Vandari.

Robin inverted the grip on his sword and leaped from the battery platform. He jumped down onto the back of a Vandari. His knees slammed into its broad shoulders, but his own armor shunted away the force of the landing. Shifting his hands to the sword's crosshilt, he stabbed the blade down through the Ram's neck, then jerked the blade left and right to sweep through the chest's interior.

The armor beneath him hunched, then convulsed. As the Vandari's spine straightened, the armor bucked Robin clear and sent him flying. Somersaulting up through the air, he flew above the forward Vandari ranks. One of the Rams flailed at him with a cloven hoof. It caught him with a glancing blow on the left hip, shooting pain down his leg. The force of the blow also tossed him higher, crashing him into several Helorians casting rocks down upon the Vandari from a rooftop.

Robin hit hard on his back and rolled across the flat roof to the far parapet. *I like flying, but these landings need work.* He shook his head to clear it, then gingerly tried to stand. He almost made it upright when a tremor shook the building and he went down again. *What in hell?*

Men screamed as the far edge of the building began to collapse beneath them. The roof buckled, timbers split, and a huge crevasse opened. It headed straight for Robin and threatened to suck him down to the floor below where Vandari were burrowing into the structure. Through the dust he heard Natalya scream, "Robin, no!" then he began to fall.

Grigory Khrolic saw Ram Thirteen collapse beneath the Wolf-priest's attack. He pushed forward to smash the priest, but Thirteen's death throes pitched the silver man high into the air. Ram Eight then swatted the man like an insect and used him to knock down some of the defenders on top of a two-story-tall building.

The knot of Vandari just beyond the gate surprised Khrolic. His plan of attack had not anticipated things being as crowded as they

were. His men were accustomed to using their speed and power to
break enemy lines and crush their troops. Here, in a city, where the
enemy hid in buildings or stood above, out of reach, the Vandari
found themselves impotent.

"Attack buildings. Bring them down!" The defenders had
suited themselves well to opposing the Vandari, but those tactics
would fail to be useful in fighting cavalry or infantry. Turning back
toward his own lines, he saw half his cavalry had moved to engage
the Khasts. He gauged their chances of success with a practiced eye,
then waved the rest of the cavalry and his foot soldiers in. Helor.
What Vandari have begun, they can finish.

Passing through the gate, Grigory heard a woman's voice
shouting in Ilbeorian. Without thinking, he turned to the right and
raised Twenty-seven's right hoof to strike at her, knowing instinctively from the urgency and horror in her words that she was an
enemy. Hoof upraised, he acquired his target with a half-glance,
then brought his hoof down.

At the last second he shifted his line of attack, missing her but
shattering the wooden magazine that held iron bolts for the ballista.
"Natalya?"

"Grigory?"

"Why are you here?"

"To stop you and your treason."

In a heartbeat Grigory's dreams started to crumble. *If she carries word of my actions back to her father, all is finished.*

He raised his hoof again. "You cannot stop what is destiny, Natalya. I shall mourn your death."

Alone in the darkness, Uriah shifted around to his knees and knelt
there. The unevenness of the stone floor dug into his kneecaps and
shins, but he found the pain easy to ignore in his frustration. *How
could they leave me here?* His right hand contracted into a fist and
liquid gold spurted out between his fingers.

"I have to be out there." He started to roll the ball into a cylinder to make a pry bar, but he stopped when he realized that even as
angry as he was, he could not force the stone doorway up. "And if I
go back through the tunnel, I won't reach the gates of Helor for two
days. How could they leave me here?"

Deep inside himself he knew the question he really should
have been asking. *How could they take me with them? What they do
out there they do for the people of Helor. They are risking their lives
to do it, and I didn't learn enough to be able to help them. Out there*

I would be a liability. They could not trust me to do what needed to be done, and they didn't need to be looking after me in the middle of a battle.

"For someone who likes to think of himself as smart, Uriah Smith, you were too stupid to see that the reason to apply yourself to a task is not for any immediate reward, but just to be ready for when your help will prove vital. I hope it's not too late to make amends and prove myself useful."

"As it is Your will, Atarax, weave through me the war magicks you have given me." Invoking his combat magick as his horse thundered toward the galloping Stranan lines, Rafiq felt his flesh flush. He felt strength flood into his muscles. His heartbeat pulsed through him, filling him with power. He saw Stranan riders shift in their saddles and raise their sabers for the first exchange of cuts. He measured them and the fear in their eyes, then chose the man he would kill first.

Rafiq ducked beneath the line of the Stranan's slash, then whipped his own sword forward. The cut caught the Hussar above his hip, but just below the wide leather belt he wore. It clipped the hip bone, chipping off a piece, but fully a third of his sword sliced through the man's bowels.

Past him Rafiq parried a saber high. He had no chance to attack that man as his horse carried him yet further in the Hussars' formation. He clove through most of one man's arm and slashed another across the face, then found himself on the other side of the Stranan line.

Reining his horse around, he saw his people fully engaged in a melee. Cuts and parries, ripostes and blocks, filled the dusty air with the peal of ringing steel. The Stranans, perhaps unused to meeting a force that had not been devastated by cannon barrages, fought hard but were being fragmented and surrounded.

He looked back over his shoulder to where the full moon was rising. "If you are to watch me die, rejoice, for this battle is glorious and a fitting place for any warrior to breathe his last. Not me, not today, but many will know such glory beneath your ivory light."

Natalya flinched as the Vandari's hoof descended. "You cannot do this." She knelt on the platform, holding her hands out imploringly to him. "You must stop."

"You are an obstacle to my dreams, Natalya, and like those before you, you must be eliminated."

The hoof fell.

But never hit her. Below, between the Ram's legs, Natalya saw a flash of silver. Robin stabbed one of the fallen bolts into the meaty part of the Ram's right thigh. Screams of agony resonated from the armored beast as it fell backward. Other Rams moved in through the gate, cutting off Natalya's sight of Grigory.

Robin rose up through the air before her, then collapsed to the battery platform. His chest heaved and he clutched at his left leg. Groaning, he lay flat on his back.

"What happened to you, Robin? How did you . . ."

Natalya heard pained laughter resonate through the expressionless facemask. "Flying is controlled falling. As the building came down, I pushed off and flew toward this battery. I landed at the feet of that Ram and skewered it."

"That was Grigory."

"I should have gone for the groin."

"For that I would gladly load."

Robin hammered the platform with a fist. "The stop blocks were a stupid idea. I should have known they'd get into the city."

Natalya shook her head as the thunder of advancing Stranan cavalrymen echoed through the gate. "It would not matter now. Nothing can stop Grigroy. There are no more obstacles to his foul ambitions. The Grigory I knew is dead, and one I hate has taken his place."

— 75 —

Helor, Helansajar
28 Majest 1687

Moving with the Tigers, Malachy paced his Wolf up the tunnel toward the northern edge of Jebel Quirana. With each step his anthropomorphic armor took, he could feel his own muscles working. He was not imparting strength or power to the Ausdari's limbs, but direction and coordination. Through his metal feet he could feel the ground and had no trouble maintaining his balance. While he felt separate and complete himself, he also felt as if he'd become part of the armor. *Or it has become part of me.*

The tunnel sloped upward, then leveled out for a short distance.

It ended in an archway that had been bricked over. From the sloppy way mortar curled out of the joints on this side of the wall he imagined the masons had worked to create it from the outside. Malachy's sense of the city told him he stood on the other side of the archway above the Alanim's palace.

The Ausdari company parted as the Dost came through. In human form he looked a bit shorter and decidedly less threatening than his lupine and feline counterparts. Even so, the grace with which he moved hinted at incredible power. "The hour of our greatest challenge is at hand. Go forth and conquer our enemies."

The Dost drummed his fingers against the wall. It shattered as if it had been nothing more than glass the thickness of an eyelash. Exploding out through the wall with the others, Malachy saw the city's shattered gate to the north, the dying sun to the west and the rising moon to the east. It surprised him that he noticed more than the battle, then it struck him that the battle was but one part of the apocalyptic event in which he had become embroiled.

Leaping forward with the same abandon he'd known running through the palace, Malachy sent his Wolf surging toward the city's shattered gate. His footfalls felt feather-light despite the actual weight of his metal avatar. Coursing through the streets, he felt his shoulders clip buildings and slight pain radiated out through his metal body, but he reveled in that sensation. It struck him that if he could feel pain, the armor made no pretense at providing invulnerability. Had it been a creation of Shaitan it *would* have made the user feel unstoppable, then the Devil would delight in the excesses perpetrated with his tool.

The Dost said this is how I am to begin my healing. Being able to see again, being in this Wolf, I feel more alive than I have felt since Glogau. He smiled. *Khrolic is out there. He stole my eyes and yet I return to defeat him. God has brought me full circle so I can undo what Khrolic did so long ago.*

Speeding down the main thoroughfare, Malachy caught sight of one of the lead Vandari. He had seen Vandari before—members of the Elephant and Wolverine companies, not the Rams—and had thought them splendid things. Now, wearing a Wolf that had not been degraded by a succession of poorly trained operators, he could see how the Rams had changed from what they must have originally been. Where once their limbs would have been full and lifelike, now their forearms and legs were I-beams. As Strana had mechanized and industrialized, the Vandari had subtly been changed to conform to the images their operators felt right and proper.

In his gut Malachy knew the Vandari possessed only a fraction of the capabilities his Wolf did, and could do even less than he was capable of handling. In his Ausdari Wolf he was to them what an armed and armored Wolf-priest would have been to the combatants in a schoolyard squabble. Defeating the Dost's enemies did not require their deaths. The Stranans needed to be driven from the city and forced back into their own realm. Defeating them could forestall future invasions while slaughtering them would only demand revenge.

Blocking a flying hoof with his right paw, Malachy slapped the first Ram in the flank. The force of the blow spun the Vandari about and sent it stumbling back into its own lines. Reaching around to the left, Malachy plucked another Ram from inside a disintegrating building and propelled it back into the milling herd of Vandari. Around him the Tigers similarly laid into the Rams, forcing them back, further and further, over the broken gate and out onto the plains again.

Chaos reigned before the walls. The retreating Vandari broke their own cavalry charge. As the horsemen slowed, they turned around and started riding to where the Khasts were overwhelming the other half of the Hussar horsemen. The 3rd Sonasny Militiamen—foot soldiers all—caught in the open in their advance, broke and started running for the safety of their trenches as the Hussars rode back toward them.

Malachy saw one Ram with an iron shaft sticking out from its right thigh. He reached out and helped the fallen Vandari up. As he did so he felt something through the armor. Shoving the stricken Ram through the gate, Malachy growled wolfishly in Stranan. "Crawl away, Grigory Khrolic."

The Ram stumbled and fell, then slowly got back on its feet. "Kidd, here?"

Malachy nodded and advanced through the gate. "I'm here. I'm your opposition once again, but this time I harbor no illusions about you being my ally."

Through the gold globe Uriah felt serenity tinged with apprehension and fear course into him. The Ilbeorian youth knew he was feeling the emotions racing through the Dost. His realization heartened him and yet saddened him. *I'm doing him no good here.*

Frustration erupted in him. He could not lift the stone curtain that kept him trapped in the empty chamber. *I can do no good here for anyone. At least out there I could do something! I could help somehow!*

A trickle of energy reminiscent of the lightning bolt tingled up through his fingertips. *This is interesting. Concentrate, Uriah. Focus yourself. If you're so good at learning, now's the time for it.*

He concentrated on the golden globe, trying to recapture some of the Dost's peace, and found himself looking out at Helor itself. He saw the Dost as the giant man slowly walked toward the broken gate. People huddled behind the armor of ballistae batteries atop the walls and Stranans were running for their trenches. The Tigers had forced the Vandari from the city and Malachy's Wolf stood menacing a wounded Ram.

I have to be out there.

The same question he had used to challenge Kidd during the tactics evaluation exploded in his head. *Why?*

Uriah smiled slowly. *I have to be there for them, not me.*

He laughed aloud and began to flatten the globe. *And being a quick learner* can *help. I remember the design for the medallion he gave Rafiq, and I remember the words* — issa hunak. *I hope I do this right.*

Even as he began to work the stars up out of the metal and trace the lines of the web, he knew his medallion would be perfect. *It will work.* Deep in his heart he knew he had hit upon the right path.

I know why I've come all this way. A purposefulness he had never known flowed into him and his work became more certain, his motions more definite. *I just pray I can meet the challenge coming my way.*

Fear tasting bitter in his mouth, Grigory Khrolic stared out at the powerful Dari Wolf. Its strength and power mocked all the Vandari. *This is not possible. Nothing can be more powerful than the Vandari.*

He slowly limped Ram Twenty-seven backward. "It is good you no longer delude yourself, Kidd. I have ever known you were no ally to Strana. Now you prove that, much as has your nation."

"You are the invader here." Kidd's Wolf stood aside. "I am here because of the Dost."

Grigory stared past the Wolf at the clean-limbed gold man stepping over Ram Thirteen and through the broken gateway. *So the rumors were true after all.* Because they had been elicited through torture he had never fully trusted them. As his advance on Helor had progressed he had come to disbelieve them. As much as thinking the Dost had not returned had brought Grigory peace, seeing the gold man disturbed him.

This is the Dost. He must die. Grigory's decision was made without conscious thought. All he had worked for would be swept away by the Dost. Childhood terrors and the pain of his dying dreams shot through him and prompted him to act. *For my Strana, the Dost must die.*

Grigory lunged toward the Dost, but the Wolf intervened, crashing Grigory to the ground with a cuff to the head. The bolt in his thigh stabbed a bit deeper, jolting physical pain through him again. The Stranan pushed off with his left hoof and leg, trying to bring himself upright again, but he could not move. Broken and weak, he lay on the ground, easy prey for the Wolf. *How is this possible?*

In front of him the Dost held a hand up as if signaling him to stop. Struggling as mightily as he could, Grigory could not defy him. His guts twisted as a wave of magick poured over him, then he saw the other Vandari Rams had frozen in place. *Is this how we will die? Trapped? Helpless? Will Strana perish this way?*

"There has been enough fighting now. Pokovnik Kidd, if you will please back away." The Dost stepped forward graciously, as if a parent separating squabbling children. "And Pokovnik Khrolic, there is no need for continued hostilities. Your fears are unfounded."

Grigory looked to the right and left, then laughed. "Unfounded? My men and I are prisoners in our armor. Our fears are fully supported."

The Dost nodded casually. "Your armor had been disabled to prevent trouble." The Dost waved a hand and the pain in Grigory's right leg faded. Looking down, he saw the latter half of the iron bolt lying on the ground. "I wish you no harm."

"But you have returned to conquer us."

"I have returned to save my people, and to plan for the future." Again the Dost gestured and into the center of Grigory's vision floated the square tile with the infant on it. "Please invoke this magick."

"No. If you wish me dead, kill me, do not make me kill myself."

The Dost smiled. "I was about to ask you to trust me, but this is foolish. So be it."

The tile reversed itself and Grigory's vision whited out as if he were in the middle of a furious blizzard. Along the edges of his sight he saw his square tiles, then hexagonal tiles flowed into his vision like snowflakes. A brilliance pushed into his brain, then, one after another, the hexagons plumped out into squares with images on them he recognized as belonging to spells that gave the Vandari abilities that he had long thought mythical.

Above and beyond that, he felt power flow through his limbs. His Ram's forearms thickened and muscles tightened. Grigory was able to straighten up without difficulty and knew his armor's limbs would grant the Vandari the sheer and overwhelming power the Tigers and Wolf possessed. The Dost had made him the equal of any of the Dari that had emerged from the city.

The Dost had made him the most powerful Vandari Strana had known in centuries.

"Why have you done this?"

"So you, Grigory Khrolic, can choose the path for your own future." The Dost opened his hands. "Fight here and you will die here. Leave here and within five years you will be involved in war that will bring you more power and glory than you are capable of understanding. The choice—"

The Dost's voice died amid a scream of metal. A black iron bolt burst out through his left breast. Unfathomable agony washed over the Dost's golden mask as the giant staggered for one step, then pitched forward on his face and lay still on the plains before Helor.

Rafiq felt fire stab through his chest. *The Dost is dying!* He looked toward the city and saw the Dost prostrate on the ground with an iron shaft sticking up out of his back. Behind him, on the city's wall, Rafiq saw the ballista battery that had shot him. *They will shoot again. I must save the Dost.*

He kicked himself free of his stirrups and leaped from his saddle. Focusing on the fragment of rampart beside the battery, the Helansajaran touched his medallion. *"Issa Hunak."*

In an eyeblink he passed from the battlefield to the walls of Helor. A wave of dizziness passed over him, then some of the stone beneath his feet broke away. He slipped, slamming his knees into the rampart. Ignoring the pain, he desperately grabbed at rocks to keep himself on the wall. *I must save the Dost!*

Then he looked up and saw Shukri Awan silhouetted by the moon. "You claim to have pledged your service to the Dost, then you come to kill him? You are a fool, Rafiq, for *I* am the Dost!" The crescent sword in Awan's hand flashed down, filling Rafiq's belly with fire.

Rafiq sagged forward. *I will not die, I cannot die.* Clutching his right hand to his stomach to keep his entrails from pouring out of him, the Helansajaran clawed at the rock with his free hand. *I serve the Dost. I cannot let myself die.*

"What in hell? Why did he shoot?" Robin didn't know who the gold man was, but he didn't need a formal introduction to know he and his companions had forced the Stranans from Helor. "He's on our side."

Natalya looked out over at Shukri Awan's battery. "He's reloading! We have to do something."

Robin dragged himself to his feet and leaned heavily on the ballista. "Load."

The Tachotha looked surprised. "The stop block. You can't shoot him."

"I know." Robin dropped the cocking hooks on the bow wire and drew it back. "And I can't run over there and I'm too tired to fly." He locked the bow wire down with the trigger lever. "Load."

"Da."

His left leg throbbed as he stepped down on the pedal and raised his shielding. Robin looked out through his cross at the ethyrines standing before the gate. "Connor."

"Sir."

"Get someone up to kill Shukri Awan!"

"MacBride, Hoskins, come with me!"

Natalya looked out. "The Alanim is sending his bodyguards to stop your men."

"Good luck to them." Robin gritted his teeth and pulled the hooks off the bow wire. "Clear."

"Da."

"Natalya, duck down. I have to see Awan." Robin leaned back, holding on to the ballista with his left hand and keeping his right hand on the trigger lever. The pain in his left leg made it seem as if it were on fire. "Natalya, can you hold the shield pedal down?"

"Da. What are you doing?"

"A gunner's trick—opportunity shot." He muttered a prayer

and the ballista began to glow a spring green. Robin could feel his strength ebb and pain begin to win the battle for his body. "Hurry, you stupid ass. I haven't got all day."

Of Shukri Awan he could only see his hand on the trigger lever, but that was enough. When the Helorian pushed the lever down, Robin did as well. The ballista thrummed deeply and jerked to the left beneath Robin's hand. The bolt shot out straight and true, slamming into the iron shaft Shukri Awan had shot.

Robin pulled himself forward, then slipped and landed on the platform exhausted. "Got it."

"How?"

He grunted. "The spell aims the bow, timing is up to me." Lying there, he stared up at the purple- and pink-streaked clouds, then shouted at the sky. "Move it, Connor! I'm done."

Malachy caught sight of the second shot at the Dost out of the corner of his vision. He turned back toward Helor, thinking to interpose himself between the city and the Dost, but Khrolic's Ram sprang toward the fallen giant. Invoking a spell, Malachy sprouted claws on his right forepaw and struck at the Ram. Khrolic parried with a fan-shield blossoming on this right forehoof, but still had to veer off from his intended target.

The fan-shield on the Ram's hoof split and grew out into curved razored extensions of the hoof's natural shape. Khrolic planted his left hindhoof and lunged back at the Wolf. Twisting, Malachy avoided the slash at his belly, then brought his left forepaw in. Magick transformed it into a round shield, the edge of which caught Khrolic's Ram just behind the right elbow. Sparks flew and metal pealed. Khrolic stumbled back, clutching at his Ram's arm, but nothing in the set of the Vandari's shoulders even began to suggest resignation or surrender.

Malachy saw enough activity back on the top of the wall to know the battery was preparing another shot at the Dost. The Wolf-priest searched his spell inventory for anything that might allow him to strike at the ballista, but none of the icons suggested themselves. Uncertain which threat stood a greater chance of finishing the Dost off, Malachy's indecision made him hesitate.

Khrolic's Ram surged forward and caught the Wolf with a head butt in the middle of the chest. The force of the blow thundered through Malachy's chest and a twinge of pain from his ribs shot through him. He knew his Wolf had been knocked flying, but he had no chance to invoke Aeromancer magick before the metal beast slammed into the ground. The Wolf landed on its back and pitched back, heels flying up over its head. Stars exploded before Malachy's eyes, then the world whirled around him. He caught a flash of Khrolic coming at him again, then the Wolf's head hit the ground and, for Malachy Kidd, the world went black.

Shukri Awan ignored the sounds of his bodyguards fighting with the Wolf-priests below as he dropped another iron bolt onto the bed of the ballista. On the plains the Wolf and the Ram fought—all around him people fought—but they would not overcome him. He was the Dost. He was destined to rule an empire. Rafiq Khast lay dying on the wall at his feet, and his own son, the abomination, lay dying on the plains.

Finish him and everything begins anew!

Shukri Awan sighted through the gathering dusk onto the golden manform's spine. "It is as it has been prophesied!"

He felt a sudden weight on his back. A blood-slicked hand and arm snaked over his left shoulder, trapping his neck. The hand pushed his face to the right and pressed him cheek to cheek with Rafiq Khast.

"Do you see the moon, Shukri Awan?"

Shukri Awan laughed at the pain in the man's question. He drove his right elbow back into Rafiq's ribs and felt the death grip begin to slacken. "Yes, it is the full moon beneath which you will die."

"It is the full moon beneath which I *choose* to die." Breath hissed in through Rafiq's clenched teeth. *"Issa hunak."*

Staining the dusky sky with its fiery death, a falling star arced down from the full moon. Natalya thought the dark shape she saw moving through the sky was an afterimage burned into her eyes by the star's death, but when the shape crossed in front of the moon, eclipsing the orb, she knew it was real and she began to shout. "Robin, it is the *Saint Mikhail.*"

Announcing its arrival, the airship shot one barrage that swept over the Stranans' cannon batteries. The remaining battle boilers exploded, casting fire and steam into the air. Metal and wood splinters *ping*'d off the ballista's shields. Glowing embers circled the boilers' grave, casting coppery highlights on the Vandari and Ausdari battling out on the plains.

Malachy shook his head to clear it and drew his Wolf's legs up, bringing its knees to his own muzzle as Khrolic's rushing Ram slowly swam into view. He kicked up and out, letting both paws hit solidly and thrust the Ram's weight aside. He felt the tremor through the rocks as the Ram landed heavily and rolled away. Malachy rolled to his right and came up, then turned to the right to face the Ram.

He pushed his sensations and gathered in yet more information. The air and the disturbances the Ram made as it gained its feet again fit Grigory into a three-dimensional matrix. It communicated to Malachy speed, direction, balance, and size. He heard wind whistling around the edges of the Ram's horns and could feel the pressure change caused by the Ram's left forehoof growing a set of blades to match those on the first.

All this and thousands of other clues flooded into Malachy's awareness, but they did not overwhelm him. On an unconscious level he had dealt with a similar wealth of information for years. *I've been in training for this moment for the last dozen years.* Malachy smiled. *You started me down this path, Grigory Khrolic. You created the instrument of your own death.*

The Wolf ducked beneath a slash at its neck and let the Ram rush past. Pivoting faster than such a huge thing should have been able to do, the Wolf thrust both forepaws into the Ram's back. The push spilled the Ram forward. Its horns gouged two parallel tracks in the stone. One caught, flipping the Ram over onto its back.

Malachy smiled. *As the Dost said, it is time for my healing to begin, and avenging myself on Khrolic is the perfect place to start.*

Khrolic continued his Ram through a somersault and came up. It spun to face the Wolf again with a bent horn and a great deal more caution. As Khrolic came in, Malachy's vision began to fade. Instinctively he cut to the right, but found himself unable to sidestep the Ram's attack. Blades came in low and up on a diagonal that tore the flesh over the Wolf's chest. Malachy hissed with pain and reflexively drove his left fist forward. It hit solidly, bouncing the Ram back a step, but Khrolic lashed out with a hoof and caught the Wolf's right knee, sending the Wolf stumbling back.

A curtain of blackness descended over Malachy, completely cutting off sight of his enemy. *What's happening?*

An invisible kick from the Ram tossed him backward. He tried to roll up to his feet again, but a third kick caught the Wolf in the head and dropped the Ausdari to its back. The jolt bounced Malachy alternately off the back and breast of the Wolf, and he tasted blood on his lips. *I don't understand! Why isn't it working?*

The Ram towered over him. "You were never my equal. You are broken now as you were in Glogau. Now the Dost dies, then Helor dies."

"You cannot, Grigory."

The Stranan laughed. "And you cannot stop me, Malachy."

The Wolf-priest snarled, and tried to get his armor to its feet, but even the locomotion spell had quit on him. *I have failed. All this way, all this time, and I have failed. The Dost will die. Is this what You intended for me, dear God?*

A distant thrum and a sharp clang told Malachy another bolt had come streaking out from one of the harpoon batteries on the city walls. Malachy heard a woman shout something from the wall and knew the target had been Khrolic's Ram. *Natalya!*

"You, too, will die, you treacherous witch."

No, I won't let you do that, Grigory. Malachy concentrated, placing Khrolic, the Dost, and the city beyond him in position within his mind. *Khrolic was the enemy of my first vision, and the Dost the charge of my second. I am in the Wolf of the third vision. I should have seen it before.*

I am the Wolf. Malachy nodded solemnly. *Vengeance is not mine to seek, I am the Wolf, I protect those who cannot protect themselves!*

The simplicity of it all stunned Malachy. Vitality flooded through him in the wake of his discovery. The world sharpened into colorful images, ringed by triangular tiles that once again reversed their colors as they became active. He saw Khrolic's Ram slowly stalking toward the Dost, could feel the tremors of each step.

Gathering the Dari's limbs beneath it, Malachy heaved the Wolf to its feet, then lunged at the Ram. With a swipe of a clawed paw, the Wolf laid the Ram's right leg open and toppled the Vandari on its side.

The Ram spun around and levered itself up off the ground. "Are you that eager to die?"

"No, I'm that eager to stop you from killing." Rising slowly, Malachy opened the Wolf's paws and sidled over to place himself between the Ram and the Dost. "I have no desire to kill you."

"You can't."

"I will. Give me a choice."

"*Nyet!* The Dost must die!" Left forehoof upraised, the Vandari Ram charged forward.

You force me to be the Wolf, Grigory! A new tile drifted into the center of Malachy's vision. It had a snarling wolf on it and he invoked it without a second thought.

The Wolf leaped forward, its body shimmering brightly as it shifted from the humanoid shape it had known to that of a true wolf. Jaws closed on the Ram's left forelimb. The Wolf savagely jerked its head left and right. The voice inside the Ram screamed as the Vandari's left shoulder stretched, popped, and slumped.

The Wolf released the arm, letting it dangle uselessly at the Ram's side. The Ram clutched the ruined limb to itself, then turned suddenly and began to run. The Wolf sprinted after it, golden teeth ringing as they snapped at the Ram's heels. Paws and hooves struck sparks from the stone as the Wolf chased Khrolic away from the Dost.

The Ram slammed into the crowd of frozen Vandari, scattering them like tenpins. Khrolic's hooves churned infantrymen into bloody froth in his blind panic. Horses reared, dumping riders, and sprinted off across the plain to get away from the fleeing Ram. The dusk hid the terror on most faces, but the screams and wails from Stranan soldiers carried it in full.

Khrolic had gained half a stride and Malachy prepared to make a push to catch him when the Ram's right hoof plunged into one of the Stranan trenches. The knee locked straight, then the body began to turn, dislocating the right hip with a thunderous pop. Khrolic shrieked in pain as he fell and Malachy knew the injuries evident on the Vandari were mirrored on the man inside it.

The Wolf leaped the trench and pounced on the Ram. Long fangs closed on the Vandari's throat, testing the metal flesh. Through it Malachy could feel Khrolic's physical agony and sense the outer edges of the man's mental turmoil.

He could feel Khrolic's dreams dying.

"You wanted too much, Grigory."

"I still want it."

"I know. And you want it for all the wrong reasons."

The Wolf's jaws closed and Vandari Ram Twenty-seven died.

— 77 —

Malachy lifted his muzzle from the body of Ram Twenty-seven and invoked the spell that again made his Wolf into a man with a lupine head. Turning back toward the city, he saw the Dost still lying on his face and knew the Dost had been still far too long. *Is he dead? Have I truly failed?*

The bolt sticking up out of the Dost's back began to quiver. The motion built, increasing sharply until the iron shaft whipped back and forth so violently that it snapped off at the Dost's flesh and cartwheeled into the dusk. The wound sealed itself over seamlessly and smoothly. The Dost's Ausdari gathered its hands beneath it and brought itself up into a kneeling position.

He lives! Malachy felt a shiver as he stopped before the Dost. "You were wrong, Nimchin. It wasn't time for me to begin healing, but time for me to realize I'd been healed."

The Dost's armor shook its head. "It was both and it was neither. It was about who you truly are and recapturing that sense of yourself. It was that way for you and"—the Dost hesitated for a moment—"that way for me, as well."

Malachy brought his Wolf down to its knees, then cast the spell that opened the armor. The rush of cooling night air chilled him as it plastered his torn, sweat-soaked, bloody nightshirt to his body. He stumbled out of the armor and sank to his hands and knees. Exhausted and hurt, he still smiled and even began to laugh.

"Malachy, you're bleeding."

He nodded as droplets of blood splashed on the ground. "Just a flesh wound. No worse than my Wolf took for me." *But I can see the blood!* Malachy looked up and saw Natalya standing over him. "You're more beautiful than I could have imagined."

She blushed, then her jaw dropped. "You see me?"

He nodded.

"It's a miracle."

Malachy shook his head and stood unsteadily. "Just a revelation, not a miracle." He reached out with his right arm and she came to him. She hugged him tightly and, despite the ache in his ribs, he'd not have surrendered that embrace for anything. "A lot of things have been revealed to me."

He looked over at the Dost. "As beat up as I feel, you must be worse."

"Yes and no."

Malachy arched an eyebrow at the golden man. "It is a function of being the Dost that prevents a simple answer?"

"Yes and no." The golden features froze as the head slid up and the chest opened. Out of the Ausdari stepped a tall, clean-limbed youth. Sharpened ears rose up through a thick mop of red hair. Mismatched eyes of amber and green shone with wonder as the Dost held his arms out and studied both them and his legs. Blue flesh formed a mask around the Dost's eyes, helping make him appear more alien, but Malachy found much about him very familiar.

"Uriah?"

The Dost looked up at the Wolf-priest. "I am, we are, Uriah *and* Nimchin." He flexed his arms, then squatted down and bounced back up. "This is incredible."

"How can you be two people?"

"How can you be seeing with eyes of silver?" The Dost shook his head. "The bolt that pierced me was killing me. I was dying, there, in my armor. Uriah had fashioned a talisman that allowed him to teleport to a place he could see, but he was alone and in the darkness. My pain and dying became his only external reference point, so he teleported into it. He came into me and we merged. We became complete in each other. In his self-sacrifice he found the belonging he had always sought. He found that subordination of self for the benefit of others is a strength, not a weakness."

"That is a lesson I needed to be reminded of, as well." Malachy slowly nodded. "I was blind because I chose to be blind."

"What do you mean, Malachy?"

He smiled at Natalya. "When I was blinded at Glogau, I began to look inside myself to see if I was worthy of my place in God's plan. That answer eluded me for all this time because there was no answer to it. Seeking the answer to that question raised me to a level of greater importance than I deserved. My quest pushed me further away from the vows I had taken to become a Wolf-priest. I had pledged myself to the service of others, to protect them, and by turning inward I abrogated that responsibility."

Malachy tapped his own chest with his left hand. "As I rediscovered here, in this battle, I am a Wolf who aids the Lord Shepherd in protecting His flock. My welfare does not matter as long as the flock is protected. When I thought to avenge myself on Grigory, my sight failed. When he threatened you, I returned to my vows and my role in life. I became again the Wolf and therein found the strength to defeat him."

"Would that be the reason God allowed the Dost to be reincarnated?" Robin Drury limped forward with the aid of another ethyrine. He pointed out toward where Helansajaran and Stranan troops had ridden in together to view the spectacle of the Dost's recovery. "The fighting all but stopped after he appeared on the battlefield. I think he could have killed the Rams as easily as he froze them. For a conqueror returning, I'd say he's saved more lives than he's caused to be taken."

The Dost nodded, then shrugged and finally smiled in Malachy's direction. "A strong Helansajar will serve as a buffer state between Aran and Strana. It will prevent war, but not without cost to all sides. We are pleased to have lives saved by our return. We also know peace will frustrate those who sought war for their own advantage."

The Dost looked off to the northwest. "In three days Duke Vasily Arzlov will be here with a force numbering three regiments. He is a threat, but not a wholly unreasonable one. Likewise the *Saint Michael* is a threat, but we think the Ilboerian Prince on board is a thoughtful man. Perhaps, in the coming days, we will be able to reach an accord what will work well for Helansajar, Strana, and Ilbeoria."

Looking at Natalya, the Dost nodded. "Tachotha Natalya, you would honor us with being our guest here in Helor. We welcome the Hussars and their Vandari as your Honor Guard. Likewise we are pleased to have Viscount Warcross here. I believe both of your nations will find your covert diplomatic mission to Helor has laid a strong foundation for future cordial relations with the court of Uriachin Dost."

He waved them toward the city. "Welcome to Helor. Please forgive the mess, but I have been long absent and things have deteriorated in that time."

—— 78 ——

> **Court of Uriachin Dost**
> **Helor, Helansajar**
> **2 Autumbre 1687**

The four days since the Dost's return had been very busy for everyone, though Malachy Kidd suspected he had the most to do of all. Not only did he have to attend the ceremonies and meetings and negotiations arranged on all sides, but he was getting accustomed to seeing again. There were times when the sights and colors threatened to overwhelm him, so he closed his eyes and took refuge in the darkness he had once hated.

The *Saint Michael*'s early return to Helor had been explained by the small armada of airships that had come north with her. Prince Trevelien had commandeered a significant number of Grimshaw airships and independents, including the *Stoat*. While the *Saint Michael* had raced north to Helor, the cargo ships sailed to the Kulang Valley and loaded coal from the stockpile for Prince Agra-sho's destroyed steel mill. Using ethyrskiffs, lines, and canvas chutes, the smaller ships were able to refuel the dreadnought in flight, allowing it to return very fast to Helor.

By the time Vasily Arzlov and his troops arrived at Helor the *Saint Michael* had enough coal to see it through weeks of battle. His flagship, the *Leshii*, had fewer than a tenth of the guns on the *Saint Michael*, so combat between them would have been ridiculous. Arzlov put his flagship down outside the city and consented to being the Dost's guest. His troops—the 1st and 2nd Vzorin Uhlans and Vzorin Dragoons—set up camp outside the city, but under orders from the Tachotha they helped the Hussars and ethyrines clear rubble and rebuild.

Tachotha Natalya and Prince Trevelien quickly found in each other allies. While neither fully trusted the other, they discovered a mutual distrust of Vasily Arzlov. That unity served to confirm their initial assessments of the other's intelligence and perception. Both of them agreed they should be able to persuade their governments to suspend hostilities. Toward that end Trevelien offered to replace the *Zarnitsky* with a ship from Ilbeoria and Natalya proposed Stranan pensions for the survivors of the dozen ethyrines who died in the defense of Helor.

Arzlov had not been pleased with the arrangements the two royals had made between them before his arrival. Natalya had already decided that Arzlov was in league with Khrolic and she saw his advance with troops in tow as proof of his intention to support Khrolic's conquest of Helor. She was looking forward to a treason trial in Murom for the Duke.

Arzlov had other ideas and presented a spirited defense of himself and his actions. He said he had come into Helansajar with his local Vzorin troops to *stop* Khrolic and rescue the Tachotha. Natalya, as he pointed out, could not cite any statement by the Duke that linked him to Khrolic's action, nor even suggested he had condoned in any way the invasion. Arzlov said he had become alarmed when the Tachotha disappeared. He assumed she had gone to stop Khrolic, so he brought his troops out to oppose him as well and bring Natalya back to Strana safely.

Natalya had been forced to accept his story, but she vowed to get him removed as Vzorin's Governor. For all of his planning, Arzlov had forgotten that Malachy had been made a Hero by the Tacier after the Lescari War. Torturing him, as offenses went, was minor, but it would be enough to allow her to convince her father that Arzlov should be guarding snowdrifts in Murumyskda. His removal from Vzorin would be in keeping with Prince Trevelien's vow to exile the treasonous Ilbeorian elements from Aran.

Standing outside the Dost's audience hall in a dress gray uniform of Helorian manufacture, Malachy smiled at Robin Drury. "Good afternoon, Brother Robin. Why the long face? When this afternoon's business concludes, you'll be heading back to Dhilica. Your winter will be much more pleasant there than mine will be in Murom."

The taller man nodded. "That's likely to be true, sir. However, after you accept your award from the Tacier, I imagine you'll be in great demand in social circuits. You'll not notice the weather."

Malachy shook his head. "The Tachotha will be in great demand after her adventure, not me."

"But you'll be with her, and I think she'll find a way to keep you warm during the Stranan winter."

"True enough, but that doesn't answer my question."

"No, sir, it doesn't." Robin's gaze flicked down and then back up. "Prince Trevelien is ordering a number of people back to Ilbeoria. There's a woman, Amanda Grimshaw—"

"The one who got my message to the Prince?"

"Yes, sir. Her father is one of the people being exiled. We'll return to Dhilica just about the time they leave for Ilbeoria."

Malachy winced. "Bad luck, that. Of course, you *are* an officer. You could ask her to marry you. If she accepted, she could stay."

Robin smiled. "I think she's the right one for me, sir, but I'm not certain she could become accustomed to living within the means my office provides me. And, given that her father hates me, the chances he'd settle a dowry on her are slim."

"Brother Robin, I have been in the habit of giving a grant to my aides and that position was recently made vacant. We might be able—"

Robin held his hands up. "Thank you, sir, but no thanks. I have no desire for charity."

"I understand. Perhaps the Dost will—"

"He already offered a reward to the ethyrines for our service. We voted to give half to the survivors of our dead and the rest to Father Ryan's Donnist mission." Robin frowned. "You see, sir, it's not a question of money, but one of character and time. I think Amanda would do fine as my wife, but I'd need time to find that out. With her leaving Aran . . ."

"Time is a precious commodity, Brother Robin." Malachy smiled slowly. "Luckily, if you are meant for each other, time won't erode those feelings. In a couple of years, when you return to Ilbeoria, she'll be waiting for you."

"I hope so, sir."

Suhayl ibn-Hakim, the Dost's new chamberlain, stepped through the opening doors of the audience hall. "You will come with me, please?"

The elder Wolf-priest nodded and waved Robin forward. They entered a broad hall that was only a quarter as deep as it was wide. A forest of columns raised the tiled ceiling up a considerable distance above their heads. Across from the door the Dost's golden Ausdari stood behind his throne and ten of the gold Tigers lined either side of the handwoven carpet linking the throne dais with the doors.

The throne dais itself had three chairs upon it. The Dost sat in the central throne. To his left sat a young woman Malachy remembered being introduced as the widow of Rafiq Khast. At the Dost's right hand sat a strikingly beautiful woman named Turikana. The Dost wore an embroidered tunic and pants woven of golden threads.

The embroidery had been patterned after a tiger's stripes and had been done in black except over the center of his chest where two pale green eyes stared out from the edges of the quasi-clerical collar. Khast's widow wore black, but Turikana had been given a long gown of gold with similar embroidery as the clothing the Dost wore.

Prince Trevelien stood on the left of the hall along with Captain Hassett. Opposite them stood Tachotha Natalya, Duke Arzlov, and the Stranan named Valentin Svilik. Both Wolf-priests stopped half a dozen yards from the throne, then bowed when Suhayl announced them to the court. "Viscount Warcross and Brother Robert Drury, as you requested, my lord."

The Dost stood. "Forgive the formality, my friends, but these are times for ceremony. Of those assembled here, save my sisters, you are the people I know best. I respect your wisdom and all you've done for me. I want to reward you."

Malachy glanced at Robin, then shook his head. "We did not do what we did for a reward, my lord."

"I know, but please." Uriachin glanced at Prince Trevelien and Tachotha Natalya. "I stand here between leaders I would like to have think of me as a peer. I must show them I am civilized enough to offer my gratitude to those who helped me return to my throne. Please?"

Malachy and Robin looked at each other, then shrugged. "Do you think, Brother Robin, that Uriah added the *please*?"

Robin shook his head. "Probably not, but it *is* he who is intent on getting his way."

The Dost arched an eyebrow at them. "Neither of you liked making things easy for me, did you? Now, as to your rewards: you, Malachy Kidd, already possess an Ausdari Wolf. To you I entrust the two dozen Ausdari Wolves hidden in Jebel Quirana. After you travel to Murom and show the Stranans how to return their Vandari to their original state, I want you to come back here and take possession of the Wolves. You will take them to Sandwycke. You will train other Wolf-priests in the way of the Dari."

Malachy smiled. "I'm honored by your reward, my lord. It will be my pleasure to do as you ask."

"Good." The Dost looked over at Robin. "That part of me which was Uriah Smith knows you will accept no reward. The part of me that was Nimchin is determined to thank you."

Robin shook his head. "Begging your pardon, my lord, but I was the one who made the ballista that almost killed you."

"You did what you did to stop the abuses of a man who had great and terrible ambitions. That another man perverted your intentions is not your fault. I don't hold you responsible for Shukri Awan's actions." The Dost waved him forward. "Please come here."

Robin marched forward with crisp military precision. He stopped at the foot of the dais and bowed his head.

"Robin Drury, you judge people by their true worth, not the money they have or their position. You demand from everyone the best they are capable of delivering. Most importantly, as you did here, you are willing to impose yourself between the powerful and the weak. For a man such as you, there can be only one reward."

The Dost reached out and touched Robin's forehead. The Wolf-priest staggered back a few steps, then blinked his eyes and smiled broadly. "Thank you for this gift and for your trust."

The Dost smiled. "You are most welcome, my friend."

Robin spun on his heel and returned to Malachy's side.

An eyebrow arched above a silver eye. "What happened?"

"You remember how the Vandari were unable to move after you drove them out of the city?"

"Sure."

Robin tapped his forehead. "He gave me that spell."

Malachy nodded. The Dari armor was more powerful than anyone could imagine, and therefore subject to abuse. The Dost had given Robin the means of stopping the Dari—all of them, including the Dost's armor. He had made Robin the judge and executioner of anyone who misused the Dari.

"He chose well."

"Thank you, sir."

The Dost opened his hands. "Prince Trevelien, Tachotha Natalya, I would ask a favor of each of you. I hope they will forward the cause of peace and our mutual cooperation."

The Dost nodded to Natalya. "Tachotha Natalya, it will be necessary for you to find a replacement for the position of Governor of the Vzorin Military District."

Natalya glared over at Duke Arzlov. "You are correct, my lord."

The Dost smiled. "I would like to recommend my friend Valentin Svilik. You know he has years of experience in Vzorin. He speaks Helansajaran and has been instrumental in my coming to understand your people and their ways. With him in Vzorin, I would not fear for my realm's safety, and I know we will begin trade that will benefit both our realms."

The Tachotha nodded. "Your recommendation will bear great weight with my father, my lord."

"Excellent." Uriachin turned toward Duke Arzlov and addressed him in Stranan. "My lord, I understand you were architect of Fernandi's defeat, yet you were not recognized for your accomplishment. Because of your subordinate's invasion of Helansajar, you will probably spend the rest of your life in a region so cold and sterile that I decided not to take it eight centuries ago. I offer you now the same choice I offered Grigory Khrolic: you may die in Strana, or you may join me as my Warlord."

Arzlov blinked. "I beg your pardon?"

"You would command the Ausdari in my name. Your reputation will cow those who think to take my realm." The Dost clasped his hands together. "If you join me you will know glory that will outlive any nation represented here today."

Robin glanced at Malachy. "What's he saying?"

"The Dost is confirming he made a good choice in his gift to you."

Arzlov nodded. "I accept your offer, my lord."

Malachy shook his head. "Made a *very* good choice in your gift, Robin."

Natalya bowed her head. "It is my wish you find Duke Arzlov more tractable than I ever did, my lord."

"Strana has no need for a Warlord to defend her. Helansajar does. In our need I think Duke Arzlov will find a challenge suited to his skills."

"I hope this is true, my lord."

Uriachin nodded at Tachotha Natalya, then looked over to Prince Trevelien. "I realize having Duke Arzlov in my service will not bring you much peace. I wish you to accept a gift that will prove I harbor no malice against Ilbeoria."

Trevelien shook his head. "I know of Uriah Smith. Colonel Kidd has spoken most highly of him. I cannot imagine him wishing Ilbeoria harm."

"Nor does he. In fact, my gift to you is based upon the feelings of your nation for you." The Dost held out his right hand and Turikana took it as she stood. "I would have you wed my sister, to bind our realms and to provide you peace. She knows of you and Ilbeoria through Uriah. She has agreed to this match if you will have her."

Only a slight narrowing of Trevelien's eyes marked the Prince's surprise at the offer. "A sister is too precious to be used to seal an alliance, my lord."

"I would agree if I meant her only to bind our governments together." Concern damped down the Dost's smile. "It was my thought that she could heal your heart. In doing that she would earn the love of your people and make the bond between our nations stronger. I am Ilbeorian and Stranan, Helansajaran and Durranian. I want the people of the world to become as comfortable with the mix as I must. They can't do that without getting to know people from my realm."

Trevelien looked up at Turikana. "Becoming my wife will not be an easy thing."

She smiled back at him. "Uriah told me of the difficulties your Rochelle overcame. I cannot hope to be her equal in your mind. I know I cannot equal her in your heart. However, your enemies will find me her twin when they seek to do you harm."

The Prince nodded. "You have chosen well for me, my lord. You make me wish I had gotten to know Uriah Smith directly, not just through his friends."

"It doesn't matter that you didn't know him, Prince Trevelien. He knew you. He knew how well your people love you. Their welfare is a sacred trust you must always hold dear, for your sake, and for theirs."

"I will." Prince Trevelien accepted Turikana's left hand in his right and she came to stand beside him.

Natalya looked over at Malachy and nodded. He smiled at her. *Yes, they do make a handsome couple.*

The Dost smiled and clapped his hands together with a relish in which Malachy recognized a piece of Uriah's self-satisfaction. "Good, our formal business is done. I know you will all be leaving my realm tomorrow, so I have arranged a banquet in your honor this evening. I want this evening to be a wake for old rivalries and hatreds. I want it to celebrate the birth of a new peace. I want it to unite us against whatever the future will throw at us."

Malachy accepted Natalya's hand on his arm. "For the future, Tachotha?"

"And a recovery of our past, Colonel Kidd?"

He glanced over at Robin Drury, then gazed into Natalya's sea-green eyes. "Can we really make up for twelve lost years?"

"The *Leshii* is *not* a fast ship, my love." Natalya gave his arm a squeeze. "Time lost is time lost. Squandering time is a tragedy, so we will have to use what time we have left to the utmost. Yes?"

Malachy nodded, letting his smile carry up into his argent eyes. "As before, Natalya, I am awed by your wisdom."

"This before I have crushed your forces on a chessboard?" Natalya's delighted laugh filled the Dost's chamber. "The future just gets brighter and brighter."

Epilogue

> **Airship *Grim's Pride***
> **East of Dhilica, Puresaran**
> **Aran**
> **9 Autumbre 1687**

So angry with her father was Amanda Grimshaw that the world out-side her stateroom made only the barest of impressions upon her. She had asked him to delay their departure from Dhilica until the *Saint Michael* had returned from Helor. Though she expected to earn her father's ire, she had gone ahead and admitted to him that she had seen Robin Drury several times since he had been a guest in their house. She added that she did not intend to leave Aran until she bid him farewell.

Her father surprised her by promising they would not leave un-til the dreadnought returned to Dhilica. True to his word, her father delayed their flight until the *Saint Michael* had appeared as a dark speck on the northern horizon. When she demanded him to have the ship turned around, he laughed and ordered the *Pride* to flank speed.

"Take this as a lesson, daughter. Defy me at your peril." Though he had reached up to stroke her hair, his voice remained rime-edged. "In time you will thank me for this."

Powerless, she fled to her stateroom and locked herself in. Tears flowed, but she refused to give in to utter despair. "This *is* a lesson, Father, and you'll rue the day you taught it to me." A million plans for revenge flitted through her mind, ranging from a delicate poisoning to her finding a man who would be able to gobble up her father's mercantile empire and marrying him.

Even as those plans salved some of her hurt, she knew she would never employ them. *Those are things my father would do and, in some ways, he would be pleased I had thought of them.* She shivered as she remembered her father's glee at withholding infor-mation that put the life of a Wolf-priest in Helor at jeopardy. "I have never desired to cause others pain and I will not do so now, even to alleviate my own."

A huge hiss of steam swallowed the second half of her state-ment. Heat and mist flushed up through the decking as the pounding thrum of the *Pride*'s steam engines stopped. Amanda heard two muffled thumps from above and her father's strident voice shouting, "Why are we stopping?"

Curious, she rushed out of her stateroom and along the companionway to the stairs. Hiking her skirts, she raced up the steps half a flight behind her father. He reached the wing deck before she did and his frustrated snarl came loudly enough to be heard from the Himlans to Vlengul and back. "How dare you!"

The wind tugged at Amanda's hair as she reached the open wing deck. Standing there, two silver angels folded their wings and looked down at her father. One angel wore an impassive mask of silver, the other's bore a regal expression. Beyond them, above and alongside the *Pride*, hovered the *Saint Michael*.

The angel on the right removed his helmet and her heart began beating faster. "Robin?"

The ethyrine nodded solemnly. "I was afraid you'd be leaving before we had a chance to speak."

"I wanted to wait."

"But the Prince's order to leave Aran left us no choice. I was merely following Imperial orders," Grimshaw snapped. "How dare you board us?"

Trevelien removed his helmet and Grimshaw took a step back. "It was done on *my* order. The way *Grim's Pride* flew from Dhilica as soon as we came within sight of the city made me think you were smuggling precious cargo out of Aran."

"You insult me."

"And I think Brother Robin finds your daughter an incomparable treasure."

Robin nodded and stepped forward. He took Amanda's right hand in his and dropped to one knee. "Forgive the armor and the drama, but I've been thinking a lot on the trip back about you and how I would feel if you were gone. You're looking at all I am, and all I'm likely ever to be. A warrior; a priest. It's not much. That understood between us, will you consent to be my wife?"

Amanda covered her mouth with her left hand, but before she could answer, her father slapped their hands apart. "Never! I will not allow it."

Robin rose to his feet and grabbed Erwin Grimshaw by the lapels of his jacket. He hoisted the man up until Grimshaw's feet dangled in the air. "I did not ask *you*."

Even struggling in Robin's grasp, her father's voice filled with venom. "If you agree, daughter, you will get nothing. No money. No property. You will cease being my daughter."

Robin winked at her. "That last item makes your dowry very attractive."

Amanda laughed aloud. "Yes, Robin, I'll marry you."

Robin dropped her father and gathered her into his arms. "You've just made me the happiest I've ever been, Amanda. I'll do the same for you."

"I know, Robin." She kissed him for as long as it took her father to scramble up from the deck, and a little bit longer.

"That's it, Amanda, you're disowned. You'll have nothing. See if you can live on the paltry sum the Church pays him."

She shifted within Robin's embrace and looked down at her father. "I can and I will. I will even work and earn money, if need be. And I will be happy because I have love."

"Nonsense. You'll starve on love." Grimshaw's face twisted into a cruel sneer. "And who would hire *you*?"

Prince Trevelien cleared his throat. "Actually, Miss Grimshaw, I understand from Brother Robin you are an educator. I would like to retain your services."

Amanda looked at the Prince with surprise. "For your children? They are coming here?"

"No, actually, I wish you to instruct my new wife in the ways of Ilbeoria." Trevelien smiled and nodded toward her father. "You already know how to deal with thoroughly disagreeable scoundrels. We have four and a half years to prepare her for Ilbeoria and I would have her ready to take our home by storm."

"It will be my honor and pleasure, my lord." Amanda hugged Robin again and kissed him. "The Prince has a new wife and I have a husband. Will wonders never cease?"

"With any luck, my love," Robin whispered as he unfurled his wings and the two of them lifted off the deck, "not until the world we know is long dead and we have passed into eternity together."

About the Author

MICHAEL A. STACKPOLE is still an award-winning game designer, computer game designer and writer who is uncomfortable about this third-person bio thing. Not much has changed since the last bio, actually, except there is a third dog in the house: Saint, the great-grandson of Ruthless and the great-grandnephew of Ember, the other two dogs living here. Growing up in Vermont, Mike only ever had one dog at a time in the house, but if all three of these Cardigan Welsh Corgis were piled into one dog, they would equal the Labrador with which he grew up.

Mike still plays soccer on weekends and is on a team with players who do all sorts of things to make him look really good. He's still riding his mountain bike—the more he rides it, the less of a mountain he becomes.

By the time you're reading this, he should have finished his final X-wing book. He'll also have finished scripting bunches of the X-wing Rogue Squadron comic from Dark Horse, which he finds to be a lot of fun. And, after all, if you can't have fun writing, there is absolutely no reason to do it—it's too much hard work otherwise. His next big project is an epic fantasy series for Bantam called the Dragoncrown War and he's really looking forward to it.

His website can be found at <http://www.flyingbuffalo.com/stackpol.htm>. It's updated every so often (okay, often is a relative term).